ENERGY WARS

THE SEQUEL TO PROJECT ANAN

ENERGY WARS

Book 2 of the Energy Exchange Series
Part 1 & 2

BY

LIONEL LAZARUS

First published in 2021 by Lionel Lazarus, Dublin, Ireland.

Available in Print and as an eBook

Paperback   ISBN-978-1-9168757-0-8

eBook   ISBN-978-1-9168757-1-5

Author Website;

www.lionellazarus.com

Email;

lionellazarus@lionellazarus.com

Book cover design by DESIGN for WRITERS

www.designforwriters.com

To Carol

BOOK 2 – PART ONE

PROLOGUE

Company Structure

Anan Corp Ltd and Mack Investments Ltd are registered in New Zealand. Our offshore companies, Anan Holdings Pte Ltd and Aknar Investments Pte Ltd are registered in Singapore. The project, engineering and security managers – Robert Leslie, Thomas Parker and Niamh Parker (nee Sullivan) with Alan Phillips, Katherine Phillips and Janet Cooper – are principal shareholders. Directorship of the organisations falls to me, General Arie Machai of the House of Aknar, named as Mack Aknar on Earth's legal documents. In my absence, on behalf of The Eight, the financial controller Alan Phillips, with company secretary Katherine Phillips, has overall control and day-to-day management of our Earth-based corporations.

• Extract from: Corporate Structure Representing The Eight's holdings on Earth. General Arie Machai

*

New Zealand, Christchurch, Anan Corp Office, 2nd April 2027

ALAN PHILLIPS SAT AT HIS desk and smiled as he scrolled through the latest financial statement his investment team had produced. To most, such pages would be lifeless but not to him and, he mused, not to Mack, the alien who had come calling with his mighty Overlord over thirteen months ago. Back then, Alan would never have imagined what was to come. Now, so much had changed, and from the reports he had finished reading, more change would arrive. The "black box", the Anan investment computer the aliens had left in their basement, continued to work its enviable magic generating enormous profits for Anan Corp. Even after the immense costs of the spaceship *Hela's* refit and the rebuilding of its base in Australia, their corporate accounts were flush with cold hard cash. At the very beginning, when he first plotted the potential profits the "black box" could generate, he realised that the real power would come with the money. Their "black box" was now a powerful financial weapon, wielding severe consequences for Earth's major banks and industries. Between four corporations, their Overlord, The Eight – even while absent in a far distant galaxy – would soon control most of Earth's financial assets.

Not before time, Alan thought, now browsing the darkness bleating from the planet's news feeds. Not a wet week after the majestic *Hela* left, the work that The Eight had done towards global harmonisation was quickly consigned to the political rubbish tip. Those who he had left in charge of the U.S. and the Great Northern Union were sideswiped by opportunist politicians who stoked the fires of fear to further their own agendas. Theological battles raged. "Are we to abandon our one true god based on the brief apparition of a blue demon from space?" they spouted, waving their Bibles and guns. He watched the live feeds of bloody riots – fanned by Muslim and Christian differences – erupting across the Middle East and Europe. Sickened by it all, he turned off his computer, leaned back in his chair and sighed. *War is coming again*, he supposed, as he heard the phone in his sister, Katherine's office ring.

A tired Katherine Phillips leafed through the C.V.s from the eager applicants submitting for Colony-2. She yawned – a deep Friday afternoon one – longing for a shower; she sat back and started to tease out her untidy brown hair. *The day's done*, she thought, as she allowed her eyes and mind to play about on the office walls. As always, her gaze drifted to the pictures. The giant golden *Hela* – departing for the New World – floating above the base in Australia, dominated the far wall. Kath, as the Human Resource Consultant, had hired the precious cargo – two thousand five hundred human colonists. *Where are you now*, she wondered? Her eyes, with a mind of their own, followed a pre-ordered procession of admiration. On to the picture taken after the first meeting with the aliens that showed, Theia Aknar, Empress of Planet Anan and General Arie Machai (Mack) positioned on each side of Kath, with Janet Cooper, their receptionist, alongside Mack and Alan. Taken on her birthday in the kitchen of Kath's house in Christchurch with Kath's fiftieth balloons and streamers in the background, it had gained iconic status, fuelling the headline 'Aliens Crash Birthday Bash' across the globe. And then on to Niamh Sullivan's wedding; the photo of the beautiful bride with her new husband Thomas Parker and their Scottish project manager Robert Leslie all scrubbed up like new pins. *Yes, where are you now?* she wondered again ... the phone rang. 'Katherine Phillips, Anan Corp,' she answered.

Kath put the phone down and sighed. It was not the news she expected on a Friday evening just before she planned a well-deserved exit. The *Hela* was gone three months, and now she was landed with this. She got up and walked into her brother, Alan's office.

'You finished for the day?' he asked, as he tidied up his desk.

'No, and don't think you are either. I got a call from Picton, it appears Bri left something behind.'

'He was never in Picton.'

'No, but a girl he met in Queenstown is.'

Alan jumped up with the shock. 'Ah shit, Kath, no. How?'

Leaning against the office door, she folded her arms and looked at him. 'Remember when he escaped from the compound over the New Year?'

'Yeah, I'll never forget that mess!' They had been looking for the young alien prince all over the South Island and he nearly missed the launch of the *Hela*.

'Now we know what he was up to. I'm just off the phone from a doctor in Picton. A young girl came into her surgery today. Thankfully, the good doctor had the presence of mind to contact us. She's keeping the girl until we get there. You need to get the plane ready,' Kath said, as she turned and left his office in disgust.

He sat back down at his desk and shook his head before calling the airport. The antics of the young alien were now legendary. He had even absconded from the office for lunchtime pints in a nearby Christchurch pub after which, needless to say, his picture appeared on the web, threatening the security of their project. *Brizo Sema, the young alien prince, heir to the Aknar throne and the future Emperor of Anan, a pisshead and a drug addict*, were the unflattering thoughts that flashed through Alan's mind as he dialled the number.

*

New Zealand, Picton

As the plane prepared to land, they could see the Interisland Ferry leave from the docks in Picton. Black smoke, from the cold diesels, revving up in its bowels curled up from the stack, drifting into the clear air above. The view, stretching before them, of the sparsely populated Marlborough Sounds, their turquoise-blue waters surrounded by green, orange and yellow covered mountains was breathtaking. Queen Charlotte and the Kenepuru Sounds sparkled in the bright autumn evening sunshine. Tourists paid lots to gorge their eyes on such sights, but Kath and Alan, preoccupied with their latest crisis, were oblivious to the stunning scenery. They quickly disembarked from their small plane and after that, it was a short drive to the surgery, located on a quiet street outside the town centre. They knocked on the door. It opened and a tall woman of about thirty stepped out. After the usual pleasantries, the doctor led them in to meet the girl.

'Kath, Alan, this is Hana,' she said, in a quiet voice.

Kath looked across the room at the young woman seated on the couch, warming herself beside a stove. As she turned to face them, her look of misery and dejection pierced Kath's heart. She was dressed in a long dark-coloured skirt and a grey fleece, both worn and faded from wear. Her long black hair was matted, and her dark Polynesian face streaked with dried tears.

Her hands shook as she pitched a wary eye on the duo from Christchurch, not expecting much else. *Boring old farts – typical office types*, she thought. *He looks like death warmed up, and she looks like she was just dragged through a hedge.* Hana was right. Their end-of-the-week, nondescript appearance in dull office attire with Kath's brown hair all over the place and Alan's pale face and creased grimy shirt, didn't do them any favours in the fashion stakes. As Kath approached, Hana turned away, looking with glazed eyes at the stove.

Kath knelt down beside her and took her hands in her own. In a soft voice, she said, 'It'll be all right, Hana. We'll look after you. Whatever you want, we'll get you.'

Her brown puppy dog eyes opened wide with surprise – not what she had expected. 'I want Bri; where is he?'

Kath squirmed at the question. *Yes, where is the little shit now? Pity he didn't miss the flight, after all,* she thought. 'Light-years from Earth, I'm afraid, on the *Hela*. They should be near the New World by now,' she said, full of hope.

Wiping a tear from her face, she turned to look at Kath and Alan. 'He said he'd take me with him. He's a real bastard.'

Yes, I bet he did, thought Kath. *And he could have taken her to the New Colony, making a life together. She would have been the makings of him. Men! The same the universe over – alien or human. O Bri, how could you?* Her thoughts waned and composing herself, she smiled across at Hana. 'What's more important now is you and your baby. We—'

'I just want to stay here, near Picton. I want privacy – if the media find out, they'll hound me. I'll become a freak and so will my baby. They'll call me "the girl who shagged the alien". You know what they're like. I want to look after my child in a safe place, that's all.'

Kath smiled and nodded at the young woman. *She's smart,* she thought, impressed with the girl's forthright manner. 'Not too much to ask, no not at all,' she said, throwing a questioning look to the doctor.

The doctor grimaced, knowing full well what it would all entail, an alien pregnancy and the first of its kind on Earth. Still, she nodded her head and then smiled at the girl. 'Yeah, I'll look after you, Hana, but I'll need help,' she said, pushing some of it back on Kath and Alan.

'Of course, we'll help; that's why we're here,' Alan said, his pale face etched with worry. *We gotta keep this quiet,* he realised. *It isn't right. Against the order of all things Anan, it is.* He sensed a grave danger. *What is that?* he wondered, as he looked at the beautiful Maori girl. This was no ordinary dalliance, he realised. It was not just her beauty – she gave off a real sense of care and softness. There was an inner magnificence, a radiance that she extruded. And it wasn't from the pregnancy. It was her. She had captivated the alien prince's heart, and he would take that with him. Like a quake, the danger they were in, what the empirical accountant within didn't understand, shook him to the core. Like thunder, it beat through his mind. *Bri, Bri, what have you done now? You toerag, you must have known there might be consequences for your actions. How could you leave this woman in such a state? And humanity, what danger have you left us in?* With such a sombre mood in the room, there was little else to say.

'Come, Hana, we have rooms booked in a guest house near here. Doctor, I'll be in touch tomorrow,' Kath said, as she took Hana's hand and lead her out.

*

The following afternoon a helicopter landed at the back of a discreet lodge on the shore of Kenepuru Sound. A transformed Hana, Kath and Alan stepped out onto the grass.

'This place is cool,' Hana said, smiling as she looked around at the lush forest enclosing the back of the lodge.

They ate a late lunch, looking out at the blue waters of the sound lapping on the nearby shore. Kath watched the young woman hungrily devour her food. She had enjoyed the shopping trip with Hana that morning. After the stress of managing such an unexpected event, it was a welcome break. At the top of the South Island and at the railhead, Picton is the main ferry port between the north and south islands. Kath loved the compact town centre, full of eclectic shops and, even in the autumn, buzzing with tourists on their way either to the North Island or coming from it. It was a busy morning in Picton – also the staging town for the Queen Charlotte Track. They took time to sit and watch the backpackers hurriedly making their way to the port for the boats that would ferry them out into the sound. Kath loved to sit, sipping coffee, in the broad deckchairs on the seafront and watch the toing and froing between town and harbour. She made the best of it with Hana that morning, cheering up the girl and bonding with her.

With her new clothes, and after a leisurely shower in the guest house, the young woman now bubbled with life and enthusiasm. Gone was yesterday's look of dejection and hopelessness. *She's incredible. The mother of a new race and a child for the house of Aknar,* Kath realised, as she admired Hana's long shining black hair, her dark eyes and soft brown skin. They sat in silence as they ate and feasted their eyes on the beauty of this isolated place and the mountains behind.

Finishing her food, Hana sat back and looked at Kath and Alan. 'Where's this place?'

'We're on the Kenepuru Sound. If you're finished, we'll show you where you can stay. It's up the road,' Alan said.

Ten minutes later, they stood on a dirt road outside the property. Kath and Alan stepped back as Hana ran up through the gate. As she went around the back, they could hear her squeals of delight. Then she suddenly appeared from behind the thick growth of plants and bushes that cloaked the beautiful cottage.

'It's fabulous! Who owns it?' she said, running back down to them.

Alan smiled, his banker's face had long since softened. 'We do. If you like it, you can have it. We'll arrange the transfer of ownership this week.'

'You're not serious. Are—?'

'Hana, I wouldn't joke about something like that. We need to protect you and your baby. This place is as safe as we can get. You'll see. It's so remote – your secret will be safe here. The only way in is by air, boat or a long drive on this dirt road. If you like it, it's yours.' He took her hand, and with Kath, led her back to the cottage door. As Kath unlocked it, he watched as Hana rushed inside.

CHAPTER ONE

Overlords

The event we know as the Big Bang heralded the arrival of our known universe. Before that seminal moment, matter, anti-matter, space, time and energy swirled together in a vast primordial soup. The bang brought order to chaos, separating matter and anti-matter, propelling it out on its never-ending journey through a freshly ordered space and time. Nothing, corporeal or entity, knows what fuelled that bang. But what a few powerful entities know is what happened in its wake. Fragments of a post-bang residue generated powerful energy called blue, giving birth to the universe's first intelligence. On their long voyage, swirling through space and time, some of those intelligent entities learned to harness the blue energy they were born into.

In the same way that corporeal beings depend on oxygen, sugars, proteins and carbohydrates to live, that pure blue energy fuels those entities. They depend on blue for their very existence. Over many epochs they evolved into what we know as Overlords, gaining strengths, forging civilisations over many galaxies and gifting others with intelligence. After building an alliance of ten of their kind, their great triumph was the creation of the Intergalactic Energy Exchange. The Exchange forms a commercial hub for our Overlords and the inhabitants of their galaxies. It functions as a universal marketplace for all commerce. This vast structure, orbiting our Planet Anan, has developed into a city in space, where all energy, physical material and produce is traded.

‣ Introduction from: The History of the Energy Exchange Part 1. Theia Aknar

*

The Hela, Intergalactic Space.
EPTS (Earth Parallel Time Stamp): A137808

SOON THEY WOULD ARRIVE BACK in the Anan Galaxy. *What will we find?* wondered the powerful entity known as The Eight. *Where is The One? Am I too late? Will all the work we achieved in Project Anan be in vain?* The questions swirled in his energy mass with the memories of how it had all started.

Leaving the Energy Exchange on the *Hela* for Earth, with Empress Theia and her cousin, Mack, General Arie Machai, was a last-ditch attempt to thwart The Sixth's energy-grabbing troika. The Eight's return to Earth, after such a long absence, was well timed. Verifying his decision to involve the humans, Project Anan was a resounding success. They had refitted the *Hela* on Earth and, led by Robert Leslie, transplanted two thousand five hundred humans across intergalactic space to a secret New World, rich in blue. While setting up their settlement and offloading the *Hela*, a small contingent of colonists had mined for his precious energy.

The fruit of the humans' labour, his energy, was loaded on the *Hela* with a bonus commissioned by the Empress, a treatment and a cure for the pure-breed's sickness. Now The Eight returned to his home galaxy of Anan with the valuable energy for The One, his companion and the supreme leader of the ten Overlords. But he had heard nothing from him – and feared the worst.

The closer he got to their home galaxy, the more intense the foreboding feeling pulsed in his energy mass. *Why has he not contacted me? What's happened? I must risk it,* he thought. Fearing their discovery as the *Hela* sped through space, faster than the speed of light, the preeminent entity, known to the crew as The Eight, focused his mind. Forming an invisible vessel of blue, he projected his thoughts out towards their destination. Dancing through the milieu of time and space, he probed for evidence of another. It was bleak – deserted – emptiness he had never experienced before. The total blackness added to his worry. Closer and closer, his consciousness travelled to the Anan Galaxy. But there was nothing; his companion, The One, lord of their kind, all trace of his presence had evaporated. He probed onwards, to a place they had shared, one of their many secrets, a site he had long forgotten. *He would have used this place; returned here to replenish,* he thought.

As the cosmic mists cleared, he peered out at a small asteroid. *A ship, there is a ship there. How is this possible?* Invisible to the biped purebreeds, he watched as they transferred the last of The One's meagre supply of blue energy – his catastrophe hoard – onto a waiting freighter, the livery of The Sixth embossed on the hull. Probing for more, The Eight's thoughts brushed against one of the precious canisters. The message his friend and companion had embedded in the energy exploded in his consciousness. *"Stay away; all is lost. Go, my friend, save yourself. For the sake of our kind, save yourself."* As quickly as it appeared, it was gone. Faster than the speed of light, his mind retreated in shock, back across the voids of space and time. And then, like the sting of a million Uldonian microbes, he felt the pulse of a faint voice resonating out in the blackness. *"Eight, is that you? Where are you? Eight, answer me. I feel you ..."*

The voice died away as he travelled ever faster and faster back to the safety of the *Hela*. Alone in his chamber on the *Hela*, his energy mass pulsed with a dark purple light. He focused his powerful mind, shutting out the strange feeling, something he had never experienced before – loneliness. *I should not feel. I am an Overlord*, he thought. *Where are you, One? What manner of evilness has descended on this epoch? I will expunge you, Six*, he vowed. As he tried to quell the purple pulsing, thoughts screamed through his energy mass. *It was he, he felt my presence. He should never have been elevated, never, never, never. A mistake, one that may cost us our universe.*

Little by little, he quelled his rage. Logical thought returned with the realisation that The One was gone and Six had nearly discovered them. *Return to Planet Anan? No, not an option – for now anyway. I am too late. Time for a new plan, but what?* he wondered.

*

The Colony. Fort Leslie, New World.
EPTS: A137808

Robert Leslie, the six-foot five-inch sandy-haired Scotsman, sat listening to the steady grinding of the blue energy rig as it poked its long curling tube into the craggy mountains behind their colony. Since arriving in this

New World, he never tired of watching the hectic moments that would come up next. The drill would stall then break through the subterranean prison, exposing the precious energy they were here for. Then, planting the deep-hole packer riding behind the bit, they would vent the tubing of drill fluid and start recovering blue. So far, from his estimates, each of the small nodes they broached had yielded between fifty and a hundred barrels of the precious energy.

After the big bang, matter cooled and fragments congealed into solids, trapping blue as bubbles of pure energy. Over time, the dense prisons – burnished by heat and pressure – formed crystal nodes rich with blue. Floating within the young planet's mantle, as prime continental drift shaped their New World, these nodes were uplifted back towards the sky they came from. Finally settling into the snow-covered mountains, the colonists were now mining. And there were more of these precious nodes trapped in asteroids, meteorites and the close-by planets. Looking up at the sky, Robert wondered at the New World's two small moons visible today. *More blue there – off-world mining, in space suits. Well, that's for another day.*

His gaze fell back to the Anan rig. Anchored to the platform, its colossal excavator arm had carved out the side of the mountain. This load would top up tanks on the rear of the rig. Then, back to Fort Leslie to transfer the cargo into the colony's tank farm. With two rigs and one support platform, the on-planet mining of blue had gone without a hitch. Before they landed, scanning the planet from space, they had pre-mapped its deposits of blue. Robert focused his attention on what he called "low hanging fruit". The vast deposits in the mountains behind Fort Leslie. It was the reason why they had chosen the colony's location in the first place. The crews had made good progress, keeping the two rigs working while staying in the following accommodation platform. With the main storage tanks at the colony near full and no interstellar ship to export on, their work had come to an end.

But that wasn't the problem. A far bigger one loomed, one never foreseen. Robert heard the noise change and die off, followed by loud shouts from the crew. From his perch on the side of the accommodation platform, he stood up and turned to watch. First, a low rumbling as the drilling fluid rushed back into its tanks through the two-inch tubing. Then, a more dramatic hissing sound as the blue energy vented up from the subterranean prison. The crew hurried around, watching the machinery as the alien auto-systems channelled blue to the near brimming tanks. The team were well schooled by now and soon had grav-powered air compressors lined up to scour out the last of the blue. Through toughened glass ports, he watched the strange energy swirl into the tank. The newer fresh batch flowed with a more in-depth blue colour, then curled into the lighter older stuff with an ever-changing hue. The process mesmerised him until a soft voice with a flat northeast brogue stirred his world.

'We're done, Robert. No more room for any more.'

He turned to face Shona. She had come over from her own rig, shut down and parked beside them on the big mountain platform, grey barren peaks rising behind it. 'Aye, we are at that,' he nodded. 'You ready?'

'I am. I'll get the man. He can leave the crew to clean up here,' she said, climbing up a ladder onto the working rig.

He watched, grinning, as a giant of a man on the prow of the rig scooped up the small woman and gave her a big kiss. Shona and Blair Hay, his workmates from a previous life in the North Sea and the European oil fields, now husband and wife, hell-bent on carving a life for themselves on the New World. He never forgot the ever-grouchy Blair was almost killed when they first started work on the *Hela*. She laughed playfully, fending off his affections. He put her down, turned, and after barking some curse words at his crew, dutifully followed his wife over to Robert.

Blair scowled. 'Well, Robert, another fine mess you have us in …'

She hit him. 'Shut it, Blair. Come on, we'll save grav an' take my rig back; it's done here and needs parking back at Leslie.'

Jumping up to the controls, she soon had the grav-powered rig hovering up above the rocky platform. Turning away from the drill site, she drove the large, graceless machine with its yellow-painted grab, brown coiled drill tube and blue tanks, back through the air to Fort Leslie.

Robert watched the mountains recede behind them. The many sites, where they had dug platforms and bored down to recover blue, scarred the desolate grey mountain landscape. *Mankind has definitely arrived*, he thought. Looking to the approaching colony, Fort Leslie's burgeoning size, behind a pristine golden beach, galvanised that muse. They had started to clear the surrounding forest. The town centre had grown with a proliferation of colonial-style wooden buildings, sprouting from the bounty the felled trees endowed them with. From this distance, the pods, the living accommodation transported from Earth, looked like giant white steps descending down the hill they were built on. The blue ocean stretched out into a dark cloudy sky from a long golden beach. The landing pads – their "spaceport" – built on the beach, cut that view in half. The wind freshened, buffeting the big grav platform.

'Storm's coming,' Shona said, pointing to dark bulbous clouds on the horizon. She landed the rig on a pad beside the blue tank farm. And then, without another word, they made their way to the colony offices.

Robert took a seat at the head of the table. Looking around, he nodded at the people, a mix of the colony's management, already seated: Janet Cooper, the planner, Thomas Parker, the security manager along with the chief colony engineer, technicians, doctors, zoologists, and the botanists. Leaning against the wall at the back was Alice, one of Tom's soldiers, a wonder medic, now entrusted with the care of the Overlord's catbears and the ever-silent Blair and Shona.

He looked at their sombre faces. 'So, what's all this about?' he asked, knowing full well their dilemma and why the chief engineer had called them here today.

The chief spoke first. 'Robert, I'm sorry, but from our calculations, at this burn rate, we'll run out of the stuff. We've been here over three months and used a third of our grav stocks.'

With a face that could chop trees, he answered, 'Did ya no think to check that before we left Earth?'

The engineer squirmed. 'We had no idea, Robert. We trusted the Anan data and what we learned from the Pilot. Grav was a new energy; we hadn't a baseline on consumption.'

With his rising rage, his arm started to glow a deep purple and, for the first time, hurt. The hairless blue limb was a gift from The Eight after Robert had helped him win the war on Earth. As it flashed and changed, he often wondered how much of a benefit it was. 'We left all the diesels – fuel and engines – back on Earth. Grav fuels everything! Now you tell me we're running out of it.'

'Not quite, Robert. We took two emergency gennies and some diesel …'

'Enough for a fart in the wind.' *What's gotten us to this, only three months after the Hela has left?* Robert wondered. They had intended to take diesel engines from Earth with tanks of the stuff along with equipment to reclaim fossil fuel from the New World. But, after finding a hoard of old grav machinery in the Australian base with grav from the Pilot's family hoard, they had elected to abandon the use of fossil fuel in the New World. To power the colony, there were submersible turbines in the river and estuary and wind turbines planted on the hills. But for transport, running portable machinery, all the lifting and carrying, they relied on grav and believed they had enough for years. So prolific was their reliance on grav, they hadn't even built roads, flying everywhere. Not the case now. 'How long?'

The chief engineer looked down at his notes. 'At this rate, less than a year.'

Robert felt a soft hand on his arm. The blue pulsing slowed, his arm quietened down and the pain subsided. It was Janet. 'Robert, it's not their fault. They didn't have data to work with on Earth. We were training new grav drivers, using different grades of the stuff with no idea of its properties. You know that. It wasn't until we got here and started to actually use it – in the machinery – that they could find out what we burn daily. Be reasonable,' she said, her hands now open on the desk before her.

There was a pregnant pause. Robert got up and started to pace back and forth. Wearing one of his old kilts, he cut a sight, with his long sandy hair and kilt swaying as he walked up and down. They were well used to it, waiting in silence for the inevitable. *She was always right*, he thought. 'Its survival now isn't it?'

They nodded.

'Alright, reports – give it up.' He looked at the botanists. 'You're first.' If enthusiasm could be bottled, in this world, those scientists had the patent for it. They had discovered new foods and developed a farming system that would have the colony near self-sufficient within months. Their chief gave a short report of where they were and the current food stocks.

Robert looked down at Tom. His men were providing an ample supply of fresh meat, enough for the colonists and their friends, the catbears. 'We'll no starve, will we Tom?'

Tom shook his head. 'No, we won't, but my guys will need grav for the security patrols and the hunting.'

The rest of the team leaders followed on with their brief reports. It wasn't as bad as Robert first assumed. Surrounded by wood – cheap fuel and building material – they had food, shelter and electric power. On their own, they could make a life here in this New World. And before leaving, if what The Eight had told him might happen did happen, they may have to do that. He held that dark thought, that The Eight might never return, or that they may be discovered by The Sixth.

Smiling now, he looked at Alice. 'The catbears, can we use them?' he said, referring to the intelligent beasts resembling a cross between lion and bear, which lived in the forest. The strong five to seven-foot tree climbers, with green and brown stripes woven together for camouflage, naturally blended into the surrounding forest. As well as that, the dexterous catbears could stand on their hind legs and use their top claws as hands.

She shifted on her feet. 'They help us now without prompting. You've seen them yourself, Robert. Fetching and carrying, pushing and pulling loads whenever they can.'

He rubbed his face in disbelief. 'Bit utopian isn't it, Alice – can't be as easy as that!'

From her wide brown eyes, she stared daggers at him. Trying to hold her voice in check after such sarcasm, she blurted back, 'Robert, you know perfectly well he spoke to them before he left. To them, the Overlord is a god. Their whole life has changed. They were facing extinction before we showed up …' Holding her tongue, she pursed her lips.

He blushed; he hadn't meant to sound so bitter. 'Sorry, Alice. You're right,' he said, thinking about how bad these beautiful catbears had looked when they arrived. Mangy looking creatures, half-starved and covered with sores. With plenty of fresh meat from the planet's wild animals – compliments of Tom's guns – basic medicines and Alice's minding, the catbears had come good, developing into the beautiful, strong beasts they were always intended to be. 'So, you think they'll help?'

'Whatever deal he made with them, I suspect they will. They worship him, and they know their change of fortune is due to him. They see us as his instruments. That's why they'll work with us.' She shifted her stance, placing her hands on her hips, addressing all in the room. In her firm no-nonsense voice, she continued, 'They're not slaves or to be abused or treated as domestic animals, you all hear that? They're sentient beings, like us…' They nodded, realising this was a significant change in how their colony would work. 'It's up to us to build a symbiotic relationship with them. Before he left, The Eight told me that they would make good soldiers for Tom as well. Go figure that one, Tom.'

'So, it's done. Park up the grav platforms, the lifters and all that stuff we don't need. Luxury it is, one we can't afford. By our own strength and the catbears' help, we'll build roads, wheels, carts and all the rest. Tom, you have what you need for security. Tanks are full. We stop the blue recovery.' He paused as a thought burst through his mind. *I cannae believe we have the most powerful energy in the galaxy, and it's useless to us.* 'How's that sound?' he said, looking at the engineer.

He doubled down with his calculator and pen. After some hasty scratchings, the man looked up and for the first time, smiled. 'We can make it last over three years at that.'

Robert clapped him on the back. 'Go away and work on a usage program with Tom. If we have to wait three years for resupply, we're on our own anyway, and we'll have bigger problems. Good, anyone seen Mack?' he asked, looking at Janet. She shook her head. The alien purebreed, General Arie Machai, The Eight's representative on the New World, was ever noticeable by his absence. *What's wrong there?* Robert wondered as he watched his team file out, all happy with the outcome.

*

The Hela, Intergalactic Space. EPTS: A137809

Back on the *Hela*, even as The Eight suppressed his rage, the loss of The One was still a shock. Usually, there was a warning, some sign that an Overlord's existence approached termination. With the critical shortage of blue, The Eight had known this could happen but when it did, he had felt it – feelings he hadn't known before. It was a reminder that, although their existence could span aeons, it was finite. There were limits to their powers! He thought about how the humans had dreamed up mythical gods to worship when he had abandoned Earth. With the religious turmoil that ensued after his return, some had believed he was a god. Nothing could be further from the truth. He was another life form, existing on a different plain, an intelligence that fed on blue energy. Without air, humans die. Without blue, Overlords die. It was a simple logic he needed to accept, along with the rest of the physical and intellectual axioms that governed their existence. It still didn't make it easier to bear, but to survive, he had to move on.

Using his logical mind, The Eight processed the options for a way forward. The first and most apparent was to return to the New World and hide away with his humans. Until an ever-strengthening Six would inevitably discover them. *No, I think not. That is a slow path to my and the human's extinction. And, I can't abandon the Anan Galaxy.* Or choose the more immediate instinctive reaction – ignore all rational thinking to return and confront The Sixth. He wouldn't risk that trap. Six had his own fleet and a cast of followers. A direct fight between the two Overlords wasn't an option either. The others frowned upon such contests. And there were risks; guaranteeing a successful outcome – to that – was a fool's game!

Despite those negative notions, The Eight's internal conflict demanded action. The Sixth could never be allowed to succeed with his unlawful coup. If The Eight deserted the Anan Galaxy, he would be abandoning all possible hope of ever reviving – his friend and companion – The One. Like siblings, they had roamed the galaxies for aeons and, as the oldest of the Overlords, had worked with the original creators of the Energy Exchange. Over time, The One had advanced, while The Eight was content running his own galaxies and assisting The One as a companion and confidant.

Moreover, he couldn't discard the people who had served them both. Nor could he relinquish the valuable Anan Galaxy and the Energy Exchange to the troika. The prized possession of their known universe. And what of the remaining Overlords, not aligned to the troika? What of them? No, he couldn't leave them to wither away in some dark corner of the galaxy. The Eight had to fight back.

He paused, allowing his blue-enriched mind to delve back into his hidden memories, far in the past, to the last intergalactic war. Led by their Overlords, the purebreeds and other biped races waged brutal and futile space battles. Fleets of star cruisers armed to the hilt pounded each other out of existence. It was the single greatest waste of resources and life forms ever recorded. And it achieved nothing. When a peace conclave convened, in the mists of space and time, none of the Overlords could remember what had started that war.

After those momentous battles, they agreed to an accord that regulated their group to a maximum of ten. Treaties were authorised that apportioned the known galaxies out amongst the Overlords. The group approved regulations governing the distribution of blue energy. Its core tenet stated that blue "could never be hoarded or controlled by one single Overlord". The spirit of that rule ensured the Overlords shared their blue energy – a significant change in their ways. The accords and associated treaties laid the foundation for the Energy Exchange and the present galactic trading system. With one fell swoop, The Sixth had crushed the Overlord's founding principles. No, he couldn't get away with that. The Eight would see to it. But conventional warfare was not the right tactic. Leading fleets of starships into battle would repeat those historical mistakes. Nor could he ever get the resources to fight back in that way. Yes, he would have to fight battles but not on the scale of the past. The Eight would have to outsmart The Sixth and his troika on different fronts if his campaign was to triumph.

With the demise of The One, the order of governance in the Anan Galaxy had altered. To begin his new project, The Eight needed intelligence on the extent of that change. His energy mass glowed with white light as to-do lists flowed through his memory: a project plan, his own fleet, crews and a channel to sell blue from the New World at the Energy Exchange. However, he couldn't build his own fleet of ships exclusively on Earth. Intergalactic ships were a mix of technology, elements and compounds from different worlds. Earth didn't have all the resources. The ideas hammered his brain – he badly needed those vessels and crews to combat The Sixth. The humans were one part of the solution but he needed much, much more to wage a smart-war on The Sixth.

The way started to form in his enriched blue mind – the Borea resources, supposedly hidden away since the demise of that outlawed family's fortune. Demard had given him a data package of it when leaving the New World, part of a proposed deal between the Pilot and The Eight. Hidden away for a generation and guarded by him and Zaval, the Pilot, it catalogued the extensive resources the family had controlled. It was a myriad of all things a multifaceted intergalactic energy corporation would hold and included illegals. *Yes, Zaval, time to sort that mess out. What secret gadgets, tech, tools and devices you shouldn't have do you and the family control? What is still on your bases?* From Demard's data, he knew sensors protected those assets from discovery, and the penultimate invasion by an Overlord. They worked by recognising blue and applying some simple logical questions. "Is it moving freely through space, on a specific course and not contained in a vessel, pipe or tank?" And "What size is it?" The computer's logic determined the threat level and sounded an alarm. If, as would be the case now, the base was not occupied, the controlling computer would detonate pre-placed grav charges destroying the facility. *Smart,* he had thought, when he first reviewed the data.

He pondered the imponderable: *uncharted waters and too many variables. But a bolt hole, a secret base, at the edge of the Anan Galaxy with resources and ships perhaps, to aid the ascension of Earth and my New World's power. A chance to gain a staging base for transhipment of blue to the Energy Exchange. No, a situation not to be merely dismissed.* He also believed there was an illegal device there, for covert links with Anan.

Such decisions always lead to a logical outcome. Or if not, prompt further discussion with The One or the group. *Not now; I am on my own. This is my end game.* No guaranteed result forced The Eight to look at advantage and opportunity for success. He must strike now, before The Sixth cemented his grip, gaining control of the Anan naval fleet. It was holed up at the Exchange's space dock when The Eight last departed it on *Hela*. *If Six can ever get a loyal crew and enough blue to fuel our own fleet, all is lost. He will control the known universe. There is no choice, I must act now.* He flashed an order to the bridge. 'Captain, I need you now. Come.'

*

The mysterious Pilot, his real name Zaval Borea, sat in the captain's chair of the *Hela*. The dim lights of the bridge hid his anxious face as he watched his niece Siba work the nav-con. *What sort of a future would the family have,* he wondered? *Would The Eight honour his promise?* His eyes wandered to the curved display that dominated the forward section of the *Hela* bridge. Suspended from the ceiling by translucent rods, it looked to be floating in the air. Straight in front, the bowed toughened glass windows looked down on the forward shuttle landing platform and out into infinite space. Approaching the Anan Galaxy, the black blurring of their faster than light speed prompted his mind to wander. He put his hand in his pocket and fingered the data crystal his father had given him long, long ago. As his fingers gripped it, his thoughts drifted back to those dark family secrets his father had told.

Generations ago, the Borea family were one of the largest Charters in the known galaxy. They were dealers in all types of energy with their own fleets, shipping bases and also, they designed and built their own vessels. They were among the very best at that time and possessed a cloaking technology no others could breach.

The family were rich in assets until the one who became known as the "gutless wonder" believed it a good idea to invest in an intergalactic bank. The Pilot closed his eyes as he recalled how his father had whispered this grim tale. The misguided youth convinced the then head of the family to branch out from their core business and get the bank. They bet vast sums at the Energy Exchange to buy a controlling interest in it – until disaster struck. A brief shortage of blue – not unusual at the time – stifled intergalactic trade, lowering profits and general asset values. Unbeknown to the Borea, in cahoots with an Overlord, the bank's value had been carefully groomed by a rival Charter. Surprising many, the worthless bank failed. It was "too big to fail" all and sundry wailed. But fail it did, on a grand scale never experienced before, sending shock waves through the intergalactic financial system. Recriminations flew backwards and forwards, with everyone blaming each other.

But it was the Borea, caught long with a worthless wager, who were left carrying the can. Their burden hid their guilty rivals and Overlord from retribution. The debt was called in by the Energy Exchange, bankrupting the Borea family. Assets were confiscated, but not enough to pay back the debt. Faced with losing everything, there followed ructions within the family. In an orgy of violence, a degenerate faction rose up. They decapitated the head of the family and while he was still alive, ripped the innards from the misguided youth, the architect of the whole mess. He was forever known as "the gutless wonder". Taking advantage of all that infighting, the Pilot's great-grandfather seized control of the family.

Throughout the ages, the Borea had always maintained a cache of hidden assets. Depots in different galaxies with ships secreted amongst them. Assisted by his son and nephew, the Pilot's great-grandfather started to build a criminal network using those bases, smuggling goods and energy between the outer worlds. The older man reigned in the violent revenge that the younger ones wanted to exert on the establishment. Yet, when he died, control passed to his son, Zaval's grandfather, who, with his brutal cousin by his side, ruthlessly expanded into piracy. With one of the most advanced ships in the galaxy, they waged war on anything or anyone who got in their way. It was robbery and terror on a scale never seen before. It took a fleet from the Anan Navy and two Overlords to finally defeat the Borea pirates. Those of the family left alive scattered. Like the Pilot and his father, some earned honest employment in the outer worlds as ship's crew while others made a living on the edges of society. Others rebuilt old criminal networks, trading drugs and any contraband that turned a profit.

The Pilot shook as he remembered the stories told about their grandfather and his younger cousin. Violence, rape and pillage were their perverse pleasure. It was said that the younger cousin, their grandfather's personal enforcer, was the worst of all. An evil monster who had bubbled with malevolent rage. Rumour said it was he who had led the attack on the clan leadership. Wielding a curved baharian blade, he slit the throat of the family's leader, dragged his bleeding body across the man's own desk and hacked through his neck to sever the head. He then turned his wrath on the young financial architect. With a quick flash of the blade, he slit the poor youth's abdomen and thrust his bare hand inside. Grabbing the screaming youth's bloody guts, he ripped them out, flinging them at the rest of his pleading followers. That was the monster they called Frike Borea.

But the stories stopped there – it was a mystery where their grandfather and his brutal cousin had disappeared to. No one in the family knew. The Pilot's father suspected that in the end, they both fell out. And that was why he had been given the precious data crystals that held details of the family's hidden assets. Zaval fingered his one, another – a copy – he had passed to Demard. His closest relative and friend possessed his own cherished data crystal with more invaluable info. They both had worked tirelessly for The Eight, sharing their family secrets to expunge their debt. It was their time now …

A message from The Eight flashed across the bridge screen. Eyes wide open, the Pilot sat bolt upright in the captain's chair. *Decision time*, he realised, as he jumped up and left the bridge.

*

'Come in. Time to discuss your proposal,' The Eight said, resting in his silver spoon-shaped container at the front of the chariot that served as his "throne".

The Pilot entered, gazing in admiration at the mighty looking Overlord. It was the chariot that Niamh made for him on Earth that did it. An engineering marvel, containing memory banks, The Eight's energy mass and his blue energy tanks. The whole affair was mounted on a small grav platform, allowing him to move anywhere without using blue. The Eight could store and access his old memories and hibernate in his glass container, reducing his power needs.

The chariot, adorned with woven golden cables and silver panels mounted with rare blue pearls, appeared as a floating throne, shining with gold and shimmering with his blue light reflected in the silver and the pearls. He looked all-powerful as the fresh blue energy from Fort Leslie, the first human colony, flashed in his energy mass.

'Overlord,' the Pilot said, kneeling in front of The Eight, 'you reviewed the data and our suggestions?'

'Yes, Pilot, I did. I am not sure I trust the others in your family.'

'They will serve you as I and my close family on the *Hela* do.'

'You must understand my concern. Your family are outlaws. I have not met them. You and your crew, your niece and nephew, came aboard the *Hela* when we first left Anan. Then, I had nothing to lose, but now it is different. There is a full cargo of blue and the cure for the Anan sickness on board – a tempting prize.'

'Overlord, you forget Demard—'

'No, I do not forget the computer technician. He served me before I met you, recommended you and your crew for this voyage. He was right about you. Unlike the others of my kind, I honour my agreements. You, your niece and nephew serve me well. You should not suffer for the sins of your ancestors. Your family debt is paid. Times are changing, Pilot – those who do not change will be left behind. From now on, you will be known as Zaval Borea. And I will allow limited dealings by your Charter.'

Wide-eyed with gratitude, the Pilot bowed his head. He had never believed he could get such a decision from an Overlord. The family name restored and the ability to trade, albeit limited, was much more than he expected. In a haltering voice stung with emotion, he said, 'Overlord, thank you, thank you. By my word, the family are bound to serve you for this.'

'Such statements are nugatory. You cannot bind the others – who are absent. I am not wholly convinced. Do they still have access to illegal technology, devices we banned?'

'No, such things should be concealed at our proposed destination.'

Should, he says, not so convincing. But no other choices left, The Eight thought, replaying his previous analysis in his mind. 'Show me the route,' he said, as he projected a map of space into his chamber.

'With Niamh's help, I've plotted a course to the edge of the Anan Galaxy, away from the main shipping lanes. We'll arrive at the destination within fifteen cycles,' he said, pointing it out on the map.

'What about access?'

'It'll be a problem. Demard and I don't have all the codes.'

'You did prepare me for that, and I have a solution. You want more?' With impatience, his energy mass pulsed – near to purple.

'Overlord, my other suggestion?' he asked, referring to plays on the future price of blue.

'I will think about it. Pilot, you inherited the family gene. Only reprobates and gangsters would suggest something as audacious. Go now and tell Niamh to visit me at the end of her shift.'

He watched the Pilot go, grinning with the knowledge that the family name was restored. *Such a simple deed*, he thought. *Oh, but if it were all so simple.* Soon they would arrive back in the Anan Galaxy. *Time to prepare Niamh.*

CHAPTER TWO

Blue Energy

At the top of the energy tree, blue – the purest form of energy – is the first choice for fast intergalactic travel. Two other energies – fusion and gravity – although slower and inefficient over long distances, also provide power for space travel. Only blue, when compressed by a dodecahedron rotor, can release the tremendous, focused energy burst required to generate a fold in space. Binding matter together, blue is the building block of our universe and is the energy that feeds our Overlords. In its concentrated form, it is visible as deep blue coloured gas and is sometimes (wrongly) compared to electricity in a gaseous form. It exists dimensionally above the common electromagnetic spectrum. After the big bang, it existed in vast clouds floating freely through space. Over time, as matter crystallised, blue was trapped within dense mineral matter and carbon crystal nodes, in some cases, saturating those crystals with blue energy. Light, high-density phaenian steel is the preferred compound for blue energy containment. The low void fraction of this metal makes it the most suitable substance to manufacture blue containment structures. The energy will leak through less suitable microporous assemblies. Spills or contamination may be contained with a simple matter depletor or cleaned by Uldonian microbes that are attracted to its colour. Those endowed with the navigation gene can manipulate this energy by use of brain generated, gamma waves.

· **Principals of Energy from: Fundamentals of intergalactic travel.**
Zaval Borea

*

The Hela, Intergalactic Space. EPTS: A137812

THE EIGHT GAZED AT HIS protégé: Niamh Parker, nee Sullivan, the smartest of all the humans he had encountered. Dressed in a grimy ship garb, with her red hair hanging untidily down over her shoulders, the engineer, now a navigator and pilot as well, looked tired after her watch on the bridge. 'My child, how are you?'

Despite her tired body, her blue eyes still sparkled with enthusiasm. At an average of five-foot-eight, she was level with his energy mass as he lounged in his chariot. 'I'm fine,' she lied, knowing full well he would know.

'No, you are not. I sense your loneliness. You miss Tom,' he said, referring to her husband, the project Security Manager who she had married on Earth.

It must be about three months – how are you now, Tom? What goes on in the colony? she wondered, frowning at the memory of such an emotional departure. He had reassured her, telling her she must go and do what was needed. Now it seemed but a distant image in her mind. 'I do, but work keeps me going.'

'I want to teach you something. It will help you in the future, enhancing your abilities. Do you want to try?' The Eight asked.

She looked intently into his deep blue pulsing energy mass. 'Of course, I'm intrigued,' she blurted out.

'I want to teach you how we moved through space – by folding it ourselves.'

'Without a blue drive? How's that possible?'

'It was always possible. My kind travelled through space without ships in the past but what I will teach you is not as magnificent. Just to move small objects, you will need your own portable tank of blue.'

'And where will I get one of those, out here in empty space?'

'Make one – you have crafting skills, use them. In the area you call the old stores,' The Eight said, referring to a compartment where Niamh had gathered all the old parts they had found lying around the *Hela*, 'there are spare flow-ports.'

'Yes, yes there are,' she said, wondering what he was about.

'Also, there are phaenian steel pipe parts, and you have gelatinous sheets.'

She nodded her head, wide-eyed with curiosity.

'You will make a blue energy tank with them. I have sent the drawings and specifications to your computer in the area you call the workshop. Go now, my child.'

Intrigued, making her way straight to the workshop, Niamh couldn't wait to open the drawings. She hardly noticed the treasured machinery she had fitted the place with before they left Earth. When he had seen the weights of it, there were full-on arguments with Tom, as usual, wanting more weapons. But Robert, knowing full well how isolated they would be, approved her order.

'If things break down, we'll no be able to call the supplier. No, we won't. You'll have to fix it yourself Niamh,' were his wise words.

She opened the file, and yes, it was a small marvel of engineering The Eight had designed. Next, she raced down to the old stores for a quick rummage. She found the four slim alien flanges first, threading her hands through them to check their size and then, on a shelf below, a flow port. The oval flow port, constructed from phaenian steel and toughened glass, was used to monitor the flow of blue energy into the hybrid engine feed. Adapted with pipework nipples, it was perfect for making the small tank. Bringing her newfound treasure back to the workshop, she retired for the day.

After her next shift on the bridge, she returned to the workshop. Mounting a flange in her pride and joy – the big Colchester lathe – she started to lap out the recess for the gelatinous seals. Wholly engrossed in work, she watched, as the tungsten carbide-tipped tool easily sliced through the phaenian steel. The shavings shimmered like polished silver as they fell into the lathe's sump.

Before she saw him, she felt the presence of the Pilot, quietly watching. 'Captain, what brings you down here, to the lower decks?' she quipped, a welcoming smile playing across her grimy face.

He had seen, on the bridge, the power coming on in the workshop and came down to check on it himself. Truth be known, he surmised it was she, and his curiosity got the better of him. 'I'm intrigued, yes I am,' he said, moving closer to watch the rotating chuck, and cocking his head as he listened to the light grinding noise and the sound of the drive motor.

'I haven't seen this machinery used before. I wondered why you had it installed; it's so primitive. Now I see – yes, so useful out here in space.'

Having worked a bridge shift already, in a grimy ship garb with her red hair untidily held up in a bun, she looked quite a sight. Wiping a smudge of cutting fluid from her face, she laughed. 'Within reason, Captain, we can repair or remake most things – although, a spherical polyhedron rotor is beyond us.' *Now is the time to get more info*, she thought.

The Pilot, as the captain of the *Hela*, out of his usual character, paid much more attention to his appearance. His light blue ship garb was immaculate, and he now kept his porcelain white bald head polished. The same height as Niamh, he bowed in deference to her skill. 'You are so dexterous; most of our people have lost that ability.'

She cast him a quizzical look. 'I've seen you and your family work on the engines before?'

'Yes, but there are limits to what we can do. General maintenance and servicing, that sort of thing you already know.' Shaking his head, he went on. 'No, no, now we cannot do this. Most of the manufacturing is done in specialist factories working at an atomic level. Pre-programmed machines generate the parts from base materials. But …'

More mystery, and what's he inferring with "now"? Not getting any of what he was saying, she screwed up her freckled face. 'But what? Aren't there portable versions, like our 3D printers?'

With envy, he had watched them use those archaic devices during the refit. They had banks of them generating replacements for the flexible composites and some non-metallic parts. "Worn out consumables", the humans had called such components, carefully measuring and copying them. 'No, such tech is kept secret by the factory owners. See, here is their logo,' he said, smiling as he pointed to a marking on the side of the flange and hoping she wouldn't detect the half-truth. *Soon I must tell her all.*

His ruse worked. *Well, that's new info*, she realised, looking at the logo. She had seen it on most other alien pieces before, believing it was part of the standards and size they were embossed with. 'And where might they be?'

'The biggest are on Hirkiv, a planet in the Kandark Galaxy.' He watched as she stopped the lathe, changed flanges and started it up again, cutting out the seal area on the second one.

'Is that where the hybrid drive came from?'

'Most likely,' he said, non-committing. Niamh had asked him the same before; truth be known, he couldn't tell and wondered himself where it was made.

She continued until all four flanges were done. Taking two, she crossed the workshop and placed them on a bench beside a TIG welder. 'You might want to watch your eyes,' she said, offering him a spare welder's hood.

Mesmerised, he watched her place another one of the hoods on her head, then make adjustments to a small machine and gas bottle beside the bench. She offered up a flange to the flow port – mounted securely in a jig. Deftly moving her head, forcing the hood to fall in place over her face, she struck the joint with the electrode. There was a hum from the machine, a crackle and flash of blinding light from the arc. He gasped in surprise. Holding the spare hood over his face, he watched Niamh manipulate the puddle of molten metal, welding the flange to the pipe nipple on the flow port.

She stopped, lifted her hood and checked it was square. 'You've seen our techs do this before, Pilot, during the refit. Why such interest?' she said, now dressing the weld.

'Yes, but not you. I thought such skills were special among humans.'

'Yes and no. I picked all this up in college, as an extra. I like making things. Go on, off with ya,' she said, smiling at his wonderment. 'They'll be missing you on the bridge.'

After he left, she continued with her work, welding on the other flange and then finishing off the workpieces with a polishing grinder. All the while, musing on the alien manufacturing processes and the maker of the mysterious hybrid drive, puckering her lips at the thought she couldn't expel: *we need to know where and who makes them.*

The workshop was split into two sections. The "dirty work" space was filled with Earth machinery, including the lathes, a turret mill, welders, metalworking presses and all the hand tools a well-fitted workshop would have. The "clean area" was just that, fitted out with Anan instruments and some high-quality Earth-sourced electrical and instrumentation tools, including their invaluable three-dimensional printers. It was in here the material he had specified was carefully stored, in clean hermetically sealed drawers, and where she brought the tank to fit the end seals.

The gelatinous sheets were made from rare Neredian frond, harvested from its deep oceans. This unique low porosity material was ideal for creating flexible blue containment seals. The clear gelatinous structure retained its molecular memory allowing the construction of the self-sealing ports. Using a flange as a template, Niamh carefully cut four round sheets of the precious material. Scoring the four discs with an eight-point star, she bolted them double, with the remaining two (retaining) flanges onto the ones she had welded to the flow port. Finally, when it was all finished, she stepped back and admired her work. The delicately made oval tank was about the size of a four-litre bottle and weighed little over three kilos.

It shone like silver, the fresh phaenian steel surfaces glistening in the harsh lights of the workshop. After pressure testing the tank and seals with nitrogen, she carried it back aft to the hybrid engine room. Carefully, she pierced one of its seals with a spigot on the blue feed manifold. Holding the tank in place over the tap, she cracked a valve, watching with interest as the energy gushed in. Its bright blue form swirled and curled as it filled the small tank. The alien seals did their job, containing the blue inside. Turning off the valve, she pulled the tank off the spigot. Amazingly, the gelatinous seals, following their molecular memory, slammed shut – not spilling a drop. *Wow*, she thought, as the tank shimmered a beautiful deep blue from the colour of the energy trapped inside.

*

After her next watch, Niamh Parker bounced into The Eight's chamber carrying her small tank of blue.

'My child, calm down. You will need all your brainpower to do this.'

'Jeez, what do you expect? I'm raring to have a go.'

'Put your pen on the floor over here, now stand away from it. First, kneel down with the tank on the floor and then I want you to put the tips of your fingers into the tank through the orifices. If you made it to my specifications, it allows your fingers in without leaking blue.'

Following his instructions, Niamh knelt down with the small tank in front of her and placed her fingers through the seals into the blue filled tank. 'Now, you know how you bring up a navigation projection – do the same with the space around the pen. Yes, that's good,' The Eight said, as a plot of the empty space around the pen appeared. Now you must fold the space – like a piece of paper.'

Focusing her mind, she projected her thoughts out into the plot of empty space. Delving deep down, into the atomic level of empty space between matter, the gamma waves from her brain mingled with the subatomic particles. But nothing happened. She didn't give up; with her hands now inside the tank of blue, she closed her eyes. This time, using the blue, she amplified her thoughts. Like waves, an invisible power flowed out of her mind, crashing into the space around her pen. She tried and tried, her stomach churning with the effort until – from the exertion – a pain developed in her chest.

After an hour, a tired Niamh finally slumped on the floor. 'I'm exhausted from that, and it never worked,' she said, as she picked up the remains of her pen. 'Look at my poor pen. It's squashed.'

The Eight, ever quiet during her efforts, finally spoke. 'I never said it would be easy, but you did well for the first day. Leave your tank of blue here and bring something more solid to move tomorrow.'

*

Niamh tirelessly worked on moving a metal ruler through folded space. Throughout her training, he was there in her mind, his quiet voice showing her how to control her thoughts and how to focus her spirit and energy.

She made a harness for the small tank which allowed her to carry it without kneeling on the floor. It was soon a relaxed part of her, and eventually, she did it, opening a small port in folded space and moving the ruler through it.

'Well done, my child. You see, it is easy when you practise. You must believe in your abilities. As the blue crystal allows you to project your brain waves to map and navigate through space, the blue energy allows you to manipulate it. You are the only biped I have seen do this.'

'Now you tell me,' she said, standing six-foot-tall and grinning from ear to ear, her brown freckles shining on her flush red cheeks. 'I'm amazed and delighted myself. Really, Overlord, I never believed I could do such things.'

'Tomorrow, we try something larger. Meet me in the main cargo bay.'

As the *Hela* travelled ever closer to their destination at the edge of the Anan Galaxy, Niamh spent all her available time working with The Eight. Her abilities and the size of the objects she moved increased. Finally, The Eight suggested she move an empty forty-foot container.

She screwed up her face. 'It's too large.'

'No, the size of the object does not matter – it needs more energy. Come, my child, try it.'

Niamh concentrated on folding the space in the large cargo hold. She opened a port, connecting two sides of an empty area she had marked out in a cargo bay. She raised the container and with it halfway through the port, she opened her mind to the infinity of space and time, something she hadn't done before. *So close to the blackness.* In the past, with the crystal fuelled navigation, it felt like her celestial mind was outside her body, travelling in space. Now, with so much power, it felt different. It was like she, Niamh, was out there, body and soul, standing alone in the darkness of empty space. Terrified, she lost concentration, and the port collapsed, cutting the container neatly in two. It crashed back down on the deck, the loud bang ringing throughout the cargo hold.

Her body shaking with disbelief and the fright from the shadowy world, she sat down on the floor. 'Ah shit, that was terrifying. And the container, I knew it was too big. Overlord, you know they weigh about two tons.'

'Yes, I do, and that's not the problem — you must believe you can do this. You must conquer your fear. We try again tomorrow.' Watching Niamh go, he had never thought she could get so far so soon. All she needed now was confidence in her abilities. And, he now knew, they would grow. But, at the back of his intelligence, something gnawed, a phenomenon he had not imagined would occur. He had watched the change in her hands, placed in the tank, stained blue from raw contact with the energy.

*

The Eight's guidance, delving into her mind, like a friend holding her hand, helped her conquered the fear. Finally, it all came together and all her hard work paid off. She connected with the blue, not afraid of the blackness. Her mind opened to it. She felt its very essence, what she could do with it. Like a moth to a flame, it sucked her in, allowing her to meld with its power, the very power the Overlords had found, all that time ago.

Her thoughts grabbed at the micro matter, the invisible particles in space between anti-matter and matter. She could see them all, quarks, fermions, neutrinos, bosons, protons and so, so many more. It was a seminal moment when she learned how the amplified gamma waves, flowing from her blue powered brain – like paper – folded the space between those particles. Standing by the edge of time and space, looking into the colourless vastness of that what scared her – it all snapped into order.

'You have it, conquered your fear,' The Eight said, pulsing with bright blue light.

'How does a blue energy drive open a port?' Niamh asked.

'By directing an astronomical powered pulse.'

Now she knew what she must do; she had approached the previous work with the blundering of a charging bull. She had some knowledge, but not it all. It was, as he said, "simple". With her hands embedded through the gelatinous seals of her tank, now an extension of her body – as if gathering the energy – she flexed her fingers. Merging every facet of her body, until the pure energy flowed from the tank into her hands, up through her arms and limbs and into her brain – with her very soul centring her life force, she generated that elusive pulse. With a crackle and a small burst of white light, it poured out through her eyes. Space folded and with the determination of a beating heart, she carved a port through it.

In her mind, she stood beside it, looking through the black void. She turned and picked up the forty-foot container and pushed it through. At the other side, with her ghostly hand, she grabbed and balanced it, setting it down on the deck. For those watching, all they saw was the port open, the container float up in the air and glide through, appearing again on the other side of the cargo bay.

Niamh stood stock still throughout, in a broad stable base with one foot in front of the other – the fighter's stance. Her hands steady in the blue tank, hanging at waist level and all the time, as if in a trance, her eyes glowed with a soft blue light. She had done it.

Some of the Anan purebreeds watched in awe as she practised moving objects through the empty space in the cargo hold. To challenge her ability, The Eight devised complicated tests, involving multiple shifts, of different items through many ports for her. Enthralling her admiring audience, with flying colours, she passed them all.

'Well done, my child. You see, it is easy. You must believe in your ability; that is all it takes,' he said.

In an excited voice, she said, 'I never imagined this possible, I really didn't. But tell me, Overlord, why did you teach me this?' Over the time she spent with him, she'd loved every minute of learning this new ability. But she always wondered why he was teaching such a guarded secret to a mortal.

'You will see. Now shortly, we arrive at our destination. Get some rest. I will see you again on the bridge before we arrive.'

*

Jora Galaxy. EPTS: A138504

In a dusty dry canyon, on the windswept Planet Natok, The Sixth looked up at the surrounding caves. Then he saw him and patiently watched, as the biped picked its way down to the canyon floor. *He is weak from hunger,* he thought.

Since touching The Eight's mind, there was an uneasiness about The Sixth. He was surprised to sense Eight at all, believing he would, long since, have expired from the lack of blue. He wondered, *what is he up to, where is he and how does he exist?* Those thoughts beat through The Sixth's energy mass. And, he couldn't rely on the Aknar army or their space fleet laid up at the Energy Exchange docks. *Treacherous they would be*, he thought. *No, keep that fleet starved of blue, with them all holed up at Anan.* He had always intended to waken the ceirim, and now the time was right. He would forge a new weapon to use with his own loyal fleet in a war with The Eight. *Eight, whatever you are up to, we will be ready.*

The six-foot-tall black biped raised his long thin arms and prostrated himself on the ground in front of his Overlord. Long thin black spikes, growing out from the ceirim's hide, glistened in the faint light of the planet's two suns. The neck – like a pin cushion – bristled with more spikes. Dark eyes peered out from his round featureless head. Small dimples on the side were all that showed of his ear canal – nothing to damage or grab on to. He opened his large mouth – sharp teeth glittered like steel barbs. 'Overlord,' he croaked, 'you return, after all this time. Why did you abandon us?'

The Sixth looked down at the grovelling ceirim. 'I never abandoned you. How many are left?'

'Sixteen thousand hibernate in the caves – they'll be hungry when we wake them. I followed your orders and left one continent with living animals – fresh meat to harvest for the awakening. But I'm ravenous, Overlord. Living on grubs and insects, I have struggled to defeat a deep desire to consume the others,' he said, daring to look up at the bloated entity's oval energy mass. Buffeted by the hollow wind, the seven-foot-high and four-foot-wide floating entity looked terrifying. His translucent mass shimmered with dark blue light, increasing in intensity at his core. The colours continually changed in tone – dark blue and purple with the occasional grey. Unusually dark for an Overlord – sporadically, his energy mass pulsed with a harsh blackness. Like unwanted tumours, dark nodules peppered The Sixth's extremity. Knowing what those nodes were capable of, the ceirim shuddered. *He has grown*, he thought, as the wind howled around them.

'Yes, I have grown in power. You did well to preserve your species.'

'Why, Overlord? Why have you done this to us and what of the promise you made to change us?'

'You did not know this, but aeons ago, your species were created to scour superfluous or malevolent life forms from our planets. They could purge a planet of all life and then consume themselves – a perfect, energy free, biological weapon.' He paused, floating closer to the ceirim his voice deepened in intensity. 'Our decrepit leader, The One of this epoch, in his infinite stupidity, believed you were a mistake. The best weapon we ever made – how could he believe you were a mistake? Do you know how hard it is to create life?' The ceirim shook his black head. The voice dropped in tone. 'No, of course, you don't. He asked me to expunge your species from the universe. I ignored him and have carefully cultivated you and your small group, the last survivors of your race.'

'And what of the experiments you did?'

One hundred Earth years ago, a geneticist working for The Sixth conducted routine tests on a group of the ceirim in the *Hela* med-bay. Some of the ceirim's DNA stayed in the test machine on the *Hela*. That was the contaminated matter that entered the unborn child of a human doctor, Alex, and Rhea, his purebreed lover, as they conducted their own tests to grow a cure for the Anan sickness. The voracious DNA of the ceirim takes over a contaminated host, quickly mutating the body into another ceirim. The perfect weapon – contaminate, transform and consume. That fatal contamination resulted in the demise of Alex, Rhea and their unborn child.

The Sixth floated away from the ceirim, dancing in the wind, his voice softened. 'We have a solution. My geneticists will alter the DNA of the sixteen thousand, inhibiting the procreative element. They won't be able to transform others. The change will stop uncontrolled expansion and the all-consuming orgy of feeding, of your species, on themselves.'

The ceirim squirmed, his dark eyes wide with surprise. 'But, Overlord, you stop our species' ability to propagate – stuck at sixteen thousand we be … unable to replace the aged or the injured …'

The entity's mass darkened. 'You doubt me. You believe I would be so stupid not to consider that.'

Cowering down on the ground, the ceirim's long claws dug into the dirt. 'Forgive me, Overlord,' he pleaded, his mouth dry with fear.

'Get up, you fool. I will make you the ceirim's androgynous leader. You'll be the only one who can introduce the transforming DNA to a host. At my behest, with the right bipeds, you will breed me new armies.'

The ceirim rose up from his prostrated position and stood before his Overlord's pulsating energy mass. He bowed his head. 'Overlord, such an honour I never imagined. When and how will you administer this?'

A shuttle de-cloaked beside The Sixth. 'Now, we do this today. My geneticists will administer the DNA-changing compound to the sixteen thousand. Your own compound is more complicated to administer. They favour oral delivery. A technique I believe will please. You will be known as Kochtos, the leader of your species, and here is the compound.'

The Sixth looked over to the shuttle – the door opened. A four-legged animal, harnessed to a cage, walked out, dragging it behind him. As they saw the ceirim, three stout purebreeds imprisoned in the cage, screamed. The Sixth had taken them from the jails of Anan. With an average height of five-foot-eight and porcelain white skin, the hairless aliens showed their ample feeding and lazy lifestyle. Scantily dressed in one-piece overalls, they shivered in the cold air as their screams pierced the deadly quiet of the canyon. With his long claws, Kochtos slashed through the animal's throat. Placing his full open mouth below the cut – as it spurted out, pulsing in rhythm with the animal's dying heart – he drank the crimson blood. He gurgled and gulped, consuming the tasty liquid. Slicing off one leg of the beast, he sat down in front of the cage and, listening to the screams and whimpers of the purebreeds, devoured the meat.

When Kochtos finished the first satisfying feed he had had in a long time, he looked at the purebreeds. 'I will savour you three,' he growled in Anan. Then he grinned as he plucked the food debris from between his long sharp teeth with his claws. Examining the small pieces, Kochtos belched and placed the morsels of food back into his mouth. With a slavering sound, a long black tongue darted out and licked the blood from around his mouth. Finally, he hacked up a ball of gristle and fat from his throat and spat it out onto the dusty ground beside the cage. 'Thank you, Overlord. I will give you your army,' he said, as he stood up and bowed again to his Overlord.

The Sixth watched his geneticists fly out of the shuttle on grav platforms. Dressed in biohazard suits, they headed up to the caves to deliver
the DNA compound to the sixteen thousand hibernating ceirim. 'Come,
Kochtos, let us go and watch the changing of your species.' *It finally starts
– in my own galaxy,* he thought, *my advancement to becoming The One.*

CHAPTER THREE

Universal Credits

To avoid inter-world disagreement on cargo values, the Universal Credit or UC, as it is more commonly known, was introduced by the Overlords after the third expansion period of the Energy Exchange. Up until then, traders at the Exchange relied on the art of arbitrage to reconcile the different values of assets, commodities and energy they bartered. That the cost of a world's prized cargo was set by a faceless dealer sitting at a desk in the far distant Anan Galaxy, sparked – on occasion – interplanetary war. The value of the UC is based on: a basket of energies, commodities and assets, availability of their supply, the demand for them and the work or effort necessary to get them. The Overlords monitored and set the value to avoid unfair manipulation of markets, or one world getting rich on the endeavours of another.

⦁ Extract From: The History of the Energy Exchange Part 2. Theia Aknar

*

Energy Exchange, Anan Solar System. EPTS: A138552

LIKE A SPINNING TOP, THE bulbous shaped floating city, tapering down to its blue drive foundations, sparkled in the shadows of space as it orbited the cloudy planet of Anan. The galactic Energy Exchange, with its vast space docks, hummed with activity, it's near half million inhabitants preparing for a much-welcomed break. Ships lined up at the docks, some awaiting clearance to leave, others waiting for a berth, and as always, the small few hoping to unload an irregular cargo in the closing minutes of the trading period.

Arb, the lead grav trader, looked at the warning flashing on his screen. He was the oldest of the ten purebreeds working in the Exchange's grav trading cell. Riddled with the Anan sickness, Arb frowned and scratched at the sores on his face. Leaning over, he whispered to the young girl, sitting at the desk beside him. 'You shouldn't have taken that trade. Before we close, quick, cancel it.'

Immaculate, with her white Anan nose in the air, she rudely replied, 'Mind your business.'

'I don't understand you,' Arb whispered. Many times he had explained it to her – the worlds, in their known universe, barter to trade energy and assets between each other. To be successful, the Exchange traders must reconcile the different energy, commodities and asset values to UC. *There's no value in what she's doing*, he believed, *unless – no, not worth thinking about.* 'It'll cost you,' he said, frowning at her. In disgust, Arb turned back to close out his own work. *Her loss*, he thought, *there will be trouble when Cylla sees this.*

Knowing demand for grav would be high, their boss Cylla Ora, arranging a supply for the post-holiday start, missed the girl's tactic. 'I'll take it all,' Cylla, the biped amphibian, said, looking at the haggard face of the old grav supplier on the viewscreen. 'No, don't say you can't deliver. You'll get your price. It's agreed then,' she said, as the old man smiled and nodded. Cylla smiled back as he cut off the transmission. *Another job done*, she thought, as she finished her preparations for the Exchange to close for the holiday. From the water-covered planet of Nered, she was a different creature to the purebreed Anans who mostly staffed it.

Relaxing back into her seat, she looked around and up at the main trading hall that stretched through four levels of the vast Exchange. She loved to stop and look at the extensive gallery. The various trading cells anchored at different levels, and the activity of the commodity and energy traders in the terminals, never ceased to amaze her.

Fortunes were made and lost in the open and the close of the market. Cylla loved this, the closing time buzz of the Exchange as the noise rose and the prices changed and flashed at each of the trading terminals.

Through the transparent domed roof, she looked out into space and the stars beyond. The planet, Anan, its surface masked by grey and white clouds, was coming into view. As their massive city in space turned, Cylla couldn't believe it was five orbits since she had first started working here. Inexperienced and naive, she learned it all from the lead trader. She glanced over at him but his look of disgust snapped her back to reality.

Cylla's tail started to uncoil and flap violently above her head as her screen flashed the reason for his annoyance. *It had to be her*, she realised. *She's been with us half an orbit and still not extracted herself from the trial period.* 'What's the problem now?'

The tall Neredian leaned over the girl's console, her nose and gills flaring in anger. The girl coughed, covering her face with her hands as the foul pheromones seeped from Cylla's gills, slowly permeating the small trading pit. The others held their noses. 'Well, well,' she stammered, 'he put in a limit order to buy a hundred cubes of grav, but didn't want to pay in UC — he has a cargo to trade.'

'You know orders are only accepted in UC,' growled Cylla, referring to the innovative Universal Credit. Instead of bartering, it was introduced to provide a more user-friendly, and fairer way, for interplanetary commerce. Mistake number one. 'So, tell me, why did you take the order if he isn't going to pay in UC? What's the precious cargo? And who's the client?'

The girl flashed the white smiling young face of the overconfident captain across her screen. 'It's him, with a cargo of chemical waste, and I have someone in commodities interested—'

Cylla shook her head. 'That foul mess is supposed to go to Javan for treating! And I told you, all orders from that cunning slimeball are to be routed to me. What were you thinking?' Mistakes two and three. Her face was now glowing golden with anger. 'Cancel it now. Yes, cancel it right now,' Cylla shouted, as a loud horn sounded.

The girl trembled as she looked at Cylla's tail, circling menacingly above her. 'No, no, I can't.' Her white complexion turned grey as fear built up in her gut. She was previously warned that Neredians use their tails as whips. 'The market's closed.'

'Of course, it is. I'll call the slimeball myself. Get him on screen,' Cylla roared. The girl, trying to control her shaking hands, called the ship, passing comms to Cylla.

'Grav terminal here. Let me talk to your captain.'

After a pause, a young, friendly face, with a polished head and immaculately pressed light green suit, appeared on screen. 'Cylla, what can I do for you?' he said. *Here we go*, the slimeball thought, *the Water Monster interferes with what she knows nothing about.*

'It's your cargo,' she said, frowning at him. 'Do you have waste permits, chemical analysis and certs of origin for each substance?' she asked, knowing quite well he wouldn't. Abruptly, the young girl tried to block Cylla's view. A surprised Cylla pushed her back down into her chair. Then she realised why; partially covered by the clutter of the captain's desk, the girl's family crest peeped out. The unmistakable logo, a green shield with three stars at its corners and two crossed swords supporting a spaceship, was mounted on the back of a family comms unit. Intergalactic conquest or greed, as most would decipher it. She took a deep breath, bit down hard and concentrated on stopping her tail from whipping the girl to death. *Now is not the time to lose it*, she thought, regaining some semblance of self-control. Anan corruption, it was why she was given this position, to stamp that all so familiar jobbery out.

Oblivious to what she had seen, the captain tried to sound surprised at her question. 'You mean you didn't get them?' he asked, his face flush with deceit.

Maintaining her composure, she continued with the expected dialogue. 'You know I didn't. You should have sent them when placing the trade. I'm closing up here.'

'Apologies, Cylla. Can we get around that and get our grav?'

'No. Your trade is illegal. You shouldn't have come to market without proper documents. You know it, I know it, everybody knows it! I'm cancelling your order,' she said, anxious to end this time-wasting charade.

His face darkened. 'You can't do that – no, we have six ships with cargo. I'll complain to the Moderator, I will. It was accepted on hold,' he argued.

'You know the rules. Go complain, see if it gets you anywhere,' Cylla said, abruptly closing the connection. Tired of this now, she turned to face the girl. It was three cardinal sins in a row – a breach of their protocol – allowing Cylla to take the action she had wanted to. She smiled within.

By her own stupidity, the girl had done Cylla a favour. She had wanted to fire her since shortly after the young one started. Now it was a simple sacking, without going through the time-wasting hassle of proving the family's corruption. In a quiet voice, she broke the news. 'As for you, that's your last day here. Pack it up and don't come back. Maybe you can get a job in commodities but don't ask for a reference from me.'

With her head slumped down over her long neck in shame, the girl got up and walked out of the hall.

Clearing what was left on the girl's trading station, Cylla cancelled the trade. Her tail was still flapping in agitated circles back and forth around her body. She was proud of it and her self-control, managing to stop the sharp tail from whipping the girl. The other traders cowered in fear as they closed up and prepared to leave. She turned around and looked at them. 'If I've told you all once, I've told you a thousand times, we don't take waste or any commodity or asset not registered. I've given you all a list of the slimeballs whose trades you're to direct to me. Don't stick your necks out. I'm here to support you – all you have to do is ask. Fair enough?'

'Yes,' they replied.

'Finish up and enjoy the break,' she said. Smiling at Arb and whispering a thank you to him as he left, she watched the rest file out. They were dodging around her still moving tail. *So young and inexperienced. Where was she to get a replacement for the young girl? I'd be lost without the lead*, she thought.

With everybody else in the Exchange, Haret, the chief blue energy trader, watched the unfolding drama. He was so proud of her. Cylla had turned out to be his star apprentice. He quietly admired her. Her long brown hair reached down to the middle of her back and her golden scales shimmered from the anger as her long tail flapped fiercely above her head. He could see her green eyes flashing and the pink forked tongue darting in and out as she spoke. She looked ferocious. That look, coupled with her beauty and elegance captivated the whole Exchange. There was no doubt – she commanded the respect she deserved.

All the traders wore the same dull blue garments that were tailored to fit over their different body sizes. It made them all look the same. *Regardless of what she wears, Cylla Ora stands out from the crowd,* he thought. He had met her on a trip to Nered and immediately saw her potential. Offering her a job as his assistant was a change to the way things were done at the Exchange, staffed by purebreeds from Anan. Without any hesitation, she accepted the offer. She had come a long way since then and soon eclipsed the Anans working alongside her. Catching The One's attention, she had amazed him with her success as a trader. As she advanced, her peers gave her the nickname "Water Monster". She was quite proud of that.

Haret watched the girl leave. Not the demure one she appeared to be, he felt no pity for her. She and her high-born family, influential owners of many assets, would not take this lightly. She would rise again with the help of her family but that didn't deter Cylla from tackling her. She treated the team equally and expected the same high standards from all, no exceptions. It was a cutthroat business with no room for mistakes. The weak fell by the wayside and were swiftly replaced. He closed out his terminal and went over to talk to his apprentice, whose tail was now coiled around her.

'Well, well, aren't you glorious today. All ready for the holiday?' Haret asked. He was small for a purebreed and always found himself looking up to her more than average height.

'Old man, don't be so patronising,' she replied. 'Except for Arb, I'm surrounded by idiots. Can you believe that?' Cylla said, looking at Haret sitting quite relaxed in her trading terminal. She wanted to tell him all but knew now was not the time. The clamour of the Exchange was dying as the traders closed their terminals and started to leave for the holiday.

'You should have flayed her alive with your tail – blood and skin flying through the air. Oh yes,' Haret said, his hands raised in the air like he was conducting the whole operation, 'your tail slashing through the intestines. Those foul smells, long time since such putrid fresh death tickled my nostrils. And the screams, yes, the bloodcurdling screams, your other traders would have shit their pants – yes, they would. It's so long since you gave a good lashing. And, you know it gives you such pleasure,' he said, as his eyes glinted with mirth and a small smile curled across his grey lips. It had the right effect.

Cylla burst into laughter, put her arms around him and gave him a big hug. Laughing, she took hold of his two small hands and looking deep into his blue eyes, said, 'I love you, old man. You know how to cheer me up. Now tell me how your three wives and those four gorgeous children are doing?'

Letting go of her hands and leaning back, he laughed as well. 'My wives are great, thank you, and so are the children. They all keep asking when you are coming around again to visit. You must. Every day they ask how you are doing. My daughters want to discuss the whole male thing with you,' he said. Wagging his finger at Cylla, he continued. 'I don't know what you said to them the last time you were over, and I don't want to know either, but they were of course intrigued. Why am I shocked at that?'

'I … I told them nothing,' she replied, shaking her head and trying to sound innocent.

'So, what have you planned for the holiday? Can you come over?' he asked. 'My wife, who cooks, will make your favourite dish. You know the white meat from Anan in spices.'

And then she got the message. *Haret wants to talk in private*, she realised. The walls here have ears. She knew enough to keep the small talk going and to bury everything in subterfuge. 'Well, I do have plans and someone new to meet. I'm quite looking forward to it,' she purred.

'Do tell, do tell,' he said, winking at her. *She got the message*, he thought. For the sake of any eavesdroppers, they would continue with this chat, and it was now getting interesting.

'I've booked a suite in the new hideaway they installed on the lower floor. You know, the Hilotes Complex, they named it after the planet, Hilote,' Cylla said. 'I'm taking my new companion there. She paused as her eyes glazed over, and said in a dreamy slow voice, 'The time there is going to be spent pleasuring ourselves.'

'Oh, do tell me more, I'm intrigued,' he said, as he slapped his hands on the table.

'No, old man, that's enough info. But I'll call over towards the end of the holiday. I'd like that; I'll tell all then.'

'Excellent,' he said, as he clapped his hands together. 'Now, come, let's get out of this place.' Continuing the small talk, they both left the great hall of the Exchange.

*

'Father, I'm afraid … I've bad news for you,' the girl said, speaking into the comms terminal from her room at the Exchange. 'The Water Monster fired me.'

Sitting in the family's plush offices on Anan, her father's grey face shrivelled with the unwelcome news. 'She can't do that. She couldn't have known it was my cargo you tried to trade.'

'That's not the reason she gave for firing me, but I suspect she knew.'

'Come back to Anan. There's trouble coming; I want you safe with us.'

'What about your waste, and the grav you need? What will you do?'

'I'll take care of it, don't worry. Come home,' her father said.

'I'll book a flight today,' she said, bowing her head in reverence as the connection terminated.

The tall purebreed man, head of the influential Svang Charter, looked pensively at the blank screen in front of him. His gaze shifted to a small glass canister of blue, placed in front of the prized possessions adorning his desk. The beautiful blue colours continually radiated out as the energy swirled in the glass prison. It was a gift, an extravagant one, its indulgence oozing wealth and power. He banged a fist on the bureau in frustration. There was no blue anymore. The Sixth had it all. How was he supposed to transport chemical waste to Javan for processing? The economics of it didn't make sense. It would be an unnecessary drain of the precious, expensive grav and time. Worst of all, the chemical leftovers, solvents from their mines on Bahar, a nearby planet, could be burned here on Anan to generate power. Yes, there were environmental issues with that – burning fuel on their cloudy home didn't go down too well. But now they had no choice. For too long, senseless regulation had stifled their trade. Times were changing – with no blue for intergalactic travel, people would have to adapt.

He glanced up at a big screen on the wall, watching the graphs and figures scroll down. The cargo index, an indicator he worshipped, was down forty per cent. Were they asleep up there in the sky on the all so high and mighty Energy Exchange? Did they not understand the meaning of that simple indicator and see reality, intergalactic trade down a massive amount. Unprecedented in this modern era. The outlying worlds stifled by the high cost of grav, and with no blue in sight, it's price was set as unaffordable. All they were interested in was the holidays, fat commissions and luxurious lifestyles, all funded by him and the Charters. He huffed a deep sigh. Now he would have to dump the cargo in space – a more significant mess to make!

Shrugging that decision off, he stood and walked across to the window, looking out at the wet city below, his faint reflection caught in the glass. The man adjusted the shirt on his broad shoulders, then touched the faint scar on his cheek. He smiled, thinking about how he had got it – a silly game with swords when they first joined the military together. They were young then, full of love and not a care in the world, all that time ago. And from that, he had married her, they were inseparable, and the two swords found their way onto the family crest. She had tried hard, year after year until finally, she had given birth to their daughter: their only child, a miracle of life.

At birth, the girl was tested for the dreaded Anan sickness, and to their joy, their only child, their miracle of life, was free of it. But, there were no guarantees with the test; the disease could manifest itself later in her life. All they could hope for was she would have her own children, continue as the head of the family's charter and pass that mantle on to her offspring. He turned, making his way back to the desk. Smiling at the happy image of his wife and daughter perched on the bureau, he placed another call, this time to the Exchange Moderator.

CHAPTER FOUR

The Anan Sickness

The term "purebreed" refers to the inhabitants of the planet, Anan. Legend has it, we were the first bipeds to receive intelligence from the Overlords. To guard that intelligence and our unique DNA, it became custom and practice for our people not to interbreed with other biped races. Aeons of interbreeding between our limited populations have diminished the ability to procreate. The Anan sickness developed over the last forty thousand orbits. Our geneticists predict purebreed DNA will continue to break down over time. So far, they are unsuccessful in developing a cure. For the afflicted, once the disease takes hold, it attacks the reproductive organs, then ravages the body until we finally expire — an early painful death. While on a voyage to a distant planet, Empress Theia Aknar employed Alex Barber, a human geneticist to develop a cure. With his colleague, Rhea Lupe, a purebreed doctor, they identified the genes and compounds needed for a remedy, generating an initial, first-stage treatment. As the disease was well advanced in me, I was chosen as a test subject. I am happy to say, once blighted by the sores from the Anan sickness, I enjoyed a period of respite, courtesy of the First Stage Treatment, developed by the ill-fated doctors, Alex and Rhea. I can only hope, from their research and samples, their work continues, and Anan produces a permanent cure.

> **· Extract from: the journal of Demard Borea**

*

The Hela, Anan Galaxy. EPTS: A138552

WITH THE HYBRID DRIVE DECOUPLED from the grav engines, the *Hela* slowed as it approached a thick asteroid belt at the edge of the Anan Galaxy. From her navigation console, 'Pilot, course is set,' Niamh said.

He watched the approaching asteroid belt, his eyes glued to the bridge screen, magnifying the view of space in front of them. 'Siba, reduce speed, fifty per cent.' A pulse beat on the side of his white temple with the tension. There was no margin for error. Five minutes later, his next order shattered the deadly silence. 'Siba, reduce speed, twenty per cent.' The asteroids loomed larger and larger on the screen as if they were bursting into the ship from the curved display. At one hundred kilometres out, 'Siba, all stop, all stop.'

The ship trembled as the grav engines fired in reverse. The deep throbbing rose, then after what seemed an age, died away. 'All stopped, Captain, and holding,' she confirmed with a nod to her uncle.

'Overlord, we are near enough now,' the Pilot said, as he moved over to stand in front of Niamh's navigation projection. 'Mrs Parker, can you bring up a view of this area here,' he asked, pointing to a location deep within the asteroid belt.

By now, her ability to map space was as natural as walking. She never forgot that first day on the *Hela*, when Theia, the alien empress, had thought her that skill. Tightening her grip on her blue crystal embedded in the nav-con, Niamh instinctively focused her brain's gamma waves until the energy-soaked pendant glowed. Through it, she projected her mind out into the asteroid belt to the location the Pilot indicated, her view mirrored in the projection in front of her. To her surprise, she was looking into a giant space station carved out of a small moon-sized asteroid. 'There's a base here, with ships as well, but I can't see a way in.'

'Overlord, I can fly the *Hela* between the outer asteroids to here,' the Pilot said, pointing to a precise location beyond the enclosing rocks. 'But that's as far as we go on a conventional drive. Is Mrs Parker ready?'

'What does he mean, am I ready?' Niamh asked, turning from her station to look at the Pilot and the Overlord. Their stony silence said it all. Looking down at her blue-stained hands, she realised what it was all about. Anger flashed across her freckled face. 'So that's why you taught me. No, it's too much. Why can't you do it, Overlord? Tell me, tell me right now. I deserve an explanation,' she said, glaring at the two co-conspirators.

'Yes, Niamh, you do. Until we are sure of our way ahead, we are safe here, at least for a short time.' He turned to the Pilot's cousin, the indispensable communications expert. 'Demard, any ships showing up on the scanners?'

Once blighted by the sores from the Anan sickness, now in respite, courtesy of the First Stage Treatment, Demard turned. 'No, Overlord, out here there is nothing. We are alone, and with our cloak engaged, we are invisible too.'

'Pilot, Niamh, we will adjourn to the ready room. Pilot, you can explain and leave nothing out.'

*

'Niamh, what do you know about my family and me?' the Pilot asked, sitting across from her in the captain's ready room at the back of the bridge.

'Not much; you've managed to hide everything. We always suspected you were more than a shuttle pilot. I know your family were energy traders and that locker in the Australian base was theirs, and yes, we're burning your grav, but the rest is a mystery.'

'I chose to remain a mystery because of my family's history. Generations ago, our ancestors, the Borea of old, were one of the largest Charters, dealers in all types of energy with their own fleets, shipping bases and also, they designed and built their own vessels – they were the best in the galaxies. The last generation was what you would call "greedy rogues". They turned a successful, legitimate energy business into a dismal failure, bankrupting the family. A violent faction took over.' He paused, as the shakes of shame fluttered in his gut. He continued, hastily glossing over the worst part. 'Demons they were, who resorted to smuggling, piracy and thievery and finally, fell foul of the Overlords. Our family name, Borea, was struck from the Register of Charters and we were cast out. We owed a large debt to the Energy Exchange and the Overlords and, in our world, the debt remains with the family. The contents of the Australian base and my family's work for Project Anan's success have expunged that debt. The Eight has restored our name and to some extent, our Charter.

As part of the settlement, I have offered our secret bases and ships to The Eight for his use. This base is our largest. It is well hidden in the asteroid belt and was used, I am ashamed to admit, to smuggle and as my Grandfather's pirate base.'

'Jeez, Pilot, that's quite a story. So, what's the problem in getting in?'

'When the family left, three hundred of your years ago, they sealed the base and protected it from intruders. The asteroids are part of the defence mechanism and form an impenetrable guard. With the right codes, they are programmed to move aside and open an access channel. I don't have those codes to open the channel remotely from the *Hela*.'

'Overlord, why can't you use your powers, find the codes or jump us through a port in space?'

'He can't, Niamh. My family knew the Overlords would try to get in. They have something that shields the base from their power. If activated, it'll destroy the space station. We need to get a shuttle into it. Once we're in, Demard can disable the protection measures and open the channel for the *Hela*.'

To their surprise, The Eight added, 'Also, you must know, I wish to stay anonymous in space and time. Such is my power, if I use it now, others may see me. You, Niamh, a mere blip, will never be noticed.'

'So, you want me to open a port for one of our small shuttles, a little larger than a forty-foot container,' she said. In her excitement, she failed to realise the significance of what he had revealed. Her happy face flushed with enthusiasm and she smiled for the first time. 'Lads, I thought you expected me to jump the *Hela* in.'

'No, Niamh. Not this time. Your ability is strong enough to do that but using so much energy may change you. Today, we need you to get the computer technician and Siba into the space station. All you do is fold space and open a port. Siba will fly the shuttle through it. It will be easier than the tests I set you in the cargo bay.'

'When do we leave?' she asked, jumping up from her seat. 'I can't wait to try this.' In her rush to leave the room, she completely missed a quick pulse of intense blue light from The Eight's energy mass.

'Overlord, was that a glow of pride?' the Pilot whispered.

'Pilot Zaval, do not test me. Remember, I can easily take what I give. But, yes, you are right, it was.'

*

Borea Base, Anan Galaxy

Sitting in the shuttle one kilometre from the never-ending three-dimensional procession of crushing mayhem, Niamh, Siba and Demard watched the guardian asteroids swirl and collide as they protected the pirate base from attack.

'That's amazing – how did they build it?' Niamh said. 'Each rock must have its own embedded grav drive and be linked to a central processor. And how is it fuelled? It never stops. Demard, will you be able to get the specs for it when we get through? I have to know how it works; I'm intrigued.'

'Yes, so I see,' he said, as he watched Niamh's head twist and turn as she gazed in awe at the swirling maze. 'Grandfather was quite the engineer.'

'Did you lads see the containers that I destroyed in the cargo bay?' she said, now looking intently at the two Anans with her face screwed up and her brow furrowed.

Siba's usually white face started to go grey with worry. 'Yes, and you shouldn't have brought that up now,' she said. 'I would appreciate it if you would concentrate on what you need to achieve, Mrs Parker.'

Looking up from his workstation in the cramped shuttle, the old Demard grinned. 'Calm down, Siba. Niamh is teasing you. Niamh, I'm ready when you are. We've a link to the base computer.'

'Siba, you ready?' Niamh asked, trying not to laugh. It was a trick she had learned from the Pilot on Earth – lighten the mood, stay confident and happy. The more endorphins her body released, the easier it would be to manipulate space.

'Yes, Mrs Parker.'

Niamh placed her hands into her tank of blue. 'Here we go.' The nav-con erupted with a split view of the inside of the station and the open space immediately in front of the shuttle. Niamh's eyes flashed with white light. Space folded, and as Niamh's mind carved it, a port appeared in the projection while one simultaneously appeared immediately outside the shuttle. 'Siba, all ahead at twenty.'

'Ahead twenty per cent, Mrs Parker.'

The shuttle advanced into the open port, flew straight through the fold and out of the port she had opened, inside the space station. 'Turn one-eighty,' Niamh said.

'Turning one-eighty.'

'All stop,' Niamh said, as they looked from inside the station back at the opening. 'We're clear.' They watched the round port close in front of them, locking them inside, the guarding asteroids continuing their procession, now behind them.

A new readout scrolled across Demard's screen. 'Niamh, we're being scanned by the base security system. It's automatic and will look at our DNA; it'll recognise Siba and me as family Borea.'

'What about me?'

'You, it will see, are a female and not of our species. Not unusual for grandfather's appetite,' he replied, smiling at her question.

'I see, some fella, your grandfather. Can we have a look around? I want to see the ships and where we can dock the *Hela*,' she said, looking around the vast area inside the space station.

*

The Eight and the Pilot watched the shuttle's progress from the *Hela* bridge. 'They're in, Overlord. She's amazing. That's history being made. There will be legends born from this.'

All the Anan crew were on the bridge to watch this historic moment. The split-screen gave them a bird's eye view of the event, showing pictures from the shuttle cameras and the perspective from the *Hela*, lying five kilometres out from the swirling three-dimensional maze.

Proud of Niamh's achievement, The Eight stayed silent. Still, he had reservations about what he had done. *She is the first mortal to manipulate space like that. The others will try to take my energy if they find out what I have taught her. I may now be an outlaw amongst my own kind*, he thought.

Suddenly the view from the shuttle changed. The Pilot jumped up with excitement at the sight that filled the curved bridge display. 'Look, look, it's still here. I wasn't sure it would be still intact. It's beautiful, formidable and fast, the most dangerous ship in the galaxy. The *Boreal*, my grandfather's battle-cruiser. Even the Aknar fleet doesn't have such a ship.' He turned and bowed in deference to The Eight. 'Overlord, it is yours, part of our agreement. It will serve you well as a flagship.' Turning back to the comms, he contacted the shuttle. 'Siba, I want to see up close, all around that ship. Look for any damage in the hull. Demard, have you disabled the base defence systems?'

'There's a temporary fix in place. It will do until we gain access to the main computer's core. There is time; we can look at the *Boreal* first.'

*

The *Boreal* was indeed a formidable looking ship. The small shuttle flew around the five hundred metre long vessel, inspecting its hull for signs of damage or a breach.

'What class of a spaceship is that?' Niamh asked.

'It's one of a kind, designed for grandfather. Those dipped wings at the aft area house blue and hybrid drives. The large cylinders house grav missiles. They're like the armoury on the *Hela* but have larger and more destructive missiles. Look at the main body of the ship. There are the outlets for the grav engines. That ship is packed with engines,' Demard said, pointing to the features on the strangely shaped ship.

'What's that below the bow, the big upside-down fin?'

'It's part of the landing structure. There are two gun positions on each side of the fin, and you see it's connected to a superstructure above. Look closely – there, you see,' he said, as he pointed to an area of the ship they were flying past. 'Those windows are an accommodation section and where our grandfather lived. Rumour has it, it's sumptuously fitted out. He lived there with the best, enjoying the spoils of his ill-gotten gains. It serves as a runabout as well. Can disconnect from the mother ship and work as a lifeboat or, as I heard, more usually, a stealthy shuttle for smuggling. Borea cloaks are the best, undetectable …'

In silence, they spent ten minutes flying around the darkened grey ship. Moored up beside the space dock, it looked neglected and gloomy, giving no sign of its power or its capabilities. *It's going to be a real challenge to power it up*, thought Niamh. After feasting her eyes on the new technology, she contacted the *Hela*.

'Pilot, it looks okay. No visible signs of structural damage that I can see. I can't imagine how we'll survey its insides. But we need to crack on. I want to look at the rest of the base and see where we'll dock the *Hela*.'

'Agreed, I've seen enough.'

The small shuttle, dwarfed by the vast ship it was flying about, turned and dived into the depths of the space station beyond. Passing three more much smaller craft, the shuttle finally reached the end of the station's structure – terminating at the curved walls of the asteroid it occupied.

Constructed half into the asteroid, a large building appeared in front of the shuttle. It held a commanding view of the space station and was connected to the main docking areas by floating gantries. Emerging at the side of the building and festooned with pipes and cables, were the space station's main storage tanks.

'That's the blue energy depot and the space station's headquarters,' Demard said, in his dull voice. 'We need to get inside there. Siba, land on that shuttle platform outside the building.'

*

Faultlessly, Siba, the Pilot's young niece, landed the shuttle beside the main door of the building. Long gone was the fear she had experienced when they first started out on this mission. The discovery of her family's past fascinated her, and that The Eight had requested her for this mission, continued to fill her with pride.

Once outside on the deck, Niamh hooked up an emergency power supply from the shuttle to a connection at the door. Now standing beside Siba, she impatiently watched Demard work at a data terminal mounted on the wall. It was the first time she had ventured out of the safety of the ship or a shuttle in a spacesuit. Another first, it was an eventful day for her, she realised, as she looked around at the vast pirate base. The new technology that surrounded her piqued her curiosity. She turned this way and that, and it took all her self-control to stay with Demard and Siba. As if he could read her mind, Demard stopped his work and turned to face Niamh.

'Mrs Parker, you must stay with us. Do not roam, do not get distracted. Stay right beside me. We discussed this. Until I disarm the base security, we're all in danger.'

'Yes, Demard. I promise.'

'Thank you. Help me open this door. The mechanism is jammed.'

It was the first sign of the mechanical state of the base. In their spacesuits, they struggled to pry the door and airlock inside it open. Sometime in the distant past, the damaged airlock let the atmosphere inside the building leak out. With light from torches mounted on their suits, they continued inside, working their way along a dark corridor. Tripping over something on the floor, Niamh suddenly stumbled. She screamed as a skeletal foot appeared in the pool of light from her helmet. They shone their torches down to the ground, illuminating the skeleton of a biped lying prostrate with its legs held together by foot-chains. The grisly discovery added to the macabre nature of their journey. Trying to settle her nerves, Niamh took a deep breath. As they continued, the grim discoveries increased, as they passed by rooms with skeletal remains still chained to the walls.

After passing the fifth skeleton, Niamh shook her head and looked across at Demard. 'This is horrible. Who were they?'

'Grandfather's slaves and prisoners. They were Neredians—'

'Neredians? What are they and how do you know?'

'They are from the water Planet Nered. You can see the remains of their tails, look there,' Demard said, pointing to one of the skeletons. 'Get used to this, Niamh; it will get worse as we explore the base.'

'What do you mean? And why?'

'Remember what you were told? They were outlaws; they had prisoners; they were outcasts. When it all came to an end, Grandfather retreated to this base. He locked himself and the slaves and prisoners in.'

'So, he died here with these poor wretches?'

'We're not sure. Grandfather left the family puzzles and codes to access this and the other assets he owned. We don't know if he escaped. Could have survived – but I think that's unlikely. If he survived, why is he not here? I don't know. Zaval the Pilot and I were left with all the puzzles and the codes to work out where everything is and how to get in,' Demard said, as his wide eyes peered out through the visor of his spacesuit.

'So, there are more secret bases.'

'Yes, there are, or were, a lot of assets. Now, enough talk, we must continue. I want to find the main computer,' he said, as he started to shuffle down the dark passage, his old back bent with the effort of carrying the air bottles.

Twenty minutes later, after working their way along the corridor and up a set of stairs, they arrived at the central control room.

'This is eerie,' Niamh said, as she looked around the dark room. 'Look, all the workstations are empty and clean. They even tucked their seats back into the recesses below their stations. It's like they knew they would never be back.'

From the control room window, Demard looked out over the space dock and the dull silhouette of the four ships. 'Yes, it does, but where did they go? The ships are still here.' He returned to the control stations and soon found what he was looking for. 'Zaval, I'm at the main computer terminal. I'll try to get full control,' he said, over his comms system as he started his work. From a pocket in his spacesuit, he took out a small data drive, one that his father had left to him. From the drive, he extracted a master code he was told would enable a hack into any of the family's systems. But he knew access was only part of the problem. Once in, he would have to reconfigure the control and the security systems. His long bony fingers, covered by the thin material of his spacesuit, moved assiduously across the keyboards as he worked his hack.

Lights started to come on in the control room. Seeing them from the shuttle's cameras, the comms bristled with Zaval's voice. 'Have you access to the computer core already?'

'Getting it now. The power link we set up from the shuttle is working,' Demard answered. 'I've also got access to the defence mechanism. Give me ten minutes to work it out.'

As Demard worked, Niamh watched the old man. His resilience astounded her. When she first met him, he was very sick; now the sores of his affliction had abated. That he had made it here, in a spacesuit, with portable air, was a miracle. No fuss; get the work done – that was Demard. Instinctively, she glanced down at the air gauge on the cuff of her suit. A third gone, between her and Siba, they had carried in three spare bottles. Enough, they had, with extra air as well. They needed it. There was no rescue here. If this went bad, they were staying here along with the other corpses. She shuddered at the thought; it would be all over and she would never see Tom again. Until Demard stopped the asteroids, the *Hela* was stuck outside. No one else would come. Through the vast control room window, she could see the shuttle below, its lights cutting the blackness of the harsh space around it. Their lifeboat – without it, they were dead. As the sounds from Siba's grunts and gasps as she rummaged in the other rooms, drifted over their comms, she made her way closer to the window.

Ignoring Siba's startling sounds, Niamh shook her head in frustration. She couldn't see where they could berth the *Hela*. There were three empty docks but they were just too small for the great ship. A lattice boom connected to the primary structure, and at its end, a docking clamp like the ones the *Hela* used. Designed to attach to the underside of a ship, Niamh suspected it could fit theirs. It could be used, she hoped, but maybe not. She'd need time and some help to inspect it first.

'Pilot,' Niamh called to the *Hela*, 'I can't see anywhere to dock the ship. And to make matters worse, the base is in poor condition with no life-support. We need resources to fix it, to rebuild the atmospheric containment. To do that, we would want an experienced repair crew.'

The Pilot got her message. The Anan purebreed crew left on the *Hela* would be of no help here. It was hard enough to motivate them to do any work on the voyage out from Anan to Earth. The ship had arrived at Earth in need of a refit. It very nearly did not make it at all. The purebreeds missed a leak in the aft section of the *Hela*, and the air was foul throughout their voyage. Niamh and her human crew repaired the hole and got the *Hela* shipshape before they landed in Australia. Her work in the refit transformed the ship from an old rust bucket into an intergalactic transporter. Excluding the Pilot's Borea family, the crew were Aknars and wanted to go back to Anan. Stopping the ship, here at this secret space station, surprised and disappointed them. The purebreed Anans were, for the most part, tired, lazy and hard to motivate. It was one of the reasons that The Eight returned to Earth to use the human colonists. *Never mind,* thought the Pilot, *we don't need to dock now.*

'Mrs Parker, we can do everything from shuttles. We'll open the channel and fly the *Hela* in. Once inside, we use the automatic docking assist to hold her in position.'

The *Hela* waited, as Demard Borea, their gifted computer tech – as his family called him – worked his magic. Using the codes and puzzles his grandfather had left them, he reprogrammed the base's computer core. Finally, after fifteen long minutes, the first sign of his success started to unveil itself in front of the *Hela*.

'Overlord, look, he's done it. The asteroids are slowing,' the Pilot said, as they watched the pirate base's guardian rocks arrest their random procession. Finally, as if by some unseen force, they stopped, forming an access channel between the asteroid belt. But there was one delinquent, stubbornly staying where it stopped and blocking the *Hela*'s passage.'Alke, go get the tractor, see if you can shift that rock out of our way,' the Pilot said, referring to their strongest shuttle. Designed as a small space-tug – with enough power to move the *Hela* – the Pilot had used it to slow the *Hela* when it first came to land on Earth. It was their only hope now to clear the channel.

'Pilot, Demard's checked the asteroid's processor – its control mechanism's shot. We can't do anything from here,' Niamh said, as her mind raced, thinking about the mammoth task in front of her trying to refurbish four ships and a full space station.

'Don't worry, Alke will move it with the tractor. Any news, Demard?'

'Yes, I have it all. Reprogramming our own codes now and Siba's found the devices. They're all in this building. We'll bring one back to the *Hela* on the shuttle.'

The Eight listened to that with interest. *What will they have, and what did they find?* he wondered.

The Pilot watched the tractor leave the *Hela* and make its way to the delinquent asteroid. Taking the controls of the *Hela*, he steered the ship into the channel. He watched silently as the tractor started to push at the asteroid. Then he smiled as it guided it into empty space between the others, clearing the three-dimensional passage. It took all his concentration to manually fly the eight hundred metre beast through the tight channel using the bridge screens and the *Hela's* external cameras. The Anan crew sat in silence as they watched. Any inaccuracy in the Pilot's calculations and commands to the engines would end in disaster. Gradually, the great ship floated along the channel and into the open space of the pirate base. He had to be sure the aft end was well clear of the passage before turning the ship. He could see Alke following in the tractor and, finally, his relieved voice came across the comms.

'Uncle, you're clear of the asteroids.'

'Thanks, Alke. Come up to the port bow and give us a nudge for a starboard turn. Then you'll have to go around to the starboard side to straighten us up,' he said to his young nephew. He was concerned; this would test Alke's skill, but there was no other way. He needed as much help as possible to manoeuvre the *Hela* into the safe haven within the space station. They heard an unexpected loud thump and felt the bridge shake. He and the crew instinctively turned to look at the port side as the tractor made hard contact with the *Hela*.

The Pilot closed his eyes and screwed up his face as he contained his anger. 'Alke, that was a little bit too much power,' he said, as he watched the bow of the *Hela* rear to starboard, heading back towards the stationary asteroids. 'I need you on the starboard side now. Hurry – and remember to engage reverse as you make contact.' If Alke didn't get around quick enough, he risked getting crushed between the *Hela* and the asteroids. The bridge crew turned their heads to the starboard side, but there was no thud as Alke gently engaged the tractor against the hull. 'Alke, are you up against the push plate?' the Pilot asked. The sweat on his brow, and his grey pallor, revealed his concern as he tried to remain calm. It was vital Alke engaged the tractor in the right place. If he didn't, he would push right through the hull walls. The Pilot knew there was only enough time for one manoeuvre.

'Of course, I am,' came back the terse reply.

'Forward. I need a burst at one hundred per cent. Yes, that's it, full-throttle, Alke' he said, as the *Hela* groaned under the tractor's onslaught. The groans turned into a shuddering as the *Hela*'s momentum to starboard finally stopped.'All stop, Alke. Disengage now and fly in front in case I need you again,' the Pilot said, as he wiped the sweat from his brow. Looking around, he could see the relief on the faces of the crew.

'What, no burst of pride in your nephew's endeavours, Pilot?' The Eight said.

'He's a good man but still very young. He dares to try anything but sometimes he gets flustered.'

Throughout the tricky manoeuvre, The Eight had stayed silent at the back of the bridge, trusting the Pilot to do his job. If it all went wrong, there would be nothing he could do without betraying their location to The Sixth. 'You did well, Pilot, and all on manual control.'

'Autopilot's no good in a tight turn. The program won't allow the *Hela* to make such manoeuvres. They never brought such big ships into this station before. Eventually, we'll need to re-engineer the channel. But that's for the future. We're here, Overlord. We made it!' the Pilot said, his voice trembling with pride. Finally engaging the docking assist, the golden *Hela* stopped, floating majestically, five hundred metres off the space station's headquarters and well hidden inside a safe harbour.

*

The Eight floated in his chariot at the back of his chamber. They filed in, Siba carrying the device she had retrieved from the Borea headquarters. With emergency lighting restored, the journey back was not so intimidating. She gasped when she saw The Eight, with a look of guilt as her body crumbled before him. On her knees, she placed the offending article in front of him. This was not what she expected; why did it have to be her that carried it? She had found it and its companions, real trouble, languishing in an armoury at the back of the control room. Tears welled in her soft grey eyes as the others looked on, wondering, as she, what he would do. A faint message from The Eight touched her mind. It was quiet and caring, not what she anticipated. 'You have done nothing wrong, Siba. Do not be afraid of me. You serve me well and I know your loyalty to me.'

The Eight looked at the small object she had placed on the floor. 'Thank you, Siba,' he said. 'Demard, how is such a small thing so potent and dreaded by my kind. It is not what I expected. And the other devices? What did you find?'

Siba stood up, looked at Demard, and he nodded. 'Overlord, I … I have pictures of what is there,' she said in a soft haltering voice, pulling a screen from her bag.

'Come, show me,' he said, turning his chariot so she could stand beside him. He looked at the pictures scrolling across her screen. They were neatly stacked on shelves, at least ten from what he could see, packed in grey bags – Uldonian cloaks. He could also see, hung on the wall, an array of weapons and guns of different types, and on the ground, crates of ammunition and armour. *A well-stocked weapons' locker; we may have a use for some of it*, he thought. Then, the view changed to a close up of something he had heard about but didn't believe ever existed. In an open case, packed in moulded foam, were six oval, grey glass devices. Through the glass, the motionless grey mass gave no clue to its deadly purpose. 'Are they Uldonian bombs?' he asked.

Siba stayed rooted to the deck beside him. The Pilot stepped forwards. 'Yes, Overlord, they are, and there are over ten Uldonian cloaks. If you agree, our first task will be to destroy them. There's a chemical incinerator in the room beside the weapons' locker. I believe Grandfather used it for—'

Demard coughed and stepped forwards. 'Enough, Zaval. We saw some of his handiwork today. Overlord, there is work to be done. You asked about that,' he said, pointing to what Siba had laid in front of him.

Flashing with blue light, he said, 'Yes, go on.' He was intrigued that so much illegal tech had bypassed The One's reign.

The old Demard tried to bend down to pick up the device. His knees cracked. Siba came to the rescue, nimbly picking it up and holding it out for him.

He pointed to the base of the cone-shaped unit. 'As we hoped, the communicator is working. It's not "so potent and dreaded" as you think. A simple encryption device, working with cosmic waves, totally harmless.'

The Eight floated up from his chariot and moved closer to Siba, now holding the small unit out on the palm of her hand. 'Amazing, such a small thing, yet we knew nothing about such tech. There are others like it?'

Demard shook his head. 'Not many. There are three here, one back on the Energy Exchange, and one on Anan – that we know of. They were used by the family to send secret messages. The cosmic waves are encrypted and then fired off in the direction of the addressed receiver. The waves travel faster than light and if detected, are seen as harmless cosmic white noise. The encryption key will only work on the addressed device, and with some booster power, they can make a video call. Very simple and safe.'

The Eight reposed back in his chariot. 'There is one on the Energy Exchange. How did we miss that? Well, by The One, I am thankful we did, yes, I am. Brilliant! Scoundrels, you are. Yes, you are. Who has it?'

'My son,' the Pilot said.

There was a long pause. Like school children before the principle, the Borea, with their heads bent down, admired the patterns on the deck. Niamh's was the only head turning and looking. Wide-eyed, the proceedings had mesmerised her. After her outing in their old home, the display of the family's past treachery didn't surprise her. She didn't understand what the Uldonian tech was but knew it was in some way dangerous to the Overlords.

Finally, The Eight spoke. 'A military man. Why does that not shock me? We stick to the plan. Make the arrangements and contact him. And Pilot, destroy the Uldonian tech. I want that done immediately. You may all go. Niamh, stay with me,' he said, as the Borea left the room.

'Well,' he said, 'here I am, an outlaw with the worst of them, hidden away on The Sixth's doorstep and with a secret comms device! Who would have thought that?'

She giggled at his light hearted comment, despite their desperate situation. 'What next?'

'My child, we are at a fork in the road. If all goes well, we end up with more ships, an operational base and resources to build more. *Boreal* is part of the way. That ship will be our strength in defeating The Sixth.'

Her mood changed as she contemplated what he had said. Realising he wasn't telling her all, she asked, 'And if it doesn't? What's the other way on the road?'

'A dark hole I cannot see. But it will not end well for me or humanity. I want to plan for that. Assemble a team to work with you. Brizo Sema, the Aknar prince, he is physically strong and has healed from his addictions. Languishing with the Empress in the accommodation is not good – he needs work. With him, use two more of the Aknar crew; the technicians you trained, they will work with you.'

'What about the Borea—'

'They have enough work fixing the base up, getting the blue depot operational and those three ships – we may need them as well. Besides, you must make a separate path …'

As she left, she sensed something strange, a feeling never before detected from him – *fear, no it couldn't be*, she thought, *Overlords, are incapable of fear.*

*

In a military base on the Energy Exchange, at the end of his shift, a tall captain closed the door of his room. Instinctively, he unlocked a metal trunk under his bed. The flashing lights on the cone-shaped device excited him. *They're back*, he realised, as he began to read the message it contained. The white skin on his brow furrowed as he digested its contents. Not so cheerful, he flashed back an acknowledgement. *The dangerous work starts now*, he thought.

CHAPTER FIVE

Blue Diamonds

Blue diamonds, recovered from a crystal node containing blue energy, are carbon-based diamonds, soaked in blue energy over time. Working as a power source, they enhance the mental capabilities of those endowed with the navigation gene, enabling them to project their mind into the physical world or, as they may do, into the thoughts of others. By the use of brain-generated, gamma waves, they can manipulate the blue energy within the crystal. The energy amplifies their mind, thoughts and feelings. Like all other power sources, the stronger the diamond, the more power it generates. Regardless of this, the extent of the celestial navigation depends on each individual's ability to thrust their mind out into the stars and their planetary systems projecting a navigational plot above their workstations

‹ *Principals of Navigation from: Fundamentals of intergalactic travel.* **Zaval Borea**

*

Planet Anan. EPTS: A138648

IN A RAMSHACKLE OLD HOUSE, shrouded in clouds on the side of a mountain, a wizened old man turned to face the door. He had heard the grav platform land outside. *Little Kake,* he thought, *it could only be him.* He gritted his worn yellow teeth as the door opened. A tall, confident Anan entered. He looked down at his old great-uncle, glaring up from an ancient pod chair. Hanging from the rafters, it would have started life as a blonde rattan, but over time, developed a dusty grey pallor, matching the crusted skin of the old man.

'Why have you come?' he grumped. 'I told you never to come. Did someone follow you?'

'No, Frike, no one followed me. So far from the capital, I checked. I always check. You should know better than to ask such a question.' The tall young man blinked as he stared down at his mentor. He caught his breath and smiled. 'I have some rare news,' he continued softly, as if others were listening. 'Intrigued me, it did.'

'Well, spit it out,' his great-uncle rasped.

'Get ready to travel; the others are planning something big.'

The short wrinkled old Frike Borea looked up from his chair. It was the tone of the statement that caught his ear. The ancient relic of the clan knew his nephew had designed it so. Very little raised the interest of the old man, but this did! His grey wrinkled skin and twisted spine was a testament to the four hundred orbits he had seen. Most believed, he was long dead, and few knew of his existence – in this secret lair. Those trusted soldiers who did, swore an oath never to divulge such a priceless family secret. If he were part of the mainstream Anan populace, long since he would have received an award for his grand old age from the office of the Empress. Yet, had a whisper that he be still alive ever crossed their path, her guards would have hounded every one of the Borea family until they caught him. Such was the fear and loathing the crime lord implanted.

During the Borea's pirate reign of terror, Frike had served the then head of the family – his first cousin – as an enforcer, devoting his life to the advancement of the family's ill-gotten gains. Tomes were written about this evil monster's deeds, his malevolent rage and ruthlessness. Now his interest was indeed piqued. 'What are they planning? Tell me more.'

'I don't know it all, but it's significant. They prepare a small transport ship.'

Expecting more, he scowled. 'So they are going on holiday. You shouldn't have come with such meagre scraps of gossip. If you continue like this, you'll lead them to me.' Disappointed, he settled back down in his pod, relaxing his tired old neck muscles, his head dropping down.

Well used to the old man's impatience, the young Kake persisted. Gently, he raised his voice. 'No, Frike, it's not a holiday. Take me seriously. It's a job – involves an asset.'

'An asset? How do you know?' he snapped back.

'Because of the secrecy and those invited. Most interesting, the family go to great lengths to hide it from me,' the young man said, smiling at his great-uncle Frike. If he didn't get his mentor's interest now, all hope of infiltrating their rival kin's operation would die.

The opportunity to meddle in the affairs of the family attracted Frike. For too long, he had languished in the shadows, like an invisible bogeyman. Now was the time to secure his seat as head of the Borea family. And when he died, Little Kake would follow in his footsteps. The assets had remained hidden, their location concealed by his cousin, the secrets passed down his own family line to the Pilot Zaval – an ultimate betrayal. Frike had lived in the hidden depots and flown in the ships, but as his cousin's enforcer – a soldier and executioner – he never knew the all-important locations or navigation data. His cousin had made sure of that! He paused, rubbing an old wizened tattoo on his face as his tired grey brain weighed the risk. *Yes*, he mused, *now's the time to seize control – grab it all. But it was so long ago, could the others lead him back there? Was it still possible?*

The thoughts mulled around in his old brain. Then, like an uncoiling snake, he sat back up in his hanging chair, his head straightened and his eyes glistened as he looked straight up at the tall young man. In anticipation of a favourable answer, enthusiasm spilt out from Kake's grinning face. 'Ah. So, you have listened to me. I suppose you think you are so smart. I see. Yes. What are they hiding? What are they hiding?' Frike said, as he continued to rub the tattoo. 'You did right coming to me, little Kake. Are any of our allies invited?'

'Yes, yes they are. And that's what surprised me – until I broke down the disciplines. Those with the best technical abilities – pilots, navigators, engineers.'

'Our so-called allies, did they contact you?'

'One did. We use her as an engineer on our transporter. Very trust-worthy, but I told her, I didn't want to know. It wasn't our business, and she should tell the others not to contact us.'

'You did well. At this age, very little excites me, but this does. I'm fascinated,' Frike grated, as his old face lit up with a grin. 'Play her along, yes do that, and keep her well-oiled. She's been a good investment. What news of the other business?'

With the shortage of blue, the drug business, their core income, was in rapid decline. 'With so few intergalactic ships on the move, the market for bawrak is collapsing.' The potent brain-enhancing narcotic augments the brainwave projection and navigation capabilities. Over time, as a side effect of the breakdown of their DNA, some purebreeds lost this ability. Many of the older navigators became addicted to the drug, which also amplifies the senses and physical abilities. Even the Aknar prince, Brizo Sema, became addicted to it.

'I expected so. The old navigators have no work. We should rebrand. Look for a different market. You were always enthusiastic about that. You keep telling me, "the drug's so versatile." Well now's your chance.'

The tall young man smiled down at his old mentor. 'Thank you. I hope you don't mind, but I invested some of my resources, and I have a plan. We think renaming it "gileyal" – strength and happiness – will be a real attraction to the younger generation. They'll love the effects of the drug. It gives everything the young want.'

'That was cunning of you, scheming behind my back.'

'No, Frike, just research in case you want it,' the young man said, his face now wrinkled with worry at his elder's response.

To the young man's surprise, Frike burst out laughing. When it subsided, the old man climbed out of his hanging pod. Looking at his pupil, he stretched up and patted him on the back. 'Little Kake, that was a compliment. Never stop scheming, always be cunning. You should be plotting how to get at my wealth and power – how do you think I have kept it?' he said, looking up into Kake's eyes.

Kake grinned at the compliment. 'Frike, you are always so good to me,' he said, as he clasped his great-uncle's bony hands.

*

Energy Exchange and The Hela, Space Station Borea. EPTS: A138672

As she knocked on the door, Haret opened it. Sticking his head out, he furtively glanced up and down the corridor. 'Come in, Cylla.'

He hastily closed the door behind her. She looked around, enviously admiring his luxurious apartment. On the upper level of their floating city, the views out into the blackness of space, sprinkled with shimmering stars, were spectacular. Her own apartment was nothing like this. But the sense of trouble spoiled her marvelling mood. It was as if he was waiting for her when he opened the door. As she looked around, something else hit her – the others were gone. She turned to face him, 'Haret, is everything all right?'

'Yes, Cylla, it is. Of course, it is,' he lied, evading her questioning gaze.

'The apartment's too clean and quiet, and I don't smell food cooking. Don't lie to me, where's your family?'

He shrugged. 'You're so perceptive; they're visiting the grandparents. My wife, who cooks, left cold food for us. I'm sorry, but you know how it is with family; something always comes up. How was your weekend?'

It was the shaky inflexion when he used the word "cold". Cylla nodded. She got his message. Something was wrong. 'Oh, you're so lucky, she left food for us. What a weekend. I'm exhausted. My new companion is divine. She's moving in with me next week. I can't wait, Haret,' she said, wondering who could be listening and what trouble brewed.

'Come inside,' he said, as he led her into a room that Cylla hadn't seen before. It was square and windowless, embedded like a secret keep, surrounded by the other rooms and corridors. Haret closed and locked the door behind her. The impervious bolt hole was finished with an illegal overlay, compliments of The One. To Haret's surprise, before he disappeared, he had provided the rare cloaking paint, impregnated with spores of Uldonian microbes. It prevented unwanted eavesdropping, even from an Overlord. This ultimate gift from The One was a testimony to the trust he had placed in the honest Haret. 'Welcome to my inner sanctum, Cylla. May I introduce you to a good friend, Captain Quriel.'

'Haret, what's going on?' she asked as she looked at the towering pure-breed in a striking blue military uniform.

He smiled and like a fish out of water, opened his mouth. Before he could utter a word, raising her hand and flicking her long brown hair, she cut him off. 'Haret, I'm too tired for all this. I thought you wanted to talk in private about work, not match-make with some well-dressed piece of eye candy,' she said, ignoring the captain.

'Cylla, this has nothing to do with your private life. I'm sorry. Over the holiday, things changed radically! I need you to meet two others. But first, sit please,' he said, as he led her to a large chair at the side of the room.

The captain sat down beside Cylla. 'Miss Ora, he speaks the truth.'

She pouted as she relaxed into the deep soft chair. 'Start with the bad news; get it over with.'

Haret started to pace up and down, wringing his hands and shaking his head. 'Oh, Cylla, there's no easy way to put this.'

'I'm fired. Yes, the little calbak's father, it was his cargo she was trying to sell. I knew it. So, the corrupt piece of Anan excrement you call the Exchange Moderator wants my head. "The Neredian, that horrible Water Monster, sack her." Isn't that what he told you, Haret?'

'Yes, he called me over the holiday. I'm sorry, it's not why I first asked you to come. There's more. For you, this may present a fresh opportunity—'

'Oh, please, don't patronise me, old man. How many times have I said those very words to those I've fired? Really, "a fresh opportunity", you say. Just at the right time. I've a new apartment, and I asked my beau to move in with me – great timing, Haret.' Her green eyes flashed with anger as she stood up to allow her tail to uncoil.

'There's no time for this,' the captain said, interrupting. 'Time approaches – the others will be online soon. Miss Ora, you must keep what you will see a secret.' He reached over and switched on the cone-shaped communicator sitting on the table in front of them.

She hadn't noticed it until now. The burst of its light pierced her anger. Gradually, a projection formed above the table. The captain stepped back, and with a look that gave her no doubt about his seriousness, said, 'These illegal comms devices are secure from the Overlord's prying ears.'

Cylla watched as the picture focused, and then when she recognised the face of the Pilot, she screamed in agony. To the captain's horror, her tail slashed backwards and forwards above her head, her golden scales glowing with anger. She growled out some words. 'Him, Zaval, the Pilot. Haret, what are you doing to me? Why is he here and what's that beside him?'

'Miss Ora, that is my father and the person beside him is a human,' the captain said, now standing in front of Cylla. 'If you wish to whip me, please do so. If it appeases your anger, get on with it. I'm sorry for what our grandfather did to your people. He was a monster. But we need to get on with this. We cannot keep the link open for long. There's much to discuss.'

Haret took Cylla's hands and looking into her green flashing eyes, he spoke. 'Cylla, please, please calm down; you need to listen to this. We need you. I knew this would be hard for you but times change. You're incorruptible, we trust you – that's why you're here. Sit down and listen and try and do something with that tail of yours. It'll scratch the paint.'

'Old man, I don't have a choice, do I? All right, I'll listen,' she said as she sat down, the violent lashing of her tail subsiding.

On the other side of the Anan Galaxy, huddled around the comms device in The Eight's chamber on the *Hela*, the shocked Pilot warily smiled at his friend. 'Haret, after such a long time, it's good to see you.' He paused and looking at the image of Cylla, said, 'Miss Ora, also, my apologies for what our grandfather did.' He pulled Niamh forward. 'Now to business. I want to introduce you to Niamh Parker of the Sullivan Parker Charter. She's an engineer and a human from the Planet Earth.'

'Did you say Charter?' Haret asked as he started to wring his hands again. 'Who authorised that?' The first message, sent to Quriel, asked for a bookkeeper. There was no explanation as to the reason why. That question was now answered!

'The Eight authorised our Charter,' Niamh said in a faltering voice, disquieted by the open display of alien belligerence. The sight of Cylla, her tail thrashing about and her forked tongue darting in and out, had frightened her.

'She speaks Anan. I'm shocked. Pilot, Pilot, this is too much. Really, just too much. When you sent the first message, I never expected this,'

Haret said, leaning forwards and shaking his finger at the projection on the table.

Hidden from the comms unit camera, The Eight watched the acrimonious start to their online meeting. He had had a hand in crafting the initial message to the Pilot's son, Captain Quriel Borea and Haret, but the appearance of Cylla Ora, as the bookkeeper they requested, was unexpected. Her availability could herald a break in their fortune. Now, he was hungry for more information; without it, they were dead. The constant bickering and the meaningless chit-chat frustrated him, but he held fast. Like a blue rock he waited, and then it all came gushing out and, as he had expected, the self-centred Haret delivered.

'... The One is missing, gone for nearly half an orbit. Much has changed since you left. It was bad then but now I fear we see the demise of whatever order we had. The Sixth's evil troika infiltrate the government and our commercial structures. He's running the galaxy with The Seventh and The Ninth supported by his political cronies. You know them all. The usual suspects and more now fight to get a piece of the dwindling pie. It's truly disgusting to watch,' Haret said, 'and it gets worse, yes, worse. The Emperor is now involved. The Empress is missing, along with your friend, General Machai. Zaval, are they with you?'

The Sixth has made his play, The Eight realised as he concentrated on stopping his energy mass from flashing and giving his presence away. *The Emperor turns traitor as well. I did not foresee that.*

The Pilot shook his head as he lied, 'No, Haret. I hear they are on a mission to another galaxy.'

'Of course, they are,' Haret said, shaking his head in disbelief. 'Here, to shorten our meeting time, you can read this after. With the latest shipping index and cargo lists, it's a secret report I prepared for The One. But now – well, that's a lost cause,' he said, as he sent the document. It flashed up above the comms device on the *Hela*.

Sickened by the awful truth, The Eight digested the message, in Haret's self-praising flowery language to his lost friend. "... as I predicted, a select group of power-grabbing conspirators manipulate the market with the collaboration of The Sixth's troika. It is corruption, graft and the worst case of price gouging I have ever seen. The outlying worlds are getting fleeced by higher prices for goods and transport. The troika lends Universal Credits to the outer planets, at low-interest rates, for the purchase of chattels their select bunch of cronies manufacture. It is a contemptible strategy, encouraging the worlds to buy goods they do not need – or could make themselves. They employ new tricks called "targeted marketing". My Lord, I predicted that would happen as well …"

"It defeats the system you created that prevented the remote world's ability to accumulate deficits. The arbitration of value we set, against the different goods they traded, protected them from that …"

"My Lord, I have projected this new financial tactic forward. The distant planets will never be able to pay back their debts and will leave these worlds exposed to financial Armageddon …"

The Eight skipped on. "The Sixth and his troika have control of whatever blue is left. They use it for their energy mass and to power their own ships. It is still quoted at the Exchange but at two hundred and fifty per cent above the price an orbit ago. No one can afford to buy it…"

Impatiently, The Eight scrolled down through the lengthy document, finally gripping the golden nugget that popped out — right at the end. "The changes are subtle. The Energy Exchange still functions as it did before, but underneath, prices are carefully cultivated to benefit the select few. They have not been able to infiltrate the underlying coding written into the Exchange computer and our Central Bank. The Charter's ordering and delivery systems are intact, and I believe, My Lord, the safeguards you and the previous Ones installed are impenetrable."

The Eight stopped reading, contemplating this critical revelation. What would he do, he wondered, if he were in The Sixth's position? *I would want to break down those codes, the very core of our galactic management and financial structure. He will try, yes, he will … There is hope.* From all that dross a plan moulded in The Eight's mind. He leafed through the shipping index. *They are gorging on grav; how long before that runs out?* he wondered. *Chaos cometh.* The information he had gleaned from Haret's report to his friend, The One, could prove to be a pivotal point in his struggle. He needed Miss Ora. The useless chit-chat had continued, belligerent and unhelpful. The Eight turned his attention to it.

Pacing up and down in his keep, Haret was still holding court. 'Grav is now becoming the propulsion of choice. Cylla Ora was never so busy, filling the orders—'

'The other Overlords – you said The One is missing – but what of the others, not part of this troika?' the Pilot asked, glancing across at The Eight.

'They tried to retreat to their home galaxies. Rumour has it some are sheltering in their ships stranded at the distant worlds. What of The Eight? Human, you must have met him if he conferred you with a Charter,' Haret said.

The Pilot shook his head as he looked at the small device in front of him. 'We don't know where he is.'

'Of course, you don't. And I don't want to know. But understand this, human. The Eight is the most powerful and cunning of them all. Pilot, we must conclude. I shortly leave, following my family to Nered. They left yesterday; it's too dangerous for us here on Anan. Human, you need a bookkeeper?'

Niamh's head snapped back in surprise at Haret's statement. 'A bookkeeper, for what? What books are you talking about?'

'She has a Charter and doesn't keep books. Zaval, why did you bring this amateur to our meeting?'

'We've a business manager on Earth, we're not amateurs, and my name is Niamh – don't you dare address me as "human" again,' she said, staring at the projection of the small purebreed.

'Niamh, then. You need a bookkeeper to manage the Charter accounts for the Exchange. I also suspect you will need a trader. With a Charter, you get a seat in the Energy—'

'No,' Cylla growled. 'I know where this is going. I'm not working for that thing with the red hair and ugly brown spots on its face. Really, Haret, is this the best you can do after sacking me? The troika will never let them take their Exchange seat. They'll stamp them out!'

'You called me a thing,' Niamh shouted back, pointing at Cylla's image on the projection. 'My name is Niamh Parker, and I'm a living being, not a thing. I love my red hair and the brown spots on my face are called freckles. If you were the last trader in the galaxy, I wouldn't employ you. No wonder he fired you. Pilot, I don't know what this is about, but I'm finished. I've an engine to fix,' she said, disappearing from the projection. As she stomped off, they could hear the sound of her feet fading into the distance.

Cylla looked at Haret pacing backwards and forwards with his back to the projection. He had missed it when Niamh raised her blue-stained hand and pointed at Cylla. She looked at the captain. He sat pensively with his hand on his chin, smiled and then winked at her. *He had seen it, but it was no surprise,* thought Cylla. *He knows more than he's letting on. There's more going on, much more and the old man doesn't see it, or,* she thought, *he doesn't want to. The more he knows, the more danger he's in.* 'Pilot, I want to work for her,' Cylla said, surprising them all with her abrupt change of mind. 'When do we leave, Captain?'

'Meet me at the old docks, airlock seven on the lower deck at the close of the cycle. But you must know you will travel with others in my family. They'll not be as polite. You have a seat in the cockpit, away from them.'

'There you have it, Zaval, a bookkeeper and a trader, and all the information you asked for. As usual, you get everything, I get nothing. We must terminate this call. Good fortune in your endeavours.'

'Safe journey, Haret. Quriel, we'll be in touch,' the Pilot said, as he reached over and turned the communicator off. He smiled to himself. *The first part of my plan in place, and the best of all traders to help, something I would never have believed possible. Her misfortune was our gain.*

'So, I am the most powerful and cunning of them all,' The Eight said, turning away from the empty projection.

'He didn't know you were listening,' the Pilot said. 'Better still, they don't know where you are.' He paused as The Eight stayed silent. 'Overlord, my plan with the Borea family's support is the only solution. I know it will take some time, but it should work.'

'Your son is a fine man – he has his father's integrity. But you and your son know what some of the rest of your family are like.'

'They have committed to this, Overlord. They will follow me.'

'We shall see. Bring me the Empress – she needs to know this sad news. She will be devastated that her husband has turned against her.'

*

'Overlord. Thank you for seeing me. Why are we stopped, and where are we?' Theia asked. She had remained in her quarters with Brizo, the Aknar prince, during the long voyage. The Eight had blamed Theia for the risks she had allowed her friend Rhea, the Anan doctor and Rhea's lover, Alex, a human geneticist, to take after their deaths on the voyage to the New World. After the sorry saga, The Eight agreed to let the Empress go back to Anan, where she could manufacture the cure to the Anan sickness that Alex and Rhea had discovered. As a condition, the Empress would work towards reforming the population of Anan, expunging the corruption, the laziness, the graft and the belief that they were a superior race.

'Empress, I have bad news. We made contact with Anan. I can't tell you where you are; the less you know, the better. We have a dilemma. Let me explain what we know,' the Overlord said, repeating the news he had gleaned from Haret.

'Overlord, I'm sorry. I know you were close to The One. As for the Emperor, he was not an Aknar and always tried to further his family's business. It's no surprise. What do you want me to do?'

'Empress, I don't have many alternatives to give you. I forgive you for what you did. Compared to our problems now, it is of little significance. You did it to further your cure, and that is that. You can stay with me, or you can go back to Anan. But there are consequences if you do that.'

'I want to return and heal my people. We have the cure. The Sixth won't interfere with its development. If he did that, it would be tantamount to genocide, and he has many Anan supporters. Besides, you are our Overlord. The house of Aknar will always support you. As long as I am alive, I will make sure of that.' Tears ran down her cheeks as she knelt before him. 'My Lord, please leave me with something from the voyage. I enjoyed it so much and have made great friends and companions. You know I always want to return to Earth, to that place north of Christchurch, where we would meet the human rulers.'

'Empress, when the time comes, I will be gentle.'

As she left his chambers, the Overlord reflected on the day's events. *I have failed*, he believed. *My friend is gone and The Sixth is running the galaxy as if it was his own personal fiefdom. The Pilot's plan is audacious; it may work in the long term, but I need more*, he realised.

CHAPTER SIX

Uldonian Cloaks

Developed by an outlaw Borea engineer, The One of this epoch proscribed Uldonian cloaks. The Uldonian microbe, a blue feeding parasite, forms the core of the mantle. The rare bacteria come from volcanic vents in deep acidic oceans on Planet Uldan, an outlier of the Tar Galaxy. Bonding together, they form an energy-hungry collective that may be manipulated to construct devices undetectable by an Overlord. The Borea engineer discovered that embedding these organic collectives within a micro net spun from grav forms an impervious fabric or cloak, invisible to an Overlord. All such covers were destroyed post-Borea campaign when the family was struck from the register of Charters.

⸰ **Extract from: Prohibited Weapons and Associated Devices. General Arie Machai**

*

Energy Exchange, Dock 7. EPTS: A138720

WITHOUT A SOUND, CYLLA WAITED, watching the throng of Borea around the entrance dock to the nondescript transporter. Leaning against the wall of a secluded recess, dressed in a long dark hooded wrap, she blended into the shadows. It was a tough goodbye to her new companion. Despite her own reservations, she had assured her she would be back soon. A soft lie! Most of all, she would miss her apartment and the recently acquired possession she had worked so hard for. From the recess, she watched the Borea mill around the ship's entrance, clapping each other on the back, as some renewed old acquaintances. She wanted to learn as much as possible of this strange family before she threw her hand in with them.

They were of mixed race. Cylla doubted even those with Anan features were purebreed. And, as she watched, the family divisions showed. The looks of suspicion, the barging and jostling and the arguments that started between the factions said it all. From what she could see, there were three cliques. The purebreeds, a separate group of mixed-race misfits, and then a group that looked purebreed, but had green skin – the product of their grandfather's mating with her own race. It surprised Cylla to see Captain Quriel embrace one of the greenskins and kiss her on the lips. *Kissing cousins, although apparently quite distant, how disgusting,* she thought. *Well, I suppose it keeps the wealth within the greater family, an Anan tradition.* She watched as they chatted and then, as the Exchange clock announced cycle end, a female greenskin stepped out of the transporter, shouting for them all to embark.

The crowd thinned out. Then Cylla noticed a group of eight swaddled in capes, standing well away from the throng. As was she, they watched the Borea. She froze as her eyes met the gaze of one, an old man with wizened features and an unmistakable tattoo on his face. And then he was gone, as the group turned and disappeared around a corner, his chilling gaze etched in her mind. It was terrifying; she felt like something evil had squeezed her racing heart. Unbeknown to Cylla, the family's evil monster, Frike Borea, had crawled out from his lair!

'Cylla, you came after all,' the captain said, walking up to her as she wrestled her mind back to reality. 'I didn't see you here. Let me take your bags. Come, meet Verteg, she'll pilot the vessel,' he said, as he led her down to the cockpit hatch. 'You'll share her flight deck and living quarters. The rest will travel in the ship's accommodation. You'll be safe here.'

'Are you not coming with us, Captain?'

'No, Cylla. I'll join you later at the destination. There isn't enough room on my small ship for you. This is a good compromise.'

'Are you sure your family will get along? I see trouble there.'

'Cylla, it won't be easy, but we're committed to this.'

Following him into the ship, a clean and tidy cockpit surprised her. Not what she expected from this rabble. Sitting at the controls was the greenskin who had ushered the family to board. He introduced her as the vessel's pilot, Verteg.

'I have one order for you, Cylla. You keep the place clean. No mess,' the pilot said, as she turned from the pre-flight preparations on her console and looked at Cylla.

Cylla turned and smiled. 'Captain, I'm sure we'll get along fine.'

*

Frike Borea lay down in the crawl space behind the engine room bulkhead. He was sorry they couldn't take little Kake, *but*, he thought, *he's too big to fit in this small space. Besides, I need someone to run the business when I'm away.* If it went wrong, and he didn't return, Kake would manage their enterprises. He looked over at the other seven, his most trusted grandsons and grandnephews. They were settling down, getting ready for the long journey. A cramped one, but their engineer had done well with the secret fit-out. He had glimpsed her outside, getting ready to board with the rest of the family. The journey from his mountain lair to the Energy Exchange was fraught with risk but Little Kake had made it happen. Smuggling was their business. Keeping an old man hidden was another cog of their well-oiled machine.

To reduce the risk of discovery, they travelled overland to an obscure cargo terminal that shipped agri-food to the Energy Exchange. A people-smuggler provided a shipping capsule, fitted with a life-hab, then loaded it onto a cargo vessel for the journey up. Once at the Exchange, shady contacts in flight control ensured their anonymity; booking their landing time in over a shift change and scheduling maintenance of the nearby security cameras at the same time. And they made sure their cargo ship would arrive at an adjacent dock. It was an easy walk to the transporter. Like Cylla, the gang remained concealed in a recess, peeping out at the rest of the family. Frike had enjoyed that, watching the usual divisional differences bubbling up – even amongst this young group. *All so young,* he thought, shaking his head. *So set on the here and now; no time for the long game.* He had caught a glimpse of a voluptuous Neredian on the space dock. Even her cloak couldn't hide her beauty. He had enjoyed locking eyes with her as he sensed her brief terror. It brought back fond memories of old. *Will I be going home?* Frike wondered.

He turned to the one beside him. 'Do we have a location yet?' he whispered as he watched strange coloured shapes moving across the man's white skin. Frike never ceased to wonder at this craze the young were now into.

'No, I can't get into the ships nav-com. But, from what I overheard, it's definitely an asset and a big one at that.'

'Good, I love this,' he said, rubbing his hands in glee. 'Such a long time since I was out and about. You make an old man happy,' he whispered as he wrapped himself in a strange-looking cloak and settled down to sleep.

*

Cylla settled down into the co-pilot's seat beside Verteg. She watched the greenskin execute the pre-flight checks with ease and confidence that shouted experience. Her blue hair was tied up in a neat bun and her brown eyes never still, as they scanned each readout. The small bridge screen, set below the cockpit's semi-circular windows, burst into life displaying an overview of the Energy Exchange's flight control. It flickered until the white face of a purebreed in a crisp blue uniform of the Anan navy smiled back at them.

'Flight plan is approved,' he said. Glancing at Cylla, he turned and spoke to someone behind him. The face of the Dock Master filled the screen – he looked at Cylla. With pursed lips, he nodded, saluted her, and then he was gone.

Gazing at the nondescript grey view of dock seven from the cockpit windows, Cylla sighed. *So now the rumour's confirmed. The Water Monster's sacked*, she thought. She had spent many a happy day discussing ship movements and docking logistics with him. Her shoulders slumped in resignation as she started this unknown chapter in her life.

On screen, the white face of the young controller returned. 'You're cleared to leave, Verteg. Channel seven is yours. Have a safe flight.' The view from the windows changed as the ship lifted from its docking pad. Turning one-eighty on its axis, the space docks came into view. Cylla hadn't realised how many ships were laid up. She had read the reports but seeing them so close took her breath away.

Along with the parked shipping fleet, was the whole Aknar navy. Over one hundred ships, most intergalactic blue-drive battlecruisers, now clamped in irons. With not enough space, some were racked out with the old derelicts in the lower part of the docks. The size of these behemoths, some near a thousand metres in length, dwarfed their small transporter. As they moved further out into the shipping lane, the blue tank farm came into view. Usually, there would be ships queued up to refuel here; not now. She watched a crew in spacesuits floating outside one tank. Vacuuming out the dregs from it, she realised. Blue was in such short supply, it had come to this. Cylla glanced at Verteg. Engaged in piloting the craft, she had missed the spectacle. Under her command, they advanced through channel seven, out into the cold blackness of space. With the Exchange and Planet Anan behind them, Verteg brought the grav drives up to speed. And then they were away, with a burst of blurred white luminosity, travelling faster than light, heading out into the Anan Galaxy.

The pilot's controls filled the forward section of the compact cockpit. In front of Cylla was the nav-con with a port for a blue diamond. One was in, but there was no projection. She realised Verteg was relying on pre-programmed coordinates. 'Where we going?' she asked

'Out past Nered. I told them we were going there for a family reunion and that I would drop you off there as well.'

'Is that where we're really—'

'You'll see.'

The journey to Nered's solar system took under a full cycle. Approaching the first planet, Verteg cut the grav engines back from light speed. Cylla watched with interest. Verteg reached out and touched her blue diamond. A vision of the surrounding planets and their moons jumped up above the control console. She changed course towards a large moon orbiting an outlying world. Like most in the universe, two useless rocks in space, devoid of any harvestable wealth, or the ability to support life. It was a subtle variation, small enough to appear as a minor error by anyone monitoring their course vector. The closer they got to the moon, the more their course deviated as if its gravity pulled the ship in. Then, when its featureless mass filled their windows, Verteg drew out a small panel from below the control console.

'All crew, all crew, buckle up. I say again, buckle up,' she barked in a voice that left no doubt on the importance of those words. Closer and closer they advanced to the moon and then she threw the small craft into a ninety-degree turn. A violent burst of acceleration took them around to the hidden side of the moon – between it and the planet. Immediately, she stopped the transporter dead in space. The grav dampers struggled to keep up with her forceful turns, pushing their bodies to gut-wrenching limits. Even some of the space-hardened crew spewed their guts up. Cylla took in a deep breath, glad she had taken Verteg's advice and missed breakfast that morning. They could hear the moans and groans from the Borea below decks, protesting at the upset.

Verteg smiled. 'That went well,' she said.

Putting her hand on the pad of the device she had opened, a synthetic voice asked, 'Identity?'

'Verteg Borea 197,' she replied.

There was a warble from the device. Cylla sensed a change in the ship. She looked out a side window – just in time – to see a translucent vibration running through the hull.

'Borea cloak,' said Verteg. 'We wait here.'

Cylla knew enough not to ask any questions. She watched Verteg scan the various ship and flight control frequencies for any sign that they were missed. Silently they waited for two-time segments. Even the lower deck was quiet, as the rest of the family knew how vital this stop was. Verteg left the comms on auto scan, but no one hailed them.

'We're gone,' she said, as she initiated a sub-routine on the nav-con. Triggered by their present position and space-time, it unlocked another set of coordinates – their final secret destination. Engaging the grav drives, the invisible ship sneaked out from its hiding place between the nondescript planet and its moon, heading back towards Anan.

*

Space Station Borea

At the voyage's end, Cylla watched Verteg pilot the ship through the asteroid channel into the secret space station. Where the Borea got the vessel from was a mystery. She had asked, but Verteg was non-committal. From its configuration, Cylla knew it was a short-haul grav passenger vessel, suitable for forty. When they arrived at the asteroid belt, it was not what she had expected. But, after twelve cycles on the small craft, any destination was welcome. Although the pilot's quarters were ample, she still felt cooped up. And the noise of the constant bickering filtering up from the Borea riffraff's cramped quarters behind disturbed her sleep. Still, Verteg was a wonder and made it quite palatable. She turned and looked at the pilot, even after their journey, dressed in a crispy clean ship garb. Throughout the trip, Verteg was the personification of professionalism. A *real gem* thought Cylla, and despite many questions, she never divulged any of the family's history. 'Verteg, you made all that look easy.'

'O Cylla, so out of character. A compliment coming from the one called the Water Monster,' she replied with a smile as she slowed the ship down. 'We'll dock soon. I don't know what Zaval has planned for me. I suspect I'll pilot one of those ships. Look, at the *Borea1*. What a vessel. Cylla, I've heard legends about her. I never suspected I could get so close,' Verteg said, as they flew past her grandfather's battleship, now docked near the *Hela*. They could hear the "oohs and aahs" from those below. A beep heralding an incoming message forced her back to her ship's viewscreen. 'You must get ready to disembark. I've received instructions to wipe the transporter's database and nav-com. Then, after you all disembark, I hand it over to an Aknar crew. Perhaps our paths will cross again,' she said, as she smiled at Cylla.

*

The Hela, Space Station Borea. EPTS: A139032

Under the Uldonian cloaks, the eight outlaw stowaways lay undetected as the ship docked. Frike listened. *the family are getting off; soon we move.* He listened to their mumbled briefing – explaining where the accommodation was and when to meet on the bridge. *More info*, he realised. Knocks and bumps from the adjacent cargo hold announced the unloading of the family's space freight capsule – with their meagre possessions and tools. A pause, then the noise restarted, as they loaded the Aknar container. Their personal belongings and Theia's all-important cure, leaving the *Hela*, on the final leg of its long journey, to Anan.

When it was all quiet outside, he raised his head and nodded. Knowing what to do, his gang stirred. Keeping covered by their magic cloaks, they started prepping for the raid. One of them, his most trusted grandson, broke open a sealed container. From it, he withdrew four grey bags, again sealed. He looked at Frike and he nodded. *No going back now*, flashed through his mind as he watched the seals on the vacuum packs being ripped. His grandson withdrew four diaphanous suits. They were the last of Frike's most prized possessions, secreted away for such a day. A day when they would defeat the most cunning of all – The Eight.

Unlike the cumbersome Uldonian cloaks, the gossamer-like suits would enable them to move quickly and undetected through the ship. It was the Borea's last engineer who had invented them. Long dead, he was a real genius in developing illegal tech. Legend says, he had bred a rapacious collective of Uldonian microbes, feeding them on a mix of grav, and an unknown cocktail of composite metals. The mass morphed into worm-like creatures. As they digested the toxic blend of grav and metal, they spun – as waste – a web of micro threads. The engineer harvested those threads and through a process long lost, wove them into fabric. Like the cloaks, the finished product, of that rare dexterous fabric, was impervious to detection by an Overlord or other scanning devices. With grav embedded in the thread, it also afforded protection against violent force. These were the last of the gossamer suits he had made from that batch of fabric. Such rare devices came with a limited lifespan. Once exposed to an atmosphere, it would be a matter of time before they decayed.

They had practised and practised what they were to do here today, but due to the suit's lifespan, putting them on was a new experience. Still, under cover of their Uldonian cloaks, four of them quickly suited up.

Wrapping their cargo bags – with more illegal tech – in spare cloaks and scouring the engine compartment for any sign of themselves, they sneaked out into the now deserted shuttle bay.

Right on cue, as they secreted themselves behind one of the *Hela's* shuttles, they heard the Aknars approach. It was a happy, noisy party that filed into the bay, glad they were going home. They headed straight for the ship led by Verteg. Frike watched with interest as she spoke with a young Aknar, then left. To his horror, Empress Theia Aknar appeared. *That powerful one, she who can kill with her mind*, he thought. Reassuringly, he touched the thin net veil of the gossamer suit covering his face. He looked at his companions; they had seen Theia as well. Their grey fear etched faces said it all, as they wondered, would the Empress's powerful mind feel their presence? They fussed the tufts of their cloaks and suits, making sure no gaps allowed their terror to ooze out.

Theia's appearance sent a cold shiver across Frike's face. Wishing her gone, he scratched at his tattoo. Yet more surprises were to come. Following Theia was a strange-looking biped. A white female, similar in stature to the purebreds, but with a head of long red untidy hair and brown coloured spots on her face – *a new species!* Dressed in the same type of one-piece ship suits as the Aknars. But hers was not the clean white they wore. More a dirty grey – well-washed – with the visible repairs of a working garb. *She actually does physical work, unlike those lazy Aknars*, he thought. What followed amazed him even more. The Empress and the strange biped embraced and there were tears. For the first time, he caught sight of Niamh's blue hands. His amazement forced a gasp, nearly betraying their hide. *What goes on here?* he wondered. *Are the rumours true? The Eight, he is breeding a super race. We must capture her. So much info, all from this little jaunt.* Relieved, he watched the end of their teary goodbye and the Empress boarded the ship.

The young Aknar reappeared and with the biped, started to inspect the small vessel. To Frike's disgust, they walked to the engine room hatch – still open. He glared at his youngest grandson, the one with the scrolling tattoos. Looks said it all; the young man squirmed under Frike's murdering gaze. It was like the monster stole in, squeezing his heart. The last out, he should have closed it. Luckily, there were no panic alarms or shouts. The two went into the engine room then, unperturbed, came out, sealing the hatch. After a short goodbye, the strange biped left.

Frike, conscious of the ever-moving time and the suit's inevitable decay, steadfastly stuck to his plan. They wouldn't move until the Aknars had departed. He had mulled on this and decided it must be so. The Aknars were the only force strong enough to overpower his men. The ship lifted off, turning for the airlock and then – again, more astonishment. A faint blue mist appeared from nowhere, covering the vessel. *Blue energy. I was right to wait*, he thought. *What did he do? Did he wipe their minds? That's it, he doesn't want The Sixth to know what he is at.* As quick as it appeared, it was gone, the ship disappearing into the airlock. Realising what The Eight must now do, Frike grinned. *He recharges his energy mass. Time, time is with us – as well – they should all be on the bridge. Now we move.* Like a ghost, he signalled his troop.

All rehearsed, two lay behind to guard the shuttle bay. Four set out for the bridge with two following to post a guard in the accommodation block. For Frike, this was the penultimate challenge – going up against an Overlord. In his final years, he would get back all they had taken from his family. *Now, when the Overlords fight amongst themselves is the time to strike back. Yes, divided we conquer,* he thought, as one of his grandsons carried him on his back towards the Overlord's chamber.

Not knowing where it was, following the ship's station bills, ones Robert had posted during the refit with clear coloured diagrams, they rushed towards the bridge. Always, Overlords picked a chamber close to it. History and the cloak's attraction to blue would give up his location. Stealthily, approaching the bridge along the central corridor from the aft section, it would be a matter of time before the cloaks betrayed The Eight's location. And they did, down the passageway from the bridge. The proximity to the Overlord's blue excited the microbes which started to glow and pulse within the grav net. With a tool they had developed for the job, one of his men deftly started a circular Uldonian cloak spinning in front of them. Outside The Eight's chamber, the living mantles pulsed, thick and long, as they strained, trying to get in.

It took all their strength and concentration to control the pulsing organic masses. As Frike stepped down from his ride, another grabbed a short, stocky gun-shaped weapon from a bag. Sounds from the bridge trickled out. Frike cocked an ear. *The Pilot, yes, it is he, Zaval, lecturing the newly embarked family. To be welcomed by that imbecile, what a waste! He couldn't wait to get them in his clutches. Good, let him lecture.*

Like the pre-planned dance move it was, they took up their positions outside the door of The Eight's chamber. Undercover of the spinning cloak, one aimed the weapon. They would have seconds. From historical antidotes, Frike estimated about fifteen of the precious time divisions. He held his hand up; starting a count, he dropped it. The loud bang that followed reverberated through the *Hela's* frame. Not from the weapon's discharge, but from the chemical reaction the charge generated. It dissolved the door and bulkhead into a neat round hole – more prominent than the spinning cloak. The explosive vibration tripped power breakers, knocking out the ship's lighting. With a shrill, the general alarm sounded. Dim emergency lights, along with flashing beacons, turned on. Oblivious to the chaos they had triggered, Frike's team rushed in, the spinning cloak pulsing ever faster. Like a flash, they had two others opened out. Though completely surprised at what they faced, Frike's most trusted did not falter, throwing the pulsating organic masses of horror at The Eight.

It's done, Frike stopped counting *Only four seconds. All our training paid off.* Over and over again, they had practised until spinning the cloak and firing the correctly sized charge from the right distance paid off. The hole, sized for the spinning cloak, completely dissolving the door and bulkhead barrier. What they had faced was not as expected. Instead of an oval ball of energy, there was The Eight in his magnificent shining chariot. Despite that complete change, they had done their work. The Eight's chariot was now covered by three foul-stinging Uldonian mantles.

'What's that thing?' one asked, in the dim light and over the noisy alarm.

Frike exhaled and gulped in a fresh breath. He hadn't realised he had held his breath since they had started. Fear and anticipation, he happily recognised. Long time since he was so exhilarated. 'I can only surmise he took a mechanised form to conserve blue.'

'Is he done?' another said.

'Looks like it. I'm not lifting the cloaks to check,' the youngest replied.

For the first time, Frike allowed himself a smile. 'If he wasn't "done" we'd know all about it. Wouldn't we? Do you think he'd let us get away with this? No, he wouldn't. We'd be dust on the deck!' Ignoring the ever-present pulsing din in the background, he took a moment to savour his victory, his greatest achievement. *The young today, do they not know how impossible it is to take out an Overlord – and the most cunning of all? Today, I, Frike Borea, become a legend; they will sing songs about me. It wouldn't have happened without Little Kake's help. Pity he had to stay behind. It was his cultivation of the good looking one that got us here. Her charms melted that boor, Captain Quriel. Yes, she did. Rubbing egos with high-born Aknars – he does – sucking their anal juices. In the military, no less, thinks he's so high and mighty, and a simple love trap snared him. All she'd to do was polish his fruit, and his secrets came gushing out. Zaval, your son's not so high and mighty now. Ha, he keeps his brains in his pants.* At that thought, he smiled again.

Checking the time, he turned to one of his troop. 'Make sure those cloaks are secure. Don't leave any chinks in and tie them to the grav platform. Yes, that's what it is, they built it on a simple old grav platform. We'll have time to dissect it later. See what he was about, maybe tech there we can use. The rest of you – time runs on – that bang will wake up Zaval. Let's go,' he said, listening to the hiss of the bridge door opening.

Grabbing six lightweight menacing grav guns from the cargo bags, slinging two each on bands across their chests, the three rushed out to secure the bridge. The black rifles started life as max-charge weapons with enough firepower to take out a shuttlecraft. To scare by their very appearance, Frike modified them by fitting shorn-short flared double barrels. With a grey grav cylindrical cartridge mounted below and a coiled auto-sight on top, they looked the part. Unknown to those they would be used against, the force of the charge was reduced to pop a purebreed's head open without damaging the ship. Holding a weapon in each hand and firing on auto sight, they could take out four in one go.

The one they left warily looked at the covered mess in front of him. Gorging themselves on The Overlord's blue, the microbes within the cloaks pulsed and writhed as they competed with each other for their newfound food. Gingerly, he touched it, recoiling in disgust at the grey slimy mess – digested from blue – they extruded. He sucked in a deep breath. Gritting his teeth, he started over. This time, wearing thick gloves, he tucked the cloaks in tight around the platform. Then, with bindings from one of their bags, he secured them to it. Stepping back, with a grin, he admired his handy work. Grabbing a grav gun, he turned to join Frike on the bridge. He didn't see the last flicker of the battery backup's multi-coloured LED lights go out beneath the grav-powered chariot.

CHAPTER SEVEN

Folding Space

The biggest conundrum faced by intergalactic travellers speeding faster than light, is the time it takes to traverse the vast distances of space. By far, the optimum approach is to fold it. Imagine space as a flat sheet. The longer route to get from A to B would be in a straight line, although we must remember, space is actually curved. Take the sheet and fold it in two, with A and B overlapping. Now, to cross to the other side, we can cut a hole between A and B and travel straight through. A much shorter distance and the same principle applies to folding space. To generate the vast amounts of energy required to fold space, we use blue energy compressed by a dodecahedron rotor in a blue drive. Once space is folded, the engine tunnels into the fold at point A, opening a hole, commonly called a port. Transportation to the other side or point B is not instantaneous. Travel time will depend on the distance, now translated to the depth of the fold, the speed of the physical object travelling through the tunnel and the efficiency of the astronomical pulses the blue drive can generate.

‹ *An Introduction: Fundamentals of intergalactic travel. Zaval Borea*

*

The Hela. EPTS: A139045

AN EXHAUSTED NIAMH LAY ON the bunk of her small cabin. Her mind was racing as she reviewed the work of the past two weeks with Bri and the small Aknar crew. The long, punishing days toiling in a spacesuit were a new experience – one her lithe body could do without. Every movement was an effort, even in the super lightweight Anan suits. But it was the work in the starboard engine room of *Borea1* that was the hardest. Moving the remains of long-dead Neredians was not what she imagined this exciting new job would entail. The Pilot's grandfather was indeed a monster. More disturbing, Niamh had found some skulls partly caved in, as if the poor misfortunates were kicked or beaten to death. She had shuddered when she learned from Siba, rumour had it, there was another – more brutal than Grandfather Borea.

As the Aknars prepared to leave from the shuttle deck, Niamh had said her goodbye to Theia wondering if she would ever see her again. But it was Theia's final words that unsettled her the most.

'Niamh, if we meet again and we cannot remember you, don't judge our Overlord or us harshly. Our ways are different from humans. But always remember this, the time I had on Earth was the best time of my life. You are like a daughter to me. I'll miss you.'

'I'll see you again,' Niamh had replied, her voice tinged with the emotion of this unwelcome departure.

Theia shook her head. 'It's possible you may not. When you see Mack, tell him to marry Janet before she gets away. He's always too slow, never realises the time differences with other species – it's occurred before. Your friend is the best thing that has happened to him. Enough, I must go.'

Niamh still remembered the tight embrace and the tears on Theia's cheeks as she turned and stepped into the transporter.

Before leaving the shuttle bay, she helped Bri inspect the small ship. 'That's a surprise,' Bri had said, as they discovered the hatch to the engine room open. 'The Borea pilot forgot to mention this.'

Taking the opportunity to inspect the open compartment, they were happy to find it spick and span, with all the signs of regular engine maintenance. Whatever else was in store for the Aknars, "You should have a safe flight back," Niamh had said to Bri, as they embraced and said their goodbyes. And then Bri was gone.

Emotionally and physically drained, Niamh returned to her cabin. Meeting the Borea and her unwanted bookkeeper, Cylla, could wait. Leaving her grubby ship garb on, she drifted off to sleep.

*

The Eight's Chamber

Touching the minds of the Aknars, a thing he rarely did and only when he must, The Eight's consciousness retreated to his energy mass. He didn't want to, but he had to – there was no way out. And, he had to do it in the safe confines of the ship, lest his presence out in space alerted his nemesis. Now he must recharge his energy. As he sucked on new blue from the glass holding tank on his chariot, mayhem broke loose. With a bang, the door and bulkhead dissolved. *Uldonian tech; I am betrayed by the Borea.* Breaking time into the smallest of movements, he bent his mind up and around the spinning cloak invading his space. On the other side were four faint grey-coloured shapes. Impervious to his power and to make matters worse, he could sense nothing from them. *What manner of subversive terror is this?* exploded in his mind.

Dressed in their one-piece suits, with veil's covering their faces, Frike's crew were indeed invisible to him. Without them, they were dead! As the spinning cloak brushed his blue, the stings of the foul microbes started – millions of them. Time and power limits dictated his action. *Niamh! At all costs, I must save her,* he realised, flashing a message to her mind as his consciousness rushed into the glass holding tank. Reaching the bottom, with microbes now chomping at the top of the tank, he split into two.

One part fled through the gold bus bars into the solid-state memory banks. The other escaped through the blue energy buffer connected to them. With the foul stinging organisms in hot pursuit – in a feeding frenzy of his now-abandoned blue – he slammed and locked closed the steel valve at the base of the tank. Upstream, as he retreated into the buffer, he closed and secured another. Decoupling the gold bus bars from the blue feed manifold, he stopped to take stock. His presence was all there, safe in the solid-state memory banks. Safe here, with double-block isolations between those horrors. There were a precious five litres of blue as well, trapped in the fall-back buffer Niamh had made from high-strength titanium alloy and installed to ease his passage to and from the memory banks. He could hear them gloating outside, and then three left for the bridge. He lay silent as another worked to secure the cloaks around his chariot, a clumsy effort that the man rushed. Satisfied with his labour, he turned and left The Eight's chamber. As he went, The Eight's mind flowed out through the cables, reconfiguring the battery backup, routing all the power to sustain his memory. A vibrant spark rattled in the Overlords consciousness; *I am not "done" yet!*

*

The Hela – Niamh

She woke to the sound of a loud bang, followed by the shrill sound of the ship's alarm. Wide awake, Niamh jumped from the bed, the adrenaline from the fright coursing through her body. She glanced at her watch – it was less than half an hour since she had laid down. And then she heard him in her mind, like a faint whisper, the voice of The Eight far away in the distance.

'Niamh, take what Tom gave you. Get off this ship, now. Go to Boreal, to the starboard engine room with your shuttle. Find Cylla, take her with you. Do not return for me. You are in great danger. Kill anyone who gets in your way. Go. Go now, my child.'

Without thinking, Niamh reached under her bed, extracting the two guns Tom had given her. So well balanced and made especially for his female agents, the perfect weapons were a gift from Chang, the Chinese spymaster who had once tortured her. Weighing both in her hands, already knowing the answer, she checked the magazines were loaded. Swiftly she attached the gun's holsters to the belt on her ship garb. The finely made pistols were not something Tom wanted her to have in space. But he had said, "If you ever need them, a hole in the hull of the *Hela* may be the least of your worries." Running from her room, she made her way to the guest's cabins where she hoped Cylla would be.

Relying on the dim glow from the emergency lighting, Niamh ran down the darkened corridors while the harsh noise of the general alarm battered her hearing. At the end of the passage, she turned right and walked into two strange creatures. With dark green skin and flashing green eyes, the bipeds looked like nothing she had seen before. Borea she suspected. As soon as they saw Niamh, with deadly intent, they raised their grav guns. Before they could fire, she ducked, turned, and ran back around the corner. Taking out a firearm and toggling the safety, she aimed it in front of her, ready for what might come. She played Tom's voice over and over in her mind. *"If you ever have to point it at someone, be prepared to use it. Remember your training to aim and fire."* Holding her stance, like a coiled spring, she waited for them to come. She heard footsteps approach and then the sound of a bloodcurdling scream echoed up the corridor. As the yelling continued, Niamh listened to the racket of someone running, followed by the sound of something like a whip. Keeping her body secure, she peeped around the corner. The sight of Cylla whipping two cowering Borea froze Niamh in her tracks.

'Human, if that's a weapon, use it now,' Cylla shouted. Above their unmerciful flogging, the two Borea tried to level and aim their grav guns at her.

Aiming at the closest one, Niamh squeezed the trigger. At the sound of the loud gunshot, the two Borea turned in shock. Off-target, the bullet embedded itself into the shoulder of one. Unphased by the shot, Cylla impaled the other through the neck with her tail. Its arrow point severed the main artery to the brain, snuffing out the Borea's life. Green blood spurted out, covering the walls of the corridor. Not done yet, Cylla forced the barb of her tail's arrow point back out through the ill-fated Borea's bloody gash, the strength of her pull near severing the head from the body. Coupled with her first shot at a living being, the unexpected gruesome sight paralysed Niamh.

'Kill him! Kill him!' Cylla screamed, as the wounded Borea tried to raise his grav weapon and shoot Niamh.

Adrenalin pulsed to her brain. Screaming, she aimed the gun and shot him in the head. Above the shock of her first kill, she thanked Tom for his insistence on her learning to shoot.

Cold hard confidence washed over her body. She remembered The Eight's orders. 'We need to get to my shuttle. No arguments. We go this way,' Niamh barked, as she passed Cylla and started to run towards the shuttle bay. Without question, the Neredian followed, close behind. Five long minutes of running along the darkened corridors brought them to a stop outside that fateful compartment where, unknown to them, the mess had all started. Niamh looked at the big golden alien. It wouldn't be easy, but she would need a spacesuit. 'Cylla, we need to get you a spacesuit.'

'Why, human? I believed we were going to your shuttle.'

'Cylla, don't argue, you need a suit. Can you wear one?'

'I'll get into a large one. Where do we get it?'

'In the shuttle bay, but I'm sure the Borea will be there as well.'

'If they are, I'll distract them; give you time to fire that weapon.'

Niamh crouched down behind Cylla. 'I'll follow you in.'

Opening the door with a loud crash, Cylla dashed into the shuttle bay. Two Borea, sitting in the centre of the compartment, got up and turned to face her. They were different from the two they had encountered in the corridor – more like purebreeds. Their white skin was adorned with strange, coloured shapes, like moving tattoos.

'What are you doing here?' the largest asked.

'Where did you expect me to go? It's an emergency. The alarms are sounding. Can't you hear them? The evac board in my cabin tells me to come here. Where's my escape pod? Where's the rest of the crew?' a breathless Cylla said as she hurried towards them.

'It's a false alarm; go back to your cabin.'

'You mean there's no emergency?'

'Like I said, it's a false alarm. Go back to your cabin, Neredian, or we'll—'

'Or you'll what? I'm breathless and excited now,' purred Cylla. Seductively, she stretched her legs out in front of her, strutting up to them. 'I hear you Borea like to play,' she said, now standing in front of the two with her legs apart and her tail poised above her. With her long hair flowing down her back, she looked as beautiful and elegant as she did that day in the Exchange. Captivated by her voluptuous beauty and lost for words, the two Borea gaped at her.

Slipping in following Cylla's diversion, Niamh concealed herself behind some boxes. She couldn't afford to miss this shot. Not like the last, she had one chance at it. Taking careful aim, the gun felt like an extension of her arm. Tom had told her a chest shot to the heart was the easier target. But now, aiming at the strange alien with moving tattoos on his torso, the location of his heart wasn't so obvious. She chose the harder target, no doubt about where his brain would be. Focusing her mind at a spot on the man's forehead, she aimed Chang's weapon. Her blue powers painted an invisible line from the barrel to her target, and then she squeezed the trigger. The loud shot rang out, reverberating throughout the shuttle bay. Red blood spilt from a hole in the side of the larger of the two alien's head. Dead, he fell to the floor. At the same time, Cylla's tail erupted in a violent assault, slashing back and forth against the other's head. Surprised by the shot, and the sudden frenzied lashing from the Neredian's tail, he dropped to the floor, cowering for mercy. Without another thought, Niamh rushed forwards.

'Stop, Cylla. Get out of the way,' she shouted, above the lashing sounds from Cylla's tail.

'Human, I am enjoying this. Nowadays, we never get to flail someone to death – the practice is frowned upon.'

'Stop! I can't get a clear shot at him. We don't have time for this,' she said, as she tried to get to the Borea cowering on the ground. She pushed past Cylla who had no alternative but to withdraw her thrashing tail. Niamh took careful aim, clinically shooting the bloodied mutilated man in the head. 'Come on,' she said, as his body slumped in a heap, 'we need to get you a suit.'

She dragged Cylla over to a rack of spacesuits on the wall. 'Here, take these two – at least one will fit – and grab those oxygen tanks, yes, those three,' she said, as she ran back to the shuttle carrying another three oxygen tanks with her. *The codes*, she thought. *If they have changed them, we're dead.* At the shuttle hatch, Niamh recited in her own personal codes, ones she had recently programmed before she started the work two weeks ago. To her delight, the hatch opened. Throwing the oxygen bottles into the shuttle, she ran back, followed by Cylla for six more. 'I don't know if this will be enough. I didn't figure you'd be with me,' she said, as they both rushed back to the shuttle.

'Is there water?' Cylla asked as they secured the oxygen bottles into the back of the shuttle.

'Yes, there is. We need to go. Strap yourself into the cockpit, that seat over there,' Niamh said, pointing to where Cylla should sit. Securing the shuttle hatch, Niamh finally stopped and looked around. Everything was as she left it. She nearly cried with joy as she saw her little tank of blue. Strapping it on, she jumped up into the cockpit beside Cylla. She looked at her watch – it was seven minutes since the alarms had gone off. If they were to get away, she needed to keep moving, and fast.

'Human, what makes you think the Borea will let us out of here? Who'll open the shuttle bay?'

Grabbing the blue diamond around her neck, Niamh stabbed it into the nav-con as she started up the engines, her hands a blur of movement as she worked at the flight controls. The shuttle rose up and turned to face the largest empty area in the landing bay. At the same time, generated by Niamh, a projection of the space in front burst out above the nav-con.

'Cylla, don't scream, don't talk, do absolutely nothing to disturb my concentration, and keep that tail of yours wrapped around your waist,' Niamh quietly said, as she placed her fingers into the tank of blue in front of her. Folding space, an opening appeared on the projection and in the landing bay, directly in front of their shuttle. With a nudge from the grav drive, Niamh moved the shuttle through the port out into open space. As it closed behind them, she fully engaged the shuttle drive flying away from the *Hela*. Her power was now so forceful, she never noticed the complications of folding space and operating a ship at the same time.

Cylla shook her head and blinked. Her heart palpitating, she looked at Niamh and then back out of the cockpit window. Her voice quivered with fear. 'Human, I'm sorry if I ever caused you offence, but I can't pronounce your name. Tell me, what did you do? How is that possible?'

Happy to be away from the *Hela*, self-belief oozed from Niamh's voice. 'Never mind, we're not out of the woods yet. Look, there it is,' Niamh said, pointing to the *Borea1*, now moored on a temporary docking boom close to the *Hela*. She looked at her watch again – ten minutes since the alarms went off. She didn't know what had happened to the *Hela*. She could see the great ship was still lying five hundred metres off the space station's headquarters. Most likely with its automatic docking assist still operational, and thankfully, there was no sign of damage to the bridge. Whatever happened, once the Borea or whoever was leading them, realised she had escaped, they would come after her and Cylla.

As she flew the shuttle up alongside the starboard aft wing of *Borea1*, undaunted, she knew the next part of the plan would not be so easy. Light filtered out through its engine room's hatch window, breaking the darkened derelict spell the ship was earlier saddled with. Sweat dripped from her brow. She had finished the engine room refurb and closed that hatch yesterday. If it hadn't been done, they'd both be dead or captured now.

Parking the shuttle facing the wing, Niamh brought up a projection of space outside and inside the engine room. She hesitated. Moving the shuttle from inside the confines of the *Hela* to the open space outside was easier. Now she was going the other way. Putting her hands back through the gelatinous seals of her blue energy tank, she flexed her fingers. She let the pure energy flow from the tank into her hands and up through her arms and limbs into her brain. Her mind focused on her goal, a tiny space inside the vast ship. With a hiss, a small burst of white light poured out through her eyes as she generated that mysterious astronomical pulse. Space folded and without hesitating, she opened a port through it, straight into *Borea1's* starboard engine room. Maintaining all her concentration, she drove the shuttle through the open port.

Holding her breath, Cylla watched in awe as Niamh's eyes flashed with white light. Her long red hair jumbled down to her shoulders shone with a faint blue hue. Cylla sat stock still as the shuttle passed through the fold. Thousands of images danced in her mind as she wondered what would happen if it closed. Would they be embedded in the ship's hull, or just sliced in two? However it went, if Niamh got this wrong, death's kiss would hastily follow.

Using the grav engines, Niamh guided the shuttle into the engine room and over an area she had previously marked on the deck. She closed her eyes and projected her mind outside and around the shuttle. *Yes, we're in*, she thought, smiling to herself, as she closed the port in folded space and landed. She hadn't noticed it, the draw of the energy deep within her brain, her growing abilities and that with one hand in her tank she could readily use the other to control the shuttle. It was that fundamental power of the energy, the one the Overlords craved, its strength and the ability of an intelligent being to harness it. Unbeknown to Niamh, it was growing inside her.

With a big sigh, glad at the vision of safety, Cylla exhaled. 'Where are we?' she asked.

'We're in an engine room of the fastest vessel in the galaxy.'

'Is that another shuttle beside us?'

Impatient to get going, Niamh huffed a terse answer. 'Yes, the *Hela* shuttle 2; it's our control pod. Enough questions, we need to hurry. There's no atmosphere left on this ship – that's why we need the spacesuits.'

Ten minutes later, Niamh and Cylla climbed out of the small airlock into shuttle 2, its cramped cabin packed with temporary equipment and control consoles. There were wire looms festooned from each panel and all running up to a sealed hole in the side of the ship. Looking out into the dim engine room, Cylla could see the cable looms connected to a large control panel.

Overawed at the alien tech, again, Cylla was full of questions. 'What are these panels? And where did you get them from?' she asked.

'They control the *Borea1* and its starboard blue energy and grav drives,' Niamh explained as she stripped off her spacesuit. She sat at one of the consoles and powered it up. With her blue diamond, she brought up a projection of space in front of the *Borea1*. There was hardly any room in the confines of the space station for what she was attempting now. The Eight had worked out the course details, programming it into the blue drive nav-com. Without that help, she wouldn't have been able to escape now.

Niamh looked at the route. She couldn't do it. She couldn't leave him. Copying the course programme, she changed the destination and re-entered it into the nav-com. Turning to the engine controls, she started a grav engine located three floors above in the central part of the ship. As it warmed up, she looked out through the shuttle windows onto the blue drive engine room floor. Checking the tanks of blue, filled from the *Hela*, were all secured around the grand drive, she smiled to herself. *Yes, they are,* she thought. Everything was as she left it the previous day. The container they transferred, with extra life support, was secured to the side of the shuttle. Inspecting the hull of the engine room, she could see the main hatch locked closed. A reassuring sight.

Cylla crouched up in the corner of the shuttle deck trying to keep out of Niamh's way. 'Where are we going?'

'First off, we need to get out into the open space outside this station. Then I need to try and find The Eight. You should sit up in one of the cockpit seats and strap in. This may be a rough ride,' Niamh said, as she strapped herself in and continued with the blue drive startup sequence. 'You should also know, I've never driven one of these before.'

'Human, I trust you,' Cylla said, smiling at Niamh for the first time, as she climbed into the cockpit and strapped herself in.

Niamh could feel that trust, shining bright like Cylla's golden scales. She opened the blue energy feeds. The ship trembled, and without fault, the blue-drive started. Eerie flashes of white light filled the engine room as it reached critical mass for the pre-programmed flight plan. Niamh throttled up the grav drive by ten per cent. She winced as the force of her throttle split the docking clamp's lock-dog shear pins. Designed for such an emergency, they allowed a ship to disconnect and run for open space. With a shudder, the grav drive forced *Boreal* out of its temporary berth.

Their vessel floated forwards. She engaged the blue drive, and with a thump, the pulse of the engine opened a port four hundred metres in front of the *Boreal*. Nudged by its grav drive, the ship entered the large port in folded space.

'Here we go; let's hope my calculations were correct,' she shouted over the shuddering noises coming from the shuttle as it bounced on the shaking deck of *Boreal*. In an instant, the great ship travelled through the first astronomical pulse it had opened in a generation. Like a massive flower, another port opened, and seconds later the vessel appeared out of folded space one hundred kilometres from the asteroid belt. 'We're safe here for the moment,' Niamh said, as she disengaged the grav and blue drives, stopping the ship. Another first for her, but again she didn't acknowledge it. Her thoughts were full of what had happened to The Eight, for without his insistence on getting the job done, she wouldn't be alive now. The blue drive's dodecahedron rotor wound down, calming the vociferous vibrations and after their desperate escape, a welcomed silence enveloped the shuttle.

Cylla's quizzical voice shattered that quiet moment. 'Where are we?' she demanded to know.

'We've stopped outside the asteroid belt, in space. It's where the *Hela* parked up after its long flight from the New World.'

'How was this possible? So much, you did so much!' Cylla asked while shaking her head in wonder.

Niamh looked across at Cylla. She needed to unburden herself. As conversation had been slim over the past while, it all came gushing out. Cylla was wide-eyed with interest as Niamh began to talk.

After that fateful online meeting with Haret, which Cylla was at, The Eight had told Niamh to make a separate path. That was why she had sensed fear from him. All along, he had suspected betrayal and "the separate path" was about planning this.

The job started when the Pilot handed over the executive codes for the *Boreal* to Niamh, and with The Eight's help, she changed them all. After that, The Eight gave her a long, tedious list of work starting with towing *Boreal* to the docking boom they had left from. Taking ownership of *Boreal*, she opened the large starboard engine room hatch. The Eight came over on a shuttle and scanned the vessel. He made a set of drawings and found out what state the ship was in. After all, it was his now. As the Pilot's family explored the space station and reclaimed the three other parked vessels, Niamh had worked on *Boreal* with a small Aknar crew. It was gruelling work, most of it in spacesuits, preparing the derelict craft for flight. The ship lacked a breathable atmosphere so they concentrated all the work in the starboard engine room, through its large open access hatch. It was Niamh's idea to cannibalise shuttle 2, damaged in a battle on the New World, and now useless. She had it towed over to the starboard engine room, wired into *Boreal* control systems, and used it as an airtight flight control pod. Always the hoarder, Niamh had kept the temporary control panels she had used to land the *Hela* in the Australian desert. Now connected to the *Boreal* control systems, they formed the nerve centre of its flight control. Her clever jury-rigging gave her command of the grav dampers, grav engines and navigation as well, all from inside shuttle 2.

Before a flight, they had to prime the engines with blue. The dormant ship had every last drop of its precious energy sucked dry, leaving the blue feed manifolds under a vacuum. The Pilot had helped with that problem, connecting hoses from the *Hela's* blue tanks to the docking gantry, allowing the energy to transfer from one ship to another. During the process, for the first time in an age, the blue energy swirled and curled through the manifolds, gaining a life of its own, as it flowed around the dodecahedron rotor. Niamh recalled that day's work; venting precious blue into space, they had waited with bated breath to see if the rotor would turn. And turn it did, free and easy, giving her comfort that today, the first time she would run a blue drive, it would work. The final part of The Eight's laborious work plan was to freshly pack one grav engine with fuel from the *Hela*. After carrying out The Eight's instructions to the letter, today she realised his backup plan was all about her escape.

Cylla sat back in amazement. *No wonder this poor creature looked exhausted*, she thought.

CHAPTER EIGHT

Grav Dampers

The speeds generated by ships travelling in space create tremendous forces on a corporeal body. Without managing those gravitational pressures, our bodies would be crushed flat. Grav dampers are the mechanisms we use to control those forces and are part of the life-sustaining systems on all our spaceships. The dampers set up a localised gravitational field on the vessel that counteracts the crushing effects of gravity generated by both acceleration and deceleration. They work in conjunction with the grav bubble that envelopes a ship when travelling faster than light, protecting it from cosmic forces, space debris and the crushing effect of a space fold.

‹ **An Introduction: Fundamentals of intergalactic travel. Zaval Borea**

*

Hela Bridge. EPTS: A139049

PURE EVIL FOLLOWED FRIKE WHEN he entered the bridge. The poor misfortunate family didn't stand a chance. He and his misfits drew their weapons, and without any other choice in the matter, the unarmed relatives raised their hands in capitulation. It was as Frike had predicted – when he revealed himself, most of the factious family switched sides. History repeated itself as they followed whoever promised the greatest reward. Immediately, he had grabbed Zaval the Pilot, his niece Siba, and nephew Alke. Once tied up, his cohorts, with poisoned zeal, dumped them on the deck. Frike hardly noticed the precious time go by as he ogled out of the big bridge window at the *Borea1*. Tears welled in his grey eyes when he first saw it moored on the gantry beside them. Admiring the three assault craft, now docked on the *Hela's* landing platform, a rare smile played on his lips. He even took a moment to recall the many happy days he spent marauding out in the galaxy in them. *Home, I am finally home,* he thought.

The silence on the bridge snapped him back to reality. Home he was, like he never left, taking command, barking orders, reorganising the family, dispatching some to relieve his own men and others to crew the assault ships. *They'd need them shortly,* he had thought, oblivious to how soon.

Then it happened, without warning. The *Boreal* broke its mooring and disappeared into a fold in space. Above the gasps of horror from the family, with thunder beating in his brain, the old man gaped at the *Hela* viewscreen. He couldn't believe it. He blinked his eyes and looked again. Walking over to the bridge's long curved window, he gazed out into the spaceport beyond. Cold empty space said it all. Their hope, his long-dead cousin's pride and joy, had disappeared! *How could that happen? Everything had gone so well until now,* he thought. *Unless …*

At the realisation of how the ship got away, his face blackened with rage and feelings he hadn't felt for a long, long time. Murder incarnate turned, looking down at the Pilot tied up on the floor beneath his feet. 'Zaval, did you give our ship to the Overlord?' he screamed. 'What right had you to do that? You gave him the codes your grandfather, my own cousin, left you, didn't you? Yes, you did.' He paused as the spittle of wrath poured from his hoary mouth. It was always a bone of contention. At the bitter end, ignoring Frike, Grandfather Borea had left all his secret codes and data to Zaval's side of the family. Now, look where that had got them. 'He would turn in his grave if he knew what you had done, yes he would,' he roared while kicking the Pilot in the stomach and face. The Pilot twisted and turned, trying to protect himself from the old man's onslaught. Frike's old boots, handcrafted for his brutal pleasure, even had his personal logo filed into their metal welt. At this ancient age, his infamous kick still packed a punch, vouched for by the wounds growing on the Pilot's battered face.

'Frike, you're a monster – like he was. Nothing but a cheap drug dealer. I hoped you were dead. I'm so sorry, I was wrong. For the next generation, I did it. Yes, I restored our good name with the deal I made with our Overlord,' he croaked, as blood seeped from the cuts on his face, staining the deck of the *Hela*. 'Your generation – thieves, murderers and rapists – tainted our family with dishonour …' His voice trailed off as he gasped for breath.

'Get him and his clan out of my site. Lock them up, well away from their Overlord, or what's left of him!'

In horror, the Pilot's bloodstained face turned up to face Frike. 'What have you done to him?' he screamed. An intense fear coursed through his body. The Eight had been right all along – he had betrayed him. *No, he* thought, *no, no, no.*

'I killed him. You supposed all the devices were here at the station. You were wrong. I always kept some. He never saw us coming.'

The old man watched as his new allies dragged the Pilot and his immediate family, bound in fetters, off the bridge. *Now to matters in hand; what's going on?* he wondered. *Who's flying that ship?* He turned to the comms console. 'Demard, what gives here? Who—'

'The Overlord's protégé; the human, called Niamh. It must be her, Frike. She has a power, some would say, she shouldn't have – he taught her. It could only be she who could escape the *Hela*. She's clever, very clever.'

A deadly silence enveloped the bridge. The loss of the *Boreal* was so shocking, Frike needed to stop and think. With its three assault craft, he had planned on using that ship. *Where was it gone? Can we chase it? Will it come back?* Over and over those critical thoughts flooded his mind. And then there was a small ray of hope, as he realised what the *Hela* was capable of. He looked back at Demard. 'The *Hela* armoury, quick, get access to it, now – right now,' he shouted.

Demard hesitated and then started to work intensely at his console, his head and old tired body hunched down over it. Alarms flashed red, while a drab machine voice recited, 'Access denied, access denied …'

Finally, Demard sat up, his wrinkled face said it all. 'No, Frike, that won't work. I cannot crack the codes. She augmented the Aknar armoury cyphers with a layer of her own, in her language. She didn't have access to the Aknar cryptograms but to stop others from getting at the armoury, she installed something she called a firewall.'

'What do you mean? Don't you speak their language?' he asked as he limped over to Demard's console.

'Yes, their main one, I do. But the human uses an obscure dialect from an ancient language spoken in her own lands. We never kept records of all Earth's languages in the database,' Demard said, looking at the old man's piercing eyes as he leaned over him. He tried hard not to wince as the stench of Frike's rotten breath wafted across his nose.

'But if it's a language, there must be some form of rhythm, a beat you can de-code?'

'It's not that simple. I tried that. The human uses local colloquialisms. Random words in a vernacular only she and her kind understand. It's easy to remember but impenetrable for an outsider. I told you she was clever; she would never let me into that secret. All her codes are based on that recipe,' he said, staring back into the old man's eyes. 'We could break the door of the armoury down but you still won't be able to launch the weapons.'

'Frike, I have news of the others,' said a breathless greenskin as she entered the bridge.

'Well, don't just stand there panting, tell me,' he shouted at her.

Trembling, she knelt down and bowed her head before the old man. 'They're dead,' she said, her head shaking back and forth.

'What did you say?'

'They're dead, all four. One critically mutilated by a Neredian's tail, and the other three were killed by a crude projectile weapon,' she said, covering her head with her hands.

The old man screamed, then beat the unfortunate messenger senseless across the head with his gnarled fists. As she slumped on the ground, he turned to face his shocked crew.

A beep from Demard's comms unit broke the frightening silence. 'Frike, long-range sensors detected the *Boreal*. It's outside the asteroid belt. Looks like it's coming back.'

Frike closed his eyes. Gripping his two hands together, he looked up at the ceiling and exhaling all his frustrations, screamed. Sitting down on the captain's chair, he broke the stillness that followed his screech. In a cold hard voice, he said, 'If those three assault ships aren't launched now, I'll start whipping people.' Finally, his stare fell on Verteg, who was working at the ship's helm in silence. 'Can we get the *Hela* moving, get her out of here, into open space?' he asked.

'There's something wrong. I can't connect to the main drives,' Verteg said, her voice trembling with fear. 'Frike, I've tried everything. I can't get a response from the control system. It's locked into the autodocking sequence.' It was true. When she had come up from the shuttle bay, Siba had shown Verteg the ship's controls. It was then that they had found the glitch. Even during the hiatus of Frike's takeover, Verteg had worked on it. Until she fixed that problem, the *Hela* was going nowhere.

The previous exertions, the euphoria of defeating The Eight and now all this depressing negativity had exhausted the old man. He slumped back in his seat. 'I'm surrounded by incompetents. No wonder we never regained our rightful place. Make yourself useful, you green-skinned calbak. Go, help them with the assault ships,' he said. As Verteg ran from the bridge, Frike cradled his head in his hands. It was going so well, and now two of his grandsons, his direct descendants and two of his closest grandnephews, were dead.

*

Boreal

'What do we do now?' Cylla asked, sitting next to Niamh in the shuttle 2 cockpit – inside *Boreal*'s engine room.

'I'm trying to find The Eight. Something strange has happened to him. Cylla, I'm not leaving until I get him. We have some time before they follow us. It'll take them a while to launch their ships.'

'We should go. You heard what Haret said of him – he is the most powerful and cunning of all the Overlords. He can take care of himself.'

Niamh turned around in her chair and glared straight into Cylla's green eyes. 'Know this, Cylla. I just said goodbye to someone who was like a mother to me over the past year. I may never see her again. That entity you refer to as "the most powerful and cunning of all the Overlords" is the nearest I have to a father. We're not leaving without him.' Taking a deep breath, Niamh paused. The silence was riveting. 'I'll use all my power and strength to get him back. Do you understand that?'

'No, human, I don't. But that makes no difference,' she said. Looking back at the strange human, she wondered how one with such a lithe body, could have such abilities. 'You're the most powerful mortal I have ever met. Whatever you decide and wherever you go, I will follow if you'll have me?'

'Jeez, Cylla, don't go all soppy on me now. Come on, you can watch that screen. It'll show any ships leaving the asteroid belt. I'll search for him.'

Ten minutes later, a frustrated Niamh stopped. *I'm missing something,* she thought.

'Cylla, they talked about a device – Uldonian tech. Do you know of anything that can harm an Overlord?'

'Yes, there was always talk of an organic device or devices. I know Captain Quriel had something that enabled us to communicate without the Overlords listening. I've heard talk of larger devices that can trap an Overlord. Supposed to cover them with its own mass. But it was gossip, such stories, you know, may not be true.'

More info, thought Niamh, who had not understood how dangerous the illegal tech could be. She had assumed The Eight was impenetrable. Despite her presumptions, she remembered how he had always maintained he wasn't infallible. *Looks like there's more meaning to that,* she realised. There was so much she was in the dark about. She needed something to go on – maybe this was it. 'Okay, let's assume that's what they used. It's probably why I can't communicate with him.' She turned to her nav-con and holding her blue diamond, projected her mind out into the space station and then right into the *Hela.*

She could see into the bridge and watched as an old man ran about ranting and raving, trying to do something to stop her. Enthralled by the spectacle, she wanted to stay and watch, but she needed to find The Eight. Starting in his chamber, surprised, she discovered what looked like his chariot, entombed in an unknown grey-coloured growth. Her first thoughts were, *it can't be that easy.* And then, as she scrutinised it, she realised it definitely was his grav platform. Her heart beat fast in her chest. 'There he is,' she said, pointing at the projection.

'There's no blue mass. That odd growth must have consumed it,' Cylla said, shocked at what she was looking at.

Through a small chink in the cloaks, she sensed his life force. 'No, not all of it. He's still there. I must get to him. I'll need more blue,' Niamh said, her fingers drumming on the console as she considered her options. Surprising Cylla, she jumped up, racing over to where her spacesuit was hanging. In seconds, she had it on and taking her small blue tank, made her way to the shuttle airlock.

'What are you doing, human? Where are you going?'

Ignoring the questions, Niamh turned and waved at Cylla before entering the airlock. Once out in the engine room, she refilled her small tank from one of the portable ones strapped down beside the main engine, and without delay, returned to the shuttle.

Knowing his life force still existed – that he was still alive – drove her on. 'We need to get closer,' she said, as she started the grav drive and set a course back to the secret space station.

'Are you sure you can fly this thing, with one engine, from inside this shuttle, into the asteroid belt?' Cylla said, doubtfully looking at the navigation projection of their course. It would take them back through the outer asteroids to where the Pilot had laid up the *Hela* – outside the maze that guarded their secret base.

'I never said it would be easy, but you're right. It's like flying a sick pig.'

'Oh, and you fly these sick pigs often, I suppose.'

Niamh grinned as she recalled landing the *Hela* in the Australian desert; it seemed so long ago. 'Well, I helped land one, twice the size of this, on Earth. It was the *Hela* before we fixed her up.'

Shaking her head while wondering what would come next, Cylla watched Niamh guide the ship around and over the asteroids from the remote helm in shuttle 2. 'Why does that not surprise me, human.'

But it wasn't all plain sailing. Niamh pushed the vessel to its limits, flying on one jury-rigged engine. As they neared their destination, failing to respond to her tight command to turn, the ship trembled with protest while heading straight towards a giant asteroid languishing in front of them. Cylla looked away, put her head between her knees and, to protect herself, her hands on her head. Fear quickened her heart. She closed her eyes while the shuddering increased, the ship objecting to Niamh's immediate stop command. Then, the unwanted effects of gravity came boring down. *There go the grav dampeners,* Cylla thought, as she was squashed down into her seat. For the next two minutes, she couldn't move, trapped with her head between her knees she felt as if the world was crashing down on her. Her body tried to vomit but the force was so intense, her muscles seized up. Blackness started to cover her mind as the pain got harder and harder to bear, and then, the big Neredian passed out.

Time passed by in degrees for Niamh. She grappled with the controls, increasing reverse thrust to the grav drive. *Boreal* sped on. The asteroid getting larger and larger in the shuttle's small viewscreen, telling Niamh, time was near the end. Miraculously, the ship slowed then came to an abrupt stop a couple of hundred metres from the rock's surface.

'Cylla, Cylla. Wake up,' Niamh shouted as she shook her back and forth.

There was a pool of green vomit on the deck between her legs, and inelegantly, dribbled down Cylla's face onto her knees. Opening her eyes and sitting back up, she wiped the mess from her face. 'What happened? Where are we?' The smell cut the stale atmosphere inside the confines of the shuttle's cockpit.

'We're stopped beside that large asteroid I almost hit, not far from the channel into their space station. You passed out. I told you, you need to strap up into your seat. I'm going to get The Eight,' Niamh said, as she reached over for her tank of blue. Before she started, she reflected back on the training The Eight had given her. To sharpen her abilities, he had devised a complicated test, involving many shifts of different items through numerous ports. His rescue would require much more than that and would take all her brainpower. She believed she could do it. 'Believe in your abilities,' he always said to her.

Placing her hands inside the full tank of blue strapped in front of her, Niamh concentrated her mind. Within seconds, two separate navigation projections, one of The Eight inside his chamber, and one of space immediately outside *Boreal*, appeared above her cramped control console. Touching blue with her fingers and concentrating on The Eight's location on the *Hela*, she embraced the blackness of space. Her thoughts grabbed at the micro matter – reaching out to him – pushing her ability farther than she ever had before. Pure blue poured from the tank into her hands, up through her arms and limbs and into her brain. A crackle and a burst of white light filled the cockpit, as her gamma waves melded the blue into a forceful astronomical pulse. Space folded, simultaneously, two ports opened, one in The Eight's chamber and one outside *Boreal*. She had done it! Closing off every other sensation, her ethereal body was there, standing in his room on the *Hela*, right beside his chariot.

To his surprise, he sensed her presence and through a chink in the cloaks, flashed a message. '*Don't touch that grey mass.*' His tone left no doubt as to the danger she was in.

Sensing the presence of her fresh blue, the Uldonian cloak's grey mass started to pulse. Warily, she stood her ground. Her ghostly presence, looking for a way in, circled his chariot.

'*You're still alive, still in there?*' she asked.

'*Yes, in the buffer, and the memory banks,*' he replied.

It was indeed a mess of throbbing bile, a horror she had never imagined. But urgency spurred her on. There were limits to her power and the blue in her small tank wouldn't last forever. She'd have to find a way to move him through the fold. Her brain broke down the vision, allowing her to focus clearly on something yellow crisscrossing the grey pulsing mass. It was the bindings, clumsy labour done by one of Frike's men to hold the cloaks in place. Now they presented an unexpected solution.

'*What about those bindings?*'

'*I cannot see them,*' was his quiet reply. '*Leave me, you shouldn't have come.*'

Not an option, she thought, inspecting the ties that ran under and over his chariot. She focused on three overlapping bindings that disappeared under the chariot, reappearing at the other side. Thick and broad, enough to provide a barrier – she hoped. Using them, with both hands under it, her eerie presence picked up his chariot.

But her arrival had not gone unnoticed. When the port opened, the thump of displaced air was felt close by on the bridge. Two of Frike's nephews had rushed to investigate. At the demolished doorway, they stood stock-still, staring into his chamber. The sight of a ghostly Niamh, standing beside a shimmering black hole in space, lifting The Eight's chariot, froze them both in their tracks. They couldn't believe it. There she was, the strange alien they had seen in the shuttle bay who had stolen *Borea 1* – back on board! Entranced by the spectacle, they watched Niamh's apparition. From the hair on her head to the tips of her boots, everything shimmered with an ethereal blue glow. Keeping clear of the pulsing Uldonian mass, she had her two hands charily placed on the yellow bindings. Then, with a deft heave, she threw The Eight's chariot right into the open port.

Realising what was happening, they raised their weapons shouting. Their unwanted noisy presence disturbed Niamh's work. She turned to look at them. Rage at what they had done to her Overlord poured from her eyes. White light, pure blue energy, flashed towards the young aliens. They dropped their guns and ran – not before a blue bolt grazed one on his shoulder. The painful burn seared deep into the bone. His bloodcurdling screams echoed down the corridor into the bridge, halting any other would-be pursuers.

Powering behind The Eight, Niamh followed him into the fold in space. With raw energy manipulated by her thoughts, she pushed him down the black tunnel towards the port at the other side.

On shuttle 2, in the *Borea1* engine room, in shock from her ordeal and trying to clean her mess from the floor of the shuttle, Cylla heard an ominous crackling behind her. She turned. The sight of Niamh's physical body, surrounded by sizzling blue energy with her eyes glazed by a soft blue light, was terrifying. Blue flashing energy surrounded Niamh's head. Cylla backed off, away from her, into the far corner of the shuttle and sat down on the floor, trembling with fear.

It was longer than Niamh imagined; she knew it would be difficult, but the tunnel seemed endless. *The distance shouldn't make any difference,* she thought over and over. *Just needs more energy.* And then she heard The Eight's encouragement, faint in the distance, but it was him.

'*It does, my child – the distance needs more time and energy. Why did you try this?*'

'*Because I love you. I will never leave you, you should know that.*'

'Where are you taking me?'

'Back to the Boreal; we're nearly there.'

'Do not bring me into the engine room. Keep me as far from blue as you can.'

She didn't need to ask why. All through their epic journey, the Uldonian microbes had strained and beat on their bindings. Trying to get out, to suck up her energy, and devour her ethereal existence. If they succeeded, she knew she would die. When the Eight's chariot appeared from the fold, alongside the *Boreal*, relief coursed through Niamh's physical body back on shuttle 2. It was thick and meaningful, so full of life and hope. But she wasn't out of the woods yet. She could sense her tank of blue was near empty.

Immediately, she scanned the ship. The safest place for The Eight was an empty ammunitions locker beside the starboard gun turret at the bottom of the great fin. *There it is*, she thought. Urgency drove her on and within seconds she had opened a port in the locker and one outside the ship in front of The Eight. The last of her blue flashed and crackled as she transported him inside the secure compartment deep within *Boreal*.

'Cylla, I have him. We need to get out of here,' she shouted. 'Cylla, what's wrong?' Niamh looked around at the Neredian, still trembling, crouched down in the corner of the shuttle.

'Look at yourself, human. You cannot see your face, but your eyes, they are blue and your hair, face and hands, you're changing.'

Niamh looked at her hands. Cylla was right, they were bluer than before. *Shit, it'll be fine*, she believed. *I need to stay focused; we have to get out of here.* As she looked at the navigation projection, she saw the guardian asteroid maze start to slow. The Borea had recovered – it had taken them some time, but they were coming. She suspected she had unseen help from the *Hela*. Looking at her watch, it was now over an hour since the alarms on the *Hela* first sounded. As she watched, three small ships made their way towards the channel. They would be on top of them within minutes. Like a demon possessed, Niamh turned to the blue drive controls.

'Cylla, there's no time to make it back to open space on grav power. We'll take a shortcut. Strap in or hold on tight.' Within seconds, she had the blue drive online and a port opened for a short jump through a fold, back to where they had come from. Simultaneously, she started the grav drive. It was an ill-timed jump. The grav dampers couldn't keep up with the changes Niamh's flight plan had exerted on the ship. Gritting her teeth and screaming as the vessel ripped through the fold in space, she managed to stay conscious. The *Boreal* appeared again, one thousand kilometres away from the asteroid belt. Niamh looked at the projection. The three ships, having cleared the deadly channel, had stopped to look for her.

Recovering The Eight's original pre-programmed course, she modified it with their present location. After loading it into blue-drive nav-com, a new fold opened in space. With the grav drives, she nudged the ship in, all the time, increasing power to the grav dampers. Before the port closed behind them, she could see the three small craft launching missiles in an attempt to stop them.

They were too late. Safe in a gravity bubble, *Boreal* started its long journey through folded space, back to the colony on the New World. Relieved and flushed with her achievement, Niamh slumped back in her seat. However, her happy feeling of success faded when she saw Cylla lying unconscious on the floor, blood seeping from a gash on her head.

CHAPTER NINE

Anan Galaxy

Our Anan Galaxy is a gravitationally bound system of stars one hundred and eighty thousand light-years wide. Although a small galaxy in the greater universe, it is our home and contains precious and bountiful solar systems, asteroid belts, gases, dust and other celestial bodies – too numerous to categorise here. At the end of the last intergalactic war, a conclave of Overlords apportioned ownership of the known galaxies amongst themselves. The Overlords acknowledged in this epoch as The One, and The Eight are the owners of our world and galaxy. Host to the Energy Exchange, the Anan Galaxy is of prime rank in the universe. The House of Aknar is bound by celestial treaty to protect the integrity of this galaxy.

‹ **Introduction from: Basic Galactic History. Theia Aknar**

*

Asteroid Belt, Space Station Borea.
EPTS: A139058

IT TOOK HIM LONGER THAN planned but Quriel Borea, the Pilot's son, arrived outside the asteroid belt in a small military ship. Quriel hadn't experienced any problems in commandeering the vessel, but it was the last-minute flight approval that caused the upset. After leaving Cylla at the Energy Exchange space dock, he had returned to his ship to find flight control had scuppered his plans. Unbeknown to him, it was Little Kake's corrupt contacts who instigated the delay. Knowing Quriel would be following Verteg's ship, with Frike's crew on board, Kake pushed hard to delay the well-armed ship's departure. And it worked. After much wrangling with his superiors and flight control, Quriel finally got an admiral, a devoted follower of The Eight, to approve the fake flight plan. Still, he lost valuable time – costly in every way.

Not knowing what they might find, and leaving folded space early, he and his crew had made a cautious approach to the Borea base. 'Captain, there's trouble at the space station. Transmission's coming in, and I have visual as well – on screen now,' the excited comms officer cried.

Mystified by the unfolding drama, they watched the three small vessels launch missiles at *Borea1*, then it disappeared into a fold in space.

'By The One, what's going on?' Quriel asked no one in particular, as he stared, transfixed, at the viewscreen. Totally engrossed in the proceedings, they listened intently to trite blather on the comms, trying to make sense of what was happening.

Then a quivering voice, laced with fear, broke through the idle chatter. '*Hela* bridge, *Hela* bridge, they've gone. They managed to open a fold. I'm sorry, Frike. We were too late.'

Interrupted by the faint hiss of cosmic noise, there followed a deadly silence. Quriel's jaw dropped. He hunched over his console in astonishment at the mention of that name. He recognised the voice of Verteg, the pilot he had entrusted Cylla with. His stomach churned while he wondered at her fate. A crackle shattered the silence, announcing someone was about to speak. And then they heard it, the chilling voice of the Borea bogeyman, Frike. His shrill speech spilt abject rage over the void of space. 'Verteg, you useless kilith, I should have you whipped. How could you let them get away? All three of you – call yourselves pilots. I, I …'

'He's cut the transmission, Captain,' said the comms officer, the shock stifling her voice. She glared at Quriel, as if to say: to what unimaginable fate have you brought us to? And, spitting out what the rest of the crew were thinking: "we need to get out of here!"

Digging deep into the well of his battle-hardened training, Quriel fought back the emotional upheaval. Logical thought prevailed. They weren't going anywhere. His solid, commanding voice relayed his thoughts. 'No. We wait. They cannot see us.' Stating the obvious, he needed to quell their fear. 'We have the best cloak available in space. No one can see us. I need to know what happened. I can't believe he's still alive.'

Quriel looked around at his crew of six. They were his most trusted followers, a toughened multi-skilled bunch from the Aknar military. Coming from the mainstream Anan populace, they had served in his unit since he made captain. Not from gilded charter families, they had to work their way up through the ranks the hard way. They shared the feeling of dread, within the Aknar military, that The Sixth might prevail. When Quriel had come to them with an outlandish proposal to help The Eight, they jumped at it.

Now rising to the challenge, they sat at their stations in the small military transporter in silence. Quriel sat on a raised dais in the middle of the cramped cockpit, his crew straddled on either side. They packed the cabin aft of the cockpit with the tools of their trade – weapons and personal transports. Not knowing what his father's jaunt would entail, Quriel had come prepared for a fight. Now it looked like it would start earlier than he had planned.

'Captain, he's on the *Hela*,' their crew chief said, as he brought up a navigation projection of the inside of the space station. 'It appears immobilised,' he continued with surprise.

The comms officer looked up from her screen and shouted, 'Captain, there's a scanning pulse – it's launched from the *Hela*.'

'It can't see us.'

'It's passing over us now. Well, I'll be – there's a signal embedded in it.'

An intrigued Quriel stepped across to comms. 'How's that possible? Can you decode it?' he asked.

'Yes, I can,' was the enthusiastic answer as she attacked the coded burst. 'That's strange, I recognise the encryption.' Comms worked at her console as Quriel stood over watching. Suddenly, a message appeared on the screen.

Quriel, Frike is back. He stole away on the transporter, split the family and took over the Hela and the space station. Your father and his people are imprisoned. Niamh and Cylla escaped with The Eight on the Boreal. The Hela is damaged – Frike's crew can't fix it. He plans to steal the blue and leave on the three vessels. You can get into the base from here, but you'll need spacesuits.

The message ended with a map of the asteroid.

'So that's how Grandfather got out,' Quriel said, as he traced his finger along a secret passage through the asteroid. 'That's where we go. Right there,' he said, with his finger on the screen.

'It could be a trap, Captain,' the Chief said.

'Yes, it could, but we have to risk it. Who would use that encryption?'

Comms looked up. 'Your own uncle, Demard. I'd recognise his work anywhere; he wrote it.'

'It's not a trap – it's his cry for help. Chief, get this ship around to the dark side of the asteroid. Let's see if we can find Grandfather's back door.'

*

The Hela, Space Station Borea

With tails between their legs, the three assault craft returned to the *Hela*. The landing on the forward deck was unremarkable. The three pilots, their heads hung low, moped on the long trudge back to the bridge. Knowing the wrath they would face, no one hurried. However, the inevitable couldn't be put off forever and, with the other two pilots, Verteg knelt in front of Frike, shaking with fear as he ranted.

'Verteg, some lead pilot you are. You couldn't even get the *Hela* going, and now this! You're a shame to this family. What else can I expect from a green-skinned kilith? I knew your mother. She sold herself to the low-life – the dregs of society. That's where you were spawned from, not purebreed Borea seed.'

His cruel words cut to her very core; she loved her mother. Not knowing her father made it worse. Her mother had always told her he was a Borea purebreed from Anan, a brilliant man who loved her and Verteg dearly. As she blinked, he lashed out with his closed fist. She never saw it coming. With an explosion of stars, it connected with her face. The pain burned into her brain but she tried to stay upright. He raised his boot – instinct took over as Verteg cowered down. He kicked her, the first soft blow to measure, then, once his body adjusted to her distance, he continued harder and harder.

'Stop, Frike! Stop, stop, stop,' she pleaded. Her voice trailed off as she rolled away from his boot. It connected with her stomach and she howled in pain. It was a long, long time since he had kicked someone to death. *Such pleasure, such pleasure*, was the rancid thought purring in his twisted mind. The more she screamed, the harder he kicked, the spittle flowing from his full grinning mouth and his eyes ablaze with fury. He stomped down on her legs and then her face. The sound of crushing bones and the sight of her blood spurting out from her broken nose spurred the other two pilots into action.

'We need her, Frike. She's our best navigator. Stop, please stop,' they pleaded, as they sheltered her from his flaying boots. The sharp points had dug into her flesh and they could see the deep welts and bruises all over her bare arms, legs and face. Ignoring Frike's screams, the two brave pilots lifted the unconscious Verteg up and carried her off the bridge.

With the loss of his prey, he turned his attention on the rest of his clan. 'Get the ships ready to load,' Frike roared, still shaking with rage. 'Start loading the blue onto them. It won't recompense for the loss of the *Borea1*, but it'll help with the restoration of our business.' As they ran out of the bridge, he looked across at Demard. 'Any sign of Quriel? He should be here soon.'

The old comms engineer sat throughout the brutal affair, always working at his comms console – as if nothing else mattered. 'No, Frike,' he cheerfully replied. 'I have the scans set up. He'll de-cloak when he arrives at the asteroid belt. We'll catch him there. And you know he cannot get in unless we open the channel.'

Frike sat down in the captain's chair and, picking up a cup, smiled at Demard before he took a long drink. Beating and torturing was always thirsty work, but now, something was off. As he sipped his drink, his mind whirled around and around. *What am I missing?* he asked himself.

Deep in thought, he never noticed Demard stand up from his chair, stretching his body and getting the kinks out of his long neck. He made his way slowly to where Frike had exerted himself. As if exercising his back, he deftly bent over. Palming a small DNA sampler, the old comms engineer surreptitiously collected a sample of Frike's spittle.

*

Quriel's ship made the short journey to the dark side of the giant asteroid that formed the Borea base. Meticulously, they scanned the clefts and caves cut into the rough wall of it until they found the space dock. It was cleverly concealed in a deep natural pocket of the asteroid's darkened wall. Ages ago, the cave provided their grandfather and his crew the perfect escape route. Quriel watched his team as they guided their small vessel into a cavern that opened out from the dark recess into the asteroid.

He had mulled it over and over in his head and now, slumped in his seat, he had come to the same conclusion. He had loved her but she had betrayed him. It was the only answer. They had kissed goodbye on the space dock and she had wished him well. "I will see you soon, my love," were her parting words. He did not trust anyone else with the details. The others were fed bits and pieces of information and never told the full story. Even Verteg, the pilot who had worked for them since she was a child, was not informed of her final destination until she was light-years clear of Anan. Despite all the security, it was she, the technician who had shared his bed – his innermost desires and thoughts – who had betrayed him. His heart beat fast in his chest as his mind mulled and churned this ultimate deceit.

A slight bump announced their arrival. 'Captain, we're here.'

Back to reality, he looked out on the dock. It was bigger than he had thought and would effortlessly accommodate one of the assault ships. His chief landed it right in the middle of the pier. Silently, they donned their spacesuits and opened the hatch at the rear of their craft. Well used to the equipment, they had their personal flyers unloaded and lined up outside their ship. Weapons were next.

'Arm up and set your grav guns to kill. Have no mercy. Anyone who fires on us is with him,' Quriel said. The grav guns checked and loaded, each slung one across their shoulder and mounted a spare in a holster on the flyers.

Sitting astride their assault flyers, they raced from the dock, up into an opening Demard had marked on the map. The secret passage started at a broken airlock and worked its way up through the deep interior of the asteroid. Illuminating the route, just wide enough for their small craft, they silently made their way into the base beyond.

*

Demard had stripped all the data from his and Zaval's crystals and amalgamated it with that of what he had decoded deep in the base computers. Yet, there was another layer he couldn't open. Their grandfather had protected it. Although he didn't trust Frike with the entire data, he had wanted him, or a section of his part of the family, involved in some way. Demard didn't understand what his grandfather had intended. The monster was what he was, and for some twisted reason, perhaps revenge or guilt for betraying him, Grandfather had included him in the puzzle. All Demard really knew was that he needed Frike's DNA to access all the files. Once he had it, he plugged the small sampler into his terminal. Like a key, Frike's DNA signature decrypted the final guarding algorithm. Demard watched as file after file opened, unravelling the last riddle. Although engrossed in his work, he never lost touch with that evil presence. Soon it would come.

His mind cleared. Frike put down his warm drink, rubbing the tattoo on the side of his face. *Time to take stock*, he thought. *All is not as it seems.* When they arrived, everything went as planned. He and his crew, cloaked from The Eight, secretly got on board the *Hela*. The strange cloaks hid them as they made their way to his chamber. They had rushed in and fired the device. Latching onto his blue energy, it covered The Eight with its dark mass. Their biggest challenge a success – they had defeated an Overlord. The explosion caused mayhem among the *Hela* crew as emergency alarms sounded and they lost contact with their Overlord. Frike and his small team stormed the bridge. *Zaval's people had no weapons and were easily defeated. What have I missed?* he thought as he looked across at Demard.

The old computer technician hunched over his console, wholly engaged in his work. As his long bony fingers ran across it, they beat out a strange rhythm as the musical sounds of his work penetrated the quiet bridge. 'Any sign of Quriel and his gang?' Frike asked.

Demard stopped, turned to look, his sizeable eyes now squinting at Frike. 'No, there's a grav transporter ten light-years away making its way to Anan, but that's it.'

'Keep looking. They'll arrive soon.' *He's lying; they're here already. That's when it all went wrong,* he thought. When he secured the bridge, he had left two of his grandsons to guard the shuttle bay. But Niamh had killed them as she escaped with Cylla. Yes, she had jumped the shuttle out into space with her powers but there was no warning when she started its engines. An alarm should have gone off on the bridge. And the armoury – it was all too convenient. Getting up from his seat, he walked into the captain's ready room. Sitting down on the desk, he called his grandson. 'How soon can you be ready to leave?'

'The vessels are prepped for flight. The green-skinned tech is loading the blue.'

'Let me talk to her.' Silence, then the voice of the girl. 'Yes, Frike.'

'How much blue have you?'

'Only about half—'

'Enough. Your boyfriend is here.'

'Frike, he'll kill us. He has six of his best troops with him. We don't stand a chance.'

'Stop the transfer and prepare those ships for departure, now.'

'Frike, please take me with you. I can navigate and I'm a good technician. He'll kill me.'

'Yes, yes. Let me talk to my grandson.'

'I heard that, Frike. We'll grab what valuables we can. How many of the family will we take?'

'Only our allies. If any of the others resist, kill them, and,' he paused, 'make an example of them. You know the drill.'

'Yes, Frike,' was the eager reply.

The old man looked out at Demard, still working at his console. *What's he doing?* he wondered as he walked back into the bridge and over to the comms console. He sat down beside him and smiled. 'Demard, it's time for us to go. I can't risk waiting any longer. If Quriel arrives, we don't stand a chance. Open the channel now.'

'As you wish, Frike,' he answered, as he started to key in the sequence. They both watched as the three-dimensional procession of the asteroids slowly came to a stop, forming the open channel.

'I was told one of the asteroids was damaged. It blocked your first entrance.'

'Yes, a delinquent. We moved it out of the way and disabled it. You see, there it is,' he said, pointing to the side of the clear channel.

Frike smiled at Demard. 'You have served me well, Demard. Before we leave, I have a gift for you.'

Demard turned away from his screen and looked at the wizened old, tattooed face of Frike. Frike bent over on his seat, so close that Demard could smell his foul breath. 'You monster! You know I betrayed you. Quriel is here. Look,' he said, as he changed the view on the big screen. They watched as Quriel and his companions sped out of the tunnel and made their way into the base headquarters. 'Soon they'll be on board. I opened the channel to give you an escape route. Your haste to escape will prevent you from killing the others. I'm timeworn, Frike, and ready for—'

With a flash of steel, Frike embedded a long dagger into Demard's heart. Grabbing his back with one hand, he twisted the knife deep into Demard with the other. 'Nobody crosses me and lives,' he said, as he spat into Demard's face.

As his red blood trickled from the side of his mouth, Demard looked up and smiled. 'Monster, I'm ready and willing to die to defeat you. Knowing that I did will make me die a happy man.'

Frike pulled the dagger from Demard's heart, rubbed it across his shoulders to wipe it clean, and then he screamed with rage. He wanted to go to the brig and kill Zaval and his clan, but Demard was right, there wasn't enough time. He knew it would take all his strength to hobble down to the shuttle bay airlock. The image of Quriel and his crew, sitting on their craft, with their weapons strapped across their chests, played on the viewscreen. Self-preservation kicked in and all thoughts of revenge evaporated as the old relic of the family hobbled off towards the shuttle bay. His ability to move surprised even him as he adopted a running gait, fleeing for his life, back along the corridors he had been carried up.

*

Quriel could never understand the designers' thinking when they had penned the drawings for these "flyers". Intended for clandestine missions, they were the most uncomfortable craft imaginable. He had a pain in his backside from sitting astride the crude device, and his spine ached! *They must have been modelled on a farm animal,* he thought as he led his crew across the small void in the Borea station to the *Hela.* In contrast to the blackness of space, the vast golden ship shimmered with light. Their journey through the dark caverns was uneventful, with an exit through another broken airlock a short distance from the Borea headquarters. *Blown away from the wall,* he thought, *most likely in haste to escape.* He dumped the thoughts of his grandfather's retreat as he led his team up towards the bow of the *Hela.*

He could see two of the assault craft had lifted off and were fleeing in the direction of the open channel. One ship was still sitting on its landing pad, light spilling out from the cabin windows. He sped up towards it, not sure what he would find. Slowing, he peered in. There were some of the family he had seen at the space dock on the Exchange, now pointing out of the windows at him and his crew. He looked at their faces, etched with worry, and although he couldn't hear, their lips betrayed their fearful shouts. Then the dynamic within the cabin changed. All heads turned towards the aft end of the craft. He sped along the windows to see what had caught their attention and gasped at his first view of the evil monster of the Borea's past. Frike himself hobbled along the corridor. That wasn't the only shocker. There she was – the betrayer – helping the old man to his seat. A black blanket of fury clouded his brain – never before had he felt such hate. He reached for the rifle, fingering the trigger as he withdrew it from the holster. Then a firm hand pressed his shoulder.

Relayed through their suit comms, the calm voice of the Chief filled his ears. 'No, Captain, we don't do this. If you blow out that window, you'll kill them all.'

He was right. Quriel stayed stock still. He watched as hate flowed from his brain. It punched her inner senses. Not so surprised, she walked to a window and looked out at him. Sat astride his flyer, dressed in a silver spacesuit with a hand on a grav rifle – half out of the holster – would put the fear of death in anyone. Not her. Scowling at him, she turned away and it was the last he saw of her.

The calm voice of the Chief returned. 'Hurry, Captain. We need to get inside – the team have found an airlock.'

Turning away, he didn't wait to watch the last ship as it lifted off, letting the evil monster, Frike Borea, free again to rampage in the galaxy.

The seven climbed down a ladder from the airlock into the shuttle bay. If Quriel had had any inkling of the macabre sight they would discover, he would have blasted the fleeing ship's window and those inside into oblivion. Five of their family lay dead on the shuttle's bloodstained deck. Two were gutted, the contents of their stomachs hanging out beside them. Two others bore the unmistakable burns from a grav gun. The fate of the last was the most gruesome of all — his head had been hacked from the body. Quriel remembered the dark tales from the family past, now back here to haunt them.

The survivors huddled together in a corner, so traumatised, they hardly reacted to the sight of the seven military rescuers.

A bloodstained technician looked up at them. 'You're late,' was her terse greeting.

Quriel stood before them, ashamed, his head hung low. He wiped the sweat from his brow, while the smell of death stung the back of his nose. 'I'm sorry,' was his lame reply. He could have prevented this. 'How many are left? Zaval is—'

'He's alive,' she blurted out, 'with others in the brig. There are more on the bridge. We don't know who's left alive. Verteg's dying in a place they call med-bay; she needs help. I'll take you there.'

Quriel split up his group. With one of the family, he went to free Zaval, the Pilot. Two went back for their ship and its medical supplies and three to secure the *Hela* bridge. It was the Chief, with the field medical kit, whom he sent to med-bay.

While the young technician hurried him along, the Chief remembered Verteg. He had met her once with Quriel. The beautiful and talented woman, oozing with intelligence, had captivated him. He had vivid memories of her smooth green skin, her long blue hair and deep brown eyes. All his military toughness melted away when he entered med-bay. Verteg lay unconscious on her back, her blue hair matted with blood. Pale purple bruising covered her smooth green skin. Bloodied bones pushed out from her body, the compound fractures piercing her tunic. And worst of all, the monster had flattened her nose down into her once beautiful face. *How, how could one do this to another?* were the thoughts that flashed through his brain. He could feel Verteg's pain; the sensation and the sheer extent of the trauma she had experienced, shocked his very core. If the Chief had known what he would see and feel now, he wouldn't have stopped Quriel from firing his weapon at the escaping monster. *He would have joined him*, he thought.

Shaking himself back to reality, he could hear her laboured breathing. He realised, if Verteg were to survive she would need expert medical attention – and now. Serving his time as a field medic, he would do all he could to preserve her life but he was far from the expert she needed. Breaking open his field kit, he pulled out the life-scanner. It scattered a thin white beam of light down along her body as he held it up over her.

While the magical instrument examined Verteg, the Chief could feel the anxious presence of the girl. 'What's this place?' he asked her, trying to put the young techie at ease.

She looked up at the tall purebreed man. He had his spacesuit peeled back over his torso, tied around his waist. The muscles on his broad shoulders rippled through the thin undergarment as he held the device aloft. She felt his deep emotions, care and empathy, and it surprised her! *A gentle giant*, she thought. Her trembling reply cut the tension. 'The Pilot told us it's a human medical facility. Apparently, one of them built it before the ship left their colony.'

Taking stock, the Chief looked around the alien room. Verteg was lying on what appeared to be a crude bed on wheels. *Primitive, but practical*, were his thoughts on the earthly gurney. To heal Verteg, he'd need much more than was here. 'Where's the Anan med-bay? We'll need a full auto-healer,' he asked, the concern now laced in his voice.

'It's gone; this is all that's here.'

Her quiet answer again chilled the tall Chief to the core. 'Nothing's ever easy,' he gasped at this unwelcome news.

Finished its scan, he put the tool down. Looking for anything that might help, he started to pull open drawers and cabinets. Futile. It was all labour-intensive stuff, primitive intruments, field dressings and alien medicines. *No time for this,* he thought, as Verteg exhaled a deep pain-ridden moan. Quickly, he retrieved a field-doc from his pack. The small medical device already communicated with the diagnostic tool. Its screen displayed Verteg's injuries – the broken bones and critical injuries flashing purple – as well as the immediate life-saving measures she needed. Chief loaded it with vials from his kit. The usual battle remedies, pain suppressants, heart stabilisers, salts and energy tonics. Holding it to her forearm, it found a vein and dispensed the exact life-saving doses. As the drugs coursed through her body, Verteg started to relax, her breathing improved and the moaning subsided.

Chief looked across at the young technician. Her green and white face was grey at the sight of her friend covered in matted blood, bruising and her nose flattened into her face. A faint, lifeless dimple, played on her left cheek, now a mask of worry.

Out of immediate danger, if Verteg was to survive, she needed much more – their work had only started. He spoke quietly to the girl. 'We have Anan plasma on our ship. My crew will bring it here; it'll help her. But,' he paused at what he was about to ask, 'in the meantime, I need your help. The tunic must come off. We need to clean and dress her wounds, and bones must be set. We can use the alien supplies. Can you do it?'

The young girl nodded and they both set to work, neither expecting they would ever have had to take on such a gruesome task.

CHAPTER TEN

Grav Engines

Basic, faster than light starships, are powered by the humble grav engine. The engine uses a malleable metal propellant with properties that nullify the effects of gravity. Pre-flight, the drives are packed with the malleable metal fuel. Instantaneous velocity is obtained by focusing the energy through apertures on the ship's hull. Directional control is maintained by synchronous modulators which translate control system dialogue through omnidirectional grav shields straddling the engine's external drive ports. To prevent accidental exposure of grav when the ship is docked, laid up in a shuttle bay or on a landing pad, the grav ports are sealed closed by steel-pinned docking locks.

‹ *An Introduction: Fundamentals of intergalactic travel. Zaval Borea*

*

The Hela, Space Station Borea. EPTS: A139078

Rapidly, Quriel and his team established control of the ship and within a time-seg, had the *Hela* and its all-important bridge secure. Two of his soldiers had returned with their small craft, landing it on the shuttle deck. A runner delivered the life-giving purebreed plasma to med-bay. The unique plasma served as a blood replacement, giving the body time to heal itself after a massive trauma wound. It gave the Chief some hope that he could save Verteg's life.

Despite Frike's departure, the soldiers didn't take anything for granted and assumed all they met were hostile until proved otherwise. But the family left on board dispelled any doubts about their allegiance. Even after their late arrival, they welcomed the Aknar troops. There was little to say when Quriel released Zaval the Pilot, Siba and Alke from the brig.

In reality, it was the safest place for them. The Pilot was overjoyed to see his son. They had so much catching up to do, but after the happy reunion, they agreed it should wait.

The logical place for all to meet up was the galley. No one had eaten since Frike had taken control of the ship and it was a favourable opportunity for the remaining Borea and their military companions to coalesce as a new crew. As they mingled, the Pilot started to take stock and count. Including Frike and his stowaways, forty-eight Borea had left the Exchange on the transporter. Nine were now dead, and fourteen had gone on the three fleeing ships. It was a family disaster, with only twenty-five Borea now left on board the *Hela*. The Eight, their Overlord, was gone, his fate unknown and Verteg, their best pilot, was lying in med-bay with the Chief desperately trying to keep her alive.

However, after the horror of Frike's takeover, it was a boisterous lot that assembled in the *Hela's* galley. Safe for the first time, they could relax and take in their surroundings. The comments were all the same: 'Why does an Aknar ship look like an alien ship?' They were surprised the station bills, and other info-boards, were in both Anan and English. 'What's that strange script?' they asked Siba and Alke. And as for the galley: 'Where are the auto food dispensers?' The technicians started to explore the ovens, cookers, fridges, dishwashers and other paraphernalia of a well-stocked earthly kitchen. 'What are those strange machines? Are those things for cooking food? Did you actually cook food here?' They were surprised at the primitive alien tech and wondered at the Overlord's wisdom in transplanting the humans at all.

Siba tried to explain. 'It was the humans who refitted the *Hela* on their home world, Earth.'

Some of the technicians had recognised the work in the engine room and the bridge. However, they still maintained it was all shoddy alien work. Hungry, they started to rummage in the pantries and cold store behind the galley. The sight of more alien food was a big upset.

'Is this what we have to eat?' one asked, as he spat out the raw rice he had tasted.

'It must be cooked,' replied Alke. 'And stop spilling it,' he said, as he started to sweep the half bag of precious rice back up. He carefully opened the top of the twenty-five-kilo bag and poured the spill back in. It was a sobering moment and revealed to them all the critical position they were in. The intention was always to bunker up in the Anan Galaxy – now that was not an option. The food that was here was all they had.

Throughout, the Pilot sat stock still, watching his niece and nephew's futile explanations. Eventually, two of Quriel's soldiers shooed the explorers out of the pantries and helped Alke and Siba as they gathered a meal of dried meat, dried fruit and nuts.

'Alien food. Is this what we came for,' they asked the Pilot. 'Is this the best you can offer?'

Although, as they got accustomed to the different textures and tastes, some begrudgingly accepted that it was okay and they might actually be able to get used to it. Then the talk turned to who would cook. Siba explained that on the passage from the New World, the Aknar crew had scheduled a roster of mess duties. The unwelcome news, amongst this prima donna group of technicians, navigators and pilots, sparked another inferno of argument.

By now, the disgusted Pilot, well used to his fractious family, turned to Quriel. 'We need to go. I need to see him on the bridge. I've put this off long enough.'

*

They looked down at the body of Demard, his head slumped into his chest and a smile left across his face.

The Pilot knelt down and looked into the face of his cousin. 'I thought he had betrayed us.'

'He saved you all, Father. I'm sorry. I arrived too late and the ultimate betrayal, that came from me.'

'You were not to know. We never knew that the demon was still alive – Frike's clan influence was unknown to us. We thought Little Kake was a small-time drug dealer. We were so wrong. Demard must have blamed himself for missing that. He always maintained he knew everything. How could he have known this? He gave his life for us, Quriel. Had you not come when you did, we'd all be dead!' The Pilot sat down in a chair beside

Demard's console, his eyes drawn to it by the flashing lights. He wiped his face with his hands and looked back up at his son. 'The demons are not gone, Quriel. Still, the Borea name is cursed. They killed five of their own family, technicians and engineers. What threat did they pose to Frike's bunch of thugs? And Verteg ...'

'Father, the Chief has done all he can. Hopefully, the plasma will stabilise her. We can only wait.'

The Pilot nodded, a deep and grave one, his lips pursed in futile recognition of their fate. What could they do now? It was hopeless. Low on food, fuel and nowhere to go? Drawn like a magnet, his anxious face looked back at the console, his eyes again resting on the flashing lights. 'What is that pattern? Look, Quriel. It's repeating itself over and over.'

They moved the body of Demard aside. The Pilot sat back at the console and, concentrating on the pattern, typed in the colour. A program, asking for an access code, started up. The Pilot punched in his own personal cypher and the screen came alive.

'Well, I'll be ... he knew. He left us a message,' the Pilot said, as he and Quriel pored over the screen.

Zaval, if you are reading this, I am now deceased. I hope my deception worked and the demon is either gone or dead. Do not grieve for me, my friend. You know I should be dead already from the sickness. That I have survived so long is a testament to Alex and Rhea's medicine. I have deciphered all our grandfather's codes and puzzles. The location of the bases and assets are in the attached files. The demon does not know what I have found. I have scrubbed the base computers, and all the data resides here on the Hela. I must go. He has finished beating Verteg. It is the worst thing in my life I have ever seen. I am so sorry. I could do nothing to help her. I have loaded up my revenge for that, to his three vessels. If he leaves as I planned, he will not get far. He forced her to work for him. He told her he would kill you if she didn't. Please look after her and give her my love. You know what to do with my possessions.

The Pilot sat back in his chair and sighed. He looked across at the body of Demard. 'That you had to witness that, and could do nothing to stop it, your own daughter. Demard, I am so sorry.'

'Father, is—'

'Yes, Quriel, she's Demard's daughter.'

'Does she know?'

'No, she doesn't,' he spat back at his son. 'We always kept mixed-breed matings a secret. We're a bizarre bunch of misfits. You should know that by now. But that's why she worked so closely with our side of the family. I taught her to fly and to navigate. Let me visit her. I must see her and then we need to plan what we do next.'

*

He sat down at the bed beside Verteg. The knot in his stomach tightened as he looked at her swaddled in a mix of Anan and Earth bandages.

'It's the best I could do, Pilot, with these primitive human medical devices. I stabilised her with the purebreed plasma and the field supplies we had on board our own vessel. She'll need medical help soon,' the Aknar soldier said.

Taking her hand, he looked back at the soldier. 'You did good, thank you. You saved her life. Verteg, its Zaval. Can you hear me?'

She flinched at the sound of his voice and nodded. She tried to speak, but only a low croak came from her mouth.

'Stay quiet if you find it hurts. You and Demard saved us all. Can you help on the bridge?'

She nodded and clapped her hands together, squeezing the Pilot's as well.

'Good, I thought you'd be happy to do something. I'll need you, Verteg. We'll help you get around.' He gently shook her hand again and left.

Returning to his room, he was surprised to see it was as he left it. *They must have gone in a hurry; no time to ransack it,* he thought. He looked under the bed. It was still there – the three crates he had packed on Earth. Two full of red wine and one full of a brown liquid. He couldn't remember the name but they explained it was a spirit, and much stronger than wine. He sat on the bed and looked down at his long bony fingers. They were shaking and the knot in his stomach tightened. He closed his eyes and dreamed of the taste of the liquid and the euphoric rush it delivered. He wanted it so bad. The shaking increased. He looked longingly at the crates, and then his brain snapped him back to reality. *No. not now. They need me,* he thought. He stood up, stripped off his clothes and entered the small water closet. He washed the grime, the dried blood and stench of death from his body. After the wash, he lay on the bed wrapped in a towel and thought of the options they had. Finally, he stood up and dressed in clean clothes. Before he left the cabin, he looked down at his hands – the shaking had stopped. *How long can I hold that devil at bay,* he wondered as he made his way back to the bridge.

*

For the first time, on the *Hela* bridge, the motley crew of thirty-one were all together. It was a sobering moment as the team looked around. The body of Demard was gone and the bloodstains washed off the deck. But the stench of death doggedly clung to the stale air. Their six companions, along with the four of Frike's guards – all dead – were stored in a refrigerated container, waiting for burial. Their presence would cast a sour shadow on the ship. The Borea family recalled when they had stood here last, listening to the Pilot's welcome speech. That carefully planned greeting so fatally breached by Frike's intervention. Tension and ill-feeling cut the atmosphere like a knife. Some wore what remained of the project Anan ship suits while others dressed in their own, well-worn overalls. Garbed in the different shabby outfits, the Borea looked beat. Only Quriel's soldiers looked sharp, wearing grey military fatigues with their sidearms strapped on. Despite the colourless rancour, they all stood by, eager to hear what their fate would bring.

The Pilot stood up and spoke. He fidgeted, his hand rubbing his brow, and most telling of all were the dark circles under his eyes. 'We've three options,' he said, trying to put a positive spin on their predicament. 'We go back to Anan.' He paused as he caught Quriel's eye.

'Not an option. We walk straight into the hands of The Sixth,' Quriel replied. The look of disdain from the elders of the Borea family caught him short. *What gives here,* he wondered. *Was he facing a mutiny?* It wasn't something he had considered. He stood steadfast beside his six armed men, but the last thing he wanted was more killing.

The Pilot felt the family unease and something he hadn't felt before – a deep-seated fear of the unknown. Unperturbed, he battled on. 'Agreed,' he said. 'The second one, we return to the New World to find The Eight and join the humans.'

'We don't have enough supplies for such a long journey,' Siba said, her face a mask of disappointment. She had enjoyed her time working for The Eight. The young Borea girl had found her time in different galaxies and meeting other life forms exhilarating. But, no matter how hard she wanted to go back, reality knocked. They hadn't enough fuel. Most of the grav was used during the flight from Earth to the New World – where they had left some behind for the colony. If they were to try and make it back on the hybrid drive, they risked running out of blue halfway there. Siba had checked the tanks, and with what *Boreal* had taken, and what Frike's crew had stolen, there wasn't enough. Nor was there enough food for such a long journey. It all came back to the one-way trip they had made to the Anan Galaxy. They had planned to bunker the *Hela* at the Energy Exchange. With The Sixth now in control, they felt beaten.

The Pilot's head hung low as he agreed with his niece. 'No, Siba, we don't,' he said in a quiet voice. After a deep sigh, he continued. 'We won't survive such a long journey. Most likely, we will run out of food and fuel in intergalactic space. A one-way trip to a cold, lonely grave.' He stopped talking, allowing that stark message to sink in. Shuffling and murmurs of dissent from the family broke the silence.

'Hush, you lot,' Quriel, in no mood for an argument, shouted.

They didn't hush. Coming from the elders of the Borea family, the murmurs grew louder. They really couldn't care which Overlord they worked for. If The Sixth were to offer them long-term contracts servicing his fleet, they would work for him – no questions asked. It was how they had survived since the family fell from grace – outcasts working on the fringes. But they all knew there wasn't a chance of that. The Sixth had his own crews. Like the rest of the Anan-based navigators, technicians and pilots, austerity cut deep. They were on hard times – no work and no money coming in. The Overlord's war and the shortage of blue had caused that. All that mattered to them was the cold hard cash of the Universal

Credit. Some had even lost their homes and had nowhere to go. When Quriel contacted them with an offer of work, despite their hatred of him, consumed by the reality of their fate, they jumped at it. It was a far cry from the family loyalty the Pilot had tried to sell to The Eight.

The Pilot held up his hands to silence them. 'Let me finish, let me finish,' he pleaded.

Not helping much, Quriel glared at them all but knowing it all hinged on this, he lowered his tone. 'Option three, Father. Explain that.' This was their last chance to convince the family to stay with them.

Before revealing what he had found, the Pilot paused as he looked at the others. Hopeful something big was coming, they stayed quiet. 'Demard found all our grandfather's assets.'

There was a collective gasp. The family had thought this was the only base left. The Pilot waited for the information to soak in. 'He left me the access codes and location of the other space bases. There's one, near here, on the other side of this asteroid belt that may provide a solution.' It was the plural, the word "bases" that got their interest. In an instant, the dynamic changed! Feeling their attention quicken, he continued. 'It's the only option left. With luck, there may be something there that might help. Besides, we should check it out. It's family property now. What about the rest of you?' he asked.

After some more shuffling and muttering, they grouped into a huddle. There were some quiet whispers, and then the elder of the group turned and asked a question. 'What do you mean, family property?'

It was the Pilot's final card. He had shouted it out to Frike on the bridge but most had missed the significance of his words. 'The Eight has reinstated our Charter. Not fully, mind – but we can trade, do business and make a living again. We can rebuild and work for our children. I know it'll be hard, and we don't even know if The Eight is still alive, but what I do know is that the human, Niamh, will have taken him to their colony. If he's alive, we throw our hand in behind his war effort. Look at us now, we've nothing; there's no future for the young ones,' he said, pointing to them. 'If we don't seize this moment, they'll always be dredging the fringes for an existence. No, I say we go. Look for our other space stations, scavenge what fuel and supplies we can, and follow the *Boreal* to the human's New World.'

To the Pilot's delight, the group smiled and nodded in agreement. They spun away and again went into a huddle. More whispers and then they turned back to face him. It was the elder amongst them who spoke. 'Zaval, we're with you,' he shouted in agreement.

'And what of Frike? What if he's there, at the next base?' Siba asked. Her low shivering voice betrayed the fear the younger ones felt.

'Demard left him a parting gift. It was his final revenge. The monster won't bother us again,' the Pilot answered.

Ever the practical one, Siba continued. 'But the *Hela*, Verteg couldn't get control of the engines. And now I've looked, I can't see any interlocks that Demard may have put in,' she said while Verteg's bandaged head nodded in agreement.

It was news to the Pilot. He had missed all that when he was in the brig and with so much going on, no one had thought to tell him. 'Now you tell me,' he said as he glared over at his niece. *What next?* he thought, as he tried to access the engine controls from the captain's station. The engines, caught in the auto-docking sequence he had set when they first arrived, wouldn't respond.

A message from Verteg scrolled across his screen. 'You see, Pilot, we're stuck here until you get this fixed. I tried everything. We've lost engine control.'

After such an uplifting moment, the whole crew looked on in disgust as the Pilot scratched his head. Not the bright future he had promised them – if he couldn't even get the ship going. *It didn't make sense. The engines are running and holding us in position, but we can't access the controls from here. Why?* He looked around, and as his eyes settled on Alke, standing on the port side, he started to laugh. 'Open that panel – that there – the control system interface,' he said, pointing to one on the port side of the bridge. He watched as the Borea technicians removed the cover, exposing the rack of cables behind. 'Alke, you saved us all,' he said, as he reached in and pressed back a connector. 'The push plate you hit with the tractor is behind this panel on the hull. The bang you gave us when we docked must have loosened it. The vibration created by the explosion of Frike's device was enough to dislodge the connections. Try that now, Verteg.'

Verteg looked down at the readouts of the ship's control system on her screen. She worked, refreshing the engine status displays and then looked back up at Siba, standing beside her.

Siba smiled back at her cousin. 'That's done it,' she said. 'We've engine control.'

In a flash, the bridge filled with loud, happy chatter as the family clapped each other on the back. They mingled about, discussing their hopes for the future, while the Pilot retreated to the captain's chair. He sat down. The knot in his belly had returned and he clasped his hands to stop the shaking. Sweat glistened on his brow as he tried to stave off the craving. Images of the liquid in his cabin filled his mind until his eyes fell on Verteg. The injured woman, swaddled in bandages, sat at Demard's comms console. He hadn't told her Demard was her father – time for that sad news later. He knew, to survive, she needed urgent medical attention, and the colony was the only place she would get it. He also believed it was what Frike had done to Verteg that had made the difference. She had a popular following within the family. The young looked up to her and the old cast her as a hardworking, intelligent and respectful role model. She had been the Pilot's pupil and they knew some credit was due there. He had no doubt that they would follow him in the hope for a better life in a distant galaxy. The prospect of failure, gnawing at his stomach, was a burden he couldn't bear.

*

Borea Assault Craft, Anan Galaxy.
EPTS: A139098

The escape of the three assault craft from the Borea base was swift. Once confronted with a force that could bite, the bully ran. Frike had remembered old smuggling contacts whose homes were on a derelict moon at the edge of this quadrant. One of the few destinations his cousin had shared with him and an easy find from the Borea base. He had spent happy times trading with the outlaws, who had since passed their business on to their children. It was his destination now, where Frike would barter the cargo of blue.

As the three ships sped on towards their destination, a surreptitious program deep in the cores of each vessel's computer measured time and distance. At precisely one light-year away from the secret Borea station, the programs sent executable commands to other files. The files opened, dispatching orders to the engines: "All stop, disengage and lock."

The first command closed the grav drive vents, smothering the burning grav's forward momentum. A feedback loop sensed the primary execution and simultaneously opened the reverse thrusters, slowing the ships until they dropped out of light speed and coasted to a stop. Finally, the reverse thrusters slammed shut.

The following orders disengaged the engine control systems from the pilot's consoles. Locked out, they could do nothing.

The last was the most terminal of all – never before done in open space. With all grav ports closed, the docking locks engaged. Steel pins only used in a spaceport and designed to stop an accidental exposure of grav. Had anyone watched the control modules in the small engine rooms, they would have wondered who's ghostly presence was controlling the ships as the mysterious commands scrolled down their module's mini-screens.

Frike was lost in thought when the young pilot beside him shouted in surprise. 'Frike, we're stopping. The engines have cut out,' he said as he started to adjust his controls.

They looked up at the bridge screen. The other two vessels were slowing as well. The comms burst with chatter from the others – the same was happening to them. Their engines had cut out too. Without propulsion, the three vessels continued to slow to a stop.

'Frike, all three are immobilised. I don't understand it,' his pilot said as he tried hard to restart his engines.

Frike got up from his seat and walked over to the pilot's console. 'What do you mean, stopped? You're supposed to be able to fly this thing. Where are we?' he demanded.

'We're here,' he said, pointing to a section of empty space on the navigation projection. 'It's a light-year out from the base. The other two vessels are reporting the same problem. We're locked out of the ship's controls.' The old man rubbed his tattoo. 'Locked out. What caused that?' He spat at the young pilot then cuffed him across the head.

Unbeknown to him, the program flawlessly continued as its maker had designed it. When the ship stopped, it triggered another file that took command of the bridge viewscreens. The image on the screen changed – displaying Frike's answer. A video of the worst moments of Frike's assault on Verteg replaced the picture of space in front of the vessel. The video played in a loop, and the piercing sounds of her screams and pleas for mercy filled the bridge. A dark coloured caption started to scroll across the screen. *My revenge for your assault of my daughter. Die, you monster.*

In milliseconds, the last file opened, dispatching microelectronic instructions to the airlocks. The ship's bulkheads and, fatally, all external doors were ordered to "open and lock". Following that, another set of pulses hit the escape pods: "close and lock". And then the program burst in one brief electromagnetic pulse, burning the command computer's core. It was the same on all three of the ill-fated vessels — their journey was at an end.

Alarms and flashing lights lit up the pilot's console. He worked frantically, trying to regain control of his ship. 'Frike, the airlocks and the ship's bulkhead doors are opening. I can't stop them.' His young voice rose to a near scream as he realised what was happening. A dark panic enveloped him. 'We're venting atmosphere. Frike, Frike, we're venting atmosphere. I can't stop it,' he screamed.

The bridge crew jumped up. 'Go, go, go! We need to get to the escape pods,' one shouted, as they all ran from the bridge, leaving their infamous leader to fend for himself.

Frike tried to follow. Hobbling as fast as he could, his laboured breathing struggled to get air. Above the ship's alarms, he could hear the screams of his crew. He fell to the floor of the bridge, clutching his chest and gulped for life-giving air as it rushed out into space. The effects of decompression started to take hold. He felt something wet on his nose. Wiping it away with his scrawny old hand, he looked down. To his horror, blood covered his hand and more gushed out onto the deck beside him. All hell broke loose as the grav dampers failed and he floated up from the floor. He turned towards the bridge and looked up into the big screen, still playing the looped video. Pain seared his chest but before he died of explosive decompression, the last part of Demard's message burned in his brain – *die, you monster*.

CHAPTER ELEVEN

Magnetic Guns

Magnetic, or mag-guns as they are commonly called, utilise an electric charge converted to a magnetic force that accelerates a projectile along the gun barrel. The output velocity is directly proportional to: the diameter and length of the gun, the number of magnetic rings mounted in the barrel and the available electric charge. The projectile's magnetic properties are paramount. The plentiful carbon steel, tipped with the harder phaenian steel, economical both in weight and cost, is the standard. Used in conjunction with an abundant local electrical supply such as a fusion reactor, the larger of these guns are formidable weapons that can fire up to a thousand mag-bolts a minute. Other custom-made projectiles are available and can include grav impregnated missiles and shells.

‹ ***Extract from: Basic Weaponry. General Arie Machai***

*

The Hela, Asteroid Belt, Anan Galaxy. EPTS: A139108

IN A DIFFERENT DIRECTION, TWO light-years away from the secret space station, the *Hela* approached a deep section of the asteroid belt. Once the Pilot had solved the engine control problem and cemented his lead, there was little else to do other than go. With the small military transporter secured to its outside shuttle deck, leave they did. He hoped someday they would return with the resources to restore the space station to its intended use as a blue energy terminal. But, from what he could see now, those days were far in the distance. Now their focus was to try and scavenge any supplies, grav, blue and food for a journey back to the New World. The exit from the space station was not as dramatic as the entrance. With the help of Alke's tractor, they made short work of getting the *Hela* through the open channel.

The journey across the asteroid belt gave the family time to coalesce as a team. Each found their own skill an asset to the group. And, despite the alien appearance of the *Hela*, the Borea along with Quriel's soldiers, settled in for the long haul. Expectations of the Borea crew heightened as they approached the coordinates of the next base.

On the bridge, the Pilot, Quriel and one of the family elders, poured over Siba's navigation projection. 'It should be somewhere here,' he said, pointing to a location within the belt.

'We won't get the *Hela* in there; the asteroids are too close,' she said. Then her view changed. 'Look, look, there it is,' she shouted. Concentrating hard, Siba increased the detail on the projection. Soon they could see a space station, like the one they had left, constructed into the back of an asteroid.

The Pilot looked at the wall of asteroids floating lifeless in space, still denying the *Hela* access. 'The guardian channel has stopped. I suppose they ran out of fuel. But you're right, Siba, it's too tight to get the *Hela* in.' He looked across at Quriel. 'We'll use your small ship; it'll easily navigate through those rocks.'

One of the family traced a finger along the asteroids in the projection. 'But, Zaval, will we be able to get any ships in there out? That's the question, isn't it?'

The Pilot shrugged. His head dropped down and he clenched his bony hands as he looked at the projection. *I knew it wouldn't be easy*, he thought. He turned to the small group. 'It doesn't matter now. We need to go in and look. We're committed. If we can't get anything from here, we're finished.' They knew he was right – if there were nothing here, it would be a bad omen for the rest of the assets. They could spend all the available resources exploring and find nothing. It was a case of "suck it and see"!

*

Quriel guided the small military transporter through the gaps in the asteroids. 'It's not as bad as I thought. We could get bigger ships out through these. Look, the channel opens up here.' The cramped cockpit was full, with a crew that included three Borea and three soldiers. Although they believed Frike was long dead, they weren't taking any chances. They watched in earnest as Siba navigated.

The Pilot looked out at the partially cleared channel. *Yes, it's possible. Dare I hope for a break?* he wondered.

'There it is. Look, we can see into it now. Siba, can you get a closer look inside that chamber?' Quriel asked, as he stopped their ship outside a massive cut into a moon-sized asteroid.

'It's dark, I can only give you outlines—'

'Let me help, Siba,' the Pilot said as he put his blue diamond into the nav-con beside hers. He closed his eyes and slowly, Siba's dim projection of the chamber's interior started to take shape.

'What's this place?' Quriel asked as he looked at what was appearing on the projection.

'It was our family's shipping base. Used in a time before Grandfather seized control. I read about it when I was young. At the pinnacle of our Charter's prosperity, it was an operations base for the shipping and energy business. The stories say, maybe five space-tugs and twenty transport vessels worked from here.' The Pilot looked across at the elder Borea, nodding as he remembered those happy tales.

'Space-tugs. Father, dare we hope—'

'That would be a lucky break, but time isn't on our side. Now we see,' he said, as the images focused, 'there are ships still here. Put your lights on and fly in. I want to look at that dock section there,' he said, pointing to a location on his projection. The small transporter advanced into the dark interior of the asteroid. The powerful forward lights pushed a white beam through the eerie darkness, revealing the ravages of time-decayed metal.

'It was as I feared. Time has taken its toll,' the Pilot said, as they passed ruined and fallen gantries festooned with broken cables, hoses and pipework.

'Look, Father, is that it? Are they space-tugs?' Quriel asked as he brought the small ship to a stop facing two strange-looking craft. The spaceships were about four hundred metres long and unlike anything he had seen before.

Both had a forward shuttle deck and an after-deck housing a strange array that mystified them all except The Pilot. 'There are two left, and they still have their tow-trammels. That's what those things are,' he said, pointing to the back end of the two tugs. 'There must be more ships here; let's have a look at what's left.' The Pilot felt a hand on his shoulder and turned to face the family elder.

Tears ran down his face as he looked out at the two ships. 'Zaval, after seeing *Boreal*, I never thought I would ever see such a sight again. But, by The One, you have done it; a repeat performance!'

Embarrassed, the Pilot screwed up his face. He looked back and then grinned at the rare compliment. 'Easy, old man. We're not out of the excrement yet.'

Engrossed by the sights, Quriel flew them deep into the cavern past two more empty docks until they arrived at its end. Moored to one of the few intact space docks were four ships. 'What are they?'

'Inter-system transporters. Like the *Hela* – but smaller – five hundred metres long with grav propulsion engines and designed to work with the tugs. You haven't seen such a system before?'

'No, Father, I haven't.'

'The big intergalactic blue drive ships – the big blue guzzlers – replaced this older system. It's one of the reasons why we are where we are today.'

Quriel peered out at the ships, turning their small craft until the light played across the port side of one of the vessels. 'That one is holed,' he said, as they looked into a long gash stretching across the hull. Looks like there are three we could use. Father, the tugs, they have blue drives? Is that how this works?'

'Yes, Quriel. The space-tugs open the fold in space. They have grav drives as well, and with their trammels, they draw the ships into the fold. We used to synchronise the grav drives on all the ships as well—'

'What do you mean, "we"? Father, you weren't alive when these were used.'

'No, not these, but when I was a boy, I worked as a junior techie, on a similar setup. It was a small company. We used to transport goods between the Anan and Jora galaxies. The ships were based on Nered.'

'I gather Demard was with you then?'

'Yes, Quriel, he was. It was a great time in our lives,' he said, as tears started to run down his cheeks. After losing his closest friend, his voice quivered with the emotion of such memories. 'We worked and played hard, not a care in the universe. There was a shortage of blue then, and the space-tug was in great demand. Enough. We need to see the tugs first. Take us back; let's see if we can get one going.'

*

The first tug they visited was a mess. The only breathable atmosphere was on the bridge, and even that was putrid. It was a physically demanding visit, using all the functions of their spacesuits. But, some good came from the tour, with the ship's engines stoked with grav, and some blue left in the tanks. *Salvageable, but not a simple task,* the Pilot thought as they moved onto the second tug.

It proved to be in much better condition with clean atmosphere right from the shuttle bay, allowing a trouble-free exploration using only the lights from their spacesuits. The Pilot stood on the bridge with Siba and Quriel, looking down through translucent panels into the vast engine room below. Similar see-through panels separated the engine room from the open afterdeck – where the trammel lay – providing those who were running the tug a clear view of their tow. Dimmed light from their transporter spilt in, eerily illuminating the tug and its decks. It was a spectacular sight, giving them the illusion that they were standing in space as they looked across the engine room and out into the great void aft of the ship.

Siba placed her hands on the glass-like panel and peered out. 'This one looks better than the last, Uncle. I'm surprised the air is clear. The other one is derelict compared to this.' She then went over to the drive console and ran her hands across the controls. To her surprise, lights started to come on. 'How is that possible, Uncle? The engines are still offline. Where's the power coming from?'

'From here,' he called, as he closed the door on a compartment at the back of the bridge. 'The backup power cells are still charged. Someone's been maintaining this. Check the logs.'

She went to the engineering console and entered the codes he gave her. 'You're right, Uncle. Someone was here over a hundred orbits ago. Before that, it was a regular visit every hundred orbits. I guess Grandfather wanted to take care of his assets.'

'That's good news for us. We need a break. Let's see what's still working.'

As they worked, Quriel looked out of the forward windows, down onto the shuttle deck where their transporter stood beside two small shuttles. *We can use those,* he thought. Then, walking back across the bridge, he noticed the lights come on in the stepped-down engine room. He watched the other Borea explore it, the elder directing the two younger technicians through the nooks and crannies of the vast chamber. The two great blue drives, mounted on their energy intake manifolds, stood proudly in the enormous engine room. The drives stretched along the length of the ship and disappeared under the forward deck. The smaller grav engines ran along part of the port and starboard side, with their power outlets vanishing out through the hull of the ship. *This ship is all engine,* he thought. *There's no room for anything else.*

The symmetrical drives were laid down along the keel of the tug. The six great dodecahedron rotors in each engine glittered in their mounting frames. The longitudinal drives stretched back aft and dominated the view of the engine room. Quriel wondered at the power pulses they would unleash – as they folded space – opening the colossus of ports for the vessels they towed. It was Siba who brought him back to reality as she shouted to the Pilot.

'Uncle! Uncle! The tanks, they're full of blue. The sensors must be broken. That's not possible. Uncle, we'll have to look,' she said, as she jumped up and down at the engineering console gesturing at the readouts.

'By The One, you're right, Siba. If the sensors are working, that'll save us. What about grav?'

'They're fully stoked, look,' she said, grinning as she pointed to the readouts. 'This one is fuelled up and ready for flight. I'll bet the other three ships are ready as well.'

Not believing their luck, the Pilot checked the central flight-control console himself. 'She was prepped for a transport run out to Raigar, right before Grandfather took over the Charter. The tow-trammel is configured for four ships. Quriel, this is a big break.'

Quriel sat down in the captain's chair and looked around at the bridge. It was spotless. From what they had seen when they entered this vessel, it was well maintained and now they knew why. The old demon was a great engineer himself and determined to keep what he had. 'Can you do it, Father?'

The clatter of footsteps and happy voices announced the arrival of the other three Borea. The old man carried what appeared to be a book. He looked at the Pilot and held out his hands, the object clutched in one. 'Zaval, she's prepped for flight, engines stoked and full of blue, and I found this, in the engineer's cabin. A Borea ledger; it details the stock and cargo of those four ships. Zaval, there's a treasure of gear on them. Includes off-world mining rigs, and the best of them. We could rent it out to the humans and The Eight – hopefully, he's still alive. Can we get the fleet going?'

'Quriel asked the same question. You're the engineer – you know the risks.' The old man was their most experienced technician. 'I won't lie to you, it won't be easy, even with all our family's best techs – there's still so much involved. Give me time to think. We can hole up here with the *Hela* hidden in the asteroid belt.'

*

Shipping Base, Anan Galaxy

Returning to the *Hela*, the Pilot's mood transformed. Uncharacteristically, he brooded on the way back. The rest stayed silent, as if they knew the weighty decisions he had to make. That all changed when they arrived on the ship. The crew, anxious to hear all, met them in the shuttle bay. Shouts of welcome and the hubbub of their happy news lifted the family's spirits. Unnoticed, the Pilot disappeared as soon as they docked. He ran to his room to hide.

The monumental size of what he was about to undertake overwhelmed him. Curled up on his bed, his brain spun a confusing web, the thoughts and feelings of a man possessed. He had worked all his life as a pilot and was one of the best in the business. However, it was always as a pilot. He had skippered ships before but it was on unassuming runs, the most complex of those being the trip from the New World back to the Anan Galaxy. He was afraid of this. Towing the four ships through a fold in space was only half of the problem. It was the project management, to get them operational and then aligned in open space to connect the trammel – that was the real challenge. No, he couldn't do it. If it went wrong, they could be squashed flat. No one would survive. Better they take only *Tug1*. With luck, they could be back in the New World, safe and sound, within fifteen cycles.

Through the turmoil in his brain, he didn't notice the shaking return, until salty sweat dripped from his brow and the knot in his stomach pressed on his heart. He gasped, as his eyes darted to the boxes of liquid. He put his hands on his head, anguish screaming in his mind as he battled his demon, looking for something, anything, to calm those raging thoughts. He wanted to hide in the soothing wash of the earthly liquid, lose himself in its calming spirit. He could taste it, such was the craving. He clasped his hands tight trying to will the shaking to stop. Thoughts of the family sprayed a fresh breath at his brain. He couldn't lose it, not now – so many depended on him.

With that fresh breath, the fog in his mind cleared and there was Robert Leslie, the tall sandy-haired Scotsman who had led the humans to the New World. It was his management style, the meticulous planning with Janet Cooper, which made Project Anan such a success. The Borea family wouldn't let the Pilot leave the ships behind. Already the old one was calculating projected profits. Greed would spur them on. He would be expected to saddle up the lot and go. Besides, The Eight needed those ships!

The Pilot had sat through many of Robert's planning meetings, watched him use the primitive whiteboards, carefully drawing lists and charts of what needed to be done. The Borea hadn't used this process before. For the ordinarily small projects they did, their custom and practice were to work from an age-old established process. Keep it simple, he realised, as the shaking subsided. He jumped up and ran to his shower. The water washed away the anguish.

Like a newborn, he dressed in a clean ship suit and made his way to the old meeting room Robert and Niamh had used as a base during the *Hela's* repair in space. During the refit, the room was refreshed, but the whiteboards were still there, and although they had taken most of the planning tools – flip charts, pens and notepads – there was enough left for what he would need. At his disposal were the best technicians, pilots, engineers and an Aknar military squad – all the ingredients he needed to execute a daring escape plan from the Anan Galaxy. He laid it all out on the whiteboards for the family. Each of the tasks were dissected into lists, with stock quantities – from the humble helium-3, the cosmic dust that fuelled the fusion reactors to the complex blue for the massive drives – all carefully laid out. As he didn't have all the answers, there were blanks on the charts, blanks for his crews to complete. Then he called them in.

*

Using the tug's shuttles to ferry the crews to and fro, the first order of business was to transfer command from the *Hela* to the functional *Tug1*. The lion's share of the team would inhabit *Tug1* with skeleton crews dispersed on the other ships. They spent ten cycles preparing the tug and three salvageable ships for flight. Working around the clock, the Borea technicians rallied around the new head of the family, following their human-shaped plans with enthusiasm. As an added bonus – and, to their delight – they discovered an abundant source of base constituents to supply the tug's auto-food dispensers. The "larder's" atmosphere had been vented to space, preserving the ingredients of carbohydrates, proteins vitamins and minerals for all time – frozen in a vacuum. Enough purebreed food for the journey back to the New World.

*

Demard hadn't lied to Frike when he told him there was "a grav transporter ten light-years away making its way to Anan". What his sensors failed to show was that the "grav transporter" had been converted into an armed cruiser. Ten light-years distant, the vessel, on patrol under orders from The Sixth, was out hunting. From their encounter in ethereal space, The

Sixth, believing his nemesis, The Eight, was close, had mustered as many loyal ships as he could. Their mission: leave no rock unturned – find The Eight. The five hundred metre warship reached the limits of its patrol and turned about. Bristling with newly fitted armaments and sensors, the vessel rivalled some of the best Aknar navy cruisers. A forward gun turret that fired a thousand mag-bolts a minute and fifty batteries of multi-cluster grav missiles would make short work of anything that got in its way.

Unlike the swish military equipment recently fitted, the captain and crew were of a different breed. From a merchant shipping background, the tedium of this constant patrol on the edge of a distant quadrant tested their enthusiasm. It took time for them to notice the intermittent ghostly signatures coming from the deep part of the asteroid belt where the Borea bases were. The comms officer assumed it was echoes of asteroids colliding – until now!

'There should be nothing out there,' the captain said, as they studied the scans.

Comms traced her finger across a blue screen. The asteroids showed up as orange and in amongst them was a faint tell-tale greyish dot. 'It must be a vessel or a cluster of smaller ships,' she said.

Not wanting to waste fuel investigating a blip, the captain shook his head. 'I'm not convinced. Where did it come from?'

'It just appeared,' she replied, 'and it, or they, go nowhere!' Unbeknown to her, she had spotted Frike's three transporters, drifting aimlessly in space. Once the engines shut-down, they lost their cloaks.

The lazy purebreed captain returned to his chair. He sighed as his fat arse sank back into his ever-so-comfy seat. 'You see, if it's a vessel, there should be movement. There's none. No, we hold our course. Watch that section closely; if you see anything else, we'll inspect.' He closed his eyes. His mind drifted as he listened to the soft hum and gentle bleeping coming from the ship's controls.

*

On *Tug1*, back at the Borea base, oblivious to the stalking cruiser, Verteg munched happily on a food bar. Siba, sitting beside her cousin, dined on nuts, dried apricots and meat from the *Hela's* larder. Although first cousins, their physical make up was different, Siba's skin, purebreed Borea, was the snow-white of porcelain and was complemented by her soft grey eyes. Her long neck stretched up from slim female shoulders, while a close-fitting ship suit showed off her attractive, feminine body. Her hands and fingers were smooth as silk.

Verteg, the child of Demard, her purebreed father and her mother, a native Neredian, was quite the contrast. Like Cylla Ora, her mother had a long tail, golden scales, green hair and green eyes. Anan society frowned upon such unions, and Demard and his wife had a terrible time of it, bringing up Verteg. It was why her mother had hidden her father's identity. Verteg was a testimony to the merits of mating with different species. Purebreed DNA languished in the cul-de-sac of in-breeding for too long. The mix of DNA, from two intelligent species, endowed Verteg with brightness beyond her father's expectation. With her mother's beauty, she inherited both her mum and dad's intelligence. Her blue hair hung down from her bandages and where exposed, her green porcelain-like skin glittered in the white light of the mess.

Her brown eyes darted about as she silently watched her cousin scoop up a handful of cashew nuts. She shook her head as Siba offered them to her, pointing her green fingers at her own food bars. The Chief had brought her over on one of the shuttles. With the young female technician, he had discovered what the primitive earthly medical equipment was for. Transferring it over from the *Hela*, he had fitted the captain's cabin as Verteg's personal-care room. The excitement of learning to pilot a new craft and the mechanics of towing vessels through folded space kept her mind occupied. She closed it off when the Chief and the techie worked on her each day, taking care of her physical needs, changing her bandages and administering top-up doses of the life-giving Anan plasma. They had hoped to find an autodoc on the tug or on one of the other ships. After a quick look and confirmation from the Pilot that such equipment was never installed on these ships, they gave up.

Similar in age, the two girls grew up, studied and flew together. It was Verteg who was always out in front. Her navigation projections were more vibrant and further than anything Siba could conjure. She could fly faster and most surprising of all, her ability for the complex calculations of folded space outpaced even the Pilot. After learning of the beating, Siba had felt sick to her stomach. She had cried a deluge until her cousin hugged her tight, wiped the tears away, and typed a short message on her comms unit. "No more tears. Work, we work to get out of this mess." After that, Siba was by her cousin's side, plotting the courses, prepping computers, calibrating engine outputs. Doing all the mandatory pre-flight commissioning checks for a newly assembled tow-fleet.

It was tense work for the Borea technicians, powering up the tug's engines, boarding the transporters for the first time and getting them habitable. Unlike the tug, their life-support systems were powered down and the atmospheres required scrubbing. Primary reactors had to be energised, filters changed, fans started and all in spacesuits in near zero-g. The young Borea technicians jumped at the work, each competing to get the hardest tasks. It was frontier labour, something they would only get to do once in a lifetime, and they relished it.

CHAPTER TWELVE

Tow-Trammel

A tow-trammel is a turned mesh that confines a fleet of ships together for a journey through folded space. Blue energy, extruded through a Zakkonain generator forms a solid web-like structure encasing each vessel within the tow. The trammel-enclosed vessels are connected together by a bulbous lead, self-generated in space, by programmed nanites. An emergency disconnect, controlled from the command tug, is contained within each connector. The concept of towing ships through folded space was developed after the third blue energy shortage of our epoch. Generating and stripping back a tow is a precision operation. To avoid catastrophic damage to the vessels, only a certified tow master shall undertake this operation.

‹ *An Introduction: Fundamentals of intergalactic travel. Zaval Borea*

*

Shipping Base, Anan Galaxy. EPTS: A139241

ONCE OPERATIONAL, TWO SHUTTLES TOWED the three transport ships out of the channel. Alke helped with his tractor, nudging them clear of the asteroids. Finally, with the three parked alongside the *Hela*, it was the turn of *Tug1* to transit the channel. Verteg plotted the simplest of routes through the lifeless guarding rocks. Without any assistance from the Pilot, the injured young woman took control of the four hundred metre floating engine. Under her tutelage, it slipped its space clamps and gently floated out towards the exit passage. Gracefully, she steered it out of its confining prison, into the open space beside their small fleet.

It was a milestone in their quest for an escape. The whole family, working with the Aknar military, threw their hearts and souls into the expedition.

Their enthusiasm even shocked the hardened Quriel. 'Father, I didn't expect our family to throw their lot in with you so easily after Frike's return. They know Little Kake will inherit his mantle and is as much of a monster.'

Gazing out the window of the *Hela*, admiring the vessels parked beside them, the Pilot nodded slowly. He was surprised that they had come so far. He broke the silence with a soft reply. 'When they saw what was done to Verteg, and the brutal killing of our relatives, they wanted out of this galaxy. She's an extraordinary pilot, and you know she commands the respect of the whole family. Frike destroyed whatever following he had when he assaulted her. They'll do anything to get away from here.' He never mentioned the elder's greed and their hope of future profits. Some things don't change. Greed spurred the elder ones on. It was what it was, and as long as they played ball, the Pilot was okay with that!

'How soon will we be ready?' Quriel asked.

'We take a rest now. The crews need some sleep. When we start again, we couple up the tow trammel, and then – we should be back at the human colony within fifteen cycles.'

*

After their break time, the crews returned to the meeting room on the *Hela* for a pre-hook-up gathering. It was a noisy affair as they all crossed off their tasks on the whiteboards and charts. Before their departure, the Pilot looked around at them. *How many will survive this?* he wondered. *Can I pull it off?* Hiding his innermost thoughts, he smiled at the well-rested crews – their eager looks told the story. They were keen to get away to the safety of the humans' New World. 'There's a risk. It's a long journey and there's no room for complacency. I'm not going to repeat it all again. You have your orders and flight plans. Any questions?'

The room erupted with all kinds of derogatory comments, followed by the usual family banter. 'All right, all right,' shouted the Pilot over the noise. 'Have a safe passage. Let's go,' he concluded.

Alke would command transport *Three*, Siba *Two*, the Aknar crew chief *One* and Quriel with his comms officer would have the *Hela*. Verteg would assist the Pilot with *Tug1*. Their technicians were dispersed throughout the fleet with most of them supporting the tug. *Will we make it?* the Pilot wondered as he watched the crews file down to the *Hela* shuttle deck. A worry nagged at the back of his mind. He put his hand on Quriel's shoulder. 'What's the chance of us getting caught? You know, when we leave the cover of the asteroids.'

The frown on Quriel's brow said it all. 'We'll be exposed to long-range sensors. We should cloak for the test flights.'

'We can do that, but for the hook-up, we must drop the cloaks.'

'How long will that take?' Quriel asked.

'About half a cycle to get the ships in line. Then another to get the fleet enclosed and underway.'

Quriel sucked in his breath. They hadn't talked about this before. 'One full cycle with no cloak, out in open space.'

'Yes, Quriel. Then we're gone. Did you see anything on your way here from Anan?'

'One ship looks like a grav transporter – light-years from here. But I'm afraid. Such a grouping of ships may attract The Sixth's attention. His followers are looking for The Eight. They continually scan deep galactic space.'

'We plan for the worst case, Quriel. Expect that they locate us soon after we start the hook-up. If Haret is right, it'll take them at least a cycle to mobilise. Once we move into folded space, we're gone.'

'But it's a cycle, Father. One full cycle. We've no weapons on the ships to defend ourselves. We can't even access *Hela*'s armoury. What if I get my chief to launch our small transporter? It has forward cannons.'

'It's a complication to the hook-up. I'm not sure your chief could get back on board under the trammel. And we need him as *One*'s captain. No,' the Pilot said, as he rubbed his head with his bony hands, 'there must be a better way, Quriel.'

*

Space-Tug 1, Anan Galaxy

The status readout from Verteg's comms console flashed across the Pilot's screen. *Fusion reactor online – ninety per cent efficient! Blue drives on idle with full fuel flow available; grav drives stoked and ready. Pilot, how you coming with the tow-trammel?*

The Pilot, immersed in his work, looked up from the command console. He turned to gaze down on the engine room and out aft at the tow-trammel, floating above the after deck like a pulsing spider's web. 'It's nearly ready,' he said, as he turned to look at Verteg. To catch a glimpse of the tow-trammel, she had also twisted in her seat. Her face was still wrapped in bandages and her legs encased in splints.

They had removed the bandages from her hands, leaving them free to operate the comms console. She looked at the Piot, opening her hands, still scarred with black welts from her injuries. She deflected her head in a questioning manner.

'Once the fleet is in position, I'll launch it. They have the coordinates?'

Leaning forwards, she nodded.

'I'm sorry, of course, they have. You've done everything for them except eat their meals.'

She nodded again, clapped her hands at him, and turned back to her comms console. He watched her work – her mental recovery had amazed him. He knew she was still scarred internally and couldn't talk. *Was it from the deep pain in her face or the pain in her mind?* He didn't know, but whatever it was, she needed help soon. Her work was extraordinary. She had calculated the flight plans, engine settings and the all-important hook-up coordinates. Working from the bridge of the tug, she was the de facto pilot of each vessel in the fleet.

The fleet had assembled in open space half a light-year clear of the asteroid belt at the edge of the Anan Galaxy. The crews used this short journey to familiarise themselves with their ship's controls. He watched a projection of the fleet as they worked their way aft of *Tug1* in open space. It was a happy moment for him, all their hard work coming to fruition.

On the side of the bridge viewscreen, the clock counted down. When it hit zero, the Pilot nodded to Verteg. The message flashed across his screen as she sent it to the other ships. *Cloaks down, cloaks down,* and then the clock reset.

*

On the converted grav transporter, harsh alarms pierced the quiet bridge. The comms console flashed red, as the long-range sensors detected the uncloaked Borea fleet. Brutally woken from his restful slumber, fat arse fell out of his seat. Picking himself up from the deck, he shook laziness from his mind. 'What's that infernal noise?' he rasped.

'A fleet, we've detected a fleet; uncloaked they are,' shouted an excited Comms.

Composing himself, the captain peered over her shoulder. 'Where—'

'There,' she said, pointing at the screen. She held back a smirk. It was in the same quadrant as the other ships she had detected. *I told you so*, whispered in her mind.

Fat arse lumbered back to his chair. In unfamiliar territory he didn't know what to do.

'We need to pursue them – now,' came the firm voice of their weapons expert, a tall, stocky purebreed seconded from The Sixth's military. A scar across his face and a twisted eye gave him a sinister look. Most wrongly thought he had earned those badges of action in military combat. Unashamedly, he let those legends linger – never telling the truth – that he got them in a fight in an edge-world brothel. 'Plot an intercept,' he shouted. 'Now, Captain. Yes, now.'

The captain nodded to his navigator. 'Do it,' he said, authority returning to his voice. Warily, he cast a look at the new addition to his crew – an unwanted soldier fostered on them by The Sixth. 'Are you ready for this?'

With a toothless grin, he laughed, a hollow coarse sound, out of step with the seriousness of the situation. 'Of course, I am. Watch!'

Happy to finally see some action, the tall military man moved to the weapons' station. With a swirl of his wrist, a translucent panel burst out above the workspace. His fingers moved like lightning and, without warning, the whole ship shuddered.

'What are you doing?' shouted the captain.

'Testing the mag-cannon; what do you think I'm doing? It wasn't commissioned after they fitted it. Got to make sure it doesn't peel off from the hull before we engage the enemy. Looks good,' he grinned. 'It's still with us.'

Another quick shuddering followed. White-hot particles of heavy metal flying from the ship lit up the bridge viewscreen. It was a sight the captain and his merchant crew had never seen before. Any vessel that those particles connected with would be cut in half in the bat of an eye. A thousand mag-bolts a minute, over sixteen of the deadly shells per-second.

The captain wasn't impressed. He would have to account for any action here. His brief was to stop, board and search in the name of The Sixth. 'Surely it won't come to that.'

'Pucker up, Captain. If we aren't allowed to board those vessels, it most certainly will. The Eight could be on board, or there may be info on where he is. This is the best lead we have. Play this tight, Captain. No quarter.' And to make his point, he sliced his finger through the weapons' actuator. The ship shuddered again as the white-hot projectiles beat a deadly path through space.

*

'Are they all in alignment?' the Pilot asked Verteg, both oblivious to the approaching danger.

She nodded, clapped her hands, and then patted her own head as she looked across at him.

'You haven't lost your sense of humour, you green-skinned wonder. Look at that,' the Pilot said, gazing back aft of the tug. It was a fantastic sight: the *Hela*, two hundred metres behind the tug, followed by the three transport ships.

'Why is *Three* so far back, Alke?' he said, into his comms unit. 'You're too far back. You should be two hundred metres behind *Two*. Follow Verteg's flight plan. You must hit those coordinates exactly for the hook-up.' He looked across at her. She was shaking her fist at the viewscreen as Alke's face appeared on the side.

'Yes, Uncle. Sorry, we're closing the gap now.'

He shook his head and grinned at Verteg, as she slapped the side of her head and pointed to the screen. 'Yes, I know, but he'll be fine. That's our most complicated manoeuvre finished, and we did it all cloaked.' He looked at the clock, counting the time they were visible in space and smiled.

'Verteg, with those flight plans, you've knocked off half a cycle from the uncloaked time.'

Moving to tow control – at the back of the bridge – the Pilot activated the launch sequence. His Borea crew watched, mesmerised as the giant pulsating web started to float up from the aft deck of the tug. With four bulbous leads, the trammel opened out. Matching the girth of the *Hela*, it tracked across the two hundred metre gap between the two ships and started to swallow the golden vessel. 'Engine room, report,' he said.

'Pilot, all good here; trammel generator one is handling the load. I've a clean flow of blue to it.'

'When the *Hela's* enclosed, switch to generator two.'

'Why? One's—'

'There are three generators. You need to share the load to stop them overheating. Usually, everyone starts number one, ignoring two and three unless there's a problem. One is always the most used.'

A small reply came back over the comms. 'How do—'

With a harsh voice, the Pilot cut him off. 'How do I know that? I was doing this when you were still growing inside your mother. Do as you're told! If you've any problems, let me know.' A stinging rebuke from the level-headed Pilot, a hint of inner turmoil that surprised even him.

The young technician bit his lip. 'Yes, Pilot,' came back his reserved reply.

He looked across at Verteg. 'Well, I was,' he said.

She shook her head from side to side then lifted one hand level with her mouth and started to snap her fingers and thumb up and down – mocking him. He looked around at the other technicians on the bridge. They all had their heads down as if engaged deep in their work.

'*Hela* to *Tug1*, *Hela* to *Tug1*.'

'Go ahead, Quriel.'

'Your status, Father. How are we on the timeline?'

'It look's good from here; already the *Hela* is over fifty per cent enclosed – on time.'

The picture of the tow-trammel flowing across *Hela* flashed on its screen. 'You were right; we couldn't launch the transporter from its shuttle deck. *Hela* out.'

'Now, we wait. This is the worst part for the Tug Master, Verteg. Watching and waiting.'

*

As the trammel worked its way over Alke's ship, the last in the fleet, the clock sounded three time segments. *Time to induce the all-important protective grav bubble*, the Pilot happily thought. *Finally, we'll shortly be underway.* His crew rushed about, checking the readouts and making the finishing adjustments. It was Verteg who noticed it first. She reached out and hit the Pilot, pointing aft at the trammel. It had stopped.

'Engine room, what's wrong? The trammel's stopped.' There was no answer. The Pilot repeated the message again, and again, shouting into the comms unit.

In a shaky voice, the reply came back. 'Pilot, I've a problem with the fuel feed. I'm trying to change tanks, but I—'

'I'm on the way. Verteg, you have the bridge,' he said, as he leapt down the ladder into the engine room. The designers had adopted a minimalistic approach when assembling such a powerhouse. He lamented the lack of a lift. It was all engine, with little space for comforts. Sliding down the ladders, he then ran along the catwalk between the two blue drives. Despite his haste, he still listened to the hum of the drivetrains as they slowly rotated the dodecahedron rotors. *Warming up nicely*, he thought, as he ran past the fusion reactor. *Pulsing raw current into the ship's grid.* Panting for breath, he slowed as he reached the generator room, at the aft end of the ship.

The young technician was on his knees, poring over a schematic of the fuel feed. He looked up as the Pilot approached, relief flowing from his eyes. 'I'm sorry, Pilot,' was all he could say.

'I never expected this to go faultless,' the Pilot gasped, as he sucked the warm air into his breathless lungs. 'I did the same myself when I was young. Look here, the controls are in this panel,' he said, slamming his hand onto a bulkhead hatch. It sprang open, revealing the elusive fuel controls. 'I should have shown it to you before.' The Pilot gulped in air as he reconfigured the fuel flow. 'I thought there would be enough in the one tank. It's the extra size of the *Hela* that's used it up. There, you see,' he said, as generator three started up. A knot pained in his stomach. *I shouldn't have neglected this*, he thought. *What else have we missed?*

They both stood stock still, calmed by the whine of the generator as it wove the last of the trammel. A small screen in the generator room tracked its progress over Alke's ship. The Pilot clapped the young technician on the back. He was about to praise the young man when a shrill alarm pierced their ears. 'What now,' he gasped, as a foreboding message flashed across the screen.

Pilot, we have company. Quriel has detected a fold opening in space. I need you back on the bridge. Verteg.

'I have this, Pilot. Go, go now.'

He ran all the way back to the bridge, taking the ladder rungs two by two. When he got there, the crew were peering out of the port windows into space.

It was a short run for the converted grav transporter through folded space. Comms gave them regular updates, but it wasn't until they exited the fold that the enormity of what they had stumbled upon sank in. Fat arse jumped up as the view of the *Tug1* with the *Hela*, and the three transport ships enclosed in a gleaming trammel, filled their viewscreen. Universal Credits, salvage rights and the hope of riches filled his brain. The same thoughts flashed in Comms' mind as she looked across at her captain's drooling face. He caught her eye and winked. It was a simple gesture but said it all: *Yes, if we pull this off, you get a big fat bonus.*

Spurred by greed, authority now laced his voice. 'They're getting underway. Quick, fire a burst from your cannon across that tug's bow.'

With combat looming, the earlier aggression drained from the so-called weapons expert. 'But, Captain, you need to hail them. They might—'

Fat arse roared, 'Do it now. Fire across their bows and under no circumstances damage any of them. I want that salvage.'

The ship shuddered as white-hot metal burst out from the mag-cannon, tracking through space towards the tug's bow. If the military man got the trajectory wrong, it would cut the tug in two.

The Pilot's heart skipped a beat. All his fears banged in his head as he watched the track of the deathly missiles through space, straight towards them. *Why have they fired?* he wondered. No notice given. If it were a warning shot, it would have been across their bows. But the imbecile that sent this hadn't adjusted correctly and was way off the mark.

On the converted grav transporter, the captain had the same thoughts. Frozen in time, he and his bridge crew watched as their prize was about to be blown to bits. And then, their bridge screen adjusted to a three-dimensional view. Relieved, they watched as the shells passed harmlessly below the Pilot's fleet. Pure emotion erupted as they cheered, a warning fired and the fleet still intact. As she jumped for joy, Comms missed a fleeting flash from the bow of the tug.

Seconds after the white-hot metal passed below *Tug1*, self-preservation grasped the Pilot. 'Back to your stations. Get ready to make way,' he roared at his crew. Then he looked up at the image of Quriel on the viewscreen – grey with fright.

'Father, they came out of a fold about fifty thousand kilometres away. We missed them on the long-range scanners – I thought they were a transport ship! How long before you're ready?'

'We're nearly done here. But I need time to form a stable grav bubble and to get the fleet under tow, before opening a fold. Who are they?'

'Looks like an armed charter vessel. They're hailing us now, listen.'

The voice of fat arse spilt from the comms. 'You are in a controlled section of space. Identify yourselves.'

'I am Captain Quriel of the Aknar Military. This fleet is under the control of The House of Aknar. We control all space in this galaxy. Who are you to be challenging us like that?'

'Captain, you do not control this section anymore. We are on patrol under orders from The Sixth. Prepare to be boarded or we will fire on your tug, and our next shots won't miss.'

Is the drone ready? flashed a message from Quriel across Verteg's screen.

Launched after they opened fire, cloaked and standing off on our port side, she replied.

Commit to intercept.

On course, the weapon's primed. Time to contact point four five.

Hold course until further orders.

'Board us – you threaten to board us and fire again on our tug. Captain, on whose authority do you take control of this quadrant of space?' asked Quriel. They were at the edge of the Anan Galaxy – Aknar space – historically ruled by The One and The Eight. That they were being challenged here, bore testament to the troika's coup.

'By The Sixth. It's his galaxy now, Captain Quriel. You should know that.'

The Pilot listened as his son stalled for time. The four bulbous leads meshed together, locking the tow-trammel over the fleet. *Finally, the weave's done.* 'All ships, all ships, we're secure. On Verteg's mark, activate grav drives,' he said, as he engaged the tug's own grav engines. The ship shuddered and groaned, as it took up the load of its tow. Slowly, the five ships made their way towards their fold coordinates. 'Verteg, in your own time, send them their engine settings.' As her orders flashed across his screen, she turned and saluted him. 'Increase grav engines to fifty,' he said to their engineering tech. 'Finally, we're underway.'

The captain of the converted grav transporter hailed them again. 'Quriel, I told you to stop—'

'Captain, I am tired of this. You have no authority here. You represent a failed troika that has no mandate to seize control of intergalactic space. There are ancient treaties in place, legalised by Overlords aeons before those who fight for supremacy now. You are embroiled in a fight that is above your comprehension. Save yourselves, turn around now, or I'll destroy your ship. I warn you – you've no time left – if you do not turn away now you will be destroyed.'

'You're bluffing. You don't have any weapons.'

'I'm sorry, Captain. I never bluff. We do have weapons. Turn away now and we will spare you,' Quriel said, as he read a message coming in from *Tug1*.

He is taking too long.

Hold its course, Verteg. Father, how long?

Quriel, we cannot rush this. I need more time. I need to extend the tug's grav bubble around the fleet, and we are not yet up to light speed.

The drone sped on, closing the gap between the converted grav trans-porter and the fleet. On its final approach, it turned, aligning its course trajectory with its target, the ship's engine room.

'Captain Quriel, as I said before, stop now or …' Comms' console flashed red, and a shrill alarm cut their ears. 'What's that? Turn, turn to port now,' screamed the captain of the ill-fated ship.

Converted to a drone loaded with grav, Quriel's cloaked military ship embedded itself into the grav transporter. Penetrating the larger vessel's hull, the small craft ruptured. Uncontained grav added to the ferocity of the impact as it flew into millions of droplets of pure energy. Quriel's military-grade cloak guaranteed the small craft's invisibility. When Comms' attack alarms sounded, it was too late. The doomed captain and his crew had milliseconds to react before the fatal explosion ripped their ship apart. Annihilation came quickly. The violent blast, created as grav mixed with blue from the ship's own engine room, incinerated all life in the blink of an eye.

It was the Pilot's "better way". The thought of sitting out in space with an unprotected fleet was too much for him and Quriel to bear. Converting the small military transporter into a drone was Quriel's idea. If it could stave off any unwanted attention, its sacrifice was a low price to pay. Once converted into a remote weapon, the little ship was parked on *Tug1*'s shuttle deck, where it could be quickly launched by Verteg.

Unable to watch the destruction she had unleashed, Verteg turned away from the viewscreen, covering her face with her hands. *How many are dead?* was the thought that flashed through her mind.

Quriel appeared on the fleet's viewscreens. 'That is the first casualty of our Energy War. Although they fired first, I take full responsibility for that. Have no doubt, had we not defended ourselves, we would have been returned to The Sixth or blown apart in space. We must leave this quadrant of the universe. There's no future for us here. We face a hazardous passage through folded space in grav ships towed by a tug. Only the Pilot has seen this done before. It is new to us all and I know we are all fearful of what we are about to do. Trust in his and Verteg's leadership. Follow your orders. I know this will work. Father, we go on your command.'

The Pilot clasped his hands to stop them shaking. The knot in his stomach tightened while his heart raced. He opened his mouth but nothing came out. Closing his eyes, he quelled the emotions coursing through his body. Surprising him, a hand rested on his shoulders and he turned to face the wizened old face of the elder Borea. The old man nodded and smiled encouragement at the Pilot, and as silently as he came, he melted away into the shadows of the bridge. The briefest of gestures returned the Pilot's composure – they depended on him, all the family and their three and a half kilometre tow. It was his show now. He opened his mouth, and as if in a dream, he didn't recognise the clear firm voice that came out, but the family did. 'All ships, all ships. When the fleet is fully enclosed in the tug's grav bubble, we increase speed. Verteg will send you the engine settings. Once fleet-speed is faster than light, I open the fold.'

A cycle later, Verteg's reports flashed across his screen. *We are up to speed and approaching the fold coordinates.*

The Pilot turned to the technicians seated behind him. 'Bring up the blue drives to thirty,' he said, as he walked back to look down at the engine room. He watched as the great dodecahedron rotors blurred from their speed and the engines flashed with blue light. The flashes dissipated, and the engines settled. 'Increase power to sixty.' Through the thick translucent walls, the pitch of the humming noise intensified. The engines appeared to distort into one mass of blue light. And then the Pilot felt it. He smiled as *Tug1* shuddered from the first power pulse. He turned around and his crew gasped in awe at the view before them. Like a giant flower, the fold opened up in front of their bridge window. He looked down at Verteg and grinned. 'Green-skin, stick with me. I'll teach you how to get around.'

She turned her head sideways, looked up at him and again brought her hand up to her mouth. He laughed as she snapped her fingers and thumb up and down as she rocked her head from side to side.

The hiatus ended as they all returned to the demands of their journey. Comms erupted as the questions on speed, engine settings, location and arrival time flowed over the video links. Memories of the destroyed grav transporter were quickly banished from their thoughts. With the Pilot as the Tow Master, they settled down for their journey to the New World.

CHAPTER THIRTEEN

Aknar City

Welcome to Aknar City, the capital of Planet Anan and the governing centre of the Anan Galaxy. The "Capital", as we call it, is home to our Overlords, the rulers of the House of Aknar, the Council of Anan and the Charter Guild. Located on the western shore of Anan's smallest continent, the city hosts the core of the planet's transportation hub. It is known for its low-rise brightly coloured buildings and their overlapping pitched roofs. To protect you from our planet's heavy rain, the buildings are connected by the typical Anan covered walkways. The glittering city centre, always illuminated by bright lights, is well known as the planet's commercial centre. You will find it an eclectic meeting place, enriched by its many and varied eating houses. City garb is informal with all-weather, brightly coloured capes or coats an essential outer layer. A visit to the Aknar Palace is...

◂ **Extract from: A City Guide, from The Aknar City Municipal Corporation**

*

Planet Anan. EPTS: A139217

BACK ON ANAN, AS HARET had told The Eight, The Sixth had galvanised his power with The Seventh and The Ninth by his side. The Emperor couldn't wait to join him, usurping the absent Empress's authority. Like a herd of hungry beasts, politicians flocked to gorge on the new trough of promised riches, worshipping the troika and its maleficent leader. With the absence of The One, the Eight and the Overlords that supported him, The Sixth's power grab was impossible to stop. Obsessed with gaining total control, he convened a meeting of the Charter Guild. It was unheard of for an Overlord to assemble such a gathering, but the charter heads rapidly realised, strange was now the new norm. Convention had disappeared like a wispy cloud.

In a plush apartment in the Anan capital, the head of the Svang Charter huffed a deep sigh as he adjusted his shirt in the mirror. His green eyes squinted as he tried to get it to sit on his broad shoulders.

His wife laughed at his efforts. 'You'll be fine.'

'Of all meetings, this is the one I have to chair,' he lamented.

Facing him, she smiled, touched the scar on his cheek, then kissed him on his lips. 'Stop fussing. They'll be so hungry to impress the new master they won't even notice you. Go now. I'll follow on.'

Grunting an agitated goodbye, he threw on an all-weather coat and hurried out. Ducking under the covered walkway in the street outside, he pulled up his hood, insulating himself from the steady rain. Hurrying down the road between the bright coloured buildings, he made his way to the centre of their compact city. The capital of Anan lay on the western shore of its smallest continent. Over time, little had changed in the planet's administrative hub. The residents were mostly from charters, the government or the Aknar palace. As usual, the grey clouds swirled over the city, dumping drenching water on the inhabitants.

Today was a big day for him, charter families took it in turn to chair their guild. And, of all days – the day The Sixth called them to order – it was his turn. Others would relish the opportunity and indeed knife him in the back to get it, but not him. He and his wife had built the Svang Charter into a multi-faceted organisation. They had always kept well below the parapet, preferring a back-channel approach to business. Forging alliances, or as some called it, "advantageous synergies". Stretching across the galaxy, their diverse business interests varied from mining to engine manufacturing.

He hardly noticed the surrounding buildings of power as he entered their guildhall. The rotunda sparkled, its polished wooden chairs, carved with each charter's crest, gleaming in preparation for the meeting. He didn't notice any of it as he made his way up to the chairman's podium. He threw on his grey robe of office and sitting in an ornate throne, gazed down at the circular hall. His quick eye now checked everything was ready, robes laid out, viewscreens on and the sweet smell of flowers perfumed the air. Drawing breath, he patiently paused.

Waiting gave him time to think, again, about the price of blue. It had become an obsession. A consuming need for fast intergalactic travel assured their society's addiction to the rare blue energy. Thoughts rattled in his brain; musings that, if an Overlord could see them, would be considered treasonous. With only three left in the Anan galaxy, chances of that were slim. *It was The One who had expanded the use of blue*, he thought. Centuries past, Overlords reserved blue for themselves and the military. Merchant ships used grav. It was the invention of the hybrid drive that introduced blue for universal shipping. Although frugal in their consumption of such precious energy, those drives proved unpopular. The merchant shipping crews found the complex navigation and engine balancing techniques a challenge. And so, they turned to the use of the mainstream blue drives. It had a pivotal role in the demise of the supply. Quick-witted, the head of the Svang Charter often took the contrarian view. *Maybe this shortage is a good thing*, he mused, always trying to profit from misfortune.

Back to reality, the heads of the intergalactic charters filed in. Hurrying to their seats, some acknowledged the man while others ignored him – their loyalties crystal clear. The hall filled up, all eager to hear what the new order had to say. He nodded at his wife, taking their own pew. Unscripted, as soon as all sat down, the troika floated in. Seven and Nine had travelled for this. Such power assembled in one place was unheard of: three Overlords and the wealthiest women and men in the Anan Galaxy.

Silence. The chairman stood, in his confident manner, and welcomed them. Not wasting words, he handed the meeting over to The Sixth.

Flashing with blue light, his oval energy mass rose up into the centre of the rotunda. Shining above them, The Sixth's voice boomed out as he claimed command of all the known galaxies. Detailing his plans, nothing surprised. The man had known what would be said. Little would change at the Exchange. Trade would continue, blue rationed while the price of grav would continue to rise. Hybrid engines would be the future. He had known that and had already changed their manufacturing priorities. The troika was prospecting for a new supply of blue. *Well, he thought, so was everyone else!*

As soon as the meeting ended, they all ran out – it was as if the last out would have to pay the bill. The truth was, they believed they could profit from the news. *As if they could,* he thought, disgusted with them all. Assisted by the anonymous functionaries, the man ignored their haste, busying himself with the mundane housekeeping duties of the meeting chair. A flash of blue light made him turn, and to his shock, he realised The Sixth had remained behind.

'I want to talk to you alone.'

Taking the hint, the staff ran from the hall.

The man made his way down to the centre of the chamber and stood in front of The Sixth. Trembling at being so close to an Overlord's energy mass, he tried to speak. Fear gripped his mind and it went blank.

'I want you to work for me,' The Sixth said.

'Why?' was the only reply he could muster.

'Because you have always remained in the shadows. You run one of the most successful charters whose influence stretches across the galaxy. You couldn't have done that without resolve and a firm hand. I need that. You will be my Shoter, you are familiar with the term?'

In aeons past, Overlords employed the services of a purebreed to oversee their interests. The position developed into a purebreed managing galaxies, influencing trade, laws and the common good. The Shoters became so powerful they could quash decisions of the head of the house of Aknar. Emperors and Empresses detested them so much that they petitioned The One to abolish the Shoter's role. And that he did, disallowing the post – until now. Knowing that history, the enormity of what The Sixth had said overwhelmed the man. He knew refusal wasn't an option. 'Yes, Overlord. I understand what you want. I—'

'You have reservations about how I and those in the Energy Exchange are managing the shortage of blue. Yes? And you are unsure if my ascendancy is desirable for the galaxy's prosperity?'

'I …' for an instant, he hesitated. 'Yes, Overlord I do.' There, he had said it. To one of the most powerful beings in the universe, he had told him he had doubts! *Now what?* the man wondered, expecting to be turned to dust. His life and love of his wife and daughter flashed through his mind.

'That is why you will be my Shoter. I want someone who is going to tell me what they think, not what I want to hear. You start tomorrow. A ship will take you to Raigar. Empress Theia has surfaced with the Aknars she disappeared with. I want news of The Eight. You will go and collect them.' With another flash of blue light, The Sixth floated out of the hall.

As soon as The Sixth was gone, the man's wife came in. 'You heard?'

'Not all, but enough.'

'I am to be his Shoter!'

'No better man,' she said, as she stretched up and kissed him.

'And the Empress is back. What do you think of that?'

'Nothing surprises me anymore,' she said as she took his hand. They walked home together, their chat full of his new position and how she would run their Charter.

*

Planet Raigar. EPTS: A139237

Leaving the Borea base on Verteg's small transport ship, The Eight entered the minds of Empress Theia Aknar and her faithful crew. Unnoticed, he took their memories of the journey to Earth and the New World. Four cycles later, they arrived on Planet Raigar. The ship's data banks, wiped clean of everything, left no trace of where the vessel had been. Theia helped her nephew, Brizo Sema and her bemused crew with the landing sequence. After that, the nightmare began. As soon as they touched down in Raigar's spaceport, The Sixth's guards arrested them like they were common criminals. Searching the ship, they seized all the Aknar's belongings and then, to their horror, the interrogation started. It was humiliating for the proud Empress, locked up in jail. She demanded to see someone in authority.

A cycle later, a tall purebreed with a scar on his face and broad shoulders entered her cell. Wrapped in a grey cloak, simply dressed below in a grey shirt and pants, he bowed in front of Theia. 'Empress, I am The Sixth's Shoter. Welcome back. You were missed.'

The use of the olden-day term shocked Theia. It showed on her face as she scowled at him. 'That post was—'

'Reinstated by The Sixth. I can assure you, I am no threat to you. I serve The Sixth. I am to escort you and your crew home. I apologise for the way you were treated here. Come now. We are to leave.'

Recognising the Shoter as the head of the Svang Charter, she trembled as she left her cell. This powerful man had tentacles throughout the galaxy and, to make matters worse, his wife was related, genealogically, to the House of Aknar. It was no wonder The Sixth had employed him. Leading her crew and family onto his ship, fear of what would become of them laced her mind.

The one-cycle journey was uneventful. The Shoter gave Theia the respect an Empress deserved and to her surprise, the best quarters on the ship. Near the end of the journey, the Shoter came to her room. 'Empress, we arrive shortly. The Captain asks if you would like to join us on the bridge.'

'Thank you, Shoter. I would like that,' she said. Seated outside, the Aknar crew bowed as she passed them by. Following the Shoter, their excited chatter about home disappeared in the distance. It was the last segment of their strange voyage. Entering the vessel's bridge, she wondered, *where did we go?*

The captain turned to greet her. 'Empress, please take my chair. We are rounding Anan now. The Energy Exchange will shortly be in view.'

'Captain, Shoter, I appreciate your courtesy.'

'Empress you are still—'

'Say no more, Captain,' she said, as she raised her hand for him to stop. Theia sat down in his command chair and looked out onto her world. The Planet Anan – she was finally home. As she watched the clouds swirl around the grey planet, she couldn't quell the thoughts running around her mind. *How long were we away?* Closing her eyes, pictures slowly formed in her brain. She was sitting in a lush green garden, surrounded by strange plants with beautiful, coloured leaves. The warmth of a sun shone down through a cloudless blue sky. *Where was that? It was The Eight – only he could have wiped our memories, and in such a gentle way. Thank you, Overlord. You have left me my most cherished memories of our mysterious trip.* Such interventions by the Overlords usually resulted in long term memory loss and sometimes, irreversible damage to the brain. Not this time. He had wiped their memories of Project Anan and the location of Earth and the New World. Only The Eight could have done that with such a gentle touch.

The sounds from the bridge brought her back to reality, and when she opened her eyes, she gasped at her first view – in such a long time – of the Energy Exchange. Tears welled in her eyes at the sight of their multi-faceted city and trading centre floating majestically in space. The dome of its vast trading hall glistened in the sunlight, and as the ship turned, the Intergalactic Space Dock came into view. 'We left from there – it must be nearly an orbit ago.'

The Shoter looked across at her. 'Yes, Empress, you did, and The Sixth wants to know where you went.'

'You were already told, Shoter. We cannot remember.'

'Things have changed since you left, Empress. You know that. He demands your presence.'

*

Planet Anan. EPTS: A139241

The ever-present clouds cleared as Theia's shuttle made its way down to the Anan capital. Closer and closer it travelled, then hovering, allowing her a rare moment in time to view her home city. Brightly coloured buildings, interconnected by the typical Anan covered paths, peppered the landscape. No tall towers or ramparts adorned the functional palaces. Instead, pitched roofs covered them, overlapping the structure to give protection from the rain. Like spokes from a wheel, people-mover tubes radiated out from the capital, connecting it with other Anan cities. Bright lights glittered in the commercial area. In miniature, Theia watched the populace rushing to and fro as they busied themselves in their daily lives. Most wore simple all-weather cloaks or covers, decorated with vibrant colours. Her subjects!

*

Shortly after Theia's landing on Raigar, to their surprise, The Sixth's guards discovered Rhea and Alex's hoard inside the Aknar shipping container. Hermetically sealed and marked with a biohazard symbol, the cure to the Anan sickness was carefully unloaded. Stored in refrigeration units, the critical purebreed and human DNA samples with a formula for a cure that could be synthesised on Anan had finally arrived. The treasure trove included human blood samples and life-changing batches of "The First Stage Treatment", medicine to arrest the initial onset of the disease.

Along with Theia and her crew's possession, they transferred the cargo to the Shoter's vessel and shipped it to Anan. Informed of a biohazard, The Sixth's Master Geneticist waited for the ship when it arrived in orbit. After the guards left with the Empress and her Aknar crew in tow, his shuttle docked with the now silent vessel. Standing in its hold, he looked over the strange alien cargo. The quality of the biohazard seals with attached handling instructions – all in Anan – impressed him. Done by purebreeds, he believed. He was wrong. It was Alex's work with clear and concise instructions, directions and formulae for all his discoveries – a human genius.

The learned purebreed traced a thin finger over the strange lettering embossed on the plastic document boxes – manufacturing part numbers, he guessed. The sample fridges intrigued him the most. Primitive alien technology modified to connect to an Anan power grid. He wondered who would do that while he tried to read the strange symbols on a fridge's maker plate, its operational parameters, complying standards and that it was "Made in China", all stamped in English by the maker. He stood back and looked at the cargo – still wondering – until something caught his eye. In a flash, an answer jumped off one of the document boxes. Stuck to the top, on a shipping wallet, was the seal of the Anan medical institute. Opening it, Alex and Rhea's handwritten journal peeped out. Rhea had kept it in their quarters, dutifully filling it out at the end of each day.

Shaking hands withdrew the book. Flicking through it, he marvelled at the neat Anan script covering the pages.

Not what he expected to find! His heart bounced in his chest when his eyes focused on the book's first page – a separately printed index and cargo inventory. The bold header cried out "Details of a cure for the Anan Sickness". A list of DNA and blood samples jumped off the page – all from purebreeds and a new species. To quell the hammering in his heart, the geneticist sat down on one of the boxes. Taking out his communicator, he called the Shoter. Leafing through the book, he read out some of the eye-catching discoveries. He ordered the transfer of the find to the quiet of his laboratory – during which, he never let the treasure trove out of his sight.

*

Back on the planet, Thea's shuttle landed in the courtyard of The One's palace. Ushered in to see The Sixth, Theia wondered at his guile – *he didn't waste any time!* His chamber was at the end of a long corridor. Outside, the Shoter positioned his desk to watch all who came and went. Except for some necessary technical paraphernalia, scanners, viewscreens and the like, the chamber was bare. The Sixth floated in the centre, his bloated energy mass pulsing with light. Delivering Theia, the Shoter bowed and left. She waited – and then it started.

The Sixth's harsh voice rang out. 'Where were you, Empress? Tell me now or I will find out for myself.'

'Overlord, I have no recollection. I'm surprised you are here. Where is The One and The Eight? The Sixth's place was always in the Jora—'

'Empress, do not test me,' The Sixth boomed. The force of his voice knocked her to the floor. 'You were briefed on Raigar of the change of order. Your husband now rules as Emperor. With the absence of The One, the Council of Anan and the Charter Guild has endorsed my rule over this galaxy.'

Crouched on the floor with her hands over her ears, the upside-down justification for his ascendancy surprised Theia. Purebreeds didn't sanction an Overlord's rule. Overlords did that! Purebreeds served them. Their advancement was far more complicated than a simple "endorsement" by bipeds. Ancient codes ruled the Overlords' hierarchy with a complex process dictating a One's ascendancy. Stored in her palace's library, she was familiar with those early texts. *Do they not understand their constitutional limitations?* she wondered through the pain of his voice.

Theia dared to look up at him. The seven-foot-high and four-foot-wide floating entity looked terrifying, his energy pulsing erratically. Overinflated to intimidate, The Sixth's translucent mass shimmered darkly for an Overlord. The colours regularly changed in tone – a murky blue and purple with the occasional grey. Unlike The Eight's smooth egg-shaped mass, dark nodules peppered The Sixth's extremity. Theia had heard of what those nodes were capable of. Bewildered, she realised she wasn't afraid of him. She wondered why? Then it hit her. The Eight – he had done that. Knowing this moment would come, he had equipped her to deal with him. She stood up and looked straight into his energy mass. 'Overlord, I and my crew cannot remember. Our memory of the journey is gone. If you dare, you may delve into my innermost thoughts, something The One or The Eight would never do. You will see, there is nothing there.'

'Empress, Empress, you are trying my patience.'

She knelt before him. 'I cannot tell what I do not know. Look into my mind, now – get it over with, please.'

Long blue tentacles spun from the nodes on his body. In a flash of light, they entered her brain through her nose, ears and mouth. She felt it, her head covered in this foul blue growth. With searing pain, The Sixth's clumsy consciousness delved deep into her thoughts. She gasped for air as the pain in her head increased. The less he found, the more he probed. He saw images of the scenery, colourful plants, a warm yellow sun and the faces of a strange biped species. But none of it told him where they were or what they were doing. Frustrated, he withdrew his tentacles from the mind of the Empress, now lying comatose on the floor of his chamber.

Calling for his Shoter, the man appeared in an instant. 'Get rid of her and bring me her crew,' The Sixth said. The Aknars came and went – he did the same to them all but found nothing.

*

Meanwhile, the Shoter dispatched Theia to her own palace with a medical team he had on standby. She wasn't going to die on his watch, he'd make sure of that. Waiting for The Sixth to finish, he inspected a discovery that intrigued him. It was part of the valuable info they had found in the Aknar's stuff. A find so startling, he felt it would change the future of the known universe. Never expecting to handle something like this when he started as The Sixth's Shoter, he continued to stare at the find – until summoned.

Frustrated, after interrogating the Aknars, The Sixth called his Shoter in. 'I cannot believe it. The Eight has wiped it all from their minds. There must be something left. Have you any news for me, Shoter? You must have found something.'

The Shoter reached into the folds of his grey robe and took out three small items. 'Overlord, my men searched through everything they brought back. We found these primitive images in the Aknar Prince's belongings. Let me—'

'Show me, now. Put them up on the screen,' The Sixth shouted, as his energy mass pulsed with flashes of blue and purple.

'Yes, my Lord,' he said, hurrying over to a console. 'There, you see,' he said, as he projected three images onto a large viewscreen.

The photos were dog-eared and scratched. The first showed Brizo Sema, the Aknar prince and heir to the Anan throne, beside a dark-skinned female biped with long black hair. Smiling, the prince had one arm around her while holding a bottle up to the camera with the other. The second photo, similar to the first, included another fair-skinned male biped with blond hair. But it was the third that had attracted the attention of the Shoter. Taken looking up from the ground, it showed Bri and his girlfriend pointing up at the stars. The clear dark night allowed the camera to capture the star-filled sky. The picture of a grinning Aknar prince, pointing up into space, was something the Shoter never expected to see. In the direction of the Anan Galaxy, he suspected. Where else would he point? Clearly, the girl meant something to the young prince. Her beauty captivated, even in this simple image. A tight, brightly coloured top with strange writing and short pants accentuated her female curves. Long shining black hair, dark eyes and soft brown skin complemented her looks. But the gorgeous face and bubbly smile shining from the picture showed the female was something special – even to the alien purebreed.

The pictures were taken in Queenstown, after the New Year celebrations, on their way back to the hostel. It was when Bri had escaped from the compound, going off on a folly of his own. His girlfriend, Hana, had delighted him when she had them printed out the next day. It was all he had left from that fateful event. Stuffed into his pocket, to be – he had hoped – cherished forever.

Despite his Shoter's enthusiasm, The Sixth wasn't impressed. 'And what do we get from these images? Do you think it's so easy to decipher their location from such scraps? They are distorted by time and space. What you see is millions of light-years away and on the other side of the space curve.'

'Overlord, it's a new species, in some way connected to The Eight. I believe we can work out the location. It'll take time but the image of the stars – it's a guide to where to look in the universe. The Seventh, Overlord, he can help with this.'

'Shoter, I know that star charts are his passion. Yes, he may be able to decipher the constellations. But it will take time. Time I do not have. What else did you find?'

'Overlord, we know they visited a planet in a distant galaxy. We have DNA samples of the bipeds you see in the picture.'

'Now you tell me this. DNA of another species; what were the Aknars doing with that?'

-'The species are related to purebreeds. It looks like The Eight's geneticists used our DNA in their first touching. From what we found we can see that the Empress was working on a cure for the Anan sickness. We found a treatment, samples of DNA from the species and purebreeds, and a formula to synthesise a cure here on Anan. It's an extraordinary breakthrough in the search for a cure for the sickness that curses our species.' He paused and looked across at his Overlord. The Sixth remained quiet, his energy pulsing slowly.

'Overlord, the Empress, her crew and cure, we should use them to advance your approval rating among the general population.'

'How will that help?'

The Shoter huffed a deep sigh, then paused. 'The Anan Council will welcome the Empress's return,' he said, with conviction. 'They'll see your release of her and her crew as an act of benevolence. After finding the Aknars lost in the galaxy – abandoned by their Overlord, The Eight – you take the credit for their safe delivery. You will also be praised for finding a cure for the Anan sickness.' Lies, but lies he could easily spin!

The Sixth was silent, pulsing with purple light as he contemplated that advice. 'The DNA from the new species, have you had my geneticist look at it yet?'

'As we speak, Overlord, he is assessing the find. The quality of the storage and the records, prepared in their own primitive technology, surprised him,' the Shoter said. He watched The Sixth's reaction, now pulsing blue. Thankfully, his temperament had eased.

'Shoter, you are so devious. There was value in employing you. Yes, release the Empress and her crew. Let her have her cure. Have my geneticists work with her and the Anan medical institution in its development. But the Aknar Prince, from those images I see he was close to a female of that species. Hold him. I want to dissect him further.'

'Yes, Overlord. And the star charts?'

'Shoter, you try my patience. Yes, I will contact The Seventh.'

CHAPTER FOURTEEN

To: The Council of Anan And The Charter Guild: Anan Constitutional Diktat

The One and The Eight rule Planet Anan and the Energy Exchange. The Overlords devolve provincial decision-making, concerning the governance of the planet's population, to the elected Council of Anan. The Council is authorised to enact laws, regulations and protocols on matters wholly associated with responsible governance of the Anan populace. The Anan Council shall not involve itself in: matters of galactic or intergalactic polity, issues concerning the Overlords including, but not limited to, the ascension or descension of an Overlord.

The Royal House of Aknar has equal executive powers as the Council of Anan. The ruler of the day, Empress or Emperor, under direction of an Overlord, may involve themselves in intergalactic and interspecies affairs. The ruler of the House of Aknar is the supreme commander of the Aknar military and shall ensure the military's allegiance to the ruling Overlords.

The Charter Guild is a commercial league of approved families and organisations. Any Overlord may grant Charter status to a new guild member. The grant of charter status gives a family or organisation the right to undertake commercial activities between galaxies and a seat at the Energy Exchange. The Charter Guild has no political or legal powers.

> *A **reminder of your constitutional boundaries.***
> *From: Empress Theia Aknar*

*

Planet Anan. EPTS: A139257

No sooner than he released the Empress, on behalf of The Sixth, the Shoter issued a top-secret briefing note to the Council of Anan. Deceitfully crafted, the report accused The Eight of abandoning the Empress and the House of Aknar. Most audacious of all, it credited The Sixth with "finding" a cure for the Anan Sickness. It included vague information about the symptom-reducing treatment and that a formula to synthesise a cure on Anan existed. Within a cycle, every interplanetary newsfeed roared with the Shoter's "top secret brief".

"Benevolent Overlord Finds Abandoned Empress", "The Sixth Releases A Cure For The Hated Sickness" and "House Of Aknar Abandoned By The Eight" were some of the catchy headlines the populace found scrolling across their comms units. The stories grew arms and legs and pretty soon they were hailing The Sixth as their saviour. The Shoter gave a rare grin as he watched the flattery – his creation – spread far and wide. Refusing to take any credit, on behalf of The Sixth, he maintained a stoic silence, driving further The Sixth's popularity.

What did not make the news feeds was the stinging statutory reminder issued from the office of the Empress to the Council and Charter members. No, it did not. They all conveniently ignored that official memo.

*

Once he had his hands on Alex and Rhea's work, The Sixth's geneticist retreated to the quiet of his laboratory. Getting old, wrinkles and worry lines crisscrossed his white face. At an average height and with an unremarkable physique, he could go unnoticed, passing as an ordinary plain purebreed. Nothing could be further from the truth. The best mind the medical institute had, and a brilliant geneticist, pushed the boundaries of discovery – often past ethical limits.

Sitting back in his chair, he closed his eyes. He had worked incessantly in his small lab, trying to understand what they had found. While resting, he wondered about the research, the neatness of the journal and what happened to the two doctors. *Where are you?* he mused.

Opening his eyes, he picked up the journal again. Leafing through it, he found the last entry, documenting Rhea's pregnancy. Hastily written in a different style, the final paragraph mentioned complications. He gasped as he realised it was in her lover, the alien doctor's own hand. Something had happened to Rhea Loupe and her unborn child. *Strange*, he thought. *What was it?* There was nothing untoward in the samples that indicated anything hazardous. He had double-checked all that before he had started working on them. He sighed, realising with all the other unanswered questions, it was a mystery he may never decipher.

Little did the geneticist know, Alex, Rhea and their unborn child had died at his own hand. Over one hundred orbits ago, he had conducted routine tests on a group of ceirim, on the *Hela*. Sneaking aboard the old derelict ship to avoid detection, he had carried out illegal experiments, past the limits of Anan ethics. Those tests were the forerunner to Kochtos's recent transformation. Some of the ceirim DNA stayed in the machine – his sloppy carelessness. That was the contaminated matter that had entered Alex and Rhea's unborn child. Their research lived on, and ironically, the man who played a part in their death would be the one to finish it!

Refreshed, he got up, stretched his tired back and loaded a set of samples into the autoanalyser. Sitting back down, he put a data crystal into his computer and began the laborious task of poring through their research. While the machines evaluated the DNA samples, he combed through the technical records and the priceless formulae. The geneticist had heard mention of Rhea Loupe. Some time ago, gossip abounded about how happy the medical institution had been to see the back of her. Apparently, she was to go away with the Empress. He always spurned such idle chatter, preferring to make up his own mind. Despite such a damming pedigree, he studied the doctor's research with an open mind.

Time ticked on, until the light of the sun poked dimly through the thick Anan clouds, heralding the arrival of another cold, damp dawn. The Sixth's geneticist stared at the autoanalyser screen. The results, flashing on the bright display, shocked him. He reran the tests, checking and rechecking the DNA samples from the alien species. And he still couldn't believe what he was seeing. Outside his closeted lab, much had changed since the arrival of the Empress, with speculation of a cure rife. Rubbing his tear-filled eyes, he got up, stretched his aching back and returned to sit at his desk. *Such a monumental discovery. Why me?* he wondered, his eyes resting on his shaking hands. *I will have to tell* him, he realised as he got up and, taking a data crystal, made his way to The Sixth's chamber.

*

'You have finished. From what I sense, there is no good news. Get on with it.'

The geneticist placed the crystal onto a pad beside the chamber console. A swirling projection appeared above them. 'Overlord, this is the alien species DNA. We have named them species-y. As you can see, it's similar to purebreeds. That's what links us to them and what generated the cure to our sickness.'

'I know that already. The Shoter told me. You are hiding something.'

'No, Overlord,' the geneticist said, trying to control his shaking hands. 'I—' he stopped talking and increased the magnification of species-y DNA. 'There, see for yourself.'

The Sixth looked up at the projection. Slowly digesting the information, he flashed with purple light. 'Is that right? Are you sure there is no contamination?'

'Yes, I am. I've verified the results on separate samples. Overlord, please spare me. I have told no one,' he said, as he knelt down before The Sixth.

'You must think me a terrible monster. Why would I kill you? I need you. Tell me how something like this could happen. You know it was always forbidden?'

'Whoever prepared the gene splice, at the species first touching aeons ago, used blue from an Overlord as the catalyst. It's the only explanation.'

'It's from The Eight. That's why he went there. I have never seen this done before. What do you think?'

'Overlord, they will have more than intelligence. I believe they have free will, and an inbuilt drive to progenerate their species, far beyond what any of us have.'

'Will that spread with your cure?'

'No, Overlord, it won't. It's what makes the cure possible – how our two species are linked. If I was working on a cure for our sickness, it is what I'd do. It's a clever mechanism to use species-y strong DNA to kick start regeneration of the old purebreed DNA.'

The Sixth paused and looked at the projection. There was no doubt, the marker from an Overlord's essence, blue from a pulsing energy mass, was visible in the sample. 'Will the cure work?'

'I think so. But, Overlord, nothing is easy with genetic change – there is always gain and loss. I need time to work with the medical institute to assess what the implications are.'

'You have that time; do what you need. As for species-y, we must work to expunge them. If what you say is true, they could take over the galaxies. You are finished with the ceirim?'

'Yes, Overlord. Kochtos's lieutenants are resurrected. A regular supply of meat, to sustain them, is arranged. I've created your army. The remaining ceirim are transformed and hibernate. The infrastructure to transport them, when the need arises, is also prepared. I'm pleased with the outcome.'

'And you think me the monster. Go,' The Sixth said. After the geneticist left his chamber, he reached out with his consciousness to The Seventh. '*I have news for you.*'

'*The image you sent – an intriguing puzzle you set.*'

'*Well, you need to decipher it soon,*' The Sixth replied, then recounted the story his geneticist had told him. He showed The Seventh the DNA images.

'*He is a traitor. Such actions were forbidden by our predecessors. How could he do such a thing? It is a betrayal of our trust and our most cherished puissance; how could he give that away?*'

'*We need to find that species' location. The Eight is planning something. Do you have any idea of what part of the universe they are in?*'

'*I will run a program now, but it'll take time.*'

'*We don't have that time Seven. What else can you do?*'

'*Scout ships. I could send them out, but I need blue.*'

'*You'll have it, as much as you want. My Shoter will arrange it,*' The Sixth said, as his consciousness returned to Anan.

He called his Shoter. 'Make sure The Seventh has enough blue. If he needs more ships, let him have them. Get me the Aknar Prince, Brizo Sema; time to interrogate him. Go now,' he said.

Sensing fear and rage from the purple pulsing of his Overlord's energy mass, the Shoter ran to do his bidding. Consuming The Sixth, the hunt for Earth – and the human race – had stepped up into gear.

*

After making the arrangements for The Seventh's blue, the Shoter summoned Bri. Guards, dressed in the dark grey livery of The Sixth, delivered the young prince, his hands bound behind him. The Shoter whispered instructions to two of the guardsmen, and they disappeared into the Overlord's chamber.

'Sit down,' the Shoter ordered Bri.

'Why am I here? You know I'm the Crown Prince to the Aknar throne, Empress Theia's nephew. How dare you treat me like this,' he said, his voice trembling with fright.

The Shoter smiled at him. 'Prince Brizo, you well know the order has changed in our galaxy. We released Empress Theia, and you will be released soon too. The Overlord wants to know about these,' he said, putting the three pictures down on his desk.

Bri looked at the pictures. A pulse twitched on his temple, betraying his anguish while his face turned grey. Images of Hana flashed in his mind. On Earth, he had gone missing on New Year's Eve, escaping from the complex where he was staying with Alex and Rhea. He had met Hana on the wharf in Queenstown while watching the New Year fireworks. Her beauty and an inner glow of warmth had attracted him. Over the four days he had stayed with her, he had never known such feelings of love. Those feelings still coursed through his body as he stared at her picture.

He could remember her, watching a white machine that floated on water with a red funnel belching black smoke. It was the TSS *Earnslaw* steamship coming in to dock on Lake Wakatipu before the fireworks started. Enthralled himself, he had asked her what it was, and that was how their love affair began. Looking at her picture, his mind recalled her soft voice and her body's sweet fragrance. His heart ached for her touch. But that was all he had. The Eight had wiped his memories of Earth's location, where else Bri had been and what he had done, over the long voyage.

Tears rolled down Bri's face. He hung his head over his long neck. 'I remember her, but nothing else.'

'She meant something to you?' the Shoter asked. The young prince's reaction to the pictures was not what he expected.

'Yes, I love her.'

The statement shocked the Shoter. A prohibited mixed-species affair, between the heir to the Aknar throne and this alien. 'You know such affairs are—'

'Banned. Of course, I do.' Bri sat up and looked the Shoter in the eye, fear gone from his voice. 'Does that matter now? No, it doesn't. I'm a prisoner, I'll never get back to her, and that monster inside will probably kill me.'

The Shoter huffed a deep sigh. He nodded at the young man's foresight. 'Try to remember. All he wants is their location. Go now,' he said, as he gestured the guards to take Bri in.

The guards led him into the Overlord's chamber. Grabbing Bri, they ripped off his clothes, turned him upside down and tied his feet to lashings their two predecessors had hung from the ceiling. His body dangled in front of The Sixth, a metre off the floor.

'Can you hear me?' he asked Bri.

'Yes, you monster, I hear.'

'What can you tell me about that alien species?'

'I only remember the faces, some of the scenery. I remember something like a vessel that floated on water. It made loud sounds and then travelled across the water. There were flashes of light in the night sky above the vessel and her face. She's so beautiful ...'

'I saw all that in your mind.'

The purple flashing oval energy mass bristled with ominous nodes. Once before, at his initial interrogation, Bri had seen The Sixth; he looked different to The Eight – frightening, oozing horror. The young prince's body quivered as he watched tentacles of raw blue energy extrude from the nodes. They stretched out towards him. Hoping death would come quick, Bri never noticed terror empty his bowel while the lethal blue tentacles hovered over him. One tracked along his bare chest and stopped.

'Overlord, you have seen every—' He screamed as two tentacles entered his nose, darting up towards his brain. Searing pain infiltrated his body, driving his heart to beat faster. Rummaging in Bri's mind, The Sixth could find nothing new. Still conscious, the young prince could feel everything. To no avail, his mind pleaded with the evil Overlord until his heart burst. Blood flooded his chest cavity while the blackness of death descended on his lacerated brain.

The Sixth didn't even notice Bri's passing. Continuing with the prince's dissection, the blue tentacles ripped him apart, organ by organ. He looked in every part of the body for any hint of a code or marker or a memory of what the prince had done. But in each sense, all he found were memories of the girl. The more he looked, the more infuriated he became.

When finished, he called his Shoter. The purebreed, gagged and swallowed the bile ejected from his stomach when he saw the sight of Brizo Sema, heir to the Aknar throne and the last of his line, lying in a pool of blood on the floor. His body was dissected in two and his organs lay in a heap on top of it. Bri, never knowing that back on Earth the love of his life had carried his child. The Shoter tried to compose himself but the thoughts wouldn't stop. Here on the floor lay, what he believed, was the end of the Aknar line. *No more children. When Theia dies,* he thought, *so does the House of Aknar!* The notion that a purebreed human child, a new species and heir to the Aknar throne, resided on a distant planet never entered his mind. Had Hana known what fate would await her prince, she most likely would never have gone with him. In the Milky Way, she was safe in the house alongside the Kenepuru sound. Alan Phillips' fears had come true, across intergalactic space – an evil entity had Brizo's crumbs. Crumbs from the Planet Earth!

A growl from the Shoter's Overlord cleared his senses. 'Get rid of that mess,' The Sixth said.

*

Exhausted after her interrogation at the hands of The Sixth, Theia languished in her quarters in the Aknar palace. The betraying Anan Council and Charter Guild had, as expected, ignored her scathing memo.

Corrupt hacks hellbent on personal enrichment and advancing their own power. When Bri died, she sensed his loss. The death of her nephew cut deep; he was like a son to her. An unwanted gloom blotted out the memories she had of Earth while she descended into a rage. Not seeing the Emperor since her return, she now realised it was time to confront that darkness. Striding from her chamber, Theia crossed the palace to her husband's rooms. She found him standing in an ornate hall, one he had recently decorated around a new throne. As she ran towards him, his guards raised their weapons until she fell at his feet in tears. She wailed, and the sorrowful emotion she projected pierced her husband's heart.

Tears flowed from her eyes. 'I'm so sorry,' she cried, burying her head in her lap. 'I should never have left.'

The guards didn't move, holding their grav weapons at the ready. They knew the power she could wield – a deadly force. Yet now, kneeling on the floor in her crumpled, once regal blue robes, she looked defeated. For an instant, she looked up at them. Her face was grey. Rivers of tears, black with viscid dirt, cut through the once white porcelain skin.

'It was The Eight; he forced us to leave,' she said, her voice quivering with pain.

Unsure, his guards looked at him; the sorrow and agony she projected pierced their hearts, her emotions washing through their minds. The Emperor nodded and, lowering their weapons, they withdrew. He knelt beside her, murmuring reassurances as he tried to lift her head.

The Emperor never saw it coming, nor did his guards. With lightning speed, Theia reached out with her right arm, clamping her hand around the long neck of her back-stabbing husband. Her left hand clutched at her blue pendant, the most powerful she possessed, one she rarely wore. As her charged crystal glowed, she squeezed his neck. Her blue eyes, flashing with the pendant's energy, bored into those of her husband's. Simultaneously, blue from her pendant rushed through her hand and with her thoughts, flooded his mind. *Betray me – you should never have done that! The monster killed Brizo; your fault for backing him.*

The room filled with the noise of crackling energy. The pungent smell of burning flesh assaulted the noses of the horrified guards. The family dispute now out of their hands, they dared not interfere. Theia looked deep into the dying Emperor's soul. Pleading thoughts flowed back from the depth of his terrified brain. Squeezing harder and focusing the blue deeper, she felt joy as his life slipped away in her hand. He fell from her into a heap on the floor, a black burn, in the shape of her hand, etched into his long white neck. His golden robes smouldered from the force of her energy. She stood up, the two guards now kneeling before her. She turned, her regal blue robes swirling with a flourish as she left the dead Emperor lying where he fell. Empress Theia was back.

*

While the dead Emperor's leaking fluid stained his marble floor, one of the guards had the worst idea possible – that he should call the Shoter and let him know what had happened.

'Tell no one,' the big man barked. The death of Bri had unsettled the cold-blooded Shoter. A walk in the cold rain washed that anguish away, restoring his orderly business mindset. Now this, another royal dead! Opening a small keep in his office, he withdrew two slim palm-sized objects; prototypes, from one of his weapons factories, untested cutting-edge tech. Setting them on his desk, he threw on his all-weather coat then passed a hand over one. A screen burst out in the air over the two objects. Deft movements of his fingers relayed instructions to the devices. Slipping them into the two deep side pockets of his coat, he hurried out into the gloomy day.

Within a seg of receiving the call, the tall, broad-shouldered Shoter arrived in the palace. He strode in, followed by his loyal Svang Charter crew, their military boots printing a wet track on the floor. Dressed in water-drenched flowing dark coats, with hoods up, the five looked more like thugs than the rescuing forces they were supposed to be. In the bright light of the room, the furrow of the Shoter's rain-crusted scar glistened on his face. Following his instructions to the letter, the faithful guards had sealed the place. No one knew what had happened here. Thankful to see him, they bowed their heads in a greeting.

Nodding, as he surveyed the grim scene, the Shoter stood in front of them – his hands in his pockets. Without warning, he withdrew them, throwing the two devices up into the air. Now activated, his instructions flowed through the deadly weapons' processor. Micro-beams of light shot out, fixing dots on the two guard's chests. A low hiss pierced the silence as the miniature floating grav guns fired two deadly rounds. In an instant, neat holes appeared in the guard's chests, marking the sanitary shot's trajectory – straight through their hearts. They fell dead to the floor, right beside their fallen boss. As quickly as it happened, his military training never forgotten, the Shoter grabbed the two devices, returning them to the seclusion of his pockets. *A successful test; much potential for these weapons,* his brain registered.

'Clean this mess up,' he ordered his men. 'With what's left of the prince, take these bodies to our chemical incinerator. Leave no trace.'

The crew of four, saluting in agreement, smiled inside. They would expect a hefty bonus for such an audacious task. Times were definitely changing.

As quick as he had entered, pulling his hood up over his head, the Shoter left. Outside, his comms unit flashed a message. Glancing down at it, he groaned. *More bad news,* he thought as he rushed back to The Sixth's palace. Awash with the calamitous events, his brain wondered how he could spin all this in a positive light. He didn't notice the short walk, his body in automatic, ignoring staff and friends as he rushed on. It was a bad day. Leaving his post as head of the Svang Charter, he expected working as The Sixth's Shoter would be challenging. But this, the death of two of the royal household in one day – no – not what he ever imagined. And, that he had to kill two innocent guards, to cover for Empress Theia's actions, hurt even his hard heart.

Before going to see his Overlord, he reread the report that had flowed across his screen. The disappearance of one of the vessels they had dispatched to patrol the far reaches of the galaxy shocked him. Long-range sensors showed a debris field where the ship had been. Destroyed – there was no other explanation. Shaking his head, he got up and entered The Sixth's chamber.

'I can feel your doubt. You have bad news. Tell me now,' The Sixth ordered.

The Shoter told him all, no embellishments, the plain facts.

'Kill the Empress,' was the first reaction from the Overlord.

'Overlord, no. That would be a mistake. Leave her be. You have the population behind you. We allow her some semblance of power. Make it look like she is back in charge. We tell them the Emperor has gone on a mission! Like she did, with the young prince. They'll lap that up. This is a good thing, believe me. They love Theia, more than they did the double-dealing Emperor. And the Aknar military, they'll do nothing!'

The energy mass pulsed a dark shade of blue. 'You think that?'

'Yes, Overlord, I do. The loss of the ship is a disaster we can't do anything about. But we present it as an act of war by The Eight. You have done nothing. Your hands, metaphorically speaking, are clean. It's The Eight who has started a war. An Energy War – that's what we tell the populace. They'll rally around you.' He was right. Purebreeds wouldn't take kindly to the destruction of an intergalactic cruiser and the loss of its crew. The Aknar military, mystified by all the changing events, would or could, do nothing. Stood down by the Emperor, on orders from The Sixth, they wouldn't be so keen to take sides.

The Sixth's energy mass pulsed with a blue light. Silence enveloped his chamber as he processed the possible outcomes. He had employed the Shoter for his devious ways and the fact that he would always speak his mind. Killing Theia was what The Sixth wanted to do. But the Shoter was right, no need to antagonise these bipeds. With blue in such short supply, he would find it taxing to fight on so many fronts. His voice cut the silence. 'Agreed. What else? I sense you want more.'

On a roll, the Shoter stood tall, puffing up his broad chest as he put across the next piece of his plan. 'Overlord, I suggest we release some details about species-y. It will come out anyway, so we should capitalise on it. Spin it a little, you—'

'What do you propose?'

'I'll cultivate the news channels. Drop hints of what The Eight is up to. Leave it to me, you'll see. It will shock the populace.' Silence and a blue flash indicated the audience was over. The Shoter turned and left. Sitting at his desk, he called an acquaintance at one of the planet's info channels.

By the end of the day, the newsfeeds were full of the impending Energy War and The Eight's treachery. Catchy headlines announced, "Rogue Overlord Breeds Super-Race" and "Threat That Galaxies Will Be Overrun By Super Beings". The story recounted how "evidence has emerged that unknown to the other Overlords, The Eight secretly bred a race of super-beings …" Salacious stuff, fuelling the rancour amongst the pure-breeds after the destruction of the transporter was also announced. The Shoter's fabrications did precisely as he predicted. The Anan population turned against their Overlord, The Eight, wondering how he could do such a thing. It was their Empress, biding her time shut up in her palace, who knew otherwise.

*

Close to one of the Svang Charters factories, a rectangularly shaped grav platform descended from the clouds. Its covered tipping-bucket, wearing the marks of the grime it shovelled, sat upright on the bow of the machine. Used to collect the planet's detritus, it stank as well. The four occupants, their noses long sensitised to the foul odour, smiled together at the sight of their destination. Huddled in a valley on the far side of Anan, the secluded factory processed the planet's waste, dissolving it into base reusable commodities.

They were expected, one of the factories' square inlet hoppers left uncovered. Flying straight in, they parked the grav dozer – like an insect, hovering over the giant box. Two power pistons upended the scoop, dumping the four bodies into the chemical digester. From the edges of the hopper, jets of acid cleaner flared up, scouring the machine and the inside of its scoop. Safe in the cab, the four watched the factory wipe the remains of the two royal Aknars and their guards from all history. The Shoter had ensured dead men would tell no tales, all traces of their bodies and DNA dissolved forever. Job done, his loyal four, counting the fat bonuses over and over in their minds, steered the machine back to its waste compound in the capital. Their idle chatter bustled with merriment and crude jokes about what delicate products the reprocessed bodies would end up in!

*

Energy Exchange.EPTS: A139355

It was Bardek, one of The Seventh's captains that located four deep-space exploration ships. Searching for anything to do with such craft, he found a dusty, forgotten report, about a deep-space mission the Anan navy had undertaken. Wondering where the scout ships were, he contacted an old friend – an elderly captain in the Anan navy. One thing led to another, and after ten cycles, he arrived on the Energy Exchange to meet his friend. The ships were lying up in the docks with the other larger derelicts. Having served together in previous conflicts, the two friends chatted amiably on the way to the space berths. Reminiscing about border wars and skirmishes with space pirates – in times past – it was hard to believe so much had changed.

'This new order will test us all,' Bardek said, as they walked along a pressurised catwalk to the scout ships. The clear poly tube stretched out to the metal dock, giving the impression they were walking in space. Lights from the Energy Exchange lit up the hundreds of vessels surrounding them.

His friend, dressed in a casual light-blue Aknar navy ship suit, stopped. The man looked straight into Bardek's eyes. 'Friend, this alters everything. We could be on opposing sides!'

'You think?'

'Yes, I do. Look out there – all our ships are laid up, in irons, we are. No fuel, it was stripped out on orders from our Emperor, who might I say, has conveniently disappeared. Empress Theia is back. If she can get her hands on any blue, she'll bunker this fleet first. And then, who knows what'll happen. Don't say I said that!'

Bardek frowned at his friend's honesty. 'No, I won't, and I hope it never happens.'

'We'll see. There are your ships,' the captain said, pointing at four vessels moored to a space-gantry, the dock's lattice supports disappearing below their poly tube, which terminated at an airlock.

Bardek gazed out at the four small exploration ships. With minimalistic cylinder design, a cone-shaped bow and two aft engine housings, they were unremarkable to look at. He had read the specs before. Now, looking at the thirty-metre long vessels, he wondered.

As if reading his mind, his friend laughed. 'Small they are! Look, they've long-range engines. Perfect for what you want. With their size and shape, the pulse generation doesn't have to be so large. They cover vast distances through small folds. Long-range tanks fitted inside too – for blue and grav. Yes, uncomfortable they are. But Bardek, you can't have everything.'

Bardek couldn't believe his luck. His friend was right. 'They're perfect. You've made—'

'Yes, yes,' his friend nodded. 'All the arrangements are made. We'll service them. You'll have to bunker them. Papers for the transfer all done as well. Where you going with them?'

'It's top secret.' He paused, then remembering his friend's honesty, he whispered, 'To search for species-y. The Sixth's orders; he's obsessed with finding them.'

The Aknar captain shook his head and sighed. 'Pity them when he finds them. He'll wipe them out – or try to. You know that, don't you.'

Bardek looked at his friend's face. It was a scared look. One he hadn't seen before – as if the man sensed something else. 'Yes, I do.' They walked back in silence, his mind filled with the awful consequences this expedition would put in motion. A word kept surfacing in his mind. He blotted it out as he focused on the job in hand.

The Seventh generated four separate star charts with quadrants to search for possible locations of species-y's planet. After maintenance, the Aknar navy moved the four ships around to The Sixth's space dock for bunkering, with blue, grav and life support. Finally, with The Seventh's crews on board, the explorers left the Anan Galaxy in four different directions to scour the universe for species-y. The search for the human race and Planet Earth was on.

CHAPTER FIFTEEN

Life Support

The primary concern of a vessel commander is sustaining life during space travel. As a rule of thumb, Anan's atmosphere contains twenty per cent oxygen, seventy-nine per cent nitrogen and one per cent of other gases. This is true for most of the rare, life-sustaining biped planets. Oxygen-deficient atmospheres can cause death. Small reductions in the oxygen content have grave consequences on the crew of a vessel. A decrease to nineteen per cent has some physiological effects but may not be noticeable. A reduction between nineteen and fifteen per cent will impair the brain's ability to think and coordinate the body. Ability to work is reduced. A further reduction, between fifteen and twelve per cent, hastens the onset of fatigue and further weakens the body's decision-making and coordination ability. Oxygen depletion below twelve per cent has devastating consequences, including death.

⸰ *An Introduction: Fundamentals of intergalactic travel.* Zaval Borea

*

Borea1, Folded Space. EPTS: A139296

On *Borea1*, ten days into their forced journey to the New World, Cylla sat idly by while Niamh worked at the ship's controls. Using shuttle 2 as a control pod for the *Borea1*, their saviour, was her genius idea. The old, damaged craft provided an airtight home in the larger vessel's airless engine room. After the initial shock of the departure from the Borea base, they settled down together, making the most of their cramped quarters. The Neredian's healthy metabolism healed the injuries Cylla had sustained during their frantic escape. Within days, Niamh removed the bandages from the alien's head. It had been a close call that shook them both and made them realise how lucky they were to be alive. Over the last ten days, they each heard the other's life story and surprising them both, bonded as friends. When not chatting, they played cards with a deck they found in the cockpit.

Shuttle 2, intended to accommodate only one escaping passenger, had two beds on the floor, a table with two chairs, a rough counter that served as their galley and a water-closet at the rear. It was a far cry from the luxurious apartment Cylla had left at the Energy Exchange. Halfway across the galaxy, fleeing from her home in this metal box, she shook her head at the change in fortune. Never had she imagined events that could dynamically alter her life like this. Despite her own predicament, she frowned with concern for her new friend.

Exposure to blue energy had altered the human. Her red hair had changed colour and was now a soft blue. Her white face – speckled with deep blue freckles – had also changed. Cylla had got used to the unnerving glowing eyes and the sizzling energy that surrounded Niamh's head. She wondered, *would it ever dissipate?* And she wondered at how such a willowy body could pack so much power and intelligence. She and Niamh were both the same height, yet, with broader shoulders, powerful arms, a long tail and a larger body mass, the Neredian overshadowed the human's size.

In a faded red T-shirt, her grubby ship suit tied around her waist, Niamh sat engrossed in a problem. *There's something different about her now*, Cylla thought, noting the human's features. Her shoulders slumped, her head sagged and most worryingly, there was an ever-present frown across Niamh's brow. *Why does she look so worried and sad?* 'Nee, you are sad; you are worried. What is wrong? Soon you will see your husband.'

Niamh stopped her work and turned to face Cylla. Her grim face heralded the bad news she had bottled up. 'We don't have enough oxygen.' She paused, letting her words sink in.

The faint hum from the ship's controls sounded like an orchestra playing a death march. Knowing more was to come, Cylla stayed silent.

Responsibility for this disaster burdening her, Niamh continued with the explanation. 'I didn't expect a passenger. I preloaded more than enough oxygen for me when I prepped for an escape. What we grabbed in the *Hela* shuttle bay is not enough for both of us.'

'How long?' Cylla asked.

'We're short a day or thereabouts. But we're short; we haven't enough.' Surprising Niamh, the news didn't seem to bother Cylla. *Maybe she doesn't understand*, Niamh thought. 'We'll die, Cylla. Without oxygen, we die. We're going to die. Dead – you understand, Cylla?' she said, forcefully.

Cylla grimaced. Now she understood what had been bothered her travelling companion. How long had the human hidden that sour note, she wondered?'Nee, I understand you. Yes, I do. Tell me, how much water is there?'

Niamh's frown deepened. 'There's a small tank in this shuttle. And a much larger one in the other, refilled with clean potable water on the *Hela*. But I don't see how that'll help.'

'Can I get into the tanks?'

'Yes, you could get into the larger tank in the other shuttle. But how—'

'I have gills,' Cylla said, as she stretched her neck and opened some small slits. This was a difference between the two species Niamh had not noticed before.

Speechless, her blue eyes crackled with astonishment. She remembered Cylla had asked about water during their escape from the *Hela*. Now she saw why!

Trying not to stare at the human's flashing eyes, Cylla stood up. She tucked her tail in around her waist, ready to put on a spacesuit. 'Come on, Nee, let's go over and check it out. We've nothing to lose.'

Ten minutes later, they both climbed out of the small airlock into the bigger shuttle they had left the *Hela* on. Niamh had extracted all the oxygen cylinders from it. Its only breathable atmosphere was what remained in the cabin. She had a plan to scavenge as much of the remaining oxygen from that, but it would still leave them short.

Wasting no time, Cylla took her spacesuit off. 'Show me the tank,' she said, hope bubbling in her voice.

Niamh opened a bulkhead at the back of the shuttle. 'There it is, that's the access hatch,' she said, pointing to a small manway secured with bolts below the top of the tank.

Cylla looked up and down at the tank and the hatch. 'How far back does it go?'

Niamh pointed to a narrow passage. 'There, you can see behind the bulkhead.'

Cylla leaned into the void and forced her head around the corner. After sizing it up, she withdrew and, with a big smile, turned to face Niamh. 'Open it up. I want to see inside.'

*

Travelling faster than light, *Boreal*, guided by The Eight's magical flight plan, approached his exit coordinates. The departure point from folded space, data Niamh made sure she never changed, flashed to the ship's guidance system. A bleeped warning, from the nav-con, grabbed her attention. A message flashed on the screen – in six hours *Boreal* would leave folded space. They had arrived and would shortly enter the New World's solar system.

The diminishing supply of oxygen had started its numbing impact. Niamh struggled to bring up a navigation projection of the New World and its solar system. Over and over her brain screamed back at the oxygen deprivation. *I need to enter a flight and landing plan.*

She didn't give up. Placing her blue crystal in the nav-con, she cast her mind out into the approaching solar system. One hand on her blue diamond, the other driving coordinates into the ship's brain, she did something she had never done before – she built a pre-programmed flight plan. The plot included a waypoint when the grav drive would take over, flying *Boreal* through the solar system to the New World. Returning her consciousness to the shuttle, she built an auto-landing sequence.

Her brain resisted; it screamed for her to lie down and sleep. She was always tired and everything she did felt like a never-ending task. To make matters worse, her eyes continuously scrutinised the atmosphere gauge she had mounted on her console. It was in the orange, reading fourteen per cent oxygen, down from the standard twenty-one. She wished she had never installed it. Although she understood the effects she was feeling were from hypoxia – oxygen deprivation – it didn't help. She looked at the screen, so blurred, she couldn't see it. Blinking and wiping away the salty sweat, she persisted. Despite the inhuman help her brain got from the blue contaminant, her physical body still needed nourishment. Her breathing laboured to gulp in more air. And, all the time, she wondered whether her calculations were right. She started again, writing it all down then rechecked every step of the eighteen-hour flight plan from the exit point. But all she wanted to do was sleep. Her head nodded and she was gone into a happy blackness.

*

Another beep from the nav-con startled her. Eyes wide open, the adrenalin rush shocking her back to reality, she used it to recheck the course waypoint and the engine settings. Finally, she plotted in the landing coordinates. *There, all done*, she thought. Glancing over at the hastily cobbled together oxygen scrubbers she had made from filters and hoses, she wondered, *will they be of any use?* Beside them, the last bottle of precious oxygen was open and empty. Her last hope at remaining alive emptied into the shuttle atmosphere. She checked the atmosphere readouts – in the orange, and down to thirteen point five per cent oxygen. *I'm not going to make it*, she thought. She lay down and strapped herself into a bed on the floor of the shuttle. Closing her eyes and holding her blue diamond, she reached out with her mind.

*

Fort Leslie, New World. EPTS: A139444

On the New World colony, Niamh's husband, Thomas Parker, lay sleeping in their pod. Situated on a hill, their home had a commanding view of the town. But now, in the dead of night, with a dark cloudy sky, all that was on offer were the dim streetlights. A brain-triggered adrenaline rush started his heart pumping like mad. Eyes open, Tom sat up in bed, wide awake. *What the hell*, he thought, as he focused his mind on what woke him. *It couldn't be. How could she be back?* Niamh had been gone six months; it would be eight at the earliest before she returned. But there was no doubting the voice in his head – it was Niamh. He would never mistake that! She was calling him.

She had done this before when she was kidnapped in Australia, linking with his mind and providing the location of her kidnappers. She was doing it now but this time it was in Anan. *Why, why was she talking to him in Anan?* And then he realised, with a cold and empty feeling in his gut, she was delirious and in trouble. But the phrases she recited were the same over and over. He jumped up, and as they came into his head, he keyed them into his tablet. Despite his lousy spelling in Anan, the translation was the same over and over again: "Tom, I am coming. Soon. I am coming. Clear the landing site. I miss you. I love you. I'm in the starboard eng–" and as abruptly as it started, it stopped. He dressed within two minutes and ran out the door to Fort Leslie's control centre.

At five o'clock in the morning, he had Robert and the base communications technicians up, poring over their screens.

'It wasn't a dream, Robert. It was real, just like in Oz,' Tom said, looking hard at Robert, whose sceptical face said it all.

'Tom, you miss her; it's natural,' Robert said as he glanced over at the techie. The young man shook his head. 'But we don't see anything on the long-range scanners,' Robert said.

Tom wouldn't give up. It was Niamh who he had heard in his head. 'What if the ship's cloaked? It wouldn't travel without cloaking. You know that, Robert.'

'Okay, suppose I believe you. What can we do?'

'Clear the landing site. It's not a lot to ask, Robert. If I'm wrong, well, I'll live with the teasing I'll get from you and my crews. She's in trouble and she's coming home. I know it, Robert, believe me.'

'Let's get them up early. If Niamh is in trouble and coming in with a ship, she'll need more than the landing site cleared,' Robert said. Reaching over, he lifted the cover from the Colony's general quarter's alarm and pressed the big red button. 'There'll be some grumpy people now,' he said, as the shrill siren pierced the quiet night.

*

Back on the *Boreal*, lying on her bed in shuttle 2, Niamh couldn't understand why she had woken up. What had disturbed her sleep? *Leave me alone*, she thought, as she tried to gulp in more precious air. *What's that beeping noise?* she wondered. Then she realised it was the atmosphere alarms from the shuttle cockpit. She wished she'd turned them off – no need to know when death was so close. She closed her eyes and slipped back into blackness.

*

Like the rest of the colonists, General Arie Machai, the Eight's representative on the New World, jumped out of bed. It hadn't happened before. Drills were always in the morning, so this was real. Fear clenched his guts as he made his way to the control building. Despite the crowds milling around, he didn't rush. Dressed in a ship suit and a thick parka, he pushed open the door. By now, the place was a hive of activity. Scanners, nav-projections, comms desks all manned, while Tom and Robert stood briefing a maintenance crew.

The six-foot-tall alien stood in the doorway, his deep green eyes piercing Robert's as he caught his gaze. The hubbub died down as the humans realised their rarely seen boss had arrived. The three leaders – Mack, Tom and Robert – approached each other. Unseen sparks flew between Mack and Robert. For an instant, Robert's arm glowed and a loathing emotion flowed from Mack. Oblivious to the standoff between his two friends, Tom recounted his news. In a voice thick with emotion, he pressed home his concerns that Niamh was in mortal danger.

In an instant, Mack grasped the seriousness of the situation. A vessel may be coming! Back in charge, the Empress's Protector threw off his parka and walked tall across the room. He stopped at Kora, their best navigator. She had a blue diamond in a nav-con and a projection of the New World's solar system hovering above it. The colony had Earth-sourced scanning and long-range radar, but it couldn't see as far as their navigators. Robert had asked that the *Hela* leave a satellite in orbit to scan for approaching vessels, but Mack had refused. "It would be like painting a target on the planet," he had said.

Mack studied the ghostly blue projection of their solar system. 'Nothing,' he said, his voice laced with tension. Deep furrows on his brow and a grey pallor made the alien appear even older than he actually was.

For an instant, Robert sensed something else. *Is that fear?* he wondered. 'No, Mack, nothing so far. We're clearing the landing site. I've lifted restrictions on grav so all the craft are in the air.'

Mack ignored him and turned to Tom, still ignorant of the strain between the other two. 'What about defences? Are we ready? Have you issued out the heavy artillery? We cannot assume it is Niamh. This could be a trick, Tom.'

Mack's clear thinking shocked Tom back to a reality he didn't want to face. He sat down on a nearby chair and called his night-shift commander. 'Break it all out,' he said, his voice trembling. 'Everything – heavy weapons, rocket launchers, armoured piercing rounds, the lot. And prep the two big boats with the fifties,' he said, referring to his and Niamh's creation, a mix between a special operations boat and an armoured personnel carrier. The colony had forty of the smaller and two large gunboats. Powered by grav, the flotilla served as their core defence force. He put his head in his hands as the irony of it all sunk in. *Would they have to shoot Niamh down with a craft she had designed,* he wondered?

A shout from Kora brought him back to reality. 'There's a ship,' she said to Mack, glued to her projection of space. 'It just appeared here,' she said, pointing out the telling spot.

'Can you bring up a closer image of the ship and the space around it?' Mack asked.

Holding her blue crystal and closing her eyes, Kora projected her mind out to the approaching vessel. She opened her eyes in surprise at what she was looking at. 'I've never seen that before. What is it?'

The tall purebreed general smiled at her naïveté. 'That, Kora, is a port from folded space. Watch, as the ship's blue drives wind down, it slowly closes. Quite rare to see, and that most definitely, is not the *Hela*.'

'How does that work, General,' she asked, intrigued at what she was looking at.

The general mellowed at the young girl's questions. Her innocence had served to quell his fractious emotions – the old Mack was returning.

'The blue we extract here is used in the engines of our big ships when they fold space. On a long journey, it's quite spectacular when they leave folded space through the port on the other side. It takes a little while for the blue drive to dissipate its energy. That's what you see now. Niamh, or someone else, is here, no doubt about it. Can you see into the ship?'

'No, General, I'm sorry. It's too far away. I'm still learning how to do this. But I may be able to plot the ship's course. It's turning now. It's fast, much faster than the *Hela*. If it follows that course and speed into orbit, it should be landing within eighteen hours.'

Mack turned to face Tom and Robert; Tom's face was a mix of elation and fear. Mack sensed his inner conflict – protect Niamh and protect the colony. 'You're right, she's back, we hope,' he said as the questions started to flash across his brain. *Where was that ship from and who was flying it?* Glancing back at Kora he smiled. 'Thank you, Kora. Teaching you how to navigate has paid off. A good move, yes it was.' He meant it. Without her skills, they'd be in the dark.

*

Failing to make any contact with the vessel, they came to the conclusion it was following an automated flight plan. Still, Mack wouldn't take any chances and ordered all weapons at the ready. It was more reason to clear the landing site and the area around it. When the ship arrived in orbit, Kora was able to scan the starboard side and found the shuttles, but she couldn't get any more than that.

'Are you sure you can't see any sign of life?' Tom asked her again.

'I'm sorry, Tom, but I was only able to glimpse the shuttles. From what I can tell, they are in what appears to be an engine room there,' she said, pointing to the starboard aft wing on a projection of the ship. 'I can't get anything else. I'm sorry, but I'm not going to give you false hope.'

'Thanks. Kora. You've done well. We know where to look first.'

*

The two heavily armed grav craft hovered above the empty landing site, ready to shoot down the approaching vessel. The flying boats, loaded with surface-to-air missiles and fifty calibre guns, were the best they had. Despite their training, the crew were on edge. This was different from everything else they had encountered. Who could imagine what was in that ship – a possible alien invasion, bringing an end to their new home? It could even be The Sixth himself. Over the preceding eighteen hours, the rumour mill ground out the stories, conspiracy theories and the like. Tension on the colony was at fever pitch. Itchy fingers stroked the triggers as the *Boreal* approached.

Mack waited for the ship's arrival with Tom and his security crew, all armed with grav guns, from a safe distance. The strangely shaped craft flew in from the sea. Powered by one engine, it listed forty-five degrees as the running drive compensated for the loss of the other. In gravity-free space, cruising on one engine hadn't affected the ship's stability, but on the planet, a different set of rules applied. It was the complication that had frustrated Niamh when she penned the flight plan. In the end, she gave up on an aerodynamic level flight, resigning herself to hanging the ship off the one driving engine. Clumsy but effective, allowing a cautious approach over the sea to the landing pad on the beach.

Flying slanted exaggerated *Boreal's* aggressive appearance. When Mack saw it first, he gasped. Pictures and stories of that ship, and what it was capable of, peppered his mind. And here it was, bristling with lethal weapons, forward guns and grav missile launchers – heading straight for them! If Niamh wasn't on that ship, the colony was dead. Their fifty calibre weapons and rocket launchers would be like pop guns! He turned to Tom. 'Stand down the big guns. Let it land. We can't fight that.'

Before Tom's saving message reached their flying boats, a trigger-happy soldier locked one of the SAM's auto-sights onto *Boreal's* forward gun turret – where The Eight languished inside in his chariot. The soldier, in automatic himself, did as his training asked – painting the target with a laser. Smarter than human tech, *Boreal* possessed an intelligent defensive system. Sensing the threat, signals flashed between the ship's computer and the gun turret. To the horror of the soldiers in the flying boat, with a whirl, the gun came to life. In an instant, the barrel pointed straight at them, all the while the vessel getting ever closer to the landing pad.

Trigger-happy swore. The gentle caress of his itchy finger became a squeeze, launching the high-velocity rocket straight towards *Boreal's* gun turret. Hidden from the pulsing Uldonian microbes, unable to do anything, The Eight sensed weapon systems arming. *Boreal's* countermeasures kicked in, shooting laser intercepts at the primitive rocket. In a millisecond, lasers hit earth's best surface-to-air missile. Exploding into tiny fragments in a ball of noisy fire, the rocket disintegrated, falling into the sea. At the same time, Tom's orders to stand down burst across their comms. 'Oh shit,' trigger-happy shouted. 'Get us out of here.'

The pilot was way ahead of him, gunning the grav throttles as he flew the boat away. The other did likewise, both flying crafts fleeing through the air for their lives. Niamh hadn't foreseen this conflict, concentrating on getting this big ship, with no pilot in control, onto the ground. The dichotomy of orders flooding *Boreal's* computer confounded its logical reasoning. Amidst the defensive commands to load the grav missile tubes, flowed Niamh's pre-programmed instruction, "turn the ship ninety degrees in preparation for landing". Fortunately, the designers had built in a weapon's fail-safe. Her executive orders prevailed, overriding the secondary countermeasure signals flooding out to the armaments. Combat came to an abrupt stop, as quickly as it started, lady luck sparing the colony a bloody end.

Dancing in the air, an inelegant mess, the big ship's rise and fall did nothing for the confidence of those watching, that it would ever land at all. The roar of the grav engine as it strained to hold the vessel aloft, added to the tension. The whole colony watched on. Believing Niamh on board, some wondered whether she would ever survive this landing. Rising and falling, until the port leg made contact with the ground, the ship's engine thundered on, blasting clouds of sand up from the beach. Sensing the proximity of land, another set of orders flooded the throttles, squeezing the grav shields until the vessel started to sink down onto the sandy base. It was a clumsy landing, the ship turning and twisting from side to side, rotating on its axis until it touched down, coming to rest on the forward fin and two aft wings.

'It was flying on one engine,' Mack said, as he waited until she had finally settled on the ground. The grav drive shut down, and then a huge hatch on the starboard aft wing opened. There was a loud whoosh as the atmosphere rushed in. The hatch lowered itself down onto the landing site, forming an access ramp into the ship. 'Tom, you're good to go,' Mack ordered.

Within minutes, the colony's flying security craft, bristling with guns and armed security teams surrounded the ship. On one, Tom, with his own team and Niamh's technicians, flew down to the ramp, landing beside it.

Without any prompting, they ran out of the craft and followed Tom up into the ship. It was a strange scene that greeted them as they filed in through the mess of cables and discarded supplies that littered the alien engine room.

'Tom, if she's here, she'll be in that shuttle there,' the colony's chief engineer said, one of Niamh's best technicians. 'That rig up, it's got Niamh's handiwork all over it,' he said, pointing to the loom of cables connecting the shuttle to the blue drive.

CHAPTER SIXTEEN

General Purpose Matter Depletor

No engine room should be without this standard cleaning tool. Developed to capture and neutralise blue energy and its derivatives, the tool is primarily used to scour the stellar drives, feed manifold pipes and tanks before maintenance. The versatile multipurpose tool can also capture and neutralise dark energies, and in some instances, maybe the only known remedy to those contaminates. All models are easily adapted to clean up blue energy spills and are effective on most substances. The mechanism operates on the principle of generating a localised black void via a portable lance at the target site. The resulting void imbibes the energy into an impermeable vessel where it is dissipated through a collorian ventricule. To adapt the tool to simply clean up blue spills or manifolds, the ventricule should be removed. Always refer to the operational manual for each tool before use.

‹ *An Introduction: Fundamentals of intergalactic travel. Zaval Borea*

Fort Leslie, New World. EPTS: A139479

As soon as they opened the hatch on the shuttle, Tom realised why he had lost contact with Niamh. The stale air hit him first. The fetid smell lingered at the back of his throat, so heavy in the atmosphere spilling out from the shuttle, he could taste it. The flashing low oxygen alarm added to the deathly feeling. The sight of her on the floor, lying comatose in her bed, spurred him on. He took a big breath of air and jumped up into the shuttle. He tried to drag her out but she wouldn't move. Like a demon, he dragged at the blankets covering her until he found the constraining flight harness. His eyes popped open. *It's my Niamh*, he told himself, while closing the shock of her transformed appearance from his mind. Determination to get her out won that battle. Not wasting any time looking for the release buckle, with his knife he slashed through the harness, dragging her out into the ship's engine room. Gulping in the fresh air, he ran with her, out and down the platform, placing her on the ground beside the waiting med team.

He looked up at them and the colour drained from their faces. Two stepped back in fear at Niamh's unearthly appearance. 'Oxygen, she needs oxygen. Don't act so surprised, you lot; it's still Niamh.'

'Leave her, Tom; we have her,' said the Doc, pushing an oxygen mask over her face. 'Come on, you lot; snap out of it. She's still human.'

Tom stepped back, as the med team rallied around their doc. Shaking his head in disbelief, he spoke into his comms unit. 'Mack, come down here. I need you.'

The noises from the medical team burst in his ears – they had found a pulse! His heart skipped a beat with that news. Then came the sound of the life-giving gas forced into her lungs – oxygen, her body badly needed. All the while, he wondered what horrors she had braved to come back so transformed?

After what seemed an age, the Doc shouted, 'Tom, come here. She's breathing; she's okay.'

Without a word, Tom knelt down beside her and took her into his arms. He fought back the lump in his throat as he tried to speak, his hands quivering as he held her. Brushing her blue hair, fighting back the urge to let her go, Tom's fingers tingled from the flashing energy surrounding her head like a halo. Closing his eyes, he swallowed. *It's my Niamh*, he told himself as he held her close. He felt the response to his touch as she stirred. He opened his eyes and found himself staring into hers, flashing like St. Elmo's fire with white light. Wiping away the tears as they seeped down her cheeks, his mind wondered again, *What trials has she faced? What evil thing forced her into such a desperate situation?*

Oxygen-enriched blood flooded her brain, feeding her corporeal needs. The blue energy that had kept her alive so far relinquished its hold, diminishing the effects of the contamination. Consciousness returned and then she spoke her first words – deliriously in Anan.

She's speaking Anan; why's that? he wondered. Overcoming the natural revulsion to her unearthly appearance, Tom kissed her. Her lips tingled.

As he explored her mouth with his tongue, he felt her stiffen. Then she responded, her hands grabbing his head – pulling him closer. Hungrily they devoured each other until the passion of their first kiss in months subsided. He pulled back, wiping the blue tear stains from her face.

'Niamh, Niamh, it's me, Tom,' was all he could think of to say.

Immersed in a cloud of emotions, she giggled a happy reply in Anan. 'Well, I hope so, husband.' Clutching Tom, her eyes focused on her surroundings: the ship behind them on the landing pad, the cloud-speckled sky and the faint shape of the two moons floating above the New World. Elation filled her as she realised she was home – or was this a cruel dream? Was she still in the shuttle, delirious, suffering from hypoxia? She didn't notice how far back the medics had withdrawn or the gasps of those who had arrived. Her mind only filled with love for Tom. Then it hit her, *The Eight and Cylla – had they survived?*

He looked into her fiery eyes, still softly flashing with blue energy. 'Niamh, speak in English. You're back on the colony.'

'Tom, I still can't believe what I'm seeing. Did I make it?' Niamh asked, now speaking English.

'Yes, you're home.'

'I've changed, haven't I?'

'I love you; you're still my wife. You're not getting out of that,' he said, looking at her. She had changed – her red hair was now a soft blue and her white face was speckled with blue freckles. Both her hands were blue but it was her glowing blue eyes that gave her the eerie look that had frightened the med team. Oxygen had diminished the effects of the blue, softening her contaminated appearance.

Abuzz with the landing, from a distance, the colonists watched the drama unfold. Sounds of hooves, growling and loud roars announced the arrival of the catbears, followed by their ever-present benefactor, Alice. In vain, she tried to contain them, unable to keep them away from the ship. Sensing his presence, they surround the bow landing fin where The Eight awaited rescue.

At the front of the growing crowd, pressing ever forwards, was Janet Cooper, the colony's planner. Alone, she watched her friend Niamh, carried by Tom, and then the uneasy treatment by the medics. Unable to stand idly by, Janet ran through the loose barrier of Tom's soldiers towards her friend. Alone on the sand, she couldn't believe what she was seeing – her friend Niamh in Tom's arms, polluted with blue. She remembered the day when Niamh had first arrived in the agency in Christchurch. Then helping Janet get the doubting Thomas and Robert onto the shuttle for their first visit to the *Hela*. Janet had been Niamh's first real friend in Christchurch, and a bridesmaid at her wedding.

A wave of revulsion washed over Janet. She and Kath had hired Niamh! What fate would await them all now after this? She turned away, vomiting the contents of her stomach onto the dark, dusty sand. Falling on her knees, she wailed for her friend. It was Robert who grabbed her, ignoring Mack as he ran past Tom and Niamh. Carrying Janet back to the colonists, all the while his voice reassuring, 'She's alive, Janet. That's all that matters; she's alive.' Handing her to a group of her friends, he returned to face the mayhem of Niamh's arrival. A question burned his brain. *Where's The Eight?*

Realising she was home, the same thoughts flooded Niamh's now active brain. *The Eight, had he survived?* 'Tom, The Eight, he's in an ammunition locker in the bow landing fin. You'll need to keep him away from blue.'

The big sandy-haired Scotsman, Robert, was close enough to hear those words. But what did she mean, "keep him away from blue"? Ever the Project Manager, always looking after his colonists, the dark thoughts and questions whirled in his head. *What comes next? All this is wrong. The One, he must be gone. We've failed.*

Standing up, Niamh watched the green and brown striped catbears surround the landing fin, roaring for the return of their Overlord. He's alive, she realised. But what about her other travelling companion?

'Cylla, she's a Neredian. She's in the other shuttle,' she said to all. The sound of shouting and a bloodcurdling scream came from the depths of the engine room. 'Oh, they've found her. Tom, don't let them hurt her – she's our bookkeeper.'

Another racket spilling from the ship's engine room added to the general mayhem. Tom's soldiers spilt out, guns pointing behind them.

Three limped and one held his arm as if it were broken. They were shouting orders to "stop, or we'll shoot", while a strange alien voice shrieked in Anan, 'Nee, Nee, where are you?'

What the hell? thought Robert, as he watched Niamh run towards the ship's gangway. Ordering the soldiers to drop their weapons, she ran up the walkway to meet the strange-looking alien, dripping in water, which emerged. Robert couldn't believe it as Niamh and the Alien hugged, while the alien's long menacing tail circled above. Arm in arm, the two walked back towards Tom and Mack. Robert watched as Mack and the new arrival greeted each other. They bowed a greeting, and then the gold-coloured alien kissed Mack on the cheek. *More intrigue,* Robert thought.

At the base of the ship, despite the chaos her arrival had caused – as if back in the pub – Niamh calmly did the introductions. 'Tom, meet Cylla Ora, our bookkeeper. Mack—'

Mack, trying hard not to stare at Niamh, interrupted. 'Welcome back, Niamh. Yes, Miss Ora and I are acquainted. Although, Cylla, why you are here mystifies me.' She started to speak, but he held up his hand. 'No, explanations will come later. The Eight, that's our priority,' he said. His eyes, hungry for info, squinted at Niamh.

Gushing out, the news didn't bode well. The instant Niamh started the narrative, Mack knew – Uldonian microbes. He had believed such weapons were long gone. Rescuing The Eight wouldn't be easy but nothing else mattered. Clearing his mind, he turned to Robert; the orders he barked were swift and precise. 'Get your man Blair, his drill crew and a grav platform. You'll also need two engineers, with what you call "the cutting gear". We'll need a tool. Get Blair to bring what he calls the "hoover". I'll look for another.' His voice softened. 'Tom, take Niamh home and please drop Miss Ora off at my pod; she'll stay there. Cylla, make yourself at home,' he said, hurrying off into the engine room.

While Robert gathered the rest, Mack looked around the *Boreal's* engine room. Ignoring the debris of the forced journey, he focused on finding one thing. Ripping open lockers and storage rooms, he searched for the specialist tool – there had to be one. The one they had on the colony wouldn't be enough. And then he found it, neatly folded in a locker, a priceless matter depletor. The Anan tool, designed to capture and neutralise energies like blue and its derivatives, and used to scour the engines and manifolds before maintenance. Before it left, Blair took one from the *Hela* armoury, adapting it to pump blue slops from the tanks. On Earth, the Aknar Prince Brizo successfully deployed it to destroy grey matter in the *Hela* base in Australia. Designed to capture and neutralise dark energy, the tool was also used to clean up blue energy spills. Effective on most forms of energy, Mack hoped it would be capable of extinguishing the organic's power. It was their only hope to capture and kill those foul microbes.

*

Managing to chase the catbears off to a safe distance, Robert opened the big hatch to the ammo locker. The cold and dark interior and the foul stench of stale air didn't bode well. 'This won't be easy,' he said to Blair, peering into the void beside him.

'What's new with that? Nothing ever is here,' his grumpy countryman replied. 'Another fine mess we're in, Robert! Let's go to a far-off land in space. Riches abound. We'll make a fortune and live happily ever after. A fairy tale, Robert. That's what that was.'

Blair was right. They were in a pickle now. Shining a light inside *Boreal's* forward ammo locker, Robert found The Eight's chariot. 'What the hell?' he said. 'How'd she get that in here? Mack, take a look at this.' The tone of Robert's voice dispelled their differences.

Mack looked in. He put his hands over his face in anguish as he realised how Niamh had become contaminated by blue. He kept those assumptions to himself. All that mattered was that she had saved their Overlord. The two burly Scotsmen overshadowed their alien boss. Mack's body language said it all. Reaching up, he put a reassuring hand on Blair's broad shoulder. He had a soft spot for this grumpy driller. Despite his rancorous temperament, the man made it all happen, working tirelessly with his crews to harvest blue. He and his smart wife Shona would make a suitable replacement for Robert! 'We get him out, Blair. Even if we've to cut the side out of this ship, we'll do it. But first, that mess has to be neutered,' he said, his voice all business-like. They agreed on a plan.

Fifteen minutes later, the void purged with air, Robert and Blair climbed into the dark locker. Sensing their end, and the proximity of Robert's blue-stained arm, the Uldonian microbes grey mass started to pulse. It took the human team an age, but bit by bit they cut away the metal mesh as the wands of the depletors sucked up the poisonous bile.

It was dirty and cramped work. Robert stayed in the void throughout. Grinding away, the alien tool scoured the microbes out from the woven fabric of the micro net spun from grav. Gorged on The Eight's blue, the microbe's growth precluded stripping the cloaks off the chariot and lifting the lot out. Mack wouldn't risk that. If they got out, like a magnet, the nearby blue energy tank farm would drive them mad. And if they got in there, the microbes would be no more. Mack shuddered at the notion of the giant blue-hungry beasts they could turn into. It had happened before, once in recorded history, on the Planet Uldan where the pesky bugs came from. A whole blue tank farm gobbled up! It took an Aknar battalion twenty orbits to clean up the mess. After that, on that planet, they stored all the blue on an orbiting space station. No, Mack wasn't letting them out here.

Throughout the work, the old and tired General stayed at the entrance to the void. To the humans, age was taking its toll on the once powerful alien. His shoulders slumped, his pallor was grey and worry lines creased his brow. Then they saw something they hadn't seen before – he was shivering. His dealings with Robert were terse – gone was any sign of friendship. Pitying the cranky General, Blair returned with a hot drink and a thick blanket. Without a word, Mack threw the blanket over himself and grabbed the cup. Blair couldn't understand what had changed. Not being the one to linger, he jumped back into the armament locker to continue with the work.

At last, with sighs of relief, they were done. All signs of the foul blue-eating microbes had been hounded out from the void. The depletors did their job, dissolving them into combustible waste. The filthy mess then burned in a pit dug beside the ship.

Still inside, beside the chariot – never leaving his Overlord – Robert wondered what they should do next. His arm glowed faintly as a welcome voice returned to his head. *'Fill my tank with blue, Robert. Pour more into the locker and I'll take it from there.'*

'Ah, you're back!' His shout startled the others. 'We need tanks of blue. Blair, get three of the portable ones from the farm. I guess he's in the buffers or the memory banks, but he's there.' It was the best news they had had since the arrival.

Sourness descended on the colony after Niamh's tumultuous return. The appearance of a new frightening species; their Overlord, trapped in his chariot covered in alien puke; and no *Hela*. And to cap it all, their chief engineer contaminated with the alien energy. A far cry from what The Eight had said to them in Australia before they left Earth. "… together, we can shape our destiny for the better. As a species, you have achieved more than I ever thought possible. This project is a seminal event in the change of order within the galaxies. You were probably not aware of that …" His seminal event had turned into a disaster. They were short of grav, reduced to living like nineteenth-century settlers surviving on the land, and now their Overlord, the most powerful being they had ever seen, had returned beaten. Morale hit rock bottom!

Having poured pure blue energy into The Eight's glass tank and from the ladder, two more of the portable containers into the locker, Robert and his crew climbed out of *Boreal's* void. Not knowing what would happen next, they all quickly withdrew from the entrance. The newly extracted blue swirled and curled in the locker surrounding the glass tank, brimming with the precious energy. The Eight's presence, split between the chariot's memory banks and the buffer, went to work, reversing the process he had used to insulate himself from the Uldonian microbes. Opening the steel valve at the base of his tank, his consciousness flowed from the buffer. Regaining power, The Eight recoupled the gold bus bars to the blue feed manifold. The rest of his presence and deep memories flowed out from the solid-state memory banks.

Coalescing in a flash of white light, The Eight roared out of his prison back to a free-floating oval energy mass, his resurrection complete. Never before had the ethereal entity come so close to extinction. His extended mind would always remember that close call. Humans and their simple engineering had saved him. The Borea family – he wondered what had happened to them. Blaming them for his near downfall didn't enter his calculated review of the event. His own fault, poor risk management on his part. Frike got at him when he had no guards. Had he taken Thomas Parker and a few of his soldiers … Yes, a different outcome.

Eager to see the colony and what was achieved in his absence The Eight's energy mass burst out through the locker's access hatch. Mack, Robert and their crew stood back in awe as their Overlord rose above them. He didn't linger, speeding down to his catbears who howled a greeting for their god. *Alice has worked wonders with them*, The Eight thought as they fawned around him. *Such wondrous beasts.* He had plans for their future. Rex and Luna's offspring was now near full grown. Others had propagated the rare species, their young mewing in fright at the sudden appearance of such a strange blue being. He sensed satisfaction with the symbiotic relationship between them and the colonists.

Moving on, impatient to exercise his new-found freedom, The Eight flew to Fort Leslie's town centre – now deserted, in the dead of night. The change startled even the dominant entity. Timber buildings had mushroomed out of the ground, dirt roads radiating out like the spokes of a wheel to the edges of the colony. And transportation, primitive carts with halters for the catbears. And then he realised – grav, there must be a shortage. *What next?* The blue tank farm brimmed full of his life-sustaining energy. *They had been busy*, he thought. Life-sustaining measures abounded. The forest pushed back, but not all. Within the human fortifications, a forest, stretching down to the beach, remained for the thriving catbears. The botanist's industry, vertical fields of newly discovered foods, began at the edge of the town. A whole new growing process, in its infancy, minimising the horizontal use of land, heralded a new dawn in human agriculture. The silver light of the two moons showed off the beauty of this jewel, surrounded by verdant forests and blue-filled mountains, beside a sea teeming with life and food. It pleased The Eight. Despite his failure in the Anan Galaxy, Fort Leslie had entered a new age.

Hope, there was hope – no logic to that. To the empirical being, who existed on equations and logical thinking, hope was nothing more than an emotional thought process. But now, with the progress they had made without him, hope was alive and well in this colony. It embodied the colony's soul. He could see it everywhere he looked, from the new buildings to the females with child, the group existed on it. It reaffirmed his and The One's decision to return to Earth. The humans were unique. With his guidance, they would rule galaxies.

Rising above the colony's continent, he looked down on his planet. The temptation for exploration titillated his new freedom. Like a blue bullet in the night, he sped off. The night turned to day and day to night as his ethereal mass travelled every nook and cranny of this beautiful world. Forests, deserts, glaciers, grasslands, oceans and blue-filled mountains, more than they had already tapped, covered this virgin orbiting haven. Space beckoned, the urge to revisit the New World's solar system, its planets, moons and asteroids brimming with undiscovered blue energy boiled in his brain.

Logical thinking prevailed – stay shrouded from The Sixth's prying eyes. The planet's atmosphere cocooned The Eight from discovery. Out there, in the void of space, Six might sense him. No, no need to take that risk to sightsee. Matters of intergalactic polity urgently pressed. Resting on the planet's northern pole, he revisited his smart-war planning. He had the advantage of being back on his New World with a formidable ship – unknown to The Sixth. The opportunity for his project to advance to a new phase lay in front of him. Time to reconsider the Pilot's original plan. Audacious indeed, but now more than ever he needed such a scheme. In all their history, the price of blue had never been so high. The Sixth controlled that dwindling supply – until now! *Here I have the answer,* The Eight thought, calculating the deliverable volume of blue in the New World's storage tanks. He possessed enough of the base commodity to set the Pilot's trap. But he required more than the blue for it, and his war project, to succeed. *I need a fleet of starships – time to go to work.* But first, he wanted to visit Niamh.

*

Eighteen hours later, she awoke to the smell of food. *Bacon, yes, it's bacon,* she realised. *I'm dreaming. I'm still on the Boreal.* She opened her eyes and looked around. She was in their bed, home in their pod. Cocooned in the thick warm duvet, she relived the hours of her return. She had luxuriated in a long shower, washing away the dirt and grime from the arduous flight. After that, they had made love throughout the rest of the day and the night. *Home, she was finally home with Tom.*

His soft voice roused her from her daydream. 'Niamh, we've a guest. He's waiting out on the terrace. I'll bring out the food.'

'You're alive,' she said to the Overlord as she stepped out onto their terrace dressed in an old boiler suit. She admired his new energy mass – a bright blue, taken from the energy recently extracted on the New World.

'And so are you. You disobeyed my orders.'

'You should know by now, the young don't always do as they're told.'

'You could have been killed. You have changed.'

'How did you get out of that thing?'

'Mack, Blair and Robert used the devices that recover dark energy. What you call the "hoovers". The matter depletors, they worked. But my chariot was damaged when they removed it from the locker. It wouldn't come out of the hatch so they took it apart. Your people are fixing it now in the workshops. My child, it was the chariot and its memory banks that saved me. I was able to do what I did on the *Hela* when I was low in blue to preserve my consciousness. You remember that, in Earth orbit, before you landed in Australia.'

'I'll never forget it. Talking to you on a computer while you lived in the *Hela* memory core.'

'The organic feeds on our blue and, as we lose energy, we start to die. When it attacked, I left my energy mass and sheltered in the memory banks you made for me on Earth. Without the chariot you and your team constructed, I would not have survived. There would have been nothing left for you to come back for.'

'Are there more of those things out there?'

'The Pilot supposed they were all at the Borea base. You remember, I ordered they be destroyed in a chemical incinerator. But Zaval was wrong. The evil Frike had more. Now, I believe there are more out there. To think they are all destroyed would be insular. Occasionally, my own kind uses the organics as well.' He paused as Tom arrived with the food. 'Tom, once again, I am in your wife's debt.'

Her blue eyes opened wide as she looked at the food on the plate. 'Where'd you get the bacon?'

'I kept some in the freezer for your return. Sit down and eat. Overlord, I gather all did not go well on your return to Anan.'

'No, Tom, it did not. We have much to do; we must plan for war. An intergalactic war between Overlords – the first in an age. But now, I am more concerned with your wife's disobedience.'

'Overlord, you should know by now she's her own woman. That's what I love about her,' he said, smiling at Niamh.

'Yes, but such a deed must not be overlooked.'

She sat back and laughed. 'Ah, go on, Overlord. Take my powers away and turn me back into a human.'

'You are still human. Niamh, I am not sure if the effects of your exposure to blue will dissipate easily. As you suggest, I cannot take your powers away. No, I have a better idea. Look at that ship down there,' he said, as they looked down at the *Boreal*, a hive of activity, surrounded by Niamh's technicians, every hatch and ramp open, grav platforms hovering and flying all over it.

'It is mine; the Pilot transferred its ownership to me. I do not need it. Yes, it will serve me as a platform until we resolve this crisis, but after that, it will be superfluous to my needs. It is yours, on one condition.'

'And what would that be?' Tom asked as he looked a Niamh, sitting back with her mouth open in surprise.

'You change the name.'

'Overlord, why?' she asked. 'You know you are like a father to me. I didn't save you for a reward.'

'Because you deserve it. It is a small price for preserving my existence.'

'Overlord, I want something, something you can easily grant, and what I should have insisted on before. We should never be separated again. Where Niamh goes, I go. That is all we want.'

'Thomas Parker, you ask so little of me. Yes, of course, you both need to be together now. You will have a family. Niamh, I have said this before, you will have gifted children. I look forward to that.'

'Jeez, Overlord. Will ya give over on the kids thing,' she said, blushing. Tom watched in wonder as her face glowed with a strange hue of red and blue.

CHAPTER SEVENTEEN

Autopilot: Drive Control

The "drive control" function on the autopilot serves to regulate the force output of the grav engines. It is particularly beneficial with two or more drives in a vessel. The subroutines prime command is to establish what the engines are actually doing, compared to the control system dialogue orders. By real time, communication between the synchronous modulators, sensors on the omnidirectional grav shields and the control system dialogue module, the computer validates gross force output and vector. Engine imbalance or misalignment is fed back to the autopilot and corrections are made. Before engaging an autopilot, the calibration of its computer, the control system dialogue module, the sensors and the grav shields must be verified.

‹ *An Introduction: Fundamentals of intergalactic travel.* Zaval Borea

*

Borea Fleet, Folded Intergalactic Space. EPTS: A139480

UNKNOWN TO NIAMH AND THE Eight, back on the escaping flotilla, the Borea family were well on their way through folded space. Travelling faster than light – for the past ten cycles – Zaval's fleet hurled ever closer towards the safety of the New World. Balancing the forces required to tow four ships through the vastness of space fell to him. Plotting the complex navigation equations was Verteg's domain. Her ability to manage the calculations proved vital. Her cousin Siba and the Pilot had helped with the ethereal navigation, but the pre-fold computations and course vectors were all hers. And now, past halfway, as they checked their position,

Verteg was right on the mark. The constant work had occupied her mind but she still hadn't regained speech and the broken bones weren't healing. Although the Borea technician changed her bandages and helped with her daily needs, the supply of Anan plasma sustaining her life force was running out. Rationing it caused Verteg's medical condition to decline. The fact was hard to conceal – without proper treatment, she would die. Approaching the last five cycles of travel, her wellbeing consumed the Pilot. He never left the bridge, sleeping in the captain's chair beside her.

*

The Pilot awoke with a jolt from the sharp pain in his face. *What was that?* he wondered as he heard the noise from something hitting the deck. As his eyes focused, he saw a beaker rolling away across the floor. He looked up. Verteg was sitting facing him, pointing at the screen. His stomach lurched as he looked into her brown eyes, etched with fear, and the only part of her face that was visible. He stood up and focused on the viewscreen. It was transporter *Three*, at the back of the tow, slewing sideways. 'What's Alke doing? Did you contact him?' he asked.

She nodded and pointed to his console.

He looked down at his screen and read the messages she had sent to Alke. 'Has he not responded?'

She shook her head.

'Hack his ship's controls, sound their general quarters.'

As she turned to her comms console, he walked back to tow control. A warning flashed from the trammel connector between transporters *Two* and *Three*. The tension gauge was at twenty per cent below its maximum. *How could that be?* he wondered. He pressed the general quarters alarm on his own ship. He needed the full crew here on the bridge. 'Any response, Verteg?'

She shook her head.

'Sound general quarters across the fleet. Get them all up and contact Siba. I need a close-up view from the aft cameras on *Two*.' The bridge viewscreen flickered and changed. 'Is that a view of *Three's* bridge?'

She turned and nodded to him.

'Where's Alke?' And then they saw him running across the bridge as he pulled up his flight suit. 'He was sleeping – during his own watch. Verteg, I don't believe it. How—'

She stomped her foot on the floor and turned to look at him. Her eyes said it all.

She was right – recriminations wouldn't help them now. The Pilot bit down hard and took deep breaths as he worked to control his anger.

*

Two point six kilometres behind *Tug 1*, the problem facing Alke, in command of *Three*, was boredom. The designers of the transport ship built in an autopilot to combat those foreseeable risks. But for such a system to work, the vessel needed maintenance. Its resurrection on the Borea base didn't cater for such luxuries. Urgency to leave the Anan Galaxy took precedence. The ships would have skeleton crews to monitor the drive outputs – it was all they had to do. Verteg took care of every other conceivable calculation. But one thing she couldn't see was what the engines were actually doing. On Alke's ship, the force manifold's efficiency waned. The two-metre diameter steel tubes from the grav engines needed cleaning, the port one more so than the starboard. From the outset, Alke spotted the imbalance. Instead of letting Verteg know, he compensated himself, making do with the situation. Following his lead, his two companions did the same. It all worked fine until the tedium of this journey hit Alke's tired brain. He hadn't slept during his last off shift and decided to grab a nap. Thinking with his arse, he set the engine speed alarms then retired to a bunk in the captain's day cabin. As per usual, the engines drifted out of alignment. And, the untested alarm sounded, inaudible to Alke, lying comatose in the land of nod!

The starboard drive output overtook the port, forcing the ship to turn. The opposing force of the tow pulled it back straight. But something had to give – and it did. The stern of the transporter, forced sideways to port, bounced along the wall of the grav bubble.

General quarters, initiated by Verteg's hack, sounded loud and harsh. Hastily pulling on his ship suit, Alke jumped up and ran to the bridge.

His two technicians followed. Their faces said it all, as they listened in to the Pilot's and Alke's conversation.

'Alke, we have a problem.'

'Yes, Uncle. I, ah, I ...'

'That's okay, Alke. Take a look at your engine settings. You need to balance them up.'

Then the viewscreen on *Tug 1* split. The view from Siba's transport *Two's* aft cameras showed it all. Alke's ship had drifted to the side of their flight envelope. The aft end was now scraping against the wall of the grav bubble. The white flashes showed the start of the hull collapse. The Pilot had seen this once before and knew what was coming next. He put his bony hands up to his face and signed. *How, how could I have let this happen?* he wondered, as he walked over to Verteg. He looked down at her console. She was trying to calculate different engine settings for Alke's ship.

'It won't work, Verteg,' the Pilot said as he put his hand on her shoulder. She shook her head and kept working. He looked back at the viewscreen. Alke, working with his two crew, were furiously trying to straighten the ship. In the background, he could hear scraping and crushing sounds coming from the ship's hull.

'Uncle, I'm so sorry,' Alke shouted, over the rising noise.

On *Three*, after those words, his two crew realised he'd been asleep at the wheel! *Three* cried a tearing screech, the noise piercing every strut and bulkhead.

'What's that?' cried one of the technicians, his face awash with terror.

'The sound of death knocking on the door,' said the other. She was older and wiser and knew what was coming. 'A shuttle. It's a long shot but beats staying here with him,' she said, loathing for Alke, dripping from her voice.

The two techs ran from the bridge, down the centre corridor of *Three*. Bulkhead doors jammed as the ship buckled under the strain of the crushing forces. Near the aft end, they turned a corner. The black void of folded space announced its imminent arrival, stopping them dead in their tracks. Like the invisible monster it was, it had swallowed the back section of *Three*. Bolts of shimmering energy marked the boundary of life and death.

Abandoning their chance to reach the larger shuttle bay, they fled back to the lesser, located mid-ship. They both knew the futility of it all, but anything was better than giving up. The small escape craft beckoned. Jumping in, the two technicians had it started and the shuttle bay door open. A gap in the trammel gave them a glimmer of hope. They might escape after all. Gunning the shuttle engine, they flew out into space, still inside the all-protective grav bubble. Not as simple as that! Opposing force fields of grav, released by *Three's* hapless gait, struggled for supremacy. The shuttle heaved and yawed as they tried to push it forwards towards Siba's *Two* and saviour.

Siba's aft camera picked them up. She shouted in the comms to *Tug 1*, 'A shuttle! They've launched an escape shuttle. Pilot, we must save them.' Zooming in on the cockpit, the view of the two terrified techies filled the fleet's big screens.

Zaval knew it was futile. The forces needed to drive that shuttle forwards within the turbulent grav bubble were far beyond its puny engine's capabilities. They were doomed. Before he could give Siba an order to cut the camera feed, bleeding from *Three's* port engine, the invisible force struck. Two opposing waves of grav crashed over the small craft. Terror-filled white faces stared out as the cockpit, squeezed like paste, folded inwards. In slow motion, the two techie's faces pressed against the toughened glass wall. Distorted by the crushing force, eyes bulged from the sockets, red blood leeched out of their noses, grey brain matter squirted from their ears, while their bones were crunched to a pulp. The devastating force continued squashing the craft flat, compressing the remains of the two Borea technicians out into space. A green and red stain of bodily remains floating in the void, wrote their epitaph.

The Borea crews watched the drama, not only of Alke's ship getting torn to pieces but of the shuttle trying in vain to reach the safety of *Two*. It was too much for some. Unable to watch the death of their family and friends, they turned away from the giant viewscreens in horror.

In anguish, Verteg slapped the Pilot hard and then rested her head in her hands. But more was to come. A loud beep sounded from the tow control and a purple light started flashing above the bridge.

One of his crew rushed over to the panel. 'Pilot, *Three's* tension alarm – it's ten per cent below max.'

'Where are the others?'

'Just starting to rise above their normal range.'

'We have to release the coupling on *Three*.' Verteg grabbed his leg and tried to hold him back as he turned to walk to tow control. 'We have no choice. It's one damaged ship or the whole fleet,' he said.

Nesting to the side of tow control, locked closed panels showing the status of the trammel connectors glowed brightly. Three of them blazed an ominous dark blue – tension above the norm. The fourth flashed purple, the no-hope state of the connector tethering Alke's *Three* to the fleet. The Pilot ripped the seal on the panel. Yanking the cover off, a machine voice toned over the bridge, 'Warning, warning, connector four disconnect sequence initiated. Warning, warning …'

Ignoring the wails of protest from Verteg and his crew, the Pilot reached inside the panel. Cold sweat dripped from his brow, his mouth dry with fear, he felt for the lever. His white bony hand was bathed in the dark purple light as his fingers closed around the cold and uninviting handle. Shutting out all the pleading thoughts from his mind, he twisted the fatal lever.

Stiff to turn, it yielded. Unfaltering, Zaval's body now in automatic, he twisted it all the way – one eighty degrees – shooting an irretrievable signal down the trammel to the connector. The machine voice changed its message. 'Connector four disconnect sequence activated. Disconnect in five seconds, four …'

Like phaenian steel, the harsh voice cut the silence on the bridge. The Pilot's heart pounded in his chest. Glued to the screen, his crew held their breath. The count reached five and a flash of fluorescent pink light burst from the bulbous connector securing the trammel between *Two* and *Three*. And the chemical cutter did its job, severing the trammel's life-giving link to Alke's ship.

'Uncle! Uncle, we have a hull breach,' Alke screamed as his ship lurched backwards.

'Increase power to the grav bubble, maximum setting,' the Pilot said, across to the engineering tech. They weren't out of danger yet. Alke's ship still rattled in the bubble, faster than light momentum, dragging it along 'Keep our engines balanced and hold our course, straight ahead.'

They watched the split screens. The last they saw of Alke was him trying to put on a spacesuit, and then the lights went out. The whole fleet watched the view from *Two*'s aft cameras. *Three*'s stern – projecting through the grav bubble – was crushed flat.

The doomed ship slipped away, embedding itself further into the grav bubble. Amongst the flashing white light and the explosions as its engines ignited, the sight of the five-hundred-metre vessel getting crushed before their eyes was too much for many of the fleet's crew. Some turned and ran from the bridge. With the debris from the ill-fated shuttle and the bloody remains of his team, the wreck of Alke's *Three* disappeared out the other side of the grav bubble, lost forever in folded space.

The Pilot looked down at the tow status. Tension readouts were healthy and stable. The release of *Three* had prevented further damage to the fleet. 'Status reports, all ships. Now,' he roared into the comms. 'I want status reports, your engine settings and course heading. Send them all to Verteg. And I want your watch rosters. I want to know who'll be piloting each vessel and when.' He turned to his own bridge crew. 'I'm sorry, I had seen that once before and hoped never to see it again. That's what happens if a ship strays from the flight envelope. We talked about that on the *Hela* bridge, did we not?'

'Yes, Zaval, we did,' they replied.

'The rest of the fleet depends on us for their very existence. You see what happens if they stray outside our course vector. We are five cycles out from the New World. I don't want to lose another. Get back to your stations now. Any problems, ask,' he said, as he sat down. He looked down at his hands – they were shaking. The hunger was back, gnawing at his gut. He could taste the red liquid. He closed his eyes and concentrated, banishing the demon from his mind. Slowly he breathed in and out and then opened his eyes. 'Verteg,' he said, 'get me the commanders of each vessel, private lines, and I want to speak to Siba first.'

*

Seventh's Scout Ship, Intergalactic Space. EPTS: A139560

Far, far away in space, for ten cycles, The Seventh's four scout ships searched their assigned galactic quadrants in vain. Based on the picture of Earth's night sky – that Bri had brought back – The Overlord wrote a predictive program of where the stars should be in the present time. With so many variables and such a crumb to work with, the results weren't promising. What The Seventh did find were star clusters, zones for the scout ships to visit.

He issued starting coordinates and a set of star charts to each vessel. They flew to a constellation where they would compare the star systems with that of the image – dull and tedious work. On top of that, the rough and ready ship's quarters tested the crews to their limits. So far, there were no matches. Before exhausting their fuel and food, three of the craft returned to the Anan Galaxy. Empty handed, they slinked into the space docks on the Energy Exchange, filed their reports and disappeared before The Sixth's wrath descended on them for wasting his blue.

It was Bardek who wouldn't give up, pushing his crew to the limit. Conscious that the use of precious blue would need a result, he knew returning with nothing wasn't an option. The small scout ship's flight performance proved its worth, but creature comforts didn't exist. The five crew, stinking from body odour – and more – longed for a shower and hot food. Taking turns to hot-bed in the two bunks, the lack of sleep took its toll.

Bardek knew it was a matter of time before they had to give up. Sitting in the cramped cockpit with the lights dimmed, the constant pinging of the scanners lulled him to sleep. His crew worked away, the star charts they were analysing projected on a big viewscreen in front of them.

The navigator's voice woke him. 'Captain, I've checked this star pattern against The Seventh's program,' she said, pointing to a display on her navigation projection. 'It's similar. We should have a closer look.'

Bardek glanced at the flight plan. 'Have we enough blue?'

'Yes, and we'll have more than enough to get back.'

'Let's go. Open the fold,' he said. This was the tenth course the small scout ship had taken. And still no result.

Flying through the fold, Bardek tried to dispel the thoughts of what The Sixth would do when they found species-y but it wouldn't deter him from the mission. The small ship skipped through folded space. There was a whine from the back to indicate their arrival as the blue drives shut down.

Despite the tedium, his crew sat up, all alert, hungry to make history. 'All right, you know the sequence,' he said. The navigator projected the star system up above her console. Bardek pointed to the projection. 'You're right, there's a similarity. That section there. Put it up on the viewscreen and overlay the image.'

'I'm not convinced,' his navigator replied with her all too familiar stinging doubt.

Bardek wouldn't give up. 'We're not going yet. Let's increase the magnification of the image and see what we get.'

They worked hard, taking different screenshots of the navigation projection and overlaying them on the image generated by Bri's picture. It was the same every time. They assumed they had something and then nothing!

It was Comms who broke the silence. The young officer turned in her chair and looked straight at Bardek. Her face beamed excitement, so much so she couldn't get her words out. She swallowed, then blurted out, 'Captain, I'm decoding strange sounds. They're coming in on our electromagnetic detector.'

Bardek stood up. This was new. 'What do you mean – strange sounds?'

'Definite communications transmitted as electromagnetic radiation. The waves are crude but simple. Listen,' Comms said, as she played the sounds over the bridge. They listened to a series of clicks sounding out a clear pattern.

A surprised Bardek sat back down. 'That's not random space noise. There aren't any occupied planets that we know of in this quadrant. Could it be them?'

'The waves are decaying, having probably travelled over a hundred light-years through space. But I've a direction,' Comms replied as she put another star chart up on the bridge viewscreen.

Bardek looked at it and hit his head with his hand. 'Overlay that with the image.'

The two pictures converged. Realising the stars they were looking at matched Bri's view of Earth's night sky, the small crew erupted with cheers.

Bardek's voice bristled with hope. 'Can we get closer to that quadrant? How much blue have we?'

Impatient, he rubbed the sleep from his face as he watched his navigator plot the courses and fuel usage. 'We could do it. But we'd only have enough to get back to the edge of the Anan Galaxy. Our grav drives will take us home, or we could get more fuel sent out. But it's just enough.'

Bardek knew that wouldn't work. He shook his tired head. It would take too long to get home on grav, and their Overlord wanted that news. It was a deep blow. So near yet so far. He looked across at Comms. 'Will we get close enough to transmit our data?'

She did some quick calculations, turned back and smiled. 'Yes, Captain, we will.'

He didn't need any more prompting. 'Do it. Plot the course to the very edge of that quadrant.'

Shortly after, the familiar whining from the two blue drives behind them announced their arrival, in a distant galaxy, further away from their home than any of them had been before. They started the same scanning and matching sequence. But this time, while his navigator mapped the space around him, the captain stood beside his comms officer.

'I have a binary sequence, Captain. It's a more recent transmission and clearer than the last.' She played a pinging sound over the bridge for all to hear.

'Can you decode it?' he asked.

'I'm working on it now. It's a message, deliberately transmitted into deep space, some time ago. Why would anybody do that?' she said.

'I suspect as a misguided need to make first contact with others. They'll regret that!'

'Here it is, Captain. They even transmitted a copy of their DNA into space. We've found them.'

Fifty-three years before The Eight's return, Earth's most powerful radio telescope broadcasted a message into space, carrying information about humanity and the planet. It was a simple broadcast, consisting of binary numbers, a series of ones and zeros, in the universal language of mathematics. Some believed it was an attempt to contact aliens, others as an attempt to show off human technology. Not all agreed it would benefit mankind. People expressed concern that Earth's location in space could be revealed to aliens who may not be so friendly. Now, five hundred trillion kilometres from Earth, as Captain Bardek's smart comms officer finished decoding that signal, those concerns – unfortunately – bore fruit.

She projected the message up onto the viewscreen, a simple communication, with the DNA and details of species-y's size and height. A number puzzled Bardek. 'That can't be right – four point three billion population?'

'Must be some discrepancies in the decoding. It's the same number as their DNA nucleotides,' Comms replied, putting more numbers and pictures up on the big screen.

'Looks like a child drew them,' their engineer said, disdain scouring his voice.

Bardek watched the primitive message scroll along. One image depicted a biped positioned over a sequence of squares; their planet's place in their solar system, he guessed. His engineer was wrong. An emerging intelligence sent this. But why would they transmit such a message? *The Eight must have left them alone for a long time*, he realised. Purebreeds don't use electromagnetic radiation to communicate in open space. Everything encrypted, point to point with emissions from a higher spectrum. No way would they transmit such data out into the open universe. Such methods were banned. There were others out there! Rumours of distant civilisations and Overlords abounded. Reports of unidentified objects tracking across the periphery of their known galaxies were common. After all, the universe was infinite. To believe they were alone was to live in a box! Species-y would regret that transmission.

He looked down at the young comms officer. Unlike some of the other more seasoned crew, she hadn't moaned about anything. Despite the discomfort of this cramped journey, it was all about the work. They hadn't considered the possibility of detecting electromagnetic transmissions. It wasn't on the radar, but she had pulled it out of the bag. He put his hand on her shoulder and nodded as she looked up at him. 'A promotion is coming. Well done.'

He didn't rush them away, allowing the crew time to coordinate all the data and mark up The Seventh's charts. The navigator plotted the most economical route she could find. Settling down for a confined journey, the happy crew of the small scout ship left the Milky Way for home – or as close as they could get to it.

CHAPTER EIGHTEEN

Grav Guns

A max-charge grav gun set at the highest range has enough firepower to destroy a standard military shuttle. The grey grav cylindrical cartridge, mounted below the barrel, stores enough fuel for one hundred continuous rounds at maximum setting. The point-seven-five-metre long portable weapon is the Aknar Military standard personal armament. The user has a range of power settings from destroying down to kill or stun. The projectile charge burns through the target forcing in, the explosive grav. Activation is by a low-resistance trigger mechanism fitted with a safety catch. The weapons are formed from lightweight phaenian steel and carbon alloy. It is the weapon of choice and more effective than the stick-shaped grav stun cannon, which is used when lethal force may not be appropriate.

‹ *Extract from: Basic Weaponry. General Arie Machai*

*

Fort Leslie, New World. EPTS: A139756

THE ARRIVAL OF NIAMH, THE Eight and Cylla on the colony, galvanised the human resolve. Hope bubbled in every corner of the human settler's life. The Eight's perception had not lied, conversations were full of optimism and the anticipation of great things to come. Even the catbears took on a new vigour, working with a fresh sense of enthusiasm. With some prompting from The Eight, and surprising the humans, they started combat training. The sight of the huge beasts learning the intricate nuances of hand-to-hand combat techniques became a welcome diversion to daily life.

To add to the distractions, Bill, one of Tom's team leaders, ran a book on the fights. Their benefactor, Alice, tried hard to shut it down, until Rex and Luna, the catbears' leaders learned of the enterprise. Intelligence has no boundaries! Once the green and brown striped furry beasts realised Bill was capitalising on their tribe's endeavours, they wanted in. Luna's grasp of trade and barter surprised Alice. And, a whole new industry of fashioning decorated armour for the beasts sprouted up. Helped on by Tom's soldiers, the catbears soon established a fighting force, dedicated to the protection of their Overlord. Led by Rex and Luna, it marked a pivotal change in their evolution.

The refurbishment of the Borea ship, renamed by Niamh as the *Monarch,* dominated the engineer's and technician's lives. All its secrets revealed, the *Monarch* proved to be a formidable change in the humans' fortune. New technologies discovered on the ship, along with a hoard of grav, hidden away in a secret compartment, added to their wealth. Even The Eight had missed it when he scanned the vessel back on the Borea base. But still, Robert wouldn't change their path. Grav was too precious to waste on day-to-day tasks that the colonists could do with the catbears' help. He added the newfound grav to their prized stock – rationing its use remaining the priority.

Over that time, The Eight broached the subject of their predicament and his hopes to gather a fleet. But, with only the *Monarch* in play, they believed it could prove to be a long road.

Amongst the new tech discovered were long-range Borea sensors, designed to protect an asteroid from invasion. Mounted at a high point on the barren rocks, the tech could see out into space, without betraying its position. The new find excited Tom who couldn't wait to get the system working to protect the New World.

Looking for a new crew for their first charter vessel, Niamh suggested their youngest IT specialists, Geoffrey Thompson, manage the project. It would be an opportunity to prove himself as the comms officer.

An odd bird, Geoff was only nineteen and one of the last colonists they had employed before leaving Earth. An IT tech from the south of England, before the Wave, he had worked as an intern in a bank in the Far East. Orphaned by that sad event, Geoff turned to cyber-crime, finally getting caught after hacking an Australian bank. The industrious youth didn't give up on life's opportunities, applying to join the colony from his jail cell in Sydney. Endowed with the mythical gene, his test results were not far below Niamh's – too good to pass up. They had agonised about taking him on but it was Katherine Phillips who finally spoke up for him, saying "everybody deserves a second chance". Australia was happy to be rid of the troublesome teenager, granting Geoff release on the premise that Anan Corp took responsibility for him. After that, the Australian press abounded with stories about New Botany Bay, the penal colony in the stars!

Geoff flourished with the newfound responsibility. To give an all-around view of their solar system, he installed the instruments on the high mountains of each of the planet's four continents. He loved tinkering with the alien machines: blue energy conduits, molecular memory and crystal powered nanotech, mysterious technologies he could only have dreamed of in the past. This project gave him something to prove himself at. The youngest of the colonists, his social skills didn't add up to much. The young single females avoided the "nerd" as they liked to call him, like the plague. With little other communal outlets, the work consumed all his waking time. After the trip to the mountains to install the sensors, he toiled on his own to get the scanners up and running. He preferred a quiet environment and took to working through the night in the colony control room. Mack also developed nocturnal habits, surprising the few on the graveyard shift who occupied Fort Leslie's nerve centre. Unknown to the humans, their elusive alien boss was taking every opportunity to escape his new house guest, Cylla Ora.

It had taken Geoff ten days from the initial hook-up on the far-flung mountains to the commissioning phase of this new blue-powered scanning device. He had sat with it in the control room, babying it along until it projected a stable spherical hologram. The two-metre – diameter sphere represented the space out beyond the planet to the edge of its solar system. Not as far as they had hoped, but enough to give them time to react from any approaching ships. It freed up the few navigators they had who were monitoring the space with blue crystal projections – a welcome break from this long, tedious work. Impressed by Geoff's scanner as it was now known, Tom had stood the navigators down.

Tonight, Geoff would make the final commissioning checks, then this job would be over. He sat watching the projection, his mind wondering what he could do next. *After this, all the other choices would be a bore.* Chopping trees, farming and colony life didn't suit him. *Escape,* he wondered, *would that be an option? But where to?* Before The Eight's return, he had heard some of the colonists talking of leaving Fort Leslie, running off and forming a breakaway group on another continent. A fat lot of good that would do them, he had supposed. They'd turn out to be dinner for the flying lizards! No, he wanted to be away, out into the stars on a spaceship. A job on the *Monarch* was too good to hope for, perhaps, after this—

An alarm from the scanner yanked him back to reality. He couldn't believe it; could it be right? He ran towards the office Mack was dozing in, shouting all the way, 'General, General, come quick.'

The commotion woke Mack, and before Geoff arrived at his office door, the tall alien was striding out. Geoff nearly ran into him. 'Calm down, Geoffrey, you'll wake the colony up at this rate,' Mack scolded. 'Show me what's the matter.'

The old alien General and the young Earthling gazed at the eerie blue ball-shaped hologram. Geoff pointed to a green-tinted vibrating spot, out at the edge of their solar system. 'What's that, General? Look, it's growing,' Geoff gasped.

Once again, Mack's heart fluttered in his chest. *A contact, deep in space, out at the edge of our solar system. Who is that?* he wondered. 'That's a space fold and a big one. It's starting to open. We have visitors,' he said to Geoff. He looked at the big clock on the wall. 'Four thirty-six – time to get them up. Sound the alarm, Geoff,' Mack said, pointing to the colony's general quarters' alarm.

His hands shaking, Geoff pressed the big red button. For the second time in the month, the shrill siren pierced the quiet night. 'How long before they arrive?' he asked.

Mack's reply carried over the worrying sound of the alarm. 'The fold will open shortly. They are cautious. Whoever it is, wants wide open space for the exit point in case of any errors. It's near two days out from here. We need to tell The Eight if he doesn't know already.'

A message from his Overlord flashed in his mind. '*I know now. I am on the way.*'

Within minutes, Niamh, Tom, Janet and Robert followed The Eight into the control centre. Others soon arrived, crewing their stations, the navigators building projections of the quadrant Geoff's scanner had identified.

Mack sat down in front of one. 'Look, here they come,' he said, tension dripping from his weak voice.

Crowding behind Mack, Niamh, Tom, Janet and Robert watched on, while The Eight floated in front of the navigator's station. Oblivious to the crowd, the diligent man kept his eyes closed as he projected his mind out into their solar system.

The giant fold opened. The first to appear was *Tug 1* with its tow-trammel shining behind it, then the *Hela* and transporters *One* and *Two*. The remains of the trammel strung out behind *Two* – ending at the empty connector.

'It's a fleet,' Mack said, as he peered at the navigation projection. 'Can you get any more detail?' he asked.

The young man concentrated; furrows crisscrossed his brow while drops of sweat fell on his desk. Then, the view of the fleet cleared. Mack gasped at what he was seeing. He sensed the Overlord's surprise as well. 'It looks like they lost one. That – that looks like the *Hela*.' He grabbed a mike from the deep space comms unit. 'Zaval, Zaval, tell me that's you.' He repeated the message, signing his own name and rank. With no reply, he switched to a more formal request for identity. But nothing came back.

The Eight watched, all the while wondering how this was possible. The *Hela* back from the Anan Galaxy with a tug and two transporters. He flashed with a burst of purple light, surprising all around with his anger. *Had Frike found them and teamed up with The Sixth? I cannot leave this to chance. No, we intercept and destroy.* His voice thundered, 'Who is in that fleet? Niamh, how soon can you have the *Monarch* in orbit?'

'We were planning a test flight tomorrow, but we'll bring it forward. I can have her up in four hours.'

'Do it,' he ordered, his tone underlining the urgency.

Niamh grabbed Geoff. 'You're on comms. Let's go.'

They both ran from the room, Geoff's brain racing at the notion of what was to come. His prayers answered, but not the way he expected! The rest waited and watched.

After a long hour passed, there was a crackle and the sound of a faint message. But it died. More silence stoked their fears. Until minutes later, a familiar voice caressed Mack's ear.

'General, it is I, Captain Quriel. Zaval is here as well. We need help. A doctor and transport. Do you have a ship?'

Relief coursed from Mack's voice. 'Yes, we do.'

A quiet question flashed from The Eight. 'Ask him where is Frike, and who is in charge?'

The reply didn't come immediately and when it did the strain choked Quriel's voice. 'Frike is gone. Zaval is our leader, but now he's, ah, unwell. We will hold up at the edge of your solar system until help arrives.'

'We'll see you there,' Mack replied, wondering what ailed Zaval. Quriel's answer seemed to quell The Eight's unease, his energy mass flashing a soft blue. The priority was to get the *Monarch* flight-ready, and so far, the repairs of his chariot weren't finished. Since his arrival, enjoying old freedom, he had floated around in his oval blue energy mass.

Another crackle disturbed their comms, and then Quriel's voice returned. 'Please, General, come quick. Verteg Borea is dying.'

This time The Eight asked the question, projecting his voice to the mike. 'From what?'

With a faltering speech, Quriel explained, "from what!" But garbled and short, it left the gruesome bits out.

Still, a realisation that the Borea had faced unimaginable terrors started to sink into Tom, Robert and Janet, listening in the control centre. And, to cap it all, a vessel lost — with crew on board, they surmised. A sobering moment, damping the cheerful return of their prized *Hela*.

The Eight's reaction to Verteg's predicament amazed them all. 'I will go. Your doctor will not be able to do much, but we will take him and his team as well.' He turned and floated out of the room.

The rest stood stock still. It was Mack who broke the silence. 'Tom, you go too. You'll need your best soldiers. A solid force to guard The Eight and the *Monarch*. This could be a trap.' Ignoring Robert, Mack got up and walked stiffly out.

*

New World Solar System. EPTS: A139780

A clumsy takeoff heralded a new age for the rechristened *Borea1*. *Monarch*, the first starship owned by the Sullivan Parker Charter, sped off towards the edge of their solar system. Niamh's ingenious modifications littered the bridge. With the vessel's repairs incomplete, the journey tested the human crew's abilities. Unable to get the advanced Borea control panels working, she had spliced in simple human substitutes.

From a primitive touchscreen computer, Niamh did most of the piloting, flying the *Monarch* and crewing engineering at the same time. Kora's charting got them to the fleet in under eighteen hours, a real feat considering she was one of the first of their new crop of navigators. Geoff crewed comms, a post he had yearned for. Now under the pressure of real-life situations, his young face screamed terror.

Supposed to be a shakedown flight, not a rescue mission, Niamh worried about what they would find and how they could rescue an alien fleet? Tom, seated beside The Eight at the rear of the bridge, worried about the possible trap they were flying into. On the contrary, The Eight didn't display any concerns at all, his energy mass pulsing a calming soft blue light. Sometimes he would ask easy questions as if to encourage the fledgeling team. His gentle approach served to calm them all, the pressure of their first space flight as an all-human crew pressing on everyone. Approaching the fleet, Niamh cut the engines, letting the *Monarch* drift closer to the Borea's ships.

An eerie sight greeted them as the fleet came into view. 'Can you sharpen that image?' Tom asked.

Geoff played about with the long-range cameras until the clear bright view of the fleet parked in space burst out on their bridge viewscreen. They had never seen anything comparable with *Tug 1*, nor had the human crew believed anything like it existed. Resembling a shimmering spider's web, the trammel stretched out behind the tug enveloping the *Hela*, transporter *One* and *Two*. The severed connection waving behind *Two* proclaimed to all those watching on the *Monarch*, "Yes, we lost a ship." A grim sight followed by gasps of surprise.

Geoff's quivering voice broke the silence. 'I've a contact, in English. It's Siba!' he remembered the quiet alien from the journey to the colony. *Polite and helpful* were his happy memories of her. 'On screen now,' he said as Siba's picture appeared on one side of the bridge screen. On Tom's orders, Geoff restricted the comms – voice only from the *Monarch*. No need to give too much away.

A gaunt and tired Siba looked back at them. Worry lines etched her soft porcelain skin, and instead of the brilliant white, her face was a pale grey. 'Geoffrey, we need help. Have you a doctor on board?'

Tom answered. 'Siba, its Tom Parker; Niamh is here as well. Yes, we have a doctor. What's happened to your fleet? How many are left onboard? Do you have engine power…?'

Like a dam bursting, it came gushing out. The young Borea pilot couldn't hold back her emotions any longer. The sorry tale emerged and between her sobs another of her crew chirped in. After the catastrophe of losing Alke's ship, the fleet had ploughed on. Zaval, the Pilot, stayed on the bridge of *Tug 1* with Verteg throughout the remaining five-cycle journey. Before they arrived in the New World solar system, Zaval had collapsed and was carried off the bridge to his cabin. The last time they checked on him, he was comatose and reeked of a foul odour.

Verteg, getting weaker by the minute, managed to get the fleet through the fold and parked where they were now. Unable to do any more, she had retired to the captain's cabin, where she was now – unconscious. The Anan plasma sustaining her life had run out, and her life signs were fading fast. None of the conscious crew on the tug had the knowledge to retract the trammel. Siba, trapped on the trammel-encased *Two*, could not help the fleet.

'So,' Siba finished, 'the vessels are locked together in the tow. No one on *Tug 1*, save Zaval and Verteg, have the experience to release it.' A sigh signalled the end of Siba's tale.

All too confused, thought The Eight. *First, Quriel's account and then Siba's.* Quriel had mentioned Verteg's injuries, but wanting to know more, The Eight flashed a message to Geoff. *'Ask her what happened to Verteg.'*

A horror movie from the *Hela* answered that question. Frike's merciless beating of the young pilot played across the *Monarch's* big screen. Verteg's screams added to the virtual terror playing in their bridge.

Guilt flowed through Niamh's mind as she realised what she and The Eight's escape had sparked. His thoughts filled her mind. *Not your fault, my child. It's the monster's doing. Where is he?*

'And where's Frike now?' Niamh asked.

Quriel answered from the bridge of the *Hela*. It was he who had played the video. Ever the soldier, he had known how suspicious their arrival was. Coupled with the unplanned stranding of their fleet, the whole affair screamed "trap". He hadn't met the Parkers but from what his father had told him, the ruthless Thomas wouldn't put The Eight or the colony in danger. Unprepared, Quriel had delivered a scant outline of the Borea's sour tale on a garbled audio feed with Mack, their first contact. Until they proved themselves, the Borea would be toxic here in The Eight's stronghold. Suspecting their Overlord was on the *Monarch*, Quriel knew his next words would be pivotal in the Borea's acceptance.

'He's gone. And it looks like Demard killed him with what few followers he had left. Mrs Parker, I must assure you, our intentions are honourable. These vessels are for The Eight's campaign against The Sixth. What happened in the Anan Galaxy is a blot on our and my father's name. We are here to rectify that. But first, Verteg's life is all I ask of you. Please ...' Quriel's voiced faded at the thought of losing Verteg when help was so near.

On the *Monarch*, Tom looked over at Niamh. She shrugged her shoulders and nodded at The Eight. On cue, Geoff muted their transmission. 'What do you think?' Tom asked

'I haven't a clue what that tow's about. But Verteg, she needs our help,' Niamh replied.

'Siba is right,' The Eight said. 'Withdrawing the trammel is as complicated as spinning it. If they don't get it right, it can rip a ship apart. I will heal Verteg. We will transfer over to *Tug1* on a shuttle.'

Shaking his head, doubting Thomas voiced his concern. 'It could be a trap.'

'I doubt it, Thomas. I sense sorrow and hurt. They are beaten. But if you are right, you have ten of your best. We take them and the doctor. Niamh, you stay on the Monarch.' With that, he turned and left the bridge, the rest, without another word, followed their Overlord.

*

Clutching his all-important ledger, the elder Borea, with the young female technician, waited for the rescue shuttle to dock. An extended version of the standard Aknar military class, it just about fit into the tug's small commercial shuttle bay. Piloted by one of Tom's soldiers, it yawed precariously above the steel deck. Worse still, its stabilising fins oscillated dangerously close to the walls of the shuttle bay. Taken aback by the pilot's rough touch, the two Borea ran for cover. With a bang, the shuttle touched down, sparks flying as it skidded on the deck. The far bulkhead flashed forwards into the pilot's view; doing all he could to arrest the clumsy landing, he closed his eyes. To his relief, yielding to friction, the shuttle miraculously stopped millimetres from the tug's hull. Its rear door burst open. Ignoring their rough landing, ten human soldiers, dressed in black Anan combat suits wielding heavy-duty grav guns, rushed out. The phalanx formed a protective guard in front of the shuttle, and to the amazement of the two welcoming Borea, The Eight floated out.

Still shaken by the ungainly landing, the elder knelt down. 'Overlord, we are sorry for what happened—'

'Enough of that. Take me to Verteg now,' The Eight boomed, his voice reverberating through the shuttle bay.

It was the young technician who reacted first; sprinting off, she shouted for him to follow. If they were to help her cousin, there was no time to waste. With his guards in hot pursuit, The Eight followed the young woman to the captain's cabin. The girl whimpered as she entered; a rotten smell permeated the air. Verteg lay in a heap on the bed, her bandages pockmarked with yellow staining from the pus leeching from her wounds.

The girl tried to talk, but The Eight shushed her, ordering her to leave and close the door.

He floated over to Verteg, sensing how close to death she was. He needed to hurry, but first things first. *How bad and how much of her body is destroyed?* A blue haze filled the small cabin and Verteg floated off the bed as The Eight started to work on her. Gently, he stripped the bandages from her body. Unseen hands unwound the poisoned bindings and cut her tunic from her body until she floated naked in the air, the remains of her discharge-stained tunic and bandages cast-off in a heap on the deck. The Eight delved deep into Verteg's cold body. Her faint heartbeat told an unkind story – she was alive, but only just. How one being could do something so horrifying to another was beyond The Eight. He couldn't fathom how a brain, created by the Overlords, could do such a deed. *Well, there was worse done in the universe*, he thought, *yes there was*, as he focused on Verteg's condition.

Sepsis had taken hold. Internal injuries that the Anan plasma had held at bay were now killing her. Racked with infection, Verteg's time had come. No human doctor could have saved her. The Eight turned off her pain receptors and got to work, rebuilding her body from the inside out. First was her heart – a bruise on the left wall from when Frike had stamped on her chest was erased. Tiny shards of plaque, in the coronary arteries, dissolved. Then on to the lungs, liver and kidneys, all suffering from Frike's boot. It was a slow, tedious job rebuilding cells from their atomic level up. The Eight never stopped, his blue shroud covering Verteg inside and out. For the two time segments that he worked on her internals, no one disturbed him. The Borea tech sat outside the room surrounded by Tom's soldiers, all the while aching for her friend and cousin's wellbeing.

After repairing Verteg's organs, The Eight paused to re-examine her. Externally, her once soft green skin was pockmarked with purple and black bruising. Making matters worse, ugly compound fractures, pierced her skin. Future existence didn't look pretty for Verteg, her once beautiful face devastated by the monster who had crushed her nose back into her head. But before The Eight started on that, he needed to heal her blood. Coursing through her arteries and veins, his blue veil sifted out festering cells, rebuilding the life-sustaining fluid. It took time, but the ethereal transfusion finally banished the infections. He felt her breathing deepen while her heartbeat grew stronger. A positive response. *Good*, The Eight thought, knowing the next part of the process demanded Verteg sustain her own life.

Ensuring Verteg's pain receptors were still inhibited and she remained unconscious, The Eight started on the rebuild of the woman's skeleton. He didn't stop at fixing or replacing damaged bones but continued with her muscles, and the other soft tissues, upgrading it all to give her a longer and fuller life. Finally, he entered her brain.

Although unconscious, she sensed his arrival. *'Who are you?'* Verteg asked her gentle visitor.

'I am The Eight.'

The simple statement shocked Verteg, spiking her heartbeat. *'Either you're alive, or I'm dead,'* was the thought that leaked from her brain.

'Verteg, we are both most certainly alive. You must relax while I repair your brain.'

'Why, Overlord? Why are you doing this for me?'

'You suffered at the hands of the one who nearly extinguished me. And, your father, Demard, served me well. It was his actions that allowed Niamh and I to escape. He slowed down Frike, let Niamh escape on a shuttle and allowed Quriel into the base. Without him, I would not be here.'

'Demard was my father?'

'Yes, he was. Now stay quiet, I have work to do.'

She allowed her brain to drift off to sleep as The Eight repaired the damage from the stress the beating had caused. Her intelligence astounded even him. Nothing wanting there, but her resilience and confidence needed some slight grooming. Withdrawing from her body back into his oval mass, he admired his handy exertions. Green glowing skin, soft and shining like porcelain, covered her body. Her long dark blue hair shone as it fell across her beautiful face. Toned muscles emphasised her feminine curves. All evidence of the monster's gruesome work was banished. Allowing her to float back on the bed, The Eight swept a coverlet over her. He left the room, surprising those waiting outside.

'Let her sleep for one time segment. Then wake her. She will need a new ship suit,' The Eight said to the young tech. The girl peeped into the room. She gasped with joy at the sight of her cousin fast asleep on the bed. Tiptoeing in, she picked up the remains of the bandages and tunic, left and closed the door.

While The Eight healed Verteg, the human doctor visited the Pilot. Lying in one of the lower deck cabins, Zaval was still comatose. As soon as the Doc entered the room, he knew what was wrong. The smell of stale booze punched his nose. Two empty bottles lay beside the drunken alien, and stains in the bedclothes showed how far he was gone. Another half-empty bottle stood on a bedside table. The doctor sighed as he examined the white label. He knew Zaval had liked a drink on Earth but didn't ever suspect how addicted he was to the stuff. He couldn't contemplate the pressures that had forced this once-proud Pilot into such a state. The Doc did as much as he could. With one of Tom's men, he stripped Zaval, changed the bedclothes and made him as comfortable as possible. After that, he set up an intravenous drip, delivering much-needed fluid, sugars and vitamins to the fallen alien.

Returning to the bridge on *Tug 1*, the Doc told Tom what ailed The Pilot. 'He'll need constant watching.'

By now, nothing shocked Tom. 'We'll see to that until we get back to the colony,' he said.

It was a long wait for The Eight to return from healing Verteg. When he did, his silence spoke volumes. With nothing else to do, the Borea crew languished on the bridge. The comms stayed still, the whole fleet and the *Monarch* waiting for nobody knew what! It was hope. Faith in The Eight filled their minds, a newfound trust that he would help them.

Exactly one segment after The Eight returned to the bridge, carrying a hot brew, the young Borea technician left to wake Verteg. Fifteen minutes later, beaming from ear to ear and the dimple on her cheek shining with new life, the young girl returned with Verteg. Dressed in a clean blue ship suit, the beautiful young woman strode confidently across the bridge. Kneeling before The Eight, for the first time since her beating Verteg spoke. Her sharp, commanding tone filled the bridge. 'Overlord, thank you for saving my life; I pledge it to your service.' She glanced around at the rest of her family. 'As I'm sure the rest do as well.'

They fell to the floor in unison. The bridge viewscreen burst into life, showing split views of the bridges on the *Hela*, transporters *One* and *Two*. The Borea crews were kneeling, and in one voice shouting over and over, 'The Eight, The Eight, The Eight …'

Even the battle-hardened soldiers had tears in their eyes as the remaining Borea family threw their lot in behind their Overlord. The Eight stayed silent.

It was Tom who brought matters back to reality. 'Verteg, how will we get this fleet back to our New World?' he asked in haltering Anan.

Verteg stood up and smiled at the human who appeared to be in command of the soldiers occupying her bridge. 'And you are?' she asked back.

'Thomas Parker. I'm The Eight's security chief.'

A cheeky smile played across Verteg's lips. 'Well, you didn't do a good job of that, did you? We nearly lost him to my great-uncle, Frike.'

That she could say his name and joke about what had gone before spoke volumes for what The Eight had done for her. Her mind was crystal clear, no animosity or fear. A new Verteg, bright as a button, oozing intelligence and beauty. She had rooted Tom. Speechless, he watched as she strode to tow control, completely ignoring him and his soldiers. Her hands glided across the console as she interrogated the system. Within minutes, she barked an order to her crew. They gathered around as the teams on the other three vessels listened in. Her instructions, swift and precise, left no doubt about who was in command.

Taking the captain's chair, she turned to The Eight. 'Overlord, we will make our way into orbit around your new planet. It will take two cycles. Then I will withdraw the tow. You are welcome to come with us, or you could return to your flagship. It will get you home faster.'

The Eight looked at Verteg; he felt a deep sense of pride. Like when Niamh first folded space. He flashed with blue light. *Yes, he would like to stay and watch, and it would show his trust in the Borea.* 'Thomas, leave four of your men here with me; they can take it in turns to watch Zaval. Return with the rest to the *Monarch*.'

Tom shook his head. It defied logic. But there was no arguing with The Eight. Not now. Ten minutes later, he was back on the *Monarch*, his face black as thunder.

'That went well. We didn't have to do anything,' Niamh chirped, happy that the fleet was back up and running itself. 'Jeez, you look like shite. What happened over there? Did somebody hit you?'

*

While the *Monarch* assisted the fleet, the colony faced a logistical nightmare with accommodating four new ships. None could stay in orbit for fear of discovery. The spaceport had been extended in anticipation of new arrivals, but no one had foreseen the coming of this fleet. At his best guess, Robert needed a square kilometre of open sandy ground along the pristine beach. Land doesn't clear itself! Reviving the four large grav dozers, the colonists worked around the clock to clear the trees, bulldozing the debris into the sea and extending the colony's boundary fence with sand and wooden dykes. Once again, mankind made their mark, gouging out the New World's primeval ecosystem in a rush of progress.

*

It took time, but with Verteg in command of the fleet, they settled into orbit around the New World. Reversing the process the Pilot had adopted when starting the tow, she withdrew the trammel without damaging their ships. Using the shuttles to get back into orbit, she set down *Tug 1*, the *Hela* and *One* on Fort Leslie's spaceport. Developing her own piloting skills, Siba landed *Two*. Robert watched each ship land, personally welcoming the Borea family and Quriel with his Aknar troops to Fort Leslie.

The human colonists happily made arrangements for the aliens' accommodation. Brushing off the usual jibes about raw insects and mice, Robert asked the cooks to rustle up something that might suit their delicate pallet. But it was Zaval, the Pilot, who caused him the most concern. As soon as *Tug 1* landed, still unconscious, the medical team took him to their hospital. After the *Hela* landed, Robert took Quriel to be by his side. He stayed in the hospital, beside his father, hoping for his recovery.

As dusk settled, the colony buzzed with the sound of new voices, trying to understand English and poorly spoken Anan. Prized voice translators, in short supply, were the order of the day. Siba, delighted to be back, rekindled old acquaintances, introducing her family to her lost friends. Mack welcomed the Aknar soldiers who soon settled in with Tom's own troops, the alien soldiers a welcome addition to their force.

Repaired in his absence, The Eight returned to his chariot. Floating up above the colony, the mighty Overlord examined his new fleet that lay on the beach. The most potent battleship in the galaxy, the *Hela*, two inter-system transporters and a tug. *Five starships! Who would have guessed it?* he thought. A few drops of rain started to fall, the black cloudy sky heralding the arrival of another squall. He watched the Borea elder, locked in conversation with Cylla Ora, his ledger open in front of him. The wheels of business were churning away, even in this dire time. As the rain started, they ran for cover. If The Eight could smile, he would; instead, he flashed a blue light, satisfied with what had transpired. Thanks to the Borea, Quriel and his loyal Aknar soldiers, he had a small fleet.

CHAPTER NINETEEN

Borea Family Order

Since the loss of Charter status and the debarring of the Borea name, a new family structure developed, providing some semblance of clan cohesion. The title, Pilot, is now conferred on the principal experienced galactic navigator and pilot. The Pilot functions as the head of the family and will make day-to-day decisions on the family's wellbeing and development. Family elders, comms officers and engineers shall assist the Pilot in all aspects of family business. The ultimate goal of the Pilot is to restore the family's Charter status, name and seat at the Energy Exchange.

‹ **Extract from: the journal of Demard Borea**

*

The Colony, Fort Leslie. EPTS: A139849

IN THE MIDDLE OF THE night, the noise of the rain falling on the flat roof of the hospital woke the Pilot. He blinked as his eyes focused on the white antiseptic room. Human medicine, he realised, while sniffing in disgust at the primitive tube plugged into his arm. Pressure on his bladder prompted him to sit up on the bed. Unbeknown to him, to get some badly needed rest, Quriel had departed a short time ago. Now alone, Zaval yanked the invasive tube out. 'Ouch,' he cried, the pain prodding his brain back into action. *They made it*, he thought. *Back on the New World. By The One, we have done it.* His dry mouth felt like crotch rot, his head pounded and his stomach growled, demanding food. His eyes fell on the end of the bed where a clean ship garb lay folded. Ripping off the scant hospital gown, he threw on the greyish suit. A pair of boots languished under the bed. He slipped them on as well. Masked by the thundering fall of the rain on the roof, he padded out of his room. And then, under cover of the downpour's sound, on past a human sleeping in the nurse's station along the corridor.

Outside the hospital, he pissed in the cover of the doorway. He sighed as the gush of yellowish liquid relieved the pain in his bladder. Food was only a stone's throw away – he needed that first. Pulling up his hood, he ran along a walkway to the colony's large canteen. The two Italian cooks were cleaning up after the welcoming party for their new arrivals. One looked at the Pilot; he remembered him – the alien who smoked and liked a drink.

'You hungry?' he asked, staring at the wet, bedraggled Pilot.

'Why do you think I'm here,' the Pilot snapped back.

The cook turned away. 'I've no time for grumpy aliens. Cold cuts are on that table over there,' he shouted, pointing to a meagre offering left out for any overnight stragglers. Ignoring the Pilot, he hurried back into his kitchen.

Stuffing food into his mouth, the Pilot took stock of where he was. Shaking from the cold, he wanted to be back in his cabin on the *Hela* – the only place Zaval could call home. He hardly tasted the meats and bread, as his mouth ground down the sustenance before his throat sent it to his stomach for processing. That's all it was to him – fuel to get him home.

Making his way back to the doorway, he watched the rain ease off. The landing pad was near two kilometres away – he'd need more than the wet ship garb he was wearing. Rummaging in a nearby closet, he stole a parka. Like a thief in the night, the once-proud Pilot scurried along the waterlogged path to the space dock.

Bathed in soft light, spilling out from the neighbouring ship's windows, the golden cylinder-shaped *Hela* beckoned him on. Two of Tom's night guards stood under cover of the ship's gangway, their presence shattering the deserted colony night.

Recognising the Pilot, one stared at the purebreed and asked, 'You okay?'

'Fine, I'm fine,' the Pilot responded, keeping his head low.

'Where you going?'

'Back to my cabin. I live here,' he grunted.

Through the night, some human and alien revellers had sparked new liaisons. Looking the other way, the discreet soldiers closed their eyes to the strange coming and goings between the ship and the town. By now, nothing surprised them. 'On you go, Pilot. Good to see you back,' came the cheery response.

Nodding in acknowledgement of the man's compliment, his head held high above his long neck, the Pilot walked up the gangway. Once inside the confines of the *Hela*, he ran to his cabin. Opening the door, the sparkling clean view shocked him. The bedclothes were changed and everything was put away. He yelled as he tried to open the lock on his closet. His hands shaking, he keyed in the code. A click and the latch sprung. He near tore the door off its hinges in anticipation. It opened and his eyes caressed the boxes stacked inside – his stash of booze was safe. Shaking with the cold, he opened the first box and pulled out a bottle of red wine. A Marlborough Pinot Noir, light and fruity, but he hardly noticed the label.

Stripping off his clothes and boots, he took the bottle into the shower. Bathed in hot water, he curled up on the ground. His wet hands gripped the screw cap and with a grunt he broke the metal seal, unwinding the cap. Raising the bottle to his lips, he closed his eyes as the red liquid poured into his mouth. The fine wine's bouquet, pierced with apricots and blueberries, was lost on the Pilot's pallet. All he craved was the alcohol within. Greedily guzzling the red liquid straight from the bottle, with two long sucks, he had a third of it gone. Happily lying back in hot water, he smiled for the first time as the alcohol buzz hit his brain and the knot in his stomach relaxed.

*

Across in the colony, the sound of rain falling on the roof of the pod woke her. Early morning, she guessed, as the grey light of dawn danced in. With heavy rain, their New World's weather announced the end of their summer. Overnight, the river beside their settlement had burst its banks while the hills around formed high cascading waterfalls. Their only saving grace was Robert's foresight in positioning the town on high ground. He was asleep beside her, his blue arm curled around her waist and his face resting on her long brown hair.

Gently untangling herself from him, she slipped from the bed. Wrapping her naked body in a towel, she went to look out the window. If it weren't so disastrous, the scene below would have been breathtaking. The *Hela* lay on its space dock surrounded by water and beside it was the *Monarch*, *Richard*, *George* and *Maeve*. The transporters were renamed *Maeve* and *George* and the tug *Richard*. The *Monarch* was Niamh's choice for the *Boreal*. It didn't look so formidable now with its pennon wings and bow-fin disappearing into the water that had engulfed their space dock. She watched as a lone figure, hiding under an umbrella, picked their way through the pools of water onto the *Hela*.

'It's still raining,' he said, sitting up in the bed and looking across at her.

'Yes, it's a mess down there.'

He pulled back the covers. 'Come on back to bed. There's no work today.'

'Robert, be serious for a minute. You think of only one thing.'

'You haven't complained about that before.'

'We need to talk about this.'

'All right, all right. I'll make the tea,' Robert said, as he got up from the bed. 'And be flattered with that, there's no much of it left.'

She smiled at him as he started to dress. 'I'm sorry, Robert, but we can't go on like this.'

They sat in silence at the small table in his pod as they sipped the last of the tea. He looked across at her. 'Janet, I really don't care what Mack thinks. He never made his move. We pushed and cajoled him, but he kept saying, "We take things slower on Anan". They have a different lifespan than us.'

He was right, General Arie Machai, The Eight's representative on the colony, had formed a bond with Janet when he first met her in Christchurch. Back then, he had said, '… you are the organiser, you do all the work. You will turn out to be our main administrator and planner, you'll see.' After that, Janet had progressed from receptionist to the Project Planner and was always at Mack's side. Rumour of romance abounded. Even the Empress had hoped for the bond to be consummated. But despite Tom and Robert's encouragement, Mack faltered. Secretly in love with the beautiful Kiwi, Robert finally wooed her himself.

From twinkling hazel eyes, Janet looked at him. 'And is that all I am to you – a lifespan?'

He withered under her gaze. 'A poor choice of words. I'm sorry,' he said. Taking her hand, his voice trembled, 'Janet, I've realised how important you are to me. I should have made that move ages ago. The first time I saw you, you remember – in Christchurch.'

She smiled and nodded, as she remembered that day he had entered the office for the interview; she and Kath had been speechless at the sight of the big sandy-haired Scotsman in his kilt.

'I wanted you then and kept that bottled up all this time. The Eight used to chastise me for not moving on after losing my family. Well, I wanted to Janet, but I was too much of a gentleman to interfere with what I believed was a developing relationship. You and Mack. Not now, Janet. I'll fight for you. You mean more to me now than anything else.'

Tears leaked down her sun-stained face. 'Robert, you're impossible.'

'Why? I'm telling you like it is. Do we break up? Is that what you want?'

Wiping the tears from her face, she shook her head. 'It's for the project, Robert; we're not supposed to be together.'

'In case you missed that part, I thought it was you I was making love to for the past month,' he said, as he reached over and kissed her.

She laughed. 'Be serious.'

'I've tried to talk to Mack, but he'll have none of it. Ignores me, he does. How's he treating you?'

'It's like nothing has happened. It's infuriating. I don't know what the answer is.'

He leaned across the table, looking intently at her. 'Once we get that mess outside sorted, a ship goes back to Earth.'

'What are you thinking?'

'Mack said he would stay here. He has work to do with the bookkeeper. Maybe she'll spear him with her tail.'

'Oh, that's terrible Robert. Cylla – that's her name. And yes, she's a lot to do and can only do it here. It's something to do with the comms to their Energy Exchange and the extraction program.'

'I need to go back to Earth. I'm not needed here. Shona and Blair can run this place.'

'What about the off-world extraction of blue – space mining?'

'Blair can do that with some of the Pilot's clan. They know how that stuff works.' He reached across the table and cupped her head in his large hands. Will you come, Janet? I want you by my side; and we'll need a planner as well.'

She looked into his blue eyes. The sound of the rain hitting the roof cut through their silence. Then she sighed. 'It's just a planner you want, you big softie,' she said, smiling.

'You'll come.'

'Of course, I'll come. You won't be able to organise anything without me.' She paused as he grinned from ear to ear. She looked at him as the sound of the rain continued its incessant patter. 'Now, Robert, I'm going back to bed,' Janet said, as she stood up, letting the towel drop to the floor.

*

On that wet morning, Quriel, hearing of his father's return, looked into his cabin on the *Hela*. He found Zaval sound asleep in his bed, snoring peacefully. Bottles hidden and his closet locked, all signs of the midnight binge erased. And, to further the illusion, the sweet smell of soap permeated the cabin's air. Satisfied the human's medicine had worked, Quriel left his father to sleep.

At the same time, a rumour reached Niamh of a post-party breakfast on the *Hela*. Impatient to be back on her old friend, she returned to the ship she had rebuilt. She shivered from the damp chill as she picked her way through the puddles, sheltering under a large umbrella. The galley was abuzz with a strange mix of humans and aliens celebrating the morning after the welcoming party. Still suffering from blue exposure, her appearance caused a momentary stir. The Borea had heard and knew what had caused the contamination. Heads bowed and eyes averted, they chose to ignore it as if nothing had happened. Glad that was over with, Niamh sat with Verteg, wanting to catch up on the *Hela's* story after she had left on the *Monarch*.

They were buried in conversation when the door of the galley burst open and the Pilot entered, dressed in a new ship garb, his head shining white, his long neck stretched straight above his shoulders and smelling of soap. Holding his head high with his white skin gleaming, he oozed with strength and authority as if to say to all, "Zaval is back". He sat down, awkwardly at the table beside Niamh and Verteg.

Amazed she was healed, Zaval looked across at Verteg. His voice quivered with emotion at seeing her for the first time. 'How is this possible?' he asked.

She smiled. 'The Eight healed me,' was all she could say, delighted to have her mentor back.

Zaval nodded as if to say, *I know why he did that.* Then he glanced at Niamh. *Blue contamination; no surprise there,* he thought. His hands stayed below the table as he sighed, lingering and pensive. A thought flashed in his mind. *I trained both of them, and still, I caused them such pain.*

Above the sweet smell of soap, Niamh could smell his fresh breath. *He's washed and had a deep clean at that,* she thought. 'How you feeling, Pilot?'

Back to life, he sat up at the table, licked his lips and announced in a firm voice, 'Good, and I'm hungry. And don't call me by that name again. I am Zaval.'

Verteg gasped in surprise but said nothing. The rest of the galley's occupants had gone silent, watching the unfolding drama with interest. No one had expected him to make such an appearance and the Borea were delighted to see him. Their saviour, head of the family recovering from his upset.

'Well, Zaval, here's some fresh bread and coffee,' Niamh said as she passed over the food. Carefully half-filling a mug, she placed it down in front of him.

He brought his hands up to the table and closing his long bony fingers around the mug, lifted it up. Then it happened. His hands started to shake, slowly at first, changing into an uncontrolled convulsion. Niamh grabbed the cup of coffee, wrenching it out of Zaval's hand before the hot liquid spilt out. 'In the name of The One, what manner of ailment is this?'

'It's called the shakes,' she said, tears in her eyes at her friend's distress. 'Zaval, you need help; you're addicted to the stuff. We call that alcoholism. Here, I'll help you,' Niamh said, as she held the mug up to the Pilot's lips. 'You need the coffee and the food.'

As the Pilot drank and ate, Niamh looked across at Verteg. There were tears in their eyes as they looked at their talented tutor. But business beckoned and it was high time she broached this subject with him – they lacked competent pilots. She had heard how Tom's soldier had nearly flown the shuttle straight through the tug, crashing it onto the deck to stop it. Flying shuttles in space was different from driving grav platforms on the planet. She had discussed the problem with Janet, Tom and Robert. Without the proper training infrastructure, no matter how many ships they had, humans wouldn't get too far in developing space flight. So far, they had muddled through with Zaval's and The Eight's help. But to make progress, they needed much more.

Niamh handed him another piece of bread. 'Zaval, we need you back; we have work for you.'

'Niamh, in case you missed anything, I am finished. I'm burned out. I've nothing left. Inside is like the void of space – black and empty. Verteg is the Pilot now. She will inherit that title in the family. She deserves that.'

Verteg shook her head and pursed her lips. *This was wrong, all wrong,* she thought.

'Zaval, you still have that deep well of knowledge. You have seen so much, had so many experiences in space. We need that.'

He sat back in his chair, sticking his nose in the air. 'And how do you propose to use it? Suck my brains out? Is that what you humans do to tired old aliens? I knew there was a darker side to you. Monsters you are.'

Niamh sat back and roared with laughter. 'O Zaval, you're still there, the same old Pilot.'

'I'm not the Pilot.'

'Well, you're still the same purebreed we met over a year ago. You are, you are.'

'Maybe, there is still some life left, but you must know I'll never fly again.'

'Don't say never, and that's not what we want you for.'

'Tell me, Niamh, what is it you want?'

'We need to train humans to fly and navigate in space and to crew these vessels. We want you to head up a space academy. And we'll need your expertise in the war effort and manufacturing. You would be a valuable consultant.'

'Ha, you think I will pass on my secrets to Earthlings so easily.'

'For the right price, I believe you will. Zaval, you could do this. We'll get you help on Earth for your addiction. It won't be easy but having a purpose in life helps. You'd make a great teacher and your expertise will be invaluable.'

He sat back and scratched his face then looked back at Niamh. 'You're serious about this?'

'Yes, it's the only way we'll get crews for the fleet. The war, Zaval. We'll never win it without good crews, no matter how many ships we build.'

'I never thought of that.' He paused and looked at Verteg.

Verteg's expression had changed; her eyes were brighter and he could sense she wanted him to do this. 'Zaval,' she started in a halting voice, 'we'll take a fleet to Earth. What you did for us, getting us away from the Anan Galaxy like that. It was an incredible feat. They'll tell legends about you. Also, you've restored the Borea name. The family owe you a debt. You should do this. Come with us to Earth, please.'

The two young women's eager eyes bore into him for an answer.

He hesitated. 'I have to think about this. Yes, I do. There would be certain conditions, contracts to be worked out. No answer yet. Now, I need more food!'

After that, as they finished their meal together, they sat in silence, the two women linked by the common bond of Zaval's expert schooling.

*

After filling his stomach, with hands still shaking, Zaval rushed back to his cabin. Once inside, he couldn't wait to open his closet's door. Hands shaking, he keyed in the code. The familiar click of the latch eased his mind as it sprung open. He looked inside. The stock of red wine depleted, he decided to try something else. Lifting out the boxes, he pushed them under the bed until at the bottom of the stash, he found what he wanted. Tearing the lid off the case, he withdrew a bottle of amber coloured spirit. The extravagant twenty-four faceted bottle, capped with a solid glass cork, contained seven hundred millilitres of whiskey. On the back of the container, the advertising blurb announced the blend of malt and grain whiskies contained "notes of orange peel and white chocolate". With a sharp twist, Zaval cracked the seal and wrenched the cork out. He sniffed the liquid, then put the bottle to his mouth, letting the fine liqueur splash on his lips. Removing the bottle, he licked them, tasting the forty-three per cent proof Japanese whiskey for the first time.

Age mellowed the harsh burning sensation a cheaper spirit would give. He smiled, put the bottle to his lips and swigged. Rolling the liquid around in his mouth he completely missed the more delicate "notes" of this expensive whiskey. All Zaval wanted was the numbing sensation of the alcohol. He swallowed, sat down on the bed and took another swig. By now, his brain was feeling the effects of the first gulp. He grinned to himself as he got comfortable, propping himself up on the bed where he could relax and sip at this earthly amber fluid.

Unburdening himself from the title of the Pilot had lifted a weight off his chest. He would take to his grave the images of the death of Demard, Alke and the rest of the family whom his ill-fated actions had killed. But for now, some respite beckoned. With the elder's guidance, Verteg would lead the family. Niamh's offer to start a training academy intrigued Zaval. He had seemed offhand about it and hadn't committed. *Wouldn't be the done thing to welcome such a promising offer from a human,* he had thought. But yes, he had volumes of notes on intergalactic travel, navigation, technical maintenance and the like. *The Borea Academy of Stellar Flight,* he mused. Yes, he would do that. This would be his last binge before he committed to it, and a new life. Tomorrow, yes, he would tell them tomorrow. From then on, no more booze.

For the first time in an age, happy in himself, he drunk away half the bottle. His alcohol-drugged thoughts wandered to the blue crystal in the bedside locker. He leaned over and with one hand opened the drawer and recovered the blue diamond. Deftly hanging it around his neck, he closed his eyes and grabbed it with his free hand, the other still clutching the bottle. He didn't need a nav-con to project his mind, only the crystal. Closing his eyes, he focused his mind on its power. With a flash of blue light, Zaval's consciousness was out of his body looking back at himself. A projection of the New World's solar system glowing with the light of the stars behind, burst out above him. His alcohol-drugged mind, drawn to the pure unadulterated fun of a trip through space, succumbed to the thrill.

In an instant, Zaval's mind leapt out into the space above the New World. An exhilarating ride as his ethereal presence circumnavigated the planet's two moons – both laden with blue energy. *More wealth for The Eight*, he thought as he gazed back at the New World. A habitable planet in the biped belt, warm and wet, teeming with life. Until they arrived, a virgin planet, devoid of intelligent bipeds, or spaceships – the galaxies around deserted. A haven of solitude, away from Anan's inter-galactic hubbub. The perfect place for The Eight to build a stronghold.

Zaval sped on, the view of the blue and green planet receding behind him. Out through the solar system, past barren planets and moons also loaded with blue. On to the last of the eleven planets where a gas giant languished in dark frozen space. Intrigued by its swirling vapour, he stopped to explore. *There's enough methane here to fuel a small universe*, he thought. The family business, always flowing through his veins. *Could be mined and used as carbon fuels.* The drug-induced flight raced him on into the next solar system, five light-years away. He paused and looked, as the planets twinkled an invite to visit.

Then it hit him. Like nothing, he had ever experienced before in all his days at spatial navigation. A bolt from the darkness wrenched him back to reality. A cold, deathly feeling gripped his ghostly consciousness. The unanswered question screamed in his mind. *What is that?* All he knew was he had to get back to his corporeal body. All else dissolved in his mind as he rushed back towards the New World. His consciousness travelling faster than he ever believed possible through the grey star-filled tube of space and time. It seemed an eternity until he was back in his cabin, gazing down at himself now lying prostrate in the bed, the remains of the bottle of amber liquid spilt across the white sheets. He screamed, but silence in the room told it all. *What is happening to me?* The answer glared back at him from the bed.

Zaval's books on spatial navigation detailed the demands such trips make on the corporeal engine. Exhaustion – it had happened to Niamh on her first flight on a shuttle to France. Knowing what would happen to her, the Pilot had brought a remedy along. A healthy body feeds the brain and sustains life when the person's consciousness is off galivanting in space. Normal fit purebreeds took for granted the ability of their body to maintain such activities. The feeble and those with the Anan sickness supplemented their capabilities by using enhancing drugs like Kake's bawrak. Unlike alcohol, it worked to amplify the senses and the pure-breed's physical abilities.

Alcohol, on the other hand, had a devastating effect on Zaval's body. The forty-three per cent proof spirit was something he hadn't drunk before. His liver, swollen from the previous binging on wine, couldn't break down the lethal drug. It continued to circulate in his bloodstream, releasing hormones that constricted his blood vessels. Zaval's blood pressure increased, and at the same time, to add to the mortal conflict going on inside his body, the whiskey distressed his heart. A deadly irregular beat – arrhythmia – plagued the life-sustaining organ. Trying to push blood to his brain through constricted vessels while suffering from arrhythmia, sent Zaval's heart into overdrive. It pulsed and pulsed ever faster until, eventually, it died. Blood flow stopped, and his brain, the only part of his body connected to his ethereal mind, started to die.

Floating outside his body, he could do nothing. He looked down at his own corporeal face, frozen in a smile, and realised his time had come. Heralding the death of his brain, the blue light in the crystal he gripped faded. He turned to look at the ghostly projection of his hands. Melting, like drops of clear water, they dripped away. He held them out from his body and watched, mesmerised, as they trickled into oblivion. He looked down at his feet, already pools of silvery droplets. The evaporating symptoms, droplets of his precious life leaching away, spread from his extremities to his torso, and finally his head. No time to think, or to contemplate on his life gone by, Zaval accepted his fate as his consciousness dissolved into nothing. His life force extinguished, the proud talented Pilot, Zaval Borea, was no more.

CHAPTER TWENTY

Extinction Weapons

Devices that have sufficient yield or force to wipe out an entire population, world or city, are classed as extinction weapons. Such armaments are typically (but not limited to), biological entities, chemical and nerve agents or fusion type weapons controlled by a nuclear fuse. After the third intergalactic war, the ruling Overlords agreed to a directive on the development, use and storage of such weapons. That directive states: only The One, following consultation with all Overlords, may issue a licence for the usage of extinction weapons. Those wishing to stockpile or develop such weapons may only do so under that licencing scheme. The full text of the directive is contained in Appendix 1 of this document.

   ‣ **Extract from: Prohibited Weapons and Associated Devices. General Arie Machai**

*

Planet Anan. EPTS: A139837

WHILE THE EIGHT BASKED IN the glory of gaining a lifeline with a scanty fleet, across the void of space, his nemesis continued to plot his demise.

'You will go with them, Nine,' The Sixth said.

'My Lord, I do not see the benefit of that. My place is here, in our home galaxy. I have much to do. We have discovered new deposits of blue to mine.'

The Sixth, not foreseeing The Ninth's objection, paused as he contemplated the young Overlord's argument. After a large flash of blue light, he replied, 'The purebreeds and the specialists you employ can do that. My Shoter will oversee it.'

'My strength is mining. Why do you not send The Seventh? He is the expert in intergalactic navigation. Not me.'

'He got the coordinates for your expedition – I need him here.'

'Why?'

'I want you to go. You are the logical choice; are you not with our troika?'

'I am, but I see why you chose me. I am the Ninth, the expendable one. If I am defeated by The Eight, he gains very little.'

'You will not be defeated by him. Direct combat amongst us is not our way. It never was.'

'So you say. But we are at war now, one you started. What do you expect him to do? Run away? I don't think so. If we meet, The Eight will challenge me.'

'Your arguments exasperate me. You will go. I need you to rule the ceirim. The purebreed crews and my geneticists will not be able to control them. Kochtos will only answer to an Overlord. You must go, Nine; I need you to go. We cannot leave species-y alone to propagate in the universe. I showed you their DNA. The Eight created an abomination that must be destroyed before it devastates all we have built. Do you not realise how important this is? That species must be wiped from the universe.'

'If it is so important, why do you not come as well? You must tell me, are you afraid of him?'

'How dare you make such baseless insinuations? After all I have done for you. I made you. You are The Ninth, an Overlord of my Ragma Galaxy – act like one.'

'I know fully what I am. I do not make idle accusations. I only ask simple questions – which you fail to answer – when I need to know how powerful Eight really is. You are not much help, Six, after asking me to undertake such an important venture.'

'You cannot fail, Nine. The ceirim is the most powerful weapon we ever devised. Kochtos will obey you. It is a simple journey.'

'Oh, spare me such baseless assumptions. Whenever has wiping out a population been "a simple journey"? Never before has this been done without the authorisation of The One. You are pushing the agenda – further than I ever thought possible. Stop, do not interrupt me, Six. I will go. I will do your bidding. But know this, when I succeed, you will elevate me, and I want my own galaxies.'

'Make this happen, Nine, and you shall have that. You will have The Seventh's best ships and crews. Some of our own people will be there as well. You will travel on the *Losh*. You know the commander. The fleet leader will be Captain Bardek. He discovered the location of species-y and is committed to our cause. You will see – this will work.'

'My Lord, it must work. Otherwise, I am finished. I will need blue.'

'There is a hoard assigned for the fleet. Go now, contact Seven. He has arranged your transport to Natok.'

*

Jair Galaxy, Planet Chaya. EPTS: A139839

The logistics of transporting the Overlord's most potent biological weapon across galaxies was proving to be a horrendous project. The Sixth lacked the skillset to plan such a mission. Previous transportations were undertaken by the Aknar Navy under the direction of The One. Since their last use, hundreds of orbits ago, the ceirim were stored in hibernation tubes on Natok. The Sixth and his team of geneticists had minimal experience in such tasks, shuffling around only small batches of the ceirim for testing and experimentation. Lying to The One that he had expunged them, he was left to his own devices in keeping them alive. Not the smartest of the Overlords, The Sixth lacked the wisdom for this, underestimating the challenges of containing the universe's most hazardous biological weapon.

Typical of his style, Six left it to his purebreed geneticists and Captain Bardek to put the plans together. If it went wrong, they would get the blame. The Seventh supplied the ships and crew, with Six providing only one, the *Losh*. The Ninth, one of the youngest Overlords, had never overseen anything like this before. Nor had he ever dealt with the ceirim. His initial misgivings were well-founded. It was Captain Bardek who had to put the whole sorry mess together. His first inkling of a problem was when the vessels first congregated in orbit around The Seventh's home world, Planet Chaya in the Jair Galaxy.

*

In orbit around Chaya for three cycles, Bardek watched the assembling fleet's efforts to prepare for the project. Standing on the bridge of his command vessel, *Chad*, his eyes kept scanning the vessel's timepiece. Always, it advanced faster than the work's progress.

It flashed, then in a drab machine voice, announced a milestone time. 'Blue fuelling complete. Departure in minus one cycle.'

Bardek cringed. Despite bunkering blue, they were light-years away from being ready. The crews that had arrived were still bedding in on the six cruisers, and still more were to come. Loading vital supplies and weapons was half done, and the drive maintenance, scrubbing the blue manifolds, hadn't even started on three of the six ships. He looked out from the bridge. The comings and goings from the vessels were like a procession of giddy children. Shuttles and transporters commuting between ships and the planet. No disciplined lanes as he had directed. And, as he looked at the schedule on his command screen, over half hadn't got authorisation. A veil of rage floated across his eyes. Heads would roll. But it wasn't like he had enough crew to drag before him to whip! He was finding it hard enough to get experienced people. He had expected to have the squad from his exploration craft on his flagship, but no. The Seventh had kept them back to crew his own vessel – the best of them all. Left with the dregs, as always. The Sixth was sending some more techs from Anan, but Bardek knew, they wouldn't be the finest!

He breathed in hard to quell his anger as he watched a medium-sized people carrier leave the *Shaqa*. Expanding the on-screen view, he could see the multicoloured livery of the *Pleasure Palace*! *What in the name of The One is that doing here?* he wondered as it started to descend to the planet.

At the same time, a similarly sized craft, that had ascended from Chaya popped up in orbit. It sped towards *Chad* then twisted upside down and turned one-eighty degrees back towards the departing *Pleasure Palace*. Bardek groaned. From the erratic flight, he guessed the pilot had lost spatial awareness. A crash was imminent. The shuttle sped on, straight towards the unsuspecting *Pleasure Palace*. Space is silent, but Bardek could imagine the bang as the two craft collided. The force of the impact sent

Pleasure Palace spiralling towards his ship. Those on his bridge ran for cover as the ill-fated vessel careered end over end towards them. It struck the bridge, at the side of the crescent-shaped viewport. Bardek stood stock still. *Pleasure Palace,* splitting in two, bounced off the thick transparent bulkhead. The brightly adorned young male and female occupants spilt out into space, their bodies disintegrating under the onslaught of space's cold vacuum. Their remains – blood, guts and the like – splattered across *Chad's* bridge window.

Bardek screamed, not at the loss of life but at the sheer loss of any type of discipline and organisation. He roared, 'Who's on that shuttle?'

His crew scuttled back onto the bridge. Frantic calls established who the culprit was.

'It's a cryo-team,' Comms offered.

With a face like thunder, he turned to face Comms. 'Are you sure?'

'Yes,' was her quiet response.

'Get a rescue shuttle to them. Now,' Bardek shouted to his crew. The cryo-techs were vital to the mission; he couldn't afford to lose any.

Half a seg later, the extent of the dramatic loss of the accident emerged – the cryo-team's transporter, damaged beyond use, and the demise of *Pleasure Palace* and its crew. And, for Bardek, worst of all was the death of seven of the twenty-five cryo-techs. It appeared they were sightseeing out the windows with their flight harnesses undone when their craft turned upside down. He wasn't surprised when that morsel of information was handed up.

But, despite his impervious skin, Bardek felt for those who had died on the *Pleasure Palace*. No fault of their own; they shouldn't have been there. The male and female crew, trying to eke out a living selling their bodies for a few UC's and, to die like that! Not good enough. He'd have someone's hide for that. When he found out who had invited those poor souls here, he'd feed them to the ceirim. Not now, the mission was all that mattered. Thoughts of the ceirim filled his mind. It was the only way to restore some semblance of discipline amongst the fleet. Put the fear of the black monsters and what they could do into everyone. That's what he'd do. It was the only way.

Making his way to comms, Bardek opened a ship-wide channel. 'All ships, all ships, this is your Commander Bardek. By my order, we leave this orbit in one time seg. I repeat, one time segment. Prepare to get your ships underway. We assemble at Natok. No excuses. Navigation and orbit coordinates to follow. End of transmission.'

Silence followed. Comms' small voice cut the tension. 'Captain, will I relay that order to our shipping base. All the remaining supplies, people and weapons, will need to be transported to rendezvous with us in the Jora galaxy.'

For the first time, Bardek smiled. At last, the urgency was beginning to sink in. No excuses, just the practicalities of what needed to happen. 'Yes, Comms, make that happen.' Walking to his day room, he listened to his crew erupt with action. Engines to start, coordinates to plot and transmit to the fleet and all the other mundane tasks to get an intergalactic flotilla out of orbit into a fold. With the noise in the background, Bardek contemplated his next move. How would he introduce the fleet's crew to the ceirim?

*

Jora Galaxy, Planet Natok. EPTS: A139863

In orbit around the windy planet, Bardek stood before The Ninth. Fortunately, the *Losh* was the last to arrive in orbit, giving the captain some valuable time to catch up on the critical maintenance. After the rushed departure from Chaya, his ships had all arrived around Natok. Not at the same time, but they had come, safe and well. It was all he could hope for. Now was the time to broach his training drill – with an Overlord he had only met.

'Overlord, I need this training. The crews have no idea what they are transporting. If we lose containment, it will be a disaster. They need to get upfront and close to the ceirim, see what they are capable of. Fear is a great teacher.'

Nine wasn't so sure. Time ticked away while The Sixth was pressing for a result. Bardek had asked for four of these sessions on the planet. True,

Kochtos favoured the idea. It gave his lieutenants a chance to run free and gorge on fresh food. Up until now, the geneticists were only able to deliver meat carcases to the ceirim. It was not what The Sixth had said when he had changed them all. No, it was not. He made a promise that the ceirim could run free to hunt on a continent with live food. But The Sixth hadn't followed through on a promise he never intended to keep. This so-called training exercise of Bardek would at least appease his lieutenants. Kochtos badly needed to placate them.

Nine could see it all. He had no reticence in reading everyone's mind before he came to a decision. 'I will allow it, but only two,' he agreed. 'Time is of the essence. It shouldn't delay our departure. You still have much to do to get the cryo-tubes and the ceirim loaded. I expected all that finished by now.' He had. The size of the project he was overseeing surprised Nine. His original beliefs vindicated. Sparing with the truth was The Sixth!

*

Half the fleet's crews assembled behind a grav fort build on a knoll on the planet's grasslands. The more boisterous nicknamed the exercise "meet and greet your friendly flesh-eating monsters". They wouldn't be disappointed. The constant whistle of the wind added to the suspense of what they were about to see. Then, released from a gate in the fort's force field, six four-legged beasts stepped out onto the grasslands. The wild gonians, twice the size of a purebreed, reared their heads and sniffed the air. Their eyes glazed over as the brown furry animals sensed the horrific presence skulking in the grass. Howling with fear, they bolted, their four long legs a blur of speed as they ran. The long grass rustled. All the purebreeds could see with their naked eyes was a flash of black spikes as two mighty ceirim reared up, giving chase. In an instant, amongst howls of pain, four beasts were killed. A drone captured close-ups of the action, beaming them to the purebreeds' comms.

Their first sight of this legendary creature made the purebreeds gasp with fear. They all realised the stories weren't exaggerated. Images of the two-metre-tall black biped danced across their comm's screens. The ceirim's epidermis, formed by long thin black spikes, sparkled in the light of Natok's two suns. Vicious claws adorned the hands and feet, while razor-sharp teeth packed the jaws. Thick black eyes peered at the drone's camera as if to say, "watch this". The next scene gathered revulsion and dread from the flaky white purebreeds amongst Bardek's troop. The beasts ripped the limbs from the four dead gonians part by part. Then, with long sharp claws, they sliced open the stomachs and yanked out the animal's guts in one fell movement. Long black tongues darted out, licking the red blood from the carcases and then the feeding frenzy started. They sliced the meat with their claws and stuffed it into their mouths. When that was gone, they used their long cutting teeth to scrape the flesh from the bone. The black demons hunched down over the carcases, never stopping. Like machines, they slurped and sucked away every morsel of flesh, blood and the guts of the animals. All that remained was the bones.

Bardek watched his crews with interest. After the initial shock, some had regained their composure while the more daring bustled with jokes and the like. Like mating laestri, strutting around rolling their shoulders, with their cocks hanging out. The final part of the demo would take care of that.

A transport ship landed outside the fort. Kochtos alighted, followed by his twenty lieutenants. The noisy crew fell silent at the sight of the twenty-one ceirim walking towards the fort. What happens now, they all wondered? Then the ceirim rushed forwards, tearing at the grav force field that protected the occupants. Long claws tore at the translucent wall. Fear coursed through their bodies as the ceirim roared and growled. A black claw managed to punch through the force field, its owner snarling in anticipation as it reached for a victim. Terrified and screaming for mercy, the crowd pushed back. Kochtos passed an unseen signal to his troops. To the purebreeds' relief, the ceirim backed away.

The crowd's reaction delighted Bardek. Some had vomited and some had even shit themselves with terror. But still, there were strutting blusterers with their dicks dangling out, laughing at the others. These were the ones he would make an example of. Yes, they would learn the hard way. Follow the rules, and if not, there would be consequences. Like lightning, with some trusted guards, he grabbed as many of them as he could. The crowd fell back, surprised at Bardek's ferocity. *What gives here?* they wondered, as seventeen of their colleagues were marched to the gate. It opened and the guards pushed the blusterers out, screaming for mercy.

Kochtos and his ceirim encircled the hapless purebreeds. Screams, roars and moans filled the air. The remaining crew, safe in the fort, cried and pleaded for their mates.

Bardek grinned. This was going well and there was more to follow.

The Ninth's blue oval energy mass floated above. The Overlord watched with interest, waiting for Bardek's signal to end it all.

The ceirim's teasing intensified, the black circle closing ever smaller until the monsters were standing above the cowering purebreeds. Long black tongues darted in and out as they licked their prey. Claws extended and scraped across snow-white faces. Tunics ripped off and tummies scratched with the menacing black talons. Some of the once boisterous purebreeds fainted. Other's burrowed under their mate's bodies, trying to get some protection. It was a writhing heaving mass of screaming fear when Bardek signalled The Ninth. He flashed a message to Kochtos. 'Withdraw.' A good test of his obedience, The Ninth realised as he watched the ceirim pull back. Kochtos had to beat some as they lingered over their prey, but withdraw they did.

Bardek walked out of the gate. Standing over the fallen purebreeds, he shouted at them and his crew. 'Let that be a lesson you never forget. Know the power you are working with. There is no room for complacency, shortcuts or downright laziness. You will give everything to this project.' He reached down and grabbed one of the purebreeds – the watchkeeper from the *Shaqa*. *A lazy impudent lump of trite if ever there was one*, Bardek mused. It was he who had arranged the *Pleasure Palace's* visit. The deaths of those innocent souls fell to him. And, below contempt, he ran a surreptitious people-trafficking business as well. His position of watchkeeper on the *Shaqa* gave him ample opportunity for such jobbery and corruption. He would pay for it now. He dragged the man, kicking and screaming, to Kochtos.

Kochtos stood still as the leader of the purebreeds approached. This wasn't part of the plan. *What gives here?* he wondered.

Surprising them all, Bardek picked up the screaming weasel and flung him at Kochtos. 'Dinner,' was all he said, as he turned his back on the ceirim and walked to the fort.

A deadly silence descended as the *Shaqa's* watchkeeper lay whimpering at Kochtos's feet. The tall ceirim stooped down and pushed his snub-nosed snout up against the face of the terrified watchkeeper. Baring his sharp teeth, he growled and sniffed the man. The watchkeeper's pheromones screamed fear and terror – sweet perfume to Kochtos. In a blur, he grabbed a bicep with his claw. Standing on the man's shoulder, he wrenched the arm from his socket, ripping through sinews, tendons and skin. Blood gushed out, the man screamed, while a collective gasp escaped from the crowd.

Kochtos stuffed the arm into his mouth. In seconds, his long teeth scraped the flesh from the bone. Holding it aloft, he grinned at the purebreeds. It was a harrowing sight, the tall ceirim, blood dripping from his mouth, his black spikes glistening in the sunlight as he held the prized bone aloft. All the while, standing on the withering watchkeeper, bleeding to death at his feet. Kochtos's final act was to throw the bone over the wall of the fort. He turned and walked to his ship as the remaining ceirim ripped the purebreed apart.

Bardek said no more. His message delivered, he nodded a silent order to his guards – ready the transports, send this lot back and summon the rest.

The second training session wasn't nearly as dramatic as the first. Scenes of the first played on all the crew's comms units. It was a demure crowd which assembled in the fort. None spoke out of turn and they all gasped in terror when they met the ceirim. Those with any attitude at all made sure they curbed it. Convinced he had made his point, Bardek began the hazardous process of transferring sixteen thousand hibernating ceirim onto his fleet.

*

Human and purebreed psychologists agree that to govern by fear never brings the best out of a population. Work is done because it has to be, rules are followed because they must be. There is little understanding or communication about the reasons why things are done a particular way.

Nor is there any buy-in from the group on achieving a common purpose. Bardek had attained his objective to implant discipline in his crews. What he failed to get was a belief in the project goals. Most of the personnel followed orders, pushing the limits of their capabilities to get the job done. But Bardek's efforts failed to arrest the progress of the wheel of misfortune. A calamitous trundle put in motion before the smash-up in orbit around Chaya. No matter how hard he tried, he couldn't do enough to stop it.

*

The Refit

On the flat grasslands of Planet Natok, The Ninth's fleet lay dormant. All the ship's hatches and ports lay open. A host of purebreeds worked around the clock to complete the refit and load the hibernating ceirim inside the project timeline. The Ninth's blue pulsing oval energy mass floated above, admiring the industrial scene below. The young Overlord had stood back, allowing Captain Bardek to take care of the nuts and bolts of the operation, giving occasional advice whenever he believed it would benefit, The Ninth established a respectable working relationship with his captain, but, for the large part, it was Bardek and the lead geneticist's show.

The fleet's seven starships were of the same class. Military cruisers with vast interiors designed to accommodate any type of cargo. At six hundred metres long and with one blue drive pulse port mounted below their bows, they looked formidable. The irregular oblong hulls stretched back from the bulbous bows that contained their bridges. The rear of the cruisers enclosed the main engine rooms with three sleek grav drives. Their energy ports, framed within a convex polygon, extended out aft of the ships. Weapons' ports projected out from the underside of the hulls. And, along both sides, were the launch bays for the cruiser's transporters and shuttles. Missile tubes, grav beams and cannons bristled on the tops of the hulls, behind their bows, adding to the cruiser's strike capability.

A fleet of planetary transporters and shuttles designed to ferry troops and equipment back and forth lay beside their mother ships. The last link in the chain that would land the ceirim on Earth. The Ninth watched as a nondescript cargo vessel touched down on the grasslands. The absence of any type of markings announced its questionable ownership. Nine was expecting it. Belonging to him, it carried an unusual cargo banned by The One – extinction weapons shipped from a secret base in the Ragma galaxy. *Coming together, at last*, he thought, as he flew down to meet Bardek on the bridge of *Chad*.

The bridge now served as the project nerve centre. Colourful project charts and timeline maps showed on its large viewscreen. With the lead geneticist, Bardek's comms officer, who had worked for one of the Charters as a logistics director, had put the plan together. She walked towards The Ninth, dipping her head in respect as he floated in. Her flame-red hair tied up in a bun on her head matched her neat orange boiler suit. Unusual for The Seventh's crews, she was Javonian. Diversity wasn't alive in his fleet, his preference for purebreeds showing in the populaces make up.

Oozing confidence, she launched into the project report, purple hands pointing out the schedules. Moving sixteen thousand hibernating ceirim from the caves in a mountain on the northern continent to the ships, was a simple strategy game to her. Like all corporate planners, it was about numbers on a board!

The move would take fourteen cycles. Two thousand four hundred cryo-tubes were to be fitted in each of the seven cruiser's cargo bays. That allowed for a limited back up in the case of in-journey failures. The geneticists had provided one thousand cryo-suits to move the ceirim. Thaw time for a hibernating ceirim was four segments, giving the team ample time to complete the transfer from the caves to the ships on the grasslands. Engineering techs would modify the fleet's cargo bays. Porters would lift and fly the ceirim from the cryo-tubes in the mountains to the parked cruisers. Meantime, the cryo-techs would disconnect, transport and reconnect the tubes. Careful use of the back-up tubes allowed the switch to be completed within the allotted time frame. And so on …

Bardek tuned out her happy chatter. It was a pity all his crews didn't have her enthusiasm. A rum lot who didn't want to be here. Numbers meant nothing to them. He scratched his bald head as he watched her charts change colour as she demonstrated the breakup of the porters, cryo-tech and engineering teams who would complete the refit and transfer. A number had played over in his brain when he had started all this. If point zero one per cent of their hazardous cargo thawed out, lives would be lost. And, significantly, it would set back their timeline. *Madness*, he thought. *Always we squeeze the schedule to fit a spurious completion date. It never reflects how long it actually takes to do the work!*

While the comms officer finished her report, The Ninth felt Bardek's unease. 'Well done,' he said to her. It was a good plan, logical to the core, making the best use of their resources. But it depended on the purebreeds to get everything right. She was one of the few out-world races amongst them. A pity. The Ninth wondered why Seven hadn't made more use of such creatures. The purebreeds were a dying race, their abilities were waning. He had doubts they could get this all done in time. If they did, it would be a marvel! His thoughts wandered to the species-y population they were planning to expunge. From what he knew, they hadn't achieved interstellar flight and were going nowhere. Regardless of The Sixth's impatience, a few cycles of time either way wouldn't make much difference.

*

No beings are born perfect. All have flaws, aliens as well as humans as was seen on the *Hela* when Blair nearly died. Bardek's crews were no exception. Despite the rigorous rules and procedures the lead geneticist had put in place to manage the transportation of the most dangerous biological weapon the known universe had ever seen, some sought to break those rules. Bardek had targeted this faction in his "training exercise". For the most part, his message stuck.

Yet, in a large group, there will always be different psychological traits. Some will strictly follow the rules. Others will seek a way around, or a shortcut whether for profit or to gain an advantage, sheer devilment or downright laziness. In most cases, it is merely to get the job done faster. A group of porters chose that option. They found they could fit in an extra two hibernating ceirim in the shuttle trip from the mountain caves.

On the other hand, the lead geneticist had based the logistics on transporting ten ceirim at a time. The cryo-techs and geneticist teams were working on that premise. Adding another two ceirim to the mix didn't fit. And, not noticing the anomaly, the techs worked on, unknowingly playing a dangerous game of catch up.

The loss of the seven cryo-techs, forcing some of the crews to work short-handed, added another click to the wheel of misfortune. With that, the lead geneticist was new to the role. The Master and more experienced had remained on Anan to work on the cure for their sickness. Now add Bardek's undue pressure to fast track the project with The Sixth's constant pushing. The wheel wasn't well advanced – it was trundling along at break-neck speed!

In all but one case, the cryo-techs managed to play catch up for the extra two ceirim. Just in time, connecting the cryo-tubes to the ship's service-grid and activating it, before the beasts thawed out. Bad design of the ship's compartmented structure let the cryo-techs move into a new section, missing two tubes that had ceirim inside. Only supposed to be journey backups and never used, the inspection failsafe overlooked them. The checkers, likewise in a rush, failed to see the closed tubes contained two hibernating ceirim.

When the ceirim woke up, they did as their makers intended, crawling out of their cryo-tubes and hiding like black ghosts in the shadows. The shortcutting porters returned to take their illegal rest time in what they assumed was a deserted compartment. A pack of cards was produced and the group settled down on the floor for a game of flake. One glanced over and noticed two of the tubes were open.

'Who left the tubes open?'

'Not me,' each replied.

'We must have missed them,' one offered.

'Leave it out and deal the cards,' another said, impatient to get on with their rest time.

The one who had seen them first was adamant. 'No, I remember they were all closed.'

'Ah, come on. Don't start that sh—'

Fear grasped the man's gut as he found himself staring into two black eyes peering out of the shadows. Nothing moved. The two ceirim had circled their group, each capturing the gaze of five in their black blinkless eyes. For four long seconds, nothing moved, the ceirim enjoying the sense of fear oozing from their dumbstruck prey. Some tried to scream, their vocal cords paralysed as their mouth moved, but nothing came out. The beasts advanced out of the shadows, showing off their full bodies: black spikes, long sharp teeth and a snub-nosed snout. Before it pounced, one leaned into the face of its terrified prey. Savouring the moment, the ceirim snorted ice-cold snot over its first dinner in an age.

Flashes from their training session ate through the ten porter's minds as the long black claws pounced. No one heard their screams as the two ceirim slashed their throats. Blood gushed out on the deck. While still writhing in the throes of death, the ceirim started to drink the purebreed porters' blood. Then, they sat down, butchering the purebreeds into equal parts for both to share. The needle-like teeth began the feeding frenzy as the two escapees gorged themselves on fresh meat.

It was Kochtos who first sensed the waking. He called to The Ninth who notified Bardek. His worst nightmare come true, Bardek sounded the general alarm. Not his best course of action! Panic ensued as crews rushed to escape the confines of the ships.

The geneticists protested. 'You must return all ceirim in transit to the cryo-tubes,' they shouted, knowing the situation could get worse. Arguing and screaming at the geneticists, the rest of the crews abandoned their posts and ran from the ships – a cluster-chaos for Bardek to unravel. All the while, time ticked away for another forty hibernating ceirim, abandoned and lying on the decks, their bodies thawing out!

*

The enemy was time. Kochtos and four of his lieutenants entered the ship. They found the two escapees halfway through gorging themselves on the ten bodies. Fat and full, they belched and grinned at Kochtos. The compartment stunk of the smell of death and ceirim excrement. They hadn't planned for an escape. All they could do was lead the two out onto the grassland to run free. Stuffed with fresh meat, they didn't go far! Meantime, more of the ferocious beasts were thawing out, running wild, trying to get a feed. The purebreed crews sheltered in the grav fort. Not made for so many, it was near to bursting at the seams.

The Ninth came to Kochtos's rescue, stunning those of the ceirim who had thawed out with bolts of his precious blue energy. Led by Bardek, a team of porters and geneticists managed to return them all to functioning cryo-tubes. Two more tubes were brought out to the grasslands on a shuttle to capture the first two escapees. Still bloated from overfeeding, they flopped inside without a murmur. The unplanned event cost a team of ten porters and one time cycle. After that, Bardek had to stop all work and call a stand down for the entire project, assembling the shaken purebreeds out on the grasslands.

It was The Ninth who delivered the rousing message of inspiration. 'One more mistake like this and you all die!' Short and sharp, it left no doubt as to the quagmire of excrement the purebreeds were in.

Bardek followed with the practicalities of getting the process back up and running. It was a subdued population that reluctantly returned to work. When the comms officer reran the numbers, it shocked her. The final turn of the wheel of misfortune cost a team of ten porters and five cycles, increasing the project timeline by near thirty per cent.

When she explained it to Bardek, he put his head in his hands and moaned. His voice quivered. 'We have to do better than this. We can't have the cargo eating the crew! There'll be none of us left by the time we get to our destination. And,' he added as an afterthought, 'we still have to load the extinction weapons and fit their launch panels.' He left the bridge and headed for his cabin. Tomorrow would be another day. Species-y would have to wait.

CHAPTER TWENTY-ONE

Off-World Colony Hab-Pods

Human habitation during the long intergalactic journey, and on the destination planet, will be in factory-made habitation pods. The pods provide a self-contained portable living compartment. Integrated with, bathroom, kitchen, sleeping and living quarters, the walls, roofs and floors are insulated against thermal and cosmic radiation. Roofs are flat, structurally integral to allow stacking and are watertight. Four corner fittings are provided top and bottom for transport and lifting. Quick-couple connections facilitate water, waste-water and electrical services. Doors and windows are triple glazed with standard heating and lighting. Numbers of single, double and family pods are set out in the detailed specification below.

‹ **Extract from: Specification "Off-World Colony Habitation Pods."** **Alan Phillips**

*

Fort Leslie, New World. EPTS: A139867

OBLIVIOUS TO THE HORRORS THE Sixth had in progress in the Jora galaxy, back on the New World, The Eight felt Zaval Borea's passing. The Pilot's reappearance with the small fleet was most unexpected. His tenacity could prove to be a game changer for The Eight's war effort to thwart The Sixth's power grab. The Eight took stock of what Zaval had provided so far. Secret bases at the edge of the Anan Galaxy, the return of the *Hela* with a space-tug, and two inter-system transporters. And, best of all, Zaval's plan to "play" the future price of blue. It was an audacious suggestion that Zaval brought to The Eight when they arrived back in the Anan Galaxy. On-site, aeons ago when the Overlords first commissioned it,

The Eight understood the inner workings of The Energy Exchange more so than The Sixth. Now the first pieces of that "play" were starting to come together. True, his project lacked a plethora of resources, but thanks to Zaval, the scheme was taking shape. If he could sigh, the ethereal entity would. Instead, he watched as his colony's populace went about enjoying their day off.

The rain didn't stop play. New interspecies friendships blossomed. Niamh returned to her pod and spent the day with Tom. Quriel took time out to enjoy the New World and bond with the human soldiers. Robert and Janet finally emerged from their love nest to meet the new additions to their team. And, with the *Hela* back, there was a special consignment Janet was keen to recover. Curious about their life and customs, a happy Borea clan mingled with the humans. The sun finally came out, warming up the wet day and the young, wholly engrossed in each other and having fun, never noticed the absent Zaval.

That evening, the elder Borea missed him. He went to Zaval's cabin on the *Hela*. Knocking on the door, there was no answer. He tried to open it, but the locked door didn't yield. That didn't bode well with the old man. Using a personal tool, no match for the earth lock, he entered the cabin. The unfamiliar smell of whiskey assaulted his nostrils. But still, he advanced into the room until he reached the side of the bed. Shocked, he gasped at the sight of the dead man's pallor. More awfulness reared as the elder gazed down on Zaval. The empty bottle with its brown poison stained the bedsheets. As he grasped the implication of the surreal scene, he shuddered with emotion. It all made sense – the blue pendant, still clutched in Zaval's hand, the brown alcohol, and the deathly grey pallor, his grey-knuckled hand frozen in rigour mortice, still grasping the now dull blue crystal. The old man had heard stories of navigators dying in mid-flight. The poison had dulled his brain and his heart had stopped! The elder's heart beat like a running gonian as he realised how their Pilot had died.

No one must know. A humongous blot on the memory of this great man it would be. Not wanting the family to experience Zaval's humiliating end, he knew he had to mask the evidence. But he needed help. Using his comms unit, he summoned the only one he could trust – the young dutiful technician who had attended Verteg. She was in the *Hela* hold with Janet and some of the other girls when the call came through. The exchange was short and terse. A cold hand touched her heart as she ran off, surprising the others in the group.

Dressed in a bright pink jumpsuit, embossed with colourful flowers and sporting a matching jacket, her appearance in the corridor outside Zaval's room shocked the old man. The clothes had come from four forty-foot containers stored in the belly of the *Hela*. The shipment, consigned to "Haret, the Trader", had left Earth on the authority of the Sullivan Parker Charter. It was samples of Earth's finest fashions and produce from Janet Cooper and Partners Ltd. With the failed mission to Anan, and the impending war, Janet had decided to break out the goods. It proved a happy shopping diversion, providing a well-needed change for the humans and their new Borea partners.

'What manner of garb is that Hyeba?' the old man cried. 'Where did—'

'O Grandpa, don't be so old fashioned,' she shouted back. 'It's casual wear! I was given it by Janet, the human planner. She has a whole store of human clothes in the cargo hold ...' Her voice fell as she noticed his grey pallor. 'What's wrong, what's wrong?' Hyeba blurted out, remorseful that she dared to shout at him.

His heart bled tears of sorrow as he looked down on his granddaughter. So young and full of life. The dimple on her left cheek had disappeared in anguish. She had endured hell and never once complained, until now. Youthful enjoyment, it was. Harmless, and what she deserved. She looked lovely in the strange human costume. It matched her own green and white complexion – and he had pulled her away from it, for this.

'It's okay,' he said, nodding reassuringly. 'Go change into your workwear, and not a word to anyone. And the incense you hold, bring it here.'

Hyeba gasped at the mention of their death mask. Shaking her head, she turned and ran.

In no time at all, she was back, breathless from the rush and impatient to know what the matter was. Clutching the small container, she looked into her grandpa's eyes, old tired and grey, the usual spark of life gone. 'Who is it?' she asked.

'Zaval, he's inside. Come.'

They entered the cabin together. She gagged at the stink but she worked on helping the old man. First, they flushed all the alcohol down the toilet. Then she helped him dispose of the empty bottles. The hard part was to come – stripping and bathing the body with the sweet-smelling mortality incense. With clean sheets, they made the bed. They dressed him in a fresh ship garb, hanging his navigation pendant round his neck. Finally, propping him up with his hands folded across his chest serene and at peace, Zaval looked like the nobleman he once was.

The incense had scrubbed the foul smell of death and alcohol from the room. Their Pilot's dignity preserved, satisfied, the old man sighed – a deep emotional one. A sigh his granddaughter felt. He smiled down at her. 'Thank you, Hyeba,' he said. 'You should never have had to do this.'

As usual, she shook off his praise. 'It's okay, Grandpa. We should call Quriel now.'

He nodded his head. She was right. He couldn't delay any more. 'Yes, we should.'

Checking their handiwork, the old man shuffled out to call Quriel, thankful he had spared him the indignity of Zaval's drunken end.

*

The Funeral

The cold hard punch of death brought reality knocking on the colony door. Stored in a refrigerated container on the *Hela* awaiting burial, the body of Demard and the other nine dead Borea added to the misery. It was a nasty job Mack believed he could put off, but not now – they would join Zaval in the ground. To add to the despair, the human doctor wanted to examine Zaval's body. He found the explanation for Zaval's death unbelievable, suspecting the old man's cover-up. The empty bottles found dumped in the *Hela's* kitchen trash didn't help. The Borea vociferously objected. To have an inferior medical team examine one of their own was insulting.

And, when they heard what a human autopsy entailed, a near-riot broke out. They besieged Robert, shouting abuse at him and the Doc.

To end it all, the elder Borea whispered about what had happened to Mack. Diplomacy won the day when Mack explained to Robert. 'To the Borea, cutting open one of their dead is sacrilege. There can be no autopsy. Death is attributed to heart failure. Not surprising, given the stress Zaval was under. It's time to move on and let the Borea bury their dead. They have suffered enough,' Mack espoused, trying hard to get the message across over the bitter feelings he held for Robert.

Considering he hadn't spoken to Robert in ages, the tall Scotsman appreciated the importance of what Mack said. He knew how close Mack had been to Zaval. Respect for the dead was paramount in Robert's eyes. *What difference did it make anyway?* he thought. *The poor man is dead. Let him rest in peace. Enough is enough.* Robert placated his medical team, and as was his nature, set about assisting the Borea with the burial preparations.

Purebreed funeral rites vary. In space, the body can be buried in that great void. On a planet, it's put in the ground. When setting up the colony, a glade had been cleared for such events. The humans prepared a plot for the Borea family in the cleared field. With replanted orchid-type flowers growing out from native woods, the botanists made the gravesite into a picturesque, forested garden – like a park. With the Borea elder and Verteg, The Eight cut a notable tombstone from bare rock. He burned a simple inscription into it. "Here lies the great Borea Pilot, Zaval" and "Here lies the great Borea computer technician Demard."

While fashioning the tombstone, The Eight asked the old man about the remaining family. *A curious question,* he mused, as he explained where he believed the rest of the family could be.

'I need crews,' The Eight explained. 'Technicians, engineers, navigators and pilots.'

As head of the family, it was Verteg's place to answer. 'Overlord, we want the family back together again. If you can get to them, I will vouch they will join us. It's only Little Kake and his gang of thugs who follow the memory of our corrupt grandfather. The rest eke out a hard-living as ship's crew. They'll be glad of such an opportunity.'

'We will see,' was the Overlord's noncommittal answer as he flashed a burst of white light. However, deep within his memory, he deposited the locations she gave him, correlating them within his battle plans.

Zaval and Demard were buried side by side, beneath their towering tombstones. The Borea murdered when Frike left the *Hela*, and those killed by Niamh and Cylla, were interred in rows below. Markers were set for the missing Alke and his two crew who had died on the journey. Thirteen souls in all, a significant loss for such a small family to bear. After assisting in laying down the coffins and covering them with the New World's dirt, the humans watched on in silence as Verteg and Quriel delivered the family's last farewell. Then it was all over. The stillness shattered by the singing birds and the roars of the distant beasts. They trooped back to Fort Leslie where Robert had arranged the wake.

The wake celebrated Zaval, Demard and regardless of their deeds, the other dead family's lives, well into the night. Legends were told about Zaval's journey across the galaxy and about Demard's computer skills. "There would never be others like them" was said over and over again.

*

Although the Borea family all joined in, appreciating the human custom in honouring their dead, Mack and Cylla avoided the wake. It was Robert's affair so Mack wanted nothing to do with it. Back in his pod, the racket from the gathering below added to Mack's bitterness. He rubbed his head in anguish. Zaval's sudden death had troubled him. He couldn't cast off the feeling that he should have done more. He looked across as Cylla lounged comfortably in a deep chair, her tail curled around her waist. 'You know, Cylla, he was drunk, all the time, on that earthly poison. I hoped he would try to get better. I really did. I fear the journey broke him.'

'That's so fatal, Arie. In his last hours, you paint such a gloomy picture of the Pilot. You don't know what happened to him or what he was thinking.'

Her tone shocked him. 'He's Borea. Quriel told me you found it hard to work with Zaval at the beginning. Now you speak up for him. Why?'

Her eyes spitting fire, she glared back at him. 'There's more life in that human wake below than in your stone-cold heart. You wallow in self-pity.

I stood on the dock with the departing Borea. With Frike's team, do you know how many Borea there were on that transporter? Do you?' she shouted.

His head hung down over his long neck. He stayed silent, guessing she was about to tell him.

'I'm the bookkeeper, remember. There were forty-eight on that transporter and with Zaval's three kin on the Hela, and his son Quriel, that makes fifty-two of the family before the killing started.'

He shuddered at what Cylla was about to remind him of. The disaster the family had suffered. What Zaval had to deal with.

'How many are left after Frike's killing spree, Demard's revenge and the event during the tow? I'll tell you, Arie, just twenty-five. Less than half arrived back here. How could any man stomach that? Zaval was probably consumed with guilt in what he had started. But no, Arie, no. Not his fault. He tried to do his best. Circumstances let to the death of over half his family. And now, under Verteg's leadership and the elder's guidance, they get on about the business while you still wallow in self-pity. Arie, you disgust me.'

'I don't' he said, shaking his head. 'No, I don't. How dare—'

She cut him off, her scathing voice piercing what had started as a quiet chat. 'Arie, look at what he has achieved. They are telling legends about that journey, below at their gathering. He'll go down in history. And he's restored his family fortune and name. They're back in business.' She put her hand up as he tried to interrupt. 'I know, it's under the Sullivan Parker Charter. We're leasing the three Borea ships he brought back, and Anan Corp has leased the space mining equipment that was on *One*.'

'*Maeve*, that's what they call her now,' he said, referring to one of the transporters docked beside the *Hela*.

'And his family are working for us. Arie, they are delighted at the opportunity for a new start. As for you, when will you snap out of this spiral of self-absorbed gloom? It's that woman – Janet – isn't it? You pine for her. I'm insulted. The brown-haired calbak, she—'

'Cylla, that's uncalled for, there was nothing—'

'You lying piece of excrement.' She stood up, tossing her head in frustration, her lengthy hair flying back. 'You think I don't see how you look at her. I'm right, Arie. It was how you looked at me when we first met. And you did nothing. The great General and the Protector. As with her, you did nothing. Finally, her patience gives out, and she's with someone who'll give her what she craves – love. The same as me, you know, a female with desires for a lover. You, on the other hand, just sink into a mire of self-pity. When will you understand simple biology – our lifespan is much shorter than yours? We cannot wait for your libido, if you have any left, to awaken. Or is it something else? Can't you bring yourself to mate with another species? Is that it? Your purebreed heritage, and your purebreed rules, is that why? You sanctimonious bigot! I'm off,' she said, as she stomped to the door.

'Where are you going, Cylla?' he said, trying to avoid the uncoiling tail now flying around the room.

'You're hopeless. In case you didn't notice, my gills are inflamed. I need a swim,' Cylla said, as she stormed out into the night, slamming the door behind her.

Rubbing his face in anguish, he allowed his brain to wander. *Of course, Cylla was right, but that still didn't excuse Robert's behaviour. No it did not.*

*

The day after the funeral, The Eight called a war council. Backed into a corner, he now had a way out – project "smart-war" was in play. Afterwards, while they all filed out of the large meeting room, the icy stare Mack gave Robert said it all. They would have sat together at these meetings, but today, as they sat apart, the rift between them was apparent for all to see.

As he stood beside Mack, Tom looked across at Robert. 'Mack, it was never intentional. We are different—'

'Would you be so conciliatory if he ran away with Niamh?'

'Mack, I married Niamh. Enough, we need to move on – we're at war.' His voice betrayed his realisation as to how unglamorous galactic wars are!

It sobered Mack as well. 'Yes, Tom, we are. I fear in my bones for our colony and Earth. The Sixth will not rest until he finds us. We need more ships and crew – what Zaval delivered is a start. You and Niamh have much to do in assembling a fleet and crews of our own.'

'We'll get them, Mack. With her flying the *Monarch* and me conducting the negotiations, they don't stand a chance.'

Mack laughed. 'Thomas Parker, you never give in, do you? You love every minute of the fight.' He paused as The Eight floated over to them. 'Overlord, this is a dark day in our history.'

'General, history will judge us, and it will be swayed by the outcome of our battle plan. If we win, we will be perceived as the great liberators. If we lose, I will be known as the evil Overlord who hoarded a galaxy of energy and bred a population of super-beings for his own gain.'

Tom grinned. 'There is some truth in that, Overlord, but you're not evil. I heard they called you "the most powerful and cunning of them all". I'm glad I'm working for you. I don't fancy the odds on the other side.'

'Tom is right, you are the best hope for the universe. Your power surpasses that of the troika. I'm glad I didn't end up working for them,' Mack agreed.

'Thank you for your endorsement, General. Now to work. You and Cylla Ora have much to do when I leave,' he said, and as he floated away he sensed the General's feeling of hurt. *Always with mortals, one may gain from the other's loss. Imperfection, we can never get it one hundred per cent.*

Escaping Mack's cold shoulder, Robert sat in silence away from the throng sipping coffee until Tom sat down beside him. 'You got what you wanted – from the meeting?'

Robert looked at him, taking a sip of his drink. 'Yes, Tom, I did. We're off to Earth. It's no how I'd like to leave here. You know, the rift out in the open for all to see. But Janet and I'll be happy together and we have a big job on our hands. More colonists to recruit, manufacturing for the war effort and all that. When you return, it'll get even bigger, I hope. We'll no have a minute to ourselves. It'll be great,' he said, as he stood up and smiled across at Janet, standing beside Niamh and Cylla. 'Come on, let's join your wife,' he said, as he walked over and stood beside Janet, smiling awkwardly. 'Ladies—'

'You're the troublemaker,' Cylla said as she looked up at him. 'We haven't formally met. I'm intrigued. Janet, is his organ's size in proportion to his body?'

It was Niamh who fired a scalding answer. 'Jeez, Cylla, you don't say those sort of things in front of the men. Will you give over. Look at poor Janet, red with embarrassment. Don't worry, lads, she's always like that. No shame at all.'

'Cylla, you should get out more. Interact with us lowly humans,' Tom said, smiling at her. 'Don't stay cooped up in Mack's pod all the time.'

Ignoring Cylla's first comment, Robert looked straight at the golden-scaled alien. 'Seriously, Cylla, he's right. You need to meet more of the colonists. We have to learn how to interact with different species. And you'll need to work with Shona and Blair; they'll want your help when I leave.'

'Yes, Robert, you do need to learn how to interact with different species and running off with another's mate is not the done thing on Anan.'

Her eyes glowing blue, Niamh remembered Theia's parting words. "When you see Mack, tell him to marry Janet before she gets away. He's always too slow, never realises the time differences with other species – it's occurred before. Your friend is the best thing that has happened to him." When she returned it was all too late; she never mentioned them to Mack. By that time, Robert was firmly ensconced with Janet. As Theia feared, Mack had lingered too long. 'Jeez, Cylla—'

'I'm joking, Niamh. Robert, get rid of the look of thunder or I'll uncoil my tail. Now, take me to see Blai and Sho; we have much to negotiate.'

Robert shook his head as Cylla held out her arm in front of him. He looked at Janet who just shrugged.

'Well, are you coming?' Cylla said as she held out the other arm for Janet.

Tom and Niamh watched the trio walk together through the town centre. A bizarre sight – the big sandy-haired Scotsman in his faded kilt linking arms with the Neredian. Her golden scales flashing in the dim sunlight and her tail coiled around her waist. Dressed in a smart blue ship garb with her brown hair tucked up in a bun, Janet flanked her other side.

'Niamh, she's amazing. You brought us back a real wonder,' was all Tom could say.

'She is. Come on, husband, back to our pod. I want some quiet time together before we leave here. I have news for you as well.'

As the couple made their way back to their home, they smiled and nodded as they greeted the passing throng: aliens and humans, busying themselves in Fort Leslie's centre for the impending voyages; the Borea family with green, white and mixed-tone skin; the purebreed Quriel and his Aknar soldiers, mingling with the humans. If the colonists had any doubt about their future, it was dispelled now. Aliens would form a part of their lives. To the aliens, the colonists, with a diverse population from Earth's continents, looked quite different. The humans' various skin tones, facial features and body shape had surprised the Borea. A strange mixing pot of diversity, and amongst them all, walking hand in hand was Tom alongside the love of his life, Niamh. Her blue hair, blue-toned face and her eyes glowing with white light declaring her blue energy contamination. The colonist's thought she looked cute, but the Borea knew better. *How much longer would she live?* they all wondered, as they smiled back at her happy face.

*

Robert and Janet's serene walk with Cylla was short lived. She wasted no time raising the tempo at the next discussion on the colony's future employment arrangements.

'You can't charge us for air,' Blair shouted across the table to Cylla who had spent the last half hour explaining how off-world mining worked.

'Why not? It's a standard arrangement – life support doesn't come for free.'

'It's slavery, nothing short of slavery. You'll no get us to work in conditions like that. We'll go back to Earth first.'

Cylla smiled. 'I can arrange that if you can pay the fare.'

'Monster, you know we can't pay that.'

Janet stood up and tried to speak, but Cylla held up her hand. 'This is how it works on all the off-world mining colonies. You are charged for everything. I've read your contracts. They are for terrestrial mining on the New World only. I was surprised at how generous they were but now we need to be realistic. Before we start off-world mining, in space, we need new agreements. Janet, you wanted to say something.'

'Cylla, we're going back to Earth to recruit more for the second colony. We're at war. We need people to crew the ships, provide an army and to mine blue for The Eight. What you propose must be acceptable to the colonists here – otherwise, we'll find it hard to attract more.'

'Your species is so soft. You're too used to an easy life—'

'What?' roared Robert, now on his feet as well, his face flushed red and his arm glowing purple. 'How dare you; you've no idea what we've been through. I'll, I'll …'

Cylla stood up and stared straight into his angry face, her green eyes flashing and the pink forked tongue darting in and out as she spoke. 'You'll what?'

Janet stepped between them. 'Can we calm it down, please. Cylla, explain what you propose again. I don't think we got it the first time.'

'Really, you humans are so primitive – I don't know why I came to work for you.'

'Probably 'cause your last boss fired you and you had to run for your life,' Blair roared.

Shona boxed him on his shoulder. 'Shut it, Blair, dinnae make it worse.' She looked down at the figures she had scribbled. 'Cylla, humour us. Go over what you propose again.'

As Cylla outlined her plans for the off-world mining, Shona wrote each segment on a whiteboard in front of them. 'That's enough, Cylla, I got the picture now. It's contract work, ye pea-brains,' she said, looking at Blair and Robert. 'Shut up and listen for a minute. Anan Corp rents us out the equipment with all the life support. We cannae afford to buy it ourselves – what part of that did ye miss? The good part is that the company is responsible for maintaining the equipment and for all our living needs. We have to mine a certain quota of blue to pay for it. We're paid market rates for what we mine above the quota. Am I right, Cylla?'

Cylla clapped her hands. 'Finally, a human with some brains.'

'It's not going to work, Cylla. We'll no want market rates. We've seen what happens with energy prices and it all depends on the tract we get to mine. There has to be a risk share clause. What happens if we hit an unforeseen problem, or the tract does nae produce the expected load?

And why are you negotiating for Anan Corp? I thought you worked for Niamh and Tom.'

The room went silent as all eyes turned to Cylla. 'Sho – human names are so difficult – that's the most intelligent statement I've heard today. Yes, I do work for the Charter. Since there's no other bookkeeper here, I'm to work for Anan Corp and the Colony as well.'

This was news to Janet. 'What about the conflict of interest?'

'Yes, there will be that. I suggest the contracts are approved by Alan and Kath on Earth.'

Shona nodded. 'That'll work; what about the rest?'

'We work out a risk share clause. That's quite normal. I'm not sure how we work out a delivery price.'

'We're no wanting today's price, just a decent living for our work. What about a price average, say over ten years?'

'Ten orbits,' Cylla corrected. 'No, too short a period, Sho. Let me think about that. But we won't fall out on such a detail. Good, that was easy. You humans are so uncomplicated. Normally, such dealings take days.'

Robert put his head in his hands as he tried to hold in his temper. 'But we're not done yet, Cylla. There's the final price to agree.'

'Robert, we won't fall out over price,' she said as she sat down, defusing the tension she created. 'That you don't want the highest price blue has ever been says a lot for your tactics. I suggest you leave Sho and me to agree on an outline contract with a price per tank. You can approve it with your colonists. Janet, you can take the contracts to Earth for review.'

There was silence in the room, and then Robert sat down as well. 'That'll work for me. Janet, Shona, Blair, what do you think?'

Blair shook his head. 'We're still working for air.'

'I dinnae ken why I married you. Did I no lay it out on that pad in front of you? We'll make a bloody fortune. Thanks, Cylla. That'll be fine.'

Cylla looked across at Janet. 'Yes, that'll work. Cylla, you might need to dial down the tension when you negotiate with humans.'

'No, Janet, never. That would take the "fun", as you call it, out of the deal.'

Robert stood up. Looking at Janet, he walked out. She nodded at Cylla and left. 'What do you think?' he asked her as they walked off together.

'She's a minefield, but she knows their business inside out. We need her, Robert.'

'What did we get ourselves into, Janet? Was I right to lead a colony here?'

'It didn't matter, Robert. When The Sixth made his move in that far distant galaxy, our fate was sealed. We talked about this in Kath's office the first day the aliens arrived on Earth. Regardless of who took the job, humans were coming here to mine blue. It was inevitable. They're our ancestors.' She paused and took his hand. It was still glowing purple from his anger. 'Kath talked of slavery; she made that argument and Mack was able to argue their case against it. Cylla did the same today. Robert, you've worked wonders protecting the colonists, you really have. I'm not sure how long you can keep that up. There's a war now. We're to start mining off-world, in space. It's a whole new ball game. Don't lose hope, Robert. We'll need you more than ever.'

He stopped and looked down at her. 'From what went on in there, they'll need you more. She makes my blood boil.'

'She does it on purpose; you need to see that.'

'Aye, your right,' he said, as he bent down and kissed her. When they broke from their embrace, he looked at his arm. He turned it over, inspecting its soft blue glow. 'I need you, Janet Cooper. I'll no be able to do this without you.'

She laughed. 'We'll do it together, Robert. Come on, we need to get packed. We're off to Earth in a few days.'

CHAPTER TWENTY-TWO

Fort Leslie, New World. EPTS: A139939

THAT EVENING, ROBERT SAT OUT on his pod's balcony, admiring the spectacle below. The *Monarch*, a hive of activity, would depart first thing tomorrow. Colonists, catbears and crew thronged in and out along the gangways as they prepared the ship for flight. Robert had stayed clear of the hubbub allowing Niamh, assisted by their Dock Master and Janet, to direct proceedings. It didn't all go to plan. One of the young catbears pooped on the engine room gangway, blocking it. Robert laughed to himself as he watched Luna cuff the young cub across the chest while Alice threw him a shovel. As quick as the jam appeared, it cleared, and the procession restarted. A noise above startled Robert. He looked up to see The Eight floating down in his chariot. Final orders had arrived.

'Yes, indeed, Robert. I am here with your final orders. I leave tomorrow with Niamh and Tom on the *Monarch*.'

'Niamh's shopping trip!'

'Crudely put, Robert, but yes, more starships, engines and whatever we can get to augment Earth's manufacturing process. We need crews as well.'

'Yes, we do,' agreed Robert. That was all discussed at their war council earlier today. But The Eight hadn't revealed his whole strategy. They knew he was gathering a fleet to challenge The Sixth's supremacy, but the goal was still unknown.

'Robert, you must know the overall plan, yes, before you leave so you can prepare them on Earth before we get back.'

The Eight laid it all out: the need to transport the blue energy to the Energy Exchange without his ships getting captured by The Sixth; Zaval's play on the price of blue; and, the ultimate prize, gaining back control of the Aknar fleet. Refuelling those ships was the key to defeating the troika. Whoever controlled the blue energy supply and that fleet would control the known universe.

'Simple, eh?' Robert mused out loud. He suspected The Eight had something like this in mind. 'And Theia, where does she fit in, if she's still alive?'

'She is alive. Of that, I'm certain. She has a role to play in all this and will rule Anan again as Empress.'

They both stayed silent. Robert contemplated the linear time involved. Once *Monarch* departed, they would empty the blue tank farm onto the *Richard*, *Hela* and *George*. He and Janet would leave for Earth on the *Richard*, towing the other two ships and so on …

'Time for me to go, Robert. Take care of my planets. If anything happens to me, you are my proxy. Heed the glow in your arm – when the time comes, let it guide you.' Without another word, The Eight floated away in his chariot down to his new flagship, the *Monarch*.

Robert, sitting in silence, contemplated that surprise. *What does he mean?* he wondered.

*

Planet Natok. EPTS: A139940

Across the space-time continuum, on Planet Natok, a disgruntled Bardek had grabbed the laestri by the tail and gone before The Ninth. 'Kill me now,' he had said, 'but if you don't, we do this my way. Time stands still, no deadlines, no targets or milestones. Everything is double-checked. We finish the project without any unplanned events, but we finish it. If you grant me that, I'll get this fleet with the ceirim loaded to species-y's home world.'

Bardek's commitment surprised The Ninth. The young Overlord knew the man was right. As usual, The Sixth had underestimated the task, something he was familiar with in the past. Well, species-y hadn't evolved to space flight. And, with his Aknar navy holed up at The Energy Exchange, The Eight hadn't got any ships. Where he was, was a mystery. But a few cycles either way wouldn't make a difference. The end result was what mattered – complete annihilation of species-y. If The Sixth had any problem with that, he could come here himself and lead the charge. The Ninth gave Bardek his time and flashed a message of the delay back to The Sixth. It included the caveat that, *'If my Overlord is unhappy with the delay, you are welcome to take over the project'.* Unsurprisingly, it went unanswered.

*

Planet Anan. EPTS: A139941

On Planet Anan, The Sixth had consolidated his hold. The Charters adapted to the new order and intergalactic trade picked up, not to the scale it was before, but any bounce was welcome. It surprised many how those savvy enough to predict such a shortage had hoarded so much grav and blue. Hybrid drives became the flavour of the cycle and the herd rushed to buy them. To keep up with the demand, the Shoter's wife, head of the Svang Charter, accelerated the manufacturing processes in their consortium factories.

The Anan populace was keen to get on with their daily lives. Unlike the outlying worlds, the struggle between the Overlords did not affect Planet Anan's occupants. On those worlds, marginal economies and the loss of their supporting Overlord left them vulnerable to exploitation. The purebreeds didn't spare them a thought, wrapped up in their own lives; the only concern they had was whether they would get the dreaded Anan sickness.

With the help of the Anan medical institute, the Sixth's Master Geneticist started to manufacture batches of The First Stage Treatment: the medicine that arrested the initial onset of the disease. Based on Alex and Rhea's work and the samples returned from the *Hela*, work started in engineering the final cure. Keen to make progress, the geneticist himself interviewed test subjects for the impending clinical trials. Empress Theia, never believing such a day would come, took an active interest in the process. Her return as Empress added to the stability of Anan and the Energy Exchange. Reaching a civil concord with the Shoter, she had little need to interact with The Sixth. Yet beneath her calm exterior, smoldered a burning desire for revenge against what he did to her family and Overlord. The Sixth, ever consumed with his desire to expunge The Eight and species-y, never sensed it. Nor did he, or any of his cohorts, notice a young Aknar lieutenant deliver a strange cone-shaped device to the Empress. Turning it on, he showed her how it worked. As he left, she secreted it in a hidden compartment in her personal chambers, its flashing lights eerily illuminating the small keep.

*

New Zealand, Christchurch, Anan Corp Office, 18th December 2027

Back on Earth, in his Christchurch office, Alan Phillips scrolled through the daily news feeds. The headlines were the same from all quarters of the globe. It didn't matter who or what their political allegiances were – hard left, hard right, liberal or religious – the stories were the same. "Abandoned By The Overlord.""Alien Ship Gets A Free Refit And Kidnap 2500.""Where Has The Eight Really Gone?" And so on, exposing a general loss of faith in the Overlord's capabilities by Earth's population. Three months after he had left, the power of the military men The Eight had left in place in the U.S.A. and Russia, was usurped. Humans couldn't grasp the vast distances the *Hela* had to travel and the time it would take. After eleven months, what little patience was left, evaporated. The old rivalries won through. Greed and power-grabbing changed the political order The Eight had fostered before departing. Predictably, regional conflicts had restarted, something Alan and Harold Addison, The Eights representative on Earth, had foreseen.

Disgusted, Alan closed down the news feeds and opened another file, freshly delivered from one of his planners. Lists of resources, supplies and components spilt out: delivery notes from factories working around the clock, manufacturing parts for alien spaceships, all based on Earth technology and requisitioned from a list Niamh had left him with. And there was more, ordered directly by Mack. Secret Anan technology only to be produced in Australia and New Zealand. Anan Corp factories were turning it all out under licence from The Eight. Mack had personally delivered the requisitions and secret specs before departing Earth on the Hela. Remembering that day, Alan didn't dare hope for the success that they had achieved now.

He opened another email, this one from Matt in the Hela base in Australia. A smile played on his face as he leafed down through the happy news. The remote desert station had grown into a town and the centre of their off-world shipping efforts by its manager, Matt. Pictures of the next colony's living pods, manufactured in Germany and laid out in the desert, burst from his screen. He forwarded it straight off to Kath who had already selected another five thousand candidates for the Colony-2 – double the size of the last.

Despite the political upheaval between the two so-called superpowers, Earth would be ready for when they came back. Alan could feel it in his bones. Come back they would, one way or another, someone or something would return to Earth.

BOOK 2 – PART TWO

CHAPTER TWENTY-THREE

CNS Headlines. Unanswered Questions.

On the 20th of December in Geneva, an important United Nations confer-ence takes place. What will the delegates discuss? Will they achieve anything? Or will it be another hopeless meeting full of empty rhetoric from a bunch of windbags?

Since the powerful Overlord called The Eight departed Earth nearly one year ago, the world has adopted none of the planet-saving measures he demanded. Old isolationist policies still prevail, frustrating any chance of the promised international co-operation.

People are getting tired – and do you blame them? Where is The Eight? The ethereal oval blue energy mass we usually see floating in his golden chariot has not returned. Are we abandoned again? Was the visit contrived to have his ship repaired and leave with two thousand five hundred human slaves? A question Anan Corp – the public face of the alien visitors – denies. As yet, they haven't been able to shed light on when the Hela and the elusive Overlord will return – or indeed, if they ever will.

> *Extract from:* **Continental News Services – Good Morning Planet Earth**

*

The Monarch, New World. EPTS: A139939

A SPECTACULAR DAWN STRUCK FORT Leslie. Red and orange light curled around the horizon, painting a breathtaking picture across the blue, cloud-less sky. The dawn chorus floated out from the nearby forest – more early morning singing birds than any human could imagine. Occasional beastly roars, a reminder of the deadly predators that stalked around outside the colony's security perimeter, cut in on the act. The light sea, mirroring a kaleidoscope of colours from the dawn filled sky, lapped at the beach.

Loud cursing, in a dulcet Scottish brogue (broad Jockenese), and the sound of shovels breaking ground, brutally bashed aside the ambience of the moment. The rain stopped, but its never-ending pouring had wreaked havoc along the spaceport's sand beach. Blair and his drill-crew laboured to dig the *Monarch's* landing gear out from the all-enveloping soft sandy muck.

"Why can't we use the bloody machines?" and "What pisshead uses shovels in this day and age?" were some of the (repeatable) disgruntled comments.

"Cause we don't want to damage the ship, ya numpties. How many times do I hae to tell ya that?' roared Blair, for the umpteen time.

A dull clang rang out, the sound of metal on metal, followed by another loud curse. An alarm sounded on the *Monarch's* bridge.

Siba Borea, up early to prep her nav-com for takeoff, looked over at the alarm. Standing tall and confident, she embodied the skills her family had brought to The Eight. Preferring to serve on the *Monarch* with Niamh, Tom and Bill, the man she was falling in love with, the purebreed girl had signed on with the Sullivan Parker Charter.

'What's that?' asked Bill, the only other person on the bridge. His face stared up from a weapons console, eyes now glued to the flashing alarm. The loyal soldier from East London had been by Tom's side from their early days in the Marines. A boots-on-the-ground man, Bill was now his reluctant second. "Glued to his duty and all-things-right", was The Eight's judgement of Bill.

'Proximity alarm. The digging crew must have hit one of the landing-gear sensors,' Siba answered. They both rushed to the comms panel, Siba activating the two-way holo-projector.

The *Monarch* came with spanking new tech humans had never seen before. The holographic imager was one. On the ground, the sight of Siba and Bill — dressed in matching navy work suits — surprised the ground crew. 'What the hell!' a man exclaimed.

'Oy, you lot,' shouted Bill, 'watch what you're doing. You'll break it even before we get it in the air.'

'Mr Hay, there are sensors all over that landing pad,' Siba said in a softer voice.

Glowing in the holo-image like a statue, the beautiful Siba, with white porcelain-like skin, standing beside Bill, the bald-headed security chief – black pockmarked face, crooked nose and all – sketched a surreal scene.

Blair tried not to laugh. 'Well, if it's no beauty and the beast!' He paused, gazing at the unreal vision. 'We know, Siba. Bill, leave it out. We'll take it easy.' Then, oblivious to the interruption, head down and arse up, Blair continued digging. The wind caught his kilt. Out on the piss all night, he hadn't time to change when the work call came through from Robert. Bare hairy arse mooned out, his tackle dangling for all to see below. Siba closed her eyes. Some human males weren't so attractive after all, she realised.

*

Two hours later, led by Niamh, the rest of the *Monarch's* skeleton crew took their places on the bridge. The starship had ample accommodation for three hundred. During the Borea tenure – split over three shifts – its space-crew compliment was near seventy-six. Niamh and Tom had gathered a skeleton crew of twenty-five to start this new phase of The Eight's war. A project within a project. After losing control of the Anan Navy, The Eight was starting from scratch again, collecting more ships, parts and crew to build a small fleet. This mission on the *Monarch* began the next phase of a master plan inspired by the deceased Pilot, Zaval Borea.

Readying the ship for takeoff, Niamh, took up her place at the captain's chair. Impatient to get going, she began the interrogation. 'Navigation, you ready Siba?'

'Yes, Captain,' the sharp purebreed answered.

'Engineering, you ready?'

The chief engineer, newly promoted – with many others – answered, 'Grav engines stoked. Fusion is up—'

'And the drivetrain?' Niamh probed, referring to the all-important blue drive's warm-up sequence.

'Drivetrain's running,' the man added. Strapped into the flight engineer's seat, the young man suddenly doubted his capabilities.

A process engineer who had followed Niamh from the construction job in France, he was one of the first to join Project Anan in Christchurch. He revelled at the tasks, studying alien tech, refurbishing the *Hela* in Australia and now their latest project – restoring the *Monarch*. But that was hands-on work: prepping the enigmatic machines and controls, cleaning the ship's interior, climbing into ducts, conduits, voids and right into the bowels of the engines. There was nowhere on the vessel he hadn't been. And that's why Niamh had given him the chief engineer's job – a far cry from the hands-on-graft he was used to. Even the short rescue mission to the Borea fleet wasn't as daunting as this. He knew then, where they were going and that they could be back at the New World in no time at all. This project was different. They were now playing in the big league.

The momentous task before him hit home; leaving the New World, heading off to unknown galaxies inhabited with aliens they still didn't know anything about on the most powerful and fastest ship in Anan-controlled space. And all to buy more alien ships and parts with a skeleton crew. The *Monarch's* shiny new chief engineer shuddered as he wondered what the hell he was doing here. Worse still, where would they get the people to staff the ships they were going to buy? It didn't make sense. He wasn't alone with that belief; others in the fledgeling human team also fielded such doubts.

By now the rest of the bridge team were strapped into command stations. Some worked traditional horizontal consoles, others, the unfamiliar transparent vertical-control systems. While they busied themselves getting ready, languishing in his chariot at the back of the bridge, The Eight watched the crew. With blue hair tied up in a bun, and blue-stained hands, Niamh's eyes glowed with soft white light, showing off the persistent blue energy contamination. By now, her body had come to terms with the pollution. The Eight wondered how long would that last. She needed help. If it was the last thing he would ever do, on this mission, he would get it for her. He noticed, on the bridge viewscreen, a shuttle fly into the forward bay – the last of Tom's soldiers coming aboard.

The shuttle's arrival heralded a change in the crew's demeanour. The Eight sensed their anxiety spike. They knew what was coming next. A daunting quest, one they hadn't signed up to when they left Earth. Crew an alien spaceship, a vessel most wouldn't have thought existed two years ago. And yet now they were operating this alien tech. *They have come a long way*, he thought. *Without the humans, Fort Leslie and the colony, I am done.*

'Shuttle docked, all crew on board,' Geoff said from comms, a posting he had dreamed about weeks earlier.

Time to go, Niamh thought. No more delays. Her face beaming enthusiasm, she issued the order that would start a project she longed for. 'Engines at ten.'

The chief engineer's hands swept across the translucent control station floating in front of him. Nothing happened! He pursed his lips in frustration. Silence descended on the bridge as all eyes fell on him. Taking a deep breath, he tried again. Slower this time, allowing the electric charge in his fingers to engage the optical-slider of the grav engine's throttle.

A greenish glow from his controls indicated success. *Monarch's* port and starboard grav engines responded, disengaging the steel-pinned docking locks. Synchronous modulators translated the bridge command into machine language. Vital orders flashed to the omnidirectional grav shields. Straddling the engine's drive ports, they opened. Grav burned, its lifting force flooding through the ship's structure. Instantaneous feedback pinged the engineering station.

Relief flooded through the young man's body. He relaxed back into his chair. 'At ten now,' he called out.

Again, nothing happened! The Monarch didn't move. All eyes on the bridge looked at Niamh. Her hands clawed the seat. *We're still stuck in the mud*, she thought, wondering how much of a difference Blair's crew had made. Maybe she needed more force to break the mud's suction. Not what Niamh wanted to do. Too much power and she'd rip something off the ship. Compromising, she waited, allowing the lifting force to soak into the muck. Time ticked on. Then, biting her lip, she commanded, 'Increase to fifteen.'

By now, the young engineer was shitting bricks. Would the first moments of humanity's endeavour to command such power be dashed?

Following orders, he stoked the engine. 'At fifteen,' he called back, voice trembling.

A loud thump and a tremor through *Monarch's* hull announced the ungraceful takeoff.

'We're up, Captain. Twenty metres and rising,' Siba said, her voice oozing confidence. Her hands were carving out a navigation projection – their course into orbit plotted – above the spectral console in front of her.

Niamh's hands spun back and forth across her command console. Like an extension of her brain, the *Monarch* turned a hundred and eighty degrees towards the ocean.

Outside, the colonists thronged Fort Leslie's vantage points. A low grumbling from the burning fuel announced the engine start. Excitement bubbled from them all. Cheers erupted as the ship rose from the spaceport on the beach and turned towards the ocean. This was another big day, a milestone for them and The Eight. The *Monarch* was off!

Following Siba's route, Niamh flew the ship out over the ocean and up through the planet's atmosphere. Thirty minutes later, as they gained orbit above the New World, she turned to face Tom and The Eight. 'We're up, Overlord, and on course. All systems healthy.'

Open vertically in front of him, Tom looked out from the luminous weapons console. The controls of the *Monarch* were quite different from the old *Hela*. Pop-out translucent vertical controls augmented each of the bridge's command stations. It had taken the humans time to adjust to the alien nature of "the touchy-feely systems" – their fitting nickname – but, with similarities to the Earth's smart-screen tech, they soon adapted. Tom smiled at his wife's enthusiasm. She sparkled with it – in every sense of the word. 'With the weapons system on-line she's a formidable ship, Overlord,' he added to Niamh's previous comment.

'Siba, coordinates for our first destination are on your navigation console,' their Overlord replied. 'Thomas, are our cloaks working?'

'Yes, they are, and more powerful than those the *Hela* has.'

'It is the latest stealth technology. I was surprised the Borea got their hands on it. No offence meant, Siba,' The Eight said.

Siba looked up and smiled. By now, she was well used to the unsettling revelations leaching from her family's past. No doubt, there would be more surprises to come. Programming The Eight's coordinates into the blue-drive nav-com, she called to Niamh, 'Navigation ready.'

All eyes turned to Niamh as her hands flowed across the ship's drive controls. The *Monarch* turned to face the stars. A thump boomed through the vessel's spine, announcing the blue drives had generated the elusive astronomical pulse. The human crew gasped as the gate through folded space opened in front of the *Monarch*.

Another confident order flowed from Niamh. 'Increase speed to fifty.'

This time the chief engineer got it right. The *Monarch's* grav engines poured pure power, forcing the ship, faster than the speed of light, through folded space. As Niamh balanced the drives, again, her human crew gasped at the view from the ship's windows. Star-filled space turned into a tunnel of stretched white light as they raced towards their first destination.

Satisfied with what the first humans to crew a starship had achieved, The Eight turned to leave the bridge. 'I go to my chamber. I will be back before you exit the fold,' he said.

Engrossed in their work and the visual spectacle of folded space, except for Niamh and Siba, the rest hardly noticed he was gone.

*

Earth, United Nations, Geneva, 20th December 2027

In Geneva, light-years across the cosmic divide, oblivious to the goings-on in faraway galaxies, Harold Addison, the Eight's representative on Earth, looked up from his scribbled notes. A year ago to the day, under nuclear attack by the Chinese and Russians, the *Hela* escaped into orbit from its base in Australia. It was a pivotal moment in Earth's history, forcing The Eight to take action, reworking world order. Harold scratched his head, wondering what improvements The Eight's visit had made. Today, it seemed there was little difference between past and present. Old arguments were new arguments.

With the *Hela* gone near a year, Harold organised this United Nations Eco-Conference. The "world-changing event" was turning into the usual adversarial gathering. Since his departure, mankind hadn't adopted any of The Eight's critical planet-saving measures. *A blot on humanity*, thought Harold. Frustrated, all Harold had written against each delegate's speech was "negative, negative and again negative". He wiped his sweaty brow as he listened to the Canadian espouse her country's opinion to the current proposal.

'We have a strong record supporting climate change initiatives. But this, banning the burning of fossil fuels, is a step too far. What do I tell our shale drillers? They're already burdened with crippling debt from the loans taken out years ago. The price has never recovered after the shale oil boom brought untapped resources to the market. You all benefitted from that, and didn't complain then. Now you want to dispense with a whole industry …'

Harold shook his head as she droned on, complaining how the introduction of free fusion energy to Earth's population would overturn worldwide economic markets. Finally, the tall woman finished. Harold's head jerked up when her voice stopped. He looked around, hoping no one had noticed he had dozed off. *Oh well*, he thought, as he pictured the headlines and the accompanying photo in the news feeds tomorrow. "Overlord's representative grabs forty winks during crucial world-saving U.N. debate." Next up was the Chinese envoy. *This will be interesting*, Harold thought, as he sat up. He smiled as a small man dressed in a neat blue suit took the podium.

The man paused and looked around at the delegates, waiting, until a deafening silence engulfed the chamber. His deep booming voice shattered that stillness. 'I am Chang Jin of The Peoples Republic of China. I serve The Eight and have promised to honour his will on Earth. Do not talk of debt. Do not speak of economic markets or your own country's self-interest. Have you not learned anything? Look at China; we have suffered. Yes, it was from the mistakes of failed leaders who chased the tail of economic miracles. As others who chased "the tail of the dragon", they found such paths wholly addictive. I have listened to some of you moan about economic deflation, the dreaded downward spiral of price. Are you not making enough profit? Shame on you all. You have missed the point, the elephant in the room. Climate change is the symptom, not the problem. You must look to the root cause to identify that. You all chose to ignore it, again afraid of the deflation that will follow.'

Shouts of dissent and abuse rose from the crowd.

Raising his voice, Chang shushed them. 'Do not bore me with the ethics of what is needed. Ethics are what you have – without any difficulty – ignored in the past. What is so different now? I will tell you! You are all more worried about the economic upheaval such deflationary measures will bring.' He stopped. Again, the dissenting murmurs began to rise, this time louder than the last, his standing amongst this gathering in question. But the gifted Chang wouldn't relent. The Earth-shattering secret he would reveal next would shock this rabble to the core.

'Quiet,' he shouted. 'Earth cannot support the population we have; you were told that, and that is what we need to talk about. It's the root cause of the problem.'

'Butcher of Beijing, you're a monster and a traitor to your nation,' Grigori, the Great Northern Union's President shouted. From the politburo class, the wiry old party-hack had waited for the *Hela* to leave before seizing power. Admiral Vasily and his young naïve military order – whom Robert had seated in the Kremlin, after killing the Russian President – were quickly swept aside. Grigori, the undersecretary of defence – knowing where bodies were buried – prevailed. The political vacuity, created by the demise of the old President, was a gift to Grigori. Rushing to fill that vacuum, he copper-fastened himself as "the people's man, a leader for change". Yes, change he promised, while he dragged Mother Russia back to the Stalinist days.

Chang, waiting for such an opportunity, railed back. 'After the destruction your nation inflicted on this planet, Grigori, you dare to call me a butcher!' His unwavering poker face hid his inner joy at the coming revelations.

Grigori sat down, his face paling with worry. *No*, he thought. *He couldn't have. There were no records …*

An unusual quiet descended on the packed chamber. Heads turned to look at the two protagonists. Harold sat up in his seat in interest. *What comes next?* he wondered.

'Don't look so surprised. I am Chang Jin. I know everything. Ladies and gentlemen, perhaps I should tell you how our great nations battle it out for supremacy. How warped and twisted the human race really is. He caused the Wave, the tsunami that killed millions, destroyed whole countries, cities, and our previous United Nations building. The one we now rebuild,' he shouted, pointing at the Russian delegate. 'The "explosion" that heralded the collapse of the island was planned by him. He planted micro-nuclear bombs in the caves below the Cumbria Vija ridge. Yes, he did that!' Chang Jin stopped as the chamber exploded with shouts of rage and "liar, liar, liar".

'Don't deny this, Grigori, you pig. You planned it and waited for the great storm to engulf the Atlantic. Oh, what a coincidence, the storm and the mountain explode at the same time. And you all believed it to be a volcanic earthquake. It was the perfect opportunity for them to grab their old land back and change the world order,' Chang shouted over the uproar. He paused, allowing the din to die down. Delegates shuffled uneasily in their seats. Chang stood still, holding the floor. Finally, he pointed at the Russian envoy. 'And you have the cheek to call me a butcher, Grigori. History will judge you. Not I. No, I won't go there. Let history decide what you are.' After that, pandemonium erupted.

The Secretary General stood up, shouting for calm. Eventually, the chamber went silent. He looked up at the now quiet man on the podium. 'Chang Jin, you have levelled terrible accusations here today. Before we go any further with this debate, can you prove them?' he asked, the rabble cheering his challenge.

'Of course, I can. I am Chang Jin. I have it all. Look and learn,' he said, pointing to the large screen in the chamber. A grainy video of Grigori sitting with the deceased Russian and Chinese defence ministers started to play. The sound quality was poor but subtitles confirmed a fiendish plot to decapitate Western Civilisation.

A speechless Harold watched as the video changed, this time to show caves inside the Cumbria Vija – slick GPS graphics confirming the location.

A group – dressed in the nondescript garb of western trekkers – were stowing rucksacks inside the cave's natural fissures. *Backpack nukes*, Harold realised, knowing full well the power those small devices would unleash. A scene showed the hook-up of electronic detonators, then the ten-minute video stopped. What wasn't shown was an earlier fit-out of a satellite-linked "seismic monitoring system". The unsuspecting contractors pre-wired the mountain for the detonation. Financed by a benevolent multi-national telco, the system contained a Wi-Fi backdoor to ignite devastation. The Kremlin hackers logged into the system and waited for the right opportunity. The rest was history.

'Do not take my word that this is genuine. Arrange an expedition to what's left of the island. They will find radioactive evidence of the explosion. You will see. I don't come here today with idle gossip.' Chang paused, his exposé knocking the delegates into silence. He had found the video deep inside a secret server in Beijing, his previous boss storing it as currency for the future, lest the Russians renege on the deal to divvy up the spoils. Common blackmail, nothing more! Now it showed man's inhumanity to man – a blot on human history.

Chang looked out at the now silent rabble and continued. 'Now to the debate. Again, I say, we need to tackle the underlying problem, not the visible symptom. We have to tackle overpopulation. Yes, it will cause deflation, and there are huge problems associated with that. The old order in China tried it, but they were defeated by economics. How do we do this? I don't have the answer but we must, we have no option …' And so he continued, over the heckling and barracking that now seemed to be the norm at these debates.

Silently, Harold thanked The Eight for the one difference he had made – nuclear disarmament. Weapons of mass destruction were no more; he had destroyed them. Yet the absence of a "mutual assured destruction doctrine" emboldened some in their warlike ways. Tit for tat border skirmishes abounded. *If The Eight doesn't return soon, war will*, Harold realised. *What's left of the United States will not take this lying down. No, they won't.* Looking over at the scowling U.S. envoy, he tried to listen to Chang's closing arguments for population control. But he couldn't, his thoughts kept returning to one worrying theme. *War was coming! No doubt about that.*

CHAPTER TWENTY-FOUR

Kandark Galaxy

Away from the main shipping lanes, the Kandark Galaxy is an out-of-the-way place. This minor galaxy located towards the edge of our known universe is not claimed by an Overlord. The sparsely populated star cluster is home to some minor edge-worlds of little economic significance, with one exception – the factory world, Planet Hirkiv.

Hirkiv, managed by a consortium of charters, hosts the most significant concentration of manufacturing facilities in our known worlds. It is the go-to place for starship and engine building, general maintenance and ship refitting.

In a neighbouring solar system, of some note is the scrapyard on Planet Lagrvth. This dry world, orbiting two suns, started out as a dumping ground and graveyard for outmoded or broken starships. This continues today, and the manged yard is the primary source of recycled hulls, engines, specialist starship parts and the like for the Anan charter houses.

‣ *Introduction from: Basic Galactic History. Theia Aknar*

*

The Monarch, The Dead Zone. EPTS: A139990

BACK ON THE MONARCH, THE dreaded part of the project that Niamh viewed as mundane and tedious, commenced. Arriving at their destination, the ship slowed. Together, Niamh and Kora brought up a navigation projection of the nearby solar system.

'We've never seen anything like that,' Kora said, surprised at the dark planets.

'It's a dead system,' Niamh replied, as they looked at close-up views of the lifeless worlds.

'It died millennia ago. Its sun is near the end of its life,' were the merge explanations The Eight offered, resting in the chariot that served as his "throne". Niamh had made the chariot for him on Earth. The engineering wonder housed memory banks, The Eight's energy mass and his blue energy tanks. Mounted on a small grav platform, the chariot let him move anywhere without using blue. The Overlord could store and access old memories, hibernate in his glass container and reduce his power needs.

Adorned with woven golden cables and silver panels mounted with rare blue pearls, the chariot appeared as a floating golden throne, shimmering with his blue light reflected in the silver and the pearls.

'You have the satellite ready, Thomas?' the powerful blue oval entity asked, more concerned with the business in hand than the curiosity of his human crew.

'Yes, Overlord. Launch coordinates are in. Geoff's programmed it with Mack's codes.'

'Anything showing on our scanners?'

'No, Overlord. We saw nothing on our way here. This whole galaxy, it's like a dead zone.'

'It is, Thomas. It was always known as that.' He moved over to Tom's command station and spent time inspecting the scans of deep space. The Eight trusted his human crew, but, on their first flight, he had to be sure they hadn't missed anything. Satisfied, he pulsed with blue light. 'Launch the first one.'

Tom worked on his control console. And then, after a small vibration travelled through the *Monarch*, an oval satellite launched into space from the ship's port bow.

The crew gasped at this strange new sight. Through the bridge windows, they watched the silver-coloured satellite disappear from view. Geoff picked it up on the long-range cameras. Mesmerised, they continued to stare at the bridge viewscreen until the satellite settled into an elongated orbit around the dying sun.

'Orbit confirmed. Geoff, can you test the comms burst?' Tom asked.

Geoff busied himself and then looked across to Tom. 'It's working. I've put the graph up on the viewscreen.' A series of alien pulses tracked across the large screen.

'Niamh, hold here for a six-hour test. Kora, the next system's coordinates are on your navigation console. I go to my chamber,' The Eight said, leaving the bridge.

After an uneventful test, the *Monarch* continued with The Eight's project, his crew launching the second and third satellites around low energy suns with similar solar systems, each in a different galaxy.

Niamh sighed and sat back in her command chair as she watched the all too familiar alien graph scroll across the viewscreen. 'Finally, the last one,' she said. 'That was long and boring. Overlord, I hope it works.'

The graphs changed, morphing into pulses that played across their large viewscreen, simultaneous low-tone sounds played from the bridge's speakers.

Bursting with excitement, Geoff looked up from his comms console. 'It's working, it's working,' he shouted. 'Look, the satellites, they've all linked – we've a coded message from Mack. From the New World!'

'What's it say?' Niamh asked, not sharing his exuberance.

'I don't understand, it's a string of numbers.'

'It's for me, Geoff. I understand it. The reply is on your console; send it now,' The Eight said. 'Niamh, we wait here for an answer.'

Forty minutes later Geoff turned from his comms console to The Eight. 'Overlord, reply is on screen. It's in Anan.'

Niamh looked at the Anan letters scrolling across their screen. 'That means "verified". We're in business, Overlord. You done with this?'

The Pilot's plan takes shape, he thought. 'Yes, you have the coordinates for the next destination. I will stay in my chamber. You know what to do from here.' As he turned in his chariot to leave, a flash of blue light betrayed The Eight's pleasure at achieving this project milestone. Untraceable despatches from the New World and the talented Neredian trader, Cylla Ora, were up and running.

Niamh looked across at Siba. 'Bring up the course plot to the Kandark Galaxy. Engineering, get the two blue drives online, ready to open a fold.' *Finally*, she thought, *we can go buy some hardware*. As she looked across at Tom, her big smile said it all.

On Niamh's command, the blue drives generated that intangible astronomical pulse. Travelling faster than light – on the second stage of its mission – the *Monarch* disappeared into folded space, leaving the dead zone far behind.

*

Fort Leslie, New World. EPTS: A140064

On the New World, after the departure of the *Monarch*, life moved forwards. Again, the disgruntled Mack went back into hibernation while Robert and Janet, planning their next move, ruled the roost. The departure of *Hela* and *George* towed by *Richard* to Earth, and off-world mining supported by *Maeve*, would happen this week.

The reorganisation, penned by Janet, took far less time than Robert had imagined. Three days after the *Monarch's* departure, *George* and *Hela* were ready to launch. Both ships, loaded with blue for storage on Earth, would turn the human home world into an intergalactic supply base.

First up, Verteg piloted the *George* – her two interfiled transporters stowed on board – into orbit, parking it ready for the tow. After that, the *Hela* took off, a sight none of the colonists missed. The vision of its golden hull rising up over Fort Leslie's spaceport raised cheers. With Verteg at the helm, it floated in reverse out over the ocean, turned one hundred and eighty degrees, gaining height out over the water, then up into orbit and parked with the *George*.

Refuelling the blue-guzzling *Richard* carried on into the night. The abundance of blue was not missed on Robert who, with Verteg and the colony's chief engineer, had to reapportion some of the precious grav to the departing fleet. *Maeve* had enough grav to support the off-world mining, and if push came to shove – in a failing world – grav could be scavenged from its engines.

'If we get to that point,' Shona said, 'we're done anyway. The Eight will have lost.' Wise words from the colony's new co-leader. Her wisdom was not lost on the others.

Early morning, five days after *Monarch*, the *Richard* took off. The colonists thronged the vantage points for a view of the ship that would spirit their two leaders, Robert and Janet, away. Last off the *Richard* was Cylla Ora, heaping final words of praise for Verteg and her Borea crew.

Before Cylla left, Robert and Janet managed a quiet word. 'What of Mack?' he asked.

Cylla sighed, her lips pursed as she tried to think of an answer. She couldn't. 'I don't know. I really don't. We have work to establish contact with the Energy Exchange. Sho calls it "on-line banking in space", whatever that means—'

She stopped as Robert and Janet laughed.

'But that's all he does. Nothing else. I try to involve him in the colony affairs but he doesn't want to know.'

Janet's head dropped, her face white with shame. Before she could utter a sound, Cylla raised a hand. 'It's nothing to do with you two. No, it isn't.' She paused. 'I'm afraid for him,' were her final words spoken in a hush. With that, she hugged Janet and Robert and left.

In orbit, Verteg distributed the crews between the fleet, configured the tow, and by the end of that day, *Richard*, *Hela* and *George* left the New World's solar system for Earth. All going well, they would return within three months, the *Hela* with a new colony, the *George* stuffed with supplies from Earth.

Fort Leslie didn't stop. Under the tutelage of the Borea elder, *Maeve* disgorged its cargo of off-world mining machines. Blair attacked it like a child in a sweetie shop, throwing questions in rapid fire at the Borea. By the close of business that day, the empty spaceport beside the *Maeve* transformed into an off-world mining "school" as the Borea revealed their secrets to the humans. Another milestone in the colony's development.

*

Monarch, Kandark Galaxy. EPTS: A140120

Taking some welcome time out before arriving at their first destination in an alien galaxy, Niamh and Tom lay together on the bed in their cabin. Fitted with a walk-in bathroom, dressing room and a separate area they had turned into an office – more like a suite, it outshone anything on the *Hela*. The warm homely place, brightly painted with soft colours, served as the couple's personal residence on the *Monarch*.

'Are you sure we can pull this off?' she asked Tom.

'Stick to the plan, Niamh. Siba has the ship prepped for a tow. She's done this before.'

'She's only done it once.'

'Well, that's better than never. Besides, you know this ship inside out.'

'And what if they're hostile?'

'We expect them to be; my guys will sort that out. Niamh, have faith; you're just looking for problems.'

'I'm worried.'

'We'll be fine. I'll look after you. You need to hide those guns. You can't walk into their world looking like—'

'Like what, Tom? They're staying.'

'No, they're not. We went over this Niamh; you agreed.'

A beep from the ship's comms system interrupted them 'Captain, we're approaching the Kandark Galaxy. Exit point is twenty minutes,' Geoff said.

'We'll be there in ten,' Tom answered, admiring his wife as she lay beside him. Love beat firm in his chest every time he held her. This time more so than ever. He sensed her natural apprehension – not a surprise, considering all that had occurred. 'We need to go.'

'It changes everything, Tom.'

He looked into her glowing blue eyes. 'No, it doesn't, Niamh. Stop worrying.'

*

Three hours later, the *Monarch* slowed as they approached Planet Lagrvth's solar system. 'Lose the cloak,' Tom said, as he pored over the navigation projection. 'Geoff, see if you can contact them. If they want visual, keep Niamh out of the picture.'

'Will do,' he replied, transmitting their pre-recorded greeting. They waited, and after what seemed an age, he responded with, 'They're transmitting visual and request we do the same.'

'Okay, Geoff, on me,' Tom said, from the captain's chair. He looked across at Niamh, seated at a station on the side of the bridge, and smiled.

'Captain, please identify yourself,' the male alien responded. Purebreed features mixed with another species and long black hair curled down around his neck, hiding his ears. Eerie pink eyes flashed as he blinked.

Tom smiled at the screen and held a hand up in a greeting. 'I'm Thomas Parker, of the Sullivan Parker Charter. We wish to negotiate the purchase of some equipment. We'll proceed into orbit and wait for landing clearance.'

'Captain, I never heard of your Charter, can you—'

Tom abruptly cut the transmission and brought up his control station. 'Cloak up now,' he shouted. 'Okay, Niamh, fast as you can get us into orbit around that planet.' He watched as she maxed out the grav and hybrid engines, flying straight towards the planet.

'They're trying to contact us,' Geoff shouted across to Tom, as they all braced from the acceleration.

'Send a message burst now; apologies, problem with our comms, we're trying to repair.'

'Message away.'

'Reply is on screen.'

An ominous signal flashed across their screen. "Drop your cloak and hold outside our solar system."

The ship entered the solar system flashing past some of its planets. After a deadly quiet, Tom broke the silence. 'How close?'

'Five minutes in at this speed. Hold on as I decelerate. Engineering, kill the hybrid drives now,' she shouted.

The ship started to shudder as Niamh applied reverse thrust to the grav engines. Strapped into their seats beside her, three engineering techs wrestled with the deceleration as they decoupled the hybrid drive. Protesting at the abrupt orders, *Monarch* vibrated from the braking force. Strapped in, the rest of the crew gripped their seats. Well prepared, those who weren't on watch, also strapped in. Despite the grav dampers holding power, they left nothing to chance, with everything tied down for this manoeuvre.

'Approaching orbit trajectory,' Niamh shouted over the noise. 'Engineering, on my mark, max power to the grav dampers, Siba – enter the orbit vector.' She waited as the ship sped straight for the planet. 'Now,' she shouted. The quaking noise rose like thunder as the protesting *Monarch* slowed and turned, entering orbit in the planet's thermosphere. Once again, Niamh's sharp flying skills had tested the *Monarch's* structure to its core. As usual, the Borea wonder-ship sailed through without a hitch. It was the human crew who felt the brunt of her actions – with some spewing their guts up. Not their usual day out!

'Message coming in, Tom; they want to know where we are,' Geoff said, his voice trembling with fright.

'Tell them we have an engine problem. We in orbit?'

'Yep,' Niamh replied, not a hint of her past apprehension. 'Right where we want to be – over their equator, up in the thermosphere.'

Tom dropped the cloak. 'Open visual comms.'

As the picture cleared, the scene from the other end had changed dramatically. There were now two more aliens looking back at them. Dressed in matching suits, their hair neatly braided, the two stood with their hands behind their backs. Swaying back and forth, one started to speak. 'Captain, how dare you invade our space in that manner. We've never heard of your Charter, and I do not recognise your species. You need to leave immediately.'

Tom stood up from his seat and smiled. 'My apologies, gentlemen. As you can see, we've had problems with our ship. We need parts to repair it and we would be keen to negotiate further with you both. I have it on good authority you are the most trustworthy surplus-parts dealers in this part of the galaxy.' Lowering his head in respect, he finished his prepared speech, 'I am a human. Thomas Parker, at your service.'

Even in this distant galaxy, flattery and reverence worked. One smiled. 'You're right, we are the best. But that doesn't forgive your uninvited approach. Who recommended us?'

'A trader by the name of Haret. I believe you know him.'

'Of course, we know him. Everybody knows him. He never mentioned you were coming.'

'No, but we've engaged his prodigy as our trader. You may have heard of her, Ms Cylla Ora. I have a message to you from her.'

'The Neredian, she works for you? I don't believe it. Send on the message.'

Embedded with her verification code and that of an Energy Exchange trader, Geoff transmitted a pre-recorded introduction from Cylla.

Ten minutes later, the same two appeared back on the *Monarch's* viewscreen. 'Mr Parker, it seems your credentials check out. We are sending landing coordinates for your shuttle.'

'Thank you, gentlemen. My wife will accompany me. We'll meet shortly.' He turned to Niamh and smiled. 'Come on, dear, let's go shopping. You see, I told you it would work,' he said, as he dodged a book she threw at him.

'Jeez, Tom, sometimes you're insufferable.'

*

Planet Lagrvth. EPTS: A140136

Niamh sweated from the heat as she stood beside Tom outside their shuttle. They had landed on the outskirts of the vast scrap yard on a hard rocky pad surrounded by a barren, dry yellow landscape. The sterile world's parched hard ground and dry atmosphere well suited the scrap trade. Nothing else flourished here. Niamh looked up at the two suns searing down on the desert. 'Jeez, Tom, this won't work. I'm sweating like a pig in this get-up; did you not think about getting a weather report?'

'I tried dear, but alienweather.com was offline.'

'You gobshite, you could have used the ship's sensors—' She turned away, bent over and vomited onto the dry ground. Standing back up, she wiped her mouth and hastily kicked some dirt over her mess.

She was right, Tom thought. In vain, he had tried to hide her blue contamination features with a scarf, gloves, sunglasses and a cloak. As the two aliens approached, she ran back into the shuttle. 'Gentlemen, thank you for meeting us. Apologies, my wife is a little indisposed. It's the heat. She'll be back soon. And also, for my command of Anan; she speaks it better than me. Thomas Parker at your service; you may call me Tom.' Once again, he tilted his head in reverence.

The aliens stared at him, one dressed in a two-piece grey suit, while the other had changed into a faded grey overall like the ship garment Tom had on. White purebreed faces, pink eyes, long black hair and at about five-foot-nine, the two looked unbelievably alike.

The one in the grey suit spoke. 'Mr Parker, I am Nolget, this is my brother Touqmat. I look after commerce. Touqmat looks after the machinery. He's an expert in his field …' Nolget's voice trailed off as he looked up to see Niamh bouncing down the shuttle ramp in a light ship garb with a small pack on her back. The two strange men stepped back as she walked up to stand beside Tom.

'How's it going, lads? Jeez, that's better, Tom. It's so hot here. Lads, I can't wait to have a look at your gear; I've never seen so much stuff in one place. There's miles of it. First I heard of this place was from a comms guy called Demard. He showed me one of your old ads. Do you remember him?'

Touqmat looked into her strange flashing white eyes, 'Demard Borea. I do. He had the sickness. How is he?'

'I'm afraid he succumbed to his ailment,' she lied.

'We're sorry to hear that. He was a legend in his own right—'

Tom butted right back in. 'Gentlemen, may I introduce my wife, Niamh Parker. She's the Sullivan in our Charter.'

'You're contaminated with blue,' Touqmat said.

'Yes, she is.' Tom replied as he took her hand and then kissed her on the cheek. 'I'm afraid she was repairing a hybrid drive some months ago when she ripped her protective suit. We're told the blue contaminate will dissipate over time. It's not harmful.'

Touqmat grimaced at the blatant lie. 'We've never known a biped to survive such exposure. Well, to business; what can we do for you?'

Without delay, Niamh passed over a tablet to him. He scrolled through the pages, turned and showed them to his brother, Nolget. They turned away, and while swaying backwards and forwards, held a whispered conversation.

Niamh looked at Tom. She grinned, and as he put his finger up to his lips, she turned away, trying to hold in her laughter at the comical sight of the two swaying brothers. He squeezed her hand and, as she looked back at him, he pointed upwards, giving her the thumbs up. She knew what he meant. Shuttle 2 floated – cloaked – right above them, loaded with his crew led by Brian, Kora's husband and one of Tom's lieutenants.

The two aliens turned and this time Nolget spoke. 'It's a lot of equipment with four ships as well. I gather you have funds?'

'Yes. Cylla Ora has arranged that. We have a commerce terminal and sufficient funds. Also, we have some commodities.'

The two brothers grinned at the mention of "commodities".

'Really? How quaint; you came well prepared,' Nolget said.

They all stood in silence until Niamh shook her head. 'Jeez, lads,' she blurted out with impatience, 'can we get a move on. I can't wait to get a look at those ships. Can we start with that bundle of four over there?' she said, pointing to four inter-system cargo vessels similar to the *Hela*.

Touqmat frowned at her request. 'You can, but they're on hold for another Charter. It's difficult, but yes, we should go. Here's the grav platform. I'll come with you; Nolget will stay here.'

*

Touqmat sat on the side of the grav platform beside Tom. They had landed in a far corner of the "yard" after inspecting eight ships. 'Your wife is an amazing woman,' he said, as she walked around the old fusion drives. They watched as she vomited again and then kicked the dust back over her mess. She stood up, waved at Tom and kept on working, inspecting the machinery and taking notes on her pad. 'I'm sorry she isn't well. That's how it starts from the blue exposure, then it gets worse. Did you know that?'

'No, I didn't,' Tom said, as he wiped his brow with his hands. *That's news*, he thought. *The Eight said she would be fine.* 'I'm sure she'll be fine. Tell me about the ships she wants,' he said, his brain in turmoil at what had just been said.

The four ships were sitting in a giant frame, two up and two down. Fitted in three segments, the frame supported each of the ship's three docking rings. The whole package was over eight hundred metres long and near four hundred metres high. With their golden hulls glistening in the sunshine, they were an astounding sight sitting in this desert scrap yard. Touqmat had flown them through each of the ship's interiors.

'We have them packaged ready for an intergalactic tow. As you saw, all the internal equipment is removed. The frames are clamped to the ship's docking rings. It's a good system. The package is lifted into orbit and towed wherever the client wants. The Svang Charter wants them. But so far they haven't paid the deposit. Here is your wife back. Come, Mrs Parker, sit and have some food and drink with me,' he said, as he opened a compartment on the grav platform.

They sat in silence as they ate and drank Touqmat's offerings. Finally, he put down his cup and looked at them both, 'I would like to sell you everything you want, even the ships, but we were recently served with a restriction by the Svang Charter. You know The Sixth's Shoter was the Charter boss.'

The expression on Tom and Niamh's face betrayed that they didn't know! This was info The Eight would relish. Wanting more, they stayed silent, casting hungry eyes at Touqmat.

Unabashed, Touqmat continued. 'Since he became Shoter, the Svang Charter – his wife actually – have demanded that they approve all our trades.' He paused as that news festered. Then, pink eyes alight with mirth, he smiled. 'We didn't want to turn you away. I gather you are not alone.'

Tom smiled back at the alien's frankness. 'No, we have company. But we didn't come to rob you either.'

'You have Borea cloaks?'

'Yes. How did you know?'

'Our scanners didn't detect your ship before you entered our solar system. Then you disappeared and reappeared in orbit. We have the codes for all the cloaks – we dismantle them – so we need the manufacturer's cypher. All except the Borea, and you mentioned you knew Demard. You lied when you told me he died from the sickness.'

Purebreed brain cognisance, he had sensed her lie. Niamh tried to speak, but he put up a hand to silence her. His voice sharpened. 'Don't tell me; the less we know, the better. The equipment – you have seen what you want?'

Not expecting such a twist, Niamh blurted out her list. 'Yes, I want six of those fusion generators and twelve grav engine housings.'

'They're all shot, no pumps with them, and the grav engines, they're housings only.'

'We can use them. Will you throw the lot in?'

'Yes, but you need to know, if you're going to have them repaired on Hirkiv, he's robbing everybody. Our business fell off once he raised his prices. It's the rush to convert to grav. When blue dried up, we had a surge in business. Everybody wanted old grav ships. Then he upped his fees and they couldn't afford the refit costs. I have his prices,' Touqmat said, passing a tablet over to Niamh.

'Jeez, Tom, he's charging half a mil credits for a new grav engine. A mil for a hybrid drive! Shit, we can't afford that. And look at the refit costs.'

Tom put his hand on her leg. Lips pursed, he scowled at her. He knew she was thinking of the competition they could bring to this market. No. Not now, that wouldn't happen. Maybe a future enterprise. They had a war to win first and too much information for Touqmat would put him in danger. She got the message and stayed quiet.

With a throw-away comment, Tom lightened the mood. 'Oh well, we'll have to hit him over the head and rob him.' Keen to change the subject, he noticed a grav platform approach from the distance. 'Touqmat, is this your brother approaching?' he asked.

'Yes, we wanted a quiet place to discuss business. You know, away from the office. The walls have ears and there's a surveillance system too.'

With a wry grin, Tom nodded. Perhaps things might go their way after all.

They watched as Nolget landed. 'Mrs Parker, Mr Parker, I trust my brother has whetted your appetite?'

'He has that,' Niamh replied, smiling at the alien as he approached.

Price negotiations lasted near half an hour, finally settling on a quarter-million credits for the ships and some of the heavy equipment. The figure delighted Tom. The Eight would pay for half, buying two of the hulls

– it was what he had agreed to as their wedding present. Their Charter would pay for the rest. With the money they had earned and the shares they had in Anan Corp, it was enough. The rest of the equipment Niamh wanted, they could buy with The Eight's commodities at a discount. Cold hard cash worked anywhere! Tom didn't want to think about where the money would come from to pay the crews and for the fit-out – that was Cylla's job. It was war, there were no other options. He would get what he needed to advance The Eight's cause.

Nolget stood up, disturbing Tom's thoughts. 'Come back to the office for the formal conclusion to our business.'

*

Earth, 27th December 2027

On Earth, Harold Addison's fear – war was coming – materialised. The United States dispatched a survey mission to the Canary Islands or what remained of them. The radiation detectors verified Chang's accusations. No doubt, the deceased Russian and Chinese defence ministers plotted to decapitate Western Civilisation. High levels of radiation confirmed a nuclear detonation had caused the Wave event, a blot on any country involved in such a heinous crime. China had paid the price; The Eight had seen to that. Chang's reforms were taking hold, seeds of a new people's government sown. In reality, Chang resurrected the Communist Party, setting himself up as lifelong president. Using existing structures of government was easier than moulding something new from scratch. The appearance of him as President helped the illusion of change.

When The Eight departed, the Great Northern Union, and the United States of America, regressed back to the old leadership. Entrenched attitudes of "make America great" and "make Russia great" pushed both countries into a downward spiral of bellicose threats. News from the survey team energised those warnings!

*

Early morning in Dolinsk, on the eastern edge of Russia, a pilot and weapons systems officer finished their pre-flight checks. In two other MiG-31s parked beside them, their comrades did the same. Clearance from the tower and the three MiGs rolled forwards, making their way to the runway. Minutes later, with a burst of raw power and sound from the MiG's twin jets, all three fighters took off. The three banked northeast, heading out to the Bering Sea to play cat and mouse with the U.S. navy. The pilot touched his – banned – good luck charm stuck in the corner of his cockpit. The regulation mystified him, for what harm would a picture of his wife and two children do? After touching it, he pressed his hands to his lips and smiled at the thought of them waiting at home near the base. He would see them tonight as he started his three-day leave. Faster than sound, the MiGs sped towards the U.S. Russian border, the limit of their sovereign motherland. The mission – at all cost, protect the border from the foreign invaders.

Too young to remember the Cold War, the pilot had never experienced such tension between the two nations. All he knew was that the U.S. had made false allegations that the Russians had started the Wave event. The party line was "American propaganda, a pretext to invading their country". Now he would do his duty, on patrol on the front line. The daily skirmishes getting ever closer – U.S. planes and navy jousting with the Russians. Today, reports of an enemy frigate sailing across the boundary line in the Bering Sea prompted their launch. The mission – stop and turn the frigate back, or destroy it. To the valiant aviators, this was a routine patrol, nothing new. A fly-by to harass the frigate until her captain tires and retreats to the safety of U.S. waters. Then it's mission over, and home.

*

The U.S. Navy frigate tracked the three planes flying towards them. The routine – follow the boundary line, sailing in and out of Russian waters. The aircraft would do the same, weaving in and out of U.S. territory, each faction never staying long enough in the other's country for their opposite number to get a shot off. Until today, when the U.S. frigate's orders had changed. Hungry politicians demanded results.

The frigate's captain re-evaluated their target options. The missile launch could be pre-programmed by the onboard computer and its guidance automated. Operational limits broadened, with automatic control assigned to the trigger mechanism. Safety systems disabled. Everything that prevented an accidental or mistaken launch of a weapon deactivated. Once the planes appeared, on a vector that crossed the border, the missiles would fire. The captain's hope, target hit as they crossed the line!

Taking the role of the mouse, the frigate started its run, treading the fine line back and forth across the U.S. Russian border. As expected, the three MiGs appeared from the south-west. Tracking systems locked onto each one, as the cats started to worry the mouse. A fast run over the frigate, into U.S. airspace, and back to Mother Russia. The frigate's computer recorded it all, predicting flight paths, speed and missile trajectory. A green light flashed on the operation's weapon's system.

A message printed across a screen: "target vectors calculated".

The captain verified the launch order.

"Missiles armed and ready" printed across the screen.

The three Russian MiGs turned to make another run at the mouse. Little did they know, they were now the mouse and the cat had sharpened its claws. The frigate's weapons' computer had multiple target solutions ready to go. From inside their motherland, the MiGs started their second run, the crews elated at the buzz of the encounter, razor-sharp senses on edge to react to any change for a life-saving course correction. Before they crossed into U.S. airspace, the proximity alert sounded. The frigate had launched and multiple missiles tracked towards the three planes.

The MiG's weapon's officers initiated countermeasures – human brains lagging behind computer-driven warheads. Milliseconds later, the surface-to-air missiles exploded. Thousands of steel particles shredded the MiGs and their occupants. Cut to bloody ribbons, instantaneous death followed. The six aviators' lives snuffed out, and six families lost loved ones. On the other side, elation for the frigate crew at their computer's success and the destruction of the three planes.

The MiG's location – where they were when the missiles hit – was for another day. Others would argue that, bending facts to fit whatever side of the argument one was on. But the drama hadn't finished. Inside the Russian border, on the floor of the Bering Sea, a submarine running on silent tracked the frigate. Another cat chasing a mouse.

Following the surface drama, a long-standing veteran of submarine warfare, the sub captain's blood boiled. Sensors showed the U.S. missiles were fired when the MiGs were in Russian airspace. The crews had no chance. The captain of the sub fired three torpedoes at the frigate.

The frigate's crew, focused on the MiGs and elated at their three kills, missed the tell-tale sign of the tracking sub. Too late, alarms rang out as three torpedoes slammed into the side of the ship. The explosions ripped through the engine room, igniting the fuel. The tanks breached, more fuel gushed out, feeding the fire that belched through the frigate, a chain reaction of burning horror exploding the armaments.

Sirens sounded and emergency lights flashed, stoking the crew's worst fears. Inside the operations' centre, watertight doors closed, failing to lock into their twisted bulkheads. In a futile attempt to save their vessel, sailors ran to do their duty trying to extinguish the fires. More explosions generated more fire and smoke – a living hell for those trapped below decks.

An order nobody wants to hear bleated over the P.A. system. 'Abandon ship. Abandon ship …'

In that smoky inferno, life choices were, burn to death, suffocate or drown. Emergency lights tried to bring some illumination through black smoke – a welcome help to those trying to escape. The pressure of the sea pushed in until buckled watertight doors burst open. Water rushed through corridors, flooding compartments where some sought sanctuary. In its death-throes, sailor's screams carried through the ship.

The ill-fated frigate came to rest on the border between the two superpowers, black smoke gushing from its superstructure. Mortally wounded, within minutes she slipped below the waves, down to a watery grave. In silence, the crew of the Russian sub listened to the frigate and its crew's death. Within seconds, they turned their attention to their own survival – for an American sub was tracking them …

Few survived that day, the majority of the frigate's compliment perished along with the Russian aviators they had downed. Brave soldiers on both sides, following orders from politician's hell-bent on pushing their own agenda. Brainwashed by numpties into thinking they were protecting their sovereignty from invaders. Nothing could justify that loss of life. The U.S. and Russian leaders traded insults, each blaming the other. Claim and counterclaims were made, as the senseless war raged on, the planet dying beneath their feet and an invasion of Earth planned by an evil Overlord. Yet, the unthinkable had happened – direct conflict between two superpowers had started.

A full-blown war, centred across the Bering Sea, the only border that divided those two world powers, erupted. Regional conflicts escalated wherever the two countries' interests collided. In the Middle East and North Africa, proxy wars intensified. As Harold feared, the absence of nuclear weapons and the "mutual assured destruction doctrine" locked both superpowers into an unwinnable conflict. Other moderate states looked on in horror at the mindless madness. World War III had started.

CHAPTER TWENTY-FIVE

Ragma and Joran Galaxies

The Ragma and Joran galaxies are twin sister star systems ruled by The Sixth. In a glorious past, both galaxies enjoyed prolific deposits of blue energy. Over the passing time, rising usage of blue exhausted the finite energy resource. The Sixth invested significant capital in recovering missed deposits from out of the way places. With his prodigy, The Ninth, he developed mines on Planet Gethsema a vast gas giant in the Ragma Galaxy. Amongst the varied and many planets within the two-galaxy system, is the windswept planet, Natok.

In the heart of the Jora Galaxy, this diverse planet orbits two suns and has one moon. Its topography varies from lush verdant grasslands to cold, harsh deserts. The Sixth has avidly guarded the world, prohibiting any biped settlements or sightseeing visits.

‹ *Introduction from: Basic Galactic History. Theia Aknar*

*

Planet Lagrvth, Kandark Galaxy. EPTS: A140162

AFTER A FLIGHT BACK OVER the vast scrap yard, Niamh and Tom filed into the two brother's office, taking seats beside each other. On the way in, Tom noticed two armed security amongst the other staff. At six-foot-tall with broad, burly shoulders, their green-skinned faces tattooed with geometric shapes, the two males looked the part but Tom suspected otherwise. Tunics untidily buttoned, grav stun-guns hanging loose over their shoulders – a tardy pair, he surmised.

Seated across the table beside his brother, glaring at Tom and Niamh, Nolget spoke first. 'We told you when you landed, uninvited I must add, we were unable to trade. As a consequence of this new Energy War, the Svang Charter restricts whom we may deal with and what we can sell. It was a pleasure to meet you. When the war is over, you should return. We would welcome your business.'

Touqmat shook his head. Swaying on his chair, he looked across at Niamh. 'Mrs Parker, I'm sorry. I know you were set on the equipment and ships but our hands are tied.'

Like lightning, Tom stretched out, grabbing Touqmat's arm. Stabbing a knife through the alien's hand, he pinned it to the table. Red blood spurted out, staining the clean white tabletop. Touqmat screamed. Tom, letting him go, grabbed Nolget, wrapping his arm around his throat. The two security guards rushed in but were stopped dead in their tracks by Niamh pointing a gun at them. 'Weapons on the floor now,' barked Tom, 'or she'll shoot and I'll crush your boss's neck.'

Shaking at the threat, the two dropped their weapons and fled. Tom dragged Nolget out the door, followed by Niamh. They looked up to see shuttle 2 de-cloak above them and land on the ground beside the office. Led by Brian, four of his men rushed into the office building. 'Secure the comms. It's at the end of the hall, on the right,' Tom shouted, as his men rushed past. Bundling Nolget into the shuttle, he tied him to a seat. 'Kim, get the med-pack and the Anan plasma. You're with me. Niamh, you stay here,' he said, as he ran out of the shuttle followed by Kim.

Back in the office, he wrenched the knife from Touqmat's still bleeding hand. 'Fix him up. We need him,' he said to Kim.

Brian appeared, leaning into the room. 'Boss, comms secure, no casualties and their security team have surrendered. There's a small lock-up at the back; we've put them there.'

'Sorry about the hand, Touqmat, but I need to let you know we mean business. We want what we agreed on. This is a clock that records Earth time. Twelve of our hours are about equal to ten galactic time segments. You've twenty-four hours to have that equipment packed into one of the ships and the bundle of four in orbit, or I'll kill your brother.'

'It's not possible. Not in that time frame.'

'Well, you'd better get cracking. Kim, how's his hand?'

'You messed it up good, boss, but with the Anan plasma and this gismo,' she said, lifting up an Anan healing device, 'I'll have him fixed up in no time.'

'Brian, you and Kim stay with him. Watch his every move. Post a guard at the comms unit and the shuttle. I'll head back to the ship on shuttle 1 with Niamh and the prisoner. Remember, Touqmat, any funny business and your brother dies. His commerce terminal, where is it?'

'In his office – next door. You won't get away with this; they'll come after you.'

Taking the commerce device, Tom left the building. In shuttle 2, he cut Nolget loose. 'Right, get a move on,' Tom said, kicking Nolget out the door. 'We're going up on that one,' he said, pointing to shuttle 1.

Niamh cringed as she watched Tom kicking Nolget all the way to the shuttle. He fell over, scraping his face on the rocky ground. Tom roughly pulled him back up then booted the poor man on. Bright red blood ran down his face. Whimpering, Nolget pleaded for Tom to stop his non-stop kicking.

'It hurts, it hurts,' Nolget cried, his body crumpling under Tom's blows.

Finally, when they entered the shuttle, Tom tied Nolget into a seat at the front of the cabin.

'When you're ready, dear, fly us home, please. And you can put that gun back in your bag. We won't need it anymore.'

The sight of her husband's brutality drove Niamh to tears. 'Ya maggot, did you have to be so rough with them?'

*

Planet Natok, Jora Galaxy. EPTS: A140163

Oblivious to where and what The Eight was doing, back on Natok, The Ninth revelled in his decision to approve Bardek's delay. Typical of The Sixth's manner, the impatient Overlord hadn't been heard of since The Ninth's challenging message: "If my Overlord is unhappy with the delay, you are welcome to take over the project." A deafening silence followed, the narcissistic Sixth sulking in self-pity.

Giving Captain Bardek the time he needed to load the ceirim and prepare the fleet for the invasion of species-y's home world, paid off. That extra time allowed Kochtos and his loyal lieutenants to hunt and feed on the animals roaming the grasslands the ships had landed on. That freedom, not felt in an age, invigorated the ceirim, ingratiating them to The Ninth – a millstone reached in fostering his relationship with Kochtos.

Today the fleet's seven starships were ready: hibernating ceirim and banned extinction weapons loaded, planetary transporters and shuttles stowed, and the last of their supplies shipped out from Anan, with some more flight crew onboard as well.

The Ninth, leading an inspection team comprising Bardek, his colourful comms officer and the commanders of each ship, made their way throughout the fleet.

The Javonian comms officer had validated the post-commissioning system checks with each vessel commander. Today, the cursory inspection demonstrated that work to The Ninth. The mission planning left for the voyage, but today – physically – the ships were ready for flight. No doubt of that.

'You did well, Bardek,' The Ninth said. 'Finally we are ready. Lift off and make all haste to the species-y galaxy. I will let The Sixth know.'

Bardek watched as the Overlord's blue oval energy mass floated over to *Chad*, disappearing up its gangway as The Ninth made his way to his chamber.

'Well, you heard the Overlord. Make ready for flight. We lift off in one cycle,' Bardek cracked to his commanders.

Back in his chamber on *Chad*, across space and time, The Ninth reached out his consciousness to connect with The Sixth. *'We are ready, my Lord.'*

'It took you long enough,' The Sixth snapped back.

The Ninth refused to react or reply to such goading.

'Better late than never, I suppose. You have everything, Nine?' The Sixth asked.

'Yes, my Lord, we do.'

'Contact me when you reach species-y's galaxy,' The Sixth replied and was gone.

The Ninth waited for the residue of their contact to dissipate in the cosmic mists. Then he reached out to another.

'So, Nine, you are ready at last. The Sixth believed you couldn't do it. Raged about your delay and incompetence,' The Seventh said.

'Yes, from his silence and terse replies, I know I am out of favour. But I have done what he asks – we hold species-y fate in our fleet's holds,' The Ninth said.

'Are you satisfied with Bardek's preparations?'

'Too late if I'm not, Seven – we go regardless. We are at war now. Bardek has proved himself – as you said – a worthy captain. I have a formidable force at my disposal.'

The Seventh contemplated his friend's words. 'Beware, Nine. Do not assume this will be an uncomplicated venture. It is a long journey, far from our home galaxies. You will be on your own and we do not know where The Eight is. Nine, I trust you will do your best – but you must remember how creative The Eight can be.'

'I have no illusions, Seven. Whatever happens, I will deliver the ceirim to species-y. If I do not return, Seven, flee. Get as far away from the Anan Galaxy as possible.'

With nothing else to say, the two Overlords broke their intergalactic connection.

Exactly one cycle after Bardek's order, led by *Chad*, the *Shaqa*, *Chesh*, *Amech*, *Tain*, *Losh* and *Abra*, took off. Loaded with extinction weapons and sixteen thousand ceirim, the deadliest armada the known universe had seen in an age, made its way to Earth.

*

The Monarch, Kandark Galaxy. EPTS: A140208

Thirty-six hours after leaving the planet's surface, Tom watched as two of Touqmat's space-tugs manoeuvred their package of four ships behind the *Monarch*. He gazed out in awe at the inter-system cargo vessels – their golden hulls shimmering in the bright light of Lagrvth's two suns. His stomach heaved at the sheer size of the eight-hundred-metre-long by near four-hundred-metre-high behemoth, overshadowing the size of the smaller *Monarch*. His wife's earlier doubts rang loud in his mind: *"Are you sure we can pull this off?"* she had asked Tom before they started this caper. His glib answer had brushed aside that valid question. Now was the moment of reckoning!

Unusual for Tom, a shaky voice betrayed his feelings. 'Are you sure you know how this works?' he asked Siba, occupied at one of the new pop-up translucent control panels she had created over the last week.

'Mr Parker, it's a different configuration to what the space-tug uses. More modern and simpler. We run the tow bridle from the array under the ship and it connects straight into the head of the package. The rest is done by grav beams and the bubble. Tow control is automated.'

Niamh glanced over at Tom from her command chair. Her smooth look, which seemed to say, "I told you so", said it all!

This was Siba's baby! The young purebreed girl loved every minute of this challenge, totally immersing herself in the newest towing tech!

Placated by Niamh's laid-back guise, Tom relaxed. 'Very good, Siba,' was all he could muster. Time for him to go – business beckoned. He glanced back at Niamh and nodded. 'Come down to me when you can.'

Making his way off the bridge, he took the lift down to a "stateroom" in the lower section of the hull. The luxurious room had been Grandfather Borea's quarters – where he had lived, and a part of his own personal runabout. During the *Monarch's* restoration, The Borea had wanted to gut it, but Niamh objected. "It's a marvel of elegance," she had said, "you'll never see the like again, on any of our ships." She was right, the décor reflected a unique alien opulence never before seen. The D-shaped room, fitted with large windows, gave an impressive view of the space outside the ship. Not only aesthetic, it had also given the old pirate a commanding view of the goings-on in his domain.

Decorated with vibrant colours – blue, orange, peach, pink, gold and turquoise – the room reeked of the Borea's previous prosperity. Bright floral displays – full of life – erupting from navy stems, adorned the white porcelain tiled floor and walls. Glazed into the walls were lavish oval images of peachy flowers with turquoise leaves, framed by navy-blue scrolling feathers, drawn in a delicate golden brush stroke. Symmetrical blue-grey hatched borders divided the porcelain pictures.

Light, minimalistic furniture complemented this lavishness. A tapered-leg soft-blue desk and matching chair commanded the view over the room. Dainty, pastel-coloured chaises longues, arranged in a semi-circle – as if in silent worship – sat in front. It was where the old pirate held court. An unlikely setting, where he planned murder and mayhem with his cruel disciples.

A small alcove, designed for living, contained some more practical furnishings. A functional table and four chairs, a couch, and the only change Niamh had made, an entertainment system from Earth they had scoured from the colony. The hard-disk contained gigabits of Earth culture, movies, music, sports and nature. And some of Tom and Niamh's own personal photographs. Waited on hand and foot by the *Monarch's* crew, Nolget had spent his waiting time exploring this foreign theatre. In amongst Tom and Niamh's stuff, he found an interesting video.

It showed a team of human girls, dressed in red and blue jerseys, running along a green field. Adorned by different coloured helmets with face-guards and holding weapon-like sticks, they chased a strange white ball. One of the red jersey girls, her teeth gritted in a fearsome scowl, managed to pluck the ball from the air. She threw it back up, and with both hands now on the stick-shaped weapon, struck the ball. Like a missile, it sailed through the air, the view of the camera following it as it fell into a net strung between two posts. The girls in the red jerseys jumped for joy, surrounding the one who made the shot. The camera zoomed in on her – red mud-splattered hair streamed from below her helmet. To Nolget's surprise, he realised it was a younger Niamh. And it was a ball game that humans played! *What manner of beings are these?* he had wondered. Mesmerised, he had watched the rest of the camogie game. *If this is what they teach their engineers, what do they teach their soldiers?* he had wondered.

Knocking on the door, Tom entered. Configuring two commercial terminals, Geoff sat across from Nolget at the table in the alcove.

'Nolget, it's nearly done. They're hooking up the package now. Geoff, you got those things linked yet?'

'Yes, boss. We just received the verification codes for both. I'll head back to the bridge.'

'Niamh will be along shortly. I need her for our codes. In the meantime, we can conclude with the commodities.'

Not a trace left of his facial wounds or the rough treatment he had gotten from Tom, a curious Nolget sat back in interest as Tom unlocked a secret panel contained within one of the elaborate floral images on the wall of the room. Taking out bags from the wall cavity, Tom sat back down beside Nolget.

'I'm sorry for the violence, but you did ask me to make it realistic.'

'We did. When the Svang Charter comes calling, the surveillance video and our staff will corroborate that. I'm so glad it was my brother you stabbed, not me,' Nolget said, his soft voice laced with anticipation.

Tom counted out four, half-kilo gold bars. 'This is for the damage we will do to your comms systems – all three transmitters. We'll take them out when we leave. It should take you some time to repair.'

Nolget watched as Tom put the bars on the table. 'At least two hundred time segments.'

'These are what we agreed on for the extra control equipment, breakers and the stuff Niamh had listed as parcel two. Fifty carets in clear diamonds and five kilos of gold.'

Nolget reached out and took the bag of diamonds, shaking them out onto a cloth he had placed on the table. He took some up, looked at them and smiled at Tom as he put them back into the pouch.

'Finally, for the eight cloaking devices and the codes,' he said, looking at Nolget.

'Yes, the codes are with the devices, and your wife has copies.'

Tom reached into another bag, took out five deep coloured blue diamonds and handed them over to Nolget. The cream of the crop. 'You're a thief,' he said. 'Such a lot for old scrap.'

'Ha, ha, ha,' he laughed. 'You got a bargain – no one else will deal with you.'

Niamh walked in. Tom looked up at her and smiled. 'You done?'

'Yep, we can pay our debts and leave. Nolget, you look happy,' she said, looking down on the pile of gold and diamonds on the table.

'I am. Come, I'll show you how to work your terminal for the credits transfer. There are two accounts, I believe.'

'Yes, there are,' Niamh said, watching as he opened the intergalactic commerce system that linked them with the Energy Exchange. The alien technology never ceased to amaze her. As the three of them entered their payment codes, she remembered what the Pilot had told her after the conference with Haret. The Sixth could never infiltrate the underlying cyphers written into the Exchange computers. Their transactions and funds would be safe from him in the Exchange Central Bank. It was what Cylla had set up – their own Charter account – using the satellite system they had launched in deep space.

'There, it's done. You are an honourable couple. You could have robbed us and left,' Nolget said.

Niamh grinned at Tom. 'I wouldn't let him do that.'

'Mr Parker, before I go back to the planet, I want to talk about something else. You are from a military background?'

'Yes, Nolget, I am. Why do you ask?'

'After your arrival, it occurred to me that you could kill us and take what you want. You saw how poor our security team are. We never felt the need for protection. We're a scrap yard, after all. With the war, that's going to change. Would your Charter be able to provide such a service?'

For the first time, Tom was at a loss for an answer. He looked at Nolget; his mouth opened but nothing came out. It was Niamh who came to his rescue.

'He's great at security, but I think he may be a bit stretched now. Tom, dear, answer the man.'

He cleared his throat. It was all running around in his mind at a hundred miles an hour – a base in the Kandark Galaxy on Lagrvth; it was something he hadn't considered. *How could we get that going?* he thought, as he looked over at Nolget and smiled. 'Yes, we are a bit stretched now, but we may be able to work on something. It's the distance. Niamh will calculate flight times and fuel, and we'll let you know.'

'The sooner the better, Mr Parker. We would prefer to throw our lot in with you. We're an independent entity, never before tied to an Overlord or

Charter. We were vexed when served with a sales restriction by the Svang Charter. Such meddling in our affairs is an outrage.' He stood up to leave, hefting the bag full of his "commodities" over his shoulder. 'Good luck to you both. Now that we have finished our trade, you can take out our comms. I look forward to doing business in the future. Is that your crest?' he asked, turning to look at their Charter Crest hanging on the alcove wall.

It depicted, positioned to the left, a silhouette of Niamh's headline to her shoulders. She wore a graduation cap, with her long hair draped around her right shoulder and flanked by a pen. Tom, wearing his regimental cap and flanked by a sword, faced her. Their family names, Sullivan and Parker, arched above them in a scrolled banner. Overlaid between them, on the lower part of the crest, was a heart. A silver fern, representing New Zealand, the land where they first met, decorated the crest. Likewise, simple black and silver colours added the finishing touch.

Niamh looked away – her eyes started to moisten. She had forgotten about the symbolism in their crest, and now, after they had concluded their first deal, she finally understood its purpose. She turned and smiled. 'Yes, it is.'

'You need to get it on the side of your ships. Next time, I'll give you an all-in price on the etching,' he said, as he walked out of the room.

*

Making her way back to the bridge, Niamh reflected on how far they had come. So much had happened since she had first told Tom she wanted to own her own ships. It was in the car on their journey to the winery north of Christchurch, after he had given her a present of blue pearl earrings when they first connected. She arrived on the bridge, a broad grin advertising her spirits. 'You guys all ready?'

Siba turned and looked at her, still smiling, eyes glowing blue. But it was Niamh's hair that mesmerised Siba – glowing blue, matching her eyes. 'Yes, yes, we are.'

'When the shuttle returns, we'll leave. You got a course plotted to Hirkiv?'

'Yes, Captain. Kora plotted it before she left on the shuttle.'

'Right,' she said, as she sat down in her chair, the view of the package dominating the bridge viewscreen. Hearing a noise behind, she turned to face The Eight.

'Come,' he said. 'Let's look from the aft viewports in my chamber.'

In his chariot, The Eight led the way. His chamber – dominated by a copious glass-like wall – looked out over the after-end of the ship into space. Niamh never got tired of admiring the *Monarch* from here. The views, down and along the hull, giant gun turret rising above the mid-ship section, and the two oval grav missile launchers nestling above the port and starboard pennon wings, were spectacular. And now, the square package of four Hela-class transporters, eight hundred metres long, glistening golden in the half-light of the two suns, dominated the space behind their ship. They floated majestically in orbit behind the *Monarch*, held in place by Siba's carefully crafted tow above Lagrvth, the yellow planet below.

'My child, a bit late but your wedding present,' he said, referring to the gift he had given them. Their right to buy trading and extraction ships, to own and develop Anan technology, their Charter — and he had funded the purchase of two of these ships.

'Overlord, thank you. You have no idea what this means to me. I know you gave us the *Monarch*, but this! We have actually bought two ships ourselves. This is our fleet.'

'The fruits of your labour; you and Thomas have worked hard for this.'

'Did someone mention my name?' Tom said, entering the room.

The Overlord flashed with blue light, turning to face him. 'Yes, Thomas, I did. You did well on the planet. They did not suspect my involvement.'

'No, Overlord, they did not. Nolget has just left on shuttle 1. He has asked us to provide a security detail for his planet.'

'A base in the Kandark Galaxy. That is an opportunity I did not envision. Complicated, but you could do that.'

'What about Touqmat's intel, the Shoter—'

Before Tom could finish his sentence, The Eight pulsed with purple light. A low rumble, like nothing they had ever heard before, followed. No doubt, this was terrible news. The two humans stayed quiet, waiting for The Eight's rant to subside.

Five long minutes of silence, then the powerful entity spoke. 'Valuable intelligence, yes. Not what I wanted to hear. That position was expunged millennia ago. It bestowed too much influence on a mortal biped. Much suffering followed those who were bestowed such power. And he restores it, he turns time back, back to the bad old days where we made mistakes. Since those days, my kind have moved forward with compassion towards our dependent populations. We advance the cause of mortal bipeds – a symbiosis where we both benefit from co-existence. Now he turns time back.'

The Eight paused. Niamh and Tom stayed quiet; such rare moments of insight into their Overlords way of life were few and far between. With a flash of blue light, he continued. 'And now, the Svang Charter gains influence and power. They were already one of the biggest but that in itself may be to our advantage. Yes, it may. The Svang Charter has only one interest at heart – the advancement of their own business. If we can change the tide, they will about-face too. In that context, the offer of a base here on Lagrvth, in the Kandark Galaxy has real merit. Yes, it does. But now, we move on.'

Bursting to ask a question, it was the signal Niamh was waiting for. 'Overlord, did you see the cost of the hybrid drives on Hirkiv?'

'Yes, Niamh, I did. They are a swindling syndicate and always have been an opportunistic caitiff. Now they bleed all and sundry for their lifeblood in their struggle to survive.'

'Is it worth visiting that world?'

'Most definitely. I want to see what they are up to, and who knows, you may do a deal.'

*

Back on the bridge, fresh from the planet, Brian confirmed the final act. 'All done, boss. We disabled their comms before we left. The Borea grav cannons pack a real punch. Better than that crap we got from the *Hela's* armoury.'

Tom smiled as he remembered how useless some of the Aknar grav weapons were in the fight on the New World against the flying predators.

The Borea left nothing to chance; no wonder they were the scourge of the galaxy. 'You did good, Brian. How's the flying coming?'

'I won't lie, boss, it's still all quite new. But I got the shuttle up and down all right with help from the missus,' he said, as he looked at Kora. She glanced out from her navigation projection and scowled at him. 'Sorry, boss. I gotta go. My turn to look after junior. He's with Bill and the lads in the armoury.'

Tom smiled as he watched his young lieutenant leave in a rush after Kora's scathing gaze. The couple had met at the *Hela's* Australian base. Brian, the young Welsh Guardsman, had come with Tom at the start of Project Anan. Kora, part of the final recruitment drive, joined the project with six of her mates. The beautiful Kiwi Māori captivated the guardsman's heart, and in the process, warned Tom of the impending exposure of Project Anan to Earth's population. The couple married, their child earning the distinction of being the first human born on the New World.

Taking Kora and Brian on this mission had exposed them all to the realities of family life in space. His team were apprehensive. "Would having his wife and child on the ship affect Brian's judgement?" they had asked. "How would they work their shifts?" and "Who would help them with their baby?" were the many questions. It was Tom who had laid the law down. "Everybody would help to the best of their ability" he had told them. There were no passengers. The colony couldn't spare anyone for simple crew duties, and they needed Kora and Brian.

The Kiwi's navigation abilities were the best of all the humans. With her, Siba and Niamh, they would always have a navigator on the bridge – and he wanted Brian as his lieutenant. The young Welshman had proven himself over and over again, and now he was flying a shuttle. There was nothing he wouldn't try. The young family epitomised everything that the colony represented – a new future for the human race. They did what humans do; fall in love, have children, work to better themselves and strive for their offspring. Tom couldn't leave the family behind on the New World. No, he could not!

Their New World colony was stretched to the limit, every facet of their war effort short-handed. The planned departure of Verteg's fleet to Earth, the starting of the off-world mining, and their own mission, all suffered the same – a lack of competent staff. Running the *Monarch* on the minimum crew, with only twenty-five on board, they badly needed more people. Secretly, he and Niamh had grave doubts about their own abilities on this mission. Traversing through areas of space they had never dreamed of couldn't be done without The Eight's help. As Tom looked across at Niamh, peering at Siba's plot of their tow, he realised failure was not an option. They were halfway through their mission. From here on, the risks would increase.

'We're ready, Captain; course laid in and tow secured. But, Captain, you must curtail your aggressive manoeuvres,' Siba said.

'Siba, that's the third time you've told me that. Engineering, grav engines at half.' Niamh watched the plot of the *Monarch* and its tow on their big screen. 'We don't seem to be making way, Siba.'

'Have patience, Captain. The grav dampers, the beams, and the bubble must all adjust before we can pick up speed.' They all waited patiently while, at a snail's pace, the ship, followed by the colossal tow, turned away from orbit. 'It's working, Captain, as I calculated. Light speed in six hours. We'll be at the edge of Hirkiv's solar system in four of your days.'

Niamh jumped up from her chair. 'This is too slow for me, Siba – you have the bridge. I'm off on my rounds.'

As Niamh left, Siba looked up from her controls. 'Mr Parker, the cloak please.'

'Yes, Captain,' he replied, the meaning of his words not lost on the crew. He understood Niamh's actions. *It was time. Siba will be our next captain. But where will we get the rest?* he thought as the view of their four ships disappeared from the screen, enveloped in the cloak.

CHAPTER TWENTY-SIX

Intergalactic Communication with the Energy Exchange

The Energy Exchange is the centre of all intergalactic commerce and banking in the known universe. Deep inside the Exchange, data storage machines execute and record the Anan world's commercial transactions, including the transfer and storage of Universal Credits. Cryptographic digital signatures guard each Exchange account, from the Charter commercials to the pocket-size personal arrangements of the general populace. A network of satellites connects the Exchange to each corner of the known universe. Coded remote data terminals utilise encryption algorithms and faster-than-light beam technology for the transmission and execution of the transactions.

Blue crystal shards power these terminals. Once connected to the Energy Exchange, the device provides a secure financial service for the populace across the vast cosmic divide. It is a reliable communication facility and is often utilised as an interplanetary news feed.

· Extract from: The History of the Energy Exchange Part 2. Theia Aknar

*

The Monarch, Kandark Galaxy. EPTS: B140232

NIAMH LOVED HER "ROUNDS". SHE always started in the port pennon engine room, working her way through the ship. It usually took her three hours to work her way around the *Monarch* with its four engine rooms. After she had landed it on the New World, it was overrun with her technicians, cleaned and vented and every system rebooted and tested. There were some minor repairs, but for the most part, the ship was intact. Finding a ready supply of grav ammunition for the high-grade weapons surprised Tom. With it, he tested some of the smaller grav cannons in space above the New World. They worked first time – a welcome addition to their war chest.

As she entered the engine control room, she smiled at their new comms tech. 'You found it, Geoff?'

'Yes,' he said, looking up from a bank of data screens. 'And a lot more besides. All the training stuff and all made by him, look.'

Niamh looked at the screens playing videos of each engine on the ship. All were presented by one person and featured assembly and maintenance instructions. 'Who is he?'

'Mzimot, that's his name. He's a designer from Hirkiv; he designed all the engines on this ship for Grandfather Borea.'

'He'll be long dead by now. He's not a purebreed. Look, he's some strange crossbreed,' Niamh said, watching the video of the small man. He had bluish skin and large hairy eyebrows. His ears were tiny but it was his six-fingered hands that were his most distinctive feature.

Geoff changed the picture on one of the screens. 'I found the plans, as well, of all the engines.'

'Shit, look at that. Where did you find them?'

'Deep in the ship's archive. I used the codes Verteg gave me.'

Niamh looked at the boy. 'You glad you came with us now?'

'It's better than jail in Sydney.'

'Geoff, those codes Verteg gave you were some of Demard's most guarded secrets.'

His face flushed. 'Niamh, I swear, you can trust me. I'm done with—'

'I know, Geoff. You wouldn't be here if I didn't believe that but you need to know the importance of what you have. Guard them with your life,' she said, as her eyes flashed with blue light.

A surprised Geoff, who had never seen his boss look so frightening, jumped up and backed away. 'Niamh, don't. Please—'

Niamh reached out and gently touched him. 'Don't be afraid – I can't control the blue. I guess I look like a monster. But remember what I say, keep those codes secure. Now, let's look at what you found. Is there enough here to build the engines?' That was her plan – copy the data and have them built on Earth, if at all possible. It was what humans had been doing for ages, copying from each other. So why not from aliens? She had no qualms about that!

The colour returned to Geoff's white face as he shook his head. 'No, there's data missing.'

'Let me guess. The alignment calcs for the dodecahedron rotors and the spherical polyhedron.'

'How'd you know?'

'It's what I'd withhold if I designed them. They're copy proof. Shit, we need that data. Right, come on, back to the bridge. Time we let you out of your dungeon.'

'I'd prefer to stay.'

'Geoff, you're part of our crew. You can't hide away forever.'

'I'm afraid of them.'

Niamh put her arm around the boy. 'I know,' she said, as she felt him tremble. 'We'll help you. You need to integrate, and my Tom wants a word with you as well.' As she led him back to the bridge, she felt for him. In his teenage years, he had lost everything, drifting into crime and despair. Now, on this close-up ship's environment, he had trouble adjusting. She hadn't delved too deep, for a muddling adolescent mess raged inside Geoff's young mind.

*

The Monarch, Kandark Galaxy. EPTS: B140288

'Geoff, you need to pay attention.'

'I am. You've been over it a dozen times. How hard can it be? We go in, meet the manager, I find a data terminal, hack it with my codes, and we leave.'

Tom sat back and sighed. He could see his team turning away. If it wasn't so critical, they would be laughing now. 'Geoff, pin back your ears and try to listen. You're playing with the adults now. You're not playing the lost child waltzing into a bank data centre to hack their codes anymore.

This is real. These aliens can sense your thoughts and feelings. Some of them can read your mind. If we get caught, it's not a cosy jail in Sydney with Amnesty International monitors.'

'I got it. I got it,' Geoff shouted back.

Niamh held her blue pendant and closed her eyes. *'Listen to every word he says. This is what they are capable of, and Geoff, they won't be as gentle as I,'* was the message she flashed across to Geoff's mind. The boy screamed, put his hands to his head and fell to the floor. Niamh knelt down beside him. 'Geoff, look at me. You can learn to—'

'You're a witch. How could you do that?' he said, as he got up and ran from the bridge.

'Leave it, boss. I'll talk him round,' Bill said, as he followed the troubled teenager.

*

Bill caught up with the nineteen-year-old in the small break room up from the bridge. Without a word of warning, the big man picked Geoff up and flung him across the room. Screaming, the boy landed in a heap in the corner, smashing his face against the bulkhead. Violent contact between the soft facial tissue of Geoff's cheek and the hard metal wall compressed multiple pain receptors. Acute pain exploded in his head, searing his delicate character. Compression of the nerves felt like thousands of needles assaulting his cheek, as burst blood vessels started to bruise. It was nothing the boy had ever experienced before. His brain refused to comprehend what had happened.

Crying, and shaking in fear, he watched the burly soldier tower over him. Bill glared down on the fair-haired boy, his pockmarked face and crooked nose adding to his ferocious look. Then he started again. Grabbing Geoff by the lapels of his ship suit, Bill picked him up and carried the boy to a chair. Unceremoniously tossing the snivelling youth down in the plastic chair, Bill whacked Geoff across the ears a couple of times.

It was a dusting down, not enough to injure, but hard enough to maintain the boy's attention. A hysterical Geoff, slumping into the chair, broke down. Sobbing with self-pity, tears streamed down his face, gasping for breath while he whimpered for mercy. Bill pulled up another chair in front of the teenager – straddling it, he sat down. His heart breaking within, the burly man put a consoling hand on the boy's shoulder.

Calming words, in a soft, soothing voice. 'Easy now, boy. Take it easy,' Bill said.

Not what the now silent Geoff expected.

In a soft cockney voice, the soldier continued. 'That was a small taste of the meat you might be served if you get caught. Understand?'

His tear-streaked face stared back as the fair head nodded.

'Good. Now listen. I'm a nobody from east London. Finished school at sixteen and went into the army. What're you, nineteen?'

Geoff nodded.

'Yeah, I thought so. I made it through life living on my wits, and,' flexing his muscles, 'brawn. Tough it was in the forces for a young black boy. What I gave you was only a taste of the punishment meted out to me. But I got on okay. Got into the Marines and that's where I met Tom. He was my C.O. Never looked back since.'

Smiling, as he remembered those combat filled days, Bill paused. Learning a lesson, Geoff stayed silent.

'You, Geoff, were born with a silver spoon in your mouth. Had everything; a fancy privileged background, all the education you ever wanted — and to boot, a healthy dose of that all-important gene. I hear your near as intelligent as our Niamh.'

It was true. Gifted with the mythical gene, his test results were not far below Niamh's.

'Geoff, you know, I never took that test,' Bill said, referring to the on-line gene test created to identify humans with the intelligent genes spliced from The Eight's essence. He cuffed Geoff again across the face – a light touch this time. 'You need to wise up and grow a set of balls. Niamh and Tom have been like doting parents to you.'

A conflicted Geoff shook his head but the tears had stopped, a good sign Bill had made some progress.

'Yeah, they have. You wouldn't be here without those magic genes. You got a talent, boy – we need that!'

For five long minutes, they sat in silence, Geoff's mind a turmoil of confused hurt feelings. In time, the boy calmed down. He stared at Bill. 'You hurt me.'

'I meant to. Took no pleasure in it, either. But you need to know what it feels like. Not good, is it?'

Geoff shook his head, his long hair flying back and forth. 'No, it isn't. What do you want me to do?'

'Put those hurt feelings aside, for starters. No place for them. Learn to control your emotions. We can help with that. Now, clean yourself up and we'll go back to the bridge.'

*

Half an hour later, with Geoff sporting a big shiner on his cheek, they returned to the bridge. There was a stunned silence as the crew eyed Geoff's bruised face.

Siba glared at Bill as if to say, did you do that? Ashamed, he stared at the floor, counting the patterns embossed on the deck plate.

Ignoring the questioning looks and gasps, the young man stood tall and looked straight into Tom's eyes. 'Show me how to block all that out,' Geoff said. He didn't see Niamh wipe the tears from her eyes.

'How do you deal with pain?' Tom said as he continued with the boy's life-skills lessons.

*

Planet Hirkiv. EPTS: B140312

A frantic schedule: hide the tow on the dark side of a moon, negotiate access to Hirkiv, gather plans of the factory and so on. All within a tight timeline, the clock ticking down on the foreseeable revelations from Lagrvth. Looking around the factory world's exhibition hall – inside its tangled web of danger – the prep-work for this deep-cover mission paid off. But would they get caught before finishing here? That question rammed the mission forward.

'They're true to form, all visible security and protocols, like any large Earth multinational,' Tom said, taking the view of this enormous hall in.

Geoff, standing between him and Niamh shook his head. 'But Earth factory guards don't have guns. This place is like a fortress.'

Tom smiled at the frightened young man, the worry lines etched across his brow. 'It's well guarded, Geoff, but we knew that.' They had landed an hour ago with their pre-approvals all authorised, following Cylla's data submission. Nobody paid them any attention as they looked at the exhibits of engines, communicators and the selection of alien technology available to buy from this factory world of Hirkiv.

Niamh studied a display of equipment, all embossed with the same logo. 'They make everything here, look even the comms units the purebreeds use.' She was, without difficulty, able to disguise her contamination with more clothing on this colder world. Keeping to themselves, avoiding the crowds gathering around the newest hybrid engine, they continued to browse.

'There it is,' she said, guiding Tom and Geoff over to what The Eight had asked them to look for. 'It's the blue drive he wants – the older model.'

The exhibit of the large drive was over fifty metres long, near twenty metres tall and ten metres wide at the base. 'It's huge,' Geoff said, marvelling at this piece of alien tech.

Niamh walked around the mock-up, peering in at cut out sections that gave a clear view to the buyer of the internals of the engine. She turned to look at Geoff. 'Geoffrey, darling, did you get the photo device and our permit?' she asked loudly.

'Yes, Mother, I did.'

'Well, don't stand there gawking at the thing, get on with it.'

Geoff sighed, hung his head, and then reached into his bag to retrieve a camera. He shook his head in protest as he started to walk around the machine, directed by Niamh, capturing the valuable images of its internal workings.

A purebreed hurried over. 'You are the Sullivan?'

Tom smiled at the man and held up a hand in greeting. 'The Sullivan Parker Charter. Thomas Parker at your service. This is my wife Niamh, the Sullivan in our Charter and our son Geoffrey. You must be Iarkhel.'

'Yes, Mr Parker. Welcome to Hirkiv. I trust our processing did not inconvenience you. We are busy today. Your arrival coincided with a group of traders from the Energy Exchange.'

Arranged on purpose, after Geoff learned of the visit from the constant inter-ship chatter. A bonus they couldn't pass up.

The salesman continued. 'They are interested in our new hybrid drive. You are familiar with it?'

'Yes, I am,' Niamh said, 'and we were discommoded by your processing. Most inconvenient. We had to leave our ship in orbit around one of your moons and travel here in a shuttle. How we're supposed to buy anything, I don't know. We wanted eight engines but our shuttle can't lift any.' She turned to face him. Taking off her dark glasses, she allowed her eyes to flash blue and white light. She replaced them again as the purebreed stepped back in horror.

'You are—'

'Niamh, darling, please, there's no need for that. My apologies, Iarkhel. But yes, we were inconvenienced by your processing. Never mind, we're here now.' Tom paused and his voice dropped as if he didn't want others to hear. 'I'm interested in blue drives. I suspect they're not selling well.'

Iarkhel looked warily at Niamh who had resumed her inspection of the engine. He could sense nothing from the strange trio. 'No, for obvious reasons, they are not. What piques your interest in them?'

'I invest in discount stock. I take a contrarian view of the market.' Tom looked straight into Iarkhel's eyes. 'You're suspicious of us?'

'No, I'm not.'

'I can sense it from you,' Niamh said, as she turned to face him. 'My apologies for frightening you. Recently, I was involved in an accident. Thankfully, the contamination is dispersing. We must look quite bizarre to you. You haven't encountered our species before.' *And as yet, no news of our escapades on Lagrvth has reached you*, she thought.

'No, Mrs Parker, I haven't, and yes you do look somewhat out of the ordinary.'

Geoff looked around at the different species in the great hall. *If we're out of the ordinary, what the hell are they like?* he thought. 'I'm bored.'

'Geoffrey, darling, have patience. We told you we were here on business. Don't be rude.'

'Oh, leave him be, Niamh. You know he hates it when you get so involved with the engines. Iarkhel, do you mind if he has a look around himself. We need to discuss business and time moves along.'

The purebreed looked at the strange trio. *They are unusual*, he thought, but their credentials checked out. The Neredian had vouched for them, and there was a deposit of a quarter of a million credits transferred from the Energy Exchange. *They're interested in blue drives. What do I care if they misread the market.* Always, when a market crashes, vultures circle for the kill. Since blue had peaked, they hadn't sold one blue drive. The way things were looking, they would have to scrap the older models. *It would cost millions.* He looked at the young human; he smelled foul and his hair was long and untidy. He had hair all over his face and an annoying habit of placing his finger in his nose. Iarkhel shuddered in disgust. He reached into his pocket and took out a square-shaped thin object. 'Here, take this. It's a visitor's extended warrant. It will allow you access to the other exhibits. There's credit for the refreshment area as well,' he said, as he gingerly handed it to Geoff, careful not to touch the young human's hands.

'Thank you, Iarkhel. Geoff, you have two hours. Meet us at the entrance; we have a factory tour, and I want you to see it. That's okay, isn't it, Iarkhel?'

The big smile on his white purebreed face betrayed how happy he was to see the back of the smelly human. 'Yes, Mr Parker, Mrs Parker, it is. To business, I can offer a discount and we can deliver into orbit around the moon for an easy collection by your ship …'

Geoff walked away, listening to the monotone voice of the purebreed salesman trail off in the background as he tried to charm Niamh and Tom into a deal. Before they left the *Monarch*, Niamh, with the help of her blue diamond, had sketched out the plans of this alien structure. Flying through the place, undetected, her ethereal mind located data terminals on the floor above the exhibits. Committing those plans to memory, Geoff knew where to go.

Walking up a flight of stairs, hungry eyes absorbing all around him, the similarity of the building to some of Earth's modern structures surprised the young man. Images and models of the equipment the factory made festooned the place – and its strange logo was everywhere. Niamh told him it was similar in shape to the dodecahedron rotors that created the pulse charges in the blue drives. "Think of them as the pistons in an internal combustion engine," she had said. He couldn't miss them, hanging down above the stairs as he made his way to the upper level.

It won't be easy, he thought as he walked past the empty refreshment area. The layout was similar to an Earth self-service canteen, with cabinets of food and drinks arranged in the consortium's dodecahedron-shaped logo. Getting his bearings, he looked around. *There it is*, he thought, *the door to the restricted facilities*. Beside it was another, with the distinct markings in Anan for "toilet". He pushed through it into a toilet area that was larger, but similar in design, to what they had on the *Monarch*.

Quickly making his way to the last stall, Geoff entered and locked it. Taking a standard Anan multi-tool from his pocket, he undid some wall fixings. Removing a panel at the back, Geoff climbed into the void behind. Silently, he replaced the board. With a small torch, the young man looked around and smiled at the similarities between the alien and human design. *Cheap and cheerful*, he thought, as he traced the pipes and cables that disappeared through the walls. The space was similar to the voids he had climbed through during his brief criminal career on Earth. He wrinkled his nose at the other similarity, the smell. *Charming*, he thought, *they metabolise food the same way, shitting and pissing as we do*.

He needed to get out quick, but there was someone in a toilet on the other side of the wall. Controlling his breathing, statue-like, he waited. It seemed an age and then he heard the welcome sound of the water flush and someone leaving the stall. Silently, with the Anan multi-tool, he removed another wall panel and climbed through into the adjacent toilet stall, within the restricted area – reserved for employees only. As he heard someone else come in, he closed and locked the door. Replacing the panel, Geoff sat down – listening to the person outside. He looked at his watch. Time was moving on; he couldn't wait much longer.

Geoff could hear the person changing clothes and washing. He looked at his watch again and smiled when he heard them enter the stall beside his. Unlocking the door, Geoff was out into the deserted toilet area. As he checked his appearance in the mirror, his eyes fell to a small, neat pile of threadbare clothes beside a washbasin and a drab-coloured bag. Brushing the dust from his hair and clothes, Geoff ran to the exit and peered out. *It's deserted*, he thought. Like Iarkhel, all the other staff were down on the sales floor with their visitors.

Like he belonged there, Geoff strode out of the toilet and made his way along the corridor into a small, secluded alcove. There they were, shining in the gloom – four data terminals. He deftly placed a data crystal, attached to a bracelet on his wrist, into a port on the first terminal. The terminal burst into life – a happy Geoff smiled to himself.

Leaning against the wall, he started his hack, deep into the files of the factory's database. Unconnected to the outside world, the data-vault contained the wealth of Hirkiv's designs. Like magic, Demard's programs, loaded on the data crystal, unlocked everything. It would take minutes to get the files, and the place was still deserted. As Demard's hacking program wormed into the factory's data, Geoff put an earpiece from his bag into one ear and started up his favourite playlist. As he listened, he watched the copy progress, his head swinging back and forth to the beat of the music. Opening an engine sales brochure on screen, he waited for the copy program to finish its undetectable steal.

He froze as he heard someone walk down the corridor. An alien female appeared from around the corner. 'Who are you?' she asked. 'What are you doing at that data terminal?'

He looked at her bluish skin. She was about his height with small ears, short blue and pink closely cropped hair, thin eyebrows and dressed in a close-fitting light pink ship garb. She was carrying the same drab-coloured bag he had seen in the toilet. His eyes fell to admire the curves of her body. 'I, ah, I was bored. Iarkhel gave me a warrant. See, I have it here,' he said, as he extracted the prize from his pocket.

She moved closer. 'You're not supposed to be here. How did you get in?'

'Through the door,' he lied.

'What you doing?'

'I, ah, was just surfing at the panel, listening to music.'

'What is surfing? You shouldn't be here,' she said, moving closer to him. Then, at an arm's length, she stopped. She brought her hand up in front of her nose, fanning it. 'Oh, you ...' She turned and backed away with her head down.

Oh shit, he thought, as his face flushed. Clinkers on his arse, crotch rot scratching his balls – he hadn't washed for three days. Sweating in the same clothes, the sickening smell of stale arse and oxter perfumed the air! It was part of Tom's plan to mask him as the petulant teenager. 'I stink, I know. We got caught in the shuttle waiting to land. I'm sorry.'

To his surprise, she turned and laughed, still fanning her nose. *Six fingers, she has six fingers on her hands,* was the thought that electrified his brain. He remembered the old engine designer, Mzimot's picture. The resemblance was uncanny. 'What's your name?' he asked.

'Mzimot H'Fazqa. They call me Fazqa, and you?'

'The Right Honourable Geoffrey Thompson the Third. But Geoff will do. I'm a human,' he said, as he felt the bracelet on his wrist vibrate. *All done,* he thought as he turned to face the terminal. Quickly extracting the data crystal, he shut the terminal down. Taking the earpiece out and placing it in his pack with the bracelet, he turned to face Fazqa, 'I have some credit on this warrant. If you can stand the smell, can I get you a drink?' *We need her,* he thought, *and I'm hopeless at this.*

She stared at him. 'That is so inappropriate. You could get in–'

'Trouble? I've been there before. Come on,' he said, as he held out his hand, gesturing her to go first.

She turned and smiled as she led him down the corridor to a door. Holding her hand up to a sensor, the door opened. A delighted Geoff followed her out of the restricted zone and grinned broadly as they entered the refreshment area from an entry to its side.

'Now, educate me on the food delicacies on offer on your world,' he asked.

Fazqa tilted her head in wonder as she looked at this strange person. 'You really are different. Pity you smell so bad.'

'Are all the girls so outspoken on this world?'

'No, only me. It's a family trait,' she said, as she led him over to the serving area. The displays looked familiar to Geoff. Automated food-dispensing cabinets with pre-made dishes loaded into individual lockers. The access hatches were a clear plastic Geoff knew was, likewise made, from oil-like substances. The multi-coloured food, individually marked with dish name and price, bore no resemblance to anything on Earth. He suspected the unappetising putty-like offerings came from a synthesiser, created from the base sustenance. Fazqa confirmed his scornful gaze.

'Those are carbohydrates, sweetened with additives.' She pointed on. 'Protein, vitamin and energy cakes, and the best of all, the multi-nourish cakes. Prepped from a mix of protein, carbs and what they call "vitamins". I call them drugs. Everything you need to finish a working day!' She had that right. Spiked with "all things good", some of the synthesised food provided stimulants for the workforce. A crude method to maintain production targets.

Geoff wondered how they'd taste.

As if reading his mind, she said, 'They taste like ...' But her voice trailed off.

'Like what?' he asked.

'Find out yourself. Swipe it there,' Fazqa said indicating where he should offer up his voucher. She led him to a dispenser, taking a beaker she filled it with purple drinks. 'I'll have one of those.'

A hungry, more adventurous Geoff choose a green fluorescent protein and carb cake. He purchased the food and sat down beside her. 'What do you do here?'

'I'm a teckadv for engines. I work with the sales team ...'

Engrossed in the exotic nature of connecting with a new species, the couple chatted away – as time slipped on.

CHAPTER TWENTY-SEVEN

The Order of Purist

Pollution of our chosen DNA by interbreeding with any other life form is antagonistic to our beliefs. Purebreeds, as the name suggests, are an uncontaminated, higher life form selected to serve the Overlords. Over aeons, our intelligence has developed to a level above all other bipeds. We are pure in body and mind. Our genes remain unchanged since we were first endowed with intelligence by our Overlords.

Interbreeding with other non-purebreed life forms is punishable by death. That is our creed and the basic tenet of our existence. As Purists, we are dedicated to the defence of our DNA. We swear fealty with a blood-oath to our order and the protection of the Anan Purebreed DNA. We are the guardians of our species' purity. A death sentence befalls all who foul that Purity …

⋅ *Extract from: The Doctrine of the Purist Creed*

*

Planet Hirkiv. EPTS: B140313

BACK IN THE EXHIBITION HALL, Niamh looked at her communicator. It was long past the time, Geoff was due back and she feared the worst; they'd caught him – red-handed. 'Where is he? I knew he should have stayed with us.'

'Give it a rest, Niamh. He'll be here soon. Iarkhel, can we give him a few more minutes? It's just past the two hours,' Tom said, beginning to worry as well.

'Of course, Mr Parker,' *after such a deal, I'll wait all day for your spoiled brat,* he thought. It was near done, and, they had agreed on four of the old model blue drives. Four consigned to be disassembled for scrap. Despite

Tom's tough negotiations, they had settled on a fair price. Although heavily discounted, Iarkhel would still make a handsome commission. They were to visit the factory and inspect the engines; after that, the Parkers would transfer the credit balance.

Relief coursed through Tom at the sight of a smiling Geoff striding into the hall. 'Here he comes, Niamh. I told you he would come. You worry too much.'

'And who's with him, Tom? Look, he's a girl in tow. Really, it's just too much. Geoffrey, how many times have I told you to—'

He put up his hand to silence her and looked straight into her eyes. 'Mother, this is Mzimot H'Fazqa. I met her in the refreshment area. I wanted her to meet you; you can call her Fazqa,' he said, as he winked at Niamh.

Niamh looked hard at Fazqa. *The resemblance is uncanny*, she thought. She gently probed the girl's mind; it was the slightest of touches, but enough for Niamh. *Jeez, he found the engine-builder's great-granddaughter.* 'Fazqa, I hope my son was polite. Do you have family here as well?'

Before she could answer, Iarkhel held up his hand. 'We must go, it gets late. Fazqa's family work in the engine compound. The area we go to is beside it. She'll explain the engine workings – that's her job. Fazqa, you will accompany us. We need to go now. The grav platform is here,' he said, as it landed beside them.

Niamh placed her arm around Fazqa. 'Please. I would like to hear more about the maintenance; how did you learn about that?'

It was a warm touch, not what Fazqa expected from such a strange species. 'Yes, I can do that. I learn about it from the family; it's what we do here,' she said, stepping onto the large grav platform.

While their ride soared up above the factory complex, the first earthlings to visit this alien world got to see how huge this place was. The largest manufacturing centre in the Kandark Galaxy stretched far into the distance. Strapped into seats in their comfy grav platform, mesmerised by the view, the trio flew over kilometres of factories and the distinct employee housing. Near their destination, the platform slowed and started to lose height. Pointing down to some miserable looking buildings, Tom leaned across to Geoff. 'Workers' accommodation, remind you of anything?' he whispered.

Geoff looked back at Tom, closed his eyes and nodded. The similarity was uncanny. They could be looking down on a factory complex in Gonghough on Earth. Geoff had spent time there in one of their banks as an intern.

The grav platform landed in a compound surrounded by large brown buildings shaped like aircraft hangars. Nets enclosed the access balconies, stairwells and flat roofs of the imposing colossus. Like fetid blemishes, small buildings, crudely assembled from wood-like material, stood out at the side of the factory.

'Staff lodging,' explained Iarkhel, as they walked past the miserable box-shaped constructions, piled on top of each other. Visible through open doorways, bunk beds with makeshift shelving – housing the cooking and living needs – amplified the spartan nature of the place.

A disgusted Tom wanted to stay quiet. However, needs must. He had to play the part of a wealthy, unscrupulous Charter boss. 'Why do you use biped labour? I would have thought it more cost-effective to mechanise all the manufacturing.'

'We're working towards that, but still, over a while, we've amassed quite a labour force.'

'Now that the market's radically changed, you've no need for such a large workforce. Do you have to pay them?'

'No, not all the time. Only for the work done.'

'And how do they survive?' Tom asked.

'We have a subsistence arrangement. It's a loan to each family on future earnings. Provides those unemployed with food and accommodation.'

'And the nets, why bother?' Tom asked, referring to the enclosing barriers on the building roofs.

'They were installed by the last generation of owners. They were busy then and couldn't afford the loss rate.'

'What were the percentages?'

'Fifteen per cent were jumping at that time. Our staff work about three-quarters of our planet's day. Some find this a burden.'

Tom could feel Geoff squirm beside him. 'Geoffrey, take heed. Such loss rates in a labour force are unsustainable. Listen now, boy. I preach on and on about loss-control. It's so important, now you see what happens. Can you imagine the struggle to get productivity and quality from such a shambles?'

Iarkhel raised his eyebrows and nodded. 'Yes, Mr Parker, you are right. Most of those were engaged in the communicator and small component factories. Quality did suffer. It was in our subsidiary, Confox Precision.

'What about the engines we're buying?'

'Different process. I can assure you quality is the cornerstone of our engines. Hirkiv Precision Industries guarantees all its engines. Ask Fazqa; her family are designers and builders. They're among the best we have,' he said, as he looked across at the girl, deep in conversation with Niamh. He was glad she had shown up. *Late as usual, but still – well-timed.* Parker's questions were too close to the mark. *He's not the simple family man he makes out to be,* thought Iarkhel. *This deal is not done yet.*

'Here are your engines,' he said, as they stood inside one of the giant hangar-like structures. They had to suit up in special garments and enter through an airlock. The interior of the building was spotless and the air dry and warm. 'I have arranged for one of our engineers to show you them. Fazqa will do the introductions. Mrs Parker, I gather you will inspect.'

'Yes. Tom will stay here and go over the figures with you. Geoff, I need you to look at the control systems. You can come with me.'

Iarkhel was unable to hide his joy at the departure of the boy and Niamh. He led Tom back to a large office with glass screens overlooking the vast warehouse. 'Have you considered the banking and reregistration we offered when you first made contact?'

'No, I haven't given it much thought,' Tom replied, wondering what this was all about.

'It could save you a fortune. I sent it on to your trader, Ms Ora.'

Intrigued by the proposal and the first he had heard of it, Tom looked across at Iarkhel. For some reason, Cylla hadn't passed it back to them. 'Explain how that works.'

'You register with us as a derivative of the Sullivan Parker Charter. We set up the bank accounts, the cypher codes and intergalactic comms systems. The derivative charges a licence or royalty fee to the Sullivan Parker Charter to mine, transport, manufacture or whatever business you do. You hold the funds in our bank. The main part of your Charter shows a loss as it pays the licence fee to the derivative. You don't pay any tax to the Energy Exchange.'

'And what do you charge for that?'

'One per cent; you pay ten to the Exchange. We save you nine.'

'Is that legal?'

'Of course, it is. The Kandark Galaxy is an autonomous region. We're not tied to the Exchange or an Overlord. It's a good strategy, Mr Parker. It allows you to shift income from the higher tax areas governed by the Exchange. They cannot levy taxes on income earned by a derivative outside their jurisdiction. With the war unfolding, now is the time to change. You could make a fortune transhipping between the worlds, tax free as well.'

'How secure is your bank?

'We have our own cyphers and a security force. Granted, it's not anything like the Overlords, but we are well protected.'

'The Sixth, how will he view this?'

'We are insignificant to him. He sees us as minuscule and of no consequence. His Shoter's Charter is a shareholder in the consortium of industrialists that owns us.'

Tom smiled to himself. More intel, and what The Eight needed to hear. 'Iarkhel, we'll consider your offer. But, as you know, we're a small Charter, recently started. It's all outgoings now. There's not enough revenue that would merit such a change.'

'Still, you have assets.'

'Iarkhel, don't take this wrong. I'm not turning you down. Once we turn a profit, I'll be back. I appreciate the offer. Now to business; assuming my wife approves the quality, how soon can you have those engines in orbit …'

When Niamh returned, the two commerce terminals were open on the desk. 'Well, darling, what do you think?' Tom asked.

She passed a list of numbers across to Iarkhel. 'I want these four.'

'Only the best. I expected that, Mrs Parker. We'll have them packaged and in orbit in twenty time segments. You see, here are the grav lifters,' he said, as the roof over the immense building started to open.

Niamh smiled at Tom as she sat down in front of their terminal. 'Shall we pay the man, dear?'

'Yes, we should,' he said, as he keyed in his codes.

As soon as they had finished the payment process, Iarkhel stood up and smiled. 'Fazqa will show you to the grav carrier; it'll take you to your shuttle. I want to stay and supervise the packing. Mrs Parker, Mr Parker, it is a pleasure doing business with you,' he said, bowing profusely.

They made their way back out into the courtyard. Niamh looked around at the place, now thronged with grey-faced people, dressed in threadbare rags. 'Jeez, Tom, look at these people. Are they the workers?'

'Yes. It's quitting time. They're on a reduced working day.'

'How could they treat people like that? What a shower of blood-sucking bastards.'

'Niamh, you've seen nothing yet. Do you know what type of place this is?' he said, as they stepped around three people huddled in the doorway. Walking to the landing pad, they pushed through a throng filing out of the adjoining building.

As they stood at the pad waiting for the grav carrier, he explained the greedy tax dodge Iarkhel had touted.

'It's no wonder Cylla didn't pass that on to you. That's the shits, Tom. Here's our transport.'

As the grav carrier settled down on the pad, Niamh turned to Fazqa, standing beside Geoff. 'Fazqa, we're here for a few days. I'd like to meet your family. Geoffrey, give Fazqa your music device.'

He grimaced at the notion of passing on his precious pad. 'It has all my playlists.'

'Jeez, Geoffrey, get with it. I'm sure she'll look after it, won't you?' she said, as he handed over his most prized possession. The scowl on his face said it all. Niamh looked at the blue-skinned alien girl and smiled. 'We'll be in touch. Tom, Geoffrey, let's go,' she said. Stepping into the grav carrier, they waved goodbye.

*

The trio had an uneventful journey back on their shuttle. Niamh tapped Geoff on the shoulder. 'Shower now, then we talk.' Waiting for clearance to take off, she scanned the data the young man had recovered. The priceless design drawings, construction methods, and the elusive alignment calcs, were all there, amongst a trove of information she didn't think was possible to get. A thought stabbed her brain; they had committed the ultimate offence – intergalactic industrial espionage. On a scale off the charts for the Anan worlds! If they got caught, execution would follow – no doubt about that! She looked at Tom.

His dowdy look said it all. 'Where's that flight clearance?'

Fifteen minutes later, Geoff came out of the shower, clean-shaven and dressed in a new ship garb, oblivious to the tension of the delayed departure. 'Are we still here?' he asked.

'Waiting for flight clearance,' Niamh replied. More upbeat, she continued, 'I looked at what you got. It's more than I believed possible – designs for the hybrid on *Hela*, the blue drives on *Monarch* and the engine settings and calibrations. We can make them on Earth. Geoff, that was outstanding. And you hooked up with the designer's great-granddaughter.'

She reached out and hugged him. 'Oh, that's better,' Niamh said. 'Tom, that was a horrible disguise you gave him.'

'Worked, didn't it?' Tom replied. A message pinged the comms console. Like a coiled spring, Tom reached over and opened it. 'Clearance! Niamh, we have it; flight clearance to leave Hirkiv. Right, what's next?'

'Back to the *Monarch* now. Arrange the pickup of the engines, and believe it or not, I want to come back here. We need to talk to the Mzimot.'

*

Aknar City, Planet Anan. EPTS: B140328

On Planet Anan, accompanied by her Royal guard and a young, loyal lieutenant, who, as of late, went everywhere with her, Theia Aknar, Empress of Anan, strode across the covered courtyard of this fashionable meeting place. Dressed in a nondescript grey suit, her presence sparked quite a stir amongst the other patrons. The hubbub of diners clinking glasses, raised voices, laughter and the sound of the servers running to and fro, died away. Heads bobbed and turned as she and her entourage passed them by. Stopping at a table – on a raised dais – in front of a long picture window, Theia smiled. A woman, dressed in a sharp blue-green dress decorated with golden flowers, rose to Theia's warm greeting.

In this prized space that held a captivating view over the city below – and reserved for the elite – the duo sat down. Early evening multi-coloured lights twinkled on the buildings. Glowing people-movers sped out from the transportation hub as they ferried those finishing up for the day, home.

The childhood friends exchanged eager greetings as both admired the view overlooking their capital. Polite talk followed, reminiscing on school and college days together before affairs of state had swallowed up their happy, carefree lives. Before The Sixth's coup, they would have been the two most powerful mortals on Planet Anan.

The woman – Admiral Enirim, Supreme Commander of the Anan Navy and Military – once had the most formidable of all intergalactic navies in the known universe at her disposal. A force dedicated to The One and The Eight and sworn to protect the House of Aknar. That she had lost that power was a craw in her throat.

A well-mannered servant delivered the sweet-smelling herbal brew Theia preferred, with an assortment of the house's best delicacies. As quickly as he appeared, he left. The drinks poured, and after indulging themselves in the treats and small talk, Theia took a deep breath and put the glass down – a gesture that turned the discussion to the serious business at hand.

'Don't blame me. It was your husband, the Emperor, who ordered us to stand down when The Sixth made his move,' Enirim said.

Theia shook her head. 'I never blamed you!'

'I was ready to move the fleet. Orders issued to escape to the Tar Galaxy. I wanted to put the fleet at The Second's disposal, out of reach of The Sixth. A logical move. But your husband countermanded those orders. Even if I had wanted to rebel against the House of Aknar and take the fleet myself, he made sure we couldn't. You know what he did?'

Theia didn't, but she suspected. 'No, I don't.'

'He flooded the fleet's command computers with Aknar executive codes, disabling every ship. Where is he now, Empress?'

'I don't know.' Truthfully, she didn't know what the Shoter had done with the body after she had killed the Emperor.

'You're a terrible liar. Even though you have so much brainpower and that blue crystal of yours, I can see it in your eyes and your body position. Theia, you could never hide your emotions from me,' Enirim said.

They both laughed.

Sombreness returned. Enirim sighed. 'I guess he is with Prince Brizo.'

Theia gasped. She didn't want to face up to this. Prince Brizo, the immediate heir to the Aknar throne, killed by The Sixth. A horrible blot on his coup. And no one knew. The Shoter had covered it up, as well as her killing of the Emperor.

'I'm so sorry, Theia. I know, I know – on the record – they're both away on a mission together. But my heart goes out to you, Theia. You and the house of Aknar never deserved that. I loved Brizo.'

A betraying tear ran down Theia's cheek. The only sign, confirming Enirim's shrewd deduction.

Staring at Theia out of deep, blue round questioning eyes, Enirim pushed home part of her agenda for this meeting. 'What of your successor? You won't live forever.'

'And now you want to talk about that!'

'Yes. It falls to me, as Supreme Aknar Commander, to anoint your successor.

Brizo was the last in the Aknar line.'

Theia sat back, shaking her head. 'Well, there are others related to the House. Mack ...'

Disgust fell across Enirim's face. 'That preening eunuch. You know, Theia, I always said there was something seriously wrong with that man. He collected the most beautiful women and did nothing with them. And he didn't prefer men either.'

Speechless, Theia's face fell.

'Don't look so shocked. A nothing, Mack is. Anyway, he's gone, too.'

'You're a horror, Enirim.'

'But you know I'm right.' For a long minute, the two friends sat in silence. Enirim continued. 'What about my niece?'

It didn't shock Theia. Deep down, she had known what this meeting was always about. Succession and family infighting! With all the purebreed inbreeding, genealogically, the families were all related. 'The one that Ms Ora fired from the Energy Exchange. It took you long enough to get to that, Enirim. I'm still alive, you know!'

'She was reinstated shortly after.'

Theia wouldn't waste words. 'Nepotism.'

'Of course, no denying that. But the boot in the backside was what the girl needed. Her mother was delighted the Neredian fired her. It refocused the girl's mind. She's running the grav trading pit, the busiest at the exchange, and doing quite well now. Her father is very proud.'

'You mean, the Shoter. Can you not understand how dangerous putting so much power in that family's hands would be?' Theia's gut tightened at the thought of the Svang Charter holding the post of Shoter and Empress – owning the House of Aknar. No, that couldn't happen. 'Anyway, their connection is tenuous.'

A determined Enirim pushed back. 'No, it's not. Through me, my niece is the closest relative in the ascendancy ...'

An alarm sounded deep in Theia's mind. Her consciousness left the table, scanning the room, looking at the other guests and the comings and goings around them. Like stale breath, she could smell it: treason, death, revenge. Those feelings enveloped her mind. In slow motion, she saw them. Two purebreed men, dressed in long white trench cloaks, striding across the floor of the meeting house.

Reaching into their cloaks, they took out two grav guns. Quickening their pace, they rushed – ill intent flashing from their eyes – towards Theia and Enirim. Grav guns raised, both pointed at Theia. A shout from the side and the loyal lieutenant was running. He jumped, with grav gun raised, throwing his body into the air. Putting his own life between the assassins and his Empress – the ultimate sacrifice. Muscles on the two killers' fingers flexed.

In that millisecond, Theia's instinctive reflex for survival kicked in, projecting her mind out into the heads of the two assassins. Mind-bending orders flowed into their brains. New targets acquired, they turned to face each other. Grav guns still at the ready, both fired at the same time. Wide-angle charges, loaded in the primitive weapons, sped through the air hitting each assassin squarely in the face. The blasts tore the faces upwards from the skull, their heads bursting open. Grey brain matter, blood, skin and bone sprayed backwards, covering the unfortunate diners sitting behind. Pressed from the skull, the four eyeballs took to the air, landing on surrounding tables. A macabre scene as the headless assassins fell to the floor, their life's blood spurting from crushed carotid arteries. Red blood flowed across the colourful floral pattern on the tiled floor.

Pandemonium, screams, shouting, erupted from the crowd. The young officer landed on the ground, unhurt, his life saved by the Empress he had sworn to protect. As quickly as he fell, he jumped up, rushing to a now standing Theia and Enirim. The rest of the guards sprang into action, surrounding their precious charges. Coats hastily thrown over them, both ran out.

Outside, in the pouring rain, secured inside a phalanx of guards, Enirim looked at her friend and Empress. 'That wasn't me, Theia.'

Despite the seriousness of their predicament, Theia grinned at her friend's assumption that Theia would blame her for the plot. 'I know, Enirim. It was the Purists. I saw it in their minds.' A fundamentalist sect dedicated to the protection of the purebreed gene. Zealots who disavowed any form of interspecies relationships and inter-breeding. Brazen violence, a mainstay of their movement, had alienated them from the Anan populace.

'Because of your cure?' Enirim asked. Incompatible with the Purist's beliefs, Theia's cure for the Anan sickness embraced the fusing of purebreed DNA with that of the humans. A genetically altering process changing their hallowed DNA forever. News of the antidote Theia had brought back, and the trials the Sixth's geneticist had commenced, dominated the planet's newsfeeds. Hope for success in engineering a treatment for the dreaded sickness now gripped the Anan population. The zealots came in from the shadows, watching for an opportunity to execute the "purveyor of doom" – their epithet for Theia.

'Yes, there are consequences. And they believe I am polluting the purebreed DNA with it. We must go.'

Enirim held back. More had to be said today, and vitally important. 'Before we do …' She moved closer and hugged Theia, whispering in her ear. 'I have started a resistance.'

Theia flinched. She had not expected anything so audacious.

'Trust me, Theia. We are prepping troops, dedicated to the House of Aknar.'

'What do you need from me?' Theia asked.

'The power and leadership you showed today. And get me blue!'

Theia nodded, their hug intensified, two old friends locked together in a conspiracy against an evil Overlord. One that could cost them their lives. They broke apart and, surrounded by their guards, went their separate ways.

CHAPTER TWENTY-EIGHT

From the Office of Hirkiv Consortia Director

Salutations Iarkhel,

Well done on the sale of four old blue drives. I understand we had to part with the best of the completed engines. FYI, I had just recently signed their disassembly order! You saved us a small fortune. Profitability in these trying times is always a challenge. Thanks to your efforts, we're well on the way to meeting this quarter's goal.

I checked up on the Charter you did the deal with. A new venture we haven't heard of before. But they must be flush with funds; the transfer (as you verified) went through immediately. I see the capital is now cleared in our account. It would be good to get them on board with our financial instruments. I have attached our standard terms contract and company flyer. Pass on to them with my compliments. On the other matter, next time you are up in the admin building, call into the office. I have something for you.

> *◦ Message Ends*

*

The Monarch. EPTS: B140336

BACK ON THE MONARCH, IN The Eight's chamber, Tom and Niamh updated him on the intelligence they had gathered on Hirkiv, presenting him with the data Geoff had stolen.

Digesting the implications of what they had unearthed on Lagrvth and now confirmed on Hirkiv, the ethereal entity contemplated the duplicities of the consortia involved. Interplanetary bullying, tax dodges and price gouging! His oval energy mass flashed with blue light as it sat in his glittering chariot. Silver, speckled with blue pearls from Earth, shone brightly as Tom and Niamh waited for his verdict.

'I underestimated the power of this consortium. Until Lagrvth, I did not know how they managed their affairs or how deep the corruption in the Anan Galaxy went. Now you confirm it on Hirkiv. Thomas, you have unearthed a deep crawling bezonian.'

Tom wondered out loud. 'Did others of your kind know?'

'Possibly. Such practices amongst bipeds are not unique. You have the same issues on Earth – greed feeds corruption. But tax havens and their governance are now irrelevant. With the energy war unfolding, we have bigger problems. Through the Shoter and his Svang Charter, this consortium is aligned with The Sixth. No doubt about that. It is not safe here. We should leave as soon as we load our engines.'

Disappointment coursed across Niamh's face and her eyes glowed. It wasn't what she wanted to hear. 'Overlord, what about the Mzimot? I want to go back for them.'

Unusual for The Eight, his voice boomed loud in his chamber. 'It's too risky. We have what we came for.'

'Overlord, please. Let us try.'

His energy mass flashed with blue and purple light. 'My child, have faith in your abilities. With what you have, you will be able to start your manufacturing plants.'

Niamh continued to argue. 'That ties me to Earth, Overlord. I never wanted a job as a factory manager. Besides, they have much more to offer and we can help them as well. We load the engines in five hours. You can be away in ten. We lay-low on Hirkiv until you are gone. Take the *Monarch* and the tow to the Tar Galaxy. We can meet you there. Wait for us in the nebula at the edge of the Zakkai system.'

He turned his chariot away from them and looked out of the large window of his chamber, gazing down at the planet's barren moon. Then he pulsed with white light. 'I am uneasy with this. It is all untested and you leave me. You will be outside my protection.'

'Overlord, we can do this. Siba is well able to captain the *Monarch* and the tow. You'll have most of the crew and it'll be a slower journey. We'll catch up with you. Please.'

'Thomas, speak up.'

'Overlord, you know she has already made up her mind. But,' he said, as he put his arm around her and kissed her on the cheek, 'I wouldn't let her go on such a mission if I didn't believe we can do it. It'll be tight, but we'll have surprise on our side. We'll be long gone before they realise what's happened.'

'My child, can I not talk you out of this?'

'Jeez, Overlord, will you give it a rest. Did you talk me out of rescuing you from the *Hela*?'

'No, I couldn't then. Very well, go. You have much to do.'

*

The Runabout. EPTS: B140337

Loaded and ready for another mission to Hirkiv, the small bridge of *Monarch's* runabout hummed with activity. The significance of this event wasn't lost on The Eight. Dividing his team in this hostile solar system was not part of his plan. He understood the logic of Niamh's strategy, but still, he didn't favour it – on many levels. But she had proved herself in the past. So, he indulged her this pursuit – poaching the elusive star-drive designers and makers from under the noses of their masters.

Siba's flat matter-of-fact voice burst out on their comms. 'Mrs Parker, all bulkheads are sealed, doors locked, and control enabled to the *Runabout*.'

A grinning Niamh looked around at Tom, Geoff, Brian and their three soldiers. 'You guys ready?'

'Ready as we'll ever be,' Tom said. A grim look back at his team, strapped in on the small bridge, betrayed his feelings.

'Okay, Siba, we have control; unlock on my mark.' Vertical controls opened in front of her. Niamh's hands flew across the ethereal dials. A soft rumble announced the grav drive start. 'Engines up, disengage locks – now.'

They felt a slight vibration through the floor and then, 'Locks disengaged, Mrs Parker. We have separation. Good luck,' she bade, as the *Runabout* glided away from its mother ship.

'Thank you, Captain Siba. We'll see you in three cycles. Tom, the cloak, please. Let's go have a look at Hirkiv,' Niamh said, her voice laced with confidence. As usual, she had her way! Her eyes flashed with soft white light and her blue hair glowed, the contamination radiating her excitement while she piloted this detachable ship down towards the planet.

The vessel had a "flying bridge", its own engine room complete with grav and blue drives. Constructed into the *Monarch's* lower forward section – designed as Grandfather Borea's escape ship – this marvel of Borea engineering included the mother ship's lower fin with its array of deadly weapons. A formidable "little runabout" that had terrorised many during its illustrious past.

The cloaked ship slinked undetected down towards the planet. *Another dry and dusty world*, Geoff thought, as he searched for Fazqa Mzimot's location. His comms panel pinged, easing the intensity of his demeanour.

'She's in that desert area outside the city. It must be where their home is. Look,' Geoff said, optimism lacing his voice.

He pulled up an expanded view of the planet on the *Runabout's* curved viewscreen. Gigantic blots carved malignant scars across Hirkiv's surface. Barren grey and black gorges scooped out from abandoned open cast mines permeated the planet's landscape. The young man zoomed their view into one of those worldly welts.

'There, look! The homes are cut back into the gorge. It's like they're reclaimed from old mines …' His voice trailed off in disbelief at what he was seeing. It was their first real close-up view of the planet's surface, the previous "shopping trip" limiting any unauthorised tours or surveys of this world.

Planet Hirkiv served as the prime manufacturing world for the Overlord's galaxies and the Anan economy. It contained the largest concentrations of factories anywhere in the known worlds. Starting its life as a planet rich in the minerals used in the alien-tech manufacturing processes, it was – ages ago – stripped bare. Opencast mining extracted precious metals, rare-earths and chemical compounds, denuding the planet of an old and forgotten beauty. Lush green forests were felled and mountains levelled. Lakes and seas once teeming with life, turned into polluted fetid ponds.

But the factories, the centre of galactic commerce, continued to thrive. The resources were shipped in, magicked into valuable components and sent back out. From the humble communicator to the mighty blue drives, it was all made here. And, with the assembly and refurbishment of starships, this planet proved a real money spinner.

As shocked as Geoff, Tom scrutinised the scene unfolding in front of them. Geoff was right. In the most unlikely place, he could see the signs of habitation. People were living there, in that wasteland.

'Not where I'd expect a chief designer to live,' Tom mused out loud.

Close to the source of the signal, unnoticed, Niamh landed their cloaked ship, hiding it in one of the many barren hollows.

Biting her lip, she set a timer on the bridge for seven hours hence. By then, *Monarch* would be long gone. And the middle of the planet's dark night favoured this clandestine steal. With the cloak at maximum and the *Runabout* set to silent mode, like burglars hiding in the shadows, the seven settled down to grab some sleep. It didn't come easy to Niamh, buzzing with adrenalin; she couldn't wait to start the mission. Failure, to her, wasn't an option.

*

Planet Hirkiv

In the dead of night, Fazqa sat up in her bed. *What was that buzzing noise?* She looked around the small cave. It was coming from her bag, the one she took to work. She opened it and there it was, glowing with soft grey light and buzzing incessantly – the thing the smelly human had given her. She was surprised his mother had insisted on the gift. She had looked through the contents, immediately stopping when she discovered pictures of Geoff and other humans. *Now, why was it doing this?* Taking it out of her bag, she touched the screen. The buzzing stopped and the screen came alive. She knew what it was as she lifted it up.

'Hiya, Fazqa. I said I'd be in touch. You busy?'

'Mrs Parker, this is a surprise. I'm actually sleeping. It's our rest time.'

'Sorry to wake you. I'm outside; any chance of coming in? I'd like to talk to the family. Your dad home?'

'Mrs Parker, you're so strange. None of our clients has ever done this.'

'Ah well, nothing ventured nothing gained. Will you come and meet me? It's cold out here.'

Fazqa stood at the entrance to their cave and looked at Niamh, dressed in a ship garb, her hair and eyes glowing gently with blue light. 'Mrs Parker, how did you find us? Oh no, the communicator,' she said, as she covered her face with her hands.

Niamh smiled at the similarity to the human gestures. 'Yes, the comms unit.'

'How did you get here?'

'We have resources. Your dad home? I don't have much time. Please, I don't bite.'

'Yes, he is. Come in,' Fazqa said, as she led Niamh back into a gloomy living space. 'Wait here. I'll get him.'

As the girl disappeared down a small passage cut out in the rock, Niamh looked around. The Mzimot dwelling had all the signs of a family living room with a cooking area in the back and a large table cut from the rock. The floor was covered with materials she had seen warehouse equipment wrapped in. What meagre furniture they had was fashioned from the waste packing she had seen outside the factory. *Have I got this wrong?* she thought. *What or who forces a senior designer and engine builder to live in a cave like this?* She heard people approaching and out of the gloomy passage, a man and woman appeared, followed by Fazqa.

'Mrs Parker, these are my parents. They–'

'—are not pleased with the intrusion. Why have you come? You put us in danger by your presence here. Can't you see for yourself how desperate things are for us? They'll punish us if they know you visited. We'll end up with more debt. Already our next generation is bound in servitude.'

Niamh struggled in the gloom to see the man's features. 'Please, listen to me. Listen to what I propose. I may be able to help. If you say no, I'll leave.'

He turned to look at his mate. She nodded. 'Jarzol, what harm will it do? But be quick, and remember, the boys are not back yet.'

'I don't like it, but come, let's sit. Tell me why I get a visit in the night by an alien woman contaminated by blue,' Jarzol said.

They sat together in silence at the strange rock table out of earshot of the other two. Niamh tried to probe Jarzol's feelings but got nothing – the Mzimot man's mind was an impenetrable wall! She had visualised these negotiations but never expected such a hostile reception. Dressed in sloppy night trousers and a drab short-sleeved top, the average-height man looked nothing like the famed engine expert she had expected to meet. Bluish skin, bare hairy arms crossed in front of his chest. Grey eyes under large bushy eyebrows peered out from a scowling oval face. He ran a six-fingered hand through short-cropped black hair, then scratched one of his small ears. *Trying to awaken his tired brain*, surmised Niamh.

She started her pitch. It sounded so hollow …

'Come to a world far away and build engines for us. We'll pay your debts here, and you'll have a wonderfully rich life in a beautiful far off land. And live happily ever after – I promise!'

In the end, Niamh cringed. It sounded like a line straight from a stale America movie.

He burst out laughing. If he had a Universal Credit for every two-bit hustler who offered such riches, he'd be able to buy his own planet now. The naïveté of it all was offensive and he told her so. 'Mrs Parker, please leave. Do you think you are the first to make us such an offer? Have you wondered why we live in such conditions? Everyone hates us. We are outcasts and we choose to be outcasts, not tied to anyone or any Overlord. We despise them!'

That news shocked Niamh. She hadn't expected it. Concentrating her mind, she flashed it to Tom, hiding in the shadows outside.

In a low growling voice, Jarzol continued. 'It's a hard life here. But the family survives. And yes, I'd leave in a heartbeat – if I could. Why should I trust you? What makes you so different? Tell me.'

Niamh knew she was beaten; her negotiating skills wouldn't break this stony man. She needed Tom, and now. 'Jarzol, trust me, we are different. My husband, Tom, is outside. He'll reassure you. Please let him in.'

Her voice had lost all the confidence she had started with and its soft, pleading manner hit the blue man's heart. Not what he had heard in the past. He shouted across to Fazqa. Taken aback, the girl opened the door to find a smiling Tom, sporting a large rucksack on his back, standing outside. Without a word, she let him in, pointing to the table where Niamh and Jarzol sat. Fazqa and her mum watched on with frowning faces, wondering whether they would still be breaking rocks here tomorrow.

The dynamic of the negotiation changed when Tom sat down. Unlike Niamh, he'd anticipated difficulties. If they wanted this family to help build a fleet on Earth, Tom, the spy, would have to spin a believable yarn. And he did, never divulging all the truth but telling most of it. The family had moved closer, all listening intently to the alien's sales pitch.

Throughout Tom's talk, the rucksack lay tantalisingly on the table. All eyes were on it. *What did it contain?* they wondered. Curiosity played in their minds. *Was it weapons to coerce them? Or worse?* As he concluded, bit by bit, he opened the rucksack. First the straps, then the flap and then the drawcord was lazily pulled open. He talked throughout – part of his enticing strategy.

Abruptly, he stopped. 'What d'you think, Jarzol?' Eyes wide open, he stared back at the blue-skinned man.

For the first time, Jarzol was at a loss. The offer was, in essence, the same as the one Niamh had made, but with substance. Contracts of engagement, time limits, freedom of choice, workers' rights, their debts paid and a guaranteed bottom-line salary – more money than they ever thought possible. But Jarzol still wasn't convinced. He looked at the rucksack. 'Prove you can do this.'

Tom upended the rucksack on the table. Gold bars and four multi-coloured cloth bags spilt out – the Mzimot gasped. Niamh reached over and started to open the cloth packets, laying four blue diamonds on the table, their deep blue colour announcing their fresh newness. The trove, a parting gift from The Eight, had come from the Borea hoard found in the Australian desert. Zaval had paid some of that hoard over to the Eight to help expunge the family debt. Now it had found its way to this stone table in a dismal cave on Hirkiv.

Tom smiled. 'A down payment on the contract,' was all he said. Silence enveloped the darkened room.

Sitting on the floor of the living space, Fazqa and her mum's eyes bore into Jarzol – he felt their gaze. Never before had such treasure graced this humble table. He relaxed and, surprising everyone, laughed. A jovial laugh, defusing the tension between the Mzimot and their human adversaries. In Jarzol's eyes, the Parkers had proven themselves. No one before had offered such wealth in cold hard currency. The engine builder knew such inducements were part of the factory's everyday commerce but up till now, his family had never seen any of it!

Now, these alien visitors would become co-conspirators in the family's daring escape from Hirkiv. Jarzol stood up and beckoned the two to join them at the table.

'You heard. The Parkers have made us an offer I would never have thought possible,' he said. His eyes caressed the loot – the gold and blue diamonds glistening on the table. 'After so many false hopes, this will never come again. We should grab it and go.'

His mate shook her head. 'It won't work. We'll never get away. The boys are still working, and what about the rest of the family? We can't leave them.'

Tom had expected that. 'How many are there?'

'About twenty.' She paused and looked at Fazqa. 'Well, you know them better than me. How many?'

'Mr Parker, there are twenty-two altogether in our family unit. Leaving without them is not an option. They would be held responsible for our debts if we did that.'

'Will they agree and can we get them?'

'Yes, they will, but it will be hard to get the two boys. The consortium makes sure some in the family unit work a different shift. It's harder for them to run off,' Fazqa answered.

Niamh took the baton and replied, this time radiating confidence. 'Tom will figure that out, won't you?' she said, looking across at her husband.

'Yes, we'll manage that. We have more resources.'

'Where are they?'

'Outside as well, Fazqa,' he said, as he keyed a message into his comms unit. He smiled at the girl. 'If you open the door, they'll be there.'

*

With Niamh piloting and Tom and his two soldiers acting as porters, it took two hours to shuttle the extended family living in the caves over to the hidden *Runabout*. As Fazqa had said, they followed without question. If it was good enough for Jarzol, they were all in. The task had worried Tom. *How many trips would they have to make?* he wondered. *And, what about their stuff?*

He needn't have worried. Bedraggled, the Mzimot family filed out from the caves carrying their paltry possessions. That sight touched even the battle-hardened Tom.

Arriving on the ship, they marvelled at the luxurious accommodation on offer. Grandfather Borea had spared no expense when he fitted out his "escape pod".

'This was a Borea ship?' Jarzol asked.

Niamh smiled as his eyes wandered over the controls. 'Yes, it was. We own it now.'

Jarzol's mouth opened, but nothing came out, then he croaked, 'The mother ship you—'

'We call her the *Monarch*, and yes, she's ours as well. Can you handle the engineering controls?'

He nodded.

'Great, we'll need all the help we can get. Fazqa, we need you with Geoff at comms. Show him where the boys are. He'll direct Tom and the shuttle to the pickup. We'll need someone at weapons in the fin. Who can do that?' Niamh asked. One of the elders put up their hand. 'Fine, off you go; take one of ours to help,' she said, pointing to one of Tom's young soldiers. 'The rest of you make yourselves comfortable. I need you all seated and strapped in. It'll get rough later on.'

*

Back in the factory, finishing a long night shift working on the packing line, the two Mzimot boys made their way down the narrow plant stairs. The younger one looked at his brother. 'I'm sore all over. There was no box to stand on. I had to overstretch all night to get the packets.'

Big brother looked down at his young sibling. He looked miserable in a grey work suit stained with grime and face smeared with dirt. He tried some futile comfort. 'We'll be home soon; you can rest then. Come on, if we don't hurry, all the food will be gone.'

Taking his brother's hand, he started to push past the others working their way down the gantry stairs. He hardly glanced at the hastily repaired cut in the gantry netting where their friend had jumped to his death three shifts ago. The personification of hopelessness and despair! Finally, they reached the ground floor and, still tugging on his brother's arm, he pushed up to a gate where a man was handing out small boxes to the departing workforce.

'Grab one,' he said to his brother.

Clutching their valuable rations, they both fled out into the courtyard with the other workers. Glad to be out, they sat down with their backs to a wall and looked around the square. Four giant factories rose above the courtyard, the faceless brown exteriors adding to the gloom of the featureless square.

A man dressed in a ragged work suit crawled up to them. 'Food, please give me food,' he muttered, eying the small parcels they clutched.

The older boy kicked him. 'Go away, leave us—'

The courtyard erupted with the sound of an explosion. Dazed from the noise, the boys watched as four black-clad soldiers jumped out of thin air in the centre of the courtyard. They ran towards the two boys, firing their weapons over the milling crowd. The older boy grabbed his brother, as two of the soldiers ran towards them.

'Grab them,' Tom shouted to two of his men as he levelled his grav weapon at four factory guards running out of a doorway. He shot them in the chest, watching dispassionately as they fell down, stunned. 'Quick, before more arrive, get them in the shuttle.'

Running back to the shuttle, they carried the two struggling boys. Tom jumped in, turning to drag the rest of his crew and the two boys inside the cloaked ship. 'Brian, ready for lift off, now,' he shouted as he slammed the door shut. 'Strap those lads in. It's going to get rough. Brian let's – shit, what was that?' he said, as the shuttle lurched to one side.

'Grav weapons on the roof. They're firing down at us, boss. I've increased power to the grav bubble, but the cloak's failing and we're losing lift.'

Out of the blue, Fazqa from the *Runabout* shouted over the comms unit, 'Help them, they're here to rescue you. The engine well, decouple the cloak, use the connector to bridge the two engines. Hurry, your lives depend on it,' she screamed.

The two boys jumped up. The older one running aft, he tried to pull open the bulkhead. 'I need a hand,' he shouted. Tom grabbed it. Within seconds the cowling opened, revealing the inner workings of the shuttle's engine compartment. Both boys hopped in and set about pulling at the cables and connectors.

The shuttle rose and fell, while the inexperienced pilot – Brian – tried to control it under the onslaught of grav weapons, firing down at them from the roof. The ship shuddered then rose above the courtyard.

'You have no cloak. All power is feeding propulsion and the grav bubble. You need to hurry. The factory guards, they have a cruiser in this area. It'll be on top of us soon,' the eldest boy shouted.

Tom grabbed the comms unit. 'Niamh, we're coming out with no cloak. You ready with the *Runabout*?'

'We're working on something. That cruiser is lifting off now.'

'Stay between the buildings. Turn this thing sideways,' shouted the boy, as Brian struggled with the shuttle controls.

'He doesn't know how to do that. Help him,' Fazqa – monitoring their progress – shouted back over comms.

He looked at his younger brother. 'Stay here – you know what I'll need.' The shuttle bucked and kicked under the onslaught of the weapons' fire. With Tom's help, the eldest clawed his way up to the cockpit beside Brian.

'Let him at it,' he said to Brian. 'From what I've heard, he'll do better than you.'

Brian looked at the strange, blue-skinned boy, dressed in a dirty ship's suit with his long pink hair tied up in a plait on his head. 'Not what I expected. Come on, show me.'

The boy squeezed into the cockpit beside Brian. Hastily grabbing a seat restraint, he roared to them all, 'Hold on!' Looping a hand around the controls, he turned the shuttle on its side. Increasing throttle settings to maximum, he shouted, 'Now!' back to his younger brother wedged in the engine well. The young boy reached down. With his long fingers, he reconfigured the power damper. The engine trembled in its mounting. The shuttle, with the boosted acceleration, streaked forwards, flying on its side between the faceless buildings.

'Oh shit,' shouted Brian as he watched the tall buildings speed by. His face contorted with the acceleration. He could hear Fazqa shouting to her brother on the comms unit.

'Stop, stop, stop! You'll blow the synchronous modulator.'

'Oh, shut up. What do you know about that? All you do is look pretty to sell.'

'I do not; I earn my keep.'

Tom breathed a sigh of relief as the calm voice of their father came over the comms. 'Children, now is not the time for that. Hold your course and speed until you exit the grid. You can hide there – behind that rise,' he said, sending a location to the shuttle's viewscreen. 'We'll pick you up there after we sort out that cruiser.'

*

The bridge of the *Runabout* hummed with activity, Jarzol and his Mzimot family pitching in to help. With split views of the shuttle, the factory grid and the dreaded Hirkiv attack cruiser, the bridge viewscreen showed it all.

'Mrs Parker, take this up to one thousand metres. That cruiser's heading right after the shuttle,' Jarzol said.

The *Runabout* sped up over the factory city. 'One thousand,' Niamh said, nodding across to Jarzol.

His hands caressed the engine controls. A slight bump announced the start up. 'Blue drive on line – coordinates are at your console. Fold is open.'

Niamh looked out of the *Runabout's* window at a small port, opened in the space immediately in front of them. Nudging the ship through, they emerged out over the factory city and behind the cruiser – forewarned by the fold's disturbance – turning towards them.

'They've seen us. Get the cloak up,' Niamh shouted across to Jarzol as she flew the *Runabout* straight towards the cruiser.

'Cloak's up. Weapon ready?' Jarzol shouted to one of the family, seated in the munitions' locker, assisted by a human soldier.

A hoary voice responded over the ship's comm. 'Weapon unlocked and ready.'

'Fire, three bursts, port aft quadrant.'

'Father, that won't be enough.'

'Fazqa, you know I have friends on that vessel. I won't kill them. It will be enough. Mrs Parker, go now to their starboard side. Quick, before they recover.'

Niamh accelerated the small ship. Turning it on its side, she flew tight around the bow of the cruiser. Flying down its starboard side, she turned and righted her own ship, stopping six hundred metres off the stern. 'Hail them, Geoff.'

'Look, they're turning,' he said. 'They're heading back the way they came. There's smoke coming from their port side.'

The comms crackled and Tom's voice came through. 'Taking fire. There's another one of those cruisers; it tracked us to this mound at the edge of the city. We're just above the deck. Our engines won't last under this battering.'

Jarzol worked frantically, then swiped a hand across the display in front of him. 'Weapons, target solution at your console, max pulse, now,' he shouted over the comms.

The ship shuddered. Deadly fire left the grav cannon, arcing up through the air then down onto the cruiser, above where the shuttle was sheltering.

On the *Runabout's* bridge, Geoff increased the magnification of the view. Grav pulses ploughed into the large cruiser. As soon as they hit, it stopped targeting the shuttle and turned to face the incoming fire.

The hoary voice of the Mzimot in the weapons' locker pierced the air. 'Bridge, we can't maintain this level of fire for long; we'll run out of ammo.'

Jarzol looked across to Niamh. 'Their grav bubble will soak up the impact. We need to get closer. Quick as you can, Mrs Parker – get behind them. Weapons, reduce fire to half,' he directed.

She moved the throttle to max. The ship streaked across the sky over the factory city, straight towards the cruiser. As they neared, she shouted across at Jarzol. 'Drop the cloak for a few seconds. Give them a flash of our ship – draw their fire, then we hit them again. Weapons, hold your fire.'

Jarzol dropped the cloak as Niamh flew the *Runabout* straight along the cruiser's port side. It opened up with its own grav cannon, pounding the small ship. Immediately past the cruiser's stern, she turned the ship around. 'Bubble is holding. Weapons, now – target their port drive,' she ordered.

The *Runabout* shuddered again as the grav cannon opened up. 'They're hit. Look, smoke from the port engine,' shouted Fazqa, as the view of the cruiser turning away and falling back to the ground below flashed across their screen.

'Tom, get ready for a pickup. We're right over you. Our cloak is down,' Niamh shouted over her comms.

Minutes later, the small shuttle appeared in front of the *Runabout*, the engine smoking as it docked in the shuttle bay hangar.

'Father, the engine's on fire.'

'Quick, go. You know what to do. Get the young ones out.'

Fazqa ran to the back of the bridge, wrenched two strange-looking objects from a compartment and sprinted down the stairway to the shuttle bay.

The voice from weapons came over the comms. 'Jarzol, we need to get out of here – ammo is gone.'

It was Niamh who answered. 'Underway now. Both of you, make your way to the shuttle bay; they need help. Jarzol, open a fold – get us out anywhere over that wasteland, well away from here.'

'Open in front of you, Mrs Parker.'

She flew the ship through the fold, arriving out over the planet's far-reaching wasteland. The disused mines, with their vast tailings, cut scars across the bleak landscape.

Within minutes, Tom appeared on the bridge, followed by the two Mzimot boys and Fazqa, the young one, black from head to toe, all covered in soot. He looked across at their father, strapped in at the engineering station. 'Jarzol, I believe these are your sons; quite handy in a fight. Their skills were wasted in that factory; we'd be happy to have them work for us.'

The two boys rushed to embrace their smiling father. 'Yes, Mr Parker, their skills were wasted in that hell hole,' he replied, with tears running down his face.

'Cloaks up, we're getting out of here. Strap those young lads, in,' Niamh said, as she turned the *Runabout* towards the sky. Her stomach heaved as she looked down at the grav fuel metre. She dialled down on the throttles. *Now we'll test your design to the limit,* she thought, as she looked across at Jarzol, strapping his sons into seats at the rear of the bridge.

CHAPTER TWENTY-NINE

To: *controlroomsuper@helabase.com* From: *alan.phillips@anancorp.com* Date: *06/01/28*

> Subject: *Impatience*
>
> *Prisha,*
>
> *Perhaps I am getting impatient, but there's nothing from The Eight or the New World. As you see from the news, the world is also getting impatient. Are the satellites we launched working? So far, they haven't picked up anything in deep space. I'm afraid we might miss something. Can you please test them?*
>
> *Regards, Alan.*

To: *alan.phillips@anancorp.com* From: *controlroomsuper@helabase.com* Date: *06/01/28*

> *Alan,*
>
> *Every twenty-four hours, the nightshift run a test routine on the satellite array. We're getting good data from the edge of our solar system. I'm confident we haven't missed anything. Unfortunately, it's not what we want to see. I'm sorry.*
>
> *Regards, Prisha*

*

The Runabout. EPTS: B140377

FRANTIC AND WELL-TIMED DESCRIBES THE *Runabout's* escape from Hirkiv. By the time they realised what had happened, the consortium couldn't react fast enough to get the Mzimot back. By then, the *Runabout* was hurtling through folded space – untraceable, at faster than light speed. Furious, the autocratic consortium director blamed everyone. Taken aback by the audacity of the raid, the director combed new news and comms for sight or sound of the renegades. It popped up on an obscure channel. A message from the scrap world, Lagrvth, reporting that they were "raided and robbed by space pirates".

"Who were they? And where did they come from?" were the questions asked.

Images of the *Runabout* seen when Niamh flashed a view of it at the cruiser they attacked, added to the confusion. The unmistakable lower fin matched that of the images of the visiting *Monarch*. Thin evidence that didn't make sense. Other ships had the same configuration.

'Why would a legitimate Charter, who paid for their goods, bother to come back to steal the Mzimot?' asked the director.

With more questions than answers, the director decided to play the whole affair down. After all, they had the blueprints, the valuable rotor settings and the ability to make the engines themselves. The newer hybrid drives involved a collaboration of different designers – all of a sudden, the Mzimot family wasn't irreplaceable.

Still mystified, the consortia needed to point the finger at someone or something. They blamed the pirates who had robbed Lagrvth, concocting a conspiracy between them and the Mzimot.

The final report, a work of art, landed on the director's desk. 'Yes, that's it,' approved the director. 'The ungrateful Mzimot planned the whole thing. Escaping their debts with the pirates.'

The story worked – for a short while – deflecting any retribution away from the consortia management. The company wazzocks were puffed-up with self-serving indignation at the thankless Mzimot's actions, until a mysterious transfer from accounts in the Energy Exchange paid the Mzimot debts. That light touch by Cylla Ora stirred up the whole pot of intrigue!

*

Space-Tug Richard, Folded Space.
EPTS: B140409 7th January 2028

On the *Richard*, travelling faster than light, it took the small fleet two weeks in Earth time, near thirteen cycles in Anan space time, to passage through folded space to Earth. A milestone in travel between the New World and Earth. Verteg's unique ability to calculate the shortest vector minimised that journey time. Robert hoped the Borea pilot's pioneering route would lay the ground for the future, permanently linking Earth with its colony. Only time would tell.

In their cramped cabin, lying together in a small cot, Janet awoke early. Crawling over Robert – waking with a grunt – she stepped into the shower. The tiny space more resembled a room in a Japanese hotel than a cabin on a futuristic starship. He sat up and admired his lover, stifling the urge to join her – there was hardly enough room for one, let alone two!

Towelling herself off, Janet spoke, excitement lacing her voice. 'Come on, Robert. Get a move on. We'll be home today.'

Within minutes, showered and dressed, both left their cabin. Grabbing a quick breakfast in the empty galley, another display of the *Richard's* frugal design, they made their way to the bridge. Slipping in and smiling at a busy Verteg, the couple sat down at the back of the bridge. Oblivious to the human's entry, the Borea crew, directed by their pilot, beavered away at the tug's controls preparing the exit from folded space.

'If it's anything like entering the fold, it'll be some sight,' Robert whispered to Janet.

The couple feasted their eyes on the alien tech before them. Inside the tug's enormous engine room, the spinning dodecahedron rotors blurred into one mass of flashing blue light. Out in space, aft of the floating engine, the *Hela* and *George*, cocooned inside the trammel and connected to the *Richard* by two bulbous leads, followed in a straight line. The two-ship tow, protected by the giant gravity bubble, proved easier and safer to manage than the four Zaval had tried.

That fact didn't escape Robert. *With Verteg in command, this small fleet's made good time*, he thought. Clasping Janet's hand, he said, 'We'll be there soon.'

'What will they think?' Janet asked.

Indeed, how would Earth react when they learned of The Sixth's coup. 'I don't know, Janet. So much has changed,' was all Robert could say as he pondered that dour dilemma.

His mind wandered as he gazed back at the two following ships, crewed by Zaval's son, Quriel, his military companions and the Borea family – a motley crew of purebreed and green-skins. The fleet would return to Earth with eight Borea and seven Anan military. Nine of the Borea, under the elder's leadership, had stayed on the New World to help with the off-world mining. Humans would have to learn quickly, Robert realised. There would be no free lunches in this galactic war. An urgent voice broke his musing.

'Captain, tension on the trammel connector between the *Hela* is rising,' one of the crew shouted, from tow control.

'Message *Hela* and *George*, increase grav drives by point seven,' Verteg said to comms.

The bridge went silent as they waited for the reply. 'Captain, message back from both, "speed adjusted and holding steady. Ready for exit".'

Verteg walked back to tow control. Inspecting the panel's readouts, she quizzed the operator. 'Well, what have we got?'

'Tension on the two connectors back at optimum. We're ready Captain.' A sharp, confident reply.

Verteg returned to her captain's chair. Dressed in a two-piece blue ship garb, the green-skinned woman shone a commanding aura. Her crew drank it up, proud to serve and learn from the master pilot.

The bridge viewscreen readjusted with split views of space ahead of the *Richard* and the view aft of the *Hela* and *George* following behind.

'Navigation, status please,' Verteg asked.

The navigator looked up from his console. 'We're right at the edge of their solar system. Nothing but clear space, Captain.'

'On my mark, cut the blue feed.' Glancing down at the readings on her controls, 'Now!' Verteg shouted. 'Blue drive off. Message all ships; prepare to exit folded space. Hold course and speed.'

The ship shuddered. Robert turned and looked down at the engines. They flashed with a fading white light as the dodecahedron rotors, starved of fuel, decelerated, their shapes slowly coming back into focus. Then it happened. With a blinding flash, a tear in the black fabric of folded space opened in front of the *Richard*. It grew into long fingers, speckled with blurred white light from the distant stars of the Milky Way. They were out, travelling faster than light through Earth's solar system.

The navigator opened a fresh plot of the solar system. 'New course heading plotted with turns through x and y-axis, Captain. Am sending to *Hela* and *George*.'

Verteg bounced up from her seat, smiling. 'Well done, well done,' she said to her crew. 'Mr Leslie, we are here, at the edge of your planet's solar system. You are home.'

'Verteg, I keep telling you, it's Robert. You did good.'

*

In the Australian desert, inside the Hela base, an alarm shattered the night shift's cosy watch. Base operatives scrambled to understand what the previously unheard-of warning meant. The initial calls of "What the hell's that?" and "Is that the fire alarm?" was replaced with one sharp order. "Turn that racket off. It's a deep space alarm."

In seconds, the noise stopped. Order restored, the four-night shift operatives interrogated their space-age control systems – raw data flashing across a wall-sized screen. Instant messages flowed from the newly launched Anan Corp satellites. Disguised as primitive telescopes, they faced outward, monitoring Earth's solar system for any sign of intrusion. Commissioned by Alan Phillips, they contained enhanced Earth-based scanning tech – Anan Corp's investment in guarding the planet.

'Shit, it's a fleet,' were the first words spoken as the big screen displayed a depiction of Verteg's approaching ships.

With the manual open on the desk, the night-shift supervisor recited the prescribed challenge – while another woke Prisha, their boss.

*

Minutes later, on the *Richard's* bridge, the message pinged the comm's terminal. 'Mr Leslie,' comms said, 'we have an incoming signal in your language. Listen, please. I believe they want a reply.'

The bridge's speakers crackled and then Robert and Janet listened to the welcoming words spoken in a soft Australian accent. 'Alien ships, alien ships, this is Earth, Hela base. Identify yourself. I say again, alien ships, alien ships …'

Robert rushed across to comms and grabbed the mic. 'Hela base, Hela base, this is Robert Leslie, onboard space-tug *Richard* with *Hela* and *George* in tow. Wake Matt McKinnon. We're back and landing three ships in thirty-six hours. Our captain will message you with an orbit and landing sequence.'

There was a pause and then, what felt like an age later, another crackle. 'Confirmed, Robert. Welcome home. Will call back with Matt. Hela base, out.'

Robert turned to look at Janet. The tears streamed down her face. 'Robert, I never thought I would be so happy to hear those welcoming words, but what will we tell them?'

'The truth, Janet, and they'll no like it either. No, they won't.'

*

The Runabout, Zakkai Nebula. EPTS: B140424

As the *Runabout* hurtled through folded space, Niamh lay on their bed gazing up at Tom, his face haggard with worry. 'Don't look at me like that,' she said.

'I can't help it, you're so weak. You know, Niamh, how much I worry about you.'

'I'll be fine, I will. The Eight said there is help in the Zakkai system.' She strained from the pain coursing through her body. He watched as she closed her flashing blue eyes, clenching her hands in agony, her nails digging into his flesh as she clung to him. 'When she first trained me, Theia warned me about the energy but she never explained what would happen. The blue is changing me, Tom. My body can't cope. Hell of a time to get pregnant as well.'

'Niamh, Niamh, I love you. I'm so sorry, I never thought—'

She laughed and pulled him down to her. They kissed slowly. He could feel her tingling from the blue coursing through her body. They broke from the kiss – he lay down on the bed beside her, cradling the love of his life in his arms.

She looked into his brown eyes. 'Sorry for what? Oh, the ravishing you gave me when I returned on the *Monarch*. You never apologised after that. Did you? Yes, it was straight to bed, and it takes two. I love you, Tom. I want this, more than anything, I want our own family.'

'Did he look?'

'No, there's a limit to The Eight's power – you know that. He was afraid he might damage the baby. That's why he didn't want us to leave the *Monarch*, remember?'

Tom nodded. 'Yes, I do.' He recalled the Overlord's words when she told him they would go back for the Mzimot. "I am uneasy with this. It is all untested, and you leave me. You will be outside my protection" was what he had said. Now Tom realised what The Eight had meant.

A low buzz disturbed their embrace. 'That's the bridge. Jarzol needs you. Can you manage?'

'Help me up. I'll have to go. We can't fly on much longer through this fold without a navigator.'

Tom lifted Niamh up and carried her to the bridge. The crew looked away when they arrived, wondering how long she would last. Both human and Mzimot knew how serious her blue contamination had become. After the mission to Hirkiv, her condition had deteriorated. When the adrenal rush, generated by the exhilaration she felt during the mission, died down, her body crashed. As she settled down at the nav-con, Niamh could feel their emotion. They were afraid.

'We'll make the rendezvous, don't worry,' she said, as she placed her blue diamond in the console. The projection burst out over the small bridge, glowing for all to see. She was the only deep-space navigator on the ship, and while she rested, they had followed a course line she had plotted. Without a pre-flight plan calculated, something Niamh couldn't do, flying through a fold needed frequent navigational corrections. She knew there would be some in-fold drift, but badly needing the rest, she took the risk. As she looked at their position, she could feel her heart thump. *Not disastrous*, she thought, *but far enough out to leave us seventy-k off course.* She looked at the fuel readouts. 'Jarzol, where did the grav come from?'

'The boys scraped it from the shuttle and then managed to pack it into the *Runabout*'s engines.'

'When we were underway? You let them do that?'

'It's quite safe, Mrs Parker. There's an access hatch. We designed it for such emergencies. There's enough grav to get us to the edge of the nebula. After that …'

She looked down at her hands. They were shaking as she tried to take control of the ship. Feeling Jarzol's gaze, she looked up.

The blue skin of his face had changed to a dark purple with the worry. His grey eyes peered out through squinted hairy eyebrows. 'Plot the course, Mrs Parker. Brian and I will fly the ship.'

'Drop out of the fold.' She focused on her projection, planning a change to bring them back on course to the rendezvous. She slumped back in her chair. 'That's it. Jarzol, have we enough grav?'

The ship vibrated and the view through the bridge windows changed as they dropped out of folded space. 'No, it leaves us thirty thousand short and we'll lose the cloak.'

'We'll hide in the nebula and use the sub-light interface to contact the *Monarch*.'

He turned the ship around. 'I hope you're right. Brian, course to the nebula is on your screen. Keep it straight as you can. I'll aerate the engines; it'll extend the grav burn.' He looked across at Niamh, and Tom, who was standing beside her. 'But you know, it will run out.' *What have I done?* Jarzol thought. *How could I have trusted them? How could I have led my family into this?*

She felt his anguish and shut it out. There'd be a bigger row when they docked with the *Monarch*. She closed her eyes, focusing all her strength on keeping the nav-projection open.

The ship lumbered on. Sitting on the floor, Jarzol's family clustered around the windows. The seven humans and twenty-two Mzimot packed the small bridge. Peering out at the approaching nebula, all wondered if they would have enough power to sustain life support. Jarzol had already shut down all but the essential services. Huddled together in blankets, their collective warmth made up for the reduced heating as each breath they exhaled condensed in the cold air of the bridge.

Some drifted off into sleep while others stared into the empty depths of space. Gradually, the Zakkai nebula filled the bridge viewscreen, giving them hope. It stretched far across the cosmos, erupting in a kaleidoscopic multicoloured display.

Tom looked out at a never-ending, changing gas cloud, its red, yellow and blue gases mixing to form different colours and hues. 'Jarzol, have we enough to get into that gas giant?'

'Just enough, Mr Parker. It leaves us thirty-k short of the rendezvous.'

'We'll hide there. Geoff, anything on comms?'

'They're not here. I should see the *Monarch* now. Even if it's cloaked, the mother ship's sub-light interface should pick us up.' He could hear Fazqa's deep intake of breath as she peered over his shoulder at the comms readouts.

'Father, he's right. The mother ship, it's not here. It's a lie; they tricked us.'

Her words sparked grumbling amongst the rest of the family. Geoff was quick to respond. 'Don't be so stupid. Why would we bring you all here if it was a trick?'

Ignoring the verbal turmoil Geoff started, Niamh reached out across space with her mind. Her thoughts mingled with The Eight's.

'My child, hold on. We are coming. I will find you,' he said to her.

She held up her hand, quelling the noisy arguments around her. 'They're coming. They know where we are; we wait,' she said, as the *Runabout* entered the boundless gas cloud.

For over twenty hours they drifted in the nebula, existing on emergency power and scavenging all available battery and life support from the shuttle. Designed as Grandfather Borea's personal attach-craft and lifeboat, supporting twenty-nine souls on board stretched the ship to its limits.

Without a break, Geoff monitored the comms console. He watched as other ships plied back and forth into the Zakkai system, well away from the nebula, but no sign of the *Monarch*.

Suddenly, his sensors picked up a distortion in space. 'Starboard side,' he shouted. 'There's something there.'

The Mzimot family jumped up and rushed to the window. They gasped in wonder as they watched a fold open. Geoff put the view from the cameras up on the bridge screen. It was a spectacular sight. Like an enormous flower, folded space opened, and the *Monarch*, with the package in tow, flew majestically out.

The sight of the package of four Hela-class transporters, frames clamped into the ship's docking rings – holding them together – astounded the Mzimot. The eight-hundred-metre-long golden hulls, mirroring the multicoloured light from the nebula, blotted out space behind the *Monarch*. More gasps and shouts of awe – then the bridge of the *Runabout* erupted in cheers. Geoff blushed as Fazqa hugged him. 'I'm sorry for what I said,' she whispered. 'You didn't lie.'

A speechless Jarzol, his arm around his wife as they both gazed out the window, wondered at the sight of such wealth. 'Does the Sullivan Parker Charter own all this?' she asked him.

He shrugged his shoulders. 'They must,' was all he could say. And Niamh and Tom did own it all – with the help of an Overlord, whom the Mzimot would soon meet.

The crackle from the inter-ship comms pierced the noisy bridge. Silence, then the welcome voice of Siba. 'Mrs Parker, apologies for being late. I had to reconfigure the tow. I see you have no power; stand by for docking instructions.'

*

A relieved Tom gazed down at Niamh, slumped unconscious in the captain's chair. The welcome sound of the *Monarch* locks re-engaging the *Runabout* provided hope for her survival. Always in command, Tom gushed the long-awaited order. 'Brian, transfer all controls to the *Monarch*.'

Then Tom turned his attention to the Mzimot. After Niamh had forewarned him that they were not tied to an Overlord and despised them (the Overlords), he had glossed over their ties to The Eight. The story he told didn't reveal every detail, referring to The Eight as a benevolent boss – or words to that effect. The murky grey world of espionage would describe it as "not a lie but not the truth either!". Now that reckoning had come. Noises outside the in-ship airlock heralded their welcoming salvation.

'Jarzol, we didn't trick you. Now you will meet our boss; he's The Eight,' Tom said, and with a gush of air, the airlock opened. 'Overlord, glad to be back, but she is very sick.'

The Eight, shimmering on his chariot, entered the *Runabout*. There were gasps of horror from the Mzimot as they fell to their knees. He ignored them, making his way over to Niamh.

'Thomas, now you know why I did not want you to leave,' The Eight said.

'Can you help her?'

'In the Zakkai system,' he said, his voice unusually quiet. Feeling the expected hatred from the Mzimot clan, The Eight turned his chariot to face them.

Jarzol spat vitriol at Tom. 'You tricked us, not telling us your boss is The Eight. An Overlord, and the worst of them all. Powerful and cunning he is.' Trembling, the clan leader knelt down on the deck, his face purple with rage. 'We were told you're an evil entity hoarding a galaxy of blue and breeding a population of super beings. Is that what the humans are? Now we are owned by you, your slaves. Mr Parker, how could you trick us like that?'

The Eight spoke, in the same quiet tone. 'I never own bipeds. I own galaxies, not mortal inhabitants.'

Silence descended. The Eight exuded calm, his ethereal oval mass pulsing with bright blue light. In a more forceful voice, he continued. 'Despite knowing what you are, I paid your debt to Hirkiv.' The transfer Cylla Ora had made, as Tom promised. 'You are free to go and work as you choose. The Sullivan Parker Charter offered a fair deal. If you think you can do better, leave now. We will drop you off on one of the many ships here. You can work your passage back to the Anan Galaxy. Back to the Svang Charter, see what that brings you.'

The gentle pulsing of blue light changed, purple hues mixed in. The Eight's voice changed, becoming louder with authority. 'Thomas, this was a mistake. I should never have allowed it. Until these ungrateful mortals decide what they want, confine them.'

Turning away from them, The Eight floated Niamh onto his chariot. 'Out of my way now,' he ordered. Taking her off to med-bay, he left the bridge.

Tom shook his head, resisting the urge to follow The Eight. He turned around and faced the twenty-two quivering Mzimot kneeling on the deck. His voice faltered with rage. 'Jarzol, I, I'm lost for words. Never ever again talk to our Overlord like that. I should have you thrown out of an airlock. After all we've done for you. Niamh risked her life for this mission.'

Bill, Tom's deputy who had remained behind on the *Monarch*, stepped inside the bridge. Coming to welcome them back, he hadn't expected such conflict.

Shaking with rage, Tom bellowed an order. 'Lock them in the brig till they come to their senses.' Pointing at Jarzol, he said, 'Hang him in Grandfather's chains. Let him see how a real monster treats his prisoners.' And he stormed out of the *Runabout*.

CHAPTER THIRTY

Welcome to the Tar Galaxy

At ninety thousand light-years across, Tar is smaller than the Anan Galaxy.
A mobile city, anchored to Zakkai-Prime, forms the galaxy's admin-hub. If
you are here to load grav, proceed to the holding zone at Zakkai-Prime. For
your vessel's safety, you must stay inside the shipping lanes.

‹ The admin-hub is within a group of planets and moons in irregular orbit
around three suns – known as the Zakkai system. The three suns subject the
moons – where grav is mined – to immense gravitational forces. This force
can tear your ship apart.

‹ It is prohibited to travel to Planet Uldan (at the edge of the Tar group).
The planet's deep acidic oceans host the rare Uldonian microbes. Access to
harvest is strictly licenced.

‹ General shipping should circumvent the Hepkaz Belt. These outlying
asteroids are home to edge-world businesses and like-minded trading posts.
Your vessel's insurance is not valid in this sector.

‹ On your arrival, you will have passed the Zakkai nebula. At fifteen light-
years across, the supernova remnant is one of the most colourful gas giants in
the galaxy. Do not enter or travel through it.

*‹ **Extract from: Application to enter the Zakkai System***

*

Tar Galaxy, Zakkai System. EPTS: B140456

THE ARRIVAL OF A COMATOSE Niamh back on the *Monarch*, with the re-
belling Mzimot consigned to the brig, turned the preceding happy-clappy
morale sour. Up until then, every task and mission had been executed
without a hitch. Planning details, down to the nth-degree, paid dividends.

From launching The Eight's untraceable commercial link – his satellites – to the buy of the blue drives, nothing had gone wrong. On the other hand, Niamh's impulsive mission, prompted by the unanticipated meeting of Fazqa, imported a group hostile to The Eight. Worse, the unconscious Niamh – on life-support – had put added strain on the frail human crew. An unwelcome dynamic that played on their minds as they travelled to the next destination – the Zakkai system.

When the cloaked *Monarch* arrived, a deadly silence enveloped the bridge. The Eight shattered it with a crackle and flash of white light. The bridge crew, already deflated, turned to look at him. 'By the One,' he said, 'the apocalypse gets ever closer.'

A hopeless statement – not what the humans wanted to hear. Fear and despair etched their faces. Even Tom was at a loss. Siba, their purebreed captain, marshalled them on. Issuing the commands to slow the *Monarch*, plotting a course for its lay-over in orbit around the system's admin-hub, Zakkai-Prime, and piloting the ship there – she did it all. The Eight felt the human's despondence. Despite all the trouble, the Borea family had proved themselves. Now more than ever, the humans needed their help and he knew where that may come from. If Niamh couldn't function, unaided, the *Monarch* wouldn't make it back to the New World.

The Zakkai system was a name applied to a group of planets and moons in irregular orbits, around three suns. The unconventional rotations exposed those worlds to a constant tide of ever-changing gravitational energy. The resultant planetary forces, exerted on their moons, pulverised them into a soft, malleable substance, with antigrav properties. The "priceless" grav that fuelled starships and grav platforms – the mundane workhorses of the purebreed technology.

The apocalypse-like act that greeted them, played across the *Monarch's* viewscreen and bridge windows for all to see. There were gasps of shock as the humans tried to take in what they were seeing. Fleets of queuing ships shone in the light of the three suns, all different sizes and shapes, from the Hela-class to the hard-up inter-planetary "trampers" with bits hanging off. The humans didn't know what to make of it all. Siba took it in her stride; she'd been here before.

Breaking the bleak spell, the Eight pulsed with a dark purple light. 'The Zakkai system, a place I rarely frequent. But in all my visits, I have never seen so many ships waiting for grav. And the moons, they are near depletion. I never expected that.'

Shaking off the dismal feeling, Geoff zoomed in on one of the moons, or what remained of it. The only sign of its previous size was a trace from the arc of its lost circumference. Machines tracked across its flat surface and a procession of small ships plied back and forth, servicing the vessels, line by line, waiting at the edge of the invisible gravitational force field.

'How bad is it, Overlord?' Tom asked, finding his voice again.

'I do not know. We thought we had an inexhaustible supply of grav. Not so. Thomas, remember this, nothing lasts forever.'

An alarm sounded from comms. Before Geoff could respond, The Eight continued. 'His ship has arrived. I will know more once I talk to him,' he said, as he turned in his chariot and left the bridge.

*

Back in his chamber, the low beep, beep, beep of the life-support system maintaining Niamh's fragile metabolism, galvanised The Eight's mind. The floating Anan med bed's mechanical ventilator and cardiovascular pump maintained her precarious existence. He could feel her body's suffering, an internal battle raging between the blue energy contamination and her corporeal life force. The mechanical interventions wouldn't last much longer – and then …

Ending up in this predicament was his doing. His fault. Deep inside his energy mass, emotion returned – unwanted. It grew inside him; deep sorrow that he may lose Niamh, the only biped he had ever called "my child". It was emotion that Overlords should be impervious to. Similar feelings surfaced when he had tried to kill humans on Earth during his war with the Chinese. Human intelligence had come from his essence, a connection that bonded him to the human race, his link to Niamh clearest of all.

He cast his mind back to Earth seventy thousand years ago when he was a young Overlord, prospecting for blue with a purebreed crew. Volcanic eruption on the plant forced mankind's existence into a bottleneck.

An old purebreed geneticist had spotted an opportunity for purebreeds and humans. With so few of the bipeds left alive on Earth, "the opportunity for a first touching shouldn't be missed", he had said.

The One approved that decision and ordered the inclusion of a genetic marker in the process. To this day, that marker showed up, stronger in Niamh – The Eight's prodigy – than anyone else.

The geneticist – on a folly of his own, breeding a cure for the Anan sickness – stole The Eight's essence for the genetic change. Engrossed in star charts, the young and busy Overlord hadn't felt anything when the purebreed man plunged the tip of a micro-matter depletor into his energy mass. The old man made the gene splice, enhancing human intelligence beyond anything that was ever done before. And, as the geneticist had (in secret) designed, linking humans with purebreeds to grow a future cure for the terminal Anan sickness.

Back in the Anan Galaxy, while transferring records from the prospecting ship to the *Hela*, The Eight had discovered the deception. Caught red-handed, a video showed the old man stealing The Eight's blue from his energy mass. The Eight told The One. After some procrastination, The One did nothing!

Life moved on, The Eight returned to the Milky Way Galaxy on the *Hela* to mine blue, building a home on Earth, the pristine planet, a haven of life. Vast forests grew down to the waterside while grassland steppes stretched across continents. The Earth itself was alive, its thick glaciers stretching from the north and south poles, carving out future beautiful lands. After the volcanic event, diverse life multiplied; animals, mammals, fish, birds and insects – large and small – roamed free. Humans co-existed in harmony with the ecosystem, living a simple life on their blue and green world's natural resources.

The Eight's visit, introducing enhanced intelligence, giving the humans free will and allowing them to propagate unrestricted, changed that.

Back then, at his home on the southern islands they now call New Zealand, birds ruled. Devoid of animals – mammals or humans – thriving multicoloured birds soared through the trees, filling the air with their calls. A natural euphony of sound; an outdoor orchestra. From the mouth of the cave that formed his home, he had spent glorious days, watching and listening to the natural show the remote island's birds put on. Time marched forwards, and after the geneticist altered the humans, the planet malformed.

And, now to this – Niamh lying unconscious, her life force slipping away. He had introduced her to blue – his fault. He knew deep down what it would do. The addictive blue energy clawed at her corporeal form, changing her. She would always want it – enjoying its power, using it, living with it – until its ultimate betrayal of the host, when the blue tried to take over. He had known this could happen, but he did nothing, allowing his own selfish needs to push her forwards.

A thought eased his guilt. The Sixth had a part to play in all of this, forcing these fateful events. Love and hurt turned to rage inside the ethereal entity's energy mass. Blue flashes became purple as the conflict raged inside him. He was powerless to help her, but he couldn't let her die.

A bump on the hull got his attention. Then, the timely hiss of the airlock at the end of his chamber, as it opened.

The Eight turned his chariot to face the airlock. 'My Lord, welcome to the *Monarch*. Too much time has passed since our last meeting.'

The Overlord floated over to The Eight. His oval-shaped energy mass about three metres in diameter, shimmering in soft blue light. 'Eight, you have taken to a machine?'

'Yes, my Lord, I have. It conserves blue, and I have found other benefits as well. Is there any news of The One? Do you know where he is?'

'I am sorry, Eight. I do not. Last I heard, he tried to flee to a faraway galaxy, safe from The Sixth. He was afraid The Sixth would take his essence and memories. That is all I know. And you?'

'I know more. My mind journeyed through the cosmic mist to an asteroid where The One concealed his catastrophe hoard. I found a ship there, with the livery of The Sixth on the hull. Invisible to the biped purebreeds – unable to do anything – I watched as they stole the last of The One's supply of blue energy. Searching for more, my thoughts brushed against one of the blue canisters. He embedded a message there – The One. He must have been desperate,' The Eight said. He paused, his energy mass pulsing with purple light as he remembered those faithful words.

'And tell me. What did it say?' the floating entity asked.

'My Lord, the message said, "Stay away, all is lost, go, my friend, save yourself. For the sake of our kind, save yourself." As soon as it appeared, it was gone. As I fear The One is!'

'I am sorry, Eight. I know you were both companions.'

'Sorry is not enough, Two. Why do you not advance to fill The One's position?'

The entity, known as The Second, pulsed a flash of white light. 'You know why. As The Second, I should never take sides. I am supposed to be a force of reason amongst Overlords. Advancing to seize power is not an option.'

Silence swamped the chamber, both Overlords facing each other, The Eight in his shining chariot waiting for Two to speak again.

The Second continued. 'What of you, Eight? Your reputation precedes you. I hear "you are now an evil entity, hoarding a galaxy of blue and breeding a population of super-beings for your own gain". You must know that rumour is now gaining traction. I guess this unfortunate biped is a casualty of your failed experiments. My, my Eight, you surprise me; what a monster you have become.'

Grumpy from his previous musings, he snapped back, 'I am not a monster. It is The Sixth that has created this mayhem. She is a human called Niamh, and not from a failed experiment. She was injured when she saved me from extinction – after an attack by Uldonian microbes. Niamh risked her life for me. I want you to help her; I know you can.'

'Uldonian microbes. You must tell me more, but first let me see here,' The Second said. Then silence while the Overlord floated over to Niamh. A long tongue of blue extended from his energy mass, gently enveloping her. 'Eight, how could you have got this poor wretch into such a mess? She is with child as well. I see you did more with this one. You taught her secrets she should not know.'

'Yes, I did. I had no option. We are at war, a war we never imagined would come. Will you help her?'

'I am not supposed to take sides.'

'You must help her, Two. Her mortal life has only begun. She has so much to do and to give. Grant me at least that,' The Eight boomed, his voice shaking the walls of his chamber.

'No need to shout, Eight. You are old and cranky. Do not let that get the better of you. When you meet The Sixth – as you surely will – you need to keep a calm dispensation. I will help your Niamh, but it will not be easy.'

'Thank you.'

'Where does her species come from?'

'A planet in a distant galaxy. When I was young, searching for blue—'

'Now I remember, Eight. I am getting old. Aeons ago, you and The One told me about humans. That old biped meddled in matters beyond him. I thought you expunged them.'

'No, my Lord. The One told me to leave them.'

'Knowing, then, what that interfering geneticist had done, he should have expunged him and the humans. A decision The One decided not to make. In this epoch, in the greater context of our change in order, humans are a welcomed resource. Use them wisely, Eight.'

The Eight pulsed with a blue light at this endorsement. *More than I thought I would get, and significant, coming from The Second,* he thought. Moving on, he asked another burning question. 'What news of The Sixth, and Anan? How was the Empress's return received?'

'One at a time, Eight. Always your impatience gets the better of you. The Sixth resurrected the position of Shoter and has given it to the owner of the Svang Charter.'

'I heard that.'

A pause as The Second contemplated the next news. 'And I hear rumours The Sixth did not expunge the ceirim.'

This was a shock The Eight hadn't expected. 'Are you sure?'

'There are rumours coming from Anan. But you know, bipeds can never hold their tongues. They ooze their leader's innermost secrets. I trust it is true. If he has done that, against The One's wishes, he is an evil that requires expunging. We should never have elevated him. You know me, I don't say such things without due consideration. In the wrong hands, the ceirim could wreak havoc.'

'Not what I wanted to hear,' The Eight said. He paused to digest it. 'What of the Empress?'

'The purebreeds welcomed her back. It was a mystery as to where she was. Your doing of course ...' The Second said, continuing with the story of Theia's return, some of which The Eight had gleaned from newsfeeds at Hirkiv, including the shock assassination attempt on Theia's life. 'I suspect the Empress's cure will have huge consequences for her subjects. It may alter the purebreed make up. The Emperor has disappeared; maybe he is dead. No loss there! And, you must also be told, The Sixth killed the young Aknar Prince, Brizo Sema.'

'The Sixth did that?'

'Yes, he dissected him piece by piece, the last in the Aknar line.'

Taken aback by such behaviour by one of their kind, the two entities floated in a hush.

Finally, The Eight spoke. 'What of your grav?'

'We do the best we can. Never before was there such an appetite for the fuel. We cannot sustain this demand – you see the position yourself. Worst of all, my stock of blue is dwindling. I fear I will not last much longer.'

'My Lord, I brought you some. I have three full tanks on the *Monarch*; two are for you.'

'Eight, you surprise me. The rumour is true, you have found—'

'Do not speak of that, my Lord. I found blue hidden in an old Borea base,' he lied. 'I need grav.'

'You shall have that, as much as you can take. I will arrange it. Before I go, tell me where you encountered Uldonian tech,' The Second asked, intrigued such tech was still out there.

The Eight told his story, far more than his encounter with the Borea, leaving out locations and any data that could compromise Earth or The New World. It filled in the blanks – vital intel – The Second knew nothing of. When he finished, more silence filled the room, signalling an end to the powerful entities' meeting.

A tongue of blue extended from The Second, enveloping Niamh and her med bed. 'I go now with your human. I will do what I can but the foetus, that will be difficult.'

The Eight watched The Second leave with Niamh. His final words left no doubt as to the seriousness of her and her unborn child's condition. Once the airlock closed, The Eight left his chamber, returning to the *Monarch's* bridge.

*

When he entered, Tom immediately stood up and turned to him. 'Overlord, how is she?'

The Eight had not expected to see Fazqa and her mother pleading their case with Tom. Despite their shared concern for Niamh, this business needed a resolution. 'Before I say anything, what have they decided?'

Fazqa knelt down before him. 'Overlord, please forgive my father. We will stay. Our future is with the Sullivan Parker Charter. We will go to Earth. On my life, I guarantee my family's support.'

'A hollow pledge.' He paused as he remembered a similar assurance given by Zaval Borea. That didn't turn out so well. 'One so young cannot fulfil such an undertaking. Parker, what do you think?'

'Niamh wanted them with us. Fazqa and the younger ones in their family have committed to work with us. Jarzol, with some of the older ones, are still reluctant, but they will honour the contract they signed. When he meets Chang, I know he will work for us. Chang will enforce the contract line by line.'

'Who is this, Chang?' Fazqa asked, her blue face screwed up in angst.

Ignoring the look of horror from Geoff, Tom smiled. 'A friend of the family. We met after he kidnapped and tortured my wife. By now he should be the ruler of one of the lands on our home planet. His people will start up the factories you will work in. Let there be no doubt, Sullivan Parker will honour our part of the contract. However, your father has chosen the adversarial way. Fazqa, it could have been so different for your family. Look at the Borea,' he said, pointing to Siba. 'One is now captain of our flagship. Those opportunities were available to your family, as well. Bill,' he said, turning to face his deputy, 'take them back to the brig, and Bill, is Jarzol still in chains?'

'No, boss. When we showed him Grandfather's torture chamber, he shit himself.'

'So you—'

'Boss, we let him shower and change. Then returned him to his family in the brig. It—'

'Didn't seem the right thing to do. Goes against everything you were taught,' Tom said, grinning at Bill as his face fell. 'You did well. You see, Fazqa, we are not the monsters your father and his followers think we are.' He waited until they had left. 'Overlord, my apologies. How is she?'

'The departing ship is The Second's. Niamh is onboard. He has organics that will treat her. We must hope for success. It is all I can do, Thomas. Siba, there are coordinates on your console; make haste there. We will offload blue for The Second, and load grav. We take as much as you can load into the four ships.'

*

Zakkai-Prime. EPTS: B140463

In the bright sunshine, she walked up the mountain holding his hand. They stopped and she turned to look at Tom. They stood together arm in arm, looking down at the bay. The old, flooded crater of the volcano glistened with the turquoise blue seawater. He bent down and kissed her. She clutched him and then a shock punched Niamh's body. Her eyes opened wide.

She gasped for breath. *Where am I?* she thought, as she looked around the white room and then down at her body. It lay naked, covered with a translucent sheet, in a curved-shaped bath, her arms and legs restrained by soft straps embedded in the tub. Then she saw him and her eyes brimmed with fear. An Overlord, and not The Eight. His blue energy mass hovered beside her.

'Do not fear me. I am The Second.'

'Where's The Eight?'

'On your ship. I am to help you.'

'We're in the Zakkai system. You're the person he spoke of.'

'Yes, I am. I'm afraid you are in quite a predicament.'

'My baby, can you save it?' asked Niamh, her voice quivering with fear.

'The question is, can I save you? Everything else, after that, is a bonus. I use organics, similar to the creature you saved The Eight from. They extravasate the blue energy from your body. Are you ready?'

'No,' she said.

The Second persisted. 'We must start.'

'I'm afraid.'

'Of course, you are. Why wouldn't you be? It might not work and you will die.'

'Jeez, Overlord, did anyone tell you, you've a shitty bedside manner.'

'I don't understand that,' the impatient Overlord said. Two dwarf-like bipeds entered the room. 'They will start the treatment,' he said, as they worked on a machine beside the bath. A strange clear gel slowly entered it.

Niamh squirmed as the warm liquid started to cover her body, then she relaxed. 'It's lovely and warm. Where's the organics?'

'In the liquid.'

'Ah shit,' she screamed, afraid of what was to come. She felt her body tremble under the warm gel. 'Overlord, I'm scared. Don't leave me, please. Talk to me, tell me what happened to me, please.'

'Relax, let the treatment work. For it to succeed, you must stay conscious throughout.'

She winced as a stinging sensation started, like small mosquito bites all over her body. Ignoring it, she looked at him. 'Theia told me the blue could change me but she never explained how.'

'The Empress was right; too much exposure will change or kill a mortal. Did you ever wonder where we come from?'

'You, the Overlords? Yes, I suppose I did.'

'We are living entities, pure energy, fuelled by blue. How is that possible?'

'I don't know?'

'Think back on how you folded space; what did you do?'

'I linked my mind with the blue and manipulated the energy with my brain.'

'Now, do you see?'

'No, I'm a mortal. I still don't understand.'

'Exactly, you are mortal. Overlords are a consciousness that use blue energy. As humans depend on oxygen, sugars, proteins and carbohydrates to live, pure blue energy fuels the Overlords. My kind depends on blue for our very existence. Over many epochs, we evolved into what you see today. We gained strengths, forged civilisations and conferred others with intelligence.'

It was a story Theia had told the humans back on the *Hela* after they first met. 'Yes, we were told that.'

'If, over aeons, we die off, how do you think our species can survive?'

Like a light bulb turning on, the answer flashed through her mind. She shivered as fear ran down her spine. 'Jeez. Oh, jeez, no, no, no,' she screamed.

'Yes, Niamh Parker. That is what you are changing into, a young Overlord. Normally we would help and encourage it. My position as The Second is to cultivate a changeling. It is a rare event in our lifespan. There are only ten and we live for a long time. This is the first reversal of a changing I have ever done. He must care for you very much.'

'The Eight.'

'Yes. You are of his essence. It is you and your child he wants to survive. He believes you have much more to give as a mortal.'

'What will my child be if he or she survives?'

'A human just like you; there are no half measures. As you found out, mortals or bipeds as we commonly call you, cannot survive a deep blue exposure. Sooner or later, the corporeal body dies after contamination. This is what's happening to you now. In rare cases – with my help – the intelligence, the person's mind ascends to another level.'

She looked up at him. His light was softer than The Eight's. Her agony increased as the microscopic organisms started to pull the blue from her body. The pain penetrated deeper and deeper. A black fog closed on her brain. Through it, she found his words captivating, each one drawing her back from the dark abyss she was looking down into. As its deadly embrace beckoned her in painless oblivion, she shook her head and looked straight into his energy mass. 'Tell me, tell me more. Where did you come from? How are you chosen?'

'It is a long story. If I tell, you must promise to listen and to stay conscious.'

She tried to ignore the pain and the gentle swirling of the gel, its colour gradually turning blue. 'I will, I will. Talk to me.'

'It started after the universe was born, what you mortals call the big bang ...'

He continued with the story of the development of the entities known to mortals as Overlords after the universe came to be. Before that moment, matter, anti-matter, space, time and energy swirled together in a vast primordial soup. An explosion, theorised as the "Big Bang" brought order to chaos, separating matter and anti-matter, propelling it out on its never-ending journey through a freshly ordered space and time – the universe as we know it came to be.

The Overlords never knew what fuelled that bang but they do know what happened in its wake. Fragments of post-bang residue generated powerful energy called blue, giving birth to the universe's first intelligence – ancestors to the Overlords of this epoch. On their long voyage, swirling through space and time, some of those intelligent entities learned to harness the blue energy they were born into.

'I get that,' Niamh said. 'Tell me, where did you come from, and The Eight?'

'I cannot tell for the Eight, but I will give you a glimpse of my past. It must be our secret.'

By now, the curious Niamh, oblivious to the pain wracking her body, hungered to learn more. 'Yes, please do,' she blurted out.

'I will show you. Open your mind,' ordered The Second.

A rush of pictures filled Niamh's brain. She tried to process it all, focusing on what she could easily comprehend. One stood out amongst all. An image of a tall purebreed man, similar in stature to Mack. Porcelain white skin, tall neck, and the unmistakable blue pendant hanging around the man's neck. But it was the robes that jolted Niamh's mind, a long blue flowing gown laced with gold braid – an Emperor, she realised.

'You were an Emperor?' she asked The Second.

'Yes, Niamh, I was. Of the House of Aknar ...'

As the crew of the *Monarch* disgorged the Overlord's precious blue and loaded enough grav for the war into the ships on their tow, The Second treated Niamh. The more he talked to her, the more he realised how right The Eight was to go to Earth. It wasn't the first time in their long history that a Second had taken sides. *Yes*, he thought, *history repeats itself. A battle between Overlords begins again.*

CHAPTER THIRTY-ONE

CNS Headlines. Anan Corp Brief

In the middle of the Australian Desert, at a dry, dusty place known as the Hela base, Anan Corp's base manager Matt McKinnon issued a short announcement.

'Last night, we made contact with a fleet of three starships at the edge of our solar system. A control room operator spoke to Senior Project Manager, Robert Leslie, who is onboard one of the vessels. I can confirm the Hela, which left Earth on the 4th of January 2027 with the first Colony, is one of the three ships.' McKinnon expects the fleet to touch down about midday on the 9th of January 2028.

With much fanfare, Anan Corp's Colony left Earth one year ago. The human race is hungry for news. Are the colonists alive? How have they fared? And the biggest question of all, is the powerful Overlord, some have nicknamed the blue pimpernel, onboard?

‹ *Extract from:* **Continental News Services, Good Morning Planet Earth**

*

The Monarch. EPTS: B140468

With Niamh dispatched to the care of The Second, The Eight contemplated available real-time. Another mission pressed his hard-worked brain. Crews – he still needed them. Deep within his blue mind were the locations of the remaining Borea family – coordinates Verteg had given him. At the edge of the Tar Galaxy, half a cycle distance was a Borea enclave working from one of their old bases. To Tom's surprise, after unloading blue and bunkering grav, The Eight ordered Siba to park their tow in orbit around The Second's home, then plot a course for the *Monarch* to leave, in search of her family.

'What of Niamh?' Tom asked.

'There is nothing I can do. We must wait. Such treatments are ambivalent. The less time pressure we put on The Second, the more chance of success. I cannot afford to squander time waiting. We are too close to the Borea base to pass up a recruiting visit.'

Tom nodded. He was aware The Eight planned to stop there on their way back to the New World anyway. Despite his misgivings at leaving Niamh, such a mission made sense and it would take his mind off his wife's plight. For the first time that day, he relaxed and smiled. It would be what Niamh wanted – advance the cause. Make progress, regardless of her condition.

*

Earth, Hela Base Australian Desert.
9th January 2028

On Earth, the fleet's landing in the Australian desert was a remarkable event. The golden *Hela*, returning to its old base, was the first of the three to touch down. The three docking posts, extended up over the desert, sparkling in the harsh sunlight, faultlessly mating with the intergalactic transporter. The *Richard* and *George* followed. From the bridge of *Richard*, Verteg coordinated everything, disseminating flight plans, landing coordinates and engine settings, allowing her crews a rare opportunity – landing a starship themselves.

The return of the *Hela*, with two more alien vessels, caused consternation around the globe. World War III took a back seat as the planet's news feeds filled with speculation about starships and space travel. Self-serving analysts poured their guts out with pure bullshit. Stories gushed of the colonists, how they had fared, what they had lived on and the old chestnut, "Where is The Eight?".

Without delay, Robert gave Harold Addison, The Eight's representative on Earth, a short statement to release. "A fleet has returned to Earth to collect Colony-2 and supplies for Colony-1. Our Overlord, The Eight, is on a mission in a distant galaxy. He will return in time." All of it true! And nothing else would be said until after a meeting Harold convened in the Australian desert – guests already mobilised during the fleet's approach to Earth.

*

Standing on the roof of the accommodation block, looking out at the vast base in the Australian desert, Robert turned to his cousin. 'Matt, I can't believe you've done so much. It's near twice the size it was when we left.'

'You did leave strict orders, Robert. The McKinnon family would never let you down. After you left, we never stopped. My boys and their families moved out here full time. We've a school, shops, all that stuff outside the base. A small town now it is, Robert.'

'What's the town called?'

He grinned. 'Kept it simple. McKinnon, after the family.'

Robert smiled and nodded. 'Well done, I know what that feels like, Matt. There's a Fort Leslie back on the New World.'

'Good on ya, Robert. Our Scottish family's getting around, first Oz, now colonising a new world.' He clapped Robert on the back. 'Yeah, success of the McKinnon and Leslie clans, we should celebrate that. You marrying the Kiwi planner? Be a good excuse for a day out.'

'Dinnae start with that, Matt. Come on, our guests are waiting below.'

*

Robert took his place, standing at the head of the table in the spaceport's conference room as the "guests" filed in. A mix of alien and human included those on Earth with close allegiances to The Eight. The news that war had broken out on Earth added to the urgency of this gathering.

Janet, seated beside Kath, stole a look at her beau. Robert looked imposing, his rough uncut sandy hair resting on his shoulders and his bare blue arm shining for all to see. A gift from The Eight, after their first war on Earth, it reminded the humans of Robert's status with the powerful Overlord. Standing in a fresh ship suite, six-foot five-inches tall, his towering body dominated the room.

419

Kath grabbed Janet's hand and squeezed it. 'I'm happy for you both; you deserve each other and some joy, after all the hard work.' She had recovered from the emotion of the reunion on board the *Richard* with Janet, her previous receptionist, and Robert, the man she had hired as the Project Manager for Anan Corp. She smiled at Harold Addison, The Eight's representative on Earth, as he took a seat beside Robert. 'He's retired from New Zealand politics, Janet, after his last term as Prime Minister. There's George Smith, he was re-elected as the Oz PM again. They love him, and he's supported us over the year you were gone. You remember Admiral Cyril Whyte, head of our combined forces? He's worked with Alan getting the manufacturing plants going.'

'Who are they?' Janet asked, discreetly pointing to two men talking together.

'They're not supposed to be here. Russia and the U.S. – their two governments – are at war. The Russians started the Wave. Don't look so surprised, Janet – yes, they did. Isn't mankind great? Welcome back.' She paused, then pointing, said, 'That's the Russian. You remember, he tried to take over the Great Northern Union. Tom's friend, Admiral Vasily they call him. Politicians beat him to it. And that's General Marsh, the highest-ranking military officer in the U.S. He's a real gent, Janet. Again, beaten to the podium by politicians. Congress and the Senate have him tied up in knots.'

'Have they a new president yet?'

'Speaker of the House, a Republican – same party as his predecessor – grabbed that job.'

'Nothing's changed since we left.'

'Yes, it has, and here he is,' she said, as she stood up to face Chang Jin. 'Janet, may I present the President of the People's Republic of China.'

Dressed in his plain blue suit, he bowed then held out his hand. 'Janet Cooper, such a pleasure to meet you. You are the famous planner who moved the first human colony across the universe. Welcome back. I am so glad to see you both. No doubt, there is much news. But I am disappointed. Where is our Overlord? All is not well. No, it is not. From your face, I see it all.'

She took his hand. 'President, congratulations on your succession. You are right, all is not well. Robert has much to tell. We will need your help.'

'China is with you, have no fear of that.' With that, Chang turned away and walked towards the meeting table.

Kath leaned over and whispered in Janet's ear. 'They call him the Butcher of Beijing. Imagine what he did to earn that accolade.'

Pursing her lips, Janet shook her head. 'Considering his history, why doesn't that surprise me! I'm glad he's still on our side,' she said. A group of aliens walked in. 'Here's the Anans. They're not all purebreed; the green-skinned ones are a mixed race.'

'None of them were here before; who are they?'

'That's Quriel Borea, Zaval's son. He's a captain in the Aknar military. Works for Mack. That's his crew,' Janet said, pointing to two purebreeds in military uniform. 'And here she is, Verteg Borea, the Pilot. She's Demard's daughter, Zaval's niece. Kath, she's amazing.'

They watched the body language as Quriel's crew chief held out a chair at the top of the table for Verteg. She would sit across from the Australian PM, a tribute to the Pilot's status. Dressed in a simple blue uniform, with her blue hair hanging freely down to her shoulders and her green skin shining, she captivated all in the room. The young Aknar chief fawned around her, embarrassing the Pilot as her green face tinted to purple.

Janet stifled a grin. 'He's mad about her. She has to beat him off with a stick.'

'No. I remember they said the purebreeds were forbidden to mate with other species.'

'They are, but, well, you know, Kath, that never works. Love has no boundaries.' The Chief retreated to the side of the room where Kath and Janet were. He nodded at Janet. 'Kath, this is Chief ah—'

'I am Chief Haldock, Janet. I am sorry I do not speak your language,' he said in Anan.

'Please sit with us, Chief,' Janet said, handing him a set of earphones. 'This will translate for you. It's about ready to start.'

Robert tapped a glass with a spoon, and the clear ringing sound silenced the clamour of their exclusive gathering. 'We're back, thanks to the efforts of Verteg and her family, the Borea. Verteg, thank you for bringing us home.' The room erupted with applause. Robert paused for it to die down, and then he started, 'I have a story to tell, and not what you want to hear ...'

*

After their long day, meeting after meeting, discussion and planning groups, Robert fell down into the deep couch in Matt's off-base house. Janet curled up on top of him. 'Robert, you look like I feel, exhausted,' she said, as she settled down in his lap, her feet stretched out on the couch.

'Must be intergalactic jet lag. Christchurch tomorrow. You're going home with Kath. Get some rest.'

'What about you?'

'He's coming with me, to Geneva,' Harold said.' He needs to tell that story to the U.N.'

Kath, sitting across from Robert, shook her head. 'They'll never believe him, Harold. They can't deal with it. Your last efforts ended in disaster; we have World War III now. Who would have believed it, U.S. and Russian fighting with each other along the Bering Strait? That's Chang's fault. He should never have opened his mouth about the Wave event.'

'He wants a world war; he believes it will cull the population.'

Robert sat up in surprise. 'No, no, no. Is that what he's at?'

'Yes, he believes he's serving The Eight in moving on with population control. He's fixated with it.'

'That's enough shop,' Matt said, as he put a tray of drink and food down on the table. 'Kath, you have much better news to tell.'

'It's supposed to be a secret.'

'They need to know.'

'All right. I'll tell them,' Kath paused, while Janet and Robert started at her. 'Early in October, last year, a boy was born in a house in the Kenepuru Sound.'

'Where's that?' Robert asked.

'It's part of the Marlborough Sounds, north part of the South Island, in N.Z.'

'And what's so special about that?'

'He's Bri's son,' Kath blurted out.

'No shit,' Robert shouted, as he sat up, pushing Janet over on the couch, 'Bri, the dirty wee fuc—'

'Robert, behave yourself,' Janet said, slapping his arm. 'You're not on the rigs now. Kath, did I hear that right?' she said, over Matt and Harold's laughter.

Kath's face paled when she remembered Hana's hope for Bri's return at the news of the fleet's arrival. 'Yes, you did. Prince Brizo Sema, heir to the Aknar throne, and previous captain of the *Hela*, has had a son. Mum and baby are doing fine. Now where the hell is Dad?'

That shut them all up. Robert looked at Janet. The expression on both their faces betrayed their thoughts. *Whoever the mother was, she may never see Bri again.* Slowly, he got up and started pacing the room. 'We don't know for sure. Last we heard – from Niamh – was that he left the *Hela* with Theia for Planet Anan. The Sixth rules it now.'

Now it was Harold who sat bolt upright in his chair. 'Robert, they read minds. The Sixth will find out where they were. He'll find Earth.'

'No, Niamh told me, The Eight scrubbed the purebreed's memory before they left the *Hela*. You know he can do that. The Sixth won't be able to find us.'

Harold shook his head. So much at stake here, all assumptions must be castigated. 'I'm not convinced. What about young Bri? Mementoes of his love – pictures – that sort of thing. How do we know he never took any with him?'

'We don't, Harold,' Robert replied.

The dynamic of their relaxed family gathering changed. Before speaking again, Harold pondered their options. Bri's last contact on Earth was Hana. 'Kath, take Janet to meet Mum and her baby. See if she remembers anything he might have taken with him or indeed, left behind.'

'What's the baby look like? You got any pictures?' Janet asked.

Kath looked at Harold. She knew his concerns. 'He's just beautiful, Janet, and so is Mum. There are no pictures, no names, nothing. They don't exist; its Anan Corp's biggest secret. Alan flew up to see her and tell her you guys were back. She'd hoped Bri would be back too …'

'We must keep that secret, protect the mother and child; that's our responsibility. It's good news, though – a happy event. We should drink to that,' Harold said, as he raised his glass.

*

Tar Galaxy, Hepkaz Belt. EPTS: B140477

After leaving The Second's home, half a cycle later, the *Monarch* arrived at The Hepkaz Belt, a collection of nondescript asteroids, revolving around the edge of the Tar Galaxy. Its sketchy location, home to vague businesses trading on the margins of legality. In a dark corner of that belt, the *Monarch* located the Borea enclave, built inside an asteroid, the entrance channel guarded by the customary moving rocks.

It was Geoff, on comms, who first shattered the silence on the *Monarch's* bridge. 'Looks like those guardian stones are working,' he said as they watched the procession of crushing mayhem, the rocks, turning and swirling, threatening to squash any uninvited visitor to the Borea home. 'Overlord, I can stop them. I've all the codes Demard left.'

'Bold move,' Tom said. 'It would send a clear message—'

'You're not safe here!' Siba said. 'He should do it, Overlord.'

'Agreed,' was all The Eight said.

Geoff worked his magic, hacking the alien base with Demard's codes. Within no time, the fruits of his labour spilt across their viewscreen, the guarding rocks arresting their parade and parking harmlessly at the edge of the entrance channel. Within an instant, a swarm of small ships flew out, forming a puny line in front of the formidable *Monarch*.

Without prompting, Siba hailed the ships. 'I am Siba Borea, Captain of the *Monarch*. We are not a threat, and unless threatened, will not fire. Hold your position. I repeat, hold your position.'

Silence. The ships stayed put and all on the bridge watched with interest at what would happen next.

A crackle on the comms indicated an incoming transmission. Then a hoary voice pierced the quiet. 'Siba? Is that you? What are you doing flying around in your Grandfather's ship? And masquerading as its captain! Stop this nonsense now. Open your shuttle bay and we'll board you.'

Abject surprise flooded Siba's face. Her mouth dropped open and she gulped, trying to reply. After such an audacious order, all else stayed still on the *Monarch's* bridge, waiting for the family reunion to play out. Finally, Siba composed herself. 'Mom, is that you?'

The face of Madam Borea, as she was known, materialised on the bridge viewscreen. Her appearance matched her voice — old and haggard, with half her nose cut off and one ear missing. 'Of course, it's me,' was the blunt reply. 'Now do as I say.'

Siba held her ground while her voice changed. Laced with belligerence her friends on the bridge of the *Monarch* had never heard before, she continued, 'It's not *Borea1* anymore. It's the *Monarch*, owned by the Sullivan Parker Charter. And Mom, I am her captain. Things have changed since you kicked me out!'

With video feed from the *Monarch* disabled, the arguments raged back and forth. The shrill voice of Madam Borea filled the bridge, castigating Siba. The quarrel surprised even The Eight. Meanwhile, Geoff, ignoring the background noise, continued scanning the Borea base. All of a sudden, he sat up, urgently gesturing for The Eight and Tom.

The Eight left his chariot, floating over to peer over Geoff's shoulder as Tom sat down beside him. He whispered his concerns. 'It's not what I've found, but what I haven't,' he explained. 'These old drawings – from Demard's database – show a hollow asteroid, with inner chambers.'

The valuable data had accompanied the coordinates Verteg had given to The Eight. They watched as Geoff expanded the screen capture of one of the drawings. In one chamber it showed – what looked like – a laboratory surrounded by circular metal vessels but the actual scan of the asteroid showed it as one solid mass.

'They're hiding something, Overlord. What can do that?' Geoff asked.

'Uldonian tech. That is what masks your scan, Geoffrey. A rare cloaking paint, impregnated with spores of Uldonian microbes, must be covering those walls.' It was the same rare paint The One had given to Haret to secure his small keep. The Borea must have had barrels of it to shield such a vast chamber. The Eight flashed with a burst of purple light. 'More illegal tech, yes, indeed. What are they up to?' he asked no one in particular.

Tom scratched his brow. It was not what he had expected. This mission was proving to be much more than a simple stopover. In the background, emotionally exhausted from arguing, Siba slumped in her captain's chair. Time for Tom to take charge. He marched over to stand beside her. Signalling Geoff to open limited video transmission, he started his pitch. 'Ms Borea, I am Thomas Parker, of the Sullivan Parker Charter with my wife, the legal owner of this vessel. We have come on the recommendation of the Pilot, Verteg—'

'Madam Borea is my title, and Verteg, a greenskin half-breed, will never be Pilot,' she blurted, her face like thunder. 'So why are you here? Pray tell. We are so intrigued.'

'We need new staff, technicians and pilots to crew our expanding fleet. As simple as that. We are recruiting. Fair pay and a new life are what we offer.'

Murmurs rose from the background while more Borea crowded into her picture. The viewscreen exploded with video from the other vessels, all questioning the offer. "How much? For how long? What are the ships like? In what galaxies?" were the eager questions the Borea family threw back at Tom. Their drab and torn tunics showed their story – rummaging on the edge of this galaxy, existing on scraps, trying to make a living. And Madam Borea's bullying orbit didn't help. A chance to escape this servile bondage was too good to be true. With one loud roar, she silenced them all. A telling moment.

Tears of pain rolled down Siba's cheeks. Tom glanced down at her. *What a sad family*, was the thought that pierced his mind. Ignoring the hurtful outburst, he continued his polite dialogue. 'Madam Borea, I must apologise if our visit caused an upset. With our offer of employment, I am sincere. And I pose no threat to you or the family. I suggest we all stand down. We will park the *Monarch* within your safe harbour and wait while you discuss the matter with your family. If you wish, Siba, or another of my crew, can visit and explain the details of our employment contracts. What do you say?'

The roar of approval from around Madam Borea, and from the other ships, left the old hag with no alternative. She mumbled her consent, and with that, the viewscreen went blank. It changed to a picture of the open channel with the Borea vessels retreating back into their home. Under Siba's expert tutelage, the impenetrable *Monarch* followed. Bad memories of her youth filled her mind. She felt The Eight's presence and Bill and Tom's closeness – her family now. When she parked the *Monarch*, Tom whispered in her ear, 'Niamh would be so proud of you, Siba. I'm sorry she's not here to see this. You're a wonder surviving that …'

*

Returning to his roots as an insidious hacker, Geoff attacked the Borea base's computer core. He traced alarms, comms and data circuits throughout the asteroid. Their outline painted a grim picture of the inner workings of Madam Borea's lair. His scans, coupled with the original drawings, exposed the deception! 'There's a secret structure within that rock,' he told The Eight and Tom. 'The main living and working quarters are all in the external services buildings – as is the computer core. The Borea live there. The inside of the asteroid appears cut off from the living area above but I found an external access hatch here,' he said, pointing to a flat section on the top of the asteroid. If one didn't know what to look for, it would appear as a natural blemish. But, with inside knowledge, clearly it was a flat landing zone with a secret entrance.

That news intrigued Tom. 'We should go in and have a look. Can you get us in undetected?'

'Of course, I can,' boasted Geoff. When he realised how bad that sounded, he hung his head in shame. 'What I mean is—'

'Don't sweat it, Geoff,' Tom said. 'You did good. Overlord, do we go in and have a look?'

'Without a doubt, Thomas. Yes, we need to know what's happening on The Second's doorstep. And, if we are to employ any from here, Madam Borea's grip must be challenged.'

*

Two hours later, in a cloaked shuttle, Tom and a scout team of four left the *Monarch*. With his genius hack and Demard's codes, Geoff disabled the Borea security alarms and locks. Landing on the flat platform, dressed in spacesuits, the team left the shuttle. Turning its simple lever mechanism, a proud Tom opened the hatch. Geoff had done his job, defeating the alien defence mechanism. A testament to the young man's growing abilities. Inside, a ladder led down to an internal platform, furnished with a bizarre hopper-like aperture and an airlock. They stole through the airlock, every movement threatening to betray them. The soft hiss of pressurised air sounding like an orchestra. *Would anyone hear that?* they wondered. No one did.

Moving like ghosts, soft-soled space boots absorbing every footfall, the human team exited the airlock. Undetected, they were inside the alien base, on a hanging walkway that stretched under the ceiling of a circular cavern. A cream-coloured paint, the Uldonian cloaking tech, covered the walls and ceiling. Hidden lights embedded in the roof and walls illuminated the cavern. The combined effect gave it a bright and clean appearance. Foldback space helmets opened and they took a fresh breath of clean and dry air. Not what the invading team expected.

Tom looked down; the sight below stunned him and his team. As shown in the old drawings, the large cave housed an alien laboratory. Shining metal vessels connected by pipework ringed the cavern. The hopper-like aperture fed one of the metal vessels through another airlock. Tom wished Niamh was here to decipher what he was seeing. Translucent pipes, cable looms, and hose bundles ran from the tanks into a square-shaped alien machine. Most shocking of all, plasma conduits connected this apparatus to something truly horrible. In the centre of the lab, propped up on a dais, lay the emaciated body of an ancient purebreed man. Sustained by a plasma conduit, a blue energy mass, like an Overlord's, floated above the alien – adding to the grim scene. Unbeknown to Tom and his team, they were looking down on Grandfather Borea's research into immortality.

Demard and Zaval's grandfather ruthlessly expanded the family business into piracy with his brutal cousin Frike by his side. With the *Monarch* – known then as *Borea1* – they waged war on anything or anyone who got in their way. Making full use of one of the most advanced ships in the galaxy, nobody stood a chance. Robbery and terror on a scale never seen before, which took a fleet from the Anan Navy and two Overlords to defeat them. The evil king of the Borea's pirate reign, the cruellest in all the galaxies, was still alive! Near four hundred orbits old, Grandfather Borea was well past an average lifespan.

Tom had seen enough. Time to call home. Taking a small comms unit from his backpack, he stuck it to the cavern's ceiling. Micro-spikes pierced the Uldonian paint, anchoring the box to the asteroid's rock, turning it into a giant antenna and opening a video link with the *Monarch*. Tom fed the damning info back to the ship's bridge. It was a shocked Eight who deciphered the criminal experiment. He had heard mumblings of such evil, but like the other Overlords, dismissed it as populace folklore. How wrong they were!

The Eight boomed an order to Bill, the Security Manager Tom had left on the Monarch. 'Immediate. Dispatch chemical weapons to the away team. Go now!' Then flashed another to Tom. *Chemical weapons are on the way. You must destroy that thing. Kill it before it evolves further,* were his blunt orders. Finally, a call for help, this time over a longer distance to his friend The Second. *You need to know this ...* were his opening words, as the video of the secret lab followed. A shocked Second dispatched his own troops with more lethal weapons.

*

Towards the end of the Borea war, some three hundred orbits ago, knowing the Overlords would defeat him, Grandfather Borea secretly planned an escape from his lair at the edge of the Anan Galaxy. He told no one, not even Frike, his most trusted enforcer. Before the deciding battle, he dispatched Frike on a bogus mission to Anan. It saved Frike who was able to disappear into oblivion, hiding on Anan until he reappeared to attack The Eight.

Grandfather Borea, the more elusive of the two, vanished into the long limbs of his pirate network. The dissemination of his precious codes and cyphers to the family completed the illusion. Travelling to outlying worlds and satellites at the margins of the known galaxy, he gathered a trove of forbidden sciences; black arts on extending mortality, genetic change, and that elusive morsel, the very source of the Overlord's power – how blue energy can sustain intelligence. After an age collecting that maleficent knowledge, he returned to this secret laboratory where his daughter, Madam Borea, or MemB as he called her, was waiting.

The laboratory was where his engineers had developed the gossamer-like suits Frike had worn in his attempt to defeat The Eight. The dead engineer was a genius in developing illegal tech. It was here where he had bred a collective of Uldonian microbes, feeding them on a mix of grav, and an unknown cocktail of composite metals. The mass morphed into worm-like creatures. As they digested the toxic blend of grav and metal, they spun – as waste – a web of micro threads. The engineer harvested those threads and wove them into the fabric cloaks Frike had worn.

Grandfather Borea resurrected the dead man's experiments. But this time he fed the microbes with living beings. Captured purebreeds and other bipeds, traded into bondage by MemB's unscrupulous contacts, were fed into a reactor tank through the hopper at the top. The worms, injected with blue energy, digested the living beings, imbibing their life force. The precious waste the larvae excreated formed the blue-grey mass nourishing Grandfather Borea's body and brain. A living pulsing mass of unnatural horror, trying to emulate the energy mass of an Overlord. It sustained the evil pirate's life while his technicians refined the process.

Meanwhile, unknown to the Borea family living above, to maintain her father's horrific experiment, MemB worked them to the bone. This project was Grandfather Borea's penultimate triumph in his delving with Uldonian and blue energy tech and his search for overlord-like status.

Lying on the dais now, his emaciated body was near the end of its ability to sustain his life. The experiments were coming to an end. Through plasma conduits, he had already transferred his consciousness in and out of the floating energy mass, exploring the essence that would house his brain. Its power had mesmerised him. Never had he believed he could control such a thing, but now it was becoming a reality. One more life-sustaining feed would cement his transformation. MemB had arranged it – the delivery of captive souls scheduled to arrive within the next cycle. But something had changed. He had placed restrictions on communications between the lab and the base. It kept prying eyes out but limited his reach into the wider world outside.

MemB had flashed him a cryptic message: 'The family are back with your Borea1. There is a change afoot. If all goes well, I will have more food for you. If not, prepare to transform yourself.'

He contemplated that. Rested after his last feed of life-giving energy, he decided to move his brain back into the blue energy mass floating above him. Best be ready for any eventuality. Through the conduits, he sent a message to the lab's control processor. A white light flashed and a low warble sounded.

*

Despite the alarms, Tom and his team lay motionless on the gantry above, watching with interest the action below. One by one, four purebreeds dressed in white suits, hurried into the lab. They gathered around Grandfather Borea until a tall, alien biped came in, clearly not a purebreed, dressed in an orange boiler suit with his red hair seeping out from the cover of a white lab hat.

The Javonian's purple hands pointed at the four purebreeds. A harsh voice drowned out the soft alarm. 'Well, you imbeciles, don't stand there; get to your stations. You know the drill by now.'

Like a whip cracked, the four ran off in different directions, taking up positions at control stations around the lab.

Tom looked across at his team. Their faces said it all; whatever was happening wouldn't bode well for them. Reluctant to move, he signalled them to stay still. They'd wait for the imminent arrival of the chemical weapons.

Below, the Javonian entered a series of commands into a screen on the square-shaped alien machine. In unison, the other four initiated similar orders into their stations. Seconds ticked by, then a flash of blue light erupted from the energy-mass floating above Grandfather. It started to pulse as life-giving power, sucked from the surrounding tanks and processed by the alien machine, flowed through the plasma conduits.

The blue energy mass expanded, floating up, over the centre of the lab. Then, the strange machined whined, and with a flash, another process started. A bolt of white light erupted from a ball on top of the machine. The light morphed into translucent tentacles of living organism extruding outwards from the flashing sphere. Pulsing and growing, they twisted up towards the energy mass and down to Grandfather's head. Throbbing and crackling with energy, the tentacles pierced his skull, connecting the old pirate's brain to the blue energy mass. To the humans looking on above, this alien spectacle was akin to the vilest horror movie they had ever seen. But all was not done. The worst was to come.

Grandfather's body started to convulse and glow with a harsh blue-grey light. The light grew stronger. With a bright grey flash, the tentacles expanded as Grandfather Borea's evil consciousness flowed from his brain into the jagged ball of energy floating above his old, wizened body. Resembling that of the Overlord's in size, the energy-mass changed colour to a harsh blue-grey light as the pirate brain moved in. With pulsing tentacles, plasma connections, and a foul greyish organic membrane, it looked like the abomination it was.

CHAPTER THIRTY-TWO

Personal Log. Captain Arie Machai, Aknar 1, The One's Flagship

We travelled from the Hepkaz Belt out across the great divide from our known universe into an uncharted galaxy. Our sensors, tracking signs of Anan technology, led us to a habitable planet in an obscure solar system. With our Overlord, I led a landing party to investigate evidence of an Anan settlement. Some unknown disaster befell the occupants as little remained, of what appeared to be, a science station.

The One scanned the area, finding a hidden volume below ground. Excavations revealed a safe. Inside we found several data crystals. I placed the first in a portable reader. What it told, shocked us. The crystals spoke of research into advancing life, as we know it, to a higher level, assisted by blue. And it included experiments in evolving mortal life to an ethereal existence, like an Overlord – banned delving into dark arts. The One turned the find and the ruined buildings to dust. I wondered, like ripples in a pond, what effect could this knowledge bring to our universe in the future …

⁃ *Extract from: Mission Log, The One's Exploration past the Tar Galaxy*

*

Borea Base, Hepkaz Belt. EPTS: B140490

GRANDFATHER SETTLED INTO HIS NEW home. Pure power encased in a binding grey organic membrane. He relished it. With the final feed, soon to come, he could disengage from the support manifolds and take an ethereal form, like an Overlord. His energy mass pulsed with his power, his greed and desire for immortality. The self-gloating subsided. Concentrating on his new abilities, Grandfather tried to project his mind out from the energy mass. Through the hazy blue-grey membrane, he looked out into the lab and at his team standing in awe at his new form. He sharpened his senses – there was more here. He could feel it. The presence of life, yes, spies here in his lab, watching him. Plotting his demise. He screamed. It manifested as a high-pitched shrill sound, cutting through the lab's atmosphere and shaking the gantry the humans were hiding on. And his voice followed. The sound of Grandfather Borea, the evil fiend who should be long dead, filled the lab. 'Intruders, who are you? How dare you infiltrate my private domain.' He paused.

Tom and his team trembled at the sight and sound of this evil alien presence.

Grandfather continued. 'But thank you for coming. You will provide me with my final nourishment of sentient life.'

The energy mass rose up towards the gantry. A faint vision of Grandfather's face emerged on the shrouding membrane. Flashing with blue-grey light, it started to grow as Grandfather sucked more precious energy from the tanks through the pulsing living tentacles and plasma conduits. A grey tentacle darted out towards one of Tom's soldiers. He screamed as the alien thing pulsed in front of his face. Grandfather, getting a good view of the human, wondered what life form they were? Like a bolt of lightning, the tentacle pierced the man's head, straight through his forehead. No blood, no mess, a clean surgical incision. Shocked, Tom and the other three watched as the soldier's body withered. Like a vacuum, the tentacle sucked the life and living matter from the man. It quivered as the man's body shrunk before their eyes, his face disappearing, his torso shrinking, his hands disappearing. A gurgling sound followed and his empty spacesuit and boots fell across the walkway. The man was gone. His life essence and biological matter consumed by Grandfather Borea.

Of all the things Tom had seen in space, this was the worst. He never imagined such evil existed. Adrenalin coursed into his brain, spurring him into action. He did all he was able to and aimed his grav weapon at the centre of the heaving blue-grey mass. Rapid-fire charges pounded into the pulsing Thing. But to Tom's horror, it absorbed the energy, growing from the grav pulses. He roared at his three remaining soldiers. 'Retreat. Go get those chemical weapons. Now.'

Needing no prompting, they rushed back along the gantry towards the safety of the airlock followed by a growing tentacle. It curled over the metal handrail, flowing along the walkway, sinister pulsing death. Tom drew a long dagger from its sheath and rushed to the rail. His three remaining soldiers, inside the airlock, frantically tried to close the door. The tentacle wrapped around the leg of one. Dragged out of the airlock, and along the walkway, she screamed. Without another thought, Tom stabbed and cut at the alien substance where it flowed over the handrail. Formed from living beings, the thing still had nerves. Pain streamed back to Grandfather's brain as Tom cut the tentacle in two. The piece attached to the woman's leg withered and died – she ran back into the airlock. Seconds later, the door slammed shut.

Trying to get higher, the pulsing blue-grey Thing pulled at its life-sustaining terminations, plasma conduits and tentacles, filling the lab with shrill screeches. Looking upwards through blue-grey light, Grandfather spied Tom standing on the gantry, pointing his grav gun at something else. Grandfather sensed danger. The biped wouldn't risk another shot at his energy mass. But what else could he do? Then it hit him as his enhanced mind traced the weapon's aim. Tom was targeting the control processor embedded in the machine where the Javonian half-breed stood.

As Grandfather calculated his options for survival in those precious milliseconds, Tom fired multiple bolts of grav towards the all-important evil life-giving engine. While the grav bolts moved through the air, Grandfather Borea made a momentous decision – to do nothing was death. The life-sustaining engine would close down all his energy feeds, his mass would wither, and he would shrink and die. But not if he made the irrevocable leap of transformation. It would be early, before the final feed of living bipeds. But, from the soldier's life force, his mass was pulsing stronger. It may not be enough, but it was hope.

Grav charges slammed into the engine – Grandfather screamed again. Valves, control systems, sensors, orifices, pipework and cables all failed. The manifold pulsed and the plasma conduits glowed bright blue. Steam and smoke rose up from the depths of the lab, signs that the force of the grav blasts had disintegrated the evil controlling machine. But within those milliseconds, Grandfather Borea had attempted his transformation. A grey pulsing hybrid energy and organic mass formed above his now inert body. It rose and fell. Tom's blast had killed two of the technicians. The other two cowered down, trying to hide. The Thing, for that's what Grandfather was now, roared at them. They ran to a shattered manifold and opened a valve. Like a poisonous snake, Grandfather elongated the hybrid mass he occupied and flowed through the broken pipework, taking refuge inside the connecting tank. Tom fired again, emptying the grav gun's charge. Phaenian steel tanks and translucent manifolds burst open and grey coloured goo flowed across the lab's floor.

Twisted metal, cables, glass and the like fell in explosive chaos. With no ammo left, Tom paused and looked down at the mayhem he had released below. Two technicians cowered in a corner while debris lay everywhere. A ladder hung precariously from the side of an undamaged tank. Sparks cascaded down the side of another while smoke and flames curled up from the insides of the energy engine, the control mechanism that drove the evil process. Grandfather Borea's empty body lay face down on the floor, covered with broken glass and metal. Tom watched the tail of the Thing disappear into broken pipework. But the Javonian was nowhere to be seen. *Where have you gone?* he wondered.

His comms unit clicked with an incoming message. 'Chem-guns are here.' He ran to the base of the airlock, signalling his soldiers to advance back into the lab. Meeting two, he ordered them to stay on the gantry, covering him while he stalked the Thing.

Hastily donning some protective gear, he strapped on a chem-gun, and secondary charges. Finding an undamaged ladder, Tom looked down at the smoking remains of the lab below. All the Royal Marine training, hand-to-hand combat, battles in war-torn regions on Earth and the like, had never prepared him for something like this – a scene from a bad sci-fi movie. Tom took a deep breath, his lungs labouring against the filters in the respirator – then he stepped onto the ladder. Every rung down was a mental battle. He shouldn't be here, but he didn't capitulate to the fear.

The Eight's last orders rung in his mind. *"Kill it before it evolves further."* Mouth dry with fear, his heart hammering a death march in his chest, Tom kept going. Down into the mayhem of what remained of the evil entity's laboratory.

Stepping on the wet sticky ground, Tom looked around. Getting used to the alien respirator his laboured breathing calmed and the crystal-clear view out of the visor was a welcome break. Much better than the primitive earthly ones he had worn back home.

The grey goo had drained into scuppers embedded in the floor but it still stayed slippery, every step an effort. Tom could see the broken pipework the Thing had escaped into on the other side of the lab. He clambered across the debris, two purebreed lab techs whimpering as he passed them by.

Never had they expected such an end to their endeavours. They watched the strange biped, dressed in a black Anan spacesuit – his face, eyes and nose protected by a respirator – wielding a chem-gun. The shining weapon had a long, flared barrel, with a reservoir mounted below. Made from pressure-hardened baharian steel, it held a deadly chemical that, when exposed to an atmosphere, dissolves all it touches. If he came into contact with any of it, Tom would die. The respirator and gloves he put on were more of a talisman rather than any functioning protection!

He worked his way towards the pipework and tank where he had seen the Thing disappear. Bit by bit, he stepped closer and closer. The tank had a gash on its side, the attached pipework buckled and split. Tom stopped at the large opening. Jagged metal edges advertised the impact from a grav blast. The tank was about six metres tall and three wide, enough for the Thing to cower in. He stooped down and peered in. Sounds of sparks, fire and the hiss of escaping steam filled his ears but the tank was deadly still. He turned the gun's torch on. Holding his breath, his eyes focused on the motionless liquid inside. The fluid stirred, its surface broke as the eyes of a worm, with teeth and glowing green eyes, gazed out from the blood-red gooey mess in the bottom of the tank. Tom recoiled with fright. Unbeknown to him, he had caught sight of one of the hybrid Uldonian worms Grandfather had bred. As quickly as it appeared, it was gone. Recovering his composure, Tom gazed further into the tank, the gun's light beam piercing the darkness.

The transformed mass of Grandfather Borea shrank at the back of the tank. The dancing light beam moved back and forth, illumination his pet worm and then coming ever closer until it dazzled his ethereal face. The Borea monster roared with fury, manifesting as that familiar shrill screech that exploded out from the tank.

Tom fired a single blast of chemical. He had no idea of what it would do. It may have been better to hold his ground first but there was no going back. The bright silver-coloured chemical sprayed inside the tank. Mixing with air, it painted one side of Grandfather Borea's mass with a corrosive gel. Like thousands of lancing insects, the gel stung, assaulting his hybrid energy mass, burning the organic membrane. Grandfather Borea screamed again. This time it wasn't a shrill sound, but the sound of a purebreed man withering in pain. Panic took over and he fled from the relative shelter of the upturned tank, flowing right past Tom who recoiled in horror at the sight of Grandfather Borea's twisted face etched on the pulsing evil malignancy.

As the Thing turned around to face him, Tom fired again. More pain seared Grandfather Borea as his hybrid energy mass tried to encircle Tom. The standoff persisted while Tom continued to fire at the grey form spinning around him. Tentacles protruded from the serrated edges of the energy mass. Tom knew what would happen if they ever got near him. Hope shone through as the smoke of burning chemicals started to rise up from the Thing's organic membrane. Blue-grey membrane turned to black burning welts, as the compound did its job.

But Grandfather wouldn't give up. This was his last gasp; death would come quick if he didn't stop this biped in his tracks. Recognising his own chem-guns, he knew they had a limited charge – Grandfather had designed them, they were from his ship and his armoury. *The ignorant biped has underestimated the power of his weapon,* he gloated. As fast as Grandfather was burning, he regenerated new membrane below the burning welts.

Time stood still. With Tom in the way, the soldiers above dared not put down supporting chem-fire. The spray would envelop Tom, dissolving him as well. Countermanding his orders, they ran towards the ladder. But as Tom's weapon fired its last charge, announced by a flat ominous bleeping, they knew they were too late.

Back on the lab floor, Tom could see the Thing grinning at him. Grandfather had him and he revelled as he watched the biped squirm.

No good killing this biped now, he thought. He wanted *Boreal's* location and intelligence as to how he could get his ship back. The evil Thing's tentacles grabbed Tom, pulling him down onto the slippery, debris-strewn, floor. First, he'd get that info from Tom's brain then suck his life force and bodily remains from this physical world.

Grappling to recharge his chem-gun, the Thing reeled Tom in – like a captured fish to the table – dragging him along towards the broken tank, back to Grandfather's lair. Tom was to be dinner! Trying to steady his mind, he took a deep breath. The stink of the burning alien compounds seeped through the respirator's filter, searing his senses. Doggedly – his body in automatic – he tried, in vain, to mount the chem-charge on the gun. *It's all over*, he realised, as memories of Niamh and his love for her flooded his mind. A roar from behind broke his thoughts.

'Get down now. Get down or I'll spray you,' came the unexpected call in Anan.

Lying back on the floor, Tom followed the startling order. A jet of clear liquid passed alongside him, covering the binding tentacles. They dissolved as the Thing screamed, and that same deep voice roared. Tom thought he could hear the Anan word for "traitor". Free from the living bindings, he rolled to the side. Surprised, he saw the colourful Javonian advance from the shadows, wielding what looked like a sophisticated water pistol! Unknown to Tom, it was one of the lab's cleaning applicators, filled with noxious fluid. Used for sterilising surfaces, pipework and tanks before a batch is cultivated, the caustic-like pre-wash kills all known organisms.

Enraged at his own technician's treachery, Grandfather Borea counter attacked. The pulsing blue-grey energy mass pressed on towards the two living bipeds, his tentacles burning, and his outer membrane smoking from the burning chem-gel. He needed sustenance. These two were nothing but food for the evil Borea monster.

His stock of cleaning fluid depleted, the Javonian tech turned and ran. But by then, Tom had his weapon reloaded and his soldiers had joined him. In unison, they doused the advancing ethereal Thing with more of the hazardous gel. Screaming and smoking, Grandfather Borea retreated back inside the broken tank.

Again, The Eight's orders rang in his mind, but Tom had failed. *It had evolved, but into what?* he wondered. It wasn't only evil but another evolutionary step down a path of alien madness Tom couldn't comprehend. *We'll achieve nothing here*, thought Tom. They'd emptied near all the chem-charges and still hadn't stopped the alien monster. Save lives and live to fight another day was Tom's only option. Taking the orange-suited Javonian as well, he ordered the retreat. He had lost one person today, he wasn't going to lose another. While Grandfather Borea licked his wounds and tried to regenerate his depleted mass in the cover of the broken tank, they made their way back to the airlock. A spare spacesuit for the Javonian was dispatched from the waiting shuttle. After that, without further delay, stinking of fear and seared alien matter, the four escaped to the *Monarch*.

*

The Javonian tech, forced into slavery decades ago by MemB, was a mine of information. He had bided his time, hoping an opportunity such as this would come knocking. He gave everything up to The Eight, including the names of those in the "know". Before MemB realised what had happened, Geoff hacked her small fleet's controls, locking the ships at dock. There were two entry points to the lab, one at the top airlock and one at the back of the base. Once secured, Grandfather Borea was going nowhere.

The alien encounter traumatised even the hardest of Tom's soldiers and when the story got out, the rest of the human crew. The loss of a man was a blow to morale. Not the first who had died. There were two others killed on the New World when out hunting, but he was the first in action and the way he went horrified them the most. The poor man's life sucked through the tentacles of an outlaw lifeform.

The event shook The Eight. The mission, supposed to be a quick visit to employ new crews, turned up an illegal den of repugnance. He could do nothing but guard the base until The Second's troops arrived. When they did, half a cycle later, he transferred down to MemB's lair to supervise the cull. For that's what The Second decreed would happen.

Execution awaited all those complicit in Grandfather's scheme. The Borea assembled in a hall within their headquarter's building. Most, the poorest and most hardworking of all, wondered what was going on. It was they who had sustained MemB's efforts to progress her father's work in becoming an Overlord. The Eight scanned them – a miserable process. Some who knew the game was up tried to run and hide, only to be cut down by The Second's guards as they fled. Others collapsed with the shock. But most accepted their fate, believing The Eight would kill them all.

The guards then marched the guilty through the lab's secret entrance. Surprised, they thought they were to be spared. To their and Madam Borea's joy, they found their leader had survived. And, better still, Grand-father had transformed.

He needed more life-sustaining energy to repair his energy mass, but he had survived, scraping out some sustenance from the slops of the broken tanks. When they came in, he floated out from his hiding place in the broken vessel to greet his daughter and the twelve other co-con-spirators. Watching them approach, he calculated how long he could live on the twelve life forms. Then he felt the hatch above open. *What's that?* he wondered.

Above, The Second's guards had opened the airlock to the feed hopper. Wearing reinforced spacesuits, they dropped decontamination canisters into the laboratory below. They were the same brand Robert had released in the *Hela* med-bay to purge the ceirim contamination from the ship. The canisters exploded, filling the lab with an orange coloured gas. The gas filled every nook and cranny in the lab, seeking out living organism and killing them. Panic ensued as MemB and her accomplices, recog-nising their demise, tried to run to the locked exit. They died where they stood, frozen by the lethal vapour. A silver-coloured nanite mist followed. Programmed to feed on the contaminates and any organic material, the substance devoured the dead Borea's tissue, bone and liquids. Dead nanites were all that remained of the family.

Grandfather watched with horror as his daughter and his family fell, killed in front of him. The ones he had earmarked to feed on, disappeared in front of his eyes. The poisonous gas invaded his organic membrane, further depleting Grandfather's precious life force. It took more of his energy to combat the nanites but, determined to live, fight them he did. When the process had expended itself, he was still alive. Life force depleted but still alive. Deep within his twisted mind, he grinned. *Even with the power of an Overlord, they can't kill me*, he thought.

Time stood still for Grandfather Borea as The Eight approved the load out of forty-one innocent Borea. Technicians, pilots and engineers who would gladly join his cause. There was only one death sentence commuted – that of the Javonian. The Eight scrubbed all knowledge of the illegal process from his mind and turned him over to Tom, a happy outcome for the enslaved tech.

With the remaining Borea family loaded on the *Monarch*, it left the safe harbour, waiting outside the channel for The Second's guards. They had one more mission. Suspecting the decon-process would unlikely kill such an entity, The Eight and The Second made sure there were no loose ends to haunt them.

Once again, Grandfather detected the hatch above open. *Now what?* he wondered. Time ticked away. Loud banging noises. *Something's being loaded into the chamber*, he realised. He sensed what it was as they closed the hatch but he could do nothing. Minutes later, the first explosion launched the weapon into the centre of the asteroid's inner secret chamber. Encased in his energy mass formed from microbes, blue, grav and living sentient beings, Grandfather Borea screamed as he watched a fusion bomb fall into his lair.

Simultaneously, the guard's shuttle fled through a fold in space. Arriving beside the *Monarch*, both ships watched as the base exploded. A fiery white flash heralded the end of the secret Borea base and to their pirate Grandfather's bid for immortality. The enhanced energy weapon reduced the asteroid and everything inside to the atomic level, forming an inert dust cloud within the asteroid belt.

Watching on the bridge of the *Monarch*, Tom asked The Eight, 'Will that have killed it?'

'Nothing survives that. So close to the epicentre of the explosion. No, it doesn't. But Two will check. Nothing will be left to chance. Come, we must go; your wife awaits.'

Across the bridge, a silent Siba stood at the captain's station. More Borea madness. Who would have thought the other monster survived the Overlord's purge. *Grandfather, even after so much time you bring such shame on this family,* she thought. Tears ran down her face, not for her dead mother but for the soldier who had lost his life. She had known him, a happy young soul, full of life and committed to their cause. Dead and gone; what a waste. 'Siba …' Her name, shouted from across the bridge, brought her back to reality. Bill, standing at the security station, was pointing across at Tom. Engrossed in her thoughts, she hadn't heard his orders.

Tom gently repeated his words. 'Time to go, Siba. Back to pick up Niamh; you know the way.'

Siba nodded. Composing herself, she barked orders to her new crew. To her surprise, they cheered and laughed. And then she realised how lucky they all were, leaving such horror behind with forty-two new souls on board. For the first time since she had heard her mother's voice, Siba, gazing across the bridge at Bill, smiled.

*

United Nations, Geneva, 11th January 2028

Ignorant of the goings-on in far distant galaxies, from his small office inside the Geneva building, Harold watched Robert make his speech to the United Nations. It wasn't going well. Delegates were coming and going, booing and hissing. There were shouts of "Why did you contact them?" and "Why did you not leave them alone?".

Finally, Robert paused. Clutching the podium, he waited for his rage to subside. Slamming his hand down on it with a loud bang, he roared, 'In case you missed the start, they came here first. They are our ancestors; they are back. A wise woman told me this. "When The Sixth made his move in that far distant galaxy, our fate was sealed." She's right, we have no options …' He continued with the text of his speech, calling for world unity and a collective effort to assist The Eight's war "instead of fighting amongst ourselves". A logical step a child would understand. But the hissing and booing continued, the delegates buried in their own self-serving interests. Finally, with his head hanging low, he left the podium and made his way back to Harold's office.

As soon as he looked at the man, Robert knew something was up. A grey pallor had descended across Harold's face and pronounced wrinkles added another ten years. It was if he had seen a ghost. And he had – it resembled Earth's destruction.

'I'm afraid I have bad news from Kath. She's in Kenepuru with the child's mum,' he said, his voice shaking. 'Apparently, there were pictures. Bri may have left with pictures of Earth and the night sky. The girl told Kath they were taken on her phone on New Year's Eve. The following day, she went into a photo shop and had them printed. Bri was enthralled with them. All he left was a note and his blue diamond for her. The pictures are gone, Robert. Do you think they are of any use to The Sixth?'

Not what Robert wanted to hear, and he knew The Sixth would have more. 'I don't know, Harold. But I do know he has human DNA from the Empress's cure. That went to Anan. We must believe he now has the pictures too. Verteg or Quriel would know. I'll call Oz.'

Robert looked at his watch – middle of the night there. Stepping out of Harold's office, he took out his phone and called the Hela base.

Half an hour later, Robert stepped back inside Harold's cluttered office. A black face told the story. Quriel and Verteg's knowledge of the Overlords, star charts and galactic time distortions didn't bode well.

Robert distilled it down for Harold. 'They said The Seventh is the custodian of all the Overlord's star charts. He's part of The Sixth's troika and will do everything possible to find Earth. It'll be hard, very hard, just with that small picture. The universe is vast; they'll need more to find Earth – maybe scout ships, Verteg said. Bottom line, Harold, both Verteg and Quriel agreed, it's possible. The picture of our night sky may be a breadcrumb to Earth.'

Harold rubbed his face with his hands, trying to banish the weary feeling of hopelessness coursing through his mind. He trembled as he voiced his thoughts. 'The alien Overlords are the most powerful entity's we've ever encountered. We know The Sixth has our DNA, pictures of humans and an impression of our galaxy. Robert, we must assume they are coming – nothing less. We plan for that.'

'Shit, and we can't even contact The Eight,' Robert said.

Facing that reality, Harold's face resembled a death mask. *We are alone now. What horrible peril can come of this?* he wondered. 'I'll tell the world leaders. It'll be a miracle if they believe me. Robert, assume the worst and prepare for war, wherever it starts – and you'd better hide those three ships in the desert. They'll stick out like three sore thumbs if anyone comes calling.'

*

Zakkai-Prime. EPTS: B140542

Back in orbit around Zakkai-Prime, with the help of her family, Captain Siba picked up the tow. In high spirits after such good fortune, the Borea family set about their duties with gusto. Shift rosters, crew duties from maintenance routines to the mundane cleaning tasks, everything the *Monarch* needed to get it back to the New World, were put in place.

The discovery of the Mzimot family living in the brig didn't faze the Borea. Hungry to learn from the legendary engine builders, Bill had to shoo away some of the enthusiastic Borea engineers.

The Mzimot's lot wasn't so bad, having turned the "brig" into a comfortable accommodation block on the *Monarch's* lower decks. Earth game consoles, entertainment systems and sports gear donated by Bill and his soldiers littered the communal space. The generosity of the humans – captors as some thought – didn't go unnoticed by the Mzimot elders. But Jarzol and a core few stubbornly refused to change their opinion of the humans and The Eight, perplexing the young.

The Second returned Niamh to the *Monarch* in a hiberpod. The miracle piece of Anan tech had sustained Niamh and her unborn child's fragile life. The Second's treatment extracted the blue contamination.

However, the effects of harsh therapy stressed the corporeal body to its limit. Truth be told, Niamh was at death's door.

Stark words from The Second rooted Tom to the spot. 'I have done all I can. Your wife and the unborn struggle to survive. They need time to heal.'

Dismissed out of hand, Tom supervised the transfer of Niamh's hiberpod to med-bay. Borea technicians connected it to the ship's systems that would, with Anan plasma supplied by The Second, provide for her survival.

Meanwhile, in his chamber, The Eight had a final conference with Two. The discovery of the Borea pirate delving into black life-changing experiments on his doorstep astounded The Second. That he was "grateful" to The Eight and his humans was an overstatement – the word "indebted" was mentioned. A weighty boost to The Eight's cause. But both knew how powerful The Sixth had become and how difficult it would be to unseat him from Anan. The Second revealed Admiral Enirim's failed plan to move the Aknar fleet to the Tar Galaxy, putting it at The Second's disposal.

'Get control of that fleet, Eight, and you will stop Six,' were The Second's final words as he left the *Monarch*.

Back on the bridge, The Eight couldn't help but feel a changing force. Despite the crew's concern for Niamh's condition, a new dynamic filled the air. Human and Borea occupied each station, following Captain Siba's crisp commands without question.

'Overlord,' she said, snapping upright to face his chariot. 'Package is on tow. Course back to the New World plotted. On your command, we're ready to go.'

He waited, feeling all the eyes of the crew on Siba. *A job well done*, he thought. Demard and Zaval Borea would have been proud of their niece. 'Thank you, Captain,' he said. 'Make way. We go home.' The emphasis of the word "home" was not lost on the crew, Borea and human.

CHAPTER THIRTY-THREE

New World, its Two Moons and Solar System

The planet named as New World with a diameter of approximately 12,100 kilometres has two orbiting moons – average diameter 2,100 kilometres each. Life flourishes on this warm and wet habitable world. It is part of an eleven-planet solar system and is fourth from its sun. The system is located midway inside Galaxy X1834M, which is the joint property of The One and The Eight.

Blue Energy deposits are present in significant quantity on the planet. The attached mining reports verify this. Prolific amounts of the energy-bearing nodes are at low depths on both moons. An earlier survey by The One and The Eight identified similar deposits of blue energy on the solar system's nine other solid planets and their twenty-one moons. These nine planets do not support life and are, for the most part, barren rocks – simplifying future mining. The outermost (eleventh) world is a methane gas giant. Its location, in dark frozen space, offers the opportunity for hydrocarbon extraction.

‹ *Introduction: X1834M New World Blue Energy Contracts. Cylla Ora*

*

Energy Exchange, Anan Galaxy. EPTS: B140546

While the Monarch made its way back to the New World, the havoc The Eight's master plan had unleashed, coupled with the mess left in Kandark Galaxy, started to unwind at the Energy Exchange. From his grave, Zaval Borea's audacious plan had reached fruition. The Eight's project smart-war trap was now set and waiting for a victim! And only The Sixth had enough resources to bite.

Zaval had incubated an age-old strategy in which energy traders buy blue for immediate delivery or storage – when the price is low – and hold it (in storage) until the price increases. The critical element of the "play" relies on the future price of blue being higher than the current market price agreed in the contract, sold at the Energy Exchange. Once the buyer commits to the deal, the price locks. The only way out is if the seller can't deliver on the due date. If the price rises (as hoped) the trader makes a profit. It the price of blue falls, the trader loses the bet – a costly outcome, sometimes ending in financial ruin.

With untraceable satellites in place, Cylla and Mack established communications with the Energy Exchange servers as Shona aptly described "on-line banking in space". Mack's Aknar codes and Cylla's certification as a Market Trader, still valid after her dismissal, allowed them to post the contracts for the sale of blue. The standard arrangement – delivery to the Energy Exchange in one orbit – provided The Eight enough time to prepare a fleet on Earth.

Inside the Energy Exchange, those contracts flashed from server to server, converting from galactic-messaging to formal Anan contracts. The vital, confidential information Cylla had to include was hidden in the depts of the auto-servers. Since blue was hardly traded, the commodity ended up in the grav trading pit, managed by none other than the Shoter's daughter. The Eight couldn't have hope for a better outcome.

The young woman couldn't take her eyes off the numbers tracking across her screen. The new contracts had popped up just before the end of this trading period. The timing of their posting neatly bypassed all, except the most eager of their greedy horde. She looked across to the blue energy trading terminal, closed and empty. *Abandoned when Haret had cut and run,* she thought. *What to do? What to do about this?* There was nobody else with resources to process the contracts except her. She looked down at her trading team. When she had returned as the team's boss, after Cylla herself was fired, she had changed their structure. To his surprise, she had promoted Arb, from lead, to principal grav trader – on a par with Cylla's status. She managed the group, collected the payments and ensured the dispatch of the grav. As Admiral Enirim had told Theia, the boot in the arse was the makings of the girl – turning her into an astute young woman.

Arb managed the trading, guaranteeing the success of their team. It left the young woman free to oversee the operation and, of greater consequence, spy on what else was going on in the vast trading hall. Now she needed him. 'Arb, have a look at this,' she said, as she flashed the numbers across to his terminal.

His white face went grey as he read the numbers. He looked back at her and shook his head. 'Not sure about this.'

Her face screwed up, bewildered by his words, 'Why?'

'Long contracts too far out in time – an orbit away. Who knows what the market in blue will be when they mature?'

She moved down beside him. 'Explain,' she asked, looking into his blistered face.

'The contracts are at current market price. Delivery isn't scheduled for one orbit. The price has never been so high. Whoever buys the contracts agrees to a delivery at today's price.'

'I know that, Arb.'

'What you don't know is the price in one orbit.'

'It will be the same or higher.'

'How do you know?'

'I don't, but unless a new source of blue is found, it will be the same or higher.'

'What if one is found, or the seller of these contracts has found the mythical new hoard of blue? The seller knows the market will fall as they produce and store their blue.'

The old Arb was right. On the New World, The Eight controlled that "mythical hoard" of blue everyone was looking for. Off-world mining had started on an adjacent moon, increasing the stock further. During his first visit, with The One, to The New World's solar system, the reserves of blue energy they stumbled upon had astounded them. Never before or since did they find such a precious "hoard". The Eight surmised an anomaly, that blue had formed into a cluster of planets and moons so close together. The stuff of old legends told aeons ago.

The young woman, sceptical of those legends, screwed up her pretty face in disbelief. 'Arb, surely you don't believe those stories.'

'I believe in price action and market forces. Listen to me. You have been good to me, despite our previous history. I despised you when you worked here first under Cylla; now you are the boss. In my dying days, you treat me well. I appreciate that. I know,' he said, holding his hand up to stop her interruption, 'your father is the Shoter. That is not why I tell you this. Whoever posted those contracts has set a trap. It's an old strategy – get some fool to buy forward contracts at a high price believing the price will increase further. Instead, the supply surges and the price of blue falls. The buyer is caught long as the energy price collapses. You have the picture?'

She nodded. 'Can you tell who posted them?'

'No. Nor will the Moderator. You will no doubt check that with him. Your father will push him to use all his authority to dig deep within the Exchange but he'll find nothing – the classified material stays hidden. Whoever had the codes to post those contracts has power.' He paused as he looked into her eyes. 'Leave them, they are poison.'

She shivered at his words. 'Thank you, Arb,' she said, as she took his festering hand. 'The new medicine we got for you, the First Stage Treatment, it's not helping, is it?'

'No, little one. I am too far gone. Heed what I said,' Arb said, smiling at her.

'Arb, what else can I do for you?'

'Nothing, there is nothing you can do,' he refreshed the terminal screen. 'I came across this news on the Exchange under-chat from the outlying Kandark Galaxy. There's rumour of a raid on the scrap world, Lagrvth.' He grinned and looked at her. 'Imagine that, little one. Who would do such a thing? Anyway, the same crew tricked the consortium on Hirkiv into selling them four old blue drives. Most intriguing is the disappearance of the Mzimot family. You know them as the engine builders. Two of the consortium's cruisers were damaged. Hirkiv's director blamed the affair on pirates working in cahoots with the Mzimot. But, to add to the mystery, the Mzimot debts and all the equipment were paid for.'

Arb paused, allowing all that to sink in. The Shoter's daughter frowned, waiting for more. She knew Hirkiv's director, a thick self-centred individual, "unscrupulous" being a flattering label!

Arb watched her, brain whirling as she soaked up his info. He continued, 'When the consortium tried to trace the source of the funds, they found nothing. The credits were legally obtained, all approved by Exchange banks.'

Her face fell; she expected more. 'Arb, you know more than you are telling.'

'No, little one. That's all there is.'

What's he hiding? she wondered. 'Go on, tell me. You know they'll ask for it,' she said, referring to her mother and father. That news would affect their own personal business interests on Hirkiv.

He scratched the sores on his neck then turned and looked at her. He could smell her sweet fragrance as he admired her dainty white face. He turned away, mad at this infernal sickness. He took a deep breath and sighed. 'I think it's all connected. The contracts for blue, the scrap ships, the engines, the Mzimot. Someone powerful is building a fleet.' The smart old trader, riddled with the Anan sickness, had figured The Eight's strategy out. A recognisable plan to anyone who cared to open their mind and look.

She waited until all had left. Looking around the empty Exchange hall, she called her father. 'I have news …' she said.

*

Planet Anan. EPTS: B140576

Pulsing with dark blue light, The Sixth's oval energy mass floated in front of the Shoter. The dark Overlord sensed fear from the man kneeling in front of him. But of what? He had hidden nothing from him, repeating everything his daughter had said. 'You are afraid?'

'Yes, Overlord, I am. It must be The Eight. Only an Overlord would have the resources for such an audacious deception.' He looked at The Sixth, his knees aching.

'Get up. Tell me what you think.'

The Shoter stood, his face wincing with pain. He stretched his sore joints and started to pace up and down. 'I looked into the depths of the Exchange with the Moderator. The transactions are all by a newly formed consortium. Its holders are veiled by layers of financial instruments. The codes and cyphers were all validated by the Exchange banks.'

'Can we access them?'

'Overlord, you know we can't. Gaining access to the deep core of the Exchange is impossible. Your predecessors put those controls in place.'

'I must change that. The contracts for blue, despite what that old and broken trader says, I have to buy them. The old fool knows only half the story. It may not be The Eight; it could be one of the other Overlords who shunned my cause.' The Sixth paused as he checked his own reasoning. A flash of white light heralded his conviction in his read of the situation. 'Buy them now and list them on the Exchange for all to see. It will generate interest among the other Charters and push the price of blue even further.' His energy mass pulsed with purple light. 'Shoter, for me to consolidate my power in the known universe, I must control all the blue that is available on any market. Understand that. Do not let this get away from you. Buy immediately, and any more that are listed.'

Right there, the avaricious Sixth committed to buying The Eight's blue energy, and any more he registered for sale on the Exchange at today's price. The dark entity's drive to control the supply of blue energy overtook financial prudence. Regardless of the power he wielded over the physical world and the corporeal Anan purebreeds, The Sixth would have to pay for that blue in Universal Credits. The Energy Exchange's autonomous banks would demand it – a requisition no Overlord could ignore. The Eight, knowing The Sixth's temperament, had hoped his smart-war strategy would suck the egomaniacal entity in. Far away in a distant galaxy, he didn't know how deep!

*

Fort Leslie, New World. EPTS: B140580

On the New World, lying prostrate on the bed of his pod, a mystified Cylla scrutinised Mack's every move or lack thereof. 'What's wrong with you? If I didn't know you better, I would say you were getting lazy in your old age. But Arie, I do know you better. Something's wrong; you are hiding it from me.'

'No, I am fine. Really, it's just tiredness I feel from time to time,' Mack lied.

'Arie, it's every other day, and you ignore my advances. That's what is so hard to contemplate. Why? I know you were attracted to me when we first met. We were close but when I tried to move it on, you spurned me. As with Janet, you avoided any physical contact.' She gasped and slapped her head with her hand. Slowly, it stroked the side of her pale green face. She stared intently, leaning over him as he lay in the bed.

The purebreed general squirmed under her gaze. 'Cylla, please, please leave now.'

'Arie, Arie, how could you have hidden that from me, after all this time. Your med-chip, what did you do?' She grabbed his shirt and pulled it up. He turned away as she gazed down at the small scar below his right nipple, revealing the depth of his deception. 'O Arie, who did that for you? Is there nothing sacred with you purebreeds? Who did that?'

The game up, he spilt out his long deception. 'It was a doctor, on Anan, a close friend. When I realised what I had, he reprogrammed the chip.'

'Does the Empress know?'

'No.'

'You stupid man. How could you have hidden it? Why did you hide it? Why, Arie? Why?'

'Cylla, I thought, it was—'

Sharp as a knife, the Neredian cut him off. 'In the "early stages". You men! You think you are invincible. That's when it should be treated. There's medicine now. You know that they call it the First Stage Treatment. The FST!' She was shouting now; he turned away as her shrill Neredian voice cut the air around them. 'Arie, why did you not get the human doctor to

treat you? You know there is no such thing as "early stages". Once you have
the Anan sickness, it's there till death. You must get the treatment now.'

Cylla was right. Millennia of interbreeding between the Anan population had diminished the ability to procreate. The Anan sickness had
developed over the last forty thousand orbits, their precious DNA continuing to break down over time. For those stricken by the disease, it attacks
the reproductive organs, then ravages the body until an early painful
death. Mack's hope that he could ride out the "early stage" was a futile
belief shared by many purebreeds. A misguided male belief of "it'll never
happen to me!". The proud, tall and strong general had his invincibility
punched in the gut! His only hope now lay in the First Stage Treatment
developed by the human geneticist Alex Barber, and his lover, the purebreed doctor, Rhea Lupe.

'I can't,' Mack protested.

'Of course, you can,' Cylla insisted.

'No, the only treatment left with us was for Demard. It's still on the
Hela.'

She sat down on the bed beside him, taking his weak hand. 'And why
did you not get the cure before the fleet left, or go back to Earth on the
Hela? I could have done all the work here.'

'No, you need me for the work. And other purebreeds might need
the cure. Besides, I was too tired and I didn't have the strength to watch
Robert and Janet together.'

Tears ran down her face. 'You insult me. It always has to be her, the
human. What has she got that I don't? You won't find her so attractive
when I flay her alive with my tail. Yes, Arie, I will.'

'Please, Cylla. There's no need for that. Janet has no part in this.'

She wiped the tears from her face. 'Arie, what a mess. You are the
Great Protector, General Arie Machai, the Aknar's beast of prey, and
look at you. You can't even look after yourself.' She grabbed him, pulling
him close, burying her head and long mane in his neck. As she sobbed, he
patted her golden scaly back. He could feel her tail falling limp behind her.

'It's not that bad, Cylla. I am prepared for it, and you know, I have
had a long life.'

She sat up. 'But I'm not. I have had feelings for you since we first met on Anan. Then, you spurned me. I got over that. But again, working beside you, you know how I feel about you. We must get the medicine, we must. You shall go to Earth.'

'No, I may not survive the journey. When I first contracted the sickness, as usual, it attacked my reproduction organs. It was slow, and I believed it would be as with most others – a measured onset of the disease over time – concluding with the usual nasty sores visible on our skin. Cylla, that didn't happen. It is a rarer form that attacks the internal organs. It has started with my heart.'

'How long Arie?'

'I don't know?'

'What do we do?' Cylla asked, contemplating that bolt from the sky, a dilemma she never expected. The work unfolded in her mind: projecting production output, certifying the energy quality, writing the blue energy contracts and the final listing of them on the Exchange Servers. Cylla could do most of it herself except for the layered subterfuge. Hiding The Eight's identity, Anan Corp and the Sullivan Parker Charter could only be done by Mack using his Royal Aknar cyphers. Only he could bury that sought-after data and company structure deep inside the house of Aknar's servers at the Exchange. And, Cylla knew, The Sixth would stop at nothing to hunt out that vital info!

Stronger now, Mack continued. 'We go on with the plan. Despite what you think, you need me here. You need my Aknar codes to access the Exchange. And Cylla, there's more I need of you.'

She withdrew from him and looked down at his grey face. 'What more do you want, Arie?'

He looked straight into her green eyes. 'I must take you as my life partner.'

She screamed and her limp tail sprung into life as it whipped above her head. 'You miserable piece of excrement; after all this time, now you ask me. You have no idea how hollow that sounds.'

'Please, Cylla. It's the only way to preserve my Aknar codes and the Anan Corp listing in the Exchange. You will become an Aknar, part of the Royal House of Anan and the proxy of the Protector,' Mack said, his logical thought process overarching any emotion.

'What of your human love? Don't look away – you still have feelings for her. Do you expect us to have a happy Anan threesome?'

'Be reasonable, Cylla; it's beyond me now. Anyway, you know such things are quite legal on Anan,' Mack said, referring to a purebreed polygamy custom. Having more than one wife or husband at the same time, although uncommon, was lawful. Herat, the trader and Cylla's mentor, had such a relationship.

'Arie—' her screams pierced the room. She clenched her hands as her tail whipped above his bed. Her scales glowed with a deep golden hue as she battled to quell her anger.

For the first time, he smiled, then waited for her screams to subside. 'Cylla Ora, from the first time I saw you I wanted you. In the throes of your anger, you are most ravishing. My biggest regret in life is that we can never mate. I will take that heartache to my grave. Now, say yes to my dying demand.'

She grinned back, as her tail came to rest behind her. 'That's the nicest thing you have ever said to me, Arie. Yes. Yes, I will.'

'Thank you, Cylla,' he said, a smile playing across his pale lips. His face changed, a stern look as his brain stepped up a gear. 'Now to business. Time is running out for me. We have amassed a stock of blue and already we've contracts for delivery. The tanks here are full. As soon as the *Monarch* returns, we can refill her tanks from the mining vessel. We need to go on, Cylla. The war depends on our success.'

'You're right,' she agreed. 'Nearly time to recall Sho's ship from the off-world mine …'

After the *Monarch* had departed, the off-world mining had commenced. Borea schooling of Blair and his drill crew, in the use of the alien technology, paid off. The *Maeve* ferried the rigs up to one of the New World's two moons where the Borea were providing more on-site teaching. The lifeless moon, devoid of an atmosphere, proved a fertile training ground for the humans. Soon enough, Blair's drill crews learned a new trade. Dressed in dexterous Anan spacesuits, with climate control and advanced life support, the humans could work in zero atmospheres for near ten hours. Blue flowed thick and fast. Easy pickings, shallow and abundant from the New World's closest moon, where Shona, Blair and their crews were now.

Mack stayed quiet as Cylla recalculated the shipping schedules.

The Neredian peeped up from her terminal, gazing at Mack. 'Arie, you'll go to Earth. It's the only way. To survive the journey, we can put you in an Anan auto-doc,' she said, her voice laced with a steely resolve,

'Cylla, I—'

'Arie, you'll do nothing. You forget, I control ship movements. Somehow, I'll get you to Earth to get your FST. If I'm to be your life partner, I'll fight hard for you to stay alive.'

*

Planet Anan. EPTS: B140600

On Planet Anan, The Sixth luxuriated in the belief that he had replaced The One. Buying every available blue contract listed on the Exchange, he fortified his position in the Anan Galaxy with his troops and warships. To guard his mines and wealth, he left the larger part of his fleet in his Jora and Ragma Galaxies. Those who had accompanied him were a ragtag bunch, without the skill or discipline of the Anan navy. Despite such an impediment, his intergalactic ships had fuel – grav and blue. As the only navy in space, with The Seventh's starships, the Troika controlled all of the known galaxies.

Early in his takeover, some brave souls had challenged The Sixth's rule, making inflammatory speeches in the Council of Anan, calling for the reinstatement of The One and The Eight. The Sixth put that to bed. Summoning three outspoken delegates to his chamber, he turned them to dust. Promptly, dissent evaporated — until now.

Unheard of in Aknar City, riots broke out in front of the Council chambers. All was not well with Theia's cure to the Anan sickness. As The Second had predicted, there were side effects that chilled the purebreeds to their bones. They blamed The Sixth as it was he who had basked in the light of its initial delivery, along with the medicine called the First Stage Treatment.

With the noise of the riots clamouring across the square outside the Council chambers, he summoned his Shoter.

The man cowered before the Overlord's purple energy mass. 'Shoter, you fail me again. The riots, it is not as you foresaw,' boomed The Sixth, the walls shaking from his wrath.

Trembling with fear, the grey-faced Shoter pleaded. 'Overlord, this is not my fault. The treatment was manufactured and tested, exactly as specified. The Anan Medical Council did not gauge the final outcome.' The blame game had started. In all ruling administrations, it was always someone else's fault!

'It was obvious. Did the people not expect some side effects? If you modify DNA, there are consequences. How many are affected?' The Sixth asked.

'One thousand test subjects. Those that have taken it have had their lifespan reduced. About a quarter will now die of old age – they are furious.'

The loss of life had no meaning to The Sixth. Only interested in his image and elevation to becoming The One, he viewed this as an irritation. 'Why do they fume? Ungrateful bipeds, they are. But they must realise Overlords are not gods. There are limits to our science – genetic engineering has grave consequences.' The Sixth paused and his energy mass floated away from the Shoter. As the entity's mind calmed, the flashing light turned to a dark blue.

He spoke again, a softer voice, like a teacher to a bold pupil. 'Do they not understand the difference in that both species' lifespans must be aggregated when mixing purebreed and species-y DNA? Shoter, you purebreeds live an extraordinarily long lifespan. Species-y, with the dominant gene, like most other bipeds, live a shorter life. Do you understand that?'

The Shoter nodded. Unaffected by the cursed sickness, he and his wife had been blessed with a daughter. He felt for those hoping for a cure, and now that hope was dashed. 'Yes, I do,' was his faltering answer, tears streaming down his white face. Despite his ruthless business methods, inside, his heart beat fast – in turmoil at this failure.

The Overlord felt that pain. 'Shoter, the purebreeds must realise there is no gain without some loss. Their lifespan will be reduced, and yes, the older of your race may die if they take that cure. Did you consult the Empress?' he asked, curious about how Theia would take this.

'Yes. However, she has forgotten all of what happened during the development. Overlord, she is pleased it works and is trying to quell the dissent. But people won't listen.'

'They blame me for this. I should never have allowed it. Stop its use; limit treatment to the FST,' The Sixth said.

There had to be a compromise. Again, the Shoter pleaded. 'Overlord, we will fade away if you don't allow us the treatment. We can limit the cure to the young, those who will benefit from a long healthy life. As a publicity campaign, my daughter will take it. Please, Overlord, please.' The intensity of his feelings for his daughter's wellbeing oozed from his mind. That she could have a shorter life, guaranteed free of the sickness, meant everything to him.

His feelings pierced the Overlord's mind and The Sixth relented. It made no difference to him either way. All he wanted was an obedient following. His gesture could help to placate his serving mortals and it would give Theia Aknar a purpose. Keep her on side and busy.

'So be it,' he said in the same soft voice. 'It will take time, Shoter. You might see out your lifetime unaffected.' Then, The Sixth's voice rose with each syllable, until he was roaring. 'Now, that is the end of the matter. All my resources are to concentrate on consolidating my power base. There will be no more distractions, do you understand?'

The Shoter cowered down under the loud onslaught. 'Yes. Yes, I do.'

A more pressing matter burned The Sixth's mind. The Ninth's silence after their last talk was deafening. He hungered for word of the fleet. 'What news of the ceirim?' The Sixth blurted out, the harsh tone conveying the importance of the question.

The Shoter breathed a sigh of relief; he had that answer. 'We received a data burst. The fleet made safe passage. They should arrive at species-y home world soon.'

The Sixth floated up in the chamber, his excitement flashing with bright white and blue light. 'A good outcome, Shoter. Yes, you have done well planning that.'

CHAPTER THIRTY-FOUR

In-Fold Navigation

Guiding a starship through folded space is the biggest challenge a navigator will face. The preferred option, if available, is to preprogram the nav-com with the entrance and exit coordinates. The direction is set, the blue drive generates an astronomical pulse, space folds and the ship travels along the predetermined route to the planned exit point. This method is used for travel along the defined shipping routes. However, over such vast distances, with everchanging cosmic tides and gravitational influences, a starship can wander off course. The navigator must verify the starship's passage against a phenomenon called in-fold drift at regular intervals.

As complexity and distance increase, the greater the need for frequent navigational checks. To ensure a vessel is not pulled off course by in-fold drift, new lengthy complicated intergalactic itineraries require more than one navigator. In particular, when traversing uncharted regions where cosmic and gravitational forces are not known.

‹ Principals of Navigation from: Fundamentals of intergalactic travel. Zaval Borea

*

The Ninth's Fleet, Milky Way Galaxy, 16th January 2028

Faster than light speed, The Ninth's invading armada of seven raced towards Earth. The fatal fleet was packed full with extinction weapons – the like, never assembled before in known galactic time.

Aboard the command ship, the *Chad*, the fleet's navigator took a long drink of bawrak, a synthetic drug that rekindles the purebreed navigator's failing abilities — another symptom of the dreaded sickness. Clutching his blue crystal, he replotted the course trajectory. The drug rushed to his brain, exploding his senses as he took a deep breath, the oxygen feeding the rush from the stimulant. So *far from our home world. I can't get this wrong*, he thought, as he closed his eyes and scanned space beyond. *There it is, their planet*, he thought, as he focused on a blue world in a solar system close to the planned exit in deep space. 'Captain, we're here. Now, we need to leave folded space.'

'Do it,' Bardek shouted to his crew. 'Prepare for exit. Comms, flash coordinates to the fleet. And you,' he said,' looking at a young purebreed, 'go get the Overlord. Engineering, ready the cloak. Comms, advise all ships. I want cloaks up as soon as we exit the fold.'

The seven ships generated a magnificent burst of white light as they exited folded space. But like a wisp, the fleet immediately disappeared into the veil of concealment their cloaks generated, invisible – they supposed – to the prying eyes of Earth's primitive optical and electromagnetic telescopes.

The Ninth floated over beside Bardek. 'You made good time, Captain. We are finally here.'

'Overlord, we are cloaked and alone. There are no other ships in this quadrant of space. Comms, scan the planet for purebreed technology,' Bardek ordered.

'Is it possible, he is not here? Where is The Eight? I thought he would be here,' The Ninth said.

'That's nothing to complain about. We move on. Navigation, plot a course for the planet's moon,' Bardek said. 'We'll hide the fleet on its dark side.'

Time ticked on, the bridge clock reminding them how critical these first segments would be. The colourful Javonian comms officer finally came up for air. Purple hands brushed her red hair back as she turned towards Bardek.

Her soft female voice calmed their tension. 'Captain, no sign of purebreed tech.' Welcome words to the rest of the crew. 'However, I see traces of energy bursts coming from the planet. They look like explosions.'

'Artificial or natural?' Bardek asked.

She shook her head. 'We're not close enough to decipher.'

Bardek turned to face The Ninth. 'Overlord, what do—'

'There are billions of them,' he said, his voice weak and garbled. 'I never expected so many.'

The impatient Ninth had cast his ethereal mind out to explore species-y's home. Flashing past three dark outer planets, then a large one surrounded with rings – Saturn. Past another. Then a desolate red rock – Mars. Until his ethereal mind arrived at a blue planet teeming with life – Earth. Without stopping, his consciousness flooded Earth's biped inhabitants for any trace of The Eight. He found it, but the young inexperienced Overlord found far more than he bargained for.

Billions of free-spirited brains, filled with emotion, images and information. Dark pictures of death: wars, genocide, holocausts, starvation, and the destruction of the planet. The images contained within each person – man's inhumanity to man – captured by Earth's population, taught to the young at school, burned into every brain, overwhelmed the ethereal mind of The Ninth. And he found far worse when touching the minds of criminals, corrupt politicians and warmongers – pure butchery he had never experienced before. A darkness – the evil that had stalked Earth's inhabitants throughout the ages – sapped his strength. The perpetrators of all that killing shocked The Ninth. The entity met those foul minds, a dichotomy he hadn't expected. Pure evil that trumped everything he'd seen before.

Setting out from the Jora Galaxy, The Ninth had hatched a simple strategy to expunge species-y. Expecting an average biped population of between one to two billion, he planned to disperse half of the sixteen thousand ceirim in the first wave of the planet's invasion. The initial ceirim attack would gorge themselves on species-y, starting the cull. After that – if needed – extinction weapons, launched from orbit at the main population centres, would augment the first cull. Finally, the remaining eight thousand ceirim would invade the planet to "mop up" any survivors.

The only problem The Ninth foresaw, would be the presence of The Eight – his absence alleviated that. The planet's infestation by so many bipeds had never been considered. Had he been told that, he wouldn't have believed it, replying, "Impossible!". Unfamiliar with carbon life forms, the ethereal entity found Earth's environment wholly alien. Yet he could see a living planet was dying under the onslaught of its people, something he also hadn't expected. *They would want to leave it, seek out another world to populate and grow their kind*, he realised.

On the bridge of the *Chad*, in that same weak and garbled voice, The Ninth spoke. 'Get Kochtos and the geneticists. We do not have enough ceirim to expunge the population.'

The Ninth's mind wandered. *Eight, what are you up to? What manner of plague is this that you unleash?* He spoke again, the Overlord's voice fading fast. 'Bardek, the energy signatures are explosions. They fight amongst themselves; a war rages between two different factions.' To the horror of the crew, his energy mass turned green as he tried to extricate his ethereal mind from Earth's populace, the condemned coming close to executing their executioner. Overwhelmed by the alien emotions, with the darkness and horror that filled the planet's billions of brains, the evil entity's life force started to slip away.

'Overlord, Overlord, what's wrong?' Bardek screamed. He turned to his crew. 'Quick, get a spare tank of blue from his quarters. Hurry, we're losing him,' he roared, as they ran from the bridge.

Within minutes, they returned. Bardek grabbed the tank. Ignoring the contamination risk, the brave captain poured the blue straight into The Ninth's energy mass. He stood back and watched. The Ninth's energy mass flickered from green to blue and back again. With renewed energy, the young Overlord's mind burst free from the Earth's human population, for that is what they call themselves, he now knew. Racing back to rejoin his ethereal consciousness on the bridge of the *Chad*, The Ninth realised how badly they had underestimated the power of The Eight. As the two parts of his mind coalesced, his energy flashed with bright blue light. He was back, safe, thanks to Bardek's efforts.

'Thank you, Captain. I looked inside the minds of the humans – that is what they call themselves. Their violent thoughts overwhelmed me. They are driven to self-destruction. The Sixth is right, we must expunge them. There is blackness in some of their minds which I have not seen before in bipeds,' The Ninth said.

'Even in the ceirim?' Bardek asked.

'I never look into the mind of Kochtos. Besides, the ceirim is our creation, made for a purpose. I'm not sure why The Eight made humans. I see evidence of his visit – he was there – but now he's gone, and I cannot find where. But the human's petty war, as they fight amongst themselves, will give us an advantage.'

Together with the geneticists, the large foul-smelling Kochtos arrived on the bridge. The young purebreed sent to get him, dodged his every move and the arc of his long thin black spikes as he walked.

An aura of horror followed Kochtos into the bridge – like the creature didn't belong to a natural world. The ceirim's leader approached. Bardek backed off, his nose wrinkling at the smell. The black biped's vicious claws were hanging down from long arms, clenched ready for a kill. A cruel grin played across the black jaws, packed with thin sharp teeth and leering at the purebreeds. A suitable pause to establish his primacy, then Kochtos knelt before The Ninth. 'Overlord, I am ready.'

'Kochtos, there are more of these humans than we expected; that's what they call themselves. Too many for your numbers; you will not be able to expunge them all.'

'Why so? How many?'

'Billions. I would estimate near to seven to nine billion; there are too many for an accurate count!' The Ninth said.

He growled and coughed. 'Thank you, Overlord. We thought we were coming for a meal; now you serve us the feast of all feasts.'

'Enough, Kochtos. Remember, we have an objective to fulfil. Geneticist, The Sixth told me Kochtos is the only one who can propagate the ceirim DNA, transforming bipeds. Can we change that?'

'No, Overlord. Not here on this ship.'

'The numbers we have just won't work. I do not have enough blue, nor am I inclined to waste it expunging the population. There must be another way.'

The geneticist walked over to the comms console. 'Let me see a map of their population distribution.' As the ship sped towards Earth, he poured over the scans of the planet, finally turning to The Ninth. 'There is a solution. We use Kochtos as we made him and centre our first operation here at this location. Let me explain ...'

*

Hela base, Australian Desert, 17th January 2028

At Hela base in Australia, inside the operations centre, a stressed Robert paced up and down. Disillusioned with humankind, he had returned from the messy meeting in the United Nations. The upbeat politician, Harold, had tried to help him get over the disappointment.

'That's always the way it is, Robert; political change takes time. Two steps forward and one back. You think you are there and then it all falls apart,' he had told him.

It didn't work. The frustration of it all clawed at Robert's mind. After the assembly, he lost hope in Earth's global leader's ability to deal with the crisis that faced them now.

Calming his mind, Robert sat down at an oval meeting table with Janet, Harold, Matt and Quriel. Verteg, standing in front of a big screen, started the stark briefing on what was coming. In a soft voice, she explained the sequence of events. The alarm was raised six hours ago when the Anan Corp satellites detected a flash in deep space – the signature of a fleet leaving a fold.

'They are here, seven cloaked ships, making their way through the solar system,' Verteg said, as she pointed to a navigation plot, projected on the screen.

'If they're cloaked, how can you see them?' Robert asked.

'I modified Anan Corp's long-range satellites; reprogrammed beam technology with Borea codes.'

Robert looked puzzled. 'I don't understand, Verteg. How's that possible?'

'Robert, our family has the technology we inherited from Grandfather. You all know his business now. He had acquired codes for the most advanced scanning and cloaking tech available. Along with your people, I remodulated all Anan Corp satellites with Borea software. We see everything now. And the underlying tech is Earth-based, so all they see is primitive Earthly comms-satellites.'

While Robert and Harold were in Geneva, Verteg had taken a shuttle up into orbit, enhancing the human technology to host the Borea mods. Meanwhile, back at the base, the McKinnons reinvented the old cover they had used to hide the *Hela* on its first visit to Earth. It morphed into a shantytown, covering the three ships under a lattice of scaffold and tarps. To that, Borea techs fitted their legendary cloak generators, hiding everything from plain sight and any incoming Anan scanning tech – a Verteg burst of initiative to protect the Borea's new home.

Robert stood back up and started pacing again, his mind awash with the worst nightmare imaginable. The gravity of what they were seeing was not lost on the silent group of six.

The sandy-haired Scotsman broke the ominous silence. 'What are they doing here?' he asked. 'What do you know about them and what weapons will they have?' he asked Verteg and Quriel.

'They look like intergalactic troop transporters,' Quriel replied.

'How many do they hold?'

'From their size, I guess about fifteen thousand.'

'What? Is that all? Quriel, Verteg, we're missing something. They're not here for an invasion. Fifteen thousand, no, you're wrong. They wouldn't come all this way, burning blue, for nothing.'

A pensive Quriel stroked his white face, then answered. 'Robert, I believe they're looking for the source of the blue. The Sixth will not rest until he finds it.'

Robert shook his head. 'That doesn't make sense. How could The Sixth know about the blue? And if he did, he'd go to the New World. And why seven ships? If they were looking for the blue, they'd dispatch smaller scout ships first.'

'Maybe they did and you missed them.'

Robert shook his head, 'I don't believe we did, Quriel. Matt maintained round the clock watches. They didn't miss you when your fleet arrived. What weapons do these transporters have?'

'Grav missiles and probably enhanced grav powerbombs; they are similar devices to your fusion bombs. It's unlikely they'll use them,' Quriel said.

'Why?' a sceptical Robert asked. So far, Quriel's read of the situation defied logic. Not what Robert expected from a captain in the Aknar military.

'The Overlords haven't used those weapons in millennia. They usually use their own power.'

'Quriel, again, that doesn't make sense. Blue is scarce. Let's assume there's an Overlord on board looking for more precious energy. He wouldn't waste what he has on us. We learned that from The Eight. I think those ships are a danger to Earth; we have to assume that.'

Verteg held a green hand up for them to stop. *We've said enough, and we really don't know what or who those ships belong to*, she thought. 'You may be right, Robert. But, unless we expose ourselves, we have no way of knowing if there's an Overlord on board. If there is one, I doubt it'll be The Sixth. It will be The Seventh or more likely, The Ninth.'

'Why The Ninth?'

'He's dispensable, one of the youngest and least powerful of them all. The Sixth can do without him.'

Robert shook his head in exasperation, his long hair covering his face as he closed his eyes. 'So what do we do?'

'We do nothing, Robert. Stay hidden until we know what they are doing. We did a good job cloaking the three ships and the base. Their scans can't penetrate our cloak. With Matt's help, I've hidden everything. We shouldn't do anything to compromise that.'

Robert nodded. Sound advice from the intuitive Pilot. 'Okay, Verteg. We wait and watch. Harold, will you brief Admiral Whyte. I guess he'll let our allies know – if they'll listen. They're all full of this futile pissing contest between politicians. World War III they call it, while an intergalactic battle for supremacy among the most powerful beings in the universe reaches Earth,' he said, as he walked out of the room.

*

New World, Moon 1, Mining Vessel.
EPTS: B140687

On the larger of the New World's two moons, Blair walked around their mining vessel, checking all was stowed for their well-earned rest period. He smiled as he looked at their strange ship with its accommodation module mounted behind, its mechanised mining clutch glinting in the failing sunlight. He never tired of this view and the spectacle of their New World from this craggy moon. He waited for the planet to rise, dominating the sky as it gradually blotted out the sun. The show over, turning his back on the myriad of colours, he stepped into the airlock.

Instead of de-garbing in the cargo bay, Blair went straight to their cramped quarters. Unlatching the hood of his spacesuit, he peeled it back. The big man looked over to Shona, the love of his life, still working at the small data terminal.

'What's for dinner?' he asked, placing the helmet on the floor beside their bed.

His wife looked up from the terminal. 'Oh, you're back safe, are you? Well, that's good to know. Hungry as well; same as ever. I suppose you think I've nothing better to do than feed you and your crew. Its dried protein and fibre powder mixed with reclaimed water.'

'That stuff tastes like shite.'

'Blair, if you can do better, you know where the galley is. How'd the job go?'

'Good, really good. Team's well-tuned into the space stuff as well. Shona, this moon is thick with blue. There are nodes of the stuff buried just below the surface. How'd you do with the reports and the finance?' he asked, as he sat down beside her, resting a big lazy hand on her shoulder.

She looked at him, his face pale and tired from the day's mining. 'Based on the survey you did, I've sent Cylla the specs and energy load we'll mine here. The detail she wants is a pain in the arse. I gather it's to do with the sale of the stuff – the contracts she issues. Tanks on the New World are full, so we'll have to hold what we mine here on the rig.'

'That'll slow us down. What about the income? You calculate that yet?'

'We're making headway. We made a tidy profit on the last two cargos, even after we paid the crew bonus.'

'Pity we still have to pay for the air.'

She shook her head, her hair falling across her face. She brushed it back and scowled at him. 'Will you shut it about that. Life support's one of the highest costs. What did you expect working in space?'

'You sold us out.'

'I didn't; you never listen. I told you we made a tidy profit.'

'What about buying a rig of our own?'

'I looked over that stuff Cylla sent on. They have a way to do that; it's based on a complex lease and buy system. We'd borrow the credits and—'

'Like at home, Shona, buying on "the never, never". We're no falling for that trick.'

'For once, grumpy, you're listening. Aye, it's just like that. We'd struggle to make the payments. Leasing this rig from the Borea works best.'

'We need another rig, and for the bairn's sake, we should own our own.' He moved towards her and, picking her up in his arms, placed her on the bed.

'Oh, is it nae a bit early for that?' she said, grinning at him.

'It's no that, I need some room. I got you something,' he said, as he moved the table out of the way. She watched as he struggled out of his spacesuit. She admired her husband's muscle-clad frame and the bulge in his crotch as he stood tall in his tight undergarments.

He reached into the front pouch of the suit and took out a bag. Opening it, he placed a small purse on the table. 'Look at that,' he said, as he emptied it out.

Shona gasped as the uncut diamonds fell out. There was nothing smaller than a carat. She reached out to touch them.

'They're no for you.'

She punched him on the shoulder. 'Who are they for, then? Hae you a mistress?'

'You know I don't. Where would I get the time for another woman? Isn't one enough? Here, these are for you,' he said, mirth dancing with his brogue, while he pulled another purse out of the bag. He tipped them out on the table.

'Holy shit,' she shouted, as three large blue diamonds bounced across the table. She reached out and grabbed Blair. He lifted her up and kissed her. They clung together as they both looked at the haul on the table. She sat back down on the bed. With tears streaming down her face, she put her hand on her swollen belly. 'That's our family's future, Blair. Where'd they come from?'

'Inside the crystal nodes we mined on this moon,' he said, pointing out the window to the bleak landscape outside. 'We always knew they'd be a by-product of the mining. They're hard to find, but once we knew where and what to look for, we got them.' He paused as they both gazed at the biggest payday they'd ever had.

'That old Borea geezer explained me how to get them,' he said, referring to the Borea elder who had helped teach them off-world mining. 'They're ours to keep as well. You, my financial wiz, had that written into the contract. I gave some diamonds to the crew as well. Shona, the blue stones are yours. You keep them. If anything goes wrong, they're your, and the bairn's, get-out money. You can even rent them to Tom and Niamh. Over time, we'll build up a stock of them. They'll be our family's core wealth. The plain ones we use as a down payment for a rig of our own.'

'It's finally happening, all that hard work.'

'It is, Shona. It wouldn't have happened without your brains.'

'What's that about?' she said, as the terminal burst into life with an incoming message. She bent over to read it. 'Cylla wants us back with whatever blue we have. *Monarch's* due in for a refuel. The *Maeve's* on the way to pick us and the blue up. We've to top *Monarch* up from her on the ground – ship-to-ship transfer.'

'For once, she makes sense. Empty our tanks and leave room for more mining. What about some food before we rig down and take off from this rock?'

'All right, after giving me this,' she said, lifting up the blue diamonds, 'I'll heat you some meat pulse. Kept it for a special occasion.'

He grinned. 'Wow, warm meat pulse.'

'If you dinnae like it, stick it where the sun don't shine, you grumpy sourpuss,' she said, still smiling as she turned the blue stones over and over.

CHAPTER THIRTY-FIVE

CNS Headlines. Aliens are Back

Anan Corp's Senior Project Manager, Robert Leslie announced, "Yesterday, an unknown alien fleet of seven starships exited "folded space" at the edge of our solar system. He claims the fleet is a clear and present danger to the human race. As yet, Anan Corp has not made contact with the ships.

A group of satellites launched by Anan Corp "to enhance Earth's defence capabilities by scanning deep space", noticed the spatial anomaly created by the arrival of the starships.

Others claim the satellites are actually sophisticated spy satellites used to prospect for valuable geological deposits in the planet's crust, such as gold and heavy metals.

N.A.S.A. has dismissed Mr Leslie's comments out of hand, claiming it is fake news based on unsound science developed for private use.

*‹ Extract from: **Continental News Services. Good Morning Planet Earth***

*

Ninth's Fleet, Earth Solar System, 18th January 2028

NEVER BEFORE HAD EARTH'S SOLAR system seen such a fleet of starships – a milestone the planet would rather have missed. Their journey followed in the Hela base, the occupants wondering what fate awaited humankind. The suspense stretched out, as Bardek's fleet disappeared, hiding on the dark side of the planet's moon.

In its cocooning shadow, preparing for the first alien invasion of Earth, The Ninth ordered the awakening of half the ceirim. Their resurrection from the cryo-tubes had been planned during the flight from Natok. Every detail was plotted to the last degree. Nothing was left to chance – from their revival to getting eight thousand ceirim strapped into the transporters. Every part scrutinised by The Ninth from the bridge of the *Chad*, until the seven inter-planet vessels depart their mother ships. It was a personal achievement for the young Overlord, his masterplan for the annihilation of Earth's population in motion.

Inside their base in Australia, oblivious to the approaching demons, Robert and his team of human and Anans watched the seven smaller ships reappear. Pandemonium broke out in the operations' centre as powerless, they watched the fleet make its way to Earth. Robert made frantic calls across the globe, but except for a few close allies, none would listen.

*

Planet Earth, India, 18th January 2028

In a small village on the Indian subcontinent, a lively group celebrated a wedding. The young groom, enthralled by his beautiful wife – his childhood sweetheart – couldn't believe his luck. The couple's parents, village neighbours, knowing their children would be happy had arranged this marriage. The wedding guests, in bright, colourful clothes, marvelled at how stunning the bride looked. The young bride, engrossed in her happy day, danced with gay abandon, soaking up the loving gaze of her groom. Guests danced and feasted while young children ran about chasing each other. The old scolded the young: "Don't touch, mind your manners, stop running about!". Courting males blustered and the females blushed. The wedding gushed with high spirits – those happy human emotions people around the globe luxuriate in during such merrymaking.

That night, the young man and his bride retired to a small house at the edge of the village. They were delighted, for they had earned enough to buy this castle. Their home – bright and new – where they would live and love together and grow their own family. Clothes fell to the floor and locked in a hungry passionate embrace, the naked couple fell into their small bed ...

*

Strapped into his seat on the leading vessel, Kochtos licked his lips. His brain was in overdrive; he had never dared hope such an opportunity could present itself to his kind again. They had escaped an extinction order from The One, all due to the benevolence of The Sixth. Despite broken promises, under The Ninth's control, the ceirim awakened again.

An ecstatic Kochtos turned to his close companions, lieutenants in his army of death. 'My stomach grumbles for a good feed.'

Back-slapping and guffawing at their leader's comment, the lieutenant's mirth infected the others on the ship. Pretty soon, all eight thousand ceirim cackled with laughter as the seven cloaked transporters made their way to Earth. Watching the blue planet get closer, their hunger increased. Thoughts of their first feeding frenzy, in such a long time, heightened their anticipation. Hungry growls permeated the cockpits, disturbing the purebreed pilot's concentration. Following a slow descent through the atmosphere, and buffeted by wind and cloud, the seven cylinder-shaped ships touched down. Dense jungle vegetation flattened like cardboard, beneath the weight of the alien transporters. Cloaked from Earth's primitive warning systems, no government noticed the first alien invasion of Earth. Most had ignored Robert's alert, dismissing it as "fake news" and scaremongering. What they couldn't see, they wouldn't believe – it was as simple as that. Meanwhile, in the dead of night, in a dense jungle in the Indian subcontinent, the ceirim prepared to taste human flesh.

The doors on Kochtos's ship opened and the monsters rushed out. No need for directions, they sniffed the air and, like wisps in the night, ran through the jungle towards the nearest village. All living things, sensing death, fled before them, leaving a dreadful stillness in the surrounding lands. Without a sound, Kochtos's group encircled the first village they came upon. Hiding at the jungle boundary they waited, drinking in the sweet human sounds emitting from the sleeping town – lifegiving breaths, inhaling and exhaling.

*

Holding her in his arms, the young man lay beside his naked wife. His heart still beat fast in his chest from her intoxicating smell, the warmth of her body and the memory of their recent lovemaking – pure ecstasy. He was loath to leave her, but another sensation tapped his brain – pressure on his bladder; he needed a piss! Bit by bit, he extricated himself from his lover; she groaned and turned, her pert, brown breasts rubbing against his chest. He paused then reluctantly turned his torso away from her. He sat up, without a sound, putting his feet on the floor and stood up. He wrapped a sarong around his waist and padded out of the house – the silence was deafening. *Where's the jungle noise?* he wondered. Fear gripped his heart as step by step he walked across the flat ground outside their hut to the jungle's edge. A foul stench, like death warmed up, punched his nose. *What the hell's that?* he wondered. As if a celestial curtain had opened, the silver moon appeared from behind a cloud. A dim white light played across the village clearing, illuminating the jungle's edge, and that living hell – Kochtos and his death squad!

The young man tried to scream. Fear froze his vocal cords; not a sound came out. His mind wanted to send him back to save his love. Thoughts of her, images of her beauty filled every part of his brain. Evil black eyes locked on his own. The young man couldn't believe what was in front of him – a creature from the depths of his worst nightmares. A monster, about two metres tall, with long thin black spikes growing out from its hide. The thing's neck bristled with more spikes. Dark eyes peered out from the round, feature-less head. Small dimples on the side were all that showed of its ear canal.

Kochtos opened his large mouth, exposing his teeth – sharp, steel-like barbs filled the human's eyes. The young man, minutes ago, filled with the ultimate human joy of love, realised his life was over. He never felt the pain as Kochtos's claw grabbed his arm in a vice-like grip. Rooted to the spot, fear coursing through his trembling body, the young man's bladder let go. Warm piss ran down his legs.

With his other arm, Kochtos stripped a piece of piss-stained flesh off the young man's leg, sharp talons slicing it from the bone, red blood spurting out as Kochtos nicked an artery. He tasted the human meat and smiled, razor-sharp teeth glistening in the moonlight. Succulent, sweet and tender – it was a long time since such a delicious morsel had passed his lips. Unable to comprehend such horror, the young man fainted. Holding the limp human in one claw, Kochtos plunged the other into the man's chest. The black talon closed around the beating heart, and with one tug, Kochtos ripped it from the dead human body. Dripping with red blood, the ceirim threw the still-beating heart into his mouth, savouring the taste of this delicacy. He licked his lips then, in a feeding frenzy, pulled the human body apart, limb by limb, and gorged on it. While Kochtos indulged himself, like a wave of blackness, his cohort flooded by, hurling headlong into the village.

Seconds later, human screams laced with terror, pierced the stillness. Evil demons appeared from the darkness, dragging the villagers from their beds. None escaped. Those who tried to run were quickly dispatched into the oblivion of death by sharp claws. The ceirim gorged themselves, pulling live people apart, limb by limb. Razor-like teeth shredded flesh and sinew from the bone, every morsel greedily consumed. Crying and wailing parents watched their children held up by the legs and eaten whole. Fights broke out between competing monsters, the poor humans ripped in two by the rivals. Blood and guts spilt out onto the once clean village ground. Drains ran red with blood, some of the monsters sitting by the easy pickings, drinking the precious human life-sustaining fluid. The horror of the night exceeded anything the villagers could ever imagine.

Under Kochtos's and his lieutenants' direction, half the screaming villagers were corralled – alive – in the town centre. They were to fulfil a particular purpose – the first test of the lead geneticist's "solution" to Earth's overpopulation.

In time past, the ravenous DNA of the original ceirim contaminated their victims, mutating the unfortunate target into another ceirim. And so on, until a living, breeding mass of evil black beings emerged, finally feeding on themselves, appeasing their insatiable appetite. The uncontrollable weapon contaminated the target population, transformed it and consumed itself, the "uncontrollable" nature of the thing, its only flaw. The Sixth's Master Geneticist's research changed that. He had altered the DNA of the last remaining sixteen thousand ceirim. By inhibiting their procreative element's ability to transform others, the geneticist stopped the uncontrolled expansion, and the all-consuming orgy of feeding, of the species, on themselves.

The Master had enhanced Kochtos as well, making him the ceirim's androgynous leader. The only one with the ability to introduce the transforming DNA to a host, Kochtos could replace the aged or the injured and breed new armies for The Sixth. It was this ability the Master Geneticist's younger pupil hoped to test – produce more soldiers of death from the human captives.

Floating above the village on a grav platform, the Master's pupil, leading this group of genetics, eagerly watched the proceedings below. His team weren't as keen; some cowered down, closing their eyes and ears at the horror unfolding below. Some wondered, *who would create such evil?* But, deep down they knew. Overlords in the past had done this, and their boss The Sixth perpetrated it. Sensing their disquiet, their leader turned towards them. His silent gaze froze molten lava – they withered under it. Nothing to say, he turned back to record the ceirim's debut. All that interested him was the science; if this worked, his star would shine – with the trappings of a successful mission.

For his glorious – post carnage – finale, Kochtos walked among the living human captives, clawing at their flesh and covering them with his puke and bile. The voracious DNA of the ceirim erupted inside the captured villagers. Their epidermis changed from soft human skin to the sharp black spines of the ceirim. Human hands turned into claws, mouths erupted with sharp teeth. Starting at the feet, working its way up the body to the head, the transformation – human to ceirim – completed in seconds.

Whimpering and crying no more, the changelings howled with hunger, snapping at each other, trying to eat anything in front of them. Kochtos's lieutenants tossed the remains of those they had killed into the cauldron of evil. Ravenous and howling, the heaving black mass of ceirim fell on the fresh meat, never realising it was their neighbours, friends and family who they consumed. Barbarism flourished as another crop of ceirim evolved. The geneticist's "solution" worked; more evil for Kochtos's army.

After they had eaten their fill, Kochtos relaxed and sat beside his lieutenants. 'I will enjoy this,' he said to his trusty followers, 'and there's a whole planet of them. Pity we have to expunge them all; it would make a good home planet to live and gorge ourselves on.'

The geneticist's grav platform landed in front of them. Dressed in biohazard suits, the purebreeds interrupted the group's post-feeding euphoria.

Kochtos called out to the lead geneticists. 'You are sure this will work?' A burning question, for if it didn't, The Sixth would cause more trouble than it was worth.

The lead nodded. 'Kochtos, it will. But I need as much of your body fluid as you can give. Gorge on the humans then regurgitate your DNA in your fluids and waste. We will mix it with an accelerant and spread it over the greater population. Before they know what has hit them, there will be millions of your species here on this subcontinent.'

Kochtos's closest friend and lieutenant whispered in his ear. 'Lord, they have heavy weapons. Once they realise what we are, humans will kill us.'

'We move amongst them, change half and eat half. They won't attack their own species. You'll see, I'm right about that. We go at night until we reach a critical mass; once we have sufficient numbers, they cannot stop us. Stick to the plan. We will prevail. Soon I change continents. You will have an army here to work with,' Kochtos reassured him.

By morning, the countryside reeked with death as Kochtos's army worked its way from town to town. Daylight signalled rest, and the now disciplined army stopped, hiding in the undergrowth. The stop enabled the geneticists to harvest the all-important changing DNA from Kochtos. In a field laboratory on a transporter – combined with an accelerant – the foul substance converted into a biological weapon. The lead geneticist's "solution" was now in play!

*

Daylight brought tales of demons and black monsters to Delhi. The army dismissed such claims as "the people's imagination playing tricks in the night". Still, taking no chances, a conscientious general dispatched a platoon to investigate. Day two of the invasion brought more tales of monsters, and to the general's dismay, all contact with his platoon disappeared. He left Delhi, leading a company of his best soldiers, an airborne strike team of two hundred.

They met with the ceirim at sunset, horror coursing through the veins of every human warrior, including their general. Duty called and the vanguard of the Indian army responded. Wave after wave of choppers attacked the ceirim. Fifty-calibre bullets emptied at the black monsters. The brave attack failed, bullets bouncing off the ceirim's armoured hide. The general wouldn't relent, adopting a scorched-earth policy by setting fire to the areas occupied by the ceirim. Shocked, the general and his airborne troops watched as hordes of ceirim rushed out from the flames, engulfing their ground support.

Aerial bombing yielded some success – the close quarter explosions dismembered the ceirim. Buoyed by the realisation that they could blow their enemy apart, the general tried to copy these tactics in the field with heavy weapons fire. A battalion mobilised, bringing heavy armaments and mortar fire to the ceirim frontline. Watching from above on the cloaked alien ship, the geneticist sprayed the ceirim-changing DNA – his biological weapon – at the troops on the ground. The general's success was short-lived. His forces were engulfed by the life-changing alien DNA sprayed down from the cloaked ships above. Nothing could stop the ceirim's advance.

*

Three days after their landing, working through the night, still harried by the Indian army, the ceirim made their way towards Delhi – a city of twenty-three million people. From cloaked ships, the geneticists sprayed Kochtos's DNA on the population. Before the world realised what was happening, the purebreed geneticists had spread the fatal ceirim DNA over millions. Four days after the landing, the world's governments took the news reports filtering out from India seriously. "A plague of Biblical proportion is unfolding on Earth", catchy headlines spouted.

Robert's team tried monitoring the situation but it was difficult to see what was actually happening on the ground, inside the jungle at night.

No one news agency could describe what had occurred; it was so bizarre, they couldn't understand it. Until a video feed, recovered from a smartphone, showed a healthy man, of five food eight, metamorphose into something from a horror movie. His hands turned into claws, then his skin changed to a black leathery substance sprouting thick black spikes that covered his whole body. But it was the change of the head that caused the most distress – it was the last to go. The expression on the man's face showed to all that he recognised what was happening, as he looked down at his body, transforming before his very eyes. Then the black epidermis covered his head and face, his mouth erupted with a set of small razor-sharp teeth – transformation to ceirim was complete. Black eyes stared at the camera, shaking with fear, its operator, frozen by the gaze of the black monster – who grinned and pounced. The picture faded as a cloud of blood erupted, covering the camera lens.

CHAPTER THIRTY-SIX

Off-World Mining

The core tool for blue mining on inhospitable asteroids, moons or planets that do not support life (commonly called off-world mining), is a Mobile Life-Sustaining Extraction Rig.

The machine comes in two parts: the life-support module (LSM) and the drilling and services module (DSM). The DSM houses the power plant, life-support services, grav engines and a flight/control cockpit. The LSM houses a pressurised accommodation block for the crew, emergency power pack and an ancillary grav engine. The two units mate into one mobile vehicle capable of limited low-orbit flight. A continuous track propulsion system mounted on the undercarriage of the modules provides local, site-to-site, mobility.

As with a terrestrial rig, the method is the same: break ground with the grab arm and recover blue energy from below-ground crystal nodes with the drill. Lack of atmosphere may aggravate pressure containment. Use an enhanced packer element, change more frequently and reduce penetration rates. Extraction in hazardous atmospheres will need additional protective measures. All personnel require specialist non-life sustaining or hazardous environment training.

‹ *An Introduction: Off-World Blue Extraction. Zaval Borea*

*

Fort Leslie, New World – The Monarch.
EPTS: B140748

PARKING THE PACKAGE OF FOUR ships in orbit around the New World, Siba set a course for Fort Leslie. The colonists came out to watch the

Monarch return. They never tired of watching this strange vessel, bristling with armaments, as it flew in low over the sea towards their space dock. Hovering over the landing pad, grav engines humming with raw energy, like a feather the ship touched down on its bow-fin and the two after legs. Like a bird of prey ready to pounce, the bow of this lethal starship faced the colony. Clouds of dust from the dry sand billowed around, adding to the spectacle. The engines shut down, the sound dying off. Then there was a loud metallic clunk as the steel-pinned docking locks sealed the engines grav ports closed. The dust clouds dissipated and a stillness descended, followed by a big welcoming cheer from the colonists.

The return of the *Monarch* represented a pivotal point in their lives. Gossip flowed through the crowd. "Yes, I heard The Eight is onboard. Got it from a friend in the ops centre. Supposed to be a successful mission." And the rumour mill wasn't still either. "There's supposed to be over a hundred new aliens on board as well!" An exaggeration, blown out of proportion.

A successful mission: more grav for the colony, four more ships, engines and parts for the war effort. But it was the rescue of the forty-two from the Borea base in the Hirkiv belt that pleased The Eight the most, Verteg and Siba's family with the skills to crew a fleet and to school the humans in Anan tech. All this along with the – although reluctant – twenty-two Mzimot engine builders bringing an extra sixty-four specialist alien beings to the fight, each, even the Mzimot boys, with a valuable skill.

A dull whirling tone added to the suspense, stilling the impatient crowd. The main hatch opened, an access gangway growing out until it touched down on the landing pad. Led by the colony's doctor, the ground crew, security and medical teams moved forwards to the base of the gangway. There were welcoming shouts from the crowd at the sight of Tom, leading a strange-looking group – the Mzimot – out through the open hatch, down to the landing pad.

One look at the exhausted Tom told the Doc all. 'Where's Niamh?' he asked.

'She's in med-bay, in an Anan hiberpod. Doc, she's human again but I'm told she may not survive the healing process.'

'What about you, Tom? You're a wreck.'

Tom said nothing, his silence and blanched face oozing stress. The Doc grabbed his boss. 'Let's get you off. Some fresh food and rest, that's what's needed, no arguments,' he said. 'We'll take care of Niamh. Come on ...'

While the Doc escorted Tom back to the colony, at the gangway, directed by the *Monarch's* security crew, the Mzimot walked away from the ship. The twenty-two gathered together on the beach beside *Monarch's* landing pad. The fresh air and the view rooted the family to the spot. Bird song from the close-by jungle filled their ears. As did the sound of the surf, lapping on the beach, where an azure blue sea extended out to meet a cloudless blue sky. In the near distance, the green jungle grew down to the golden sandy beach, extending for miles around their natural harbour. Behind the colony, tall mountains, some wearing white caps of snow, reached up to the sky. The Mzimot had never seen anything like this before. Mesmerised, they gawked and wondered at the lush green planet.

Accompanying the Mzimot, Kora and Brian, carrying their child, gulped in the fresh air and the view of their world. Hand in hand, the couple paused to admire their new home, teeming with life and beauty.

Brian broke their silence. 'This is our New World, Fazqa. It's beautiful, like our Earth. You should work with us. You'd have a good life on a planet like this,' he said, his lilting Welsh accent laced with conviction.

'Maybe,' Fazqa replied, as she watched the medical team load Niamh, cocooned in the Anan hiberpod, onto a grav platform. They left, flying off to some strange buildings that she realised comprised the human settlement. Then, to Fazqa's dismay, another security detail of humans carrying, what she realised were weapons, marched up and surrounded her family. 'But we would be your prisoners, like we are now,' she said. A jealous pang crossed her mind as she watched Kora and her child play with the waves at the water's edge, free to enjoy the planet's natural delights.

Before Brian replied, Fazqa's skin crawled at the approaching apparition. A dark-skinned woman rode down on a strange hairy beast, followed by five more of the offending animals. The woman smiled and waved at Brian and Kora. 'What manner of beasts are those?' Fazqa asked, pointing at the group.

Brian never got to reply as the first of the catbears, ridden by Alice, stopped immediately in front of the Mzimot. It roared and clawed the ground. 'Steady, Rex, steady,' Alice said, as she tugged at his reigns. She jumped off him, trying to pull the beast back but Rex continued to roar at the Mzimot. The other catbears growled as they corralled the strange family into a circle. The Mzimot screamed in terror, shouting for someone to restrain the catbears. Alice pulled and tugged at Rex, trying to yank him back. Her body couldn't match the catbear's immense strength. Rex won, confronting the oldest of the Mzimot.

Without warning, the old man's face contorted and he started to grow more hair. His eyes bulged out as his front teeth extended down from his mouth. Before their eyes, he grew into a large grey-coloured beast, his six clawed hands slashing out at all in front of him. He roared, as his claw tore into Alice, rupturing her arm in a crimson explosion of blood and tissue. Rex sprung forward. Rearing up on his hind legs, he grabbed the strange Mzimot in his talons. The old one slashed at Rex with his claws, embedding them into the catbear's shoulders. Both beasts, locked in a deadly embrace, fell to the ground, rolling together and snapping at each other's neck with their jaws.

Then Rex broke free. Jumping up, he encircled the Mzimot from behind, locking a great paw around the old one's neck. Roaring with rage, he increased the deadly pressure – the old one's eyes bulged out. Digging his claws into Rex's paw, he tried in vain to loosen the catbear's grip. His loud growls subsided into a whimper as his strength ebbed from the lack of oxygen. His head slumped down onto Rex's paw. But Rex never faltered. There could only be one outcome, and not until he felt the last breath of life leave the treacherous beast, did he release his deadly hold. The old Mzimot, transformed into his true form, slumped to the ground – dead. Rex turned to look down at Alice, now surrounded by humans. They were pressing down on her wounds to stem the flow of blood.

'Easy, Rex,' one shouted. 'We'll take her to the hospital.' A med team surrounded her. Not waiting for a grav platform, they lifted her up and ran from the scene.

Enough tension to split stones erupted between the humans and the Mzimot. The security team's guns rattled and cocked.

'What the hell are you, Fazqa?' Brian asked as he stood in front of his wife and child, protecting them from the unknown.

'We're Mzimot, that's what we are,' she said, as she and her family metamorphosed into their original alien form.

Fazqa's soft bluish skin transformed into shiny blue fur, her short blue and pink hair sprouted out from her head, growing fast until it cascaded down her back. The small human-like ears grew upwards, protruding through her hair, forming prominent triangles of soft blue flesh and fur adorning her head. The nose and facial features stayed the same, except for the growth of delicate blue hair. The transformation accentuated her female curves while a small tail curled down from behind. Unlike the elder Mzimot, Fazqa's six-fingered hands didn't grow into claws, while some of the other elders' did.

The Mzimot's changing shapes drew gasps from the human watchers. The colour of their fur ranged from a deep blue to grey – age being the primary factor. The deep-blue coloured fur of Jarzol's two young boys to the grey of the elders showed that difference. The elders' sharp claws contrasted with the youthful human-like six-fingered hands. All ended up with triangular ears and tails.

Rex growled through the change, then backed off, content that they had now revealed their secret. Apart from gasps and some murmured curses, in disbelief, the humans stayed quiet.

Brian's voice broke the shocked silence. 'You and your family are full of surprises. Why did you hide that?'

Fazqa's head hung low. Thoughts of what they were and how they got to this place swirled in her mind. The first steps on this world were wonderous. Geoff had told her of its beauty, even showed her images of it. But to see such beauty and experience its intoxicating wonder was more than she had ever hoped for. It all changed at the appearance of the foul beasts. As their elders had foretold, the Mzimot were, and would always be, changeling outcasts. The humans' looks and murmurings said it all. The rest of the Mzimot stayed quiet, harbouring their disparaging feelings, some more than others, ranging from disappointment in the young to bitterness and hatred in the elders.

'Look at us. Would you have wanted us with you if you had known what we look like?' Fazqa said, her voice quivering as she tried to hold back the tears. 'We're outcasts. We were a mistake, but we adapted. We are the best at what we do because of our strange abilities. Maybe that's why the Overlords endowed us with intelligence. I don't know. But look at him,' she said, pointing at Geoff who had arrived down from the ship to see what the commotion was about. 'Your expression says it all, Geoff. You're horrified at my appearance,' she said, as she glared back at him.

Mouth open, a gobsmacked Geoff ogled Fazqa, her soft blue fur gleaming in the sunlight, tears brimming in her eyes and glinting on the blue hair on her face. With her back now straight, her female curves pushed out at the fabric of her tight ship suit. The elegant small tail curved behind her. She was a vision of classic beauty Geoff could never have imagined.

'On the contrary, Fazqa, you are – without question – beautiful. All of you,' he said, looking at the family. 'What a wonder you are. But yes, I'm horrified. Not by your appearance, but by your deceit. Why, Fazqa, why?' he shouted. 'Why did you not tell me before? I told you everything about my past – that I was a thief and a criminal. And you, you never told me about this. After all, we …' he turned and ran.

The strange family huddled together with the body of the old one lying in front of them. The two boys clutched at Jarzol, floods of tears staining the blue fur on their face. But, for some reason, Jarzol's expression didn't fit with one who had lost a valuable member of the family. Dispassionately – ignoring the body of the old one – with his wife by his side, he attended to the needs of his two boys.

'They're so cute,' Kora whispered to Brian, as Jarzol tried to console them.

'Yeah, the boys are, but I dare say the rest are deadly. Strange, they don't seem too concerned at the death of the old one,' he whispered back.

'No, they don't. That might work for us. We need them, Brian.'

'You're right, my love, we do.' He turned to Jarzol. 'Follow me. We all need food. I'll bet your boys are hungry.' He smiled as the two small ones nodded. 'Yes, they are. Come on Jarzol, that's enough aggro,' he said, trying to reduce the tension that engulfed them all. 'We've some good cooks here. You'll get a taste of Earth's finest.'

The Mzimot hesitated. They looked suspiciously at the security team who still had their weapons at the ready. That changed when one produced a tarp. The young soldier's signs, asking if he could cover the body, raised eyebrows. The Mzimot elders nodded and one helped. A simple gesture, but enough.

'Thanks, lads,' Brian said. 'You can drop the guns as well.'

By now, the Borea family were filing out of the ship. The sight of the changed Mzimot didn't surprise any of them. Some nodded a greeting, others made their way to Fort Leslie's town, the covered body on the ground ignored. Happy chatter in Anan filled the air and oohs and aahs at the surrounding beauty. No small spat between the humans and Mzimot was going to spoil the Borea's first day on the New World, news of the feast the legendary human cooks prepared for them chewed over during the run-in from orbit. Siba teased them all with that story.

The passing Borea dialled the tension down another notch. Again, Brian faced Jarzol and, switching to Anan, said, 'Come on, Jarzol. Time to go. Follow me.' Kora did the same, coaxing the family along. Subdued, they followed the Borea up to the colony, the dead Mzimot left where he fell, covered with a camouflage tarp.

*

The Eight took the laid-back approach to the arrival, waiting for the anxious humans and Borea to disembark from the *Monarch*. He sensed the fight between the Mzimot and his catbears. Rex had done well feeling their hidden abilities; another reason to adopt the catbears as his personal guard. They were ready. From now on they would be by his side.

But it was Alice's mortal wounds that alarmed The Eight. The human medics stemmed the blood loss and were now prepping an operating theatre to amputate her arm. He wouldn't allow that and began making his way through the now quiet Fort Leslie to the hospital. Inside, he dismissed her medical team, taking matters into his own ethereal "hands".

Leaving his chariot, The Eight's energy mass floated over to Alice, lying still conscious on a treatment couch. Unaware of the plan to amputate her arm, she watched the blue pulsing energy float above her. A tentacle of blue extended, covering her damaged arm. From one tentacle, thousands of micro tentacles extended, stripping her bandages away, repairing blood vessels and bone, down to the fragile human cells that make up the arm's muscles and tendons – closing and healing her wounds.

Mystified as to why she was getting this royal treatment, Alice asked, 'Overlord, why are you doing this for me?'

'In return for what you have achieved with my beasts, Alice. You have worked wonders with them. That company will go with me as my protective guard. Will you lead them?'

'It would be my pleasure, Overlord. They mean everything to me,' she said, as she watched his energy mass pulse with blue light. She could feel nothing; no pain. It was so eerie and quiet as he finished working his magic on her wounds. Without any warning, his energy mass flashed with a strange purple light. She felt a searing pain, like a lance, in her arm and then she was overcome with a feeling of death. Blackness shrouded her mind and a sound, like a screech of agony, filled the room. 'What the hell is that, Overlord?' she screamed, as she closed her eyes and tried to shut out the pain from her mind.

'Alice, Alice, I am sorry,' he said, as he tried to quell the disturbance coursing through his energy mass. 'There is death on Earth. I sense it. An extinction event not caused by nature. Alice, we must go. Now, we must go,' he said, as he returned to his chariot and left.

In the same building, dozing beside Niamh's capsule, The Eight's message erupted in Tom's brain. '*Ready the Monarch. We leave as soon as you can. Make haste, we will need a full crew. Do what you must.*'

'Overlord, what's happening?'

'Earth is attacked, death is there. He has found them.'

*

The strange feast, with human, Mzimot, Borea and the Javonian had near finished when the news of Earth's attack came through. Tom briefly stepped in and whispered it to Bill and Brian. Brian smiled and nodded, hiding the gloomy news from his wife and those around him, as Tom and his deputy Bill left. Some noticed the look on their faces, others didn't. Digesting their food, the post-dinner chat continued.

Kora, finishing her food, watched Jarzol's two boys, seated on each side of him. She tried not to laugh as they tucked into bowls of ice-cream, the white melted cream sticking to the blue fur on their faces. 'Seems we have similar taste, Jarzol. Your boys love that.'

By now, Jarzol had a good understanding of English, preferring actual speech to the voice translators others were using. 'You are alien to us and we are alien to you; nothing will change that, regardless of how well you feed us. We are different from other biped races, and we know we are despised by them.'

'Why?' she asked.

'We can change our appearance. People don't trust us.'

'I can understand that, Jarzol. Amongst our human population, we have many races,' Kora said, pointing at her Welsh husband. 'Brian's from a Celtic race. Long ago, the Celts were considered barbarians. I'm a Maori. When Brian's ancestors first met mine, they thought we were savages. Now, look where we are,' she said, smiling as she held up their child.

'Can I hold him?' Fazqa asked.

''Course you can,' she said, as she stood up and passed her child over to the delighted Fazqa. The baby gurgled with pleasure as she cradled him in her soft arms, his small brown hands clutching at her fur.

Brian watched as Kora and Fazqa left the table, both fussing the child. 'Would my wife give our most cherished possession to a Mzimot if she thought we could never trust you?'

Jarzol squirmed under Brian's gaze. His young son jumped up, wiped the ice-cream from his face and ran after Fazqa. Jarzol shook his head. 'No, it'll never happen.'

Brian leaned forwards and looked straight into Jarzol's dull grey eyes. 'Listen now, Jarzol. The human race's history is filled with atrocities. We call it "man's inhumanity to man". Look around at our people. Different colours of skin, various facial features and body size. Did you notice that?'

Jarzol's eyes dropped. He had noticed the diversity amongst the humans, something he'd never seen before and not understanding it, stayed quiet.

'You know Bill, Tom's black-skinned deputy – he just left?'

Jarzol nodded. Bill was the rock who had transformed the brig into a home for the Mzimot, making their voyage a pleasure.

'In a dark time, on our planet, Bill's ancestors were kidnapped, transported across the world and sold into slavery to my ancestors. Eventually, many years later, his family made it back to our country to face hatred and abuse. Alice's family, the girl who was injured, were also unwelcomed immigrants.' Bill paused, the intensity of what he was saying was not lost on Jarzol. With cocked ears, the Mzimot's eyes stared intently at Brian.

The young Welshman held the Mzimot leader's gaze as he continued. 'And that, Jarzol, is only a drop of the barbarism humans did to each other. Know this, on our colony, and within Anan Corp on our home world, everyone is equal, regardless of colour or creed. You are no different. Our diversity binds us as a family.' Brian paused for that to sink in. 'By the way, on the journey back, your boys made it to the engine room. They helped the Borea techs managed the fuel feeds. Delighted with the help, they were! You didn't know that, did you?'

'No.' He didn't. He had thought they were off playing computer games.

'They're fine lads, you should be proud of them. Jarzol, we need you and your family, and you need us. You need to – what we call – lighten up and get with the program.' His voice dropped to a quiet and chilling whisper. 'Minutes ago, I heard from Tom. There's a shit storm brewing on Earth, and we're leaving this planet. Right now, back into space. This intergalactic war just got a whole lot hotter. Jarzol, you need to choose a side and you'd better make it quick. There's no time left for passengers or prisoners!'

Jarzol stared back at Brian. He could feel the fear of what was coming etched in the young man's face.

Brian got up from the table, abruptly turned, and strode out. His mind whirled with everything he had just said. He wanted to say so much more, but time was up. Others got up as well – bad news travels fast. Earth needed The Eight and the *Monarch's* help.

Outside, Fort Leslie burst into life, bunkering *Monarch*, the ship-to-ship refuelling of blue from the *Maeve* well underway. The rest was done in record time as the race to save their home world began.

CHAPTER THIRTY-SEVEN

The Ceirim

Ages ago, Overlords created the ceirim to scour redundant or malevolent life forms from their worlds. In those days, the ceirim purged planets of all life and then consumed themselves. A perfect, energy free, biological weapon, viewed by some of those Overlords as the most efficient weapon they had ever made. As the Overlords advanced, new additions to their elite ten formed different opinions. The ceirim were a weapon of last choice until an age went by without their use. Maintaining such hazardous living beings as a viable weapon, ate resources and proved problematic. Plus, the ethics of keeping such evil troubled some. In particular, those who had ascended from a purebreed background. The One, judging the ceirim to be a "mistake of gargantuan proportions", ordered The Sixth to expunge them. Stored in his Jora Galaxy, he didn't, instead, conducting secret experiments on improving the monsters. They are alive and loaded on a fleet commanded by The Ninth, destination unknown.

  ‹ *Extract from Intelligence Brief: Admiral Enirim*

*

Earth, 22nd January 2028

ON EARTH, THROUGHOUT THE CEIRIM'S invasion, World War III raged on, each act of provocation goading the other side into another deed legitimised by the prodding of their enemy. Their superiors arrested General Marsh and Admiral Vasily after returning home from the secret meeting in Australia, increasing diplomatic tension. "Treason and conspiring with the enemy" were the baseless charges laid before the two brave men. To Harold's dismay, less able men, with misguided allegiances to an old failed order, replaced them.

War had started at the end of 2027 when a U.S. frigate shot down three Russian MiGs patrolling the Bering Sea. "It violated the sovereignty of our borders" was the lame excuse. The Russian's immediate retaliation resulted in the sinking of the offending U.S. frigate. War escalated into a full-blown naval conflict, as both countries went head to head in World War III. Using conventional weapons, both rushed to re-arm the nuclear arsenals they had decommissioned on The Eight's instructions.

All the news feeds and diplomatic efforts focused on the unfolding global war. The United Nations occupied itself with meetings and initiatives to halt the conflict. Europe, caught between the two great powers, resisted all efforts to be drawn into it. Despite having lost the most to the Wave and being signatories to old treaties, they steadfastly refused. Some pundits said, "They just can't agree on which side to fight with." and "They're waiting for a clear winner to emerge, then they'll join the fray – on the winning side, of course.". It was a cynical world that watched two global powers battle it out to bolster their politicians' careers. The diplomatic furore and the news frenzy the conflict generated, gave The Ninth the tactical advantage he needed to root the ceirim's hold on Earth.

*

The Chad, The Ninth's Flagship, 22nd January 2028

On The Ninth's flagship, hidden behind the moon, Captain Bardek bowed as his Overlord entered the bridge. *Report time*, the captain realised. 'Overlord, it's working; we have over twenty million ceirim established in the subcontinent. They are making their way through the big population centres. There are about one point six billion humans on that small landmass. Soon, we can transfer Kochtos to another continent.' This was the second part of the geneticist's strategy. Kochtos would lead the remaining eight thousand ceirim in a second invasion on another continent – building another army. A change to The Ninth's original plans, designed to expunge billions.

'The geneticists, how are they coping?' The Ninth asked.

493

'Pleased with the work so far.' These were slim words to describe the lead geneticist's elation at his team's achievements. The lead's plan turned out to be an overwhelming success in building a ceirim army for The Ninth.

'And Kochtos, can he produce the amounts of DNA we require?'

'He is enjoying every moment of this, Overlord. I shudder when I see the delight in his black eyes every time we communicate.'

'Enough Bardek. He has a job to do. You did not see into the minds of those he kills; I did. Look at their war – they still fight amongst themselves, even though news of our arrival filters out. You have the calculations?'

'Yes, Overlord. Best estimate for population termination is half an orbit of their planet.'

The Ninth paused as he processed that. Time moved on and The Ninth had another agenda he wanted to pursue. 'It takes too long. What of The Eight, where is he? What if he returns?' the Overlord mused out loud. 'Bardek, there are too many unknown variables and risks. Everything we can do to hasten the extinction must be done. I will give Kochtos five cycles, then we move the fleet into Earth orbit,' he ordered. 'Prepare for that now. Arm the extinction weapons. Make ready to launch on the main population centres.'

The captain of the *Chad* sensed the feelings of his crew. They knew what this meant. Already the Javonian comms officer was preparing the fleet's new orders, a command they begrudged, for it would involve added effort and risk for them. Blood red rage crossed Bardek's mind but ever the pragmatist, he swallowed it.

As expected, The Ninth sensed the crew's unease. *Not surprising*, he thought and said nothing.

Like a slap of a grav gun, the barked order from Bardek cut the hushed bridge. 'Comms, message the fleet: prepare extinction weapons for launch. Flight vectors and target coordinates to follow. Navigation, send them that data. Targets are all major population centres …' And so Bardek continued, rousing the hiding fleet. The Ninth's plans to exterminate mankind moved up a notch.

*

Hela Base, Australian Desert,
22nd January 2028

In a corner of the base's ops, unaware of the next part of hell to visit, Robert was trying to interpret the ceirim expansion in India. He stopped a video, taken from a cloaked Borea shuttle over Northern India. The graphic scenes of the ceirim's infestation of Delhi repulsed him. He shuddered as he remembered the day in the *Hela* med-bay when he first saw one. The fatal images left him in no doubt as to the peril the Earth faced.

Robert turned to the Aknar captain who had gathered this precious data. 'You did good getting those pictures, Quriel. Now we know why they're here. They want to wipe us out – it's as simple as that.' Others in the ops centre listened in, a deadly quiet descending on the normally noisy nerve centre.

The self-critical Quriel, disappointed in his previous attempts to shed light on what the invaders' intentions were, had risked his life to get that info. Launching a cloaked shuttle with Chief Haldock, he spent a night spying on the ceirim and their support ships.

With Quriel's intelligence and garbled news coming in from the region, Robert knew he had to take action to stop the ceirim's advance. "We can't hide here and watch. We have to do something,' he said, a steely determination bubbling in those words.

Quriel shook his head. 'Robert, we can do nothing; they're unstoppable. We must get off the planet. Leave now, before they get to Australia.'

'No, Quriel. We're not leaving. If you want to leave, take the *Richard* and go to the New World. Warn them. But we fight. Look, I want to show you something,' he said, as he opened up some old video files on the screen in front of them. 'See these guys here. They grabbed two countries with nothing more than the weapons they captured from others. Mounted them in the back of pick-up trucks. Look,' he said, pointing to the grainy video pictures, 'they terrified a whole region with these tactics. With nothing, they set themselves up as the kings of terror. It took Earth's armies years to make any headway against them.'

The Aknar captain couldn't see any bearing this primitive land grab had on their present situation. 'What's your point, Robert?' he asked.

'We have spaceships, weapons, blue and grav. Our Earth allies have weapons we could use as well. Quriel, we need to do something – guerrilla tactics we call it – to slow them up, until The Eight returns.'

'If he returns. We don't know where he is,' Quriel responded.

A disgruntled Robert rubbed his two hands on his face, trying to hide his frustration. *There had to be something*, he thought. Biting down hard, the Scotsman fought back the weariness. Eventually, he spoke in a pleading voice. 'Verteg, you and Quriel, look through Demard's old files from the *Hela*. The stuff he gathered during the first purebreed survey of Earth. There must be something we can use,' Robert said, clutching at straws. A horrible realisation scratched the back of his mind, one he kept pushing back. *What if Quriel's right?* Robert wondered. He remembered, after a failed attack by the combined Russian and Chinese forces, when a nuclear warhead exploded near the *Hela*.

Caught with their pants down, during the loading of the first colony, the Hela escaped into orbit. Niamh extended the grav bubble out to its maximum. With that shield in place, the nuclear blast tore into the *Hela*. The impact sent the eight-hundred-metre-long ship careering through space like a boat in a storm. But, shrouded inside the grav bubble, they and the Hela survived – undamaged! The grav bubble absorbed most of the energy from mankind's most powerful nuclear weapon. And now, decommissioned under the orders of The Eight, those weapons are gone. Disgruntled, he walked out of their operations centre.

Verteg and Quriel watched Robert's departure; the big man's shoulders slumped and his usually rod-like back bent. The stress of Earth's predicament was taking its toll on him. Quriel sat in silence. He watched Verteg start to scour her father's files from the *Hela* database. He left her to it, wondering what Demard would think of that strange turn of events – his daughter combing his records for help.

Emulating his own dead father, Zaval, Quriel sat in his chair with his feet up on the desk. Unlike Zaval, Quriel didn't smoke so he just sat there letting his mind drift. Soft background noises from operations lulled his brain until he started to play the scenes of the ceirim over and over in his head. He closed his eyes, concentrating on the images, and then he saw it. Startling Verteg, he jumped up, shouting, 'Play those sequences of the ceirim again …'

*

Deep Space, 22nd January 2028

Ignorant of the efforts underway on Earth to frustrate his attack, hiding behind the moon, The Ninth retreated to his chamber. He left Bardek to prep for the next operational phase of his mission. To get the ceirim to Earth, Bardek rammed his crews hard to get every detail right. That same cudgelling planning erupted on the bridge now. The fleet had five days to unpack, load and program the extinction weapons. An intricate task but one The Ninth had confidence Bardek would manage. The enhanced fusion weapons, nicknamed "city-busting mini-suns", would vaporise the planet's largest cities.

But now, a burning need to contact The Sixth before advancing to the next stage consumed the young Overlord. It wasn't to get approval or buy-in from The Sixth to breed more ceirim, or for final permission to use banned weapons. The unfeeling Overlord had his orders, and that was enough. No, there was more, something else – his own agenda! When the fleet arrived in the Milky Way and found Earth, The Ninth's attitude to the project completely changed. A wealthy galaxy and a home base teeming with carbon life, it was an alien world to the young Overlord, but one whose beauty he recognised. He craved to expunge the humans and take over the planet for himself. Pure greed on a scale of The Sixth! Parked behind the moon, with the ceirim in play, The Ninth, in secret, contacted the captain of the *Losh*.

'Did you see the planet and that rich galaxy?' he had asked. 'Could we use it?'

'Yes, most certainly. It would be what we always hoped for. Once you cull the humans, our people can disappear in that world, subjugating what's left of the population. They could make a slave army of workers for a new home planet. What we always wanted,' replied the captain of the *Losh*. Not what The Sixth ordered – another greed-filled agenda!

The Ninth projected his mind out into the cosmos, travelling across galaxies and the darkness of space. Faster than light, galaxies whizzed by, looking like long white pencil lines surrounding his spectral passage.

When halfway, he fired a message to the mind of The Sixth. '*Meet me now*,' The Ninth called, continuing his ethereal flight.

On Anan, The Sixth heard his plea. Believing it had all gone wrong, The Sixth's mind rushed out of his energy mass to intercept Nine. His energy mass, pulsing blue, remained in the Overlord's chamber, as did The Ninth's while their ethereal minds – their very being – met in deep space between the Anan and Milky Way Galaxies, an area of the cosmos devoid of star systems, nebula, or black holes. The occasional outcast flashed by, orphaned stars, comets or planets cast out from their home system. In this blackness, the two powerful beings met, their minds mingling in the cosmos.

'*Why did you call? What is wrong, Nine?*'

'*We found the planet, my Lord. There are well over six billion of them.*'

Back on Anan, The Sixth's energy mass flashed with white light. '*Impossible, that's impossible. You must be wrong.*'

'*I am sure of it. Do not think I would waste precious energy on idle talk. Get used to this, Six. I estimate there are near to seven billion of species-y; they call themselves humans.*' He paused as the consequences of that sunk in. '*You must also know I found more – a blackness in their minds …*'

In a millisecond The Ninth told his tale of the violence and evil that blighted the humans. The Eight had been on the planet but was now gone. Now Bardek's comms officers fruitlessly scanned the planet's news feeds and databases for evidence of what The Eight was up to and where he had gone. But the humans generated vast amounts of information in a short time frame. They filled countless servers with petabytes of useless material!

What the aliens had stumbled on was Earth's "connected world". Social platforms, blogs, websites with all sorts of conspiracy theories, fiction, movies, the entertainment media and so on. Buried in that lot of raw data was the information that the *Hela* had landed, was refurbished, and had taken off with a colony. Without the skills of a "Demard", Earth's data banks overwhelmed Bardek's comms, stumping even the clever Javonian. All they were able to do was set up the search engines and let them crawl through every byte on every server on the planet. Like looking for the needle in the haystack!

'*... my Lord, there is so much; it is like a tower of incessant meaningless drivel,*' The Ninth recounted, finishing his report.

'*Are you not powerful enough to deal with them, Nine?*' asked the belligerent Six. All he had gotten was excuses. And The Eight's location still remained a mystery.

'*You forget, Six, I am younger than you. If you remember, I did say you should have come yourself,*' replied The Ninth, again pushing everything back on his boss.

'*Nine, do not leave that solar system until every last one is expunged. Our civilisations are finished if they ever get off their world,*' The Sixth ordered.

Now was the time. The Ninth hadn't called this meeting to update Six. There was more at stake. '*I have a strategy and a new ceirim army to do that but, before I commit, I want something, Six.*'

The Sixth's mind flashed with one thought – betrayal.

'*No, I'm not betraying you, Six,*' Nine said. '*I want that galaxy, solar system and planet for myself.*' He didn't mention that he'd keep some of the humans as slaves.

The Sixth couldn't believe the audacity of The Ninth. To have summoned him here to demand that! Then the realisation hit him. He had trained The Ninth well – greed and extortion on an intergalactic scale. Nine showed promise, after all. '*Yes, you can have that. But you must get on with it, Nine. You must,*' The Sixth said, retreating back to Anan.

*

Planet Anan. EPTS: B140778

Back on Anan, troubled by the news that there were so many humans, The Sixth summoned Theia. 'Empress, we found species-y. They are called humans. Did you remember how many of them there were?'

'Overlord, all I remember is what I told you. You may look yourself. I find it difficult to be in your presence after what you did to my only nephew. You took everything from me – my heir, my people and my planet. Do not think you can bring me here to discuss humans so easily.'

'Silence,' The Sixth roared.

At this point in her life, nothing worried Theia Aknar. The thing that was in front of her was evil incarnate. No doubt about that. A dispatch from Enirim told he had resurrected the ceirim and loaded them on a fleet. The destination was, until now, unknown. They were gone to expunge the humans – The Sixth confirmed it now.

Standing tall, Theia replied to his roar with her regal tone. 'And what will you do? Kill me? Do that. Go on and put me out of my misery. Six, you have gone further than any of your predecessors. You are an abomination. Now you expunge a whole population without the approval of The One.' Her tone and confidence surprised even Theia. Part of her destiny, planted by The Eight when he wiped her memories, that assertion came from deep within.

'I am The One,' he said in a moment of narcissistic delusion.

'You are not, and never will be. There are forces you do not comprehend that will align to defeat you,' Theia said. Her knowledge of Anan and Overlord diktat outstripped many, even the Overlords. One of the many reasons The Eight had chosen the Empress for a higher purpose.

'You dream, Empress, of my demise. Never ever will that happen. What else do you remember of those bipeds?'

'I remember one. You have seen the young woman in my mind. She has red hair and a fair complexion with brown spots on her face. She was like a daughter to me. Intelligent, very intelligent, is all I remember. But know this, Six. Her species has intelligence I had never seen before. That I do remember, and you sense that too.'

His energy mass changed to a deep purple colour as her voice chilled him. Even as an Overlord, it triggered a feeling of fear, fear he had never felt before. 'Go now. I will keep you alive. You serve a purpose. When I am done with you, then we will talk about your fate,' he boomed as she walked tall from his chamber.

Outside, the Shoter watched Theia leave the Sixth's chamber. He had heard everything. Nothing shocked him now. That Empress Theia had spoken to The Sixth like that, and walked out as if nothing had happened, said volumes. He cocked his brow as she passed him by, the faintest hint of a bow of his head. Theia raised her eyes as she passed him. Nothing said, but an acknowledgement of the respect he offered.

CHAPTER THIRTY-EIGHT

CNS Headlines. Have Aliens landed?

Worrying news reports of "flesh-eating monsters" are flowing out from India. Horrific social media posts of humans morphing into demons are creating widespread panic. Unverified reports say Delhi, a city of twenty-three million people, is overrun by the black creatures. While this horror ravages the subcontinent, the U.S. and Russia engage in a pointless war, ignoring the plight of some of the world's poorest people.

The two superpowers' corrupt leaderships arrested General Marsh and Admiral Vasily after the two men's alleged clandestine attendance at an Anan Corp meeting in Australia. Reports from that meeting shed light into a deteriorating galactic polity, which may explain the arrival of a hostile fleet of starships in our solar system.

Calls for help, from the Indian government have gone unheeded as the "Leader of the Free World" describes the horrifying stories of the massacre as a hoax. Meanwhile, the two failed superpowers prosecute their border war, calling it World War Three, a fight for freedom, truth and sovereignty.

‹ **From: Continental News Services. Good Morning Planet Earth**

*

Hela Base, Australian Desert, 22nd January 2028

ON EARTH, VERTEG AND QURIEL played images of the ceirim, with their supporting ships, over and over.

The night video proved hard to see but, with crafty alien tech, the grainy imaging cleared, exposing the callous nature of The Sixth and his follower's invasion. The all-seeing Borea camera, recording on multiple wavelengths, captured the elusive pictures of a cloaked support ship spraying the human population on the ground. And then, their grotesque transformation to hungry ceirim was finally exposed. Quriel had figured it out; he didn't need to see any more. The support ships spray ceirim DNA onto the human population, creating an unstoppable ceirim army. Where the DNA came from, or who made it, was a mystery.

'No matter,' Quriel said. 'Destroy the alien ships, and the ceirim's ability to procreate is stopped.' A strategic piece of the puzzle was solved.

But this was still not enough. On Earth, they didn't have access to weapons strong enough to pierce the ship's grav bubble. Using missiles from the *Hela's* armoury wasn't an option. The golden vessel was no match for the invading fleet's superior armaments. The risk of detection during the *Hela's* takeoff was too high, even with Borea cloaks hiding it. A chance Verteg and Quriel wouldn't take.

Verteg and two of her techs returned to combing through Demard's records of the Earth survey in the *Hela* database. It didn't take as long as Quriel had thought. Even in death, Demard, the distinguished computer tech, provided his daughter much-needed help. His files were meticulously sorted from access codes to Earth's stock markets to manufacturing specifications for the latest smartphones. And, amongst it all, were files of data on the superpowers' secret weapons' research. Two designs stood out, with experimental prototypes manufactured as well.

The Borea delved deeper, hacking government computers in Russia and the U.S., confirming Demard's discoveries. There was more good news, the prototypes survived The Eight's decree for nuclear disarmament. Overlooked maybe, it didn't matter. Their existence on Earth offered a slim possibility!

Weapons weren't Verteg's thing, that was Quriel's department. He, and the two techs, pored over printouts of one of Earth's top-secret experimental weapons. At an empty desk beside them, Verteg worked on another drawing. Her speciality – flight.

Hours ticked by, but for the four Borea dedicated to their Overlord's success, time stood still. The intensity of what they were working on was not lost on the ops centre's nearby human staff. Food and drinks were delivered in silence. Empty plates collected, requests for stationery and printouts fulfilled. Bit by bit, the wall of the corner section they occupied filled with what most humans would see as abstract Anan art. Notes scribbled here, and drawings added there, morphed the blueprints into cutting-edge alien-human hybrids.

After six hours, the tired four reviewed their work. A short conflab, then Verteg announced the conclusion. 'Time to call Robert,' she said. 'You two can go get some rest, and well done,' she said to the techs.

Head dropping down over her green neck, and untidy hair falling on her shoulders, the wary Pilot, waited with Quriel.

*

Arriving back at ops with Janet, one look at the tired Borea duo and the late hour – near twenty-three hundred – told Robert the tale. They hadn't stopped work since he had left earlier in the day.

Together, Verteg and Quriel explained their findings and the proposed solutions. After which, they showed Robert and Janet the ceirim videos. The big man's face turned to thunder. Tears rolled down Janet's face as the realisation of what the human race faced sunk in. And then, they pored over the plans on the wall – a possible solution, a thin thread at slowing the ceirim advance.

'Verteg, Quriel, you've done better than I ever hoped. I knew both your fathers and they would be proud of what you have come up with for us and The Eight.' Wise and emotional words. Robert was right. The tenacious nature of the Borea family shone through Verteg and Quriel. The tall purebreed captain put a consoling arm around his green-skinned cousin. After the slog of the day and Robert's wise words, tears ran down both their faces. Spontaneously, for the first time, the two cousins stood and embraced. An emotional moment, their whispered words of comfort in Anan leaked out. Clutching Robert's hand, Janet turned away. Memories of the two legends flooded both their minds. Demard and Zaval, their spirits embodied in these designs and their two children.

Wiping tears from their eyes, the four turned to matters in hand – the practicalities of putting drawings on a wall into action.

Verteg phrased that dilemma. 'But, Robert, we will need help. That human technology is in northern hemisphere countries. And they are both at war. Your friend Chang can't help with this.'

To his surprise, Robert's arm started to glow blue. Throbbing, the glowing arm surprised the others. Not Robert, he remembered The Eight's final words when he departed the New World on the Monarch.

"Time for me to go, Robert. Take care of my planets. If anything happens to me, you are my proxy. Heed the glow in your arm – when the time comes, let it guide you," The Eight had said.

That order rang in Robert's mind; his time had come! The predicament of where the Earth-saving tech was – in Russia and the U.S. – was easy to overcome. He would bash heads together to get it.

Robert's voice dripped with confidence. 'Don't you worry about that. I'll get you the help we need.' Looking at his watch, he calculated the time differences around the globe. Calling Harold, he asked for locations of who would be where and when?

A quick answer put a shape on his plan. 'Time for some quick shut-eye' he said to them. 'We meet here in five hours.'

Together, the four left, both couples arm in arm. Verteg and Quriel felt united by familial love and respect, a new feeling neither had experienced before. Another milestone for the once-wealthy family of intergalactic energy trader's return to prosperity and status.

While they rested, Harold called contacts across the globe. Diplomatic promises of secret intelligence and help to defeat each opposing side was given to Russia and the U.S. It was subterfuge and lies that both sides swallowed in the hope they could defeat the other! The subsequent meetings, summoned in their command bunkers, prepped the way for Robert.

*

At an early hour in the Australian morning, the four assembled in the ops centre. This time, in front of a nav-con.

'Can I borrow a blue diamond?' Robert asked Quriel.

Wondering what would come next, Quriel took a deep-blue coloured stone from his pocket and handed it to Robert. His white purebreed face wrinkled with questions he didn't ask.

Robert hung the crystal around his neck. 'Verteg, plot a projection of the U.S. military base. It's under here,' he said, pointing out the Cheyenne Mountains on a map pinned to the wall of their meeting room. With a burst of ghostly blue light, the projection opened above the nav-con. 'Can you get inside?' he asked Verteg.

Banishing the questions from her mind, she nodded, her green face furrowed with the concentration, and soon a picture of a busy operations centre opened up.

Robert checked the people seated at an oval table and the man at its head. Harold's call delivered the goods – they were all there. 'Hold that projection, Verteg,' he said, gripping the blue diamond hanging around his neck with his hand. He focused on her projection and as his arm and pendant glowed bright blue, he found himself standing inside the operations centre, looking at those seated around the table.

They jumped up, surprised at the apparition of the tall Scotsman they had seen addressing the U.N. the previous week.

'Shoot him,' came the cry from the head of the table.

'Oh, don't start that now. You know who I am. I'm Robert Leslie, I represent The Eight. Have you not seen what's going on? Do you not know aliens are here to wipe us out? Think of how you would treat an infestation of cockroaches. Well, that's what this bunch think we are, cockroaches. And if you guys don't get your shit together, we'll be expunged. Now, where's General Marsh?'

'You have no right to be here. I'm the Commander-in-chief,' the would-be U.S. President said.

Robert looked across at the man standing at the head of the table. He recognised the Speaker of the House who had grabbed power and, with his opposite number, Grigori, in the Great Northern Union, another power-hungry politician, plunged Earth into World War III.

'I'll show you what these monsters are capable of,' Robert said, as he reached into his darkest memories. In a millisecond, he was standing at the door of the *Hela* med-bay when he arrived that fateful morning to find Alex operating on Rhea, with the baby ceirim biting at his hands. Through the glass walls of the treatment room, he could see Rhea lying restrained on the treatment table covered with blood. A dark-shaped object appeared half in and half out of her cut-open abdomen. As Robert watched in horror, Alex grappled with it as he tried to extract it. The thing turned and something like a head and a small mouth opened, biting Alex's hand. Then its claws withdrew from Rhea's stomach and started slashing at Alex, who finally let it go. The baby ceirim retreated back into her stomach.

As they played in his head, Robert flashed those memories into the U.S. President's brain. The man gagged and spluttered as his mind filled with the horror Robert had seen. He could feel Theia's screaming, "let them go, let them go" and watched as Alex mounted the words "thank you" when Robert finally activated the decon process. Then the President fell to the floor, retching and vomiting. "He'll need medical help. I believe he might be having a heart attack.'

The man turned and looked back up at Robert. 'Release Marsh,' he croaked. 'Swear him in as Commander-in-chief.' Then he lay back on the ground, surrounded by medics.

'Now, here's what's going to happen. I want Marsh in command within one hour. I'll be back in a cloaked ship with an Anan delegation. Their experts are Verteg Borea and Captain Quriel of the Aknar military; he works for General Arie Machai, our Overlord's Protector. You will welcome them and work with them, and the Russians, as a team. They'll help us build weapons that will slow down that vicious hoard of monsters. Is that clear?'

'Crystal clear,' a woman in a navy uniform said.

'I'll be visiting the Russians next. They know what to expect – I was there before. I'll make sure Admiral Vasily takes control. Also, you need to keep some remnants of that pissing contest going between you both. We don't want to let the aliens know we're all working together again, do we?'

Before Robert could continue, the Secretary of State stood up. 'How dare you come here, telling us what to do and calling the war we have to protect our sovereignty a pissing contest. We are the most powerful—' He screamed, covering his face with his hands, as the visions of the ceirim crawling out of Rhea's stomach burst out in his mind.

As if nothing had happened, Robert's ghostly apparition continued. 'Ladies and gentlemen, I apologise if I am brash and uncouth in my dealings with you today. I am here because your knowledge offers our civilisation some hope for survival. You and the Great Northern Union have the most advanced human developed weaponry and some of the brightest people on Earth in your military. We must channel those resources into a combined force to hold off this threat.'

'Robert, that all sounds fine, but where is The Eight? If what you say is true, we're finished without him. And, if those ships and aliens are as powerful as you make out, surely they'll see we're working together and are preparing to attack them. We know they can access our comms. Think about it, Robert. This doesn't make sense,' the woman in the navy uniform said.

Finally, a smart one, he thought. *There's hope after all.* 'I don't know where he is, Admiral. I do know he'll be back. You're right about the technology difference. But we have an advantage – superior alien comms tech that the invaders can't detect. We proved it before. They can't see our ships or access our comms. Two techs from Captain Quriel's family will install it here. I'll send them in a shuttle first.' Robert stood still, his blue ethereal appearance lighting up the room. As he had elaborated on the complexities, he felt the dynamics change amongst the group. Already, one was calling with the order to release Marsh.

'I'll accept that, Robert,' the Admiral replied. 'You won't find us wanting. But if those beasts are the threat you say, we can't beat them without The Eight.'

'You're right, Admiral,' Robert replied. 'We must slow them up until The Eight returns. That's the objective. Put our petty differences aside. What happened in the past is in the past. If we don't do that, there'll be no future here on Earth for humankind. If we continue to fight amongst ourselves, the aliens that are here now, will wipe us out.' Then he left, his ethereal presence returning to the Australian base.

*

One hour later, in a bunker below the Kremlin, The Great Northern Union's rulers were again treated to the apparition of the fair-haired

Scotsman. This time, memories of his last appearance dispelled any dissent. No puny politician prepared to die for the propaganda "the cause" promoted. It spoke volumes for the empty "cause".

Robert repeated the speech he had made to the U.S., this time, demanding the return of Admiral Vasily as President. 'Are you okay with that?' he asked.

The politicians didn't answer. A young man, in military uniform stood up with Robert's answer. He shouted some orders in Russian and in double-quick time, armed guards appeared from the shadows. With guns pointed at the politicians, they stood – and under arrest – were marched out.

'Welcome back, Robert. We wondered if you'd show up. What happens now?'

'Keep the skirmish between you and the U.S. going. You can both scale it back, but whatever happens, we mustn't let these aliens know we're working together. You and the U.S. have tech we need to combine it. It'll help us stall for time until The Eight returns. The ceirim can move at sixty kilometres an hour. Soon they'll hit a choke point. We may be able to halt them there. But we need to work quickly together. In the meantime, Chang is getting in touch with the aliens, offering his services as Emperor of Earth.' He paused, waiting for their laughter to subside.

'Will they not see through that? And what about our comms? They have access to it with their advanced tech. You did that when we attacked you on the *Hela* in space,' the young commander said.

Good thought, Robert. The same questions I got in the U.S. As long as the smart ones keep thinking and questioning, there's hope. 'We have alien tech that will hide our comms. It'll be installed in the Cheyanne Mountain base as well. You'll get a visit from a Borea team in a few hours. They'll install their comms tech here as well.'

'How do we know they're friendly?'

'Some are white-skinned, some are green and maybe a mix of both. They'll be wearing blue uniforms and they don't eat humans. Trust them, they serve The Eight.'

More laughter. Robert liked the Russians; they bled a stoic resilience. *Time to go,* he thought. With a thumbs up, his ethereal appearance disappeared.

Back in the Hela base, Robert opened his eyes. He looked at the exhausted Verteg, slumped in her chair. 'You did well, Verteg. Let's get a move on, Quriel. They're waiting on us.'

*

The intensity of what followed even took the ever-pushy Robert off step. The amount of work in so short a time frame seemed an impossible task. Install the Borea comms at strategic locations in China, Russia, and the U.S. Create a manufacturing team to build a viable weapon. Move the Anan tech from their base in Australia. Meanwhile, collect the Russian tech and people – shipping it to the mission centre in the U.S. And, to complicate matters, keep it all a secret from The Ninth. As if he didn't have enough to deal with, Harold added an item Robert didn't want on his "to-do list". Get approval for the mission from the United Nations. Robert baulked at it and a full-blown quarrel erupted between the two close friends. Meantime, the ceirim advance continued to consume the human population of the Indian subcontinent, making their way towards Asia.

The U.S. military base in the Cheyenne Mountains was the logical mission centre. It contained everything they needed. Secrecy, workshops, a command centre and some of the most critical parts for the mission, the top-secret Earth technology they needed.

The missile idea, a mix of advanced Earth and Anan tech, came from information Verteg found in Demard's files. Before the purebreeds arrived, the U.S. and the Great Northern Union were developing an advanced fusion weapon. Unlike the conventional hydrogen bomb, they both wanted a missile that would deliver a focused fusion-sized explosion without radioactive fallout. Its nickname was the clean bomb – a mythical resurrection from the past! In days reminiscent of the old Cold War, both countries locked horns in a competition to be the first to develop these new weapons. As with fusion reaction, containment was a problem. This was easily solved with the help of the Borea technicians, Anan technology and the introduction of grav to the bomb's containment.

With all his ducks in a row, Robert never believed they would jump in unity to attention. His brief brush with global politics had taught him that. Nothing would go as planned, expect the unexpected, and the ducks never march straight!

*

Siberia, 23rd January 2028

The project kicked off by dispatching a shuttle to the Cheyenne Mountains with Borea techs. After that, one of the *George's* inter-field transporters flew to an air base in Siberia to collect more top-secret Earth technology – missiles and an Aerial Launch Platform from the Russians. As planned, the pilot made contact with the division commander, and the doors of the base's hangar opened. But when they landed inside the vast building, armed guards surrounded the alien ship.

The Russian commander wouldn't allow the transfer of their most secret tech to the heart of their enemy's country, the U.S. Arguments broke out between the mystified Borea and the commander. A frantic call from the transporter's pilot to the Hela base alerted Robert to the problem. Robert called Admiral Vasily, a risky move over unsecured comms. A one-word reply, "Betrayed", told Robert all he needed to know.

The commander argued that the orders did not reach him. Or, as Vasily intimated, were deliberately ignored – it didn't matter to Robert. Just another fly in the ointment to deal with. With the help of Verteg, a pissed off Robert made another ethereal journey. This time he had no mercy – his wrath turned on the Russian commander and his guards.

The appearance of the ghostly blue Scotsman terrified them. Some dropped their guns and ran, but the commander and four others opened fire on Robert. He closed his eyes as the bullets cut through his ethereal body, continuing on into the wall of the building. He raised his blue arm and pointed at them, while his other gripped the blue diamond around his neck. Pure anger flowed from his hand. Five bolts of blue lightning flashed across the hangar, striking the commander and the four guards. Their bodies ignited, cold blue flames engulfing the screaming men from the inside out. The men withered inside their uniforms and within seconds turned to dust. Empty uniforms and weapons fell to the floor.

A roar from Robert filled the hangar, the sound reverberating around them, terrifying even the Borea, hiding in their ship. But the message sunk in. Miraculously, the orders from Admiral Vasily appeared, loyalties changed, and as night turns to day, the base erupted with enthusiastic help. Or, as Robert sensed, they were quaking in their boots to get rid of him after the failure of their double-dealing scum-bag commander. The dead man's loyalties were laid to rest with the ousted political order. *Nothing comes easy*, Robert thought, as his ethereal consciousness retreated to the Hela base. The Borea got what they wanted and left for another military facility to install their secret comms and pick up Russia's best – technicians, pilots and weapons experts.

*

Cheyenne Mountains, 24th January 2028

Robert, Verteg, Quriel and his six Aknar soldiers travelled on the last shuttle from the Hela base to the project headquarters in the Cayenne Mountains. The reluctant Russian visitors, U.S. generals, commanders, technicians, pilots and armed guards assembled inside the underground base's hangar to meet their new "alien allies". Steel doors opened to allow the cloaked shuttle entry, the humming of the grav engines alerting the crowd to the arrival of the invisible craft. Inside the cathedral-sized chamber, Verteg killed the cloak and the shuttle landed, its rear door facing the waiting delegation.

The door opened out onto a ramp and led by Chief Haldock, six Aknar troops filed out. Dressed in blue uniforms, each carrying a grav gun, they formed a protective guard at the shuttle's entrance. In the blue Aknar uniforms, the tall white-skinned purebreeds, long necks extended proud above their shoulders, grav guns at the ready, displayed that "no-nonsense look" Robert wanted. Their guise said, "We're here, to get a job done". Robert knew – despite General Marsh's ascension to Commander-in-chief

– a welcome wasn't on the agenda. Their first appearance inside this hidden lair must show superiority and control, everything Robert, as The Eight's proxy on Earth, demanded.

Quriel followed, checking around – and not for show – Verteg's safety his biggest concern. Closing his eyes, he cast his mind out for any sign of danger amongst the gun-toting humans. Confusion, suspicion and fear were what he felt. He turned and nodded at Verteg, waiting inside the shuttle. She marched out tall, for her five-foot seven-inches. Her blue hair tied neatly up in a bun, toned muscles emphasised her feminine curves. Her brown eyes scanned the crowd as her green skin glittered in the harsh artificial light. They didn't realise the sharp-minded Pilot sensed their suspicious minds. *More distrustful aliens, nothing new*, thought Verteg, here to serve The Eight and restore order in the far-away Anan Galaxy.

Robert followed last. Dressed in faded jeans, an old shirt and a grey tweed jacket, untidy sandy hair touched his shoulders. The six-foot five-inch-tall man towered over his alien friends. Although most had seen him on television at the U.N., none here had seen the big man in the flesh. He wasted no time pushing his project forward, marching out to stand beside Verteg and Quriel.

His commanding voice silenced the empty greetings. 'In case you haven't noticed, our plant is under attack by creatures designed as the universe's most dangerous biological weapon. They eat a planet's population. Right now, they are decimating the Indian subcontinent. A billion people will die; real people who live life and love as we do. Those unfortunate people are some of the poorest on the planet, hunted down into extinction by the ceirim. The ceirim's next destination is Asia. If they succeed, the human race is finished. We must work together and try to slow that advance. We'll never stop them, but with some smart guerrilla tactics, we can slow them up until our Overlord, The Eight, returns.'

Robert paused. A dead silence fell across the cathedral-sized space. His voice rang out again. 'This is the Borea Pilot, Verteg and her cousin, Captain Quriel of the Aknar Military ...'

And so he continued with the introductions, handing over to Verteg and Quriel to explain the nuts and bolts of the project. The suspicious crowd's mood changed, questions were asked, groups formed, materials inspected, designs disseminated. And, as Robert stepped back, before his eyes, humans and aliens set to work.

*

Verteg designed the vehicle, cannibalised from one of the *George's* transporters. The inter-field ship wouldn't have the aerodynamic capability to get the speeds she needed in the atmosphere – a problem solved by mating the propulsion end to an experimental plane warehoused in the Cayenne Mountains. To add to the hybrid vessel's off-the-wall appearance, they bolted on the Russian ALP. Using grav, the Borea technicians modified the fusion missiles containment. With ingenuity, Quriel crafted and combined the best of both country's fusion bombs and missiles with Anan tech. Working around the clock, the best engineers from Russia and the U.S. had the vehicle ready in six days, a feat Robert couldn't fault. When the top brass inspected it, they thought it would never get off the ground.

'The beauty of grav, oh ye of little faith,' Robert had replied to their negative comments.

Harold, back from a U.N. meeting in Geneva, interloped with the top brass – the visit timed before the craft's launch. He wanted to get the ever-elusive Robert on his own, and the Scotsman knew he couldn't avoid this meeting forever. So, in a small store Robert had purloined as a makeshift office, the two friends sat together.

There was no small talk. Harold got right to it. 'Robert it's a step too far.'

Robert shook his head, his long hair hanging over his face. 'Harold, we have to do something.' He stopped as he pushed his hair back and sat up, staring at Harold, the intensity of the conviction flowing from his blue eyes. 'Once they pass that chokepoint, the ceirim are into Asia. They'll disappear into the jungles of Myanmar, Laos and Cambodia to breed a larger army – then it's all over.' Robert was right. If the ceirim got across the Brahmaputra river, they were out of the Indian subcontinent and it was game over for Asia.

Harold shook his head. What Robert was contemplating flew in the face of everything humans considered sacrosanct. 'But millions of people will die – at your hand. The Security Council left me as their scapegoat to approve this plan – so typical of their political wrangling. "Whatever you decide, Harold." That's what the spineless bastards said. Robert, as The Eight's representative on Earth, I cannot authorise it.'

Robert held up his arm, glowing bright blue. 'When The Eight left me with this, he said to me it was my "reward for your help, Robert". Before I left the New World, he told me to take care of his planet and, if anything happens to him, I am his proxy. He said to heed the glow in my arm. When the time comes, it would guide me. Harold, since Verteg and Quriel presented me with this opportunity, it hasn't stopped glowing. This is our only option.' He pulled out a map of Northern India and the Himalayas. Again, explaining his plan in detail, jagged lines drawn on the map indicated how he hoped to push the ceirim northwards. Bridges across the great river marked for demolition, and in a semi-circle in red, the ever-increasing advancing line of the ceirim.

Harold shook his head. 'Robert, they will judge you as a war criminal if you do this.'

'So be it, Harold. Those spineless gits can chop my head off if they wish. And, if I can slow up the ceirim until The Eight gets here, I'll give it to them on a plate, if that's what they want. But you're too late to stop me. The plan's already in motion. World War III, the phoney war, has stopped. And a combined air force is bombing the bridges–'

'Who gave that order?' Harold asked, jumping up from his seat.

'I did.'

'No, Robert, we should wait,' Harold pleaded.

'By The Eight, I want this done. It's my responsibility. I will live with it and answer to him.'

The fire and fury in Robert's voice shocked the level-headed Harold. 'Robert, what have you become? You would never have done something like this before.'

'I am his planet's guardian, and Harold,' he said, holding up his blue arm, 'I wish he never ever gave me this.'

They were the last words Robert said to Harold before the start of the mission to save the planet.

CHAPTER THIRTY-NINE

CNS Headlines. Aliens Have Landed.

Harold Addison, The Eight's U.N. representative on Earth, confirmed the black creatures massacring humanity in the Indian subcontinent are alien "ceirim". A rival Overlord called The Sixth, dispatched these demons to Earth as part of his intergalactic dispute with The Eight. Addison starkly warned, "Humanity faces an extinction-level event." He failed to shed light on defensive measures other than, "We are doing everything we can with the weapons we have."

The Chinese Prime Minister, Chang Jin, has called for global co-operation in fighting the menace. "We must unite and do everything possible to defeat this evil," he said, in an interview today.

In a related matter, social media is quoting unverified reports about a regime change in the U.S. and Russia and an end to their border dispute. Both governments refused to comment …

▪ From: Continental News Services. Good Morning Planet Earth

*

The Dem-Zav1, 31st January 2028

'We're clear, Mr Leslie,' Verteg said, as the *Dem-Zav1* climbed steeply up over the Cheyenne Mountains. The hybrid craft, powered by two grav drives, mated to the back of a sleek plane, flew like an aerodynamic bullet. With short angular wings and stabilising tails mounted on the engine module, drag was minimal. Below the vessel hung the all-important ALP, loaded with four precious fusion missiles – weapons of mass destruction – the fruits of their collective labour.

'Missile systems are active, Captain,' a young man, seated in the cockpit beside Verteg, said.

'Lieutenant, configure human guidance systems with Anan navigation projection,' the Borea Pilot replied.

'Yes ma'am,' he said, in a southern drawl.

She stole a look at Robert, sitting behind. He grinned. 'You should be used to their ways by now, Verteg. They're all spit and polish, no bullshit, just get it done. That's the U.S. military,' he said in her ear.

'It's the accent, Robert. It's so different to yours and Janet's.' She turned to the Aknar military chief, his blue diamond inserted into the nav-con beside Robert. 'Haldock, let me know when the human system syncs with your projection.'

With his eyes closed, he nodded as he focused his mind on maintaining the complex projection of the Earth below.

Quriel had wanted to come on this mission but Robert had told him to stay. If they lost *Dem-Zav1*, more than ever, Quriel would be needed on Earth. Verteg had also banned his participation. If she didn't come back, Quriel would lead the family. Together they came up with the name for the crossbreed craft they pinned their hopes on. *Dem-Zav1*, named after their two fathers, Demard and Zaval. Both, who to this day, inspired their children with the legendary deeds of their past.

Dem-Zav1's command centre hummed with activity as the mixed crew of alien and human synchronised their systems.

Verteg looked over at the young human sitting in the cramped cockpit, admiring his smart and crisp flight suit. *A far cry from Zaval's old and worn ship garb*, she thought. 'Lieutenant, course is plotted. You have the ship,' she said, as she stood up.

'Yes, ma'am.'

She pursed her lips, looked down at him and put a green hand on his shoulder. 'Don't be the first human to crash an alien ship, please. Just follow the course and speed I set.'

Like a kid with a new toy, he grinned up at her. 'No ma'am, I mean …'

'I know what you mean, Lieutenant,' she said, as she walked back to join Robert in the ship's command centre.

'Is that the first of our new crop of pilots?' he asked.

'He has some ways to go, but yes, Mr Leslie. If we win the battle for the planet, we'll continue with his training. What news from Earth?'

'Chang Jin made contact with one of their ships. They told him: "Humanity will be eradicated; it's the will of The Sixth. We should bow down to The Ninth, and accept extinction." It's golden intel from Chang; now we know who we're dealing with. As you said, Verteg, it's The Ninth – the expendable one – who is here.'

'How did he contact them?'

'Flew a drone over this country here,' he said, pointing to a map of Bangladesh. 'It's where the ceirim are now. They're heading towards Asia major. Close to Chang's borders, he managed to hail one of those ships spraying DNA.' An audacious plan the master spy had hatched – fly a drone right into the thick of the ceirim advance and hail any airborne ships in the vicinity in Anan. The simplest of plans worked!

'And the primitive weapons your allies use – are they having any effect?'

'We have that on screen now, Verteg,' he said, as the tactical monitor lit up with a scene from the battle that raged below.

It was like something from the Blitz in World War II. Abandoning their phoney war had paid a dividend by surprising the ceirim. Plane after plane from a combined force flew in over the Indian and Bangladesh border, dropping tons of conventional armaments on the advancing line. Cutting a black swatch across the landscape, the planes demolished the bridges forcing the ceirim northwards to the narrow strip of land between the Himalayas and the great rivers meandering across the lowland plains. Robert's plan to push them into a choke was working in real time.

Dem-Zav1, bristling with Borea and human technology, tracked the movements of The Ninth's transporters as they continued to spray Kochtos's DNA on the population. Robert and Verteg watched as the blasts from the conventional bombs bounced off the alien ship's grav bubbles. The bombers couldn't see the cloaked alien ships, but from the devastation below, they could guess where they might be. It was enough of an effort to frustrate and slow the advance.

'Your allies don't have the resources to sustain that level of bombardment, Mr Leslie, do they?'

'No, Verteg. It's the tonnage; there are limits to what they can drop. But it does slow them up.'

She turned to face a group of humans huddled over a bank of screens. 'Are your launch systems functional?'

A young woman looked up from her screen. She blinked as her eyes met Verteg's, 'Captain, we're ah …' she began with a Russian accent. Her voice faltered as she put a hand over her nose.

'Get used to it, human. I'm half Neredian. I have gills – see,' she said, pointing to pink glands on her neck. 'The hot, dry air on the ship makes them sweat and, yes, it smells. Don't ever make me ask you a question twice.'

The young woman blushed, her eyes falling down to the readouts on her screen. 'I'm sorry, Captain. We're running some tests on the guidance system interface. So far, so good; we're on schedule for the first launch.'

Verteg leaned over the woman, sliding her hand under her flight harness. 'Your harness is loose. Did I brief you about that on Earth?'

'Yes, Captain, you did.'

'Tighten it up, human,' she rounded on them. 'All of you, your flight harnesses need to be tight. There's no room for what you humans call "sloppiness". Those flight harnesses mean life to you. The grav bubble will afford some protection but once we start moving, you will need those restraints.' Except for the hum of the grav engines and the occasional beep from the instruments, the cabin went quiet.

Robert took a deep breath. He sensed the crew's resentment. It was one of the reasons why he was here, on the maiden flight of *Dem-Zav1*, their last hope to contain the ceirim. From the outset, it was difficult getting humans to trust the alien Borea. He had to knock heads together to transcend the mistrust that had sprung up after the arrival of The Sixth's fleet. He knew some would find it hard to accept Verteg as the captain of this ship.

'I know this is all new to you, but to survive this run, you've got to listen to and trust Verteg, the Pilot. Not wanting to be melodramatic – mankind's hope is with us. This mission has to succeed. Do your best, we'll follow the plan and hopefully get back in one piece. Is that fair enough?'

'Yes, Robert,' they shouted back.

'Come on, Verteg, we've got time for a brew in the back,' he said, leading Verteg aft.

'Is this what you call tea?' she asked, sipping the hot liquid he made.

'Aye, it is. Came from India, that land those monsters have destroyed,' he said, as he leaned against a bulkhead. 'Our world is changed forever, isn't it?'

'I'm afraid so, Mr Leslie.' They sipped their tea in silence. Minutes later, the voice of the lieutenant, came over the ship's comms. 'Fifteen minutes out, Captain to the cockpit.'

'Time to go, Mr Leslie. Now we find out how the hybrid ship and weapons perform.'

*

In the dead of night, the invisible *Dem-Zav1* descended from the stratosphere. Verteg looked across at the navigation projection. The Ninth's three cloaked transporters worked their way from east to west, spraying the ceirim's DNA. The sky below was clear, the combined air forces' planes now gone.

'Three targets acquired,' came the voice of the young woman at the launch console.

'Lieutenant, they're too close together; we hit the two outer ships,' Verteg said, pointing to Haldock's navigation projection. 'I don't think we can outrun the blast from three missiles.'

'Reconfigure to targets A and C. I repeat, reconfigure to targets A and C,' the Lieutenant shouted to the missile crew behind.

Their strange ship sped on down towards their mark. Over the eerie hum of the grav engines, Verteg could hear the missile crew change the target resolution. 'Lieutenant, targets A and C acquired.'

Verteg nodded to the young lieutenant seated beside her. 'Launch when ready.'

'Fire one and four. I repeat, fire one and four,' he shouted to the missile crew behind.

Their hybrid craft jumped as the two heavy missiles released. Verteg watched them on screen, their engines igniting, as they dropped clear. She looked over to Haldock, his hand wrapped around his blue diamond embedded in the nav-con.

The big broad-shouldered purebreed, cramped in the small cockpit, cast his mind out with the power of his blue diamond. Splitting his thoughts in two, he connected with the missile's guidance modules. They had sacrificed a blue crystal to make these modules, embedding a shard of the precious diamonds into each of the four units. Blue energy conduits connected the crystals to the missile's guidance control electronics. Green LED lights flashed on, confirming Haldock's connection. Electronic commands flowed to the missile's engines and flight fins. Piloted by Haldock, the deadly weapons flew down towards their targets. On the bridge *of Dem-Zav1*, his three-dimensional navigational plot projected the course vector out into the air above the flight controls.

Verteg checked the calculations over and over before this flight. Until the missile's earth-tech guidance system locked on to the grav distortions of the ceirim's three transporters, Haldock would have to fly them using his blue diamond nav-link.

*

On the bridge of one of the three transporters, the lead geneticist watched as they sprayed the contaminating ceirim DNA over the humans below. A recent risk analysis had deemed they were impervious to anything on Earth. By now, he had stopped counting the size of the army he had created. Kochtos and his lieutenants followed at a distance, gorging on some of the new ceirim his own DNA had created. A heaving mass of human suffering ran for their lives before the alien onslaught. The apocalypse arrived at their doorstep, dispensing a fate worse than death – transformation into a dark monster. Some consumed, eaten whole, by the voracious ceirim – they were the lucky ones. Others escaped, but in such a populous area, they couldn't get far. The weak were trampled underfoot in a terror-powered stampede. Ignored by the purebreed transporter's crew and their geneticists, fear-filled every corner of the land. That's what they had created, far beyond the bounds of Anan decency and ethics. Shutting their minds to the horror they had unleashed, they immersed themselves in the gruesome task at hand.

The constant harrying from the high-level bombers didn't move them from their course. However, the bombers' destruction of the bridges on the great rivers delayed the advance. They had discussed restarting a fresh crop on the other side of the rivers, ferrying Kochtos over with the transporters, but it would divide the army and his controlling faction. Besides, it would disrupt the workflow, something the lead geneticist was keen to preserve. Ignorant to the cloaked ship and the two missiles bearing down on them from above, the geneticists planned their next DNA-replenishing stop.

*

Grav bubbles create distortions, some more than others. From their original scans of the three DNA-spraying vessels, Quriel discovered the distortion's harmonics. Verteg built a sensor from earth-tech to pinpoint them – the only downside was the short range of the sensors.

The final seconds of this flight depended on all her calculations and designs being right. With seconds to go, her brain worked in overdrive, questioning and calculating.

Verteg held their course bearing, plotted by Haldock and following the missiles he steered. This, the most critical phase of the mission, demanded the most from Anan and Earth tech. Ready to rain apocalyptic death on the apocalypse, Verteg could feel the tension in the cabin. The pressure on her crew was pushing them to the limits of their newfound skills. Fear of early death scratched at the back of her head. What if they got too close to the blast? *Vaporised in an instant, they wouldn't even feel the end*, she thought. It took self-discipline to fight her desire to pull the ship up and get away from here as fast as possible. But she couldn't, not until the missiles found their mark; only then could Haldock relinquish their command. The three targets were getting closer and closer but pursing her pink lips, she flew on. Until she heard the shout from behind!

'Missile lock, we have missile lock …'

Verteg didn't wait for the rest of the report and pulled up hard on *Dem-Zav1*'s flight controls. The missiles, close enough to their cloaked targets for their Earth guidance system to take over, locked onto the grav bubble's tell-tale distortion.

Increasing the hybrid craft's grav drives to maximum, Verteg pointed the ship straight up towards the moon, shining brightly in the night sky above. 'Lieutenant,' she shouted, 'grav dampers to max. Increase output to the bubble by seventy.' She could feel the buffeting of the air on the hull as the ship's speed increased.

'Dampers on max; bubble at seventy, ma'am.'

She looked over at his flight station. He had stuck up a picture of a young woman holding a child. 'Is that your family, Lieutenant?'

'Yes ma'am, it is,' he said, as he reached out and touched the picture.

'With a bit of luck, you'll get to see them soon.'

He smiled. 'Captain, with you flying this mongrel, I have no doubt of that—' The ship sprung forwards as, travelling faster than the speed of sound, the shock wave slammed into them.

*

Unknown to The Ninth and his crews, the missiles, locked in a deadly embrace, accelerated down to their targets, exploding on contact with the two outer ship's grav bubbles. Like an invisible hammer, the fusion blast collapsed the bubbles, compressing them down onto their vessels. The occupants didn't feel a thing. Crushed flat, death came instantly – then they burned to dust.

The two blasts cut through the third ship's grav bubble, vaporising it. The heat from the fusion blasts rolled down onto the Earth below and, like a tsunami of pure energy, scoured the land as it radiated out from the two epicentres. It was a weapon never seen before on Earth. The force and heat of the explosions rolled across the land, burning everything in its wake. Robert had unleashed mankind's last hope to hold the ceirim at bay, a simple scorched-earth policy, and incinerate everything contaminated by their foul DNA. And the catastrophic collateral damage – the local population not yet consumed by the ceirim or the life-changing DNA, also died.

With all her strength, Verteg concentrated on keeping the ship pointing skywards. Before the explosion, Haldock collapsed his navigation projection, withdrawing his mind to the ship's safety. She was steering by sight, looking out of the cockpit window, focused on flying straight up towards the moon. Firing corrective pulses from rocket thrusters, she managed to stop the ship from spinning out of control. Like a child's rattle, the machine vibrated and chattered, Its structural integrity pushed to the limit, the skills of the manufacturers sorely tested. The acceleration and violent shaking pushed Verteg's crew's tolerance to their physical limits. Some blacked out, others moaned and screamed, their fear-filled cries filling the command cabin behind her. As the light began to filter into the dark sky in front, she realised they had survived. Levelling the ship off in the stratosphere, she turned to the lieutenant. 'Reduce grav dampers and the bubble to optimum and, Lieutenant, what is that strange smell?'

'Puke, ma'am.'

'What is puke?'

'It's vomit; contents of the stomach.'

'Yes, yes, I know what that is. Haldock, can you get a navigation projection back up?'

'Yes, Captain.' Gripping his blue diamond, he closed his eyes and a projection of the space around, with Earth in the background, burst out above flight control. Their position was marked straight above the Indian subcontinent in the thermosphere.

'We have two missiles left. Mr Leslie, we should hold in a low earth orbit and see what our options are,' Verteg said. Her voice was deadpan with no sign of elation at their first victory.

The crew responded likewise – this wasn't a victory; it was only the beginning.

*

On the dark side of the moon, it took some time for Bardek's repeater satellites to relay back the news to The Ninth's fleet. When it did, pure fear erupted in the minds of the *Chad's* bridge crew. A malodorous odour flowed from their scent glands, staining the air they breathed. The one dour thought pierced their brains. *What will The Sixth do to us now?*

Seconds after the explosions erupted on the viewscreen, Bardek shattered the sudden numbness. 'What was that?' he screamed. 'Comms, what ships do they have in the area?'

'Nothing, Captain. I see nothing. The explosions just erupted above our three transport ships.'

'You missed something. Replay those images in slow motion and try to contact our three ships.' He turned and shouted to a young purebreed, 'Go get the Overlord.'

'There is nothing, Captain. I did not miss anything, look,' the comms officer said, pointing to the picture running in slow motion on their viewscreen.

'Any word from our transporters?'

'No, Captain.'

The Ninth floated onto the bridge. 'What is it, Bardek? What is happening?'

'Overlord, there was a fusion explosion right over our ships, along the advancing line. I fear we have lost them. The geneticists, they were all on board those ships.'

'What of Kochtos?'

'I don't know, Overlord. We are still reviewing the incoming data.'

*

In the moon-filled night, the flash above blinded Kochtos. All his senses came alive, filling his black brain with the feeling of death. He remembered the river. Breathing in deeply, he ran towards its sweet, pungent smell. As the blast erupted, he dived in, sinking fast into the deep waters of the Brahmaputra. Through the water above, he could see the white light and felt the searing heat and the force of the explosion as it ripped along the great river. Down he went until he was on the riverbed. He rolled along, pushed by the river's life-saving current. He looked around, turning himself over in the murky waters. He could see dark shapes all around. *Dead ceirim,* he thought. *How many did they kill? Where did they get such a weapon?* he wondered. Some naked bodies floated by. *Humans, there are humans killed as well – not possible. I never believed they would kill their own to protect their planet. Who would give such an order? At least their bodies will sustain me,* he thought, swimming over to grab the nearest one.

Sitting on the riverbed, he gorged on the soft flesh of the dead young male. His strength replenished, Kochtos struck upwards towards the light. As he broke the surface, the dark night sky had turned into a glowing blood-red day. Fires burned on the river and all along its banks. The air was hot and sticky from the blast. The harsh sound of the crackling flames and the intermitted explosions drowned out the soft sound of the flowing river. As he looked up in the sky, red glowing clouds swirled in a never-ending mass of energy created by the wind of the blast. He swam to the northern bank and crawled out. The ground, downriver from the blast's epicentre, was still hot. Hearing a noise behind, he turned to see his trusted lieutenant crawl up behind him onto the riverbank.

'I told you, Kochtos – they have weapons and I said they would use them.'

'No, friend, this is different. This is Anan technology. Come, we go back. I will contact The Ninth. He will move us to their dark continent. We will hide in the jungles; they will never find us.'

*

From the safety of Earth orbit, shrouded by the Borea cloak, Verteg's crew analysed the data their sensors had gathered.

'Mr Leslie, we got the three transport ships with the two missiles and look,' she said, pointing at the devastation, 'the Earth's scoured, the ceirim are gone. But I'm afraid we killed what was left of the human population.'

'Verteg, I knew that would happen.'

'But such destruction, I didn't realise how powerful the weapons would be,' she said. That was Quriel's forte; he understood and had discussed the yield with Robert. It was a blunt conversation, both with no delusions about the ferocity of their weapons.

'I had no doubt of that, Verteg. There was no other way.'

'Who of your leaders gave the approval to use such power?'

'They left it up to me, Verteg. Spineless lot they are. My decision. My responsibility and I will answer to our Overlord for that.'

She looked at him; it was out of character for him. His arm glowed bright blue. *He's devastated at the loss of life, despite its colour,* she thought, as she watched him run his hands through his sandy hair in anguish. 'What next?'

'Let's wait and see what the opposition do. We're in no hurry; we've stopped them. The Ninth won't be too pleased about that. If we wait, we might get a shot off at one of their intergalactic vessels.'

'Mr Leslie, we wouldn't penetrate their grav bubbles. We talked about that.'

'Maybe two missiles would.'

Verteg shook her head. She left him looking at the screens and walked aft to the small galley. She sat down beside Haldock and the human lieutenant. 'Chief Haldock, Lieutenant, well done. It seems the first part of the mission went to plan. Hard work pays off.'

The relaxing comment, appreciated by those who had heard it, was soon the scuttlebutt of their strange craft. Like ghosts, they waited and watched for The Ninth's reaction.

*

Back on the *Chad*, The Ninth cast his ethereal mind out beyond the confines of their veiling moon. A glimmer of hope touched him, enough to make a difference between total failure and the ability to recreate another army of death.

'He is alive, Kochtos is alive. You must retrieve him,' The Ninth said. 'I can feel his thoughts – he is making his way west. Captain, we stop hiding the fleet, order all ships to Earth orbit.'

'Overlord, we should—'

'Should what?' he boomed. 'Wait for another attack? No, we move now.'

'Overlord, the technology for that attack, it has to be Anan.'

'Of course, it's Anan. Do you not think The Eight left some defensive mechanism here? What do your scans show?'

'Nothing, Overlord. We cannot find anything. It's well concealed, whatever it is.'

'Bardek, you have advanced cloaks and scanning tools onboard?'

'Yes, Overlord, we do. We should see everything.'

'Who can hide from us?'

'There is nothing that I know of that could defeat our technology.'

The old navigator stood up. 'Captain, there were stories my father told me. He worked on an intergalactic transporter.'

'And?'

'Captain, he said they were attacked, travelling in empty space, when pirates came from nowhere. They appeared, right on top of them. After they plundered the vessel, they left and disappeared. There was no trace of them, before or after the attack.'

The Ninth floated over to the old navigator. He trembled and knelt down, looking at the deck and wishing he had kept his mouth shut. 'I remember those stories and that outlaw family. They are gone, and so is their outlawed technology. What made you think of them?' he said, circling the old purebreed man. 'It is their drug you take, the bawrak. We know the remains of that smuggler's family manufacture and distribute it. The One chose to ignore common criminals. He believed it was a matter for the Anan Protective Guard. You are addicted to it – I see that. What treachery have we here? Bardek, how many of your crew use the drug?'

'Overlord, you know many do. Our abilities fade due to the Anan sickness but they are loyal, I can assure you.'

'Silence,' boomed The Ninth. He reached out with a tentacle from his energy mass and delved into the mind of the navigator. It was an unwieldy approach. The man withered in agony as The Ninth reached down deep into his consciousness. 'What are you hiding? Who else in the fleet is with you?'

'No one, no one,' screamed the navigator.

'So, you admit you're the traitor.'

Whimpering in agony, he curled up in a ball on the deck. 'No, no, Overlord. I'm not.'

The Ninth delved deep inside the navigator's mind and found what he was looking for. Images of a large young man smiling at the navigator played in the old man's mind. The Ninth projected the scene out over the bridge for all to see.

'Kake, I'm out of credit. I need this for me and the crew,' the navigator said.

'This one's on the house,' Kake replied, as he handed over a package. 'You're a good customer. I trust you.'

'Thank you, Kake. I'm in your debt.'

'Well then, tell me, where you're off to?'

'A secret mission for The Sixth …' They watched the vivid images playing from the navigator's mind, as he told the drug dealer the outline of their mission.

Kake smiled and slapped his customer on the back. 'Good luck with the hunt.'

The Ninth twisted his tentacle of blue and the image faded. The old man screamed. Blood burst from his nose and his ears as he collapsed on the deck of the bridge, dead. The crew stayed silent. The Ninth sensed their hatred and fear. Some were on the drug and completely addicted to it. How many of Bardek's crew have betrayed me? he wondered.

'Bardek, this was our biggest secret and your navigator told it to his drug dealer. This is not what I expected. Where are we now? Tell me, don't hide it from me.'

'Overlord, there is no treachery here. We are all loyal to you. Ask The Seventh; contact him, he will assure you, we are his loyal subjects.'

'Explain this mess. Why did you not locate the Anan technology? The Eight knows we're here. He knew all along.'

Bardek knelt before The Ninth. 'Overlord, they were able to hide from you as well,' he said. It was a blatant castigation of The Ninth's accusations against the allegiance of the captain's crew. Whatever their failings from a technical level, Bardek wouldn't countenance an attack on their loyalty. Overlords could sense most danger but as The Eight had found, and repeatedly told Niamh and Robert, Overlords were not infallible. There were limits to their power. Recognising those limits and taking responsibility for their own failings crafted an inner strength – a skill The Ninth lacked.

Knowing Bardek's comments were wholly justified, the ham-fisted Overlord blustered on. 'Silence, Bardek. Don't doubt my abilities. We must move on now. You waste too much time arguing,' he said, heaping more blame on his loyal captain.

The crew stayed silent. Bardek, the proud purebreed, continued to kneel in front of the ethereal being's blue energy mass. His head was bent forward over his long neck, exposed in a position of servitude to The Ninth, as if to say, "Take my life now if you doubt me".

Ignoring Bardek, The Ninth paused as he contemplated a way forward. A flash of blue light as a backup plan materialised. They still had Kochtos and another eight thousand ceirim in the fleet. And the extinction weapons. Time to use them and reduce Earth's population centres to uninhabited rubble.

His voice boomed out across the bridge. 'This is a setback but, whatever happens, we fight on. Make way to Earth orbit – now. Then we transfer Kochtos to another continent and land the remaining ceirim there. Bardek, we must do that while we still have transport ships. We start the second phase also. Make sure all our ships are ready to launch extinction weapons.' He turned and left the bridge. *Bardek is right,* The Ninth thought. *We're missing something. There is no sense to this. I will scour Earth until I find it.*' His ethereal mind buzzed with the possibilities of what he had missed, churning data over and over.

On the bridge, the exact same thoughts flooded the Javonian comms officer's mind. *I've missed something,* she thought. Ignoring the frantic activity around her, she built a scanning program, this time with a very different set of criteria. Within minutes, the array on the *Chad* lit up as waves of her hunting program scanned the Earth. As night approached Oceania, New Zealand passed through her piercing scan. Her smart rays penetrated everything, seeking out a tell-tale signature – one she should have looked for earlier. The previous probes had looked for Anan tech, powered-up and working machinery. This was different, and with a faint ping she hit the jackpot, discovering The Eight's home at Milford Sound. Although powered down, deep inside the mountain his hidden store of blue energy bounced back the faintest of signals.

Crouched over the comms console in her signature orange boiler suit, the Javonian's purple hands glided across the controls as she reran the scan. She stayed still, holding her breath until the answer returned. Without a doubt, she had detected a blue energy signature. Her heart beat fast in her chest as she realised something was hiding there.

The location pointed towards a mountain on a large island in the southern quadrant of the planet. But still, she said nothing as she modified the program, bombarding the area with a penetrating ray. Minutes passed, the Earth rotated and before out of range, the answer returned. The mountain was hollow, screaming evidence of a secret structure. Again, she stayed silent as she analysed the signals, confirming what she had found. To rush now served no purpose. Over and over, she examined the data.

As darkness arrived over Australia, the Hela base tracked through her scan. Reverted to hunting for blue, the waves trickled down over McKinnon. Under the jury-rigged tarps and inside the ship's tanks, blue energy turned and swirled with kaleidoscopic bursts of blue-tinted colour. However, working their magic, the Borea cloaks did their job, masking the hidden ships and their fuel. The Earth continued to turn as the Javonian comms officer scanned the planet. But she found nothing else. A smile played on her violet face; what she had seen was enough. Satisfied with her discovery, she called Bardek.

CHAPTER FORTY

CNS Headlines. Armageddon arrives in Northern India.

Reports of two explosions over the Northern Indian subcontinent, their size never seen before on Earth, are as yet, unconfirmed. Scientists speculate the overwhelming airbursts are from an unknown weapon, most likely fusion-powered.

The detonation's epicentre, directly over the centre of the alien ceirim, add to a developing theory of a human attack on the invader's army of death. The vast explosions vaporised the alien monsters, and we regret to report, the remaining human population. The death toll is unknown but fear is growing that hundreds of millions of innocent people are dead.

Aerial pictures taken from high altitude and leaked from an unnamed source, show the blast scar covering Northern India, Bangladesh, Bhutan and Nepal. Seismic measurements, as yet uncorroborated, put the blast force beyond anything ever attempted by the human race. The U.N., Anan Corp and all government agencies have refused to comment. The source inferred that a secret plane commanded by Robert Leslie, the Anan Corp Senior Project Manager, was in the area at the time.

‹ **From: Continental News Services. Good Morning Planet Earth**

*

The Dem-Zav1, Earth Orbit, 1st February 2028

MEANWHILE, THE SOURCE OF THE Ninth's problem – what he refused to believe when the old navigator hit the nail on the head – hid in Earth orbit shrouded in its Borea cloak. The *Dem-Zav1* scanners, pointing at the moon, watched Bardek's fleet emerge.

At the back of the hybrid craft, Robert woke from the exhausting forty winks he had grabbed while they waited. Washing the remnants of a bad dream – the last conversation he had with Harold on Earth – from his mind, he opened his eyes. They focused on Verteg, leaning over him as he lay in one of the small cots. Robert looked at his arm; it still glowed blue. *We're not finished yet,* he thought. *When will it ever end?*

'Mr Leslie, they appear to be on the move. We need you.'

'The crew?'

'All rested, fed and watered, as you asked. The young lieutenant is "itchy for more action". Yes, that's what he said. Mr Leslie, you humans have such a strange language.'

He got up, rubbing the sleep from his eyes, and looked through the open doorway of the compartment into the ship's main cabin. The crew were relaxing together: American, Borea and Russian, alien and human, happy with the success of their first mission. Haldock, sitting with the missile crew, shook his head as one of the young women showed him her hand of cards. He threw his down and smiled at her. The group chatted and laughed. He could hear more noise and looking aft into their small galley, he watched as another group gossiped together while sipping hot drinks. 'Seems like they're getting on fine, Verteg. What did you do to start that?'

'Nothing, Mr Leslie,' she said, handing him a cup of coffee. 'Shortly after we made orbit, they all set to and cleaned the ship. "I want this place shipshape" was what the Lieutenant ordered. Then they relaxed. It's been like this since then.'

'What of the Ninth's fleet?' he asked before supping his coffee. Life returned to his face.

'They did nothing for some time and then they started to move out from behind the moon. They're on a course for Earth.'

His brain, alert from the coffee rush hungered for more info. 'Anything from Earth?'

'As you ordered, comms between our allies on Earth are silent. But the news media is full of our strike. Mr Leslie, it's not very flattering.'

'I never expected it to be, Verteg. I suppose it's filled with millions killed, that sort of thing.'

'Yes, Mr Leslie. The Lieutenant says, "We're not the flavour of the month".'

'I like that, Verteg. He's right, but the killing will no end here, will it now?'

'No, you'll have to purify all the lands touched by the ceirim.'

He nodded. Finishing the coffee, he crushed the cup and dumped it in a wastebasket.

'Let's go,' he said, making his way into the main cabin. The noise from the crew diminished. Returning to their workstations, they prepared *Dem-Zav1* for battle.

*

The Ninth's seven intergalactic cruisers approached Earth, shattering another milestone in the history of the planet. An alien invasion, predicted by many unheard voices, was now a reality. The six-hundred-metre-long military cruisers, powered by three sleek grav drives, made short work of the passage from the moon. Unheard in the vacuum of space, the starship's engines hummed with raw energy. Their drive ports, framed within a convex polygon, extended out aft of the vessel. The blue drives, mounted below their bows, were not needed for this short passage. From the bridge in their bulbous bows, orders flowed, prepping each vessel for war. Busy crew, running backwards and forwards turned the irregular oblong hulls into a hive of activity. Missile tubes, grav beams and grav cannons were readied for action. Inside their mother ships, The Ninth's remaining planetary transporters and shuttles lay ready to ferry the ceirim to Earth.

It fell to the *Losh's* chief engineer to coordinate the ceirim's transfer to Earth. Finishing the vital calculations, checking thaw time and vessel numbers, he called his captain.

'They'll fit on the three transporters, all eight thousand of them. They'll be out of hibernation soon,' he said, over the comms system.

'You did that in quick time. When the ceirim leave, get ready to prime the weapon. We'll need that next,' the captain replied.

He turned to his second. 'Did you hear that? The city-busting mini-sun, we're using that next!' There was no answer to such a statement.

Ignoring the silence, the chief engineer changed the subject. 'I heard the humans destroyed three transport ships. They've got Anan tech; got it from The Eight I'll bet.'

Taking no notice of his boss, the second engineer sat down on the deck, cradling his head in his hands. The pain throbbed in his brain. 'Have you any left?' he asked, his voice trembling with agony.

The Chief looked down at his old assistant. Knowing what he was going through, he handed him his silver flask. 'It's running out; that's the last I have.'

His hands shaking, he took a small drink, concentrating hard not to spill the precious liquid. The pain subsided as the drug hit his brain. He looked up at his boss. 'I heard that Overlord killed the navigator on the *Chad* for using bawrak.'

'Yes, he did,' he said. 'I told you, when we left our home world, this mission was doomed. That Overlord, The Ninth, he's bad news. No good will ever come of him.'

*

On the bridge of the *Chad*, The Ninth poured over comm's discovery. No compliments, no acknowledgement for her outstanding work. Instead, he admonished the talented officer for not finding it earlier.

'A structure or base with blue, how could you miss something like that?' he shouted.

No one dared think the obvious. Why didn't The Ninth discover it when he scanned the planet? After all, Overlords sense blue; it's their lifeblood.

He would visit the structure, that was a must. *Maybe it is Eight's base*, he mused. But who or what hit the three ships? A question that still remained unanswered and burned in The Ninth's mind — so deep, he tuned his ethereal brain to solve it. He focused the other part to the impending plan: land the remaining ceirim, unite them with Kochtos and meantime, destroy Earth's major population centres. Nothing would detract him from that.

*

As the cruisers neared their journey's end, petrified, the crews of the *Losh*, *Chesh* and *Amech*, herded the remaining ceirim onto three transport ships. The Ninth had kept them for Kochtos's move to the vast jungle continent. He had planned to hide in the rainforests while his ceirim fed and he assimilated a new army. The continent contained fifteen per cent of Earth's population, and it was a move Kochtos looked forward to. With the loss of the geneticists and the devastation caused to the advancing ceirim mass, this was The Ninth's last hope to build a second army.

Reaching the thermosphere, the cruisers took up geosynchronous orbits above Earth's most inhabited cities. The *Chesh* and *Amech were* over the Americas; at the same time, the remaining four, joined Bardek's cruiser, the *Chad*, in orbit over Asia. Finally, the three transporters left the fleet, their course trajectory – the centre of the African continent.

*

At the tracking station on *Dem-Zav1*, Robert and Verteg watched the unfolding scene.

'Look at the course. They're headed to Africa. Shit,' Robert shouted as he realised the implications. 'If they land on that continent, we'll never find them. They'll hide forever.'

The rest stayed quiet, knowing how bad a situation that could be.

Robert voiced their thoughts. 'We will have to burn the whole continent down if they get loose. Verteg, we need to intercept them now. Can you do that?' Robert was right. In the African jungle, the ceirim would disappear. Kochtos could build an army himself – The Ninth's fall-back plan.

'Yes, Mr Leslie, but they fly further apart than the previous targets, and we've …'

'I know, only two missiles. Lieutenant, make those missiles count. Those ships can't land on Earth.'

Another learning by Bardek – keep the ships apart, move fast and make any unseen attacker work to acquire a target. The second attack run would be harder than the first.

The Lieutenant turned to his missile crew. 'You heard the man. Target resolution now.'

The noise levels increased as *Dem-Zav1's* crew rushed to devise the most important firing solution they would ever work on. It was Haldock who finally came up with a course and trajectory.

'Mr Leslie,' he said, pointing to the projection, 'we hit them here, high above the continent. The blast will definitely hit the three.'

'Go for it,' Robert ordered.

In a replay of their previous action over India, Haldock tracked the three ships on his navigation projection. In the stratosphere above the African continent, they unleashed their last two weapons. The cabin of the *Dem-Zav1* was silent as they guided their missiles down towards the ceirim menace. Before they hit, Verteg turned *Dem-Zav1* around and made their dash to safety up into space. With blinding explosions, the deadly missiles struck two of the transporter's gravity bubbles. The force collapsed them down onto their ships – vaporising ceirim and purebreed. The third transporter, hit by the blast, flipped over out of control. Badly damaged, but still intact inside its gravity bubble, the pilot managed to restore command. With one engine on fire, the cloak disabled and the flight crew injured, he plotted a course to the continent below. Up in the thermosphere, after avoiding the post-impact blast, *Dem-Zav1* – without weapons and too far away – could do nothing.

'Mr Leslie, they've lost one grav engine and their cloak. They'll crash land somewhere here,' Verteg said, pointing out a location in the depths of Africa's vast continent.

Robert grabbed the comm's unit, calling Admiral Whyte and General Marsh. After the conversation, he turned to Verteg. 'They've aircraft in the air. They're on the way, with enough conventional weapons to scorch a two-hundred-kilometre radius.'

'It should stop them, Mr Leslie, but you know what that call did?'

'I'm sorry, Verteg, it couldn't be helped. How bad is it?'

'One of the intergalactic ships is headed for us. They've got our location and I suspect they have grav beams.'

'Can you outrun them?'

She had already maxed out their engine speed. 'I'm trying.'

*

On the *Chad*, The Ninth watched the drama unfold. 'Again, Bardek, they managed to kill the ceirim. Two ships down and one damaged. What of Kochtos? How do we rescue him now?'

'Overlord, we've a shuttle left – that's for you. I had planned to use one of the three transporters we dispatched with the ceirim to pick him up on the subcontinent. He's stuck somewhere here,' he said, pointing to a location in Northern India.

'You failed again, Bardek. You missed something.' He paused, then with a flash of purple light, the oval entity continued. 'The Eight must have left defences behind. It's the only explanation. I need to visit that structure we discovered. Perhaps I'll find something there …'

The other half of The Ninth's brain lit up as he sensed Robert's call for help. His voice cracked and then he boomed with what he had detected, 'There's a communication signal coming from space – close to our quadrant. Make way, Bardek. Coordinates are on your console. Comms, you should have it as well. Quick, Bardek, hurry. Get the grav beams ready.'

Excited shouts filled the bridge as the purebreed crew rushed to capture the ship they believed had caused the demise of their mission. As the great cruiser pulsed forwards under the power of its three drives, it directed grav beams at the coordinates The Ninth had given them. The beam's tentacles, forming a cone-shaped beating mass, rushed outwards from the cruiser. As one of the limbs brushed past *Dem-Zav1*'s grav bubble, alarms sounded on the *Chad*'s bridge.

'We have its location, Overlord. It's cloaked but we have it.'

Verteg twisted and turned *Dem-Zav1* as she tried to escape. In a last-ditch attempt to evade them, she spun the ship around, charging straight back towards Bardek's cruiser. But, like a fly to the light, the beams, attracted to *Dem-Zav1*'s grav bubble, turned and twisted around her. The tentacles wove themselves into a net, closing around her grav bubble, capturing the small ship.

Bardek jumped up from his chair in excitement. 'Overlord, they're captured in our grav beams. They're going nowhere.'

The Ninth floated back and forth across the bridge, his energy mass glowing a bright blue. 'When will you have them on board?'

'It will take some time to pull in their ship. Their engines are on max, fighting our beam. Soon they'll overheat and shut down. We'll have them then. Overlord, you should go as planned to that base on Earth. The attackers will be on board when you return,' he said, grinning at the change in their fortunes. *Finally*, he thought, *we make some progress*.

*

Robert closed his eyes and hung his head in his hands as he listened to the ship's alarms and the shouts from the crew, as they tried to evade capture. The cabin lights dimmed and flashed from the power overload to the engines. He could smell burning as the bus-couplers were manually recycled in an attempt to maintain power flow to both drives.

Verteg stood and faced her crew. 'Stop, stop,' she shouted, with outstretched arms, her green skin flashing in anger. 'They have us; there's no escape. All I can do is make it harder for them to reel us in. De-couple one engine and shut down all non-essential systems.' They looked at her. No one moved. 'Now – do it now,' she roared, surprising even Robert. They rushed to their tasks. Soon the sound of the alarms faded and the cabin settled to the low glow of the emergency lighting.

For the first time she smiled at her crew, trying to put them at ease, the fear etched on the faces of the young human technicians. There were tears and sobs as well as the realisation that they would face their alien foe sank in. 'We're not done yet,' she said, in a soft voice. 'I have some tricks left. This is what we do …'

*

The chief engineer on the *Chad* tried to boost the cooling flow to the beam generator. *It's not working*, he thought. His hands shook as he remembered the fate of their navigator. *We'll lose them.* 'Captain Bardek,' he called over the comms, 'we have a problem with the beam generator. It's overheating.'

'What do you mean – overheating?'

'The small ship, it's started a slow swirling movement. It twists and breaks the net our grav beams form.'

'Regenerate the beams. The tentacles will rebuild the net.'

'As we reel them in, I'm trying that. But the beam generator overheats
– it's an old one, not designed for dual action.'

'We can't lose them. You must have a solution.'

'We slow down the recovery process. Wrap a deeper net around them.
Eventually, their engines will overheat or burn all their grav. Then we reel
them in.'

'What about a boarding party?'

'Not possible, Captain. Not with the grav net around the small ship.'

'Very well, we wait. Above all, keep that craft in the net. They must not
escape. If you don't have them by the time The Ninth returns, he can help.

*

'It's working, Robert. They've stopped trying to pull us in. They're focusing
all their energy in maintaining the grav net.'

'How long, Verteg?'

She looked down at her engine controls. 'We can hold these evasive
manoeuvres for twenty of your hours. Ten on each engine at full throttle,
until we run out of fuel.'

'What happens then?'

'Without our engines, they'll reel us in.'

'You've done us proud, Verteg – given them a fight to the end.' He
turned to look at the crew, all seated in silence at their stations. The
horror of the unexpected capture by their alien enemy had now passed,
the soothing hum of the one running grav engine giving hope.

*

Ninth's Fleet, 3rd February 2028

The fleet followed through on Bardek's orders to unpack, load and program
the extinction weapons. The Javonian comms officer issuing out the target
coordinates and launch sequences left nothing to chance. All she had to
do was transmit a final code, a safety mechanism preventing a premature
or treacherous launch of the "city-busting mini-suns".

As scheduled, after the ceirim departed, weapons crews throughout the fleet removed steel locking pins, priming the fusion bombs for use. During his rule, The One had banned the use of these extinction weapons, limiting their availability. It didn't stop The Sixth, who had secreted away a pile in one of his bases in the Ragma Galaxy. The Ninth did the dirty work, shipping them to Natok for the load out. Never before seen by the fleet's crews, these legendary bombs could vaporise a planet's largest cities – Earth's wouldn't stand a chance.

Bardek issued the starting order to comms. 'Hail all ships, I want commanders on screen. You have their launch codes ready?'

'Yes, Captain. All I need is your DNA authorisation,' she replied.

Bardek placed his hand on a scanner beside her console. A flicker of dim white light was all it took and then a yellow beacon started flashing on the bridge. The bridge viewscreen lit up with a visual of Earth's largest cities overlaid with the missile's target vectors.

'Set up the comms link,' Bardek ordered.

The colourful comms officer's purple hands glided across the translucent launch panel that appeared in front of her. Meantime, the fleet's commander's faces appear on screen.

Bardek relayed their good news. 'We've caught the Anan ship that destroyed our transport vessels.' He waited as shouts of victory rallied back. 'Now, we move to the final phase, our last chance at completing this mission. The weapon's coordinates and arming sequences are pre-programmed. You must hold your orbit for the firing mechanism to activate. It's all automated, control is with the *Chad*. Commanders, verify you are ready.'

They sounded off in quick succession, each confirming "weapons ready". Six starships ready to fire at six cities. Bardek's ship, the *Chad*, coordinating this volley, would lead the next barrage of seven, with a bulkier bomb.

Devoid of any emotion, the fleet commander carried on. 'There's no mystery to this; follow your orders. After the first wave, reload your launch tubes and proceed to the next target. We launch in twenty seconds.'

His comms activated the countdown on the bridge viewscreen.

Coupled with the activation codes, the computer did everything. A machine voice counted down from twenty.

*

On Earth, unaware of the impending doom, people went about their daily lives. Some in night-time others in daylight. Earth's cities didn't sleep. Visible from space, their urban night-time sprawl twinkling like mini galaxies. Most of the population were caught up in the daily drudgery of survival. Some with long commutes through polluted streets; others living above or at the back of their shops or businesses. Some in luxurious apartments, or houses and others in ones not so flash. All were united in a common cause – to live life to the full, love each other, providing food and shelter for the family. And raise their kids, hoping for a better life for them.

One young mum shepherded her toddler, straddled on a colourful red bike, as he heeled his way along. She stopped at the traffic lights. Struggling, carrying two cold drinks and some shopping, she pressed the crossing button. The lights changed. Hurrying along, her child dutifully followed, his mind on the promise of a cold milkshake; her mind on getting him across the road safely. She never contemplated that death for them both would come so soon.

Throughout all this, connected to the *Chad*, *Dem-Zav1* continued to wrestle with the grav beam. Robert and his crew trapped and unaware of the impending slaughter to hit the planet below.

*

The countdown moved through the final numbers. Aborting the delivery of Armageddon to those populated cities never crossed Bardek's mind. Nothing deterred him from this mission. Wrinkles on his white brow furrowed by the stress of the moment; drops of sweat hung above his pursed lips.

The machine voice counted. 'Zero. Sending launch codes. Missiles activated. Launching now.'

The automated firing sequence initiated. Machine codes opened ports below each cruiser. Feedback was verified. "Ports opened." Another instantaneous command started engines, launching the weapons. Six shuttle-sized missiles flew out down towards Earth. The on-board cloaks rendered them invisible to the planet's primitive radar. No one saw what was coming. The two targeting the Americas were the first to hit, incinerating Mexico City and São Paulo in a fusion flash. Along with millions of people, the young mum and her carefree son vaporised in a blaze of white light. Both cities disappeared into craters over eighty kilometres across, taking some of the surrounding urban sprawl with them.

Four Asian cities – Shanghai, Guangzhou, Manila and Soul – were next, as The Sixth's fusion bombs exploded above Earth's most populated cities, focusing the force and heat of a small sun down on the ill-fated populace. Nothing and no one survived. In a few short minutes, The Sixth's weapons exterminated near two hundred million people. Destruction never before seen on the planet. The power unleashed by one of these weapons completely eclipsing anything the human race had seen before.

A collective gasp of fear, revulsion and horror reverberated around the world. Reaching out into space, it pierced The Eight's energy mass. A flash of purple rage electrified his resolve as he prepared for the fight back.

On the *Chad*, devoid of any feeling of remorse, Bardek sent the second set of targets to the fleet. This time the *Chad* would fire its first weapon. As he programmed their target sequence for Tokyo – Earth's largest city – Bardek lamented their mission's failings. *Unless The Ninth makes some ground-breaking discovery in the base on Earth, we'll never fulfil The Sixth's goal. There are too many of them,* he thought. He ran the calculation over in his mind. *Even with the remaining weapons, we don't have enough firepower. Kochtos and the ceirim are crucial. Without them—*

A shout from his comms officer disturbed his thoughts. 'Captain, I'm detecting an energy burst in our forward cargo hold.'

'Put it on screen.'

They watched as large blotches of colour disrupted the picture. 'It's distorted, Captain. I can't get a clear view.'

At his command station, time ticked on while Bardek analysed the energy signature. 'By The One, it's a fold. Someone's opened folded space in our cargo bay. Security, security!' he shouted over the PA system. 'Prepare to repel boarders, we have hostiles—'

Too late. Bardek's security team was already overwhelmed. The bridge doors burst open and six beasts, followed by a human female, rushed in.

'Have at them,' Alice shouted, over the roars of her catbears.

Bardek froze with shock at the intimidating sight of the giant beasts, covered with green and brown striped fur. The stripes, woven together, blurred in unison when the creatures moved. Fitted with black Anan combat suits, headgear and anti-grav breastplates for protection, the company of two female and four males rushed forwards. As their long manes shook from side to side, the six one-hundred-and-ten-kilo beasts reared up on their hind legs. About the size of a large purebreed, they growled and bared their teeth. Leaving no doubt as to their function, two long glistening white fangs protruded down from their mouths.

Two of his bridge security team raised their grav weapons and fired – the shots bouncing off the catbears' black combat armour. Rex lashed out with his right claw. With a burst of crimson blood, he gouged the unfortunate purebreed's face from his head. Maxim's left paw punched another guard, sending him flying across the bridge. The company rushed the remaining crew, grabbing them with their claws from their bridge stations and dumping them down in a heap in the centre. It was all over in seconds.

'Secure that weapon now,' screamed Alice, 'or you all die.'

Bardek stared at this lithe human. She had long black hair, and her dark complexion matched the Anan combat suit she wore. A strange percussion weapon was slung over her shoulder with another stowed in a pouch on her side. He shivered as he looked into her dark eyes which flashed pure hatred.

The Javonian comms officer stood up and pointed to the weapons' console – Alice nodded. Her purple hands shaking, she ran to the console and hit the abort button.

Alice's dark eyes bore into the frightened comms officer. 'What about the rest of the fleet?' she asked.

The comms officer's violet face paled under the scathing gaze. She owed the purebreeds nothing. Deep down, she had quelled feelings of revulsion for the genocide happening before her eyes. Hiding those feelings from

The Ninth was difficult, but with an intelligent mind, she had managed it. Now seeing a human in the flesh, she realised how alike they are. Purple hands flew across the translucent command console. With a deft swipe, the Javonian comms officer sent cancelling commands to the other six vessels. The launch clock, counting down on the side of the bridge viewscreen, froze, as did the weapons on the other six cruisers.

A weight lifted from Alice's mind as that clock stopped. 'Who's in command?' she barked.

Bardek stood up from the floor. 'I am.'

She rushed at him. Launching herself through the air she hit him straight in the chest with her right boot. The blow sent him sprawling across the floor, rolling to a painful stop at the nav-con. Before he could stand, she was at him, dragging him up and pummelling his face with her bare fists. 'You bastard. How many cities have you wiped out? Millions are dead, and now you were readying another volley. What manner of monster are you?' she said, as the blood spurted from his nose.

She started to hit him again. A gentle paw wrapped around her waist as Luna pulled Alice off the bleeding Bardek.

Regaining her composure, Alice gazed around at the defeated bridge. Her company of catbears had surrounded the petrified crew. Rex grinned then growled in the air. The sound grated the sensitive purebreed ears. They cowered at the noise of his roar. Those that had weapons, threw them aside.

'Put me down, Luna, now,' Alice shouted, as she turned to face the catbear. As she looked into Alice's brown tear-filled eyes, Luna shook her head, her green mane swaying from side to side. 'All right – I'll control myself. Now put me down.'

The protecting mother catbear set Alice down. With a low growl, she leered at Bardek, exposing her long fangs. She took one threatening step towards him.

He backed off from Luna's fighting stance till the bulkhead behind trapped him.

'Who are you?' he blurted out, his voice trembling.

'I'm Alice, and these catbears are The Eight's guardians. You have one choice. Accept the Eight as your Overlord or get off this ship.'

'We need time.' It was an audacious answer but it was all Bardek could think of. He still believed The Ninth would find some magical solution in the hidden base on the planet below.

Alice's itchy finger had found the trigger of her grav gun, now pointed at Bardek. 'You have none. I wanted to kill you all but The Eight wants this ship and crew. What'll it be?'

Fear of The Sixth governed Bardek's brain. 'Never will I bow down to The Eight.'

Alice turned to Rex. 'We'll drag them to the nearest airlock. Come on,' she said, as she started to secure the prisoners with tie-wraps.

Bardek's crew – shouting and pleading – showed how hollow their loyalty to The Sixth really was. 'What do you want of us? Spare us, please,' they begged, while she and her catbears secured the lot within minutes.

Then she spoke, a harsh voice filled with hate. 'There's a ship in your grav beams. Release it now,' Alice demanded.

Ignoring Bardek, the chief engineer stood up and gestured to his control station. Alice nodded and cut his bonds. He walked over to it and as he worked, the picture on the bridge viewscreen changed. *Dem-Zav1*, shrouded in a grav beam, came into view. Soon the confining grav net dissolved, releasing the small hybrid craft.

For the first time, Alice smiled. 'That's what we want.' She flung over a piece of paper to him. 'Land this ship at these coordinates on Earth.'

'I'll need help,' he said, pointing out three others including the comms officer.

Alice cut their bonds and within minutes they had vital controls stations back online. Comms was first to the mark as the image of the bridge viewscreen changed to show Robert and Verteg, sitting in the cockpit of *Dem-Zav1*.

'What took you so long, Alice?' Verteg asked.

'Nice to see you too, Verteg. I see you got another ship. Looks like a piece of junk.'

'Thanks, Alice. Where is he?' asked Robert, not noticing the happy banter between Verteg and Alice.

'He's here, Robert. You need to land back at base – orders from the boss. I'll see you there.'

He understood – no tactical chat. He put his thumbs up, nodded and cut the transmission.

'You heard the lady, Verteg. Set a course for the Hela base in Oz. We're going home. Lieutenant, you guys are welcome, but if you want out here—'

'That's okay, Mr Leslie. Australia is fine. Never been there before and, Mr Leslie, who was that?'

'That's Alice and her pets.'

'What are they?'

'Inhabitants of our New World; we call them catbears.'

'Are they intelligent?'

'Sort of. It's complicated, Lieutenant. They're The Eight's wee friends. He wants them as his guardians. I didn't expect to see them on Earth.'

CHAPTER FORTY-ONE

The Story of Bawrak

Bawrak is an age-old drug used to enhance the brain cognisance for interstellar navigation. The potent mind-enhancing narcotic augments the brainwave projection and navigation capabilities of the purebreeds. The popularity, and commercial success, of the drug, mirrors the increasing infection rate of the Anan sickness, which inhibits the abilities of the starship navigators and other technical crew.

Grandfather Borea, recognising the drug's commercial viability, procured the guarded recipe from a family who lived in Anan's Northern Alps. The now-deceased household sold the field-caves of unique flowers that the drug is distilled from to the Borea. Those irreplaceable secret flowers are an age-old import from a lost world.

‣ **Extract from: Family legacies, Little Kake Borea**

*

The Chad, 3rd February 2028

IN ORBIT AROUND EARTH, WITH Alice and the catbears in command, the *Chad* set off for the Hela base in Australia. One hour later, the captured crew landed their command ship in the Australian desert. Hostile human marines marched them off to a makeshift prison. Like Alice, the Australian soldiers itched to cut alien throats – with bets made on what colour their blood would be. The captives, issued with auto-translators, understood every word. White faces turned to grey. In the heat of the Australian desert, some snowflakes collapsed. With no sympathy coming from their captors, their mates had to carry them on.

Alice dragged the Javonian comms officer by the hair, kicking and screaming, away from the purebreed crew. Out of earshot of Bardek, she picked the girl up and dusted her down. 'You're Javonian. Is that right?' she asked in Anan.

A surprised nod, questioning eyes and confusion as tears ran down the girl's violet face.

Alice's voice changed. 'One of your people is crew on the *Monarch*; he saved my boss's life,' she said in a softer tone. 'You're to stay here.' she said, locking the girl in a room of her own.

Maybe she will be of use, Alice thought. *Better she's away from the pure-breed mob of war criminals.* Walking away from the prison, she watched as the odd-shaped hybrid landed with Robert and Verteg. *Catch up time,* Alice thought, as she ran to welcome Verteg back.

*

The Monarch, 3rd February 2028

On the *Monarch*, after transporting Alice and her catbears through folded space onto the *Chad*, The Eight relaxed into his energy mass. It was a long time since he had done that. *Too long,* he thought.

The human suffering from the devastation on Earth had cut him deep. He felt every life passing, building a well of emotion that threatened all his logical thinking. He walled it off inside his mind, in a place he would visit in the future. The Sixth would pay for his crimes, The Eight would see to that. But now was not the time to wallow in it. *The human race and the universe need me,* he thought. How he handled today would shape events in the future.

Contemplating that, The Eight watched the battle for the *Chad* unfold. He sensed Alice's victory and *Dem-Zav1* landing back in the Australian desert. *But where is The Ninth?* he had wondered throughout until a warning touched his mind. It answered his question.

His energy mass crackled and flashed. 'The Ninth is here, in my island base. The nerve of that young pup. My home on Earth – he dares to desecrate my house. I will terminate him for what he has done here,' he said to a surprised Tom. 'Ready me a shuttle. You know what must be done with that murdering fleet. Try to salvage as many ships as you can,' he said, as he turned in his chariot and left the bridge.

*

Milford Sound, New Zealand, 3rd February 2028

While his murdering missiles rained down on Earth, the Ninth's shuttle hovered over The Eight's mountain lair. On a bright cloudless day, Fiordland's mountain peaks stretched into the distance. Cliffs carved by glaciers during a past ice age rose out of the clear blue water, reaching up to the sky. Waterfalls cascaded down those cliffs, cutting a sparkling dash through green and grey crags. The white spray, rising in the windy updraft, created an illusion of the water flowing back up. A thin mist filled the valley, refracting sunlight into a multi-coloured rainbow. Sheer rock bluffs and green forests adorned the mountainsides, their colours reflected in the waters of the sound that shimmered like a vivid mirror. The occasional boat, filled with tourists, unaware of the evil monster above, plied through the turquoise waters. The beauty of the surrounding peaks and the Milford Sound fiord was not lost, even on The Ninth.

Such beauty is rare; no wonder The Eight kept this place hidden, he thought, as he scanned the entrance to the base.

Abandoned when they left Earth – after the second touching – The Eight's "island base" had remained hidden and undiscovered for near three thousand years. The choice of its location – inside a mountain behind the deep fiord – ensured that. The fiord was now an international tourist attraction in an uninhabited wilderness, with access to the base only by shuttle or by climbing the steep mountain cliff.

Designed as a secret store, secluded and away from the main population centres, The Eight had taken it as his home in this galaxy. It was near two years since one of the project teams had re-entered it – with difficulty – requiring them to manually activate the entrance controls from the cliff face. After that, they installed batteries and a generator, for remote access, to open the base's doorway.

From the shuttle, The Ninth explored the entrance chamber. With tentacles of blue, he started the generator. His energy flooded the operating system, bypassing the need for secret codes and opening the hydraulic valves on the pumps. The purebreed pilot watched as the main access door powered up and opened. Without hesitation, he flew straight inside the cliff face, one thousand metres above the blue waters of Milford Sound, landing on the floor of the dark entrance chamber.

'Wait here,' The Ninth said, as his energy mass floated out. He couldn't wait to see what his nemeses had left behind. Floating into the control room, he made straight for a panel he suspected would access the data storage. His blue energy danced across the console, light filled the room, but nothing else happened. He tried again, this time, attempting to bypass a DNA scanner and the codes installed to protect the computer core. He got nowhere. Frustrated by the primitive security systems, he stopped. Focusing his mind, Nine explored the mountain lair with his consciousness until his energy flashed through a small chamber cut into the rock.

He froze. *It can't be*, he thought, as his mass rushed down the corridor to what he had found. *His backup hoard; I've found The Eight's store of blue*, he thought, as he floated into a small room packed with tanks of blue.

He flashed a message to the purebreed shuttle crew: '*Come quick.*'

Entering the dimly lit room, the expression on their faces betrayed their surprise at what he had found.

'Open three now then load the rest on the shuttle,' The Ninth ordered.

He hovered impatiently as they tore the tanks open. Gorging on the fresh energy, he greedily vacuumed the contents out, expanding his mass. In fear, the purebreeds backed off, waiting until The Ninth's engorged form left to explore the depths of the base inside the mountain. When he left, the puny purebreeds abandoned all contact with their shuttle as they struggled to move the blue energy canisters out and up from the storage chamber. Pissed off by the manual work, they lost contact with their mother ship, failing to learn what was happening on the *Chad*.

With his new bloated mass, The Ninth floated down into the lower caves that housed the primary data banks. Ripping off a thick steel door, he flooded into the room. The ancient data banks, installed over three thousand years ago, were built inside domed hollows, carved out of the solid rock. His blue energy crackled and flashed, illuminating the darkened caves, as he tried to read the data. Inside the data banks, he flew from millennia to millennia attempting to make sense of it all. *How do I read so much?* he thought and stopped. *The Seventh, he will know.*

The Ninth gathered his energy mass. Focusing his blue, he attempted to project his ethereal mind out into space. Nothing happened. *What manner of chamber is this?* he thought as he tried again. He got nowhere, stopped by a defensive mechanism The Eight had installed when he first built this inner sanctum.

The Ninth realised he'd have to go up to the surface or just keep looking. The greedy Overlord chose to stay. Again, he flooded the data banks with his energy but this time he quelled his excitement and started with a much smaller section. Time stood still for him, as he meticulously worked his way through the data until something of interest popped out. He watched some of the first touching. *So it was a mistake, not of The Eight's doing,* Nine thought, as he watched the old purebreed geneticist steal The Eight's essence.

It doesn't change anything. Eight should have expunged the humans when he found out what had been done, Nine thought.

From there on, it was all boring: mining details in this quadrant of space, records of locations of The Eight's mines in this galaxy and what they had recovered.

There is no blue left here in this galaxy, he grasped. *Where are the weapons? What did he leave here?* More questions than answers!

Like a frenzied demon gnawing inside him, the veiled mystery of The Eight's secrets spurred Nine on. The deeper his search, the more insignificant the data he found. *Nothing, there is nothing,* screamed in his mind.

Immersed in a spiteful desire to discover The Eight's secrets, Nine lost contact with the war in orbit. Isolated inside the mountain lair, he didn't even notice the arrival of another.

He stopped and drew back. *There must be something,* he thought. And then, as he looked back at the storage devices, deep down, he found one not connected to the computer's core. He had missed it during his first pass, his energy tracking through the bus bars that connected the data framework. This one stood alone, unconnected. His energy floated over it, trying to get access. It was big, made up of blue crystals he had never seen before. *These are old*, he thought. *Who made them and what's in them?* he wondered, as he tried to flood them with his energy. As if they had a mind of their own, they repulsed him, the chamber flashing with blue light. The more he tried, the more the crystals glowed, absorbing his own blue and using it to defend themselves.

*

The Monarch, 3rd February 2028

The *Monarch* uncloaked as The Eight left on a shuttle for his home in Milford Sound. Its crew, under the tutelage of Siba, ready for a battle. Borea, Mzimot and human had coalesced on the two-week journey to Earth to give the ship and The Eight the best chance of defeating whatever was there. Drills, weapons tests and command briefs, pulled it all together into a skilled multi-racial crew – the likes of which the *Monarch* had never seen before.

Like a hungry bird of prey, it swooped straight into the middle of The Ninth's fleet over Asia. At the sight of the *Monarch*, chaos erupted on the bridges of the four cruisers. To their horror, they watched the flashes from its gun turrets as the *Monarch* strafed the *Shaqa* – their sister cruiser – with grav shells. From that fatal broadside, projectiles pierced the vessel's protective bubble, embedding themselves into its hull. Then they released their grav payload. Pent-up energy exploded, causing a chain reaction within the confines of the cruiser. The intergalactic ship exploded in a flash of white light, its hull ripped in two, as the unchained grav mingled with blue energy and fuel in the vessel's bunkers.

In Anan, a chilling voice with a strange accent, hailed The Ninth's routed fleet. 'This is the *Monarch*, under the command of The Eight. Surrender now. I repeat, surrender now, or you will be destroyed,' Tom said.

Video footage of the demise of their compatriots accompanied the message sent to the *Chesh* and *Amech* over the Americas. Tom's freezing voice and the images of the blown-up *Shaqa* was enough from them. "Cut and run" was the order their captains issued.

'Tom, the two over the Americas are powering up their engines; they're making a run for it,' Geoff said.

'Launch four grav missiles; target their engines,' Tom ordered.

Within seconds, they felt a soft vibration through the deck of the ship. 'Missiles away!' shouted Fazqa, from weapons control.

'Navigation configured,' Kora said, her blue diamond glowing with her confidence. Her projection flickered as it updated the missile's trajectory, the speed of the two ships increasing as they tried to leave Earth orbit.

Siba looked out from the translucent screen floating in front of her captain's chair. 'Mr Parker, the other three cruisers are powering up their grav weapons. They're underway and heading straight for us.' A deadpan voice, devoid of fear or panic.

'What do you suggest, Captain?'

She smiled. 'I believe we should wait for them. No sense in wasting grav.'

There was a flash from Kora's navigation projection. 'Missile strike – one ship hit. It's disabled. The other's opening a fold in space. Boss, it's getting away. Ah shit, the missile's detonated at the close of the fold. It's away; it's escaped.'

The *Chesh* had made it, escaping into a fold. The crew were that bit quicker than their sister ship *Amech*, who lay immobile with damaged engines in orbit over South America.

Kora's navigation projection flickered as it updated with the position of the remaining cruisers. 'Captain, three ships closing on our starboard side.'

Siba turned the *Monarch* to face the rapidly approaching fleet head on. Flying side by side, the three enemy cruisers fired six grav missiles at the *Monarch*. As the projectiles sped towards her, the *Monarch's* guns opened up, targeting them in mid-flight. With blue and golden flashes, the six missiles detonated in front of The Ninth's last operational fleet.

The bridge crews reacted to the failed strike, slamming the engines into reverse. The three intergalactic cruisers trembled and vibrated as they tried to evade the destructive debris cloud of grav from their own missiles. Grav bubbles glowed pink and red as they diverted all their ship's power in an attempt to save themselves.

In an immortal vision playing across the viewscreen, the bows of the three cruisers emerged from the debris cloud. The crew of the *Monarch* cheered as, little by little, the ship's hulls appeared out of the grey and dusty white cloud. The remains of the fleet stopped short in front of the *Monarch*. Black smoke billowed from the rear of one – they were done!

'Comms from all vessels, boss,' Geoff said. 'I'll put them up on screen.' The view on their big screen changed as three separate scenes emerged. The purebreed commanders stood on their smoke-filled bridges, their crews working behind. Noisy clamour invaded the transmission as they extinguished fires and tried to regain control of their ship's systems.

Tom spoke first. 'I asked you to surrender and you gave me your answer by launching six missiles. Are you ready now?'

'What are our options?' one commander asked.

'You have none. You have committed war crimes that surpass even those of mankind's worst. Your mindless genocide has killed over two billion of our species. Don't interrupt,' Tom said, as they tried to object. 'We follow The Eight; we chose to do that. Like you, we are endowed with free will. Unlike other species, purebreed and human can object and follow our conscience. Clearly, you never did that.'

The commander of the *Losh* knelt down. 'Human, whatever you do with me, spare my crew.'

'A noble deed, Commander, one I'm sure The Eight will consider. You will all answer to him. For now, power down your engines and park your vessels in orbit. You will be boarded shortly. If any one of you disobeys my orders, all three ships will be destroyed,' Tom said, ending the transmission. 'Geoff, message Admiral Whyte. Tell him, all clear and to dispatch marines on the shuttles. We'll need them to secure those four ships.' He stood up and walked over to the engineering station. 'Well, Jarzol, how're our engines?'

'Fine, Mr Parker. Mzimot drives last forever. You should know that by now. I am sorry, Mr Parker, that billions of your species were killed. This is unprecedented in the history of our worlds. Yes, populations were extinguished, I do remember old stories, but never in these numbers and in such a vindictive way. But before, Mr Parker, it was on agreement by all the Overlords and sanctioned by The One. Time changes for the worst.'

'I'm glad you joined us. With your help, we got home in under two of our weeks. You've got this ship humming, Jarzol. I and The Eight appreciate that.'

The head of the Mzimot family bowed his head in acknowledgement. When they realised The Eight was running the show, Jarzol and the family elders had rebelled, claiming they were tricked by Niamh and Tom. Before they set out for Earth, discovering their secret of transformation, Rex had killed one of the family elders. More fuel for the rancorous distrust between Mzimot and human. On the New World, Kora and her husband, Brian, set the foundations for this new relationship. This battle drew the curtains back on the solidity of that bond.

Jarzol continued, 'Seeing this carnage, I'm glad we did. The Sixth is a monster never seen before in time. This story will be the start of his demise. When word gets out to the outlying worlds of what he did here, they will all join The Eight. We will fix these ships for you but, Mr Parker, you need crews. The Borea family and mine isn't enough. We will train mankind. And, Mr Parker, do not use The Ninth's crews. You cannot rely on those you capture today. They are polluted.'

'Why, Jarzol? What makes you say that?' Tom asked.

'Mr Parker, I wondered why we conquered them so easily. Even with the *Monarch's* superior weapons and cloaks, those cruisers are capable of much more. Old they are, but still they pack a punch with more weapons than they used. Geoff,' he said, walking over to the comms console, 'replay the comms from their vessels in slow motion.'

Tom watched with interest as the pictures from the three cruisers tracked across their large viewscreen frame by frame.

'There, stop there,' Jarzol said. 'Look at their eyes. The colour is gone and the pupils dilated. Move it on, Geoff. Watch those men,' he said, pointing to a group working behind one of the commanders. 'See the twitch in their faces?'

He was right. In the white flesh below their colourless eyes, a subtle twitch worked across some of the purebreeds' faces. 'What's that about, Jarzol?'

'Mr Parker, they are suffering from lack of bawrak. They're addicted to it and their supply has run out.'

Tom drew a big breath. 'Withdrawal symptoms, that's what we call it. Shit, nearly half the crews look like that. That can't be, Jarzol, on such an important mission. Surely they would have used their best crews.'

'They are their best. I'm afraid the Anan sickness has taken its toll. It is no secret. Over time they have lost the capability to navigate and some of the other techs have difficulty as well. You know that drug enhances their abilities, enabling them to work. They fall apart without it.'

Tom nodded as he thought of Brizo Sema, the Aknar Prince and at one time, captain of the *Hela* until they discovered he was using the drug. It ended the poor prince's military career. 'We did see that before but not in such numbers,' he said, shaking his head as he wondered what they would do with so many drug-addicted aliens. A revelation they wouldn't have discovered without the famous engine builder's collaboration.

*

Milford Sound, New Zealand, 3rd February 2028

In Milford Sound, with his ethereal mind, The Eight watched The Ninth attempt to access his oldest data crystals. When his shuttle arrived outside his base, with a deadly thought he killed the invading crew, turning them to dust for stealing his blue. As soon as it landed, his energy mass floated out and down inside his mountain. The Eight stopped on the level above, watching The Ninth. *We are supposed to be above this*, The Eight thought, trying to understand what drives an Overlord to such depths of depravity. *Now it ends.*

Like a missile explosion, it pierced The Ninth's energy mass. White-hot pain exploded in his mind as The Eight delivered his message. 'How dare you violate my home? My most treasured possessions; what right have you to delve in them? Have you no shame? What manner of entity were you before you ascended to an Overlord? You steal my blue. What I store here is to sustain me when I have none. My last life support system in this galaxy and you plunder it, like a common thief.'

The Ninth squirmed under The Eight's attack. Withdrawing his energy from the crystals, he immediately focused on the doorway. *I must get out, out,* he thought, as his energy mass burst through the narrow opening. Blue lightning flashed up through the central access column of The Eight's mountain lair, as Nine's engorged energy mass poured up it. Wanting him out of his home, The Eight let him pass, following him up to the entrance chamber. With a screech, the two Overlords' blue energy masses flashed out through the entrance. Pure blue energy spectacularly flashed above the mountain as they flew to the skies above Milford Sound. It was there that The Eight made his move.

It was fear, something he had never experienced before, that drove The Ninth out. As he burst free into the sky, he felt something else invading his energy mass. *No,* he screamed within, as he sensed The Eight's energy penetrating his own. He stopped, realising what an advantage he might have. Concentrating his mind, he focused his force. 'I have more than you. My mass is stronger. I will defeat you.'

'It is never about magnitude; there are differences in how you use it,' The Eight said, as he wove his oval energy mass into a chiliagon. As the multi-faceted engine of death – with its thousand sides – formed, The Eight lowered his pulse rate.

The Ninth compressed his engorged mass around The Eight, crushing down on him. 'What is this you do, Eight? Some old ritual? Is this how Overlords prepare themselves for extinction?'

'Nine, you impudent upstart, you are not, or never were, entitled to be an Overlord. You are a product of The Sixth's blunders. Know this – in far distant time, Overlords once fought between each other. The winning group developed an algorithm that works as an energy conduit. I will show you how it works.'

The whistle of the wind in the clear skies above Milford Sound pierced the resounding silence between two of the universe's most powerful entities. The sight of the pulsing blue energy dominated the sky, as Eight and Nine struggled in a fight to the death. The tourists watching below from the Visitor Centre wondered what was happening, as the colours of the energy masses pulsing blue, orange and red, dominated the sky over the fiord.

Routing all the power of his pulsing mass and compressing it around Eight's chiliagon, Nine struggled to crush him. With his pulse lowered, The Eight dialled down the pressure of his essence. One thousand sides of his chiliagon erupted with white flashes, sucking life essence from Nine's energy mass. Filling the sky with white light, The Ninth's screams of agony pulsed out across intergalactic space.

'Now you understand the meaning of life, Nine. You should never have ascended. I was against it from the start. Overtaking Ten, it should never have been allowed. I always wondered where The Sixth found you. Show me, show me what evil corporeal form you came from.'

'No, Eight, no, please,' he said, as he felt his essence flow away.

The Eight expanded his mass before he completely absorbed Nine. He needed to see his origins. Like fingers of white light, he pried open what remained of Nine's consciousness, flooding it with his own. He looked deep into Nine's existence, absorbing all his data. 'There it is. What manner of being were you? I have never seen such creatures,' he said, looking at an image of a metal-grey coloured biped, the face and head knurled with rock-shaped bumps.

'The Sixth created us. He gave us life. Please spare me.'

'You are not from a pure carbon lifeform. What are you, Nine?'

'He made us!'

The Eight looked deeper inside Nine's data core, quelling the pressure spike at the shock of what he discovered. 'Never did we think such abomination was possible. Your species are a crossbreed from carbon life and metal – from gadolinium. Why?' He looked deeper, poring through the data of Nine's pre-ascension existence, his innermost secret revealed. Their home lay on the edge of The Sixth's galaxies, on a moon orbiting a vast gas giant that held deposits of blue energy. The Sixth had used the gadolinium metal of the moon to fortify a primitive carbon lifeform he had transported there. Giving them intelligence, he had deployed them as miners in the gas giant. Nine was their leader, pushing his species to the limit for his Overlord.

It answered The Eight's burning question: "How could Nine, without The One's proxy, with no hesitation, work so hard to expunge so much life, killing so many?" It was why The Sixth had sent him – he had no soul, no innermost feelings or the ability to distinguish the difference between good and evil. *How many of those foul creatures still exist? What other monsters has The Sixth created?* Eight wondered as he consumed the last of Nine.

As Nine withered and died, his final essence – the filth The Eight rejected – erupted in a multi-coloured explosion, filling the darkened evening sky with light. Across the universe, his dying screams scorched the senses of the Overlords as they felt the pain of his extinction. The Sixth crackled with fury, and The Seventh shivered as his core temperature dropped with fear, their troika now reduced to a duo.

Restoring his pressure and pulse, The Eight changed his enlarged energy mass from the deadly chiliagon to oval. He would revisit Nine's data package and send it to The Second. He must know the laws of creation were broke and what vile intelligent life exists in the universe.

His huge energy mass flowed in through the open door of his island base, swirling past the shuttles. His crew, in awe of his size, watched as he filled the chamber. 'We must clean this place,' he said. 'Let Robert and Tom know what happened. They will send you help. I go. There is more mayhem I must fix.'

By now, news of the destruction of six of Earth's largest cities had filtered through to the Milford Sound Visitor Centre. The people gathered there, watching the bright, colourful lights in the sky, put two and two together, realising they were witnesses to a battle between Overlords. What they didn't know was that such a fight hadn't happened in this epoch. They watched The Eight return, enlarged from consuming Nine, his engorged blue energy mass blazing brightly as he entered his home.

When he left again, they glimpsed another treat. The sight of their Overlord's blue energy mass flowing out from the darkened mountains and up into the night sky. It was so bright, it lit up the fiord, blue colours dancing across the water. The Eight disappeared northwards, on his next mission, a luminous blue ball of fire flashing into the night sky.

CHAPTER FORTY-TWO

CNS Headlines. The Eight is Back.

As Earth's population reel with the shock and horror of unimaginable death, Anan Corp spokesperson, Katherine Phillips, confirmed the sightings in Milford Sound, on New Zealand's South Island, is The Eight. The Overlord returned to Earth on a recently acquired battleship renamed the Monarch. Phillips stated, "The Eight's purpose on Earth is to defeat the remaining ceirim and The Sixth's invading fleet.".

A stark comfort for the loss of the Indian subcontinent and the billions of innocent people who had inhabited it, and for Shanghai, Guangzhou, Manila, Soul, Mexico City, and São Paulo. Cities that disappeared in fusion flashes by bombs generating the heat of small suns – an evil power we never before imagined. As the death count nears 1.7 billion, humanity cries tears of blood for those lost souls.

Incensed people are asking awkward questions. Where was The Eight when Earth needed him? Why did he ever come here in the first place? When will this destruction end?

• *From: Continental News Services. Good Morning Planet Earth*

*

Hela base, Australian desert, 3rd February 2028

WHILE THE BATTLE RAGED IN space and The Eight and The Ninth battled it out over Milford Sound, a tired and smelly crew alighted from *Dem-Zav1*. Verteg was last. Alice ran to her, throwing her arms around the Pilot. They hugged, both thinking they may never have seen the other again. The crew stood back, allowing them their time together. Robert, engrossed in the same greeting from Janet, savoured that moment. They were safe, had slowed the ceirim advance and against the odds, returned alive.

The moment passed; Alice started to cry. Her soft emotional sobs turning to a loud wail. Holding Alice tight, Verteg felt all the human emotion around her.

The tired catbears, suffering from the heat, padded up. Luna stroked Alice's hair, the other five lay down their paws over their eyes, trying to shut out the feelings the humans projected.

The planet's population was ravaged by death. So many dead; a feeling of failure. Questioning thoughts of "What if we had done things differently? Why did we welcome The Eight? How could something like this happen?" flowed from their minds.

Verteg yanked them back to reality. 'Stop, Alice! Stop it, all of you. This was The Sixth's doing. Those who follow him bear that consequence. The war continues.' She paused as the humans around her composed themselves.

'You're right, as usual, Verteg,' Robert said.

'Did anyone think to get the command codes of The Ninth's fleet?' Verteg asked.

Silence followed that question.

'It's useless without them. We'd have to rebuild the command systems,' Verteg said.

A light bulb went on in Alice's head. 'The Javonian comms officer – go get her,' she shouted to one of the Aussie soldiers.

Within minutes, he appeared back with the colourful girl. Verteg explained what she wanted. The girl nodded; she would help, but she couldn't do it on her own.

'I'll need Bardek's handprint and DNA,' she said.

'Left or right?' Alice asked.

The girl shrugged her shoulders. 'It doesn't matter.'

'That's not a problem. I'll meet you on the bridge,' Alice said to them as she ran back towards the cells.

Two minutes later, Bardek watched as the lithe dark-skinned woman approached. She had a primitive object in her hand. A weapon of some sort he believed. A soldier at the prison unlocked the gate. Alice grabbed Bardek and dragged him out, the six-foot-tall purebreed no match for Alice's strength. It astounded him how such a small person could be so strong. But it's what happened next that shocked the man to his core. With a boot in the groin, Alice paralysed him. Continuing her kicking onslaught, Bardek fell to the ground.

Kneeling down beside the moaning purebreed, Alice grabbed one arm below the elbow. He didn't see the fire axe raised in the other hand. Alice had grabbed it from the emergency station outside the makeshift prison. In a red blur, it swung down, severing his right hand at the wrist. Red blood spurted out, settling soldier's bets on its colour. Bardek screamed in agony, while Alice stomped off, carrying her prize.

'Better get a medic to wrap him up before he bleeds to death; we might need some more parts from him if this doesn't work,' she shouted back at the gobsmacked soldiers.

Back on the bridge of the *Chad*, the Javonian comms officer's eyes popped out of her head as Alice threw Bardek's hand on the floor beside her. The girl gagged as she tried to hold down the vomit.

'Well, what are you waiting for? Unlock that bloody ship and the ones in orbit so we can fly them,' Alice said, an icy calm laced through her voice.

Verteg looked on. Her green face paled at the sight of her blood-stained beau. Her mouth opened, but nothing came out. Like a hammer blow, it hit her. *The humans are in shock at the loss of so many of their species*, she realised. Detached from the emotion, she looked around. Robert and Janet, two people whose behaviour norms would shun such actions, just stood there waiting for the job to get done – as if nothing was wrong. The guards who had followed Alice back were chatting and joking amongst themselves.

Verteg stepped forwards, reached out and stroked Alice's face. Their eyes met. Tears flowed from both. Alice put her blood-stained hands out in front of her. Her lip quivered but she held back the wails, bottling them up for another day. Putting her hands down, she whispered to Verteg, 'I'm okay.'

Verteg smiled at the lie. *She isn't okay; none of them are*, she thought.

More soft sobs, this time from the Javonian comms officer as she worked on unlocking the command codes for the fleet, Bardek's blood still leaking from the hand she had placed on the scanner.

*

The *Monarch* landed on one of the hastily constructed concrete pads on the desert floor. The crew, elated from their victory in space, were eager to touch down. For most, this would be their first visit to Earth; as for the humans, they were happy to be home. The Hela base at McKinnon, the town's new name, was turning into Earth's first space port. As soon as the hum of her grav engines died, two ambulances, mounted on grav platforms, landed at her port side. A doctor and four paramedics jumped out. They waited as, after the usual burst of air from the pressure seals, the door opened. The gangway hit the sandy desert floor, and the team, met by Tom, hurried to the ship's med-bay.

'That's Niamh,' Tom said, pointing to a white capsule. 'It's an Anan hiberpod. Crew call it the coma-capsule. It induces hibernation, preserving the body. You have the support systems we specified?' he asked, referring to the intermittent top-up of oxygen and power, the only external help the device needed.

The alien capsule, supplied by The Second after he treated Niamh, sustained her life during her recuperation from his treatment. Expunging the blue contamination from her body had triggered a profound shock to her system. Vital organs fought for survival as her body tried to shut down – killing her and her unborn child. Strapped into this white capsule, Niamh stayed in a medically induced coma as her organs healed. The hiberpod contained an all-encompassing therapy, feeding Niamh with oxygen, Anan plasma and the essential nutrients to sustain and cure – automatically administered in a shrouding life-giving gas.

'Her support system is ready in the ambulance Tom,' the Doc said. He examined her vital signs, as they tracked across a data screen on the pod. 'How long has she been like that?'

'Doc, we measure time differently in space, but I suppose in Earth terms, maybe a month. The Second returned her to us like that. I sent you his care program; is that ready?'

'It's set up in Christchurch and a shuttle is prepared to take her there.' he said, confidence oozing from his voice.

Exhausted, Tom slumped down in a seat beside her. *Finally*, he thought, *she has a chance*. With a deep sigh, he replied, 'Okay, Doc, she's all yours.'

'You have another patient?'

Tom rubbed his tired brow, pointing. 'Next room. He's conscious but fading fast.'

Mack lay in the bed, the black fog closing around his eyes as the pain in his chest increased. He remembered leaving the New World; Cylla had insisted on it. He had stayed here in med-bay, hooked up to the Anan auto-doc, throughout the uneventful journey. But on arrival in Earth orbit, as the *Monarch* entered the battle, the dynamics of the mission changed. The increased tension, the g-forces and the ship's changing speed took its toll on his frail body. He looked out from the black fog. A man stood before him, leaning over his body. He held his wrist and then, gripping a primitive device, the man put it on his chest.

Human doctor, he thought, as the man turned and spoke to Tom. Mack couldn't hear what he said, but the soft tones of the doctor betrayed his anxiety. *I'm dying*, he thought, *and there's nothing they can do*. He tried to speak, opening his mouth, but nothing came out as the black fog finally closed around his mind.

'Take him to the base hospital,' the Doc said to the paramedics. Without a word, they transferred both patients to the ambulances outside.

*

Mack opened his eyes. He was in a white room. He could hear a low beep, beep, beep from something beside him. Searing his brain, a deep crippling pain in his head had woken him. He managed to turn and watch his heartbeat track across a monitor above his bed. Looking down at his torso, he realised there were wires connected to his chest. The old General reached up with his weak hand, trying to scratch an itch on his nose. He touched two small tubes. *They're in my nose*, he realised, as he retched in disgust. The grunting sound disturbed the two humans and they turned to look at him. 'You okay, General?'

No, he tried to say, but nothing came out.

'General, we have given you the treatment for your Anan Sickness. The First Stage Treatment; there was some on the *Hela*. Also, we found Rhea and Alex's research and formula in the database. We can manufacture more on Earth.'

Mack tried to understand what the doctor was saying. 'Pain in my head,' he managed to say.

'Yes, General, I'm sorry. It's a side effect of our drugs. We use it to open the vessels to improve blood flow. I'm afraid your heart's not getting enough oxygen,' he said, as he pointed to the drip beside the bed.

Mack looked at it. *More tubes*, he thought, as he watched the saline drip carry the medication into the vane on his wrist.

'Let me die.'

'General, I realise our methods are primitive, but give us a chance, please. We're trying to treat your other organs and with a new heart, or a pump, you'd survive.'

He gasped as he realised what they were planning. 'No. Tom, get Tom.'

'He's away to Christchurch. I'll get Robert.'

*

Mack shook his head as the last human he wanted to see walked into the room.

'What's the prognosis?' Robert asked the doctors.

'He'll die if we don't give him a pump or a transplant. His organs are failing but we might be able to treat or substitute them.'

Robert knew enough about the aliens to tell how that would go down. 'You'll no want a human heart or a pump, will you, Mack?'

Mack managed to shake his head.

'You know you'll die.'

'You'll be happy with that.'

'No, I won't, you grumpy bastard.' Mack's heart rate jumped. Robert watched as the beep's increased on the monitor. Attempting to calm him, he put his blue hand on the General's chest.

To his surprise, his arm glowed. A thought flashed in his mind. *"Squeeze it, Robert, you must squeeze it."*

Overlord, where are you? But there was no answer; engrossed in scouring ceirim detritus from his planet, The Eight stayed silent. Trusting his Overlord, Robert closed his eyes and pressed his blue arm down on Mack's chest, feeling his heart, now barely beating and near to death. *What do I do now?* He opened his mind and gently squeezed. He watched as, at the cellular level, the muscles regenerated, repairing some of the damage caused by the Anan sickness.

Mack groaned, his mouth opened and shut as he gasped for air and the pain in his head increased. He managed to grab the tube in his arm, pulling it out. He gulped in air as he felt his heart pump, harder and harder, so much so that he thought it was going to jump from his chest. The room was full of noise as the alarms on the monitors sounded off.

The two doctors shouted at Robert. 'Stop! Stop! You're killing him!' They tried, in vain, to pull his arm from Mack's chest. As quickly as they started, the alarms stopped. His heart rate calmed and the turmoil on the screen subsided to a gentle rhythm, accompanied by the calming beep, beep, beep of the monitor.

Robert took his hand off the General's chest and smiled. 'Looks like that did something. You feeling any better?'

Mack took a deep breath. The headache was subsiding. The pain in his chest was gone and he could breathe easier. He removed the tubes from his nose. 'A little, no thanks to you.'

Robert turned to the medical staff, still fussing around Mack. 'Leave us. I need to talk to him.' He watched them leave, still protesting at Robert's intrusion, shaking their heads and muttering obscenities. He looked down at Mack. 'I'm no looking for thanks but we need you. There is someone—'

'Robert, I'll never work with you again.'

'Mack, will you get over it. So much has happened.'

'Never. Get out. Get out.'

'There's news about the war you need to know. And, you've a grand-nephew on Earth.'

'What nonsense is that? A grandnephew?'

'Mack, you need to know now. Brizo has a son, here on Earth. A boy; you need to meet him. It may be the last thing you do. What I did, it's not enough to save you. I cannae do any more but it might give you more time. Time you need to meet your own grandnephew.'

'A child, how is that possible?'

'Will you listen if I tell?'

His curiosity aroused, he looked at Robert from his tired grey eyes. 'Robert, I hate you and always will. This changes nothing – but tell me.'

He pulled up a chair and told the ailing General all. Tears filled the alien's eyes as he listened to Robert's story of the sadness of war and the human suffering from The Sixth's attack. It took all his strength to control his emotions as the graph on the monitor betrayed him, calling out every heartbeat, with the alarms occasionally sounding. When Robert finished, Mack sighed and relaxed down in the bed.

For a few minutes they sat in silence, then Mack spoke. 'Thank you. I am a stubborn old fool. I am sorry about your world's loss. What you did is heroic, Robert. If our war failed here, the consequences for the known universe would be incalculable. Earth and the New World are the battlefronts, I always knew that. The loss of one would lead to the inevitable loss of the other.'

Mack rested as he thought some more. Robert stayed silent, allowing the old purebreed his headspace. 'The Anan galaxies and the House of Aknar owe mankind a debt. Yes, we do, Robert—'

'And the child?' Robert asked, more concerned about him than talk of gratitude or debts owed.

'Yes, Robert, I see it all. A human has provided an heir to the Aknar throne; I never believed that was possible. One that will be free of this cursed sickness.' Urgency crept into Mack's voice. His tone dropping to a near whisper. 'Robert, you must keep it a secret; no one must know.'

'We did that, until now, you stubborn alien. You made me blurt it out. I hope the docs didn't hear. Don't worry – if they did, they'll keep your secret. Mack, while you still have life, you need to go see him.'

Mack grunted and glared at Robert. Concern at what the fair-haired Scotsman said, pushed him on – he sat up. 'How, when?'

'We're prepping the *Monarch*. Soon as you can. I'll no go with you. Janet and Kath will meet you there.'

'You had this planned, while I was near death.'

Robert wiped a tear from his eye as he looked at the man who was once his close friend. 'With all the death and destruction on Earth, I didn't want you to die without seeing your new family. The only happy event in this dour time.' He paused as he wiped tears from his eyes. The shock of what had happened to the Earth's population was raw in his mind.

Composing himself, Robert continued. 'Your grandnephew and his mum; they say she's beautiful – a real princess. The baby should grow up with something from you. You know we haven't heard from The Empress Theia. What are we to do with him? It's a responsibility we know nothing about. While you still draw breath, Mack, you must make arrangements, for his sake and for your planet, Anan. He needs to know his own kind, where his family came from.' He turned away from Mack and pursed his lips as he tried to quell the emotion, his own heartbeat pounding in his chest as he thought of the family he once had. 'Life's too short, Mack. You've got to make the best of it,' he said, as he walked out.

*

Northern India, 4th February 2028

Kochtos had gathered those of his closest lieutenants that survived *Dem-Zav1's* attack. Together, they had worked their way westward, feeding on what humans and animal remnants they could find. There were more ceirim survivors than he had imagined. Gathering the stragglers that formed a small army – backtracking towards Delhi – Kochtos marshalled them towards fresh food on India's western border with Pakistan. It was there that The Eight found them. Surprised at how many had survived after Robert's first strike, he watched, as Kochtos's army of near one hundred thousand marched across the already blackened land.

They shuffled along, bent over with their spikes flattened down on their epidermis. Their hands hung down, lifeless, with their claws retracted. There was no sign of the sharp teeth, their jaws remaining clamped shut. They trudged along through the land, blindly following their leader. Their stomachs grumbled with hunger but still they moved, following a smell on the wind, the aroma of freshness and food. That scent kept them from turning on each other, giving hope for another feast.

Kochtos felt it first. Turning, he looked up at the sky as The Eight bore down, straight towards the black army of death. Blue balls of fire shot out from his energy mass. They sped earthwards, fanning out and flashing and crackling with pure power. By the time they reached Earth the energy had stretched out, forming a vast blue cloud, engulfing Kochtos's army. The ceirim, touched by the deadly blue vapour, disintegrated, falling to the burning ground as dust. It was over in minutes, as The Eight expunged The Sixth's biological weapons.

But there was still more to do. The Eight looked down on the land. He could see it all. Spores from the fatal DNA that the geneticists had sprayed over the subcontinent lingered in the Earth. He tracked backwards and forwards across the land, burning all until the subcontinent was aglow with a blue fire that penetrated deep into the ground. Armageddon had come to these lands again, as The Eight's blue inferno sterilised everything the ceirim had touched.

Taking to the skies again, The Eight could feel pain at what he had done. He made a vow: *I will take his energy, his data and all of his galaxies, wiping all knowledge of him from the face of the universe.* Yet he knew, deep down, it was empty rhetoric, a vow he couldn't keep. Already he had killed one Overlord. Others would judge The Sixth – and perhaps, him as well. He dumped those thoughts.

Moving on, The Eight scoured the crash site in Africa. Fires from Admiral Whyte and General Marsh's airstrikes still burned. Despite the military's best efforts, some ceirim had survived, crawling off into the jungle and feeding on whatever scraps they could find. The Eight fired his blue energy, sterilising the land within a three-hundred-kilometre radius, wiping the last of the ceirim from the universe.

The quick actions of Robert and the humans had saved this continent. A green jewel, teeming with such a diversity of life, he thought, as he powered up into the stratosphere and turned to look down at the devastation. *The Sixth has changed my planet forever. Always it will bear those horrible scars.* The images of the charred Indian subcontinent and the six craters, where some of the planet's largest cities had stood, were seared in his memory. He would present those images to The Second and any surviving Overlords as a testament to The Sixth's atrocious lawbreaking actions.

He turned for the southern hemisphere, back to Australia to meet with Robert and to return to his chariot and his beasts. They were waiting for him, stretched out by his chariot, grooming their fur when he touched down at the Hela base, outside the operations centre. The six catbears stood up and growled a welcome to their returning Overlord. He flashed them a greeting, then turned to Alice, watching over them. 'Thank you, Alice. They look magnificent, and they are so happy. I believe Luna had to restrain you.'

She had recovered from her tempest and feelings of remorse stung her mind. She had shown Verteg a side Alice never knew existed. And now, in front of her Overlord, she felt shame. 'I'm sorry, Overlord. I nearly killed the Captain.' Alice said. 'Then I chopped off his hand.'

'More's the pity you did not kill him. It would have saved me the effort. You did well, Alice, taking that ship like that. You saved millions. As for his hand, he won't need it.' A stark hint from The Eight on Bardek's future.

Robert bounded out of the door and looked up at his Overlord. 'I'm glad to see you. You've grown.'

'I was bigger, Robert, when I left my island base in New Zealand. I have used much energy since. But it is done, thanks to your efforts. Again, I am in your debt. Robert, your quick actions saved this planet from much more horror and pain. You saved two continents and countless millions of people.'

Robert hung his head. 'Overlord, that's not how our human population see it. I'm wanted as a war criminal. You need to see the news. They say I sacrificed the poorest people in the world to save the rich and Chang's China.'

The Eight flashed a purple light. 'You didn't choose the ceirim's landing coordinates. You were following my orders. Always there is more, such a waste of valuable time. Who are these imbeciles?' The Eight asked, his voice laced with an unfamiliar fury.

'Earth's ruling politicians and the U.N. council,' Robert replied.

'Where is this council? I need to address it. Times have changed; they need to know that. But first, is Alan here and what of Tom and Niamh?'

'Alan's inside waiting for you. Tom's in Christchurch. I believe Niamh has regained consciousness. Mack is with his nephew. He has little time left,' Robert said as The Eight returned to his chariot.

They made their way inside the operations centre. The mood inside changed as he appeared. Loud cheers and clapping rang out. He was back – their Overlord had returned. The Eight felt the emotions, hope, trust and more …

Inside it was a happy Alan, their financial controller, who briefed Robert and the Overlord on Anan Corp's holdings on Earth. Anan Corp owned most of the world's leading corporations and the large property portfolios amassed by its hedge funds. Those funds had consumed properties distressed by economic downturns and by the Wave. They had bought the abandoned cities and the vast tracts of lands, including Europe's western islands once flooded by the Wave.

Despite complex stock market rules, Alan had accumulated the holdings in dummy corporations held in offshore accounts – all legal. Now it was all owned by Anan Corp and controlled by The Eight. He had bought back his planet!

CHAPTER FORTY-THREE

CNS Headlines. Anan Corp leader accused of War Crimes.

Today, the U.N. confirmed Anan Corp's Robert Leslie commanded the secret warplane which dropped alien-human hybrid bombs on the populations of the north-east Indian Subcontinent. The scorched-earth attack was not sanctioned by any Government or by the U.N.

Leslie is accused of developing the weapons and the plane, fusing alien and human technologies in an amalgamation of horror designed to maximise the bomb's yield.

Off the record, U.N. leaders described Leslie's act as a war crime eclipsing that of Earth's worst protagonists including the age-old Genghis Khan. Multiple governments and the U.N. issued warrants for his arrest for crimes against humanity. Social media is full of calls for his immediate execution. Anan Corp denies the charges and speculation that Leslie's strategy sacrificed poor and destitute people to save Chang Jin's China.

On a related matter, the U.N. has agreed the crews of the alien attack vessels face Earth justice for their heinous crimes.

‹ *From: Continental News Services. Good Morning Planet Earth*

*

Kenepuru Sound, New Zealand, 7th February 2028

HOLDING HER YOUNG SON IN her arms, Hana watched from the door of her cottage. The hum of the *Monarch's* engines grew as it dropped out of the sky. She gasped at the sight of this formidable alien ship, its grey hull glinting in the sunlight, rays bouncing off the pennon wings. Ten metres above the blue waters of the Kenepuru Sound, the vessel stopped.

Turning in towards the bay, it tracked in over the sand flats and, like a feather, touched down. A grav platform flew out from an open port in its side, flying straight to the cottage's garden, where it landed. In the sparsely populated Marlborough Sounds, few noticed the arrival of this starship.

Siba jumped out. Walking straight up to Hana, she bowed her head and knelt before her. 'Princess Hana of Aknar, I am Captain Siba of the *Monarch*. General Arie Machai asks your permission to meet with you and the new son of Aknar.'

Hana blushed and looked around at Janet and Kath. 'Oh, for heaven's sake, Mack, will you cut the bullshit. You're scaring the poor girl. Siba, this is Hana and her son, Ariki Sema. Does Mack need help?'

Still looking down at the ground, Siba stood up. Gradually, she lifted her head to look into the dark eyes of Hana, 'Princess, I'm pleased to meet you.'

'Aliens, do they ever listen?' Kath said, as she marched over to the grav platform. 'Mack, do you need help? You do – well, why didn't you say so? We have a wheelchair. Simple earthly tech that doesn't have grav.' She looked at the two nurses standing beside him. 'Go get it.' Then turning to the general, 'you'll be okay in it, won't you, Mack?'

Dogged to the end, he tried to walk as they lifted him into the chair. 'Mack, will you stop. You're insufferable. Try to accept some help in your dying hours. Really, don't look so surprised; we've been briefed,' Kath said, as she directed operations. 'Come on, take him into the house.'

Kath, dispelling the formalities, gathered them inside. In quick time, the two nurses lifted Mack into a big old armchair. After that, Hana placed Ariki on his granduncle's lap. A smile played across the General's lips, his white face beaming, skin glowing with a newfound joy. For the first time he managed to speak. 'Hana, you make an old man happy. I'm sorry for your loss. You were told what happened to Brizo?'

'Yes, General, I was. I'm sorry too. I know how much you loved him,' Hana replied. The loss of her love and the father of her child was a body blow to the young girl. She had cried for the memories of Brizo. But the soft touch and sweet smell of her child served her a dose of reality. More than ever, Ariki needed her.

'Mack, call me that. I loved him like a son. It was a great loss to our House – devastating news. Yes, it was, until I heard about you and Ariki. You give me hope for a new beginning for our Royal Family. Now you are a Princess of the House of Aknar, and a beautiful one at that,' he said his head nodding on his long purebreed neck.

Hana blushed and looked away from him. Tears welled in her eyes and she put her hand to her face. 'That's a responsibility.'

'It is,' Mack said, steely confidence playing in his voice. 'One you will handle easily. I ask you one thing, only one.'

Hana looked at the powerful purebreed and her lips trembled. This was what she had feared when she first heard Mack was coming. What would he ask for? How could she deal with this? 'What is it you want?'

'Love him and teach him to be a good person. As purebreeds get to their adolescence, they become difficult. Be patient with him and always teach him where he came from. When the time comes – if we ever win this war – he should be ready to take his place as the head of the House of Aknar. Prepare him for that.'

Kath clapped her hands together in glee. 'Mack, that's five things. You said, "only one". I thought you aliens were more advanced than us. Can't you count?'

He smiled at Hana. When they first met, Mack could feel her fear. All trace of it was gone now as she tried to stop laughing. 'Hana, we are not demons. The House of Aknar is one of the oldest Royal Families in the galaxy. You will do us proud, that I am sure of.' He frowned; there was something else. Robert had said, "arrangements were to be made". He would never know how valid those words were. Mack looked across at Hana and his tone changed. 'Did Brizo leave you anything?'

She sat back in surprise. His expression had changed and his frown puzzled her 'Yes,' she said, as she jumped up.

Minutes later she returned with the blue diamond pendant and the note Brizo had left her in Queenstown – now sealed in an envelope. His parting gift to her before returning to the *Hela*. She handed them to Mack.

He turned the blue diamond over and over in his hands, then looking at the envelope, he said, 'You never opened it?'

'I put it away when he left. Since then, I haven't touched it,' Hana replied.

'Open it now, please,' he said, passing it back to her.

Hana held it in her hand and with a small knife, neatly sliced through the top of the envelope. She looked in and pulled out the crumpled note Brizo had left all that time ago. She had never read it, putting it away in the envelope for safekeeping. Unfolding it, her eyes opened in surprise at the strange symbols scratched on the paper. She couldn't read it. *Whatever is that?* Hana wondered, handing the paper to Mack.

He gazed at the writing, trying to keep the paper away from the baby's outstretched hand. 'Do you know what these represent?'

Reaching over and taking her baby back, Hana shook her head.

Mack scratched his bald white head in wonder as he stared at it. *The boy knew*, he thought. *How could he have known what his fate would hold? How could Brizo have been so sure this woman would bear his child?* Clutching the letter and the blue diamond pendant, Mack looked at Janet. Tears welled in his eyes. 'Thank Robert for what he did for me. Truly, Janet, I am sorry. To be here and to witness this, I will die a happy man.'

Mack turned to face his new niece, bouncing the young prince on her knee. 'Hana, these were Brizo's most valuable possessions, given to him by my cousin, Empress Theia, when he was born. They are what you might call "the keys to the kingdom". That's what they are.' He handed them back to Hana. 'Keep them safe together, here with you. When Ariki becomes of age, give them to him. When the time comes for his ascension on Anan, he will know what to do with them. There may be resistance to a mixed-race Emperor – he will not have it easy.'

'Mack, will you not tell her more?' Kath asked. 'That's all so mysterious, so alien of you.'

'It's enough. No need for more. Kath, their wellbeing – how is that managed?'

'Mack, really, you should know better. They want for nothing. This cottage is Hana's and they both are share-holders in Anan corp.'

He nodded and thought of the share and code transfers he had made to Cylla Ora. 'Hana, there is another; she will help. She is my wife—'

Janet jumped up. 'Wife? You have a wife. Why didn't you tell me that?' she said. With her hand on her hips, she glowered down at him.

The rest got up and hastily left. 'Come, Siba, let me show you how we make tea,' Hana said, as they disappeared into the kitchen.

'Janet, please, we were recently married when I got sick. Let me explain …'

Ten minutes later, Siba carried in a tray of tea and muffins while Hana followed in with Ariki. Janet looked at Hana and smiled. 'I'm sorry, Princess, but sometimes prince charming ends up with rust on his armour. Go on, Mack. Tell her.'

'Yes, well, before I was interrupted, I was about to say—'

'Get on with it, Mack; you could die any minute,' Kath said.

'My wife is Cylla Ora, the Neredian trader. She works for us. Hana, she holds the Aknar codes and my controlling shares in Anan Corp.'

'What does that mean, Mack?' Hana asked.

Janet closed her eyes and shook her head. She had never expected to have to explain this. 'Princess, it means uncle here signed over the access codes of the family fortune to the most argumentative alien creature we've ever met.'

Hana grinned. 'It can't be that bad, Janet. We've a simple life here in the cottage. We've all we want.'

'Tell that to your son when he grows up and has to fight with his evil step-aunt for funds to power his intergalactic ships,' Janet said.

'What ships? Mack, what's she talking about?' Hana asked, her dark Maori face alight with curiosity. Intrigued by tales of starships and Neredians – whatever they were – her brown eyes bore into her uncle's white face.

Mack yawned. 'Too many questions all at once. Janet, that will never happen. No, Cylla would never do that. Hana, believe me, Cylla will help you, and when the time comes she will help Ariki. The ships Janet speaks of, the House of Aknar has one of the biggest intergalactic fleets in the universe. Most are now laid up in the Space Dock, at the Energy Exchange – all out of blue. Now, enough business. I am tired. I need to rest.'

They left him to sleep in the big chair, watched by the two medics. Siba took Hana for a tour of the *Monarch* as Kath and Janet sat in the garden with Ariki.

'She's a treasure, Kath. Brizo was so lucky.'

'Yeah, Janet, he was,' Kath said, fussing the baby. 'Is she that bad, the Neredian?'

'Kath, she's okay. I can deal with her, but she just loves to argue for argument's sake. Fast forward sixteen years, when she's confronted with a young prince looking to usurp her, well, who knows how she'll react.'

'Our Empress Theia will help him.'

'If she survives this war, Kath. I miss her. I really do,' Janet said, her voice quivering as she realised how long it was since they had seen Theia.

With the help of his two medics and Hana, Mack spent the last week of his mortal life in the cottage on the Kenepuru Sound. The Eight came to see the General for the last time. A treat for Hana who, in her wildest dreams, could never have imagined meeting such a powerful entity. With his new family around him, Mack slipped away in the night, dying happy in the belief that the great house of Aknar would rise again.

*

United Nations, New York, 15th February 2028

Vexed with the planet's political leaders and their reaction to the ceirim invasion, The Eight instructed Harold to convene a full meeting of the United Nations. Begrudgingly assembled in New York, the world's delegates – seated for near an hour – impatiently waited on him. They had heard the sound of the *Monarch* landing – then silence. A sudden roar from the crowds outside announced their wait was near over. The Eight was coming!

His entourage marched from the starship across a recently built concourse to the refurbished U.N. building. Evidence of construction works, to reclaim the once great city of New York from the ravages of the Wave, surrounded the alien and human delegation.

They walked inside, Alice leading the group. In front of her were six catbears, surrounding The Eight. Taking no chances, on each side, black-clad Anan security guards flanked the catbears and the Overlord's chariot. The Eight's energy mass beamed out bright blue light, glistening in the polished gold and silver of his floating chariot.

Trying not to run, a guard approached. 'Ma'am, I'm sorry, but I'm told to tell you, they don't allow animals in the building, only guide dogs.'

She smiled at him as she kept walking. 'Well, that's okay, then. They're not animals and don't let him hear you call them that,' Alice said, as she walked across the entrance hall, still filled with scaffolding for its ongoing renovation.

The procession continued into the assembly chamber with Robert and Harold walking behind The Eight. The onlookers looked shocked to see the man they had christened "war criminal". The tall sandy-haired Scotsman dressed in a kilt and an old Project Anan jacket chatted with Harold. Both ignored the calls and questions from the noisy press bystanders, baying and hounding at the sides, trying to get "the quote of the year".

The Overlord, floating in on his chariot, stopped. 'I am The Eight, the owner of this galaxy. I gave you intelligence, and I am your Overlord,' he boomed, his voice filling the assembly hall. An apparition of the Milky Way burst out above the delegates. They gasped in awe as the stars glistened in black space below the ceiling of their meeting hall. 'This man on my right, Harold Addison, is my representative on Earth. He negotiates on my behalf at this council. The man on my left, Robert Leslie, the one you accuse of war crimes, is my proxy on Earth. He follows my orders.' The Eight paused for the gravity of what he was saying to sink in.

'In my absence, under my direction, he has taken measures to protect my planet. You believe he transgressed in his fight to stop the ceirim. Let me show you what evil things they are,' he said, as the pictures of the stars changed to one taken by Quriel, of the ceirim gorging themselves on live humans. There were groans and moans as the gory sight lit up the chamber. Then the image changed to a map of Earth. 'These vile things can run at sixty kilometres an hour. In five days, with a human population to feed on, they would have overrun the Asian continent. If Robert had not acted as he did, this is what Earth would look like.' The map reformed, showing a blacked-out Africa and Asia. 'Billions more would have died, and these two continents would need sterilisation.' The Eight floated over beside Robert. 'You owe him a debt of gratitude. He is the saviour of two continents and you will commend him as that. Now to business,' The Eight said, as he left Robert and Harold, floating up above the speaker's podium in his shining chariot.

The delegate for Qatar scratched at his wrist; it was hot from his watch. *What's that from?* he wondered. With tears in his eyes, he felt the wristwatch burn his skin. At once, he pressed the clasp, opening the latch on the solid gold bracelet, shaking it off. It fell on his desk, smoke started to rise, as the hot metal burned into the veneer.

'Delegate,' roared The Eight, 'how much did that watch cost?'

'I, ah, received it as a gift.'

'Yes, you did. You have so many large palaces. We could see them from space. I believe the watch cost three-quarters of a million dollars. How much did you pay the workers when they built your big circular palaces?' The well-dressed portly delegate squirmed, lowering his head as he fiddled with his thick moustache. The Eight continued, 'Why do you need so many palaces? Why do you need such an expensive watch? I understand time; it regulates the universe but it was never that expensive.' Titters of laughter filled the hall.

The Eight paused until it stopped. 'Before I returned in 2026, over half of your world's wealth was owned by one per cent of the population. You are all well aware of such inequality, discussing it many times at your economic summits. Yet you do nothing. How many of you think that is fair?' he waited.

Rex, prostrated on the floor with the rest of the catbears, sat up. He yawned, scratched at his mane, and then farted – the noise breaking the awkward silence. The fetid stench wafted over the well-heeled delegates seated nearby. The Qatar delegate choked on the smell from Rex and the alien beast's bloated bowel, and wondered, how wise was it to bribe the house manager for a front-row seat?

The Eight continued, 'I feel all your mixed emotions – some shame, some guilt and some indifference. I have news for you – all that changes. I will restore the balance I originally intended when I gave you free will and intelligence. Once again, I control Earth.'

The murmur of voices increased as the delegates turned to each other. "What does the Overlord mean? How can this be so? How did he do that?" they asked.

Again, listening to their chatter, he waited for silence. 'I bought it through your financial systems. Bought back what I owned through your own corrupt and greedy schemes.' This time they stayed quiet. No one moved, no one spoke, all eyes were on The Eight after this shattering revelation. He raised the power of his voice. The deep sound penetrated the doors and walls, the crowd assembled outside listening to every word. 'Earth's existence has changed forever. I need my planet back! Mankind will serve me. You think the visit from the ceirim is over. That The Ninth's defeat here on this planet will change the order in the universe. This was only the first battle!'

The Eight paused for his words to sink in. A dead silence gripped the meeting hall. All eyes now on him, he continued, 'History shows, one battle never won a war. There will be more. The Sixth created evil beyond what we Overlords ever imagined.' He stopped again and listened. Nothing – they were all silent and heeding every word he said.

In a softer voice, he continued, 'I do not know if that evil will come here, but I do know The Sixth will not rest until he has control of the universe as we know it. The day-to-day lives of the general population of this planet should not change significantly. Some will experience a lift in living standards. I am not a monster; the population's wellbeing will be protected. After my first return to Earth and the war I fought here – your own wars, the ceirim invasion, and the destruction of your largest cities – the population has fallen to over four billion. It is a terrible loss to mankind and something that can never be forgotten. This day we will mark in commemoration, and for future generations to remember, the genocide perpetrated by The Sixth on mankind.'

Murmurs of approval and the odd hand clap cut the silence.

The Eight continued. 'Together we can protect the planet by restricting the population to that number. There is another planet available for colonisation, the one that is called the New World. Between this planet and the New World, there is enough wealth for all of mankind to exist in a comfortable and sustainable way. I will help you manage the destruction caused by climate change – you will survive that. But you will work for me, sustaining my war effort, on my terms. We will bring order to chaos, there is no other option. We fight The Sixth or die.'

He turned his chariot and floated back down to his six beasts. They stood up and followed his shining chariot out of the hall. When the doors closed behind him, the chamber erupted with the sound of over a thousand disgruntled politicians, shouting together, as they tried to comprehend what he had said.

Harold turned to Robert. 'Time to go, Robert. You'll be late. Let's leave that lot to fight amongst each other. There's time enough to unveil his master plan.'

CHAPTER FORTY-FOUR

The Story of Bawrak

With the shortage of blue and so few intergalactic ships on the move, the market for bawrak collapsed. The family's drug business declined. Following market research, we have rebranded the drug as "gileyal" – strength and happiness. It proves a real attraction to the younger generation. They love the drug's brain-enhancing effects and the intoxicating amplification of all their body's senses. Rumours of the drug's enslaving properties are untrue. The research demonstrates low addiction rates amongst our clients.

The drug is taken orally as a drink. We distribute the base product as transportable powder. Before use, it is mixed with any water-based beverage. I have marked the field-cave's location on the attached map and included the recipe for the drug. If I die, guard this with your life.

> ◂ *Extract from: Family legacies, Little Kake Borea*

*

The Amech, Earth Orbit, 15th February 2028

IN ORBIT AROUND EARTH, TOM stared out of the window of the shuttle at the captured fleet. Back on the planet, The Eight laid down the law — upending centuries of buccaneering. But for Tom, political intrigue was irrelevant to his task today.

So far, nothing had gone to plan. Except for Bardek's ship – the *Chad* – four of the five captured vessels remained in orbit. Even with the Borea and Mzimot families, Anan Corp hadn't the resources to manage the aftermath of their victory in space. The endless list taxed them to the limit.

The *Monarch* had parked the package of four ships – bought on Lagrvth – in Mars orbit before flying on to attack The Ninth's fleet.

Retrieving the four ships and landing them back in Australia required the *Richard* and *Monarch* working in tandem. Not an easy task, one Verteg didn't relish. She and Siba planned to share the load between the two vessels and simply lower the package down to the planet. "Brute force and burn grav," was how they described their time-consuming plan.

There weren't enough pilots and crews to land what remained of The Ninth's captured fleet on Earth. Assisted by Admiral Whyte's Australian marines, Tom's security forces had taken possession of it, guarding the hostile purebreeds – a plan Quriel had come up with.

'Leave the four in orbit until we're ready to repair and crew them. Verteg's changed the command codes, immobilising the fleet. They're going nowhere,' Quriel had said. 'It's the only sensible solution.'

They transported all of The Ninth's crews, including Bardek's on Earth, to the *Amech*. Crippled by damage, it made the perfect prison ship. A "knee-jerk" reaction, born out of necessity and risk management. No one in Anan Corp wanted any of The Ninth's surviving crew on the planet.

But now, decisions had to be made. The *Amech*'s life-support systems were failing. And to heap more on their stretched resources, the U.N. security council requested the alien crew face trial for war crimes on Earth. Getting them there now was Tom's problem!

At the last minute, this shuttle had collected Tom from Christchurch. With Robert in New York, there was no one else to deal with the issue. Waiting for his instructions, Verteg stood off from the fleet in the *George's* inter-field transporter – their only one. It was up to Tom to figure out what to do with the prisoners. Transferring the hostile crews to the *Amech* was a nightmare. The *George's* inter-field ship – a mining transporter – wasn't designed for that. With no bawrak, they were strung out and suffering from withdrawal, near half were unstable and violent, causing ructions. As time moved on, locked up on *Amech* without their drugs, the purebreeds' mental stability declined. Fighting amongst themselves and goading the guards was a regular thing.

Tom ran the journey permutations over in his mind. The risk to Verteg and the security guards was too high. *It won't work*, he thought, as he scratched the stubble on his face. *I just don't want to be here.* His mind wandered back to Christchurch where Niamh lay in a hospital bed. At least she had been conscious and taking solid food when he left. Breaking his black humour, the memory of her hairless head and white face sipping tea made him smile.

Parked together, the four six-hundred-metre-long ships looked nothing like the formidable fleet that had arrived. Their irregular oblong hulls and bulbous bows bore the blackened marks from the battle they had lost. The *Amech's* wounds were clearly visible along the port side, where it sustained structural damage to some of the launch bays. Tom turned to the purebreed flying his shuttle. 'They don't look so good, do they, Chief?'

'No, Mr Parker. They were never The Sixth's best option. The *Losh* is his, the rest belong to The Seventh. They're much older than what we have back at the Energy Exchange. Our Aknar fleet is newer and fitted with better weapons. Good job he didn't help himself to them.'

'Why didn't he?'

'Loyalty and crews. He would never let a fleet loose in space with an Aknar crew. They would come and join us.'

'And those drugged-up failures couldn't fly them?'

'No, Mr Parker, they couldn't. I've clearance to dock on the starboard side of *Amech* from your team leader, Bull.'

'Bill, his name's Bill,' he said, as he watched Haldock manoeuvre the shuttle in through the starboard side landing bay. The sizable airlock closed behind them and the shuttle touched down.

Bill gasped at the sight of Tom as he jumped out, his ordinarily neat and clean ship garb replaced by jeans and a grubby shirt. The untidy hair, unshaven face and black circles under his eyes, said it all. He had to ask, 'How's the missus, boss?'

'She's conscious, Bill, and eating. She's lost weight and all her hair.'

'Look on the bright side, boss, she's alive and in good hands. She'll come good, boss. She's the most determined woman we've ever seen. You ready for them?'

'Let's get this over with. Where are they?'

'In a makeshift brig, port side shuttle bay. Come on,' he said, as he led the way through the darkened corridors of the *Amech*. As they made their way along corridors with flickering lights and the foul smell from the failing life-support system assaulting his nostrils, the journey reminded Tom of his first visit to the *Hela*.

There were forty-eight of them, huddled together in the damaged shuttle bay guarded by Anan Corp security. The twenty-something addict's condition had deteriorated, becoming more violent, their shouting and fits of anger aggravating the grim scene. To protect the guards and their fellow prisoners, their wrists were still secured by tie wraps. As Tom approached them, their shouts turned to howls. The Commander of the *Losh* stood up, quelling their unease, then walked straight over to Tom. 'Human,' he said, with his head bowed, 'we need help, and I ask you to have mercy on my crew.'

'I'm not sure how that will go, Commander.'

'At least spare the young ones – the adolescents not tainted by bawrak. There are eight. They are our sons and daughters. We train them this way.'

'They'll turn on us; we can't trust them.'

'Human, they will kneel before The Eight and swear allegiance to him. That I vouch for.'

Tom looked across at the prisoners. 'Where are they?'

'Here,' he said, calling to the group. Eight young purebreeds stood up. Their heads hung down over their long necks and with shoulders slumped, they shuffled over to Tom. Avoiding any eye contact, they stared at the floor. 'There will be no trouble, I guarantee it,' the Commander assured Tom. Then turning to the group, he said, 'Go with them, obey them and serve them well. You will atone for the sins of your families. Rebuild our good names.'

Tom put his hands up to his face as he looked at this group of young purebreeds. Lifting their heads, young, tear-streaked, white faces peered back at him. *No more than teenagers*, he thought. *They deserve a chance. The Eight can judge them.* He leaned over and whispered in Bill's ear, 'Get two of the lads to take them to the shuttle bay – keep the cuffs on them. Best they don't see what happens here.'

'Right, boss. Follow me, you lot – no monkey business either,' he said to the young purebreeds, as he handed them over to two of his men.

Tom looked around. The prisoners watched as he examined one of the airlocks. 'Is that working?' he asked.

'Yes,' one answered.

'Okay, inside, all of you. We've a transporter coming to take you to Earth. It'll dock with this airlock.'

'I don't think that'll work, human. The seal rings are buckled,' another said.

'We'll give it a try. I don't want to transfer you lot to the starboard side. Get on with it. Inside, now,' he said, pointing his carbine at them.

They grumbled and protested.

Tom leapt forwards, striking Bardek, their fleet captain, on the back with the butt of his gun. The grey-faced Bardek, cradling his bandaged stump, whimpered.

With icy steel in his voice, Tom roared, 'I said, now.'

Some screamed as they ran into the open airlock. With a bang, Tom closed the door behind them. Slamming his hands on an orange button, the metallic click of locks engaging and the hiss of seals pressurising tumbled out. His crew watched as he examined the controls. Some turned away, not wanting to witness what was coming next. Coloured purple and fitted inside a recess, Tom found what he was looking for. Lifting a transparent cover, he reached inside the compartment. The purple handle beckoned. Tom explored the mechanism – nothing complicated. Pulling a securing pin, he closed his hand over the purple lever then yanked it down.

People jumped as purple lights over the airlock flashed and a siren warbled. Screams of panic permeated through the thick inner door. The outer door of the airlock shuddered as its holding pins disengaged. An uncontrolled release of the pressurised air blew the door open, out into the vacuum of space – followed by The Ninth's crew. The force of the life-giving atmosphere leaving the chamber sucked the forty out. Not wanting to miss any of the action, Bill stood by one of the wide viewports. Nothing prepared him for the gruesome sight unfolding in front of the large window.

'Holy shit, boss. They're exploding. There's blood and gore everywhere. Look, come look, boss …' The rest of the crew stood stock still.

Tom walked over to the window and looked out. It was what he had expected. 'It's physics, Bill – the vacuum of space. Your body's like a pressurised vessel, full of liquid. Our atmosphere stabilises it – balances the pressure. Take that away and boom, the blood and liquids, in the sunlight, boil off into a vapour. Body blows up, like that,' he said, turning away from the window. 'Right, let's go,' he said to the rest of the crew as he walked towards the exit.

Bill remained, engrossed in the spectacle outside. 'Hang on a mo, boss.'

'Come on, Bill. Leave it.'

'Hey, boss – after what you said – how come physics don't work on that fella there? He didn't explode. Look, he's still floating in space.'

Tom froze and turned. A shiver ran down his back and his heart thumped hard in his chest as he looked at Bill peering out of the big window, pointing at someone floating outside. The force from the other purebreeds' decompression had pushed him back towards the ship. Tom sprinted back to the window.

'Look, boss, he's still alive. His head and eyes are bulging, and he's going all grey – like metal. He's looking straight at us. Oh, look at that face. He's pissed off. Don't think he expected you to do that.'

Tom blinked his eyes and shook his head, trying to shake off the horror he was looking at, as the Commander of the *Losh* glared back from the vacuum of space. He turned and barked orders to his crew. 'Go now, find those purebreed kids. Knock them senseless and drag them back here.' *Too late*, he thought, as the sound of a grav weapon spilt from the corridor.

They ran as fast as they could. Around a corner, they found five ill-fated purebreeds and their two guards. Two of the young purebreeds were kneeling down beside one of their guards, crying as they tried to push his stomach back into his body and staunch the blood flow from his wounds. Two others were tending to the other guard and one of their own, sitting dazed on the floor, stunned by blows to the head.

Tom knelt down beside his injured guard and felt for a pulse. *Nothing*, he thought, as the bright red blood flowed out from the soldier, pooling on the floor around him. A deadly wound had sliced up past his stomach, severing his arteries. He looked at the two purebreeds, one male and one female, both now covered with the dying man's blood. 'Leave him, he's gone,' Tom said in Anan. 'Did they say anything?'

The girl sobbed but between the gasps of shock, she blurted out, 'The shuttle, that's where they go. They changed; they are not purebreed or human. We thought they were like us. They did this with their bare hands,' she shuddered, as the memories played across her mind. 'They turned into grey monsters. We've never seen such demons before.'

Tom jumped up and grabbed at his comms unit. Haldock and his men! He had to warn them. He couldn't let them get to Haldock, kidnap him or worse, kill him. They couldn't afford to lose an experienced pilot like that. Making contact with them, he gave the order. 'Get out of there and hide. Don't try to fight. If they want the shuttle, let them have it. Do not engage. I repeat, do not engage.'

While he and his crew pursued their quarry, he called Verteg, explaining what had happened. 'Standoff the fleet. Stay cloaked with weapons armed. Call Robert – tell him to warn The Eight.' The sound of staccato gunfire announced their arrival at the starboard side landing bay. He rushed to the front of his crew, taking cover behind some cargo boxes.

'Got them pinned down in front of the shuttle, boss,' Bill said. 'But, boss, they absorb bullets; no effect on 'em at all.'

'Haldock and our men, where are they?'

'Safe, over there, look,' he said, gesturing towards a pile of cargo where the three were huddled down, taking cover.

'Keep down. Get the men to fan out and keep their distance,' Tom said, as he stood to face the three aliens. 'Ceasefire, ceasefire,' he shouted to his men. Pointing the grav weapons they had taken from his guards, the three aliens stared at him. 'Go, take the shuttle,' he said in Anan. 'The other, your Commander, is still alive outside the port side airlock in space. If you hurry, you can save him.'

In a rush to join their leader, without a word, they turned and ran into the empty shuttle. The door closed behind them. Within seconds, the sound of humming filled the landing bay as the ship lifted off.

'Out, everybody out,' Tom shouted, over the noise of a shrill alarm. They ran out. His men battened down the main access door as the landing bay master airlock started to cycle open. Through a viewing port, they watched the giant hangar open, the impatient shuttle hovering until there was enough room for it to squeeze through, out into space.

'Bloody hell, boss. Never thought I'd be so glad to see three prisoners escape. You lot, you did okay,' Bill said to his crew. 'Poor Micky, he was doing a line with an Aussie back on the base. Shit, what'll I tell her? Your man had his guts cut out by some alien monster. She won't like that, boss.'

'Best let me tell her, Bill.'

'Thanks, boss. What part of hell did they come from?'

'I don't know, Bill. What about you, Haldock?' he said, looking at the Aknar chief.

'Never before, Mr Parker. This is a new evil. They absorbed the metal from your percussion weapons. Impossible for our class of life form to do that. Even the ceirim, once you pierced their armoured skin, were damaged.'

They backtracked, recovering the injured group of young purebreeds and the surviving soldier. Two stayed back for the grim task of retrieving Micky's mutilated body. The group hurried on, arriving back in the port landing bay in time to watch the three aliens pick up their Commander from space. Without a care for the vacuum, they just opened the shuttle door and pulled him in. Turning it away from the damaged *Amech,* they flew straight over towards the *Losh.*

Tom called Verteg, standing-off in the cloaked transporter. 'Verteg, can you try to stop them. We can't let them access the *Losh.* But you need to stay well back – our weapons don't harm them.'

'Yes, Mr Parker. I can.' Turning her ship, she flew straight towards their enemy. One kilometre out and from below, she launched two small grav missiles, targeting the shuttle's drives. Embedding themselves in the engine ports, the weapons detonated, damaging the two grav drives. The explosive trajectory – calculated by Verteg – pushed the shuttle away from the fleet, out into empty space, where it drifted with the four demons, helpless and alone.

Tom's next call was Robert. 'Where is he?' he asked, after finishing the update.

'On his way. When I told him, outside the U.N., he left his chariot and flew straight to space. Spectacular exit, Tom. He left in a blue-fired trail, straight up and over New York. We're on our way up in the *Monarch*.'

The Eight arrived shortly, transferring to Verteg's transporter as she kept watch over the deadly group. 'Overlord,' she said, 'they haven't moved. We caught sight of them floating outside in space, trying to fix the engines. They're still trying to get to the *Losh*. It was their Commander's ship.'

'You did well, Verteg; quick thinking to put them out here. Stay and watch them. I go back to the *Monarch*.'

An hour later, on the *Monarch*'s bridge, Tom, Robert and The Eight watched the disabled shuttle drift in space. 'I cannot see them or sense anything from them. It's like they don't exist,' The Eight said.

Tom rubbed his darkened eyes. 'How is that possible, Overlord?'

'They are not carbon life forms. They are metal-based, something we have never seen before. I didn't think such evil would be here already.' He explained what he had seen in The Ninth's mind before he expunged him.

They sat in silence, listening to the hum and bleep from the ship's control systems. Tom jumped up from his seat. 'Overlord, you say they're metal-based; half carbon, half metal.'

'Yes, Thomas, a mix of carbon life and gadolinium and whatever else he put in. I did not get The Sixth's process from Nine.'

'They absorb bullets; who knows what'll happen if we blast them apart. Perhaps millions of sentient particles floating in space, ready to gobble up whatever they make contact with?'

'Despite your fatigue, you may be right, Thomas.'

'Overlord – chemical weapons – that's what we need. Something strong, like acid or alkaline. That'll dissolve them.'

He floated over to Tom. 'Black mood you are in, Thomas, consumed with annihilation. You were to take The Ninth's crew back to Earth and hand them over to the authorities for a trial Harold had agreed to. What possessed you to do what you did to them, venting them from an airlock?'

Looking at his Overlord's pulsing energy mass, Tom's face fell. 'I'm sorry, Overlord. I disobeyed your orders. But I felt something – at the last moment – it just didn't feel right to take them to Earth.'

'Imagine what would have happened if those things got loose on Earth. Perfect spies for The Sixth, invisible to me, they were his fall-back plan if the mission failed. Thank you, Thomas. Always follow your feelings. Earth and I owe you a debt. You suggest chemical weapons. How?'

'Give me twenty-four hours and the *Monarch*. I need to talk to Chang.'

*

The Monarch, Earth Orbit, 16th February 2028

With Chang beside them on the bridge, they watched the four alien metal-men working on the hull of the disabled shuttle. 'They're still trying to rebuild the drives. They started soon after you left, Overlord,' Verteg said over their comms system. 'They use materials from inside the shuttle, reforming it to replicate the damaged parts. They were even able to use the missile casings.'

'How far on are they?'

'They increased their pace when you arrived. Unless you have a new weapon, I need to disable their engines again. I believe they'll finish soon.'

'We have something, Verteg. We will try it now. Chang Jin, may I ask how you got such weapons?'

'Overlord, when you first arrived, my previous masters asked me to devise a weapons program to combat different life forms. I did not limit the research to carbon life; we considered metal and silicone-based entities as well.'

The delicate weapon, hidden away from the world, was loaded into one of the *Monarch's* launch tubes in China. Chang worked alongside Tom at the weapons' console, getting it primed and ready to fire.

'It's armed. Launch when ready, Parker,' he said, a satisfied smile playing across his lips.

They watched as a small missile, scribed with red Chinese characters, tracked away from the *Monarch*. Chang translated. 'It says, "gift from The Peoples Republic of China".'

Before hitting the shuttle, the missile exploded, forming a widespread superheated gas cloud in space. The four aliens turned from their work, pointing at the approaching menace. The corrosive gas made contact with the four grey monsters. Withering in agony, it was clear they knew their time was up. The scorching sulphuric acid vapour attacked their metal bodies, eating away at the gadolinium and reacting, at the molecular level, with the other compounds that made their corrupt bodies. The deadly cloud consumed them, bit by bit they disappeared, their soulless existence dissolving into space. The hungry gas ate at everything it came in contact with. Soon there was no trace of them or their shuttle. When the cloud finally dissipated, out into the vacuum of space, nothing remained.

They watched in awe, afraid to comment on the efficiency of Chang's chemical weapon – lest they jinxed it. Finally, as they watched it disappear, The Eight floated over to Chang. 'Chang Jin, how many of those weapons do you have?'

He shook his head. 'Not many, Overlord. That was a prototype. Containment of the acid is a problem.'

'You will start manufacturing more. I will help with the design. Come, we must go.'

CHAPTER FORTY-FIVE

CNS Headlines. Alien Captives Killed.

In a shock press release, Anan Corp announced that "due to an unforeseen accident in Earth orbit, the captured crews of the alien attack vessels are dead. Four of the invaders escaped during the incident".

There are no details as to what caused the accident, or the death toll. The event happened "during a routine ship-to-ship transfer of the detainees to another vessel for passage to Earth".

After the decisive space battle, a damaged alien ship, parked in Earth orbit, served to incarcerate the captives. Speculation about a broken airlock on that starship may explain the crew's sudden death.

Anan Corp's Security Manager, Thomas Parker, was in charge of the transfer. Other than that brief statement, Anan Corp refused to answer any questions and refrained from further comment.

Some will say "a timely ending for such murdering monsters" but their loss deprives the people of Earth of justice.

In another development, The Eight's hurried departure from New York may be connected to the incident.

‹ **From: Continental News Services. Good Morning Planet Earth**

*

Kenepuru Sound, New Zealand, 17th February 2028

FROM THE VERANDA OUTSIDE, NIAMH watched the *Monarch* land on the sandy flat behind the trees. *He would be here soon,* she thought, as she feasted her eyes on the view. Seated in a deep armchair sipping coffee, she looked out at the waters of the Kenepuru Sound, the mountains of the

Queen Charlotte Track, framing the Sound's far shore. Listening to the water lapping on the beach, she watched a boat fly across it. Approaching their jetty at speed, the noisy engine soon drowned out the quiet lapping sounds. A group of people disembarked. Waving a greeting, they made their way up from the jetty to the lodge. *They arrive*, she thought, *but where is he?* Standing and peering up the dirt road, she shook her head and returned to her chair. Then he appeared, walking briskly around the corner in front of the lodge. Tom waved as he walked up to her. She smiled and tears flowed down her cheeks as she looked up at him.

Tom knelt down beside her, kissing her gently. His arms pulled her close and his tongue explored her mouth. They parted – she smiled, wiping the tears from her eyes. He gazed at her white hairless head. 'You look good, Niamh. How you feeling?'

'Better, much better. Food here's great as well. You look like shit. Hard day at the office?'

'Something like that. I did something I'm not proud of – but it worked out. I need a shower.'

She watched as he disappeared through the patio doors into their room. Gulping her coffee down, she ran in after him.

He admired her naked body, her bump starting to show, as she stepped into the shower beside him. 'You're beautiful,' he said, as he caressed her. 'I missed you.'

She closed her eyes as he touched her. 'I'm like a bald bag of bones.' It was true, she had lost weight; her bones poked through her hairless skin and her bald head shone white.

'I loved you when you flashed with blue, and I love you now. You're the same Niamh Sullivan I met in Christchurch,' he said, as he pulled her to him.

*

IN THEIR LARGE LUXURIOUS BED, she awoke in his arms and watched as he still slept. Although she didn't have her blue diamond, she could feel darkness from him. *What has he done?* she wondered. As she listened to his deep breathing, she thought about her own health. While she was in the hiberpod, although unconscious, she had had flashbacks. The white cocoon haunted her and she remembered once waking up, feeling the capsule's smooth shape enclosing her. Now she remembered The Second's treatment; she shuddered at the thought of the organics eating her hair and skin. Tom's eyes popped open wide with the surprise of her shivers.

'You okay?' he asked.

'Yeah, I remember some of it.'

'You want to talk about it?' Niamh had told him some of what had happened, but not it all. She had still found it hard to accept that she had nearly changed into an Overlord.

'Jeez, no, not yet. But I've changed, Tom. I'm harder, much harder. You remember when Mack joked about throwing us out of the airlock if we didn't sign our contracts – on the first visit to the *Hela?*'

He remembered that day. It seemed an age ago. 'I do. You were incensed at my questions and what I'd do with any undecided or deserting colonists.'

'Yeah, I accused you of being a murderer. Well, look at me now. Since then, I've killed. I won't go anywhere without the guns Chang gave me. Here' she said, as she took one from under the pillow. 'I know we're safe here in the lodge but I still want them close. And you, Tom, there was a darkness about you when you came back. What happened?'

'I did what Mack joked about, without any hesitation. Niamh, I was never that bad. Even my own men turned in disgust.'

'Tell me about it.'

He held her close as he told her all. She listened, never interrupting. 'There, that's it. I did the right thing. But still, I'm racked with guilt that I did it so easily.'

She kissed him. 'The Eight was right, you probably saved our war effort, Earth and the New World.' They lay together in silence. She looked up at him. 'We have to move on, Tom. Enjoy our lives together, whatever it brings. We need to live for life and happiness together.' She put his hand on her stomach. 'More than anything, I want this child; it survived so much.'

He held her close. 'So did you. I thought I'd lost you – again. You nearly died this time.'

They lay in silence, happy to be together, safe in the soft bed. Niamh tracked a finger across the scars on his chest. 'What next for you?'

'The Kandark Galaxy. Remember Nolget and Touqmat, your friendly scrap dealers from Lagrvth? They want a security team. We need to set up a base there, or did you forget about that?'

She grinned. 'No, I didn't, and I'm coming too. I fancy a shopping trip. We've much more to do now, and before we left, they said they were getting in more stuff.'

He sat up and looked at her. 'What stuff?'

She shook her head and laughed. 'Jeez, Tom, how do I know? Lighten up, would ya. It'll be more scrap ships and parts.' she said, as she pulled him down on top of her.

*

The following morning, a small group met in the conference room at the back of the lodge. The Eight hosted this informal gathering with his personal allies, now Earth's most powerful leaders, all loyal to him. They had come to pay their respects to Arie Machai, the powerful Aknar pure-breed whom they all knew and respected. His passing was a reminder that the new visitors to Earth shared mankind's mortality.

The Eight took the time to brief the group on the new threat that they faced. Their Overlord pulled no punches! The arrival of the soulless metal life on the planet's doorstep added another level of intrigue, accelerating the prerequisite for a fightback. It moved the necessity to unseat The Sixth from the Anan Galaxy to a whole new level. The debased entity had displayed a level of uncaring indifference never before seen in Overlords. What he had done on Earth was an intergalactic crime.

The effect would test humanity further, adding layer upon layer to the ever-growing war plan. After this first battle, which it seemed they had lost but, in fact, won – despite the humongous cost in lives – The Eight painted a grim picture for the future.

'Earth and humankind are changed forever, yet the war rages on. And before it is over, another battle will come. We must prepare for that,' The Eight said.

'There is so much more to do. Nothing like it was done before, in all the time I remember as an Overlord. We must reshape Universal order. That is enough for now. I need to think. We meet again to forge a stratagem.' That word spoke volumes about the depth of his intelligence. The Eight paused. In silence, the glum group digested his brief.

Sensing their dour mood, he ended their meeting. 'Come, let us go and honour General Arie Machai in his last journey. We should celebrate his life.'

*

The purebreeds, led by Captain Quriel, officiated at Mack's funeral ceremony. Transported on a grav platform from the garden of the small cottage to the *Monarch*, the funeral party, which included Hana and Ariki, accompanied the body into orbit. There, Mack's sarcophagus was loaded onto a missile and projected out towards the sun. The funeral party watched from the bridge as General Arie Machai, the cheerful purebreed they knew as Mack, sped out into space on his last journey towards Earth's sun. The missile, visible on Kora's navigation projection, soon accelerated past the speed of light. With her blue diamond, she tracked him on his final ten-minute journey, out into the fusion fire that had given primordial life to Earth.

*

Energy Exchange, Anan Galaxy. EPTS: B141622

Across time and space, while Earth tried to heal its wounds, in the Anan Galaxy The Sixth fumed and raged. He had felt The Ninth's passing and with that, the loss of contact with the fleet. A brief encounter with Seven didn't go well either. He demanded more blue energy and recompense for the cost of his five ships and crew. The loss of Nine didn't hurt Six as much as the mission's failure and the inability to thwart Eight. To make matters worse, The Seventh had received news from the *Chesh* – the only ship to escape – confirming the ceirim invasion and the use of the extinction weapons had failed.

More confusion and rancour developed between Six and The Seventh – who felt he had lost the most. His most experienced captain, Bardek, and the best of his intergalactic fleet were gone. The Sixth, on the other hand, had kept the lion's share of his fleet back in the Jora and Ragma Galaxies – hiding from the action.

Only the Overlords felt The Ninth's passing – Six and Seven kept that quiet. From The Sixth's black mood and the constant raging flashes of purple light from his energy mass, the Shoter guessed something was up. Then there was the regular posting of new contracts for blue energy at the Exchange. The price of blue started to fall. The Shoter kept his council, staying clear of The Sixth as much as possible. Until a roar from his chamber shattered the palace's stillness.

'Get me a shuttle and load it with blue. I'm going to the Energy Exchange,' was all The Sixth said.

Inside his black mind, he had to do something to change the course of events. Engorging his mass, he would take control of the Exchange. His new mission: find out who was issuing those contracts and where they were. If he could locate the source of the blue, he would grab it for himself. He still had a fleet, and with the Aknar navy locked in irons, no one would oppose him. *Yes,* The Sixth thought, *I still have an advantage.*

*

The dealers watched his large energy mass float down through the Energy Exchange hall. His untimely appearance, near the end of the session, quelled the closing time clamour as the traders rushed to consolidate their positions. The young girl looked up and gasped at the sight above. Silhouetted against the transparent domed roof, The Sixth's energy mass glided down, blocking their view into space. 'Have you seen this before, Arb?' Her father, the Shoter, thought it best not to warn her. A wise decision.

'No, little one, never ever have I seen an Overlord in our trading hall. I thought there was an unwritten rule barring them from this sanctum.'

'He's increased his energy mass. Look, it's huge. What's he doing here?'

His wizened old face glowed. 'Maybe he has come to settle his account. I told you those contracts were poison. He kept buying them – now the price of blue is falling. He's overdrawn, caught long without a hedge, unheard of for an Overlord of such vast wealth.'

'Shush, Arb. Don't say such things.'

'Why, will he kill me? Little one, I'm nearly done; I will die soon.' he said, as he rubbed the sores on his face.

She put a hand on his shoulder, pulling him close. Tears welled in her eyes. 'I'll miss you, old man,' she said, as they both watched The Sixth's pulsing energy mass float down to the top of their central shaft. The round shaft, glowing with blue light, extended down through the floating city to its very base where the Exchange's core and the autonomous drives that keep it in orbit, reside.

The Sixth ignored the traders as they watched. He didn't notice the stillness he had created as his energy mass passed by, but he did feel their surprise and fear. He paused at the top of the shaft, hovering in the air above. Looking down at the soft blue light, reshaping his mass into a cylinder, he entered it.

As he floated down, he watched the colours in the walls pulsating in synchronous phase with the hum of the majestic drives beneath. Then it all changed; he sensed something else. *Voices, I hear voices. That cannot be,* The Sixth thought.

He stopped, the rising whispers clouding the hum of the city's engines. They grew louder until a babel of different voices erupted. *'Who is it? Why are you here? What is he doing here? He shouldn't be here. Overlords are prohibited from this place. We should take his energy. Who are you?'* And then they stopped.

'I am The One,' the delusional Overlord lied. 'Who are you?' he asked.

'You are not a One. You lie to us. We are The Ones. You shouldn't be here; it is forbidden. Why are you here?' The voices cried back.

'What do you mean, "we are The Ones"? How is that possible?' The Sixth asked.

'We are the consciousness and memories of The Ones past. Since the Exchange was built, we reside here. You are not a One. Who are you, and why are you here?'

Trying to justify his power grab, he pressed on with his hustle. 'I am The One. I am in charge of the galaxies now.'

'*You are not. He is a six, The Sixth of this epoch. I know why he is here. You thought you could access the codes of the Charters, the other Overlords and those with accounts in our Exchange. That is why you are here. You want to change the order we created.*'

'No, that's not true,' The Sixth lied again.

'*Tell us then, why are you here?*'

The voices stopped. Once more, the hum of the drives filled the enormous shaft. The Sixth tried to retreat back up it, but he couldn't move. An unseen force held him down. *What is this?* he wondered.

The Exchange's core contained blue energy and the engines that powered the floating city in space. Every one-thousand orbits, it was replenished with blue. But he never knew what else was there. *The Empress, she knew about this.* He remembered what she had said. "*There are forces you do not comprehend that will align to defeat you.*" *Why did I not see that in her mind*, he thought. *I need to get out, escape …*

A different voice interrupted his thoughts, much deeper, resounding up from the depths of the shaft. '*I know why he is here. I am The One in charge of accounts. You are The Sixth. You are overdrawn. You have bought all forward blue contracts.*'

'Yes, I have done that, but the settlement days are in the future. The contracts are purchased with my credit.'

'*Yes, you are entitled to do that, but price falls, your long positions are at a loss, well below what your assets can cover. Something we rarely see in an Overlord's account.*'

'But I haven't taken delivery of the energy. It is fictitious. It does not exist.'

'*How did you come to that conclusion?*'

'It's The Eight, trying to trick me. The blue does not exist. Never before have we seen such large quantities available.'

'*You seem sure of that?*' the voice responded.

'I am. It is totally fictitious. The Eight will fail to deliver and be forced to buy from me to honour the contract,' The Sixth said, voicing his empty hope.

'*That's why you came here, to see who issued the contracts and to fraudulently rework them in your favour.*'

'No,' he lied again.

'Six, you are a liar. Protocol does not allow me to tell you who issued those contracts, but I can say it was by more than one trading house.' The voice paused, the silence interrupted by the hum from below.

The Sixth squirmed, his energy mass shaking.

The voice continued. 'Two charters – one old, one new – a Royal house and an Overlord. All with verified codes and legal protocols, tendered before the contracts were approved and issued.'

This priceless info was Cylla Ora's masterpiece and contained; the specifications of the energy, a production profile, and a geophysical report with the location of the New World. A risk, but The Eight had confidence The Sixth couldn't get access to that data. His faith in the system was tested now!

The voice continued. 'The energy exists and there is a considerable amount in storage. We have mining and tank reports all verified by a licenced trader. Consequently, the price of blue falls. Knowledge that a new energy source is available is enough. Delivery is a technical issue. Six, what about your account? You received a recent data transfer about this. We have a receipt from your Shoter. How will you pay? Can you submit more assets? Perhaps one of your galaxies?'

The Sixth railed at this poisonous update to his status at the Energy Exchange. Requested to relinquish a galaxy for payment of something that didn't exist, in his mind, was too much. The Eight would have to deliver that energy. With all his lies and bluster, that fact kept The Sixth going. The Eight would have to provide the blue energy. One way or another, ships with blue had to dock at the Exchange – otherwise, The Eight would be saddled with The Sixth's debts! A reversal in their fortunes and a phase of the war The Eight knew he would always have to play.

Elongating his energy mass, The Sixth tried to move. He gained some upward traction. Whatever was restraining him was coming from the walls of the shaft. Slowly, he continued to lengthen his mass upwards.

'I need time,' he pleaded, all the while elongating his energy mass.

'Time is relative. We have plenty of time, Overlords have millennia …'

The babble of voices returned. 'Don't give Six any time. What of his trespass? He should never have come here. Where is The One of this epoch? What have you done with her?'

'Quiet,' interrupted the voice in charge of accounts. Silence descended, broken by the constant hum. The deeper voice continued. 'You hear them, Six? They are not pleased with you. And what of The One? Where is she?'

Suddenly he was free, his elongated energy mass sped up the shaft, faster and faster, the voices shouting after him receding in the distance. Like a long blue tube, his energy mass shot out of the shaft into the deserted hall. He let it relax back into its oval shape. The voices were silent. He looked around the darkened exchange, illuminated by starlight seeping in from the clear domed top, and then he saw it, scrolling across the trading screens. "Six, we are not pleased."

No, he thought, no, it cannot be. After the loss of Nine – now this. I will kill him, I will. Cursing The Eight, he flew from the chamber, his energy mass flashing blue and red. The dead Zaval's audacious plan had worked, trapping the greedy Overlord into a rising spiral of debt.

CHAPTER FORTY-SIX

Jair Galaxy. Planet Chaya, The Galactic news channel.

Friends, the Chesh appeared at the edge of our solar system today. I have it on good authority it's to "quarantine" in orbital parkland. It is the only one of The Seventh's battleships, from a fleet of six, that has returned. The rest, under Captain Bardek's command, are missing.

A close confidant told me that The Seventh is fuming at the loss of five of his best starships and fleet commander. I fear a disaster befell them carrying out a mission for The Sixth. Our Overlord has ordered a news blackout and a lockdown of the whole affair – cold comfort for the families of the missing crews.

I made contact with a source on the Chesh before its lockdown. I got sketchy whispers of war and breaches of intergalactic protocol. I wanted to run the story on main feed, but our boss squashed it. I trust you will keep this in confidence …

‹ From: Chaya Commschat_Anonrep@under-chat

*

Hela Base, Australian Desert, 24th February 2028

ON EARTH, LIFE CONTINUED. WITH the resilience mankind had displayed in the past, the population, still reeling from such a catastrophic event, picked up their lives and moved on. In McKinnon, as the first light of the dawn kissed the desert floor, Robert climbed the steps to the watchtower above the base. 'What're you two doing here?' he said to Tom and Niamh, entwined together, looking out at the view.

She turned and smiled at him. 'Same as you. Came to watch the sunrise and to admire our fleet.'

Standing beside them, he looked out at the ships parked on the desert floor. 'How many are yours?'

Niamh started to point them out. 'That's what we brought back from the Kandark Galaxy, those four there, Robert. They're inter-system cargo vessels similar to the *Hela*,' she said, pointing at four golden hulls lined up in the distance – each about eight hundred metres long.

Verteg and Siba had recovered them with the *Richard* and *Monarch* over the previous week. With arduous grav-burning work, the *Richard* made short work of dissembling the package, laying the four golden hulls out for their rebuild as blue energy transporters. Finally, after its long journey from a scrapyard in Lagrvth, the eight-hundred-metre-long behemoth came to rest in the Australian desert.

'They're stuffed with grav from The Second and spare parts for a rebuild.'

'What else do you own?' Robert asked.

'The *Monarch*. She's a gem and a real money-spinner,' Niamh replied.

'How's that work?'

'Every time she moves, Cylla charges Anan Corp.'

'Who owns the rest?' Robert said, pointing to two more.

'The tug *Richard* and her smaller cargo vessel, *George*, is owned by Verteg's family, the Borea. They're on contract to us with the other cargo vessel, the *Maeve*, working back on the New World.'

Robert looked down at the *Hela*, docked on the three service posts. 'Niamh, I always wondered, who owns the *Hela*?'

Niamh smiled. 'The house of Aknar; it was Theia's ship. I wanted to buy it but we're broke.'

Tom laughed at her comment and slapped Robert on the back. 'The joys of marriage, Robert.'

'It's no that bad, Tom.' Robert pointed at the intergalactic cruiser, The Ninth's command vessel. 'What about the *Chad* and the other four parked in space? Who gets them?'

'Spoils of war, I guess. They're The Eight's now,' Tom replied.

Niamh shrugged her shoulders. She had wondered about that herself. 'Unlike some of the other Overlords, he never owned ships,' she said. 'And before you ask, I don't know why. As soon as Zaval gave him the *Monarch*, he gifted it to us.'

A smile played on Robert's lips as he remembered that time. 'That's because you saved his life, girl. That's why he gave you the best ship in the universe.'

'I suppose you're right, Robert. Jeez, lads, once we refit our four cargo ships and fix up what's left of The Ninth's fleet, The Eight controls fourteen spaceships. We'll be a small trading hub in the universe.'

Robert's eyes opened wide at that analogy. 'Once the new factories get going, we should be turning out three of those beasts a year,' he said, pointing to the *Hela*. 'Mankind's time has come.'

They stood in silence as they watched the orange ball rise above the desert, its rays glinting on the starships parked below. Niamh broke the silence. 'Better go. You have to get ready, Robert.'

*

Dressed in his formal kilt and full regalia, Robert stood in the shade, outside McKinnon's small town hall, watching his guests file in.

In his gleaming chariot, The Eight floated down. 'A big day for you, Robert.'

'It is that, Overlord,' he said, as he ran his hands through his long sandy hair. 'I'm looking forward to it. She's a lovely woman.'

'She is, Robert. You will be happy together and have—'

'Don't start with the kids again, Overlord, please.'

'I'm laughing inside, Robert. You deserve a gift. I believe it is customary at this time. You know I gave the Parkers a Charter when they married.'

'Overlord, I have what I want, and Janet's the icing on the cake.'

'Janet deserves a gift for your future. You will both have a Charter. I will discuss it with her. I know she shipped containers on the *Hela* when it first left Earth. She was involved with Katherine, Alan and Harold in building a company to trade goods from Earth. They lost their investment when we never reached Anan. Such opportunities are available now. They deserve that chance. We will get a foothold in the Kandark Galaxy. In time, after this war, they can open up trading hubs on the surrounding planets.' The Eight paused as though he had remembered something else.

'On another note, Robert, The Second has thrown in his lot with us. He was distraught when I told him of what The Sixth had created and his genocidal actions on Earth. We have an advantage now, Robert. Hard pressed to get it But, yes, we have, thanks to you. What else, Robert? Something lingers in your mind – ask while you have my good ear, as you would say.'

'Overlord, I never paid much attention to who owned what in the universe or how your Energy Exchange works. But now I wonder where you get your wealth from? You wield so much power, yet, unlike the troika, you don't own any ships. Why's that?'

'An interesting question, Robert – yes, it is. Unlike the others, I do not own spaceships. I have always used the Aknar fleets for transport. They are the strongest in the galaxy.'

'I heard that from Tom. And now they're laid up in the Energy Exchange.'

'Yes, Robert, they are. I own galaxies – many of them. That's my wealth.' He paused, his energy mass flashing with blue light. 'I control the most galaxies of all the Overlords. The One and I are the oldest. Some of my galaxies generate taxes, and what you call rent, that is collected and managed in the Energy Exchange. Over time, they have generated capital that is measured and stored in the Exchange as Universal Credits. You must know this. I also have wealth in precious metals, stones, and blue diamonds. They are stored in my homes on my worlds, including my island base here on Earth.'

'I didn't need to know so much.'

'But you do, Robert. I did ask you to be my proxy.'

'Yes, Overlord, you did that, and I did my best.'

'You did more than your best, sacrificing millions for the sake of humanity and the planet. You followed my cause with your soul. You will continue as my proxy, understand my wealth and know where it is held. With good guidance from you and Janet, your family will inherit this function.'

'That's a tall order. You're full of surprises today.'

'Again, Robert, I laugh inside. Soon I go to my island base with my beasts. Once you are ready, join me there. We have much work to do. Go now, join your guests; your bride will soon arrive.'

*

Janet and Robert had chosen McKinnon as their venue because of its close family connections. They had both played a part in the base's development and the town that had sprung up around it – giving them a feeling of home. Its seclusion in the desert was a bonus, with the privacy to exclude Earth's media. That frenzy still burned bright, with headline stories taking opposing views. Captions of "war criminal to marry in secrecy" and "fairy-tale marriage of Earth's two heroes" peppered the world's news.

It was a small ceremony and the first marriage officiated in the McKinnon town hall. The guests, with the Cooper and McKinnon families, Robert and Janet's friends and the Borea, packed in to watch a beautiful Janet walk down the aisle. After the ceremony, Matt organised a beach barbecue at their artificial lake, inviting all at the base. It was a large gathering of human and alien that assembled for the celebrations.

The Eight watched as his ever-growing army of close followers revelled into the night. The different courtship rituals intrigued him, as the males and females, from all species, sparred with each other. Although they fought at every meeting, Fazqa the Mzimot and Geoff the human were never far from each other. She pouted, he turned away, ignoring her. Eventually, he relented, and they danced the night away, happy in each other's company. *The circle of life begins again*, he thought. *New families will grow and prosper.* He heard Ariki cry. Swaddled in blankets on Hana's lap, the cold desert air had assaulted his tiny face. *One destiny fulfilled already*, he thought, as he listened to Hana soothe the Aknar prince.

Tom and Niamh fussed the Mzimot boys, their fur glistening from the water as they learned how to swim. Niamh made the family welcome, making sure the shy Mzimot enjoyed the party. Never having experienced such a free lifestyle before, The Eight wondered how they would adapt to human ways. *The young will adjust, but the older ones, they will need watching,* he thought. *Still, it was the right decision of Niamh to return for them,* he conceded that. *Yes, their skills are wanted.*

'Overlord, we are ready. The shuttle is prepared,' Verteg said, as she walked up to him, accompanied by Alice.

'And my beasts, they are loaded?'

Alice nodded. 'Yes, Overlord. Fed and watered as well.'

'I am taking you both from the party.'

Verteg shook her head in surprise at his statement. 'No, Overlord, you're not. Some quiet time in New Zealand will be welcome. I need a rest. Overlord, you're a hard taskmaster.'

He didn't answer. Thoughts of her father – the great Demard – bubbled up in his energy mass. *He would be so proud of what she has become, a force to be reckoned with.*

As he followed them into the neatly loaded shuttle, he looked around. A place for his chariot and beasts, already stretched out, cleared, and a cargo of food for them secured. And, at the back, was an old covered-in grav platform, taken from deep down in the Hela base. He had not seen one like it for some time. 'Are you planning overland journeys?'

Alice turned. 'I'm going to show Verteg the South Island. You know parties are not my scene. We're glad to get away.'

'Do you have travel documents, permission to fly that device over New Zealand airspace and a passport for Verteg?'

'You're joking.' The words came out before Alice realised what she had said. Dropping to her knees in front of him, her black hair fell over her face as she bowed. 'Overlord, I'm sorry, I, I—'

Verteg laughed at her friend's innocence. 'Alice, he's joking – get up. Help me in the cockpit.'

He parked his chariot beside his six beasts while he listened to the idle chatter from the cockpit.

'He does that with Niamh, jokes with her sometimes. He has a sense of humour. That's where we inherit our attributes from, you should know that. Take the controls, hands in there, like that …' Verteg said, continuing to instruct Alice to fly.

He watched the two females, happy together in the soft light of the cockpit, Verteg's blue hair tied up neatly while Alice's tousled black hair streamed down her back. Verteg's green skin glowed in the half-light from the controls as she explained their workings to the dark-skinned Alice. *Both of similar size but such different appearances,* he thought. *The diversity of the life I foster.* He mused on the part of his wealth he had not explained to Robert – the life forms.

A large part of The Eight's wealth, built up over many epochs, consisted of the intelligent life he carefully cultivated. With the right nurturing, they advanced his wealth and power. He had made a mistake by abandoning the humans. He would not do it again. He thought about how his essence had ended up in the population. The old purebreed geneticist, who meddled without his consent, had, unknowingly, done him a service.

He started the calculations, deep in his energy mass, contemplating time, population expansion, the addition of DNA from other species and the metaphysical variables. Startling all in the shuttle, he flashed with white light when the answer arrived. *It will work,* he thought. *Possibly in one, but more likely two generations, but I could succeed. I never thought it possible in so short a time,* he mused.

With over four and a half billion humans, two planets for them to prosper and a limitless supply of blue, he had the resources to control the known universe. There would be some changes in the human's management. He thought about the plan he had mentioned in the U.N. meeting. It wouldn't go down well with Earth's ruling classes. There may have to be a cull, but it would be short-lived, brutal and swift. He had talked to Chang – he would attend to that soon. When the general population realised living standards would equalise out, overall for the better, the initial shock of a change in order, would pass. He had learned the hard way – in bygone times – a satisfied working population produces the most, staying loyal to their Overlord. Loyalty and respect from his life forms earned, not demanded, as The Sixth would inevitably find out.

But first, The Sixth must be deposed. The Eight started another set of calculations, this time much shorter. Again, he flashed with white light – a smaller burst – when a plan emerged. Time never stopped, and now he was up against the Exchange's clocks. Delivery of the New World's blue energy was crucial. He had an orbit, but to be safe, he would get it there within half that time, displacing The Sixth at the same time. Take the war to Anan. The Eight couldn't leave it any longer.

Following that decision, The Eight relaxed his mind and listened to the soft tones of Verteg Borea – the Pilot – teaching Alice to fly. Despite everything, Zaval Borea and his close family had served him well. It was Zaval's plan that had made all this possible. His audacious strategy, delivering a masterstroke, financially crippling The Sixth. 'Verteg,' he said, 'your family shall have two of The Ninth's cruisers – spoils of war. Consider it a reward for your family's contribution to my cause.'

It left Verteg speechless. Two warships! *What would she do with them?* she wondered.

*

Back in McKinnon, Robert couldn't sleep. Without a sound, he slipped from the bed and walked out of the new house on the beach. He could see Niamh sitting on a chair, her bald head silhouetted by the soft light of the moon.

'Can't sleep either, Robert?'

'No, and you? What's up?' he said, as he sat down beside her.

'I can't get it out of my mind.'

'Did you talk to Tom?'

'No, I'm afraid to tell him.' she said, as she slipped her hand under Robert's blue arm. His arm started to glow as did her blue diamond.

'Tell me, lassie, tell me what happened.'

Leaning against him, she told him everything she could remember of her time with The Second. It all flowed out: the Overlord's history, what she was changing into, and why The Eight wanted Niamh to remain human. When she finished, they sat in silence, illuminated by the blue glow from her pendant and his arm.

'You're telling me you were changing into an Overlord,' Robert said.

'Yes, I was. but apparently, my time has not yet come. The Eight believes I have much more to give as a mortal. Go figure that out, Robert.'

'That's easy, Niamh. You have ships to refit and build. And you're with child, making a family with Tom. That's your destiny. Always, he speaks about children. When he gave me this,' he said, flexing the arm, 'he said I would have gifted children.'

'What's he in store for you, Robert?'

He told her of his conversation with him before the wedding. 'I'm to be his proxy; manage his affairs, that sort of thing and the position will be passed down to my family.'

Again, they sat in silence, Niamh wondering at how much The Eight had changed their lives.

'I remembered how you walked me down the aisle at my wedding,' she stretched up and kissed him on the cheek. 'Today you married my best friend. The four of us met at the start of Project Anan when the aliens first arrived. Somehow our destinies are linked by The Eight. I wonder what he has planned.'

He stood up and laughed. 'Only he knows that. Could be a higher calling for one of us. Now that Nine is gone, there's a vacancy at the top.'

She punched him on the chest. 'Don't joke about that. Be serious, Robert.'

'Sorry, you're right. Talk to Tom. Tell him what happened. He deserves to know. Come on, we'd better get back,' he said, as they walked along the beach together.

As he climbed back into bed, Janet turned to face him. 'How's Niamh?' she asked.

He felt his face warm, as he blushed. 'How do you know I was—'

'I'm a woman, your wife and planner. I know everything, and you smell of her perfume.'

'I, ah, we met and talked.'

'And?'

'It's complicated.'

'Try and explain. Before you freak out, I know nothing's going on,' Janet said, as she rubbed his hairy chest and kissed him. 'She's my best friend. If I had thought that, I would never have married you. Would I? So, tell me, what's on your mind?'

Wrapped in his arms, he told her the gist of their conversation. When he finished, she lay still, thoughts of what the future held for them all running around in her head. Eventually, she broke the silence. 'That's so scary, Robert.'

'What is?'

'The destiny of our two families entwined by an Overlord.'

CHAPTER FORTY-SEVEN

Jair Galaxy. Planet Chaya, The Galactic news channel.

Friends, I have the story. After some digging here on Chaya, and with some arm twisting, my source on Chesh spilt the beans. A firm specialising in cryo-tech dispatched engineers to Bardek's fleet. I found shipping orders tracing the fleet to Natok, in the Jora Galaxy. That's where The Sixth kept a secret army of ceirim!

They took the ceirim to an alien planet in a distant galaxy. Billions of bipeds inhabit that world, owned by The Eight. The mission's objective: kill them all – unheard of genocide, perpetrated with the buy-in of our Overlord, The Seventh.

The Ninth led the invasion, releasing the ceirim on the unsuspecting population. They fought back. Would you blame them?

Next up, The Ninth dropped the banned city-busting mini-suns on the planet's largest population centres. They killed millions until The Eight showed up. Chesh escaped a space battle and doesn't know what happened to the others in the fleet.

Keep this quiet. I will work on getting corroborating data …

‹ From: Chaya Commschat_Anonrep@under-chat

*

**Milford Sound, New Zealand,
26th February 2028**

Two days after arriving in the old Aknar base in Milford Sound, The Eight summoned the Anan Corp managers and his closest allies for a planning meeting inside the antechamber of his home. Once again, Niamh, Tom, Janet, Robert and Geoff set the place up as a makeshift meeting room with screens hastily hung from the cave walls and enough chairs and tables to accommodate the group. Amongst Alan, Kath, Harold, General Marsh and Admirals Vasily and Whyte was Chang Jin. The Anan contingent included Quriel, Verteg, Siba, Chief Haldock and a surprised Jarzol and Fazqa Mzimot. The two Mzimot thought it a mistake when the invitation had arrived until Robert left them in no doubt as to the importance of this event.

'We'll be discussing the future of the universe, so get a move on, Jarzol,' he said to the blue-haired alien.

The rough and ready cave cut into the mountain, with the catbears lounging at the back, provided a humble setting for such a momentous meeting. Earth's most powerful men and women, perched on chairs and benches, analysed every word The Eight spoke.

Floating in front of the silent group he laid out the details of his master plan: building a fleet, setting up a base on Lagrvth, mining more blue with a second colony, transporting the blue to the Energy Exchange and gaining control of the Aknar fleet. The restoration of galactic order by reinstating Empress Theia and the House of Aknar – and so on …

When he stopped, a lone voice piped up from the back. 'How long we got for that, Overlord?' Matt McKinnon asked, in his broad Aussie accent.

'I need to be unloading blue energy at the Energy Exchange in six Earth months,' The Eight said.

For one long minute, Rex's loud snores were the only sound that disturbed the air.

Then the questions burst out. "What if? How will we fit and build so many ships in such a short time? Where will we do it?"

And then the obvious military question. "How many ships does The Sixth have?" Earth's top brass asked together.

A flash of blue light from The Eight silenced them. They waited, then in a firm voice he answered. 'I believe he can muster a fleet of fifty.'

General Marsh asked what everyone else was thinking. 'Overlord, what do we do when The Sixth sets up a blockade?'

Admiral Vasily agreed with him. 'Overlord, it's what we would do in his predicament.'

Chang Jin followed. 'It is a standing operational procedure – a blockade. We will have to fight our way through his fleet. Unless …'

'Unless what? You have the answer, Chang Jin?' The Eight asked.

'A Trojan Horse, Overlord, or a derivative of it. That's the standard stratagem. But still, we have to get it past the blockade,' Chang said, scratching his head.

'Yes, we will have help, I am sure of that. But getting anything past the blockade is the problem. The Sixth has the ships and the forces to secure the Energy Exchange. In the past, Overlords had engaged in enormous space battles, pitting mortals in warships against each other. It never ended well, resulting in needless loss of life and resources. I do not want to go that way. Nor do we have the time to build a bigger fleet to combat The Sixth face-to-face. There must be a method to wage a smarter war to defeat The Sixth, without wasting precious life and starships we don't have.'

The Eight paused. The silent audience watched his energy mass pulse with blue light. Such a powerful being and yet they knew there were limits to his ability. Today he tested their intelligence to the limit.

'There is a way to do this, I know it. And you will find a way for me. Take fourteen days off for a holiday. You all deserve that and so do your peers. Take stock and rest. We meet again here in two weeks.' Without another word, The Eight retreated into the back of his home.

Mystified, the Overlord's guests looked around at each other. The vibe changed as the talk relaxed into idle chatter. Some reflected on his speech; others espoused solutions.

Tom approached the two Mzimot. 'Well, Jarzol, Fazqa, what'd you think?'

'Mr Parker, I am still mystified as to why we were invited,' Jarzol answered, his eyebrows raised in wonder.

'Jarzol, you're to project manage the refit and the rebuild of the fleet. Didn't you understand that? You're the Refit Supervisor. I told you at Robert and Janet's wedding. The job and salary details were sent to you,' Tom replied, the look of astonishment blanched his face.

Fazqa put her blue face into her hands and shook her head. She looked back at Tom and then to her dad. 'He did tell you that! But you were, what the humans call, "drunk" and thought it was a big joke.' Her two ears twitched, something Geoff had learned was a sign of frustration.

Gripping Fazqa's hand tight, Geoff asked the inevitable question. 'Where's the paperwork now?' He feigned a stern look, inside, trying not to laugh at the absurdity of it all. Their legendary engine builder – Earth's hope to build a fleet – drunk!

Pointed ears still twitching, Fazqa glared at her father.'I told you, the woman who set up our bank accounts and pays us, Katherine, dropped off the contracts – the next day. Mum told you too.'

She waited for a reply. Jarzol shook his head, his thick blue eyebrows still raised in wonder. Paperwork was never his strong point; his wife took care of that. And, he now remembered, she had mentioned something …

'You left them back in McKinnon, didn't you?' Fazqa hissed, trying not to make a scene at this critical gathering.

Rescuing the bemused alien, Tom clapped him on the back. 'Well, Jarzol, you'd better get a move on. Sign the contracts, have a holiday with the family and start to rebuild a fleet for The Overlord. You've plenty of time. I'll need the *Chad* in about sixteen days, and the fleet in, say, five months. Here's Chang. You'll be working in China as well …'

To the amazement of Fazqa and Jarzol, Chang Jin, the President of the People's Republic of China, approached. Smiling from ear to ear, dressed in his usual blue suit, one of the planet's most formidable leaders grabbed Jarzol by the hand.

Pumping a cheery handshake, Chang gushed a greeting.'Jarzol Mzimot, I am happy to meet you. We have so much work to do …'

Languishing in a chamber at the back of his home, The Eight felt the optimism flowing from the diverse crowd. The conclusion to his war was underway. As Chang Jin aptly said, "So much work to do." And The Eight thought, *time ticks on, while The Sixth is scheming and prepping his troops for war. Yes, he is.'*

*

618

Planet Anan. EPTS: B141635

Back on Anan, The Sixth, bruised from his disastrous meeting with the ghosts of The Ones' past, licked his battered ego. Scheming wouldn't adequately describe the machinating rage that whirled in his purple energy mass. Returning on a shuttle from the Energy Exchange, he locked himself in his chamber, ignoring approaches from the Shoter or the other mortals outside. With The Ninth gone and The Seventh in mysterious isolation, he was alone. Despite that, he still had and controlled the only blue energy in these galaxies.

There was one course of action left; his last stand and something he had steered clear of in the past – not a necessary strategy. Casting his mind out to his home galaxy, he summoned his army and fleet. Leaving them in the Jora and Ragma Galaxies, to guard his wealth and blue mines, had been the right decision at the beginning of this conflict. With the deceased Emperor's help and a small garrison of his own troops, without difficulty, he had grabbed power on Anan. Fear of his raw power helped – after all, he had, and still could turn any dissenters to dust. The Charter Guild and the Council of Anan followed in step, neutralising any hint of an Aknar uprising. Or so The Sixth thought.

Circumstances have changed. The Eight has to deliver ships of blue to the Exchange. If that happens, I am done. My reign is over, The Sixth thought. But such an event would present a one-off opportunity. He would reap the fortunes of war, grabbing whatever cargo The Eight shipped to the Exchange. The Sixth, with a big enough fleet to fortify the Anan Galaxy, would search every ship for a hint of blue or for The Eight – siege tactics in reverse.

His energy mass changed to blue as his commander answered. 'Overlord, a fifty-strong fleet of our best is on the way.'

As The Eight's war team predicted, the blockade of The Energy Exchange had started.

*

Earth, 27th February 2028

On Earth, true to his word, The Eight insisted his crews and managers take time off. Niamh and Tom didn't argue with that, bolting back to the Banks Peninsula outside Christchurch where they had spent their honeymoon.

Robert objected to taking time off but Janet dragged him off to Queenstown, the adventure capital of the South Island and close enough to the Milford base to placate Robert's unease at being away from their Overlord.

In the beat-up old grav platform, Alice and Verteg continued their tour of New Zealand. Staying in Department of Conservation huts, their arrival at some of the more popular occupied destinations caused quite a stir. It wasn't every day an alien vehicle dropped out of the sky to park up beside the backcountry huts. Nor did the surprised guests they shared bread with realise the green-skinned woman was a famed starship pilot and head of an intergalactic charter.

The McKinnons took over an exclusive resort on the Bass Coast, south of Melbourne, for the Mzimot and Borea families. Anan Corp spared no expense on their wellbeing, the relaxed seaside resort proving a winner for the once impoverished aliens. After an evening walk on the beach with his wife, it took Jarzol no time at all to appreciate the simple things they had missed. Having come from working longs days as child labour in the Hirkiv factories to this, their two boys took to the place like there was no tomorrow. To their parents' delight, their sons flourished.

Halfway through the break, Jarzol put his mind to plan for the war effort, idle doodles setting the bones of his refurb plans whiling away his days. Amongst that tangled web, words about a Trojan Horse played on his mind. Jarzol laughed to himself when he read the old Greek tale from a history book sent down from Melbourne. The Greek fable played on his mind, influencing the scratched scribbles. But however hard he tried, he couldn't crack the problem of a defensive blockade. Whatever way the designer approached the problem, nothing worked. The calculations didn't lie – they didn't have enough ships. If The Sixth showed up with his projected fifty, he'd rout The Eight's paltry numbers.

Disgusted with his efforts, Jarzol threw his pad on the ground. Time for a break. Lazily he watched his young son, squatting on the floor in front of him, play a video game. Jarzol hadn't taken to this Earth tech easily, limiting its use to a few hours in the evening before bed. Imprisoned on the *Monarch* on the way back to the New World was a little different. Here, with so much outside, stricter playtime rules applied.

The toys they had here were more advanced than what was given on the *Monarch*. A new device that covered the face like a helmet brought the game closer. V.R. his son called it – virtual reality gaming had caught up with the Mzimot! That tech Jarzol had used in control systems' interfaces; the wasteful idea to include it in toys hadn't occurred to him! The young boy's arms flew in and out, his fingers pressing on virtual control systems. Immersed in the game, his excited shouts and calls, the oohs and ahs, told their own tale.

There was a loud curse then the helmet was torn off and thrown on the ground. The room erupted with shouts from those around. Jarzol's wife, disgusted with the use of so coarse a word, admonished the boy. Tears welled up in his eyes, his lips trembled, and then he wailed. Head in his hands, he shook from side to side. The emotion of being beaten by the game and then scolded by his mum was too much. Jarzol couldn't look at the sight of his tear-stained son's face anymore. His blue fur was black from his dirty hands trying to rub them too much. He picked him up, grabbed the helmet, and set him on his lap.

His wife shook her head and walked out. 'You're too easy with those boys,' she shouted.

Jarzol soothed the boy then put the helmet on to try it for himself. His son thought this was great. His demeanour changed, banishing the sour tears, and in an excited, happy voice, he explained the game's rules.

It didn't take Jarzol long to get the gist of the challenge. Focusing his eyes and brain on the images, a white light of an idea exploded in his mind. A new design concept, born from this humble video game and his drawings, ran riot in the designer's head. Once again, the helmet was ripped off and dumped with the controller on the ground. With his bemused son under his arm, Jarzol rushed out to the veranda. Fazqa and

Geoff lounging together, making happy watching the sunset, jumped up at the intrusion.

'Tell them,' Jarzol ordered the boy.

'What?' the youth asked.

'The game, tell them how it works, what you've to do …'

CHAPTER FORTY-EIGHT

CNS Headlines. Earth On A Wartime Footing.

From the Gobi Desert in China to the Simpson Desert in Australia, Earth is undergoing the fastest mobilisation of resources in the history of the planet. Factories in our world's industrial powerhouses are gearing up to produce everything from specialist power conduits, plasma relays, "translucent static stimulated control interfaces" – whatever they are – to bathroom pods and dried prepacked meals. An unprecedented manufacturing boom to support The Eight's war against The Sixth is in progress.

That intergalactic war landed on Earth with an invasion of living death. For humankind to survive, we must win this war. That was the message our Overlord spelt out to the U.N. Never before experiencing such a seminal event, people have embraced that message. The pictures from the Gobi and Simpson deserts, of alien starships undergoing a rebuild, illustrates, to our fragile existence, how serious this situation is.

‹ *From: Continental News Services. Good Morning Planet Earth*

*

Earth, 12th March 2028

AFTER THE HOLIDAY IT WAS all hands on deck. The desert base in McKinnon turned on its head to commence the final phase of The Eight's war. First up was the strip out of *Monarch* and *Chad* to transport a forward garrison of humans to the Kandark Galaxy. Janet put together a fourteen-day plan for the audacious load out. Chang Jin provided the troops and the portable pop-up military bases. Between the two ships, they would transport one thousand of China's crack military, the first human army to depart Planet Earth.

To add to the mayhem of loading the *Monarch* and *Chad*, work to prep the *Hela* and the *George* for loading Colony-2 commenced.

Before she could leave Earth on the *Richard*, Verteg landed the empty *Thain*, *Losh* and *Abra*, parked in orbit after The Ninth's defeat, in the Gobi Desert at the Chinese Jiuquan Launch Centre. An army of workers waited for the starships. They couldn't believe their eyes when each one arrived. All skilled from work on the Chinese mega-projects, this task surpassed anything they had seen before.

Equally overwhelmed, it took Jarzol Mzimot, the refit supervisor, days to grasp the scale of the project he was running. But the wise man boxed clever, appointing his wife as document coordinator, with Fazqa and Geoff as his deputies. The rest of the family fell in below them, pouting that a human had earned such an accolade.

'That's 'cause he's screwing the boss's daughter,' they gossiped.

They were wrong about the reason Geoff had got the job. He was heading a top-secret part of the project. In a covert factory in Australia, the core of Jarzol's battle machine was born. But the gossiping Mzimot were right about the other matter. Fazqa and Geoff were inseparable, the love they felt for each other growing by the day. The young man couldn't believe he had such a beautiful, intelligent woman as his partner and Fazqa felt the same about him. Despite the interspecies prejudices, Jarzol and his wife accepted the relationship. From Jarzol's point of view, Geoff's intelligence and grasp of alien tech astounded the old designer and he was happy to have the young human as part of the family.

Fazqa's mum revelled in her daughter's happiness. But in the early days of the developing relationship, she had warned Geoff – bearing her claws – 'break my daughter's heart and I'll slit your throat.'

The tone left Geoff with no illusions – this was no idle threat, from a powerful Mzimot.

*

The *Monarch* and *Chad* departed on time, but the frantic loading of the *Hela* and *George* didn't go to plan. In the end, Robert called a halt to the never-ending procession of goods packing both ships.

'Have we enough to feed Colony-2 for a month?' he asked the loadmaster.

Scanning the readouts from a multitude of containers, the man couldn't give a straight answer.

An impatient Robert pushed him on. 'Give me a ballpark figure for food and medicine,' he demanded.

The man dithered at the screens, his second came up to help, and between the two, a consensus emerged. 'Maybe two months—'

'That's it. Lock 'em up; we're finished. I want the crews and Colony-2 ready to go in two days,' Robert ordered. 'Get the *George* ready first. Verteg can have her encased in the tow and wait for the *Hela*,' he said, knocking off as much time as he could from the journey.

And that's how it went. Verteg spun the trommel over the *George* in orbit. A day later, the *Hela*, loaded with Colony-2, arrived and once inside the trommel, set out for the New World. Unlike Colony-1, towed by the monstrous *Richard* through folded space, Colony-2 had only to endure two weeks in intergalactic transit. On the bridge of all three ships, humans trailed the aliens, learning new skills and preparing for their time as starship crew.

*

Planet Lagrvth. EPTS: B142688

On the *Monarch*, alongside The Eight, Niamh plotted the shortest route from Earth to Lagrvth. She captained the *Monarch* and Siba, with Bill as her Security Chief, the *Chad*. Together, the two ships made it to the Kandark Galaxy in sixteen days. The Chinese troops spent their time training in alien tech and in understanding Anan ways. The humans quashed their cultural differences, as they strove to learn about Anan technology, language and conventions.

Their arrival in the Kandark Galaxy sparked curiosity from Nolget and Touqmat on Lagrvth. The aliens hadn't expected to see two ships, under the Sullivan Parker banner, return.

With the *Monarch* and *Chad* parked in orbit, Tom and the Chinese commander took a shuttle down to the planet. An excited Nolget and Touqmat turned out to meet them. Broad smiles lit up their white pure-breed faces and their pink eyes were wide with anticipation as they watched the shuttle land. The two brothers scrubbed up, both in clean suits, with long black hair combed neatly back. However, the sight of the military commander and her armed guards was not what they expected. Their faces fell, lips pursed, and the white faces turned grey with fear.

'Before you fly off the handle, let me explain,' Tom placated.

'Yes, Mr Parker, you should,' the two aliens shouted together.

Standing on the landing pad, Tom made the introductions, 'Nolget, Touqmat, this is Commander Li Ping of your guarding garrison. She and her troops are at your disposal and will ensure your sovereignty and independence is maintained in this galaxy.'

Not waiting for an answer, Li Ping and her troops bowed. Then, at attention, her troops presented arms in a salute to the two strange men.

In fluent Anan, Li Ping spoke, her firm voice conveying a resolute determination not lost on the group. 'Nolget and Touqmat, on behalf of the people of Earth, thank you for welcoming us to your planet. My garrison's primary mission is to guard your planet from pirates, and others, who threaten your sovereignty and your business. Do not fear my troops or I – there are one thousand of us at your disposal.'

Nolget and Touqmat blanched at the numbers. Like fish out of water, their mouths opened and closed. Silence, broken by a whistling wind flowing across the desert planet, descended on the group.

Nolget finally stuttered a reply. 'You tricked us!' He paused as he shook his head in rage. 'It's The Eight, isn't it?' he spat out.

Tom stayed silent as Li Ping worked her charming magic. She took off her hat, shook out her long hair and smiled at the two aliens. Her five-foot-six-inch demure features hid a steely resolve. She would disarm these aliens and pretty soon have them on her side. Still smiling, she walked up to face the two.

'You are, of course, right. It is The Eight we work for. And in case you didn't notice, an intergalactic war is raging around your planet. One way or another someone is going to grab your wealth. You said that to Tom on his last visit; you are vulnerable.'

She stopped and turned to gaze out at their vast yards of ships and scrap disappearing into the horizon. 'Such wealth, and you don't have any protection. How you have lasted so long is beyond me. Anyway, we are here, we are not going away – so get used to us. But know this, when we win this war, your business and independence are guaranteed to survive.'

Touqmat glared back at the demure woman. He had no illusions as to the ferocity she could unleash; he sensed it from her. She oozed charm and danger. 'And what if you don't win?'

'Life in this galaxy and business as you know it will not survive. You will be subsumed by allies of The Sixth, an inevitability you always feared. I am right, yes?' she stated, matter-of-factly.

Time for Tom to end the argument. 'Nolget, before we left, you told me that after our arrival, it had occurred to you that I could kill you and take what we wanted. We saw the weakness of your security. You didn't feel the need for protection as you're a scrapyard. Who would rob a scrap yard?'

He paused as Nolget cringed at his words being thrown back at him.

Tom pressed on. 'You knew, with the ongoing war, all that would change. And it has. You invited the Sullivan Parker Charter to provide you with a security service. Well, here we are Nolget. One thousand of Earth's crack troops, armaments, an inter-field troop carrier, two shuttles and a portable field base for the troops. Will I go on?'

'And how much will you extort from us?' Nolget spat back.

'Nothing, absolutely nothing. You get this for free. All we want is the use of a base in this galaxy. That's the price, Nolget and Touqmat, you pay for this service. The Eight picks up the tab! And by the way, you need to know, The Second is with him and The Ninth is no more.'

That morsel of information wiped the aggro from the two aliens faces. They melted. Even Li Ping could sense the emotional shift from the two strange men. That The Second had chosen a side, and The Ninth was slain, was a monumental game-changer, an event neither had witnessed in their lifetime.

'Come inside,' Touqmat said. 'I'll show you where you can build your base. And I'm sure after the long journey some refreshments are in order. And yes, Commander, you are right. We do need the help.'

Inside Nolget and Touqmat's office, Tom reviewed the recent ship movements. The shortage of blue and the rumour of an impending war had taken its toll. Intergalactic trade had fallen off a cliff, denting the brothers' business. With little passing traffic, they were in virtual isolation in this galactic backwater. Tom nodded to himself. It was as he had thought – they would be safe on this out-of-the-way world, away from the main shipping lanes.

*

Back on the *Monarch*, Siba stood before The Eight with one of the Borea comms devices, the very same instrument he had marvelled at when they took refuge on the *Hela* in her Grandfather's home base.

'The message is ready, Overlord, as you instructed,' she said.

'Send it,' he confirmed, still marvelling at how such a simple device could bypass the most sophisticated security protocols in the known universe. The Borea engineers were a wonder.

Siba ran her hand across the device, touching unseen switches. The cone-shaped device flashed with multicoloured lights and a faint hum sounded. She withdrew her hand. The light and noise faded and the message blasted across the galaxy, igniting the next phase of his war.

*

Planet Anan. EPTS: B142692

Across the space-time divide on Anan, Theia Aknar languished in her personal chambers. The pot of discord was bubbling at a boil. The Sixth's visit to the Energy Exchange set alight the underlying fear that the Charter Guild and the Council of Anan harboured. Up till now, as long as they profited, they went along with The Sixth's actions and his Shoter's lame explanations.

However, a visit to the internal workings of the Exchange by an Overlord was unheard of before. It smacked of desperation. Already the price of blue was falling. Rumours of The Sixth's exposure to the long contracts abounded. "He's a financial wreck," they whispered.

The appearance of his fifty-strong fleet silenced those rumours. Hot from The Sixth's galaxies, the warships formed a strategic position around the Energy Exchange. The whole of Anan knew the game, lock down the Exchange with a blockade. It would hamper trade, they screamed, bickered and blustered. Theia had no time for the greedy Charter bosses, but deep down, she knew The Eight would make his move and she would be ready.

A bright light seeped out from a crack in the door of her keep. She rushed over, throwing it open. Inside, the light spilt from another opening. She sprung the lock on the hidden compartment and, mesmerised, gazed at the cone-shaped instrument spilling multicoloured lights in all directions. Then it stopped. She remembered the instructions the young Lieutenant had given her. Caressing the device, the message responded to her DNA. A page filled with coded orders shimmered above the cone. Within seconds, Theia deciphered the message, committing the secret orders to memory. With a press of her finger, the note disappeared and the cone flashed again, sending one word back to The Eight. "Confirmed."

Locking it all back up, Theia reached for her communicator. She would have to act fast if they were to skirt this developing blockade.

*

On Anan, The Eight's orders to Theia played out. He didn't have the luxury of waiting for a human starship-crew training program. On the far shores of the planet, in an old deserted Aknar base, Admiral Enirim briefed the assembled team. Gathered surreptitiously in the dead of night, the Aknar space crews tried to hold in their exuberance. Purebreeds, all of them, from long-serving military backgrounds, they had waited for this call since The Sixth had grabbed power. Now they had their chance; sixty of the best pilots, technicians and engineers, gathered from the mid-range nondescript vessels of The Eight's Aknar fleet. Never believing they would see action before the prima-donnas who crewed the behemoth starships would, they thanked the luck-star watching over them.

An old beat-up transporter landed on the cracked pad. The dents on its dirty brown side and the splutters from it grav engines proved its pedigree. Purloined from a smuggler by the Energy Exchange's Dock Master, the craft's paltry appearance disguised sophisticated speed and cloaking abilities.

The sixty Aknars wasted no time in piling aboard. The dim and dowdy interior never phased the group. Throwing their bags into a makeshift hold, they strapped themselves onto benches, lining the hull of the craft. Minutes after landing, the ship took off, heading up into space on the dark side of Anan and away from the prying eyes of the Energy Exchange. Shrouded by a cloak, it slipped away from the mainstream shipping lanes, heading towards the Anan sun. The Sixth's blockade, still forming up, didn't notice, and if they had, such a shabby old vessel wouldn't have rung any alarm bells.

The ship looped around the next planet in their solar system, a deserted rock, burned by their sun. Only then did the smuggler pilot engage the supercharged grav drive, heading out, faster than light to the Kandark Galaxy.

*

New World. EPTS: B142799

Meanwhile, towed by the *Richard*, Colony-2 sped through folded space, arriving in the New World fifteen days after leaving Earth. By now, Verteg had this whole process down pat, parking the tow in orbit and withdrawing the trommel within hours of their arrival.

Janet and Robert's celebratory return to Fort Leslie was short lived, the news of the catastrophe on Earth killing off the joy of seeing both of them again and meeting a whole new batch of colonists. The unloading of *Hela* and *George* took a week. The inhabitants of Fort Leslie had prepared a site across the bay for their new neighbours, Colony-2. The colonists had already chosen its name – São Paulo Nova – and their continent – New

India. Other names, in memory of those who died during The Ninth's genocide, were penned to populate future settlements.

The frantic war effort extracted a costly fee. Unlike the unloading of Colony-1, there were three deaths amongst Colony-2. A stray lizard ate one, and a pod fell from a grav lifter, crushing two. Others suffered from a series of work-related injuries synonymous with the hectic work pace. Robert, followed by a complicit Blair, cracked the whip –— no doubt of that. After the first week and counting the cost in death and injury, Janet called a shutdown.

'Robert,' she cried, 'enough is enough. They'll be dead or burned out if you continue this pace. We've enough done. The two ships are empty. Give them some time off to regroup.'

She was right, people were hot bedding in Fort Leslie and in some of the makeshift pop-up camps they had established on the beaches. Adding to the mayhem, Colony-2 was twice the size of Colony-1 with five thousand people striving to survive their first week on an alien world, after a fourteen-day intergalactic journey cramped up on the *Hela*. It was hapless luck only three died, as hungry lizards and other peckish animals stalked the perimeter of the new settlement.

Janet's halt saved Colony-2. Exhausted from their war-effort and establishing their new home, they downed tools and regrouped. Cylla Ora, an unexpected ally, backed Janet in pushing for the stoppage. The Neredian never expecting to see Mack again, wasn't surprised at his death. However, the news of an heir to the throne did. Janet had watched Cylla's reaction and wryly whispered to Robert, 'Time will tell on that.' But most startling of all was the usually argumentative golden wonder's change of demeanour. Her pushing for the stoppage was totally out of character. It took Janet one day into the shutdown to unravel that mystery.

Groups gathered and formed to celebrate their arrival and the stoppage, or "Janet's Weekend" as they christened their holiday. Bonfires burned along the beaches, music sounded, and the smell of barbequed meat filled the air. On that bright night, the two moons cast a silver light across the still waters of their home bay. The lights of both colonies twinkled across the water from each other. Mankind had stepped out again, building another bridgehead on the New World. The new colonists drew breath, the still-ness and wonder of the pure air and the sounds from the nearby jungle mesmerising them. The incessant clatter and banging of construction was now stilled. They revelled in the New World's purity.

In one of the groups, Janet and Robert sat across from Cylla. Janet noticed a glint in the Neredian's eyes as a tall soldier walked into the group.

'How are you, John?' Robert asked, a happy lilt in his voice at seeing the man. 'Long time no see.'

Sitting down beside Cylla, the fair-haired man nodded at Robert. He couldn't take his blue eyes off the golden wonder in front of him. John had been Tom's deputy back on Earth. He had befriended Brizo and was cut up when the young prince's drug addiction surfaced. Always the coach, when they reached the New World John stepped back from leading, deciding instead to coach and groom others. Amongst his many successes were Bill and Brian, both now taking the reins of leadership.

He grinned at Robert. 'Fine, just fine,' was all he said before kissing Cylla.

'O you harlot,' Janet shouted. 'And you dared to criticise Robert and me! Mack's hardly dead a wet week, and there you are, warming someone else's bed …'

Janet's voice trailed off as Cylla grinned and shrugged her shoulders.

Across the fire, seated beside Blair, Shona hugged her new baby. 'Life's for living, Janet. There's no telling what horrors tomorrow brings. You know that.'

The ever-grumpy Blair echoed his wife's words. 'You're right as always, Shona.' He held up his mug of beer. 'To Cylla and John.'

The shy soldier blushed while Cylla said nothing. Despite the warm moment, thoughts of work whirled in her mind: contract due dates, delivery of blue to the Exchange, off-world mining to get going, ships to load with the precious energy, and much more. Their success depended on this colony taking root on the New World. She glanced along the beach. Fires burned brightly as the humans celebrated their landing. Behind the shoreline, the foundations of their new town peered out in the moon's dim light, the pods spotted on terraces carved out by Fort Leslie's occupants before they came. Trenches were dug for services and pads laid for the blue energy tank farm. Another ten days would see the end of the new build.

Cylla couldn't believe the amount achieved in so short a time by the humans. The Borea provided technical assistance with grav platforms and off-world mining. The pace of change astounded even them when the new group of humans arrived. She put her head on John's shoulder, her long hair spilling down his broad chest. She felt his arm wrap around her and leaned back into his warm body. Home: this was Cylla's home now. She had no doubt they would succeed. The blue would flow from here but would The Eight's war at Anan triumph? That was the burning question. If he failed, all this was done. The Sixth would consume them! The stark news from Earth confirmed that.

*

Planet Lagrvth. EPTS: B142908

Back on Lagrvth, another group of humans had completed the building of Anan Corp's first garrison in another galaxy. The pace of the work and the speed of the construction astounded Nolget and Touqmat. They took a video of the around-the-clock work. One day there was nothing, five days later a small town sprouted out from the desert. Humans had arrived, and unless The Sixth thwarted The Eight, they were going nowhere.

After that, the *Monarch* and *Chad* were ready to leave for Earth. But to Nolget and Touqmat's wonder, they lingered. Human anxiousness showed, trying to look busy doing nothing, while they waited for a covert arrival from Anan.

Relief materialised when a nondescript dirty brown ship arrived in orbit. Tom had purposely kept the ship's imminent arrival from Nolget and Touqmat. When it appeared, he had one thing to say. 'What you don't know, won't hurt you.'

Wisely, the two brothers left it at that! Before long, while the humans busied themselves getting ready to go, the mystery ship landed on the planet alongside the new garrison.

The Aknar crews disgorged and transferred to the *Monarch* by shuttle. Their billeting, on the fastest ship in the galaxy, after the dull smuggler, was an unexpected bonus. And then they left for Earth, leaving Li Ping and her garrison behind ensconced in the Kandark Galaxy.

*

To the Aknars, the highlight of their adventure started on the *Monarch*, reconnecting with their Overlord, The Eight. The emotional sight moved Tom and Niamh to tears as they watched the purebreeds sink to their knees and cry at the sight of The Eight.

'We feared you were dead, Overlord,' their commander said. 'We adjusted our mindset to that, trying to put aside the feeling of loss at your and The One's disappearance. It was hard for us to grow accustomed to that.'

For Tom and Niamh, it reminded them of the deep bond between the Aknar purebreeds and The Eight, forged over millennia, as they served him in a symbiotic relationship. To be brutally fractured by The Sixth!

'I am very much alive, Commander, as you see. Now that you have joined my war effort, we will succeed. I will restore the galactic balance,' The Eight said.

Tom sensed a quivering in his voice; he was right. Despite The Eight and The One's assessment of the purebreeds as lazy and corrupt, the Overlord felt their communal bond. The Eight realised it now. He missed them. He missed Theia Aknar, the Empress, and now, her emissaries had rekindled that relationship. Seated in his chariot, he said nothing, just gazed at the purebreeds, a slow blue pulse emitting from his energy mass.

Finally, he spoke. 'Commander, the Sullivan Parker Charter and the Borea family serve me now. They have both saved my essence from extinction. You will work with them and teach the humans your trades. When we reach Earth, you will get to crew some of the vessels in my new fleet. And before you judge it, it is nothing on your Aknar armada, but will be a means of getting it back.'

They cheered.

*

Planet Anan. EPTS: B142919

On Anan, Theia bided her time. The next phase of the plan wouldn't be so easy, but with forward-thinking, she and Admiral Enirim were ready. All she needed was another signal from The Eight. Long days and nights of waiting took their toll. The Sixth consolidated the blockade, so much so, that trade withered from the delays of searching ships.

Eventually, The Shoter complained to The Sixth. 'Overlord, the economy is suffering from these tactics. You could continue the blockade but with selective searches.'

'How do you propose that, Shoter?' The Sixth asked. The Anan economy wasn't one of his priorities, but so far the Shoter had kept the Anan people on side. His advice had merit.

'Not all ships are capable of transporting blue. Refining the inspection process would be more beneficial. The Shoter begged, 'Alienating the Anan Charter families and the guild serves no purpose.' He paused.

'Go on,' encouraged The Sixth.

'Also, the blockade is now affecting purebreed populations on other planets. It limits their trade, putting pressure on hard-pressed incomes. Overlord, I know they are disgruntled and are hatching plans to go their own way.' There, he'd said it. 'Plots are afoot, Overlord. If you want to keep the Anan order in place, you have to ease off on the severity of the blockade.'

What the Shoter didn't mention were the rumours that leaked from Planet Chaya – The Seventh's home world. Dark news, with stories of genocide on a distant planet, scared the populations of the marginal worlds fanning the flames of discord.

A long silence, then The Sixth responded. 'Let me look over your proposals. You will get an answer first light tomorrow.' And they left it at that.

The following day, the Shoter's efforts and lobbying worked, The Sixth allowed him to introduced an import/export licencing system. The Shoter knew nothing of Theia's plans and made sure he and his family stayed clear of any such plotting. What he didn't know, he couldn't reveal. His wife made sure her cousin Enirim knew that. But the efforts to ease the blockade served another purpose, paving the way for Theia and Enirim's plans.

*

Earth, Lagrvth, New World, 20th April 2028

While the *Monarch, Chad, Richard, Hela* and *George* serviced the colonies and the garrison on Lagrvth, the rebuild and refurbishment of The Eight's fleet on Earth gathered pace.

Factories all around the world worked twenty-four-seven, turning out the complex components for the starship fleet. The Hela base at McKinnon turned into a factory site. Air-conditioned hangars built over each of the package ships transported from Lagrvth. The ships weren't named, marked instead as *Pac-A, B, C* and *D*.

In the Gobi Desert, three and a half months after the start of their refit, *Abra, Losh* and *Tain* were ready. Well before then, the *Monarch* had brought back an Aknar crew. The size of the operation on Earth astounded the purebreed Aknars. Once ready, they had the *Abra, Losh* and *Tain* in orbit and put through their commissioning checks. Inside, the ships were unrecognisable. Jarzol Mzimot gave them a new lease of life, updating every part of the vessels from the galley to the bridge. Up-to-date engine management systems based on the Borea translucent controls reduced the bridge's old clutter.

But it was inside the ships' holds where Jarzol's changes made the difference. New weapons' racks were bolted in with twin launch tubes piercing the hull through diaphanous airlocks. New panels at the bridge weapons' stations controlled the system. And in the secret weapons' factory in Australia, Geoff threw his life and soul into the manufacturing process he and Jarzol had pioneered. The Mzimot designer pinned all their hopes on this untried, secret human-alien hybrid weapon – a weighty gamble for such a calculating man.

The rebuild of the four ships in Australia took six months. *Pac-A,*

B, and C got the royal treatment inside and out, restored as blue energy carriers and fitted with grav and blue energy drives. *Pac-D* comprised a separate project, turning out as an intergalactic multi-cargo carrier.

*

The *Chad* and *Monarch* ferried vital parts that Niamh and Jarzol needed for the projects back on Earth while bolstering the garrison on Lagrvth. It saved time, and in some instances saved their bacon, for Earth's factories couldn't make everything. The two brothers, Nolget and Touqmat, tried to ignore the comings and goings of the humans and the constant drills Li Ping pushed her soldiers through.

When asked for a dilapidated ship to use as a training rig, Touqmat put his face in his hands. 'What are you trying to do with it? And anyway, we can't allow you to wreck one of our ships. That wasn't in the agreement,' he said, frustration seeping through his shaky voice.

Li Ping smiled. 'What you don't know, can't hurt. But we are prepared to pay rent for a derelict—'

'That'll be fine,' Nolget said. 'After all, business is business. Any damage you might do will be covered by the rent.'

'It's a beat-up old hulk,' Li Ping said. Earlier in their relationship, she found the two alien scrap dealers' affinity with Earth business practices uncanny. Tom had given her a fat budget of UC to keep them on side. She didn't squander it but knew whenever an argument arose, it was the brothers' way of getting more jam on their bread!

'Also, I want spacesuits. Can you get them? Military-grade, preferably Aknar,' she asked in a matter-of-fact way, not believing they would have access to such tech. *But hey*, she thought, *if they have any old ones, they'll serve as training props in the exercises.*

It was Nolget who answered. A big smile played across his white face. He puffed up his chest as he spoke. 'No, we can't get them. But we do have old military surplus. Last time the Aknar fleet changed their suits for new, we got the old ones. Some were never used – they're like new. Touqmat can have them inspected and tested. You'll get a good deal, certified and working. How many?'

'A thousand would do, and my people will help you inspect and certify. They need to learn how to do that themselves anyway,' Li Ping said, masking her inner surprise at such an offer.

Touqmat's white face went grey at the number. His mind boggled at what they were getting themselves into. The war was lumbering on at a breakneck speed. His only hope was that they were on the right side. If The Eight lost this war, they were finished! No double-dealing or sneaky secrets passed over intergalactic comms would save them. He and Nolget had discussed this at the outset. No, they were all in and the less they knew about the plan, the better.

But they weren't stupid either. What the humans were planning here, on their planet, was an invasion and he could guess where. This drill, the smart commander had designed, smacked of it. He looked at his brother, his face still smiling, numbers running through his brain. War was a profitable business, Nolget had long since realised.

He blurted his answer out, following with another question. 'A thousand we have, no problem. What about weapons? We have those as well – old surplus stock. But those grav cannons still work and may be more suitable than your primitive percussion weapons.'

Li Ping couldn't believe what she was hearing. She had discussed tactics with Tom and Quriel. They had spacesuits and grav weapons from the *Hela* armoury and the Borea base. Not enough for all her troops but they had planned to get by with their own human tech. Nolget's offer was a game changer, solving a problem the three had mulled over – their final attack numbers.

Li Ping cocked her head; by now a wry smile played on her lips. 'Nolget, you never cease to amaze me. Let's see what you got. And it'll be from Tom's budget.'

CHAPTER FORTY-NINE

Royal Statement: A Cure For The Anan Sickness.

Thanks to the patronage of The Sixth, the genetic cure for the Anan Sickness and the all-important therapy known as The First Stage Treatment, is a resounding success. This astonishing breakthrough would never have happened without the fantastic work of The Sixth's Master Geneticist and the resources The Sixth provided.

Not only did The Sixth personally take an interest in the cure and treatment development, but he also provided the means to manufacture and deliver this medicine to the Anan population. I never dared hope for such a cure. I am eternally grateful to The Sixth for his help and wonderful, generous gesture in healing the Anan population.

‹ From: Empress Theia Aknar

*

The Monarch

SIX LONG EARTH MONTHS PASSED while The Eight built his fleet and developed his battle plan. During one of the commutes between Lagrvth and Earth, a new child was born on the *Monarch*. Welcomed to an uncertain future, Niamh gave birth to a son. Amongst the mayhem and gloom, his arrival was a happy moment in time. For days, The Eight shone with blue light. The birth of their son lifted Niamh and Tom out of a wearisome drudge dedicated to work and war. For the first time in their lives, another person depended on their love, attention and care. A dramatic, joyful change that neither expected in this grim time. Throwing convention to the wind, they named the boy Zaval, after the great Borea pilot whose life had touched their own.

Siba, impatient to see the new baby, transferred over to the *Monarch* from *Chad*.

'What's his name?' she asked, cradling the newborn in her arms, her porcelain white face beaming down at the gurgling baby.

'We've named him Zaval. Is that …' Niamh couldn't finish the sentence, for the two burst into tears at the memory of the Pilot, Zaval Borea, who had tutored them both.

Finally, Siba calmed and looked across at Niamh, tears still staining her cheeks. 'You have honoured our family. In a way, no other ever has.'

When word got out that the powerful Sullivan Parker Charter had named their first born after the legendary Pilot, the Borea family were ecstatic. It cemented the alliance between the two Charters, and more importantly, between humans and their alien allies.

*

Planet Anan

TIME AND BOREDOM ERODE A blockade. Even after the Shoter's changes, pressure from Anan Charters and the constant political bickering that grew a head of steam from the diminished economic output, took its toll. Unbeknown to The Sixth, holes and smuggling back channels weaved their way through his cordon around Anan and the Energy Exchange.

His own loyal troops, unfamiliar with Anan graft, didn't see the full picture. Corrupt officials and those with underlying loyalties to the house of Aknar abused the licencing system, rerouting ships and disguising some docking vessels. Theia and Enirim exploited these holes and backchannels to their fullest, exporting a second Aknar ship's crew to Lagrvth.

*

The New World. EPTS: B147156

The arrival of the refitted, four Hela-class energy transporters from Earth heralded a milestone in the New World's war effort. It was the end of a hectic six months. Colony-2 had hardly settled when the off-world mining kicked in. Under the tutelage of Blair and the Borea, shifts worked around the clock, mining the precious energy. By the time the four transporters arrived, the tank farms were brimming with new blue, riches the galaxy hadn't seen in a millennium. When they landed, the golden hulled *Pac-A, B,* and *C* caused quite a stir. Shining bright in the New World's sunlight, with the livery of the Sullivan Parker Charter embossed on the hulls, they looked like fresh new starships.

But it was *Pac-D* which raised the most eyebrows. "What happened to that?" and "Has our Overlord run out of money?" were some of the many questions the beat-up old transporter raised. A dirty brown lacquer dulled the golden hull. Dented panels, and an illegible, faded logo, from a defunct galactic trading company crossed out with white paint, capped the illusion. Inside was no better, the bridge fitted with old parts, cannibalised from the other vessels. Hanging cable looms, wire, tape, and jury-rigging stuck the whole mess together. The fabric stunk of age and poverty. Old lights flickered in the corridors and strewn around the cargo bay, a mirid of broken parts added to the general malaise.

All four were loaded with blue energy, emptying the New World's tank farms. Powered by a hidden blue drive, *Pac-D* set out for Lagrvth. The other three took a slower passage through folded space to the asteroid belt at the edge of the Anan Galaxy. Amongst those desolate rocks, away from the shipping lanes, they rendezvoused with the battleships, *Abra, Losh* and *Tain.* Under the command of Aknar crews, the three powerful battleships took a welcome drink of blue from the *Pac-A.* Stuffed with so much of the valuable cargo, refuelling three ships hardly registered on its inventory gauge. Synchronous clocks counted down on the bridge of each vessel, as their crews settled down to wait and watch time go by.

*

Planet Anan and The Energy Exchange

Meanwhile, on Anan, an Aknar navy engineer arrived at the Shoter's office. Admiral Enirim had arranged this meeting. All along, the dedicated engineer had warned of the consequences of mothballing the Aknar armada in haste. Keeping him in the dark – from the behind the scenes plotting – bolstered his machine-driven principles.

When he heard all the blue was to be scoured from the engines, his rage and rants grew in intensity. 'The blue drives will rust if not vented properly. Moisture ingress to the manifolds will cause havoc to the intake valves. And I haven't even started on the consequences to the controls and drivetrain,' he had roared to Enirim. 'The ships will be useless,' he predicted.

She communicated her concerns to the Shoter, enlisting his wife – her cousin – to help. Granted an audience, today, the engineer was to put a case forward for maintaining the two flagships – the giants of the Aknar Navy. Plans to move them to the maintenance dock required The Sixth's permission. Despite his verbose ways, The Sixth understood the consequences of doing nothing. Valuable resources, hard to construct, would waste away. Also, he knew the purebreed kneeling in front of him was talking about The One and Eight's flagships. The greedy Overlord desired those for himself.

Two of the most powerful battleships in the galaxy, the man was right. The like of them would never be built again. 'I approve your plan. Submit your documentation to the Shoter. He will issue the endorsing stamps and the codes for the docking clamps,' The Sixth said.

It was more than the engineer had hoped for. Amongst the deep pile of project plans, languished a blockade licence for a transporter to dock and assist the project with waste removal. Sanctioning the paperwork, preprepared by Enirim, the Shoter handed over the all-important clamp codes for the two behemoths to the engineer. Knowing nothing of the plot, both men were innocent of any deception. It was a welcome distraction to the Shoter, who idly chatted with the engineer about the merits of the venture and how it could continue throughout the fleet.

'Regardless of our current situation, one day we'll need those ships. They can't be allowed to rust away,' he said.

Within two cycles, Exchange flight control had the codes to release the destroyer's restraining irons. Keying in the cypher, tears welled in the Dock Master's eyes as he watched the clamps open. A collective sigh of relief ploughed through the Aknar navy while a fleet of tugs moved the vessels around to the maintenance dock. Under the supervision of the engineer, a group of Aknar technicians transferred to the Exchange, starting work on the destroyers. In the secret keep, behind her chamber, Theia and Enirim plotted the next phase of their rebellion, guided by incoming messages from The Eight.

*

It took *Pac-D* three days to load out at Lagrvth. Then it made its way to Anan, crawling along at light speed powered by grav engines. In a forward compartment, disguised as a slops tank – behind a false bulkhead – *Pac-D's* blue drive lay dormant.

The evening before the ship's pending arrival, the Dock Master threw a long-planned party for The Sixth's inspection and management team. He chose the Hilotes Complex on the lower floor of the Exchange. Not a "bribing" party but a "small get together to foster working relationships and team building!".

It was nothing short of a full-on knees up bawdy event, showering The Sixth's Exchange administrators with sex and drugs. Holed up on their ships in the Jora and Ragma Galaxies, the cloistered purebreeds had never imagined such pleasures. To the delight of the Dock Master, they made total animals of themselves.

*

On-time, *Pac-D* arrived at Anan, slowing from light speed as it tracked through Anan's solar system. On a flickering viewscreen, Quriel scanned the fifty blockading ships.

'The Sixth's locked this place up,' he said to no one in particular. It was the first time any of The Eight's followers had laid eyes on the Sixth's fleet. But, to preserve their secrecy, Tom had banned all comms with Lagrvth or The Eight. As far as the crew of *Pac-D* knew, the others didn't exist. They were the crew of an old waste transporter. And to complete the ruse, they couldn't risk any intergalactic contacts.

'Hail the Exchange's flight control. Let them know we're here,' Quriel ordered comms.

'Instructions to park off the Exchange received. Inspection in six segs,' she said after a communiqué came through.

'We wait,' Quriel said, as he sat down in an old beat-up armchair screwed to the bridge floor. 'Pass the message to the others.'

*

The following morning, on the Energy Exchange, The Sixth's inspection and management team failed to turn up. An urgent call from the Dock Master reminded their chief of a scheduled inspection to a waste bucket called *Pac-D*. Shit rolls downhill and, after a while, the orders arrived at the lower rank trainee. Hungover from overindulgence, the young purebreed resented – with every fibre of his sick body – that he had to go to work. Reeking of stale perfume and body odour, in a huff, he travelled to Quriel's ship on a shuttle.

On the short journey, the Dock Master smiled at the young man. 'Enjoy yourself last night?' he asked.

The youth grunted as he tried to hold in the contents of his stomach. He knew he shouldn't have eaten so much. But the filleted Anan lizard in fruit sauce, chased with laestri eyeballs marinated in Helotes wine, was too good to pass up. The images of what followed spun in his mind – drug-fuelled erotica he would never have dreamed of. Gileyal, they called the narcotic. An intoxicating substance that amplified all the body's senses. Despite the hangover, youthful impatience burned his brain. He had booked a repeat – a personal session tonight with one of the hostesses, compliments of the generous Dock Master.

Four purebreeds met them in the shuttle bay on *Pac-D*. Dressed in grimy ship suits, with dirt-strewn faces, they matched the vessel's dishevelled appearance.

With limited introductions – knowing the form – the group set out on the blockade inspection. No blue, no contraband, no weapons, a crew of ten, and here to pick up waste from the Aknar navy's maintenance operation, was the ship's mantra, entered in the licence and repeated here with conviction by the team's leader, Quriel.

They started in the grav engine room.

A *miracle they got here at all*, thought the young purebreed as he tried to stay upright.

Then on to the cargo hold, stinking of stale rubbish. The young man retched at the smell. Biting hard on his mouth, he swallowed the bile back down to his churning stomach. He could taste the half-digested lizard as he regurgitated it again. His breath smelled foul as he belched.

Leading him on his important inspection, the others tried not to laugh or wrinkle their noses. He didn't notice the bits and pieces of old engine parts which had been dumped to help along the illusion. Eventually, he couldn't continue. His stomach heaved, then his throat gagged with the vomit. Spying a grating in the floor, *a drain*, he surmised; the young man leaned over it and puked his guts up. The ship's crew turned in shock, watching the youth vomit his half-digested meal down the grating. Bits of brown masticated lizard and red fruit particles, bound in yellow foul-smelling goo, poured from the inspector's mouth down into the depths of the ship below the grating.

The Dock Master held up his hand to quell their rage. Reading his gesture, their faces and emotions miraculously changed to display concern.

'How are you?' they asked. 'Can we get you anything? Come, there's a bathroom through here,' Quriel's crew said as they hurried the inspector away from the offending grating.

It wasn't a drain! Below the air vent, five hundred Chinese soldiers, dressed in Anan spacesuits, hid with two Aknar navy crews. Packed in the false compartment, they dared not move a muscle, even the three below the vent who were covered in foul-smelling alien puke. Helmets off, the yellow goo seeped up the nose of one. He gagged at the smell and tried to clear his nose by exhaling hard but it didn't work. Unwittingly, he sucked some puke into his nasal passage then down the back of his throat. The two beside him, realising what would happen next, burst into silent action. One grabbed his legs while another clamped a hand over the unfortunate soldier's mouth and nose, holding the coughing eruption in.

The relieving cough stifled, the man's face went red as he rasped. His chest heaving for life-giving air, the brave soldier didn't struggle. Any sound from below the grating would betray their position. As seconds turned to minutes, he felt the suffocating blackness descend on his oxygen-starved brain. A final thought flowed through his mind, *Let me die rather than reveal my comrades.*

Above the hiding soldiers, the rush to lead the inspector to a toilet, outside the cargo-hold, succeeded. One of the crew doubled back and whispered an all-clear down the vent. By now, the soldier was unconscious. Leaping into action, the poor unfortunate's companions revived him.

He coughed and spluttered, dispelling the puke from his mouth and nose. Water appeared, he flushed his mouth, throat and nose, but the foul alien taste lingered. His face told the whole story as his muscles twitched and his lips puckered with anger. His mates laughed, relieving the tension. Rags appeared, and as quickly as it arrived, the foul-smelling mess disappeared.

Li Ping moved through the ranks, bolstering morale and encouraging them on. It was a resounding thumbs up for the polluted soldier. She knew, rather than reveal their position, he had embraced his own death. A thought flashed through her mind. *He'd be the first human soldier to get a medal for valour, after breathing in alien vomit!*

Following his loss of face, the young inspector couldn't wait to leave. Quriel's crew were all over him, trying to clean him up and help in any way. Back on the delipidated bridge, a cup of hot Anan tea was produced, the grimy cup screaming "dare to drink me!". The inspector couldn't refuse and gingerly sipped the tea. Ignoring the cup's stains and greasy feel, he savoured the hot drink.

Quriel presented the all-important licence. And with a flourish, the inspector signed it, nodding to the Dock Master who, with a wry smile, stamped the useless piece of The Sixth's officialdom.

On the shuttle flight back, the young inspector flashed a message to the Exchange's flight control. 'Nothing to report. *Pac-D* cleared to dock.'

The Dock Master kept quiet, his face and emotions a mask of subterfuge. That was the easy part, he realised. The hard part was yet to come.

On the bridge of *Pac-D*, Captain Quriel downloaded the docking sequence from the Exchange's flight control. A smile played on his lips as he read it out to his crew. 'We're cleared to take on the Exchange tugs and proceed to the maintenance dock! And, better still, the orders include a note for four auto-tugs to park up at the maintenance dock.' He paused as they cheered. 'I couldn't have planned it better myself.'

As quickly as they felt it, the elation passed by. The work had only just started. Any leak or hint of deception would doom this venture to failure. The Sixth had eyes everywhere. Although seconded from the navy, price gouging spies – ready to make a fast UC – infiltrated The Dock Master's own crew.

All hands turned to maintain the ruse as they entered the belly of the beast. Vital maintenance must begin before they could refuel the two Aknar destroyers. There was no question of that – the engines wouldn't start otherwise. Their hidden troops and Aknar crews would have to hide for another while.

*

At the same time as *Pac-D* waited for the imminent arrival of the blockade inspector on Anan, The Sixth languished in his chamber, calculating variables for his success. For the intolerant Overlord, the waiting game, and scanning space for any sign of The Eight, proved trying. After a hundred and fifty cycles, the blockade hadn't turned up anything. Ships came and went, inspections done, and all proved to be on legitimate charter business. He suspected plotting, graft and corruption would fester amongst the bipeds. Yet, so far, nothing had proven disruptive to his rule.

The Empress, Theia Aknar, occupied herself with the wellbeing of her people. Despite its drawbacks, she persistently promoted her cure for the Anan sickness. Regardless of the earlier riots, after persuasion from the Shoter, The Sixth had allowed her that indulgence. He believed it gave her purpose. As a courtesy, despite previous acrimony, she provided him with regular updates on the program's successes.

The Royal announcements of the treatment's triumphs were full of tributes to The Sixth. "Our new Overlord had generously provided for the manufacture of …" and "I thank The Sixth for allowing the distribution of the cure to our population. Without his unwavering support, we wouldn't have been able to conquer the sickness …" And so on. Empress

Theia made sure the planet's news feeds were full of upbeat stories and included "her appreciation for The Sixth's help".

The Overlord scanned her latest report. Take-up of the cure was increasing amongst the young purebreeds. Theia's numbers didn't lie. Faced with a sterile lifespan of three hundred orbits coupled with the likelihood that they would develop the Anan sickness, taking Theia's cure was a no-brainer. That their lifespan would reduce by near a hundred orbits, was of no consequence. The young embraced a healthy short life with children rather than a barren old age contaminated with the disease. The older infected purebreeds, instead of dying early, eased their symptoms with the "First Stage Treatment".

This was an all-round success Theia had never dared hope for and she made sure she profusely, in public, thanked The Sixth "for his unwavering support". Unknown to him, promoting the cure for the sickness gave her a cover for her movements – coordinating the resistance.

All of a sudden, he realised the planned upkeep of two Aknar navy flagships had started today, an event that raised his interest. Without blue, they weren't a threat to his rule but once finished, he would staff them with crews from his navy. He had enough blue to fuel the two destroyers. They would serve as his backup in case he needed to escape. The transporter to scour their waste was arriving today.

'Six, are you there?' a voice in his consciousness interrupted. 'Meet me now; we have business to discuss. It is I, the Second.'

A stunning interruption, one The Sixth had never banked on. What does he want? he wondered, casting his mind out into ethereal space to confer with the reclusive Overlord.

'What do you want, Two?' he asked, his mind swirling in the cosmic winds of space and time.

The Second launched an outburst of verbal mush. 'We haven't talked in a while. You need to know we are running out of grav. I predict a shortage will come in perhaps two or three orbits of Anan if new stocks aren't found. Six, I see you have taken over. What did you do with The One and where are the other Overlords? I did feel the passing of Nine. What happened there. Six, since you are running the show, you must know all this.'

'*I don't. And The Eight killed Nine, you must have sensed that—*'

The Second cut him off. '*No, I did not,*' he lied. '*You will need to point me towards new stocks of grav. Can we discuss that? I see no merit in discussing politics. It tires me, as you know.*'

'*No, I didn't know,*' replied The Sixth, still digesting the news about the grav. He had heard rumours and it was no surprise, considering the number of ships that were using it.

The Second continued in the same monotone. '*I believe there are some deposits in our known galaxies, but I need The Seventh's knowledge of star charts and planets to investigate. You know the magnetic phenomena that create the conditions for grav to form. The Seventh should as well and be able to predict where we prospect.*'

It wasn't a ruse, but a genuine conversation and the truth from Two. With The Seventh on board, the potential was there to discover more grav-bearing worlds.

'*Can we go over that now? Can you summon Seven? Here, look at the charts …*'

'*Yes, we can,*' answered a bemused Six.

'*Sorry, have you somewhere else to be?*' asked The Second.

'*No, you are right, we should do this now,*' The Sixth answered as he reached out and called on The Seventh. A quick reflection as to why Two had called him with this problem flashed in his brain. "*I see you have taken over,*" Two had said. *He sees me as The One. I have trumped them all and am perceived as the go-to Overlord by the others! Their leader,* his over-inflated ego called out to himself.

*

Back on the *Monarch*, parked beside the *Chad* on Lagrvth, the Eight could feel the ongoing ethereal conference. No internal smile, no emotion, just continuing calculation. His grasp of the space-time continuum, with help from The Second, had set this trapping diversion. He flashed a message to Tom. '*Message the fleet; rendezvous as per plan. And time stamp it. We leave now.*'

CHAPTER FIFTY

Galactic War

Galactic war between Overlords is a foul business. No matter the outcome, there are no winners. We mortals get caught in the middle, following the Overlord who granted us intelligence or controls our world.

The last war of such magnitude raged for near a millennium. Mortal beings were born and died, only knowing war. Massive starships, space stations and armada destroyed in vain. Countless mortals killed – or culled. Whole populations left to fend for themselves, as colonies on the outer worlds were abandoned to the ravages of hunger and degradation.

I was born and fought through the end of that last war. I witnessed the devastation and the post-battle debris fields. The waste of so much life and precious resources turned my stomach to bile. I remember stepping back on the ground of what was once a lush life-sustaining fertile world, turned into a charred remnant of its previous life. One of many planets transformed into barren rocks.

As a Prince of the House of Naritanjs, I dedicate my life to peaceful coexistence with others, and if I ever ascend, I will perpetuate that quest on the higher plane.

‹ **From: *The Annals of the House of Aknar. History of Galactic War* by Prince Gtherandek of Naritanjs**

*

Anan Galaxy. EPTS: B147600

SPEEDING THROUGH FOLDED SPACE TO Anan on the *Monarch*, The Eight's internal clock counted down. Perched in his chariot on the darkened bridge, he could feel raw tension from his silent biped crew. Emotions nibbled away as their brains tried to concentrate on the job in hand. Thoughts flowed back and forth like an ocean current, while wisps of feelings – as a puff of wind – bled from their turmoiled minds.

"Would they succeed in this, their final battle? Would this war between Overlords end? And how would the end affect them?" were some of those fractured feelings.

And yet, below that emotion, The Eight sensed a steely resolve. They would fight to the end of their corporeal bodies for their Overlord. They knew, if he lost, The Sixth would wipe any memory of The Eight and his followers from the universe. The plan unfolded in his mind like a spider's web, each facet reliant on the next. He had no control of it now, the different parts moving forwards in an unstoppable momentum. Each aspect was an independent cell, some not knowing what others were doing, preserving their secrecy in a hidden maze of duplicity – all in plain sight of The Sixth.

Near the asteroid belt at the edge of the Anan Galaxy, out of sight of the planet and the Energy Exchange, the *Monarch* and *Chad* exited folded space. Away from the shipping lanes, if anyone was looking, they would have put it down to cosmic irregularity or another indistinctive energy burst. Nearby, amongst the desolate asteroids, *Pac-A, B, C, Abra, Losh* and *Tain*, had patiently waited for this moment.

In concert, the synchronous clocks counting down on the bridge of The Eight's fleet reached zero. There were no welcome comms bursts at the arrival of the last two ships – just a silent fleet rendezvous. All knew too well the consequences of discovery.

One minute later, a new set of orders unpacked on the fleet's nav-coms. Hidden in plain sight by Borea cloaks, one-by-one the eight starships made their way to Anan at sub-light speed. Halfway through the Anan solar system, the three Hela-class energy carriers parked up behind a nearby moon. The *Monarch, Chad, Abra, Losh* and *Tain*, continued on – five deadly warbirds hunting for the kill.

*

The New World

As The Eight's small fleet sped towards their final battle, ignorant of where the attack force was, the inhabits of New World got on with a very different daily life. At this critical time, all mining activities had stopped. Work focused on gathering food and making ready for a hasty escape from their new homes. Laid out on the spaceport, the *Richard*, *Hela*, *George* and *Maeve* glistened in the sunshine. The colony's lifeboats made ready for an escape if The Eight lost to The Sixth.

The Eight knew the New World was where Six would come first. Seize the blue energy source – that would be his goal in consolidating his power and wealth. After that, the evil entity would be unstoppable. The energy tank farms were empty, the last of their precious fuel loaded onto the four escape ships. After all, there was no sense in leaving any for The Sixth – if he came!

The goodbyes were hard. Robert and Janet stayed behind and worse, Niamh, Tom, Kora and Brian left their children in the safety of the New World with Janet. Unsaid words – 'if we don't come back' – haunted them all.

The final goodbye to his Overlord rung hard in Robert's mind. 'This is it, Robert; the day of reckoning. Cylla will listen out on her commerce terminal for news. You will have plenty of warning. If I lose the war, load the colony and leave. I have given Verteg coordinates of an out-of-the-way world where you should survive. Also, you will find one of my bases there, with commodities that will fund the colony. It will not be easy, Robert, but it is all I have to offer …'

And that was it! The *Monarch's* takeoff was watched by Fort Leslie and their new neighbours, São Paulo Nova, across the bay. All wondered whether this was the last time they'd see this beautiful bird of prey. Would they come back? And what would the outcome be for humankind and their Borea friends? So concerned was The Eight about the effects of a defeat, he left his catbears on the New World. If he failed, they would endure, living their lives out in the jungle.

Alice and Verteg watched the takeoff together on the balcony outside their pod, an emotional event as they watched the culmination of friend and family's work head out into the stars to do battle for their very existence.

*

Planet Earth, 2nd November 2028

On Earth, Chang Jin, Harold and The Eight's closest allies took a more stoic approach. If their Overlord lost the final battle in the far distant galaxy, there would be no escape. They knew The Sixth would return and finish the humans off.

In the meantime, with Chang and Harold at the helm, the ruling body forged on, consolidating the world order The Eight had imposed during the preceding six months. A harshness some found unpalatable. After his departure, driven by misguided political hacks, people rioted in hedonistic, alcohol and drug-fuelled rebellion.

"The end is nigh" and "Armageddon cometh again" was the flavour of the misguided slogans.

In The Eight's absence and the ambiguity surrounding his safe return, Chang and Harold clamped down hard. Vowing war wouldn't erupt again, they stopped short of imposing an Orwellian-type order. Under that uneasy calm, the planet waited and hoped …

*

Anan Galaxy

Back on Anan, dressed in rags, Theia Aknar, Enirim and ten loyal Aknar troops boarded the dirty brown smuggler-vessel. An obscure cloaked route took them to the Exchange, where they arrived as "migrants" from the nearby Javan. Without drawing breath, the Dock Master assigned them a berth in a cheap, run-down section of the maintenance docks.

'That'll have to do until we find a better place,' the Dock Master mused

653

aloud to the others in flight control. None paid any attention that the vessel had docked below the Aknar navy's maintenance operation.

That job was well advanced, with poly-com tubes and transfer hoses connecting *Pac-D* to the two destroyers. After the initial shock of meeting Li Ping and the Aknar crew, the engineer and his technicians threw their heart and soul into getting the destroyers up and running. Engines vented, blue flowed from secret compartments in the beat-up *Pac-D*.

Techs warmed the all-important drivetrains for flight and stuffed what grav they had into the engines. Quriel and his crew, alongside the Chinese soldiers, assisted where they could. Engrossed in their work, they didn't notice the arrival of a nondescript group of people floating outside an airlock until comms raised the alarm.

'Who are they?' the suspicious Chinese commander asked.

The Aknars sensed something but refused to believe it. Armed guards functioned the airlock. The twelve, dressed in used, dirty spacesuits, crossed life-support's threshold. It seemed to take an age as they peeled back their spacesuits to reveal the rag and dirt-covered contingent. To Li Ping's astonishment, the Aknar guards threw themselves on the ground, kneeling. Theia pulled down her hood, revealing her shiny bald head. Opening her cloak, her distinctive blue diamond shone like a beacon of hope. And beside her, the Admiral of the Aknar forces – Enirim – did the same. Tears flowed down Theia's face as she felt the emotion from her loyal followers.

'You, you are Empress Theia Aknar,' spluttered Li Ping as she lowered her weapon.

'I am. And you are our human allies …' There was so much she didn't remember but the facial features of this woman and her troops reminded her of someone. Soon she would regain those memories. But first, they had a war to win.

*

In the early hours of the morning, while most on the Energy Exchange slept, a series of commands opened inside the flight-control computer. Digital orders flowed to the tugs parked up at the maintenance docks. The automated craft linked their controls to the bridges of the Aknar behemoths. Comms poured back and forth between the six ships. Then, to Admiral Enirim's delight, clamped between two tugs apiece, the destroyers docking locks disengaged.

'Make way to open space,' she ordered, hardly believing their carefully crafted plan had come to fruition. With enough grav for the impending battle and blue for one emergency escape into folded space, the two giant battleships slipped away.

Sleepy Exchange flight controllers didn't notice. Nor did they catch the cohort of soldiers led by Theia, Li Ping and Quriel, climbing out of the poly-tube gangways. Dressed in their spacesuits – toting a mix of weapons – the deadly force clambered along the outside of the Energy Exchange to two airlocks located in the under decks.

*

The destroyers pressed on with their escape, through an unwatched channel girdled by docking arms in the old section of the Exchange. Derelict space gantries and moorings festooned this deserted section of timeworn space-berths, most of them unserviceable, abandoned for a newer construction at a higher level. Even so, Enirim knew it wouldn't be long until someone raised the alarm.

'Hard to hide these monsters,' she said out loud to her crew on the dark half-light of the bridge. Time ticked on while they watched their instruments track the snail-like progress of the kilometre-long vessels.

Stripped of grav and blue, the abandoned *Pac-D* stayed behind, its crew split between the battleships and Theia's invading force. The carefully crafted deceptive Trojan Horse's job was done. If they were to win today, it would be proclaimed as a hero; if they lost, The Sixth would no doubt crush it to dust.

*

Inside the Energy Exchange, Theia's invading force almost hit a snag. They got in, but during their travels outside the floating city, someone had called in a complaint to the Exchange's flight control.

'There's a maintenance troop outside my window,' said the lightly sleeping individual. 'I don't know what they're doing. They were crawling past my window and woke me. Strange faces as well. They look like aliens. I didn't know you hired such people!'

'What do you mean?' asked the night-shift supervisor.

'They've yellow-tinted faces and black hair. Definitely not purebreed or any other species I've seen in our galaxy.'

'Thank you, we'll look into it,' the supervisor said in a soft understanding voice. Then he cut the call.

'I think we should call general quarters,' he said, roaring with laughter. 'There's yellow-skinned aliens crawling around the lower section of the Exchange!'

The small night-shift crew collapsed in their seats laughing. They didn't notice the airlocks' warning flash across the security screen.

'Dispatch a medic to check on her ...' his voice trailed off as the Dock Master entered flight control. *Early for his shift; what gives?* wondered the supervisor? 'Can't sleep?' he asked.

'No, I've reports to collate for the Shoter,' the Dock Master lied, sitting down in his command chair. His eyes scanned the room and the all-important security screens. So far, this crew had lived up to expectations. *They haven't noticed a thing*, he thought.

Not for long, though. Seconds later, the night-shift supervisor's mouth fell open as he focused his eyes on one of the security screens. A camera in the lower deck had picked up the invasion.

'What the—'

The supervisor – from The Sixth's troops – didn't get another word out, as vapour poured from the barrel of the Dock Master's grav gun. The charge ruptured the man's brain, covering his command console with grey matter and blood.

'Anyone else?' the Dock Master asked. 'This is the Aknar rebellion.'

Two grinned a reply, while one traitor frowned. The Dock Master's gun spat again. He had expected as much.

'Right,' he said. 'We wait for Empress Theia and her troops. Do whatever you can to slow down The Sixth's guards.' A quick glance at the dock's status readout showed Enirim's two destroyers' undetected escape making progress. *On time*, he thought, with a grateful sigh.

From then on, the Dock Master and his two loyal crew, played cat and mouse with the Sixth's guards, remotely closing and sealing sections of the Exchange, trapping them. Outside flight control, when the two guards realised what was going on, they tried to batter the impervious door down. Despite the Dock Master's efforts, more arrived to bolster that contingent, fortifying the corridors outside Exchange control.

*

Using two separate airlocks, Theia and Li Ping had divided their forces. Local knowledge was everything, so Quriel and his two companions, accompanied Li Ping's group, while Theia and her Aknar guards headed the other. It led to a speedy invasion, and within minutes of clearing the airlock, Li Ping's and Quriel's group arrived at the corridor outside flight control.

Although Li Ping had prepared her troops for this moment, she hadn't expected the ferocity of the full-scale battle that erupted. Quriel did; he hadn't overestimated the capabilities of The Sixth's crack troops. Rumours of their abilities spun around the galaxies. Stories of their brutality and their prowess with baharian blades abounded. Never verified, it played in the back of his mind.

The initial contact was vicious. Leading her group, with Quriel by her side, Li Ping rushed The Sixth's guards. She had trained her troops to use grav guns but after blasting a hole in the corridor's ceiling, she realised they mightn't be the right weapons to use here. In the sterile environment of a war game, the surplus grav guns performed flawlessly. However, under the testing pressure of battle, the old weapons provided by Nolget and Touqmat faltered. The temperature of the weapons' power modules increased, affecting the gun's output. Left with no other option, with screams and shouts, Li Ping's troops launched themselves into hand-to-hand combat using knives against their alien opponents. The ferocity of their defence surprised her.

As Quriel had suspected, The Sixth's troops were well versed in using baharian swords. The cutting action of the swords ripped through flesh, bone and earthly steel like butter. Blood flowed along the corridor as the

Chinese soldiers fell under the onslaught of the swish blades. The inferior Earth weapons couldn't match such superior tech. Abandoning previous caution, again, they tried to fire their grav guns. But, like a swarm of killer insects, an attack of tiny blades shot back – cutting more humans down.

Not giving up, Li Ping led another assault, rallying her troops to follow. They rushed along the corridor, knives, and this time, small automatic pistols, at the ready. Quriel tailed the Chinese Commander. He sensed the danger before her. In a recess in the passage, he felt the rising blade, could feel the intake of breath from its bearer and then the force behind the sword as it swung through the air. With his right hand, he grabbed Li Ping, throwing her back. His left hand raised to parry the blow, veered around and in front of her. He knew the outcome before it struck, hearing the rush of air as the baharian sword sliced downwards. Quriel never felt the pain as his left hand was cleaved from his body. Red blood spurted out of his severed arm, covering him and Li Ping. They fell in a heap together. Like greased lightning, her soldiers had the pair dragged back to safety, the sound of their small-arms fire and the salvo of lead pushing the defenders back.

Quriel's ever-present companion, Chief Haldock, sprang into action. Spraying an Anan field bandage onto the severed arm, the transparent substance flowed across the open wound, then congealed. The Chinese watched on, in awe of this alien tech. Within seconds, the coagulated fluid sealed the stump, stopping the bleed. A deft jab with a needle into a vein by the Chief and a bag of the life-giving Anan plasma was attached to Quriel's arm. The precious fluid did the rest.

Quriel's eyes opened. 'Chief, the others, save them – as many as you can,' he rasped, as he tried to stand.

With the fight in stalemate, The Sixth's guards withdrew, leaving a trail of human casualties along the corridor – arms, limbs and heads severed from their bodies. Likewise, Li Ping had no choice but to order a retreat. Over twenty lay dead, either decapitated or bled out from multiple slashing wounds. The guts of some, hanging out from their stomachs. The stench of death followed the retreating group. Chief Haldock saved as many as he could, but the carnage quickly exhausted his field supplies.

When Theia arrived, the sight of the bloody battlefield and Quriel standing cradling his stump, numbed her brain. 'What happened?' she asked, the pain dripping from her voice. Her blue eyes darted everywhere, trying to comprehend what was before her.

'Not enough room to fight and their steel swords cut through our knives. I owe my life to your Captain Quriel,' Li Ping blurted. The strain was testing her voice as she tried to hurry on with the explanation. Not what she wanted to do. "When you are explaining, you are losing," her mentor had told her many times in days gone by.

Quriel added two words, 'Baharian steel.' It was all he needed to say.

Composing herself, Li Ping continued, 'We used some of our own weapons but couldn't get a clear shot with them. At the start, we tried the grav guns but did more damage than is merited. Look, see,' she said, pointing to the hole in the ceiling above.

As Theia gazed at the dead and blood-stained wounded, Captain Quriel among them, the depth of the problem hit the Empress like a hammer. She touched Quriel on his maimed arm, her warm glow filling his heart with hope. Then Theia's commanding voice pierced their silence. 'Baharian steel cuts through all other metals. Earth tech won't match their swords.' She paused for a moment as an idea formed in her mind. 'What if we get behind and above them?'

Li Ping realised what Theia was at. She smiled and nodded. 'That'll work. Show me how we get there.'

A quick call to the Dock Master, a set of orders to the troops and the fight moved on. Soldiers were dispatched to start the other two fronts while the rest held the fort.

But it took time to weave back and forth through the Exchange, doubling back and getting behind and above the Sixth's troops. As time marched on, the impending space battle got ever nearer to the celestial Energy Exchange.

*

Oblivious of the approaching danger, the blockading warships never noticed The Eight's five deadly vessels approach.

Onboard the blockade's command vessel, the captain listened to reports of a skirmish on the Energy Exchange.

'Flight control says they're under attack,' relayed comms.

'Can you raise our troop commander?' asked the captain.

'I'm trying—'

'Well, keep trying,' barked back the captain.

Engines slowed as The Eight's paltry fleet advanced on the blockade. Five against fifty, those numbers singed the crew's minds! Maintaining a comms blackout, the stealthy vessels broke formation, taking positions at equidistance around the blockade. On the bridge of *Abra*, Geoff's hands flew across a translucent panel. Behind, Jarzol and Fazqa watched. They hardly dared to breathe as their critical weapon came online. Failure here would hasten their demise.

Inside the cargo holds of *Abra*, *Losh* and *Tain*, newly installed weapons' racks whirled into life. Jarzol's creation hummed, primed and ready to launch. Below the cargo holds – on each vessel – steel plates retracted, exposing gelatinous windows to the dark vacuum of space. Twin launch tubes lowered down through these ingenious diaphanous airlocks. Then, with a swipe of Geoff's hand, ninety drones flew out – thirty from each ship.

Back in the holiday resort near Melbourne, while trying to play one of his son's video games, Jarzol had developed this concept. In that virtual reality game, there were monsters everywhere – some real some imaginary. The game's challenge was to extricate the real ones and kill them!

The simple game concept formed the basis for their secret weapons' system – holographic ship projectors. In Australia, they manufactured a hundred ball-shaped drones, two metres in diameter, with miniature grav engines and a holo-projector. Designed to replicate a battle fleet, the drones had simple cloaking tech and the ability to appear and disappear in an instant.

On the bridge screens of The Sixth's starships, they saw an invading armada appear in the space around them. Fluctuating drone cloaks added weight to the illusion of real battleships, trying to mask their signature.

The captain of the blockade command vessel cursed as she connected the skirmish on the Exchange with the appearance of this enemy fleet.

'The Eight is here,' she shouted.

Those words filled the comms channels, shrieking panic throughout The Sixth's ships. Waiting for so long for this instant had diminished their zeal. Vital minutes ticked away as they tried to compose themselves – a gift to the Aknar destroyers. More time made for them to escape the Exchange's space docks unnoticed.

The trap worked, drawing the blockading fleet away from the Energy Exchange to engage the arriving enemy. Meanwhile, the other five, real-cloaked battleships hunting The Sixth's navy, prepared to make the whole deception convincing.

On the *Monarch*, Tom had identified their adversary's command vessel. Subtle changes to the craft betrayed its function: its broader girth, more comms arrays peppering the hull, and the unmistakable addition of extra weapons, were a dead giveaway. Under the command of Niamh, the stealthy *Monarch* moved ever closer. At a hundred kilometres away, Tom flashed a one-word message to the other four vessels.

'Attack.'

All at once, the cloaked *Monarch*, *Chad*, *Abra*, *Losh* and *Tain*, pounced on their prey.

The *Monarch* unleashed two missiles at the command vessel. Another Earth-alien hybrid, the weapons relied on primitive chemical explosives. Powered by a grav engine and shrouded by a Borea cloak, the invisible missiles targeted the enemy's aft engine ports. The first missile, five seconds ahead of its mate, exploded on contact with the vessel's grav bubble. The shockwave, travelling through the protective bubble, shook the ship like a child's rattle, astounding the captain.

Thrown across the bridge like a toy, she screamed her final orders. 'Weapons online now. Damage report—'

The captain never finished her sentence. Flying at the speed of sound – seconds after the first – the following missile sailed through the hole blown in the grav bubble, embedding itself in the engine port. One thousand kilos of Earth explosive detonated. The resultant force, like giant knives, peeled the engine room open, releasing its grav. The chemical explosive, combined with the grav, created a devastating chain reaction, ripping through the ship. The crew never knew what hit them – none survived. The explosion vapourised most and the rest blew apart, their body parts consigned to float in space with the debris.

Likewise, *Chad*, *Abra*, *Losh* and *Tain* unleashed the same deadly force, their missiles blasting another four of The Sixth's vessels into oblivion.

All hell broke loose inside the blockading fleet as The Eight's war erupted around them. Fear clamped the stomachs of the defenders at the sheer size of the invasion. No one had foreseen this. They viewed him as "an old has-been" and "a spent force".

"Where could The Eight get such an armada?" and "How did the Aknars hide them?" were some of the frantic questions that clogged the comms.

Pulling themselves together, the ill-fated Sixth's captains burst into action. The initial seconds of the surprise over, they targeted the invaders with returning missile fire. But, to add to the erupting mayhem, Jarzol had added more deception. The holo-ships could also simulate an explosion if "hit" by a missile.

While The Sixth's captains wasted precious time and ammunition targeting the holo-drones, The Eight's five warships picked them off like fish in a barrel. The battlefield descended into a maelstrom of exploding missiles and ships. Bits flew off into space, engines targeted, ships devasted, dead crew pouring out into the cold vacuum of space. Others ran to the escape pods screaming for mercy.

Not what The Eight wanted but at this late stage of his smart war, a necessary evil. The captains of his five vessels shut their minds to the size of the rout, the devastation and carnage. They knew their supremacy in this battle wouldn't last long but some help was coming. The Sixth's captains, immersed in their own survival, didn't notice the two approaching Aknar destroyers.

CHAPTER FIFTY-ONE

Galactic War

I was born during the final orbits of this millennium, the period we named "Exhaustion".

It was that feeling that befell the known universe's inhabitants, both mortal and ethereal. Overlords and mortals had had enough of war. When they tried to heal their differences, the Overlords couldn't remember what had started the war in the first place. At that moment in time, bipeds and their Overlords shared a common purpose: unite or tear the very fabric of a shared existence apart.

With one floating city surviving, the choices were stark. The Overlords settled their conflicts while the surviving mortals, of purebreed race, settled theirs. As a Princess of the House of Akjivi, I dedicate my life to peaceful coexistence with others. Together we must rebuild and relocate our last floating city, forging a future legacy for our descendants. If I ever ascend, I will perpetuate the quest for peaceful coexistence on the higher plane.

‹ **From: The Annals of the House of Aknar. The Rebuild of the Energy Exchange by Princess Theia of Akjivi**

*

The Seventh's Galaxy. EPTS: B147648

IN ETHEREAL SPACE, THE SECOND and The Seventh grovelled with Six. If the energy entity had an arse, the two others would have crawled up it. They fawned and flounced under the Overlord's narcissistic ego. Despite that, The Second and The Seventh, eager to discover new deposits of grav, steered their ghostly get-together along. As a group, their ethereal minds explored from one corner of their galaxies to another.

Inside the border of The Seventh's galaxies, the three stopped to examine a new discovery. Amongst a planetary system soaked in the gravitation pull of four surrounding suns – on moons and asteroids The Second never knew existed – a rich deposit of grav had formed. The Second, new to this quadrant of the universe, was taken aback by the sheer size of the find.

'It will take us through the next millennium,' he communicated. His words were not lost on Seven.

The disgraced Overlord wouldn't profit from this. It would be his pay-back – penance for aligning with The Sixth. Unknown to The Sixth, a deal was struck by the wavering Seven before this jaunt. Now that it bore fruit, Seven was free. If the rebellion succeeded, he could continue his existence, holding his position amongst the Overlords.

As quickly as The Sixth's elation in the discovery arrived, it vanished. His ethereal mind burst with messages of help and images of his battered and defeated ships.

The battle had moved on, with twenty immobilised and seven destroyed, the casualties painting a stark picture. The debris field, from blown apart hulls, clouded his view of the battle. The Sixth concentrated his mind, projecting it out around the Exchange. He focused on one of his cruisers – his flagship and fleet command – the after-end split, the grav engines hanging out below their energy ports, dangling in open space. The blue drive fared no better, its dodecahedron rotor impaled like a misshaped javelin in the pulse port below the bow. Sparks and fires flowed from the damaged hull, illuminating the blackness around.

Tricked was the thought that ploughed his brain. These two treacherous wisps of energy have sprung a trap, The Sixth realised, as his mind raced back to Anan. Meantime, he flashed a message to his commanders. 'Target the Energy Exchange.' If he couldn't have it, no other would!

In the milliseconds it took him to return and reunite with his energy mass on Anan, he saw something else, the reason for his ship's defeat. They were being duped by holographic illusions. He flashed another message to the remaining twenty-three ships, containing the locations and signatures of Geoff's drone engines. The Sixth's crews scrambled to reprogram their scanners. Within minutes, like a curtain opening, the drones appeared out of a fog of cloaked mayhem. Even with the enhanced Borea cloaks – for the first time – whisps of engine signatures from The Eight's five battleships also appeared.

On the *Abra*, Geoff screamed as one of his drones, struck by a laser beam, flashed and died.

'They have us,' he cried, over the comms to the other four ships – the first message since Tom had ordered the attack.

Multiple lasers flashed from the remainder of the Sixth's fleet, cleaning up their opposition's deceptive drones. Along with the Aknar destroyers, it was now seven against twenty-three. Tom didn't panic. The tide hadn't changed, he realised. It had stopped going out for The Sixth. They knew this time would come. Yet, with the previous success, and Enirim's two ships now joining the battle, the overwhelming odds had come down.

'Those destroyers pack the punch of four cruisers,' he said. 'With them at our back, we can outfox the remaining enemy.' He sent a coded message burst to Geoff. 'Send to all ships: EM-codes to oscillate our cloak frequencies.'

Geoff shook his head. *Why didn't I think of that?* he mused while he flashed the emergency codes across their small fleet.

The wonderous Borea tech worked its magic, continually changing the cloaking frequency of the *Monarch*, *Chad*, *Abra*, *Losh* and *Tain*. They made the most of their advantage, knocking out another eight of The Sixth's battleships. The accompanying mag-projectile bombardment from the two destroyers played havoc. Like giant swords, the metal shells sliced through the enemy ships, cutting them clean in two.

Back on Anan, The Sixth's energy-mass awoke to a barrage of bashing on his door. He didn't wait to open it and burst through, knocking the Shoter to the ground.

'Overlord,' he screamed, 'a shuttle is waiting …'

Ignoring him, The Sixth barrelled on, flying into the waiting shuttle. His mind projected out to the battlefield, just in time to witness the demise of more of his ships. And worse, the destroyers had formed a grav shield around the Exchange, blocking his ship's missiles. Like balls, they bounced off the powerful barrier, exploding harmlessly in space.

His ethereal mind examined the shield. Then he saw it, gaps at the lower quadrants, where the arcs of the barriers dissected each other, patches left exposed at the four intersections of the grav shield. Small indeed, but enough for missiles to penetrate. Better still, they were level with the lower extremity of the floating city, where the engine room, and he surmised, those ethereal wisps of the ghosts of the Ones past resided. If The Sixth could smile, he would have. Gloating, he flashed the locations to his remaining captains.

'Target all missiles to these coordinates,' he ordered. His shuttle sped on, ready to meet his fleet. After firing its missiles, one ship peeled off to meet him.

On his way into space, an Aknar barracks below caught his eye. The spectre of evil diverted his mind to the troops inside. Grey smoke curled from their bodies, piercing screams filled the air as terror and pain burned their fragile existence. Then silence as The Sixth turned the Aknar garrison to dust.

I should have done that at the beginning, he mused. A show of power he had wanted to exercise but his Shoter had talked him out of it.

'You need the Aknars on side, Overlord,' the purebreed had advised.

That time's long past, thought The Sixth. A burning desire to wipe the rest of the population from the planet flashed in his evil energy mass. *Turn them to dust,* he had thought over and over during his escape from Anan. Craving for revenge – and survival – forced his brain to calculate the blue he'd expend culling the Anan population. *Not enough energy,* was the numerical reply. He had three pods of his life-sustaining energy here on this shuttle – and that was it.

Enough for an escape and to survive, The Sixth realised. He blotted out the thoughts of how much of his precious blue was wasting away, spilt in space by The Eight's attack.

*

Energy Exchange

Meanwhile, on the bridge of the *Monarch*, the ongoing battle tested Niamh's flying skills to the limit. So intense was the fight, to protect her brain, Kora pulled her blue diamond from the nav-con. Relying on sensors and cameras to fly, Niamh twisted and ducked the space debris as she piloted the powerful warbird through the battlefield. A shrill proximity alarm sounded – one they were well used to by now.

Before anyone could say anything, the image of another priceless dodecahedron rotor – blasted from an engine – speeding end over end through space, appeared on the bridge viewscreen. Deftly, Niamh ducked the *Monarch* underneath the deadly projectile. It flew on, embedding itself through the hull of one of its damaged sister ships. Breath sucked in, the crew returned to their duties, hunting out another target for a kill …

The Eight's thoughts thundered out, shocking the crew to their core. A stomach-churning risk previously foreseen, debated and planned for, now realised. All senses aroused, watching every millisecond of the battle on the *Monarch's* bridge, The Eight heard The Sixth's fatal orders.

'He targets the Energy Exchange.'

The booming warning scared his biped crew to their very core. For an instant, even the unflappable Tom buried his head in his hands.

Continuing, The Eight tempered his voice.'He tries to collapse all we Overlords have worked for, over aeons, in our known universe.'

The next words he projected out into the battlefield for all to hear. 'Here and now, I will deal with you, Six. This ends today.'

There was no mistaking the booming voice of The Eight. It played out over the bridges of every vessel in the battlefield and into the mind of The Sixth.

Taking matters into his own hands, The Eight sucked at the store of blue on his chariot. Growing in size, he extracted all the blue in the tank. Gorged on fresh energy, his swelling mass looked terrifying. Floating away from his chariot, he grew in size. His bulky energy mass took up one side of the nav-con and stretched to the ceiling of the bridge. With the occasional crackle and spark, the energy he radiated flashed erratically.

Shimmering with a deep blue and white light, their Overlord gave a foreboding impression of pure anger, scaring his biped crew – except for Niamh and Tom. They had seen this before, back on the *Hela* on Earth, when attacked by nuclear weapons. They both remembered they had wished never to see him like this again – war took its toll.

Entering an airlock at the back of the bridge, the engorged Overlord raced from the *Monarch*, speeding through space into the ongoing war. At the same time, commands flowed from The Eight's mind to his battle-ships. He was running the show now. Autonomous fire targeted The Sixth's missiles pouring towards the holes in the Aknar destroyer's grav bubbles. The shields, projected out at the limit of their massive tech, could grow no more.

The Eight split his mind into six, directing all his ships' firepower at the incoming missiles. Two segments of his ethereal brain entered the control computers of the destroyers. With precision no biped or machine could muster, he moved the two destroyers' locations and boosted their grav bubble's output, closing off three of the four intersecting holes in the shield. Missiles exploded, their destructive force absorbed by the grav bubbles, bouncing off into the surrounding vacuum of space.

Like ghostly lightning, blue energy flashed across the control panels of The Eight's fleet. In awe at their Overlord's power, his loyal biped crews stood down. But Tom never gave up, scanning the battlefield, analysing the incoming data, until he realised that The Eight's intervention wouldn't be enough. Moving the two vessels in closer to the Exchange and adjusting the bubbles, still left one gap in the crucial barrier.

Floating in the centre of the battle, his engorged energy mass bursting with blue light, his brain in overdrive as he managed every facet of the fight, The Eight missed it. And The Sixth exploited that to the extreme. Taking a leaf from his adversary's playbook, he sent new coordinates to the missiles' guidance systems: the target, the one remaining break in the protective shield.

Tom gazed across the bridge to Niamh, the love of his life, mother to his child, seated in the captain's chair, her face a mask of horror. The last twelve missiles flew towards the hole in the protective grav bubbles – level with the Exchange's engine room.

They both grasped the reality of the situation – their lives flashing before them. The consequences of the Energy Exchange's engine room exploding hit them hard. Near a half million souls would perish in a blue flash, taking the nearby vessels out as well. Their lives would be over, and nothing would ever be the same again. Life in the known galaxies would change forever, with humanity wiped from the universe. The Sixth would win, regardless whether The Eight survived or not. The loss of the "jewel in the galaxy's crown" was unfathomable.

In the flash of time it took the two lovers to compute that together, Niamh had the *Monarch* turned around and headed straight to the hole in the grav bubble. It flew on its side, offering the maximum-sized shielding target to the twelve missiles raining in. Covering fire from the *Abra*, *Chad*, *Losh* and *Tain*, took out seven, blasting them into pieces. But five stubborn weapons sped on, heading for the one hole in the shield where they would end the Aknar's way of life in their known universe.

On the destroyers, Enirim furiously spat orders to her captains and weapons officers. In vain, she knew. The Eight's efforts had maximised their output. Guns, red hot from firing, and the missiles so close they couldn't get an accurate bead on them. The smaller close-range weapons put down covering fire, but still not enough to take out the remaining missiles.

Like the sting of a thousand Uldonian microbes, The Eight sensed the danger – imminent catastrophe loomed ever closer.

A voice scratched the Overlord's brain. '*Gtherandek, you have tried so hard, but alas I fear we are done.*'

It kindled a memory of long, long ago, before the time when he was a – he couldn't remember. It was like his kin had called from the past and he couldn't let them down.

From the battlefield's centre, travelling at the speed of sound, The Eight's energy mass converged back on the *Monarch*, enveloping its hull in a covering cloud of blue energy. Seconds later, in a flash of white light, three grav missiles detonated along the vessel's hull.

Good fortune smiled for the *Monarch* as The Eight absorbed most of the shockwave. However, he couldn't get it all, as part of the blast blew a pennon wing off. Like a giant invisible blade, the dissipating explosive wave ripped through the port aft-quarter, slicing the pennon wing from the vessel's hull.

The force of the blast ejected the severed wing and its engine room, along with hybrid and blue drives, out into space. A lucky escape for the fastest ship in the galaxy. Flown on its side to absorb the blast, and cushioned by The Eight, the all-important port-side missile tubes, stabiliser and rear gun turret, remained intact.

The loud bang shook the ship to its core. Alarms raged and pandemonium broke out as Niamh strived to lock down their life support systems. Bulkhead doors closed, sealing the rift on the port side. Commands flowed from the bridge, switching power conduits and control looms. *Survive this*, was Niamh's mantra as she shut down every redundant system she could find.

Outside, in the vacuum of space, The Eight cocooned the ship, deflecting it away from crashing into the Exchange's protective grav bubble.

*

Through the vivid spectacle, The Sixth, watching from afar, revelled at his adversary's weakness in trying to save the mortals' starship.

'Eight, I will exploit your feeble compassion for the mortals,' The Sixth roared across space. He had won; nothing could stop him. He focused his ethereal mind, guiding the surviving two missiles towards the last remaining gap in the Energy Exchange's protective shield. Precious seconds ticked by as the missile's engines roared on, bringing death and destruction to the Overlord's celestial wonder. Never before had their floating city, the centre of their galaxies, faced such peril.

*

While The Eight battled to save the *Monarch*, back on the Exchange, Theia pursued her own fight. With guidance from flight control, she and Li Ping planned to surround The Sixth's troops at each end of the corridor and from above. The designers did everything they could to enhance the security of the all-important control room, the narrow passage outside built with an attack in mind. That worked both for and against Theia.

The Chinese, realising they couldn't storm the narrow corridor without taking heavy losses, led by a wounded Quriel, barricaded the Sixth's crack troops in. As the Chinese soldiers settled down and waited, their pure-breed opposites wondered what would come next. Anticipation played on their minds but the feeling of the closeness of the approaching Sixth bolstered their mood.

'The Sixth comes,' they shouted at the invaders. 'Soon, he will prevail. Surrender now.'

Unbeknown to his faithful followers, their Overlord had plotted the demise of the very space station they were trying to defend – their mortal lives insignificant to him and a microscopic price to pay for victory.

In the corridor above, the hole blown in the floor by their soldiers told Theia and Li Ping they'd arrived above their enemy. A soldier sliced through what remained of the deck with a grav gun. Sparks rained down on the foe below. When they realised what was happening, they launched a shower of steel blades through the opening above. The knives missed their targets, passing by Theia's troop, embedding themselves in the ceiling and walls. A fatal few fell back on those who fired them.

The Sixth's troop commander, provoked by their desperate situation, tried to break out from the siege. But Quriel and the Chinese soldiers had fortified it well, heaping anything to hand to form a barricade. Chairs, tables and beds littered the corridor, trapping the enemy behind. With the last piece of metal cut through, the ceiling fell on top of them.

Trapped, there was nothing they could do. The ill-fated group fell under a barrage of automatic gunfire. 'Just in case,' Li Ping had packed some of Earth's primitive tech. The ear-splitting sound of percussion weapons, and the lead salvo, panicked the purebreeds. Fatal bullets embedded themselves in The Sixth's guards.

When the firing stopped, Theia stole a look. The smoke cleared, revealing the carnage below. Amongst the twisted metal lay near a hundred dead purebreeds. Red blood flowed along the corridor and the stench of death defiled the air.

But there was no time to go back around. Theia could sense the tension from the battle outside. The Sixth's orders to target the Exchange burned in her brain.

Adding more pressure, a message from Enirim sparked from her wrist comms.

'Hurry, Theia, there are two missiles—' But, the heat of the battle cut Enirim's voice off.

Time drips away, Theia realised. She shouted down to Li Ping's soldiers. 'Hurry and catch me now.'

Although they didn't understand Anan, her body language said it all as she poised at the edge of the hole. That spurred Li Ping's troops on. Climbing over the dead purebreeds – soaked in blood – three soldiers looked up at the Empress. 'Jump,' they shouted in Chinese.

Theia needed no prompting, leaping from one deck to another. In seconds, strong human hands caught her. Quriel arrived to see the Aknar Empress of the galaxy dressed in brown bloodstained rags, with a grav gun hanging over one shoulder and a captured baharian sword over another, flying through the air. She mesmerised her followers, sparking a legend for the annals of time.

*

Inside the *Monarch*, bit by bit, Niamh regained control until she was able to fly the ship herself.

Kora shouted out the all-important damage assessment. 'Life support intact in crew quarters and the bridge.'

A silent Niamh nodded at the welcome news.

It was Tom who asked the inevitable question. 'And the crew, Kora? Any news from below?'

Her smile said it all. 'Talking to Brian, they're all fine. They felt the bang. Couldn't miss it really, and he's asking how we are?' she said, tears of joy running down her face.

They had secreted all but the bridge and gun crews in the mid-ship armoury. Fitted as a keep with crash-pods, the safest part of the ship could also be jettisoned like a lifeboat. Another recent Mzimot modification.

Tom exhaled a sigh of relief, but as yet the battle wasn't over. 'Tell him we're not out of the woods,' was his grim reply, as the shrill alarms still sounded. 'And, Niamh, can you mute that noise?' he asked. 'We know we're in trouble!'

*

Outside the Exchange's flight control, without another thought, jumping over debris and dead bodies, Theia rushed to the open door. A thankful Dock Master pulled her in. Li Ping and Quriel followed – the high-tech control room was what the Chinese commander expected. Wall-to-wall screens displayed pictures from inside and outside the Exchange. Status readouts of the battle scrolled along with displays of the number of damaged or destroyed ships circling the Exchange. But what Li Ping didn't expect was the smell of death. Hidden in a closet, the bodies of the two dead traitors' foul odour lingered.

In a rush, the wounded Quriel beat on a wall panel. With a welcome click, it opened. There were shouts of relief as Theia placed her hand on the Aknar control pad, keying in her royal codes.

Without warning, the wall opened, revealing a hidden control room. Theia and Quriel ran inside as the lights flickered on and a control panel lit up. She stabbed her blue diamond into a console. Blue energy flashed across the board, and the Exchange's security system burst into life. Brushing aside all thoughts of the approaching missiles, Theia's hands glided across the controls, her vital orders triggering a rarely used part of the Exchange's electronic brain.

*

On his shuttle, with his ethereal mind, The Sixth guided the two missiles past the hole in the grav barrier. Flying them himself, he pushed the weapons straight towards the Energy Exchange's engine room. They raced closer and closer to destroying everything that would get in his way. If he managed to get those missiles through, he would win – regardless of whether The Eight survived or not.

Tear it down, he thought. *If I don't rule, no one will. Chaos and mayhem, that's what the insignificant mortal bipeds will get. And they'll blame The Eight for the attack. For it is he, not I, who started this war.*

Brainwashed by their self-loving Overlord, his purebreed crews blindly followed this futile groupthink.

*

Inside the Energy Exchange, alarms blared out a chilling warning. 'Emergency! Emergency! The Exchange is now closed. All personnel return to your quarters. Again ...'

The Aknar security system rumbled on as automatic commands awoke the Exchange's defences. Phaenian hardened steel shutters started to close on all the windows. In milliseconds, the clear dome above the trading hall metamorphosed into a black compound stronger than steel.

With a swipe of her hand, Theia woke another defensive layer. Gun turrets extended from the exterior of the Exchange, their laser cannons scanning incoming threats. Above the lower engine room – the powerhouse of the Exchange – sensors registered the danger.

Again, the metallic voice sounded off in the control room. 'Missile alert. Missile alert ...'

A.I. laser beams stalked the ever-shortening expanse between the oncoming missile and the Exchange. In a flash of white light, the two missiles exploded, their retaining casings burned through, guidance and targeting systems turned to molten metal. Thousands of droplets of grav escaped, expanding in a sunburst of light, burning up in space.

Theia slumped into the command chair. She felt Li Ping beside her and reached out to hold her ally's hand.

The Chinese commander had one burning question. 'What of our Overlord, The Eight? Is he alive?'

It was the tone of the question and the emotion that touched Theia's heart, and the use of the word "our". She had forgotten so much, but now realised these humans were family.

His voice solid as steel, Quriel answered, 'He survives, Commander.' Still in battle mode, he scanned the incoming data, routing it to the comms speakers. For the first time in an age, Quriel smiled as shouts of victory filled the comms channels. 'You hear that? We've won. It's over ...'

*

Outside, with The Eight wrapped around it, the *Monarch* had escaped from the fray. Feeling Niamh's voice in his head, The Eight relaxed his grip on her ship.

'Overlord,' she asked, 'are you all right? What of the battle? How many are left?'

Five of The Sixth's ships had survived. The two formidable Aknar destroyers, with their small but deadly allied fleet, arrested them. Gunsights lined up, with steel missiles loaded in the mag tubes, left The Sixth's captains with no option but to capitulate.

'Move and be destroyed,' Enirim told them, and to nail that order down, *Abra, Chad, Losh* and *Tain* trained grav missiles on them as well.

'It is done, and Empress Theia controls the Exchange,' The Eight told Niamh. 'But there is unfinished business.' Sensing the approaching Sixth, revenge boiled in his brain.

The Eight floated away from the *Monarch*, watching The Sixth's shuttle dock with one of his ships.

From the depths of the Energy Exchange, the voice from a ghost of One's past, returned. '*Gtherandek, you have killed one of our kind; don't do this again. It is against our ways. You know this.*'

The memories came rushing back, like tears down the face of a corporeal being, a rush of emotion in his energy mass. A multi-coloured flash of light emitted from The Eight's energy mass as he recalled his previous existence. The light shining brightly in space illuminating him like a small sun.

'You were—'

'*Your mentor. Yes, I was, and The One of this epoch. Your companion, where is she?*'

'I do not know. Is she still alive?'

'*Yes, we have not felt her passing. Let this monster go. We will punish Six.*'

The news that somewhere out there The One survived washed through The Eight's mind. The Sixth didn't matter; revenge would serve no purpose but to tarnish The Eight with more death. His goal now, to find The One. Another thought flashed in his charged brain. *What I did to Nine was inevitable and after I found out what he was …*

The voice of his ancient mentor returned. *'Justified, Gtherandek. The Second sent us his report on the matter. What Six did is unpardonable. Nine should never have been elevated. Had we found out, we would have ordered his termination.'*

The voice paused as if the being was contemplating something worse. *'And the mindless destruction on Earth. Nine was a soulless stone and deserved to die for administering The Sixth's orders. He had a choice, knowing it was wrong and against our way and our established tenets and morals. Only a One, in concord with the other nine, may sanction such annihilation. As Overlords, we have a responsibility to the wellbeing of the corporeal beings we give intelligence to. I taught you that – something I see you never forgot. We live in symbiosis with them. It is our way.'*

'And Six?' The Eight asked.

'We have made a decision. As we speak, adjustments to Six's accounts and assets are being processed. Six is banished, and his galaxies repossessed. That is our judgment.' The voice rested as The Eight digested the monumental changes taking place within the Exchange's computers. Nothing like this had happened in his existence.

The voice of his mentor returned. *'Find The One and the other Overlords. Put this alliance back together, Eight – that is your task. Repair the damage he has done and expunge any remaining monsters he has created. Use your humans wisely; they are a force we need. We pay tribute to you, Eight. Of the fifty ships, five survive. That was nothing compared to the last war. I remember the decimated armadas. Space stations as well. It was close, but your plans worked out in the end.'* And then the voice was gone, and The Eight knew this mystical out-worldly consultation was over.

On the bridge of the *Monarch*, control of the ship regained, they watched their Overlord make his way back to the airlock.

When The Eight arrived on the bridge, he felt their emotion. He had sensed their readiness to sacrifice themselves for him and his cause. *Giants they were, all of them*, he thought, before speaking. 'Six is to be left to go in peace. Let the fleet know.'

Such an order surprised his crew. It was Niamh who asked their collective question. 'Overlord, who gave—'

'A higher authority, Niamh. And don't ask any more questions.' His voice conveyed the significance of that statement.

She and Tom sensed emotion emitting from their Overlord. A multi-coloured burst of light sporadically radiated from him; something he never did before.

Daring not to speak, another question flashed in Niamh's mind. *Is that happiness?* she asked herself.

'*It is, my child,*' came back his voice in her brain.

CHAPTER FIFTY-TWO

Invitation by Royal Decree

The Empress of the house of Naritanjs and The Emperor of the House of Akjivi invite you to the joining as Life Partners of:

Princess Theia of the House of Akjivi and Prince Gtherandek of the House of Naritanjs at the Royal Palace on Planet Anan.

After the joining ceremony, the Princess and Prince will be sworn in as the first Empress and Emperor of the newly constituted joint House of Aknar.

Time and landing details are …

· From: The Annals of the House of Aknar. Origins of Our Royal Dynasty.

*

Planet Anan. EPTS: B147652

SAD NEWS OF THE SIXTH's final destructive act on Anan dampened the post-victory euphoria. More tears flowed down Theia's face as she read the casualty list. Over two thousand loyal Aknar military turned to dust by The Sixth's vengeful wrath. Part of the rebellion's follow-up guard, they were among the best troops she had.

Knowing how vital the next few time segs would be, Theia turned to Li Ping. 'He killed the best of my guards. Commander, I need you and your troops in Aknar city. A mop-up operation. Bloody it will be.'

'We are with you, Empress,' Li Ping replied, issuing orders to her lieutenants. 'Four hundred transfer to Aknar City; the rest stay here and guard the Exchange.'

*

Two time segs later, a packed transporter landed outside the Royal Palace, led by a one-handed Quriel and his soldiers; Chinese troops dashed into Aknar City. Still dressed in bloodstained rags, with a baharian sword hanging over her shoulder, the Empress of the known universe – looking anything but regal – hurried to her palace, burning with a ferocity they hadn't seen before. Her loyal guards welcomed Theia who set the scene for what would follow.

It didn't take long – shouts and screams announced their impending arrival. Li Ping's troops, sent to the houses of purebreed traitors, returned. Standing on raised steps with her palace guard, Theia watched. Driven by the Chinese soldiers, thirty-six protesting purebreeds formed a semicircle in front of their Empress.

Pleading, whimpering cries and moans filled the palace garden as the Chinese troops stood guard behind the group. Li Ping hurried up the steps. Bowing to Theia, she took a stance beside Quriel. The pleading moans stopped, and apart from the sound of the gentle rain falling on the garden's cover there was silence. Li Ping drank in the scene. The brightly painted royal palace, a simple structure, wrapped around the square. Lush, vibrant flowers grew thickly around the covered courtyard. The bright design cut through the grey Anan rain with a joyous, colourful feeling. Theia shattered that!

Her voice thundered out. 'You urged on the vote for The Sixth's ascension, participating in his takeover, and supporting the dead Emperor in locking our Aknar fleet in chains. Treason to The One, The Eight and The House of Aknar is immediate death for the guilty families. That is our ancient law.'

These were the core traitors from the Anan councils and their families. Enirim discovered secret comms where the group had canvassed for The Sixth and urged the Overlord on. Some were greedy Charter bosses, others political buccaneers trying to advance their families' wealth and status.

Hanging around her long slender neck, Theia grabbed her blue diamond. Floating up off the ground, the Empress tightly gripped the baharian sword. She flashed a message to the Chinese Troops – *step back*. They jumped, putting a four-pace distance between them and their prisoners.

Like a spectre of death, with her raised sword flashing blue light from her pendant, Theia sped through the air. Flying past each guilty person, her blade severed their head. In an instant, she flew past them all, the baharian steel blade cleaving their heads from their bodies in milliseconds. The first severed head hit the ground at the same time as Theia's sword severed the last. Blood spurted from their torsos as their hearts beat out the final death rhythm. Li Ping's soldiers blanched at the bloody mayhem as the bodies collapsed in a heap. Red blood flowed across the squeaky clean courtyard.

As Theia returned to the stepped dais, her loyal lieutenant spoke up. 'What about the Shoter?'

'No,' she answered. 'The Shoter was recruited by The Sixth to do a job. His wife gave us valuable intel and help with the rebellion. They'll survive. Give him a call; he can clean up this mess. He's good at that.'

*

Under Tom's orders, a relieved *Pac A*, *B*, and *C* left their seclusion behind a dark moon, making their way to the Energy Exchange. In space around the Exchange, the *Monarch* recovered its severed pennon wing, nudging it into *Chad's* cargo bay with a shuttle. After that, accompanied by *Chad*, *Abra*, *Losh* and *Tain*, Niamh set a course to land the damaged *Monarch* on Anan.

Clouds buffeted the unstable starship as she brought it in on one engine, Kora's navigation projection guiding them down. On a remote spaceport, the purebreed ground crew wondered at the sight of the lopsided *Monarch* appearing out of the clouds alongside four starships. Followed by the other four, like a feather, *Monarch* touched down.

With a sigh of relief, Niamh opened the doors and, led by The Eight, they set foot on Anan. Another human first! The Aknar ground crew knelt in front of their Overlord, the sight of his glistening chariot only served to grow their wonder. That moment – his return to Anan – was embedded in The Eight's memory.

A fleet of ground transporters ferried The Eight's crews to Aknar city. The humans and Mzimot strained at the windows, trying to get a glimpse of the colourful city through the clouds. The Aknars and Borea couldn't believe they had returned to Anan, their bubbly chat drowning out the others in the cramped grav buses.

*

By the time The Eight's crews reached the royal palace, the Shoter had done his duty – not a trace of the bloody execution remained. After that interlude, Theia had returned to her chambers. She stripped off, throwing her bloodstained clothes and sword on the floor, disappearing into her bathroom to scrub the smelly stains of death from her body. Unseen, her trusty lieutenant took her bloodstained rags and sword to the palace museum. They would be on display for all of time, as a relic of the Aknar fight back — the hero Empress's fighting garb.

*

In Aknar City, unseen hands rushed to prepare a victory welcome for The Eight and his liberating followers. Colourful lights festooned the palace gardens, tables were set with all types of delicacies and the proud Aknar house banners hung throughout the city and palace. Even the incessant rain thinned to a soft mist for the day.

Theia ordered the celebrations, and her reunion with The Eight was to be transmitted live, far and wide, throughout the galaxies. There wasn't room for everyone in the palace but The Eight's ship-crew were to the fore. Others congregated outside in the gardens, the order of events carefully orchestrated to show off those who had helped The Eight. Behind his chariot, alongside Tom, Niamh and Li Ping, Jarzol the blue-furred Mzimot – the architect of The Eight's winning weaponry – clutched his wife's hand. His grip tightened in awe at where they were. Behind them, Fazqa, her pointy ears twitching in amazement, gripped Geoff's hand. Then came some of the ships' crews led by Siba Borea, holding the hand of her security officer Bill. Returning here was a milestone for Siba. Her family name was restored and the warship she commanded, owned by them. The colourful diversity of The Eight's close followers was not lost on the surrounding purebreed glitterati of Aknar City. Politicians, Charter families, loyal servants and soldiers wondered at the mixed species and races on show in this chamber – previously, the inner sanctum of pure-breed culture.

Supplementing the purebreed royal guard, Li Ping's Chinese troop's features stood out. The stories of how they had saved the Energy Exchange vibrated around Aknar City. Amongst the most avid followers of these fearless Asian troops were the powerful Charter bosses. That The Sixth had targeted their priceless space city infuriated them. Li Ping had to field offers of "life partnerships" for her and her troops from them! The Eight's win, and this victory parade, consigned purebreed single species culture to the bin!

The spectacle of this vast multicoloured chamber and its beauty dazzled the new arrivals. Mirrors interposed with vibrant pictures of ages past, decorated the walls. Illuminated by the bright lights hanging from the roof, gold and silver statues – of long-dead rulers – adorned the hall's deep alcoves. The brightly coloured murals continued across the porcelain-like floor. The images of star charts, solar systems and technical drawings of the Aknar starships were included in the vivid pictures.

Theia, standing on a raised dais, welcomed them in. Dressed in a regal blue gown with a blue pendant hanging around her neck, she looked glorious. Before she could speak, a blue mist, radiating out from The Eight's chariot enveloped her.

The Empress's memories of her trip to Earth on the *Hela* came flooding back. And, alongside Mack, her first encounter with humans, at the busy junction of Riccarton and Hagley Avenues – after they landed in Christchurch – played in her mind.

'You are right. It is very different,' Theia had said to Mack. 'They appear to be working on the roadway. What do we do?'

'We can't go back; we need to make this meeting,' Mack had replied.

They had watched as orange-clad human roadworkers continued with their site set up, installing cones and traffic diversions to the junction.

One of the friendly workers turned to them and asked, 'Do you guys want to cross?' It was the first human words spoken to Earth's alien visitors.

'Yes, thank you,' Mack had said. Then he hurried Theia on to that fateful meeting with Kath, Janet and Alan.

Amongst those flooding memories was that of Niamh's wedding and the beautiful gardens of the winery in Canterbury that Theia had loved. They were the memories the Eight had left, cherished for all time, now back with context. In addition to that, The Eight included recent updates. Mack was gone – died from the Anan sickness. And Theia had a grandnephew, Prince Ariki of Aknar, son of Hana and Brizo. The sheer joy of knowing that flooded Theia's heart. Tears ran down the Empresses white face as she cast her eyes about. They stopped at Niamh, who rushed to her friend and mentor – the woman she thought of as a mother.

Embracing Theia, Niamh spoke in a bubbly voice. 'Theia, it's me, Niamh. Do you remember me?'

'Niamh, Niamh, yes, I do. I know what has happened to Earth. A crime we never imagined.' She paused at the thought of such devastation. 'And Mack is gone. But these are tears of joy for the arrival of Ariki. A miracle after such sorrow. We have so much to catch up with,' she said, not knowing where to start.

On the coveted dais, behind Theia, the head of the Svang Charter's daughter stood beside her aunt. Enirim whispered the unfolding rumour in her ear. 'There's an Aknar prince born on the human planet.'

'You mean I won't be Empress,' the girl said, making eyes at the broad-shouldered Chief Haldock standing behind Siba and Bill.

'No, you won't.'

'Auntie, that's the best news I've heard all day,' the girl chirped back.

'What do you mean?'

'Power is best wielded from behind – like my dad. He was The Sixth's Shoter. Now with our Charter's help, he has organised this festival – amongst other things! Who's that man there?' she asked, pointing discreetly at Haldock.

Enirim nodded at her niece's sophistication. Of course, the girl was right! 'That's Chief Haldock, part of Quriel's hero group. They've been to Earth and back serving The Eight,' Enirim replied, noticing the Chief returning her niece's flirting gaze.

'Well, Auntie, you'll have to promote him. And I couldn't do this if I was Empress-in-waiting,' she said, bounding off the dais in pursuit of the handsome hero.

Theia admired the familiar faces shining out from the smiling crowd. Tom, Kora, Brian and the others, and there was the Borea. Siba, standing beside Bill, but no Zaval and Demard. Theia had got that sad update. Then a murmur started and the crowd backed away, circling their Overlord. The murmur rose, until the chamber rang out with cries of, 'The Eight, The Eight, The Eight.' The celebrants outside took up the chant, until the whole of Aknar City proclaimed the return of their Overlord.

When it died off, The Eight boomed a short response. 'Thank you. To all of you, what you have done helps restore galactic order. It is good to be home.' Then he rose up above the crowd in his chariot and left the palace to explore Aknar City, showing himself to the people who had waited for his return.

While the celebrations continued with the reunion of The Eight's followers, the live stream pinged across space to Cylla Ora's commercial terminal on the New World. Revelries mirroring those on Anan started there. The next day, Cylla dispatched the *Richard*, towing a *Hela* filled with blue, with Janet and Robert and the two children they minded to join their parents on Anan.

*

Two days after the celebrations, The Eight dispatched the *Tain* to Earth with an Aknar emissary delivering news of the end of the war, and to collect a delegation from Earth. The emissary carried a top-secret invite from Empress Theia for Crown Prince Ariki and his mother, Princess Hana of Aknar – not quite a royal summons, but close.

Enirim's destroyers cleared a path through the debris field for the long awaited arrival of *Pac A, B*, and *C* at the Energy Exchange. Supervised by The Dock Master, The Eight's cargo of blue energy berthed beside the tank farms. The expanding tanks groaned under their first fill of blue in an age, a momentous moment not missed by The Eight. He had done it, put an end to this energy shortage and the war it sparked.

To locate the missing Overlords – his next quest – he ordered the reconstituting of the Aknar space fleet. The time-consuming tasks began: mobilising crews, maintenance, bunkering and the rest …

The impatient Overlord didn't wait around for all that – he had a fleet ready to go. Refuelling the behemoth destroyer, *Aknar 1* – The One's flagship – for deep space flight, alongside *Abra, Chad and Losh*, The Eight left Anan to search for The One. Travelling with him on *Aknar 1*, Niamh and Tom left Jarzol to repair the *Monarch* on Anan. It wouldn't be a permanent fix, but enough to get them back to the Jiuquan shipyards on Earth.

The hunt for The One caught a break when they traced a freighter to the Ragma Galaxy. During his previous search for The One, in ethereal space, The Eight had seen that ship stealing his companion's hoard of blue. Commanded by Admiral Enirim, the fleet made all haste there.

*

Ragma Galaxy. EPTS: B147852

The culprit was parked at a space dock in orbit around Ragma-main, The Sixth's home world. The Eight didn't expect to find Six gone. He believed he would have to evict the evil entity – hence the show of strength. But Six had done the unimaginable – he had left. Maybe he had obeyed the orders of superiors – or, more plausibly, he had grabbed whatever he could and bolted.

Stripping every serviceable starship part, grav bale, blue energy and tradable commodity, with food and water for his small fleet's crew, The Sixth had left his planet's population destitute. The impoverished purebreeds, once proud servants of an Overlord, begged for help when The Eight arrived in orbit.

Eager to curry favour with the winning Overlord, without delay they led The Eight to a dungeon below The Sixth's home. The bare concrete structure, devoid of any type of decoration or warmth, didn't surprise The Eight. In that dark, damp basement, his purebreed guides stopped at an innocuous-looking five-metre square steel container standing on the floor.

'We think what's left of The One is here,' the leader of the group said. 'But we don't know how it works or how to get inside. That was what his close guards did …'

The Eight's senses couldn't penetrate the box. 'Uldonian paint, it's lined with it,' he said to Niamh. 'How did I not think of that?'

With a drill, Niamh cut a hole through the box big enough to see in. A solid square-like object, glistening with silver skin, floated in its centre. Translucent red grav beams, projecting up from the floor, suspended the silvery object in the middle of the container.

'I know what that is. Get me four canisters of blue and cut a larger hole. And be careful we don't damage that object,' the Overlord ordered.

Niamh and an Aknar tech toiled to cut a hole big enough to climb into the prison. To protect the contents, she chose slow, laborious drilling. It was all hands on deck to lift the cut piece away. Wasting no time, Niamh and the tech climbed inside. Examining the container's internals, she discovers controls embedded in the wall. With the tech supporting the silver object, from the console, Niamh disabled the grav beams. Both holding it together, they handed it out through the opening, into the arms of a waiting group, who laid it down in front of The Eight's chariot.

Flashing with blue light, the Overlord's oval mass floated over the object. All his biped followers stood back to watch. With blue tentacles, The Eight poured the canisters of blue energy into the square silvery object. The energy flowed mysteriously from the tanks through an invisible opening, disappearing into nothingness. The second the last drop of blue vanished into the inert object, it burst with white light, blinding humans and purebreeds.

The light-burst died away and after what seemed an age, the biped mortals' sight returned. Refocusing their eyes, the oval shape of The One appeared in front of them. The ethereal Overlord's energy mass radiated light-infused power. A shimmering single elliptical gold band framed a multicoloured pulsing core of blue energy – The One's heart; her engine of life beating again.

'Welcome back, my Lord,' The Eight said, his energy mass pulsing with deep blue light.

'Eight, I am not your Lord; I am your companion,' The One said in a soft feminine voice.

'I never thought I would see you again,' The Eight responded.

Rummaging through reconstituted databases, The One paused. Images of past lives flashed through the Overlord's mind. 'You are Gtherandek.'

'Yes, I am. You remember that,' The Eight answered. 'You are Theia. I also remember, millennia ago, when I took you as my life partner.'

'You never abandoned me, Gtherandek. You must have fought a war for me, a galactic war, one we swore never to do again.'

'A war I had to fight, One. Yes, we both took an oath, and I fulfilled that oath purging that monster, Six. I fought for what we rebuilt and the goodness and fairness we created in the universe. This is what that monster did,' he said, as he showed One what happened on Earth. For an instant, her core flashed purple as she saw the images of the charred Indian subcontinent and the six craters, where some of Earth's largest cities had stood. Then the ceirim, and the rest of the horror story …

A minute ticked by. The mortals knelt in silence as the two powerful beings reviewed the horrors of The Sixth's reign. The contrasting colours of the two Overlords floating beside each other mesmerised the mortals.

Turning to his followers, The Eight broke the silence. 'One, these are the bipeds that helped me. You know our loyal Aknar followers and the Borea family. These humans are from the planet, Earth. And there are many others – not here – to whom we owe a debt of gratitude.'

The One floated through the group, her multicoloured light illuminating the melting pot of ethnic human difference – Chinese, Caucasian, Asian, Indian, African, Polynesian – who knelt down before her. The Eight had brought as many as possible to the planet: Niamh, Tom, Li Ping, Bill, Kora and Brian alongside some of the crew of the *Chad* and *Losh*. Siba Borea clutched Bill's hand tightly as she felt the pulsing, powerful Overlord beside her.

In a soft feminine voice, The One spoke. 'Eight, the humans are the same species but different. Why is that?'

'We left them for so long on their own, that humans evolved that way.'

The One sensed something, a voice amongst the group, beside her. She felt it coming from the big black male human clutching the female purebreed's hand. 'Speak your mind,' she said.

Bill cleared his throat. Never in his life did he imagine he would get to speak before such incredible power. He felt Siba's reassuring gaze, her warmth and love. He opened his mouth, and in a gush, it came out. 'Overlord, our diversity binds us as a global family. But it wasn't always like that.'

In an instant, The One read the suffering, the hate and the prejudices that had blighted the human race — the hard slog against racial hatred, slavery, ethnic cleansing and man's inhumanity to man. In flashes and whisps, it flowed from the minds of the humans. A data burst from Eight to One provided more context and images of Earth's history.

One's silence said it all. She flashed a message to Eight. 'We made a mess of that!'

'We did, but it worked out in the end,' replied The Eight. 'We must go,' his voice boomed out. 'Admiral, we take as many of these poor souls with us as we can,' he said, referring to the planet's occupants. 'If there is extra food in the fleet, leave it for the rest and dispatch emergency relief from Anan.'

It was more than the impoverished purebreeds, who The Sixth had abandoned, dared hope for. After those wise words and the happy reunion at Ragma-main, packed with refugees, *Aknar 1* and the accompanying vessels set out.

'Unfinished business,' The Eight explained to The One on their short journey to the gas giant Gethsema. The emotional catchup over, business and galactic polity took precedent.

In orbit around the gas giant, The Eight got another surprise – The Sixth had abandoned his blue mine. A drone survey of Gethsema's moon revealed more discarded servants. In his haste to escape, The Sixth left his grotesque creations behind – his miners, the metal men. The multi-sensor drones discovered they had adapted and changed into rocks to hide.

Inside *Chad* and *Losh*, ceramic containers disgorged Chang's chemical weapons. The unassuming launch fired fifty missiles at the surface of the moon. The One and Eight accelerated the attack, cloning the chemicals with blue. Their intervention generated enough of the toxic substance to scour the land, reducing the moon's surface to boiling acid. Nothing survived that!

The depth of The Sixth's depravity and his ability to circumnavigate the norms of the Overlord's existence had shocked The One. 'What else will we find?' she asked, as they watched the moon's surface boiling in acid. 'You know, Eight, this isn't the end.'

'It is for now, One. It's all we can do. Admiral, orders to the fleet – we return to Anan.'

*

On the journey back to Anan, Niamh spent the time exploring *Aknar 1*. With the mission over and a full crew on board, she had nothing else to do. Crawling out from under a hybrid drive, she found The One and The Eight watching.

'My child,' he said, 'always you are curious. What are you doing now? You cannot have one of these destroyers, nor can you build one.'

She grinned, her dirt-stained face bright as a button, her ship garb soiled from the grime. 'Overlords, no, I don't want one of these. I was looking at the hull's support frame. I thought we could build some super-sized space transporters on Earth. They'd be great for the colonies. We could even use removable drives and leave the ships behind, or transport modular cities, that sort of thing ...'

The two powerful entities stayed quiet. One flashed a message to Eight. *'Eight, we never thought of that!'*

'No, we didn't,' he replied.

'When will she be ready to ascend?' One asked.

'I have been through this before, One. Not yet.'

EPILOGUE

Planet Anan. EPTS: B148525

ALL SHIPS CONVERGED ON PLANET Anan. From the corners of the known universe they came to pay allegiance to The One. Amongst them, the returning Aknar navy dispatched to find the missing Overlords, the *Tain* from Earth, and *Richard* and *Hela* from the New World. Alice led a contingent of catbears on the *Hela* – part of The Eight's personal guard.

Accompanying The Second were The Third, Fourth and Fifth, found by the Aknar navy hiding in stasis on their home worlds. Blue, given by The Second, revived them – as Eight had done for One. The Tenth, the youngest of all, didn't survive, expiring shortly after the process. A sad day for the powerful ethereal entities; more misery doled out by The Sixth's power grab.

The Seventh slinked in on the *Chesh*, gushing profuse contrition. Inter-galactic politics prevented The One from admonishing Seven. Instead, she replied with a brief burst of praise for the help in defeating Six.

Guarded by the catbears, in an empty building on the far side of Anan, the remaining Overlords met. It was the first gathering of minds since they had congregated in ethereal space to discuss the blue energy crisis before The Sixth's troika took over. So much had happened since then, cumulating here with The Eight winning the war and delivering their life-sustaining blue. But Six lived on, in the worst possible way – outside this alliance. Foremost in their minds today was how this law-making conclave could approve the ascension of other beings to the Overlord's level.

'Never again can we let a thing like The Sixth or The Ninth ascend to our plane of existence,' The One ordered.

'I did not groom The Sixth or The Ninth for ascension. Whoever assisted The Sixth is lost in the mists of time, but without doubt, Six elevated Nine without my help or any approval. It was a fait accompli!'

The Second said. 'I will not prepare a biped for ascension without the approval of all Overlords. And, no other may delve into such a complex matter. It should be I alone,' The Second stated

Without hesitation, the conclave agreed.

'Before we move on, our group is at seven Overlords,' The Eight said, unusually for him as he had typically stayed quiet during previous ethereal meetings. 'There are three vacancies. I propose these three mortals for ascension when their time comes.'

There were no objections.

*

Across the planet, Aknar city was abuzz with activity. The guildhall welcomed two new Charters and embraced the Borea family back in. Their first non-purebreed members, Verteg, Niamh, Tom and Janet, admired newly carved crests in their seatbacks as they claimed their place in the Anan Charter Guild.

After that, it was back to the Aknar palace for Theia's welcoming celebration of their Overlord's restoration. Walking down the main street, Verteg, Niamh, Tom and Janet stopped outside a shop. "A prime corner property, extending to two floors over basement" was the agent's flowery description. The sign, "K&J Everything Earth" was already up.

Katherine Phillips had packed the *Tain* with containers full of every conceivable Earth luxury before it departed. With the launch of their brand planned in two days, interest in the goods from Planet Earth skyrocketed. Due to demand, as people prepared for the Charter Guild's ball, pre-orders for ladies' clothes and jewellery had closed.

'Looks good, Janet,' Niamh said, as she peered in through the windows at the workers hurrying to stock the place. 'You're going to have to take me in there,' she said, nudging Tom, drawing a mock gesture of frustration.

'Yes, Tom, you will. I'm taking Alice there. And to miss the crowds, you'd better book your slot,' chipped in Verteg, with a smile that lit up the street.

Before Tom could say anything, a group of four appeared from the crowd.

Haldock, with a young girl at his arm, introduced the Svang Charter family, husband, wife and daughter – fresh from the Charter meeting.

Niamh, Tom, Janet and Verteg were at a loss for words, as the man – once The Sixth's infamous Shoter – touched a scar on his face, then smiled at the group.

His wife broke the ice. 'Sullivan and Parker, you're the pirates that stole our Mzimot engine builders and you have the cheek to bring them here. I hear they're patching up your warship. It used to be called *Borea 1*. Didn't it, Ms Verteg. A pirate's battleship.'

A shocked Verteg nodded. Her mouth opened, but nothing came out.

The woman continued, 'I'm delighted to meet you all, and your baby,' she said, smiling at the tiny Zaval swaddled in a blanket in Tom's arms. 'You are blessed, Niamh.'

Wide-eyed with wonder, Niamh nodded, her mind questioning how they would square this circle.

The woman continued. 'The grapevine tells you have starship yards on your Earth, fitting out that old junk Nolget and Touqmat peddle. Competition for us!'

Tongue-tied, Niamh nodded at the purebreed woman.

Smiling ear to ear, delighted she had their adversaries at a loss, the woman's head bobbed on her long neck as she continued. 'I banned them from selling to you. No matter, that's what won this war, a good outcome. Come, we're all off to the palace. Walk with me.'

Haldock and his new beau discretely walked ahead, as the four powerful women, all Charter bosses, walked together.

Tom and Svang followed behind. 'Tom, may I call you that?'

Tom, with young Zaval in his arms, wondering what this family wanted, nodded.

'A question I need you to answer, and be honest, please,' Svang asked. 'If I can, I will,' Tom replied.

The purebreed cleared his throat, then huffed – like he was choking on the question. In a rush, Svang blurted it out. 'Chief Haldock, what sort of a person is he?' the man who had headed a prime galactic Charter, and had served as The Sixth's Shoter, asked.

Tom grinned. Of all the queries, business intentions, competition, war and the like, Svang's biggest concern was his daughter's welfare. He wasn't so bad after all. 'Haldock is what we call a rock. Honest and dedicated to the cause. He saved Verteg's life and navigated the hybrid ship that defeated the ceirim invasion on Earth. Believe me, if she were my daughter, I'd be happy for her.'

With a beaming smile, Svang turned to face Tom. The five-foot-nine tall human with his broad, muscular body was slightly shorter than the purebreed.

All the man's tension disappeared as he asked another question. 'Now, tell me how you stole our consortia's engine builders, grabbed four blue drives, and built a military base on our doorstep in the Kandark Galaxy.'

Looking into Tom's brown eyes, he wanted to ask more. *Is it true you dumped a star fleet's crew out of an airlock?* That question would wait for another day. The depth Svang saw in Tom's eyes told a hard tale. It was as if the human had been to the edge of the universe, stared death in the face, and come back.

There was no doubt in Svang's mind, The Sixth was right. The Eight's humans would change galactic history. They had seen more "action" than all the purebreeds put together. A formidable force had landed on Anan's doorstep, and Tom and Niamh were at their fore – better they be friends than enemies.

Oblivious to the man's wandering mind, Tom hugged his son and answered back, 'We paid for the drives and the Mzimot's debts …'

*

Inside the palace, Theia's celebration gathered pace. Robert, polished up in a new Anan-style suit, stood tall beside Janet. She fielded all the business questions about her, Kath and Alan's Charter.

'Nothing to do with me,' was Robert's denying reply. The business was hers!

Theia spent the time beside Hana, fussing Ariki for as long as she could. By now, the toddler had a mind of his own, trying to meander off himself. With the horror of war, stories of marauding ceirim, genocide and the like, Anan purebreeds welcomed Hana and Ariki. Humans were the source of the cure to their sickness and had helped The Eight restore order in the galaxy. The young prince was a living memory of Brizo Sema, brutally murdered by The Sixth. No manner of prejudice could prevail after such harrowing times. "Give thanks for what we have," was the catch-word of the day.

Only The One, Second and Eight came to attend their bipeds' welcoming. The other four Overlords took leave of Anan, heading back to their home galaxies. The crowd opened out as, surrounded by the catbears, the powerful entities, their oval energy masses flashing with light, floated into the palace. The clapping and shouting started again: The One, The One, The One, spilling out into the city beyond, heralding the population's relief that order was restored.

Finally, The One boomed out a 'thank you', quelling the raucous welcome. Outside and inside the palace, Aknar city's crowds settled back to their celebrations.

Flashing a message to Robert, The Eight called him and Janet over. 'Janet, Robert, this is my companion, The One, the lord of our known universe. One, without their input, I would have not succeeded.'

The One flashed with colourful light as she scanned the two mortals in front of her. 'You chose well, Eight,' was all she said, then floated away to Theia Aknar.

The Eight continued his praise. 'I owe you both. Janet without your planning and Robert, your leadership and tenacity, we wouldn't be here now.'

Ignoring all praise, Robert asked his burning question. 'What next, Overlord?'

'We fix Planet Earth for the human race. They have suffered for this victory. The One is backing that effort all the way. Niamh wants to build mobile cities on Earth and transport huge swathes of Earth's population to the New World. I have said it before, there is enough room on both planets to give Earth's population a chance for a new life. That is what we'll do. And, Robert, I must visit my other worlds. You need to see them as well. Also, that corrupt mess on Hirkiv must be reformed. And there is more; we will be busy.'

A small purebreed, dressed in a colourful coat approached.

The Eight continued. 'And here is Haret. Janet, he will help with running your Charter on Anan …'

The One floated over beside Theia. *'Empress, how is your nephew?'* she flashed to Theia's mind.

'Overlord,' Theia replied without speaking, *'he is a miracle. I couldn't have asked for anything else — to be here beside you, my namesake, with my heir.'*

'Hana,' The One said, calling the young girl over.

Hana had met The Eight, but now she was to meet The One, the most powerful being in the universe. The young Maori girl couldn't imagine what had gotten her into this predicament. Carrying Ariki, she walked over and knelt down. The was a hush as the whole palace watched. A thin beam of coloured light weaved its way from The One's energy mass to Ariki. The toddler giggled and tried to grab the light. He missed. Then, with the sound of a ringing bell, it touched his nose. The baby prince's brown face lit up as a multicoloured aura ringed his face. He giggled as he tried to catch the light. Hana clutched him for all he was worth, her mind in turmoil as to what The One was doing to her precious son.

In her mind, The One answered with a soft voice. 'Hana, do not fear me. This is my welcome kiss to your son. Fear not, he is well and will grow up strong and intelligent.'

Then she spoke, a loud booming voice for all to hear. 'Welcome, Princess Hana and Prince Ariki into my House of Aknar.'

As suddenly as they had arrived, surrounded by The Eight's majestic catbears, green and brown striped fur shining in his light and long manes swinging while they padded along, the three Overlords floated out – leaving the mortals to party on.

12th December 2028/ EPTS: B148573

The End

ABOUT THE AUTHOR

With no academic background, Lionel Lazarus picked up his writing skills while working on the North Sea Oil Rigs. Following a long career working off-shore, Lionel returned to work on-shore in the Health and Safety profession. He retired to work full time on his writing. When not writing, Lionel loves to travel and to walk in the mountains. He lives in Dublin, Ireland.

ACKNOWLEDGEMENTS

ENERGY WARS, THE 2ND AND 3rd parts of the Energy Exchange series, was six years in the making. After Project Anan, which I found hard to write, this was a mountain! I couldn't have done it without help from the book professionals, my family and my friends. Thank you.

To Cate Baum, editor at Self Publishing Review who edited the original manuscript in 2016. You pushed me on to finish the series. https://www.selfpublishingreview.com/.

To Julie Hoyle, the proof-reader at Jericho Writers, you did a fantastic job. I couldn't believe the work, and I learned so much from wading through the corrections! https://jerichowriters.com/

To Design for Writers for your patience, a remarkable cover, book format and website design. https://www.designforwriters.com/

And finally, to my extended family and friends. To Carol for putting up with me, to Brendan for the encouragement, my son Jonathan for the awesome critique and Suzie, my editorial daughter in Christchurch, New Zealand, who kicked the whole series off.

AUTHORS NOTE

To MY READERS, THANK YOU for buying the books; I hope you have enjoyed Energy Wars. If you enjoyed this book, please consider leaving a brief review at your online bookstore. A good review is important to authors and helps readers find a book worth reading. It needn't be long – a short sentence detailing what you enjoyed and a star rating is enough. Many thanks to those who have left reviews — I am humbled.

Check out my website for news and more info on the characters and story.

http://lionellazarus.com/

Or drop me a line at

lionellazarus@lionellazarus.com

Printed in Great Britain
by Amazon

10835178R00401